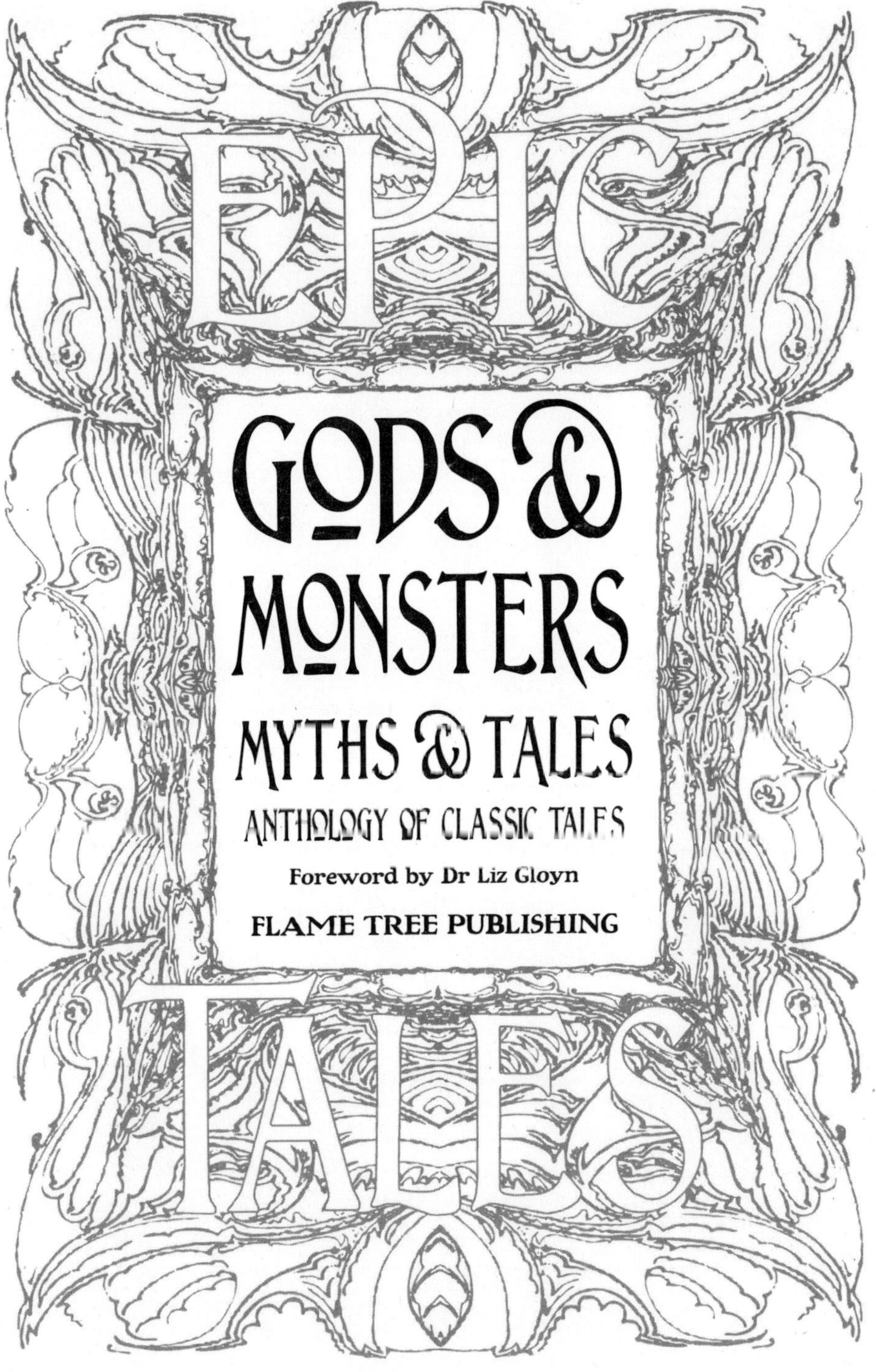
EPIC
GODS & MONSTERS
MYTHS & TALES
ANTHOLOGY OF CLASSIC TALES
Foreword by Dr Liz Gloyn
FLAME TREE PUBLISHING
TALES

This is a FLAME TREE Book

Publisher & Creative Director: Nick Wells
Editorial Director: Catherine Taylor
Special thanks to Federica Ciaravella and Taylor Bentley

FLAME TREE PUBLISHING
6 Melbray Mews, Fulham,
London SW6 3NS, United Kingdom
www.flametreepublishing.com

First published 2021

23 25 24 22
3 5 7 9 10 8 6 4

ISBN: 978-1-83964-475-7
Special ISBN: 978-1-83964-711-6

The cover image is created by Flame Tree Studio
based on artwork courtesy of Shutterstock.com.

Incidental motif images courtesy of Shutterstock.com:
sacilad and Masterlevsha.

A copy of the CIP data for this book is available from the British Library.

Printed and bound in China

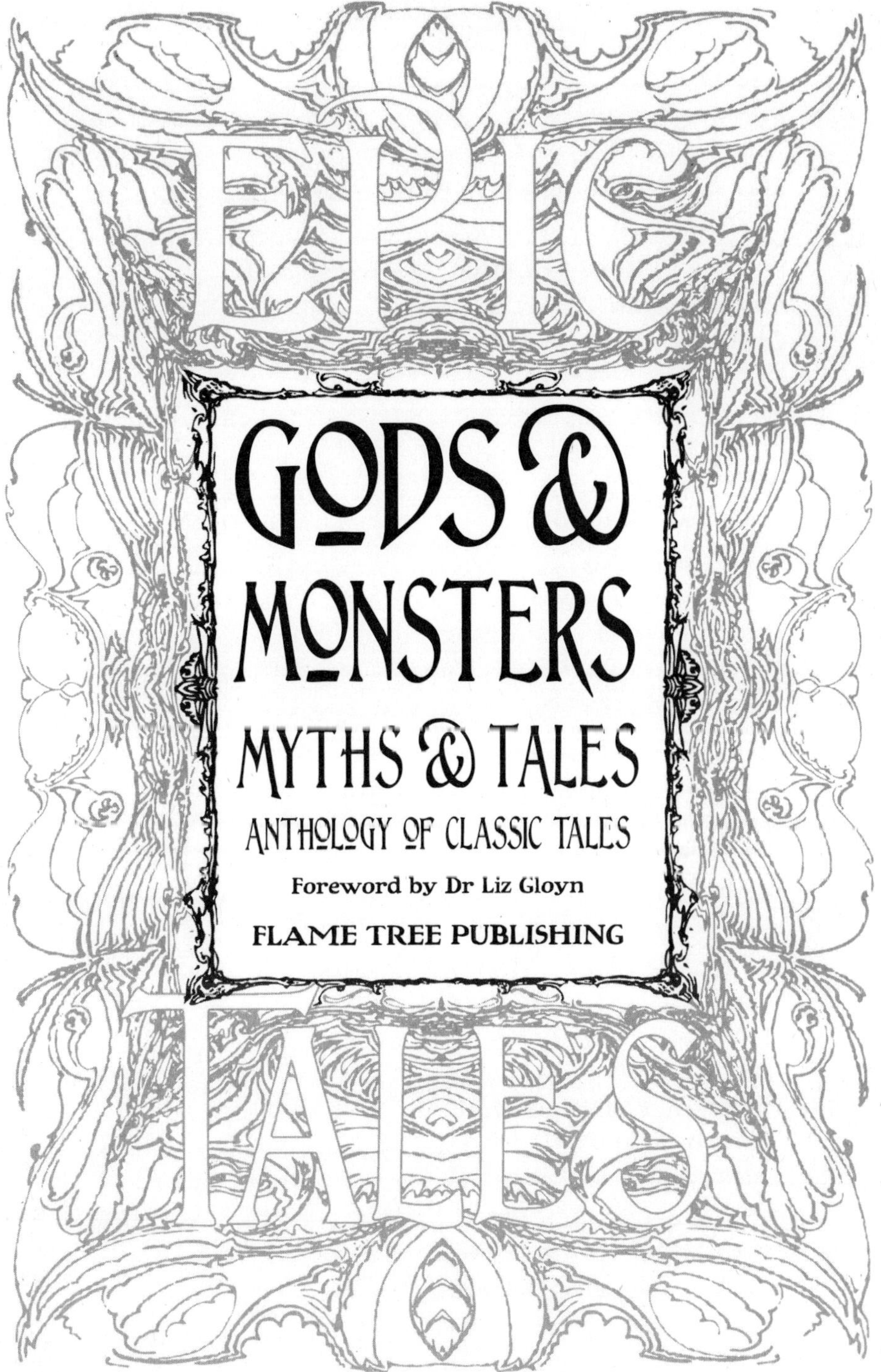

GODS & MONSTERS

MYTHS & TALES

ANTHOLOGY OF CLASSIC TALES

Foreword by Dr Liz Gloyn

FLAME TREE PUBLISHING

Contents

Heroic Encounters with Fearsome Beasts

Monstrous Gods & Divine Monsters

Beastly Beings, Malign & Benign

Foreword

WHAT DOES IT MEAN TO BE DIVINE, and what does it mean to be monstrous? Humanity sits at the hinge-point of a spectrum, with gods at one end and monsters on the other; where are the borderlands? Which boundaries do people break, on purpose or by accident, which take them outside being human and into the danger zones at either end?

It is these questions that tales of gods and monsters help us to grapple with, responding to cultural contexts across the world to explore what happens in the shadows and in the heavens. Humans who cross the line often end up in danger, whether through the presumption of ascending to heaven or over-confident bravado in the face of scales and teeth. The myths collected here firm up the unspoken rules of what happens to people who don't follow the rules, and what beings who exist outside those rules can and can't get away with.

Monsters are guaranteed to be sub-human, and so need to be controlled and conquered; when the (usually male) hero slaughters the monster, he acts as the agent of civilizing culture, removing the dangerous uncivilized force from the world. The monster is the shadow side of the human, representing all that is fearsome and fearful; monsters which are half-human, half-animal, like centaurs and the Minotaur, represent the bestial forces inside us. However, monsters also take on characteristics associated with marginalized groups such as women, people with different colour skin or ethnic backgrounds, people with disabilities, people with different sexual orientations – whatever is not considered 'normal' becomes the sign of the monster. It is no accident that in Greek creation myths, the ordered male is challenged by the chaotic female – Gaia seeks to overturn Ouranos through their children, Rhea repeats the pattern with Chronos, and Zeus celebrates his final victory over Typhoeus, a monster created by Gaia. When the hero kills the monster, his victory reinforces our sense of what is 'normal' and emphasizes who or what does not belong.

Gods, on the other hand, often wreak divine vengeance on humans who dare to doubt or offend them – yet sometimes their behaviour does make you wonder whether they really are so far away from monsters after all. When Arachne challenges Athena to a weaving competition and produces a tapestry of the gods' sexual misdemeanours, Athena cannot find fault with the quality of the work but beats Arachne and turns her into a spider for daring to show what (Athena thinks) should not be shown. Medusa, that archetypal symbol of the monstrosity of female sexuality, is, so Ovid tells us, transformed by an angry Athena after the god Poseidon rapes her, an early example of victim blaming. When the hunter Acteon accidentally stumbles upon the goddess Diana bathing, she turns him into a stag and has him ripped apart by his own hunting dogs. Both gods and monsters stand outside of the rules that control human behaviour – but the gods seem to get away with it.

The stories in this collection, from Ancient Greece and cultures all around the world, use the uncanny and the supernatural to explore these tensions around human identity and how we relate to the world around us. They ask us to consider who we see as like and unlike us, and their powerful storytelling challenges our definitions. Gods and monsters both tempt and terrify us. Through the strength of stories, the fascination of monsters, the awe of gods, readers are drawn into a centuries-long conversation about what it really means to be human.

Liz Gloyn
Senior Lecturer in Classics, Royal Holloway, University of London

Publisher's Note

AS TALES FROM MYTHOLOGY AND FOLKLORE are principally derived from an oral storytelling tradition, their written representation depends on the transcription, translation and interpretation by those who heard them and first put them to paper, and also on whether they are recently re-told versions or more directly sourced from original first-hand accounts. The stories in this book are a mixture, and you can learn more about the sources and authors at the back of the book. This collection presents a thoughtfully selected cross-section of stories from all over the world, though some countries may seem more heavily represented than others since their cultures more readily define characters with a divine or monstrous status. For the purposes of simplicity and consistency, most diacritical marks have been removed, since their usage in the original sources was sometimes inconsistent or would represent different pronunciation, depending on the original language of the story, not to mention that quite a sophisticated understanding of phonetic conventions would be required to understand how to pronounce them anyway.

We also ask the reader to remember that while the myths and tales are timeless, much of the factual information, opinions regarding the nature of countries and their peoples, as well as the style of writing in this anthology, are of the era during which they were written.

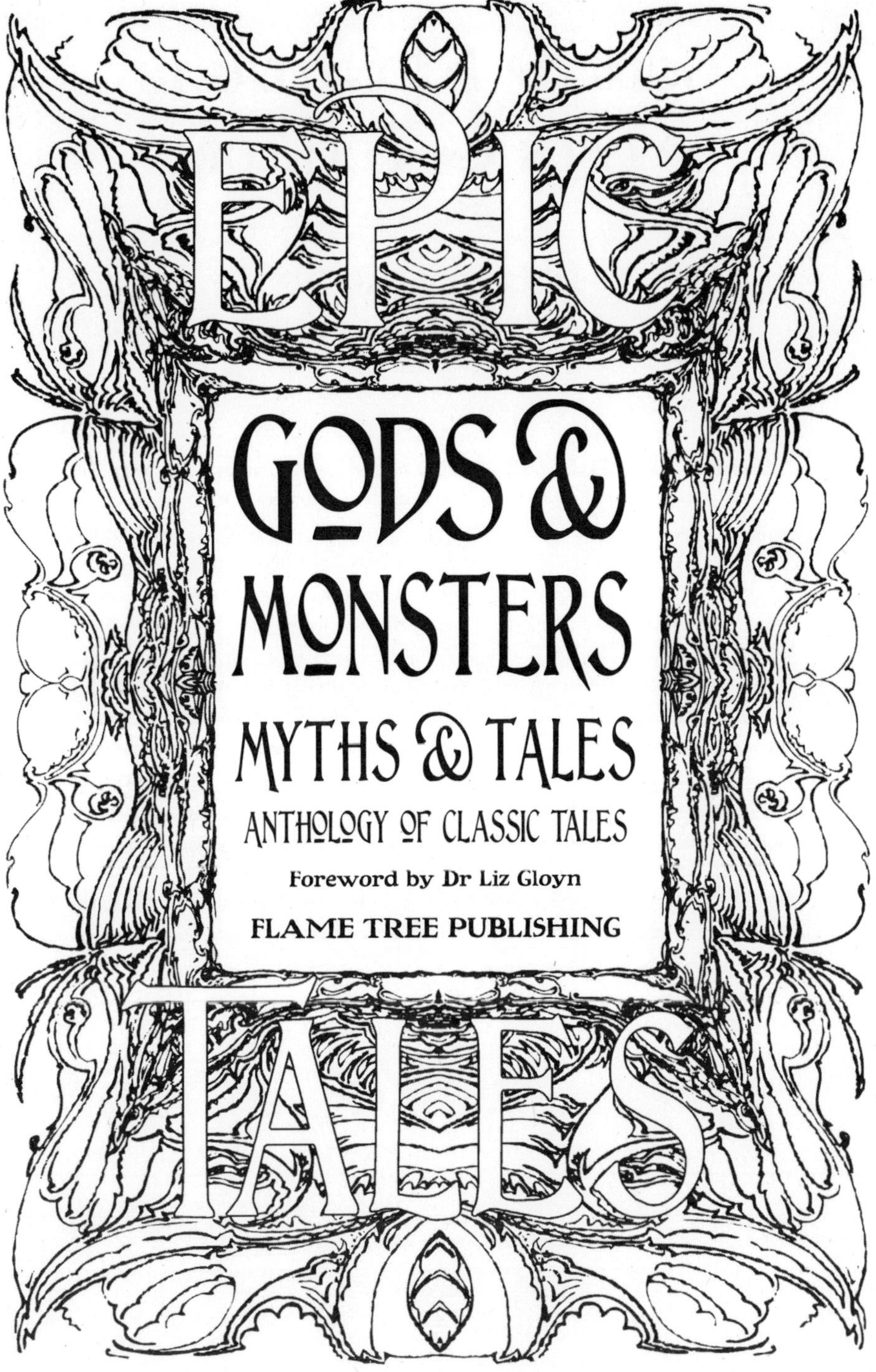
EPIC
GODS & MONSTERS
MYTHS & TALES
ANTHOLOGY OF CLASSIC TALES
Foreword by Dr Liz Gloyn
FLAME TREE PUBLISHING
TALES

Gods & Monsters in Myth & Folklore

Introduction

'MAN IS QUITE THE IDIOT,' wrote Michel de Montaigne (1533–92). 'He wouldn't know how to make a mite, and yet he makes gods in dozens.' A little harsh, given the enormous variety and vividness of the collective human pantheon as represented by the deities in the stories here, a testimony to the endless ingenuity of the human mind. A judgment, moreover, that misses the astonishing extravagance of the monsters we have made for ourselves in comparable quantities.

The great Renaissance essayist was of course quite modern in his view that gods and goddesses are the creations of their believers. Monsters too, he felt, were expressions of human fear or feeling. 'I never saw a greater monster or miracle than myself,' he noted. Divinity and depravity were just two sides of the human coin. If myths map out our imaginative world and the way we see ourselves in it, gods and monsters have represented our twin poles.

From the inspiring to the outrageous; from the glorious to the grotesque; from the majestic to the terrifying: the gods and monsters here span the far extremes of human life and originate in every corner of the globe.

Greek Mythology

Olympian Gods

Ancient Greece had its cosmogonies, myths of how the world began and other stories of the gods. Although the gods travel far and wide, they always return to their homes beyond the clouds on Mount Olympus. Hence they are known as the Olympic gods or Olympians. Each god has his or her own home, although they usually come together in the palace of Zeus, father of the gods. There they feast on ambrosia and nectar, served by the lovely goddess Hebe and entertained by Apollo on his lyre. It is an immortal world of feasting and discussion of the affairs of heaven and earth.

Zeus, though known as the father of the gods, has a beginning. His father and mother are Cronus and Rhea, of the race of Titans, themselves children of heaven/Uranus and earth/Gaea. They, in turn, sprang from Chaos ('the yawning abyss'). Zeus and his two brothers, Poseidon and Hades, shared out the world, with Zeus taking the heavens, Poseidon the seas and Hades the underworld.

The lame god Hephaestus was architect, smith and artist for the gods; he even forged thunderbolts which Zeus hurled at his enemies. In gratitude, Zeus gave him Aphrodite, goddess of love and beauty, as his wife. Some myths say that she was born of sea foam and clothed by the seasons. Eros, god of love, is her son; armed with his bow and arrows, he fires his love darts into the hearts of gods and humans. Athene, goddess of wisdom, sprang fully adult from the head of Zeus; it was she who gave her name to the city of Athens and to the most famous of all Greek temples, the Parthenon (built between 447 and 438 BC) or Athene Parthonos (Athene the Virgin).

Hermes, messenger of the gods, is usually seen wearing a winged cap and sandals. He is also the god of trade, wrestling and other sports, even thieving – whatever requires skill and dexterity. Dionysus, god of wine, presides over sacred festivals to mark the grape harvest, wine being sacred and its drinking ritualized. Dionysus is often portrayed with male and female satyrs (horned creatures, half human, half-goat) and maenads (fauns). Since he is also the god of passion, many temples were named after him and festivals held in his name.

The nine Muses, who were daughters of Zeus and Mnemosyne (Memory), were originally goddesses of memory, but later each becomes identified with song, verse, dance, comedy, tragedy, astronomy, history, art and science. The three Graces (also Zeus' daughers) bestow beauty and charm on humans and preside over banquets, dancing and all elegant entertainment.

The three Fates control every person's birth, life and death. Also known as the Cruel Fates, they spend their time spinning the threads of human destiny and cutting them with shears whenever they wish. Finally, the three Furies punish all transgressors mercilessly, usually with a deadly sting. Greeks preferred to call them the Eumenides (Good-Tempered Ones), as it would have been bad luck to use their proper name.

Human Heroes and Demigods

The distinction between heroes and demigods is unclear. While some heroes, like Jason and Oedipus, are sons of mortal parents, others, like Heracles, Perseus and Achilles, come from the union of gods or goddesses with mortals. Zeus and Alcmene produced Heracles (his name 'Glory to Hera' was meant to appease Zeus' wife, the goddess Hera);

Zeus and Danae produced Perseus; Peleus and the sea-nymph Thetis were responsible for Achilles; while rumours of divine intervention surround both Theseus (Poseidon is his putative father) and Odysseus (the putative bastard son of Sisyphus, offspring of Aeolus, god of winds).

Many rival states claimed a hero as their founder and protector, no doubt embellishing their origins: Theseus of Athens, Jason of Iolcos, Ajax of Salamis. Noble families also asserted a hero as their ancestor. Alexander the Great, for example, claimed descent from both Achilles and the Egyptian god Amon (Ammon) and insisted that his own semi-divine status was recognized throughout Greece. The bards, including Homer and Hesiod, who sang for their living, often took care to extol the ancestors of their patrons and audiences.

The catalogue of ships in Homer's *Iliad* leaves no Greek state off the roll of ancient glory; the 50 Argonauts are each attributed to a noble Greek family.

The figure most akin to a national hero is Heracles. He never settled in any one city that could take full credit for his exploits, and his wanderings carried him beyond the bounds of Greece – far into Africa and Asia Minor. He was one of the earliest mythical heroes to be featured in Greek art (dating from the eighth century BC) and on the coins of city states (on which he is usually depicted strangling snakes while in his cradle). As a symbol of national patriotism he is the only hero to be revered throughout Greece; he is also the only hero to be granted immortality.

What makes Greek heroes particularly interesting is their depiction by bards as deeply complex characters. Typically, they follow a common pattern: unnatural birth, return home as prodigal sons after being separated at an early age, exploits against monsters to prove their manhood and subsequent kingship or glorious death. Super strong and courageous they may be, mostly noble and honourable, but all have to contend with a ruthless streak that often outweighs the good. Heracles, for example, hurls his wife and children into a fire in a fit of madness and his uncontrollable lust forces him on King Thespius' 50 daughters in a single night. Nor is he averse to homosexual affairs (with Hylas, for instance), though Greek pederasty is mostly excluded from the myths.

Despite recapturing the Golden Fleece for Greece, Jason never finds contentment; he deserts his wife Medea and dies when the *Argo*'s rotting prow falls on him. Theseus is also disloyal to his wife Ariadne, abandoning her on the island of Naxos; he kills his Amazon wife Antiope and causes the death both of his son Hippolytus and his father Aegeus. Even the noble and fearless Achilles, the Greek hero of the Trojan War, a man who cannot bear dishonourable conduct, violates the dead hero's code by desecrating Hector's corpse and refusing to hand it over to the Trojans.

Like the heroes, therefore, cities that turn their hero's burial places into shrines (and oracles) receive good fortune, but they also risk invoking the hero's unpredictable temper.

Creatures and Monsters

Many are the horrifying monsters sent to test the strength and guile of Greek heroes – Jason, Heracles, Odysseus, Perseus, Theseus. They all have to journey to the very edge of known civilization and beyond into realms of fantasy where, time and again, they have to overcome giants, dragons, many-headed serpents, sirens, huge bulls and sea monsters of every sort.

The creatures of Greek myth are the archetypal villains of the European consciousness, rich material for the fertile imagination of artists, poets and children.

Some monsters, notably the giants, differ from men mainly in their size and ugliness. The human giants, such as the Cyclops (with one eye in the middle of their forehead), King Amycus of Bebryces (covered in thick black hair and beaten by the Argonaut Polydeuces in a boxing match) or Antacus (who is defeated by Heracles at wrestling) resemble ordinary mortals in proportions, and join in love and war with them.

Superhuman giants, on the other hand, war even with the gods and are of vastly grander proportions: Typhon, with his 100 arms, makes war on Zeus who slays him with a thunderbolt. He is so huge that it takes Mount Etna to cover the corpse. His brother Enceladus provides the flames of Mount Etna's volcano with his breath. For his part in the war against Zeus, the Titan Atlas has to hold up the heavens on his shoulders. It is Atlas' three daughters, the Hesperides, who bring Heracles the magical golden apples.

It can hardly have been coincidence that many of the monsters who test heroes are female. Oedipus (who has further troubles with women, unwittingly marrying his own mother) has a trial with the Sphinx, which has a woman's head and breasts, a lion's body and a bird's wings. The Harpies, fierce winged creatures with sharp claws, possess women's faces. These filthy beasts snatch food from the blind Phineus during Jason's journey to Colchis. The three Gorgon sisters, led by Medusa, have writhing snakes for hair and can turn their victims to stone with a single glance. With divine aid, Perseus cuts off Medusa's head while looking at her reflection in a polished shield.

Not all female monsters are ugly brutes. Beautiful femmes fatales out to trap unwary heroes include the Sirens, half-women, half-birds, whose song so bewitches sailors that they throw themselves overboard and drown. The Argonauts escape by having Orpheus drown out their Siren song with his lyre, while Odysseus has himself bound to the mast while his sailors fill their ears with wax.

Norse Mythology

The best-known of the Northern European deities were Odin, Thor, Loki, Balder, Niord, Frey and Freyia. These had the most distinct and vivid personalities, though there were other, more shadowy figures such as Tyr, fearless god of war. Niord, Frey and Freyia belonged to a sub-group of fertility gods known as the Vanir, while the others belonged to the main group of gods known as the Aesir.

The myths deal in conflict between the gods and giants, representing the constant struggle between chaos and order. An intense sense of fate also permeates Northern mythology: Odin chose those who would die in battle; and Ragnarok, the final great battle between the gods and the giants, was unavoidable. The people believed that their destiny was not within their own control and their myths helped them accept this, following the example of their gods. Mirroring the strong family ties of Northern society, the gods were a close-knit group that helped and supported each other, with very clear loyalties to their own kind.

Northern mythology takes us from the formation of life from the fusion of extremes – ice and fire – to the end of the world, when fire and water will again claim the life they have engendered.

Yet existence does not finish there completely: the earth will reappear after Ragnarok has passed, washed clean and renewed, when the sons of the gods will pick up where their fathers left off and life will begin again.

Cosmology – the Structure of the Universe

The dramas of Northern myths were played out against the background of a complicated cosmology, peopled with diverse races of beings. In the course of the mythological narratives, the gods would travel from land to land over differing terrains and vast distances, and a rich and varied picture of the world emerges.

The Northern cosmic structure consisted of three different levels, one above the other like a series of plates. On the top level was Asgard, the stronghold of the gods, where the Aesir lived in their magnificent halls, as well as Vanaheim, home to the Vanir, and Alfheim, land of the elves.

On the level below lay Midgard, the world of men, and Jotunheim, mountainous realm of the giants. Svartalfheim, where dark elves lived, and Nidavellir, home of the dwarfs, were also here. Asgard and Midgard were connected by a flaming bridge, Bifrost, which was very strong and built with more skill than any other structure. Humans knew Bifrost as the rainbow.

The lowest level was cold Niflheim, which included Hel, the dwelling place of those who died of sickness, old age or accident. Warriors who died in battle were received into Odin's hall, Valhalla, or Freyia's hall, Sessrumnir, on the top level in Asgard, where they became part of Odin's personal army. Those dying at sea went to another place again: the hall of the sea gods Aegir and Ran, at the bottom of the sea.

The axis and supporting pillar of the universe was an enormous ash tree, Yggdrasil, also known as the World Tree. This gigantic tree formed a central column linking the worlds of gods, men, giants and the dead, and also protected and sheltered the world. Yggdrasil's fortunes mirrored those of the universe it sheltered; it suffered alongside the world at the same time as sustaining it under its protection.

Besides gods and men, the Northern cosmos was also inhabited by dwarfs, elves and giants. There were two types of elf in Northern myth. Light elves, living in Alfheim, were thought to be more beautiful than the sun. Dark elves were blacker than pitch, and unlike their light counterparts in nature. The dark elves lived underground in Svartalfheim, and appear to have been similar to, and perhaps interchangeable with, dwarfs.

Dwarfs were not in fact thought to be particularly small, but were believed to be ugly. They were famous for their extraordinary craftsmanship, particularly in working precious metals, especially gold. They were able to fashion remarkable objects with magical powers. Most of the treasures belonging to the gods, including Miolnir, Thor's hammer, were made by dwarfs. Dwarfs were thought to have been generated from the soil: they first took form as maggots in the flesh of Ymir, the primeval giant whose body became the earth, and the gods then gave them consciousness and intelligence.

Giants, certainly thought to be of great size, played a significant part in the mythology. They represented the forces of chaos and negativity, and were usually hostile. The gods continually strove to maintain the order of their universe against these unpredictable external forces. The relationship between gods and giants was not always straightforward, however. Giants were not invariably the enemy – many gods had affairs with or even married giantesses, or were descended from them – but more often than not dealing with them involved the crashing down of Thor's hammer, which could both punish and protect gods and ordinary mortals.

Odin

Odin was the most complex of the Northern Gods. Although known as 'Allfather', he was not a benevolent father god, but a powerful and fickle character, as treacherous as he could be generous. He was respected and worshipped – particularly by kings and nobles – but was not entirely to be trusted.

Odin, head of the Northern pantheon, was a terrifying figure. The awesome god of magic, war and wisdom, he was invoked for victory in battle, but could be faithless and was often accused of awarding triumph unjustly. Bloody sacrifices would sometimes be necessary to appease him.

Odin's mastery of magic was legendary. He could change his shape at will, or be transported instantly to distant lands while his body lay as if asleep. His magical abilities made him a formidable opponent; with mere words he could calm or stir up the sea, extinguish fires or change the winds.

Odin went to great lengths to acquire magical learning. He had only one eye, as he had pledged the other as payment for a drink from the well of Mimir, which gave inspiration and knowledge of the future. Another story relates how Odin gained this wisdom and information from the decapitated head of Mimir, the wisest of the Aesir, which he kept after it was cut off by the Vanir, a group of fertility gods. Odin preserved the head with herbs and chanted incantations over it, making it able to speak to him.

While he was particularly favoured by kings, Odin was also god of poetry, which perhaps explains the prominence the poetic sources accord him. It was said that Odin himself spoke only in poetry and that poetic inspiration was his gift. Odin was also god of the dead, particularly of those who died in certain ways. Casualties of battle, especially those killed by the spear – a weapon sacred to Odin – were seen as an offering to him, and fallen enemies could also be dedicated to him. Hanged men were also sacred to Odin; he could bring them back to life. Hanging and gashing with a spear were sacrificial rites associated with Odin, and a mysterious and fascinating myth concerning the god tells of his own self-sacrifice, hanging on the World Tree for nine nights without food or water, slashed with a spear and "given to Odin, myself to myself", to win the sacred runes, source of wisdom and magical lore.

Odin owned two particular treasures that had been forged by dwarfs: his mighty, unstoppable spear, Gungnir, and a gold arm-ring, Draupnir, from which eight other rings of equal weight and value would drip every ninth night. Odin also possessed an extraordinary horse named Sleipnir, which had eight legs and was the fastest of horses, able to carry Odin on his errands through the sky and over the sea.

Odin was regularly portrayed walking amongst men as a sinister, one-eyed old man, cloaked and wearing a broad-brimmed hat or hood. He was married to Frigga, queen of the gods and goddesses, who shared with him the ability to foresee the future, although she did not make pronouncements. Frigga was beautiful, gracious, stately and possessed of deep wisdom. She was highly respected, both in Northern mythology and by the population, and as a maternal figure was invoked by women during childbirth and by those wishing to conceive.

Thor the Thunder God

The best-loved of the Northern gods, the mighty figure of Thor, strode the cosmos, fighting the forces of evil: giants and trolls. He was the protector of Asgard and the gods could always call upon him if they were in trouble – as could mankind – and many relied on him.

Ordinary people put their trust in Thor, for Thor's concerns were with justice, order and the protection of gods and men. Ancient inscriptions on rune stones, such as 'may Thor bless these runes' or 'may Thor bless this memorial', or sometimes just 'may Thor bless' are common. Sometimes Thor's protection was invoked merely with a carving of a hammer. Thor's hammer as a symbol of protection is also seen in miniature version in the form of little hammers of silver or other metals which were placed in graves alongside the buried bodies.

Thor's mighty strength excelled that of all other gods. He was huge, with red hair and beard and red eyebrows that sank down over his face when he was angry. Thunder was thought to be the sound of Thor's chariot driving across the sky, and his fierce, red, flashing eyes befitted the god of thunder and lightning. Thor also had an enormous appetite, regularly devouring more than a whole ox at one sitting.

Thor's most important possession was his hammer, Miolnir, which could never miss its mark, whether raised up or thrown, and would always return to Thor's hand. With this weapon Thor kept the forces of evil at bay, protecting the gods and mankind. Furthermore, Miolnir held the power to sanctify and could be raised for the purpose of blessing. As well as Miolnir, Thor owned a belt of strength which doubled his already formidable might when buckled on, and a pair of iron gloves, without which he could not wield Miolnir.

Thor's main occupation was destroying giants, a constant threat to the worlds of gods and men. Thor actively sought them out, with the express intention of their annihilation, and seldom hesitated to raise his hammer when he encountered one. If any gods were threatened, Thor would instantly appear. Famous stories tell how Thor defeated the giant Hrungnir, strongest of all giants, in a duel; and how he destroyed the giant Geirrod, in spite of Geirrod's attempts to attack him. The situation was not always clear-cut, however. Giants were occasionally helpful – although Geirrod and his two daughters made many attempts to defeat Thor, another giantess, Grid, chose to forewarn Thor and lent him a staff and some iron gloves. Thor even had two sons, Modi and Magni, with a giantess, Jarnsaxa. Nevertheless, Giants were usually Thor's hostile adversaries.

Many tales of Thor are affectionately humorous, attesting to the fondness the populace had for him. When Thor's hammer was stolen by a giant demanding Freyia as his wife, Thor, to his horror, had to agree to be dressed up as the bride and delivered to the giant in order to destroy the giant and thus reclaim his hammer. Gentle humour is also evident in the tale of Thor's encounter with a magical giant king, Utgard-Loki. Thor's brute strength is not enough when pitted against Utgard-Loki's magical wiles, but even so the giants have to retain a healthy respect for Thor for trying.

Thor's ultimate adversary at Ragnarok – which according to the myths is yet to happen – will not be a giant, but the World Serpent, and one myth (*see* 'Thor's Fishing', page 89) tells of an encounter before this final one.

Loki the Trickster

One of the most extraordinary characters in Northern mythology, the strange figure of Loki was not a god, yet he was ranked among the Aesir, and was the blood brother of their chief Odin. There is no evidence that Loki was worshipped as a god, but he appears to be an essential character within the mythological kinship. His presence is pivotal to many of the mythical events. He was both the constant companion and great friend of the gods, and at the same time an evil influence and a deadly enemy.

Loki was handsome, witty and charming, but was also malicious and sly. He was descended from giants – his father was the giant Farbauti – but his wife Sigyn was a goddess, and they had two sons, Narfi and Vali. Loki plays a crucial role in Northern myth, although he is not one of the gods. He takes part in most of the gods' escapades and it is his presence that causes many of the events in the myths to happen.

Loki was full of mischief, and often caused the gods great trouble with his tricks, but equally as often it was Loki's artfulness that saved them again. Loki caused the theft of Idunn's apples, yet also reversed the disaster. To keep from ageing, the gods had to eat golden apples guarded by the goddess Idunn. At the behest of a giant, Loki lured Idunn out of Asgard, where the giant abducted the goddess together with her apples. Without the apples the gods quickly grew old and grey, but Loki found Idunn and brought her home, and enabled the Aesir to kill the pursuing giant.

Loki could take on the shapes of animals, birds and, in particular, insects, reflecting his insidious nature. He became a fly when trying to distract dwarfs from their work during the making of Thor's hammer and a flea in an attempt to steal the Necklace of the Brisings from Freyia. He used the form of a fly to enter Freyia's house and when he found Freyia asleep with the clasp of the necklace beneath her, Loki became a flea and bit the goddess. She turned over and Loki stole the necklace.

The conflict between Loki and the gods was serious and far-reaching, however. When Loki brings about the death of Balder, most beloved of the gods, his true malevolence shows through, and the gods no longer tolerate him. They shackle him until Ragnarok, when he will break free and is destined to show his true colours – fighting on the side of the giants.

Loki also produced three monstrous children with a giantess, Angrboda: Jormungand, the World Serpent; Hel, guardian of the realm of the dead, and a huge wolf, Fenrir. These three terrifying creatures all played significant roles in the myths and it was believed the wolf and World Serpent would ultimately destroy Odin and Thor at Ragnarok.

The gods were all afraid when they discovered Loki's three children were being brought up in Jotunheim (Giantland). Odin had to decide their fate and sent gods to bring the monsters before him. He threw the serpent into the ocean, where it grew until it encircled the world, biting on its tail. Hel, Loki's hideous half-dead, half-alive daughter, Odin cast into Niflheim, the land of the dead, charging her with giving food and lodgings to all those sent to her – those who died of sickness or old age. The wolf, Fenrir, the Aesir decided to restrain in Asgard, to keep an eye on it, though only the god Tyr was brave enough to tend it.

The Fertility Deities

In the constant struggle with difficult terrain and climate there was much cause in Northern mythology to rely heavily on fertility deities. A group of gods known as the Vanir were especially associated with fertility, peace and prosperity. The population looked to these gods for bountiful harvests, plentiful fish, wealth, increase and peace.

The most prominent of the Vanir were the sea god Niord and his twin children, Frey and Freyia. These were the offspring of Niord's union with his sister. She is not named, but such unions were apparently permitted amongst the Vanir. When Niord and his children later came to live amongst the Aesir, Niord married a giantess, Skadi, in a myth that has been seen as the joining of a fertility deity with the cold and dark of winter represented by Skadi, who lived high up in the mountains, wore skis or snowshoes and was known as the ski goddess.

Niord was worshipped in his own right, but relatively little information about him has survived. Best known as god of the sea, he was invoked for sea travel and success in fishing as he controlled the bounty of the sea and the wind and waves. Like the other Vanir, Niord was closely associated with wealth. It was thought he could grant land and possessions to any who prayed to him for them, and a rich man was said to be 'as rich as Niord'.

Frey, Niord's son, was the principal god of fertility and plenty. A radiant god of sunshine and increase, Frey ruled the Sun and the rain, holding sway over the harvests. Marriages were also occasions to invoke Frey, as he was not only responsible for increase in the produce of the earth, but for human increase too – an important aspect of fertility gods. Furthermore, Frey was considered to be the bringer of peace. Weapons were banned in his temples and the shedding of blood or sheltering of outlaws in his sacred places was taboo. Peace and fertility appear to have been closely linked in the Northern psyche: sacrifices were often made for fruitfulness and peace together, and the fertility gods had special responsibilities regarding peace.

Frey owned two treasures made by dwarfs. The first was Skidbladnir, a ship which was large enough to hold all the gods, yet could be folded up and kept in a pouch when not in use. It would always have a fair wind when launched and so could travel anywhere at will. The other was a golden boar, Gullinbursti (golden bristles), which travelled through the air and over the sea faster than any horse and would light up its surroundings, however dark, with the light shed from its bristles.

Famous myths tell of both Frey and Niord's marriages. Frey's union is the productive relationship between a fertility god and the earth. Frey saw the beautiful Gerda, who had giantess blood on her mother's side and whose name is related to 'gard' (field), from afar and fell hopelessly in love. Gerda was in the clutches of the giants, representing winter, but eventually Frey's servant Skirnir, 'the shining one', personifying the Sun, brought them together.

Niord's marriage was not so successful, demonstrating the incompatibility of a fertility god and the barren cold of winter. Niord and the giantess Skadi tried to live alternately for nine nights in her mountain home, and nine nights at Niord's home, Noatun, (enclosure of ships, harbour), but eventually had to admit irreconcilable differences, just as winter must give way to fertile spring.

Ragnarok – the End of the World

The concept of inescapable fate informs all Northern mythology: destiny is preordained and unavoidable. It culminates in Ragnarok, the expected destruction of the world, of which all the details were known. This apocalypse must be faced, but will not be the end of everything; afterwards a new world will begin.

For the gods, and perhaps for the population as well, Ragnarok was both a cataclysmic event in the future and, because all the elements were understood and anticipated, something they lived with in the present.

The gods could not stop Ragnarok – it had to come to pass as prophesied – and their spirited bravery in the face of inevitable annihilation reflects the Northern sensibility concerning pre-destiny. Fate was a fact of life, something that could not be avoided or changed. Even one's death was already decreed and must be faced with calm and brave acceptance. To laugh in the face of death was one of the greatest achievements a Northern warrior could attain, and such a warrior would be long remembered by his peers.

Ragnarok will be preceded by fierce battles raging throughout the world for three years. Brothers will kill each other and no ties of kinship will prevent slaughter. Next a bitter winter, Fimbul-winter, will last for another three years with no summer in between. The sky will darken and the sun will not shine. The wolf chasing the sun will finally swallow it and the other wolf will catch the moon. A terrible earthquake will uproot all trees and bring the mountains crashing to the ground. All fetters and bonds will break. Fenrir, the huge wolf, will become free, and so will Loki. The World Serpent, Jormungand, will fly into a giant rage and come up onto the shore, causing the ocean to surge over the land.

A ship made from dead men's fingernails, Naglfar, will ride the wild ocean, filled with giants, with Loki at the helm. Fenrir will advance with his mouth gaping, one jaw against the sky and the other against the earth, his eyes and nostrils spouting flames. Jormungand, spitting poison, will bespatter the sky and the sea. The sky will open and from it will ride Muspell's sons, led by Surt, the fire-flinging guardian of Muspell, holding aloft his flaming sword, surrounded by burning fire. They will all advance to the plain, Vigrid, where the last battle will take place.

Sensing Ragnarok's approach, the watchman of the gods, Heimdall, will then stand up and blow mightily on Gjallarhorn, the horn used to awaken all the gods and alert them to danger, so that they can hold counsel together. The ash Yggdrasil will shake – and all heaven and earth will be terrified. The gods will arm themselves and, with the Einherjar, will advance onto the plain. Odin will ride in front brandishing his spear, Gungnir, and attack Fenrir. Thor will be unable to help him for he must fight the World Serpent. He will vanquish it, but will step away only nine paces before succumbing to the poison it will spit at him. Fenrir will swallow Odin whole. After a fierce fight, Frey will succumb to Surt, and Loki and Heimdall will slay each other.

Then Surt will fling fire over the whole earth. Flames, smoke and steam will shoot up from the burning earth to the firmament. The sky will turn black and the stars will disappear. The earth will sink down into the engulfing sea.

Gods & Goddesses of Ancient Egypt

Solar Myths

With the union of Upper and Lower Egypt under the pharaonic kingship in about 3100 BC, myths focused on the king as a solar being began to circulate. The most complex and enduring of these myths concerned Osiris, supposedly first of the pharaohs and an incarnation of the sun god Amen-Ra.

The principal centre of sun-god worship for Ra throughout Egypt's ancient history was at Anu (or Annu), called Heliopolis ('city of the sun') by the Greeks, and now a suburb of modern Cairo. He was depicted with the body of a man and the head of a hawk, the latter symbolizing height in the sky. In his nocturnal post-mortem journey through the watery afterworld, the god-king, Ra-as-sun, was constantly menaced by the primordial serpent Apep, the emblem of chaos, who was most powerful at the darkest hour of night. It was then the special duty of the sun god's priests to recite a long liturgy of curses detailing Apep's dismemberment and destruction by fire.

From early in the dynastic period the pharaoh was held to be a child of the deified sun. From time to time this solar blood-line was renewed by the god assuming the form of the reigning pharaoh, visiting the queen in her bedchamber and fathering her son. After the child's birth it was ritually presented to Ra in his temple, when the god was supposed to accept and acknowledge his divine offspring.

The long-dominant priesthood of Ra, a name meaning 'sole creator', displayed great ingenuity and political acumen in preserving and incorporating the older cults of Egypt in their rituals, insisting only that their priests acknowledge the overall sovereignty of the sun god. Thus Osiris and Isis, the great goddess of the Nile, became absorbed into the pantheon of pharaonic Egypt. However, the more ancient myth of the dying and reborn Osiris proved eventually to exercise most appeal to the Egyptian imagination. This was because the powers of Osiris as king of the afterworld included the ability to confer immortality on the souls of deceased humans. During the Later Dynastic Period the Osiris cult took on many of the attributes of the sun god. His perennial appeal could also relate to the fact that his myth reaches back to the prehistoric, pre-dynastic Egyptian Osirian myth-ritual of the divine king, whose sacrificial death and reincarnation in his young successor were held to guarantee the prosperity of the land and people.

Osiris, God of Death and Rebirth

Although Egyptians held that Osiris was the first to occupy the throne of the Pharaohs, his cult seems to have already existed in pre-dynastic times, particularly associated with the town of Abydos on the upper Nile. Later his identity became fused with that of the sun god Ra into a being known as Amen-Ra.

The many myths focused on the person of Osiris, the perpetually dying and reborn god-king, can be thought of as a collective meditation through five millennia of Egyptian history and prehistory on the theme of continuity through change and the pervasive patterns of cyclicity in human and cosmic existence. The most spectacular and most frequently recurrent of these cycles is the daily progress of the sun through the heavens, its dramatic disappearance at sunset and no less dramatic reappearance at dawn. Egyptian mythical thought saw this diurnal sequence of events as the ever-repeated birth, middle age (his highest point in the sky, at noon) and eventual death of the sun god. To achieve rebirth at the beginning of the next day, Ra travelled through the other world where Osiris had established himself as judge and king.

Thoth the Intellectual God

Among the cluster of divinities brought into being at the time of Creation, the god Thoth, together with his consort the goddess Ma'at, was particularly involved in the establishment and maintenance of order in heaven and earth. The duties of Thoth went much further than these matters, since he was responsible for the mathematical calculations behind the regulation of the cosmos. It was he who invented all the arts and sciences known to humankind; he was 'the scribe of the gods' and 'the lord of books'. Thoth measured and regulated the times and the seasons, in which role he was known as the moon god. He is also described as 'the tongue and the heart' of Ra the sun god himself. Some later Greek texts portray Thoth as the animator of human speech, giving him a nature similar to that of Plato's Logos. At its simplest, the term Logos means 'word', though in Greek philosophy logos encapsulated a general notion of reasoning or intellectual thought, expressed through reading and writing. In Greek philosophy reason was considered to be one of the guiding principles of the universe. Logos, therefore, embodies this principle as well as the expression of metaphysical knowledge. The ancient Greeks identified Thoth with their own Hermes, describing the Egyptian god as the inventor of astrology and astronomy, mathematics and geography, medicine and botany.

In hieroglyphic texts Thoth is sometimes portrayed as an ibis, sometimes as a kind of ape. The main centre of his cult was at Khemenu, or Hermopolis as the Greeks called it.

Mighty Goddesses: Isis

There were many powerful goddesses in the Egyptian pantheon, some of them fearsome, like Neith the goddess of hunting and war, and Sekhmet, the solar deity with the head of a lioness, who was associated with smallpox and other contagious diseases. The greatest of them all, however, was Isis, the consort of Osiris.

One of the most interesting myths about Isis tells how she tricked the sun god Ra into revealing to her his secret name, and thus the source of his power. Apparently, the goddess was ambitious to become the equal of Ra in his mastery of heaven and earth. At this time Ra had become old, and dribbled on the ground. Isis collected some of his spittle and made a venomous serpent out of it, which she laid in Ra's path so that when the sun god passed that way, he was fatally bitten. She consented to use her healing words of power to expel the poison from Ra's body and allow him to live, but only after he had told Isis his secret name. The story implies that Isis did indeed realize her ambition to become the sun god's equal.

Hathor, the Great Cosmic Mother

Another goddess who shared many of the powers and attributes of Isis was Hathor, 'the Egyptian Venus', patroness of lovers. She also blessed singers, dancers and artists. Like Neith – mother of Isis, Horus and Osiris, and guardian goddess of men and gods – Hathor was already known in the pre-pharaonic period, when she was worshipped in the form of a cow. She was also identified with the sky and recognized as the principal female counterpart of Ra; as such, Hathor was the Great Cosmic Mother, a divinity with roots in the Palaeolithic era. Her most famous temple was at Dendara, south of Abydos.

The loving Hathor contrasted with the ferocious Sekhmet, who was sent by the gods to destroy humankind when they began to plot against the aged Ra. After many had died, the sun god decided to spare the rest. To distract Sekhmet from her orgy of slaughter, Ra ordered the high priest at Heliopolis to make a vast quantity of beer and to stain it red. When Sekhmet saw it she lapped it up, thinking it was blood, and became so drunk she forgot her murderous mission, and was transformed into the beautiful and pacific Hathor.

Eventually, however, it was the fame of Isis that became supreme. After Alexander's conquest of Egypt in 332 BC and its subsequent occupation by Rome, the cult of Isis and her infant son Horus spread through the Empire, including France, Britain and Germany. The image of the nurturing mother and the divine child was eventually mirrored in popular imagination with the image of the Virgin Mary and the infant Jesus.

Foreign Influences

Another powerful female deity in dynastic Egypt was Bastet, the goddess of love, sex and fertility, who was usually depicted with a cat's head, and earlier in the pre-dynastic era with the head of a lioness.

The influence of Near Eastern culture on Egyptian society and culture is evident in a myth that has Seth, the divine 'destroyer of boundaries' and embodiment of chaos, being given two foreign goddesses in compensation for ceding his right to the throne of Egypt to Horus, son of Isis and Osiris. The goddesses were Anat, sister and consort of the Canaanite deity Baal, and Astarte (Ishtar), the great Semitic goddess.

Female Power

Neith could well be the oldest of all the Egyptian deities, because images of this goddess of hunting and war, whose insignia was a bow, two arrows and a shield, have been found at the major site of pre-dynastic settlement at Abydos, suggesting that her cult was introduced by the aboriginal Palaeolithic immigrants from the Sahara. Later, Neith's main cultic centre was in the Delta city of Sais.

Archaeological work at the huge prehistoric burial ground near Abydos has also unearthed a remarkable and aesthetically powerful representation of a triumphant female figure who could also be Neith or perhaps a more generalized image of the Earth Mother. Examination of the graves has shown that the largest and most richly furnished were those of females, suggesting women had high status during this prehistoric period, contrasting with their political obscurity during the pharaonic era. Royal women were the exceptions to this rule in the pharaonic era, and included the historically famous Nefertiti, the fourteenth-century-BC consort of Pharaoh Akhenaten, and Cleopatra (70–31 BC). Nevertheless, an Egyptian, married, commoner woman of the pharaonic era was substantially better off than, for example, her counterpart in nineteenth-century England, in so far as she could own property and initiate divorce.

Babylonian Gods & Monsters

Babylon became the centre of the ancient Mesopotamian kingdom of Babylonia. The earliest Babylonian religious ideas – that is, subsequent to the entrance of that people into the country watered by the Tigris and Euphrates – were undoubtedly coloured by those of the non-Semitic Sumerians whom they found in the country. They adopted the alphabet of that race, and this affords strong presumptive evidence that the immigrant Semites, as an unlettered people, would naturally accept much if not all of the religion of the more cultured folk whom they found in possession of the soil.

There is no necessity in this place to outline the nature of animistic belief at any length – it is sufficient to state here succinctly that animism is a condition of thought or belief in which man considers everything in the universe along with himself to be the possessor of 'soul', 'spirit', or at least volition. Thus, the wind, water, animals, the heavenly bodies, all live, move, and have their being, and because of his fear of or admiration for them, man placates or adores them until at length he almost unconsciously exalts them into a condition of godhead. Have we any reason to think that the ancient Semites of Babylonia regarded the universe as peopled by gods or godlings of such a type? The proofs that they did so are not a few.

Spirits and Gods

Spirits swarmed in ancient Babylonia. And here it is important to note that the determinative or symbolic written sign for 'spirit' is the same as that for 'god'. Thus the god and the spirit must in Babylonia have had a common descent.

The manner in which we can distinguish between a god and a spirit, however, is simple. Lists of the 'official' gods are provided in the historical texts, whereas spirits and demons are not included therein. But this is not to say that no attempt had been made to systematize the belief in spirits in Babylonia, for just as the great gods of the universe were apportioned their several offices, so were the spirits allotted almost exactly similar powers. Thus the *Annunaki* were perhaps regarded as the spirits of earth and the *Igigi* as spirits of heaven. So, at least, are they designated in an inscription of Rammannirari I. The grouping evidently survived from animistic times, when perhaps the spirits which are embraced in these two classes were the only 'gods' of the Babylonians or Sumerians, and from whose ranks some of the great gods of future times may have been evolved. In any case they belong to a very early period in the Babylonian religion and play no unimportant part in it almost to the end. The god Anu, the most ancient of the Babylonian deities, was regarded as the father of both companies, but other gods make use of their services. They do not appear to be well disposed to humanity. The Assyrian kings were wont to invoke them when they desired to inculcate a fear of their majesty in the people, and from this it may be inferred that they were objects of peculiar fear to the lower orders of the population – for the people often cling to the elder cults and the elder pantheons despite the innovations of ecclesiastical politicians, or the religious eccentricities of kings. There can, however, be no doubt as to the truly animistic character of early Babylonian religion. Thus in the early inscriptions one reads of the spirits of various kinds of diseases, the spirit of the south wind, the spirits of the mist, and so forth. The *bit-ili* or sacred stones marking the residence of a god were probably a link between the fetish and the idol, remaining even after the fully developed idol had been evolved.

Totemism in Babylonian Religion

Signs of totemism are not wanting in the Babylonian as in other religious systems. Many of the gods are pictured as riding upon the backs of certain animals, an almost certain indication that at one time they had themselves possessed the form of the animal they bestrode.

Religious conservatism would probably not tolerate the immediate abolition of the totem-shape, so this means was taken of gradually 'shelving' it. But some gods retained animal form until comparatively late times. Thus the sun-god of Kis had the form of an eagle, and we find that Ishtar took as lovers a horse, an eagle, and a lion – surely gods who were represented in equine, aquiline, and leonine forms. The fish-form of Oannes, the god of wisdom, is certainly a relic of totemism. Some of the old ideographic representations of the names of the gods are eloquent of a totemic connection. Thus the name of Ea, the god of the deep, is expressed by an ideograph which signifies 'antelope'. Ea is spoken of as 'the antelope of the deep', 'the lusty antelope', and so forth. He was also, as a water-god, connected with the serpent, a universal symbol of the flowing stream. The strange god Uz, probably an Akkadian survival, was worshipped under the form of a goat. The sun-god of Nippur, Adar, was connected with the pig, and was called 'lord of the swine'. Merodach may have been a bull-god. In early astronomical literature we find him alluded to as 'the bull of light'. The storm-god Zu, as is seen by his myth, retained his bird-like form. Another name of the storm-bird was Lugalbanda, patron god of the city of Marad, near Sippara. Like Prometheus – also once a bird-god, as is proved by many analogous myths – he stole the sacred fire from heaven for the service and mental illumination of man.

The Great Gods

In the phase in which it becomes first known to us, Babylonian religion is neither Semitic nor Akkadian, but Semitic-Akkadian: that is, the elements of both religious forms are so intermingled in it that they cannot be distinguished one from another; but very little that is trustworthy can be advanced concerning this shadowy time. Each petty state (and these were numerous in early Babylonia) possessed its own tutelar deity, and he again had command over a number of lesser gods. When all those pantheons were added together, as was the case in later days, they afforded the spectacle of perhaps the largest assembly of gods known to any religion.

The most outstanding of these tribal divinities, as they might justly be called, were Merodach, who was worshipped at Babylon; Shamash, who was adored at Sippar; Sin, the moon-god, who ruled at Ur; Anu, who held sway over Erech and Der; Ea, the Oannes of legend, whose city was Eridu; Bel, who ruled at Nippur, or Niffur; Nergal of Cuthah; and Ishtar, who was goddess of Nineveh. The peoples of the several provinces identified their prominent gods one with another, and indeed when Assyria rose to rivalry with Babylonia, its chief divinity, Asshur, was naturally identified with Merodach.

We will see how Merodach gained the lordship of heaven. The rise of this god to power was comparatively recent. Prior to the days of Hammurabi (the all-conquering sixth king of the First Babylonian Dynasty, who reigned from 1792 BC to 1750 BC) a rather different pantheon from that described in later inscriptions held sway. In those more primitive days the principal gods appear to have been Bel or En-lil, Belit or Nin-lil his queen, Nin-girsu, Ea, Nergal, Shamash, Sin, Anu, and other lesser divinities. There is indeed a sharp distinction between the pre- and post-Hammurabic types of religion. Attempts had been made to form a pantheon before Hammurabi's day, but his exaltation of Merodach, the patron of Babylon, to the head of the Babylonian pantheon was destined to destroy these. A glance at the condition of the great gods before the days of Hammurabi will assist us to understand their later developments.

Mythological Monsters and Animals

Tiawath was not the only monster known to Babylonian mythology. But she is sometimes likened to or confounded with the serpent of darkness with which she had originally no connection whatever.

This being was, however, like Tiawath, the offspring of the great deep and the enemy of the divine powers. We are told in the second verse of Genesis that "the earth was without form and void, and darkness was upon the face of the deep," and therefore resembling the abyss of Babylonian myth. We are also informed that the serpent was esteemed as "more subtle than other beast of the field," and this, it has been pointed out by Professor Sayce, was probably because it was associated by the author or authors of Genesis with Ea, the god of waters and of wisdom. To Babylonian geographers as to the Greeks, the ocean was a coiling, snake-like thing, which was often alluded to as the great serpent, and this soon came to be considered as the source of all evil and misfortune. The ancients, and especially the ancient Semites, with the exception of the Phoenicians, appear to have regarded it with dread and loathing. The serpent appears to have been called Aibu, 'the enemy'. We can see how the serpent of darkness, the offspring of chaos and confusion, became also the Hebrew symbol for mischief. He was first the source of physical and next the source of moral evil.

Oher animals and monsters had their place in Babylonian cult, including the gazelle, who represented Ea, and the goat, embodied in the god Uz. Adar, the sun-god of Nippur, was in the same manner connected with the pig, which may have been the totem of the city he ruled over; and many other gods had attendant animals or birds, like the sun-god of Kis, whose symbol was the eagle.

Gilgamesh

We must also not forget that hero of Babylonian myth, Gilgamesh. The Gilgamesh epic ranks with the Babylonian myth of creation as one of the greatest literary productions of ancient Babylonia. The main element in its composition is a conglomeration of mythic matter, drawn from various sources, with perhaps a substratum of historic fact, the whole being woven into a continuous narrative around the central figure of Gilgamesh, prince of Erech. It is not possible at present to fix the date when the epic was first written. Our knowledge of it is gleaned chiefly from mutilated fragments belonging to the library of Assur-bani-pal, but from internal and other evidence we gather that some at least of the traditions embodied in the epic are of much greater antiquity than his reign.

The epic, which centres round the ancient city of Erech, relates the adventures of a half-human, half-divine hero, Gilgamesh by name, who is king over Erech. Two other characters figure prominently in the narrative – Eabani, who evidently typifies primitive man (but also, according to certain authorities, a form of the sun-god, even as Gilgamesh himself), and Ut-Napishtim, the hero of the Babylonian deluge myth. Each of the three would seem to have been originally the hero of a separate group of traditions which in time became incorporated, more or less naturally, with the other two.

Gilgamesh may have been at one time a real personage, though nothing is known of him historically. Possibly the exploits of some ancient king of Erech furnished a basis for the narrative. His mythological character is more easily established. In this regard he is the personification of the sun. He represents, in fact, the fusion of a great national hero with a mythical being. Throughout the epic there are indications that Gilgamesh is partly divine by nature, though nothing specific is said on that head. His identity with the solar god is veiled in the popular narrative, but it is evident that he has some connection with the god Shamash, to whom he pays his devotions and who acts as his patron and protector.

Mesoamerican Gods and the Spirit World

In Mesoamerica (the historical lands of the Olmecs, Toltecs, Maya and Aztecs among others), gods and myths emerged from an Amerindian worldview, reflecting a natural philosophy where ideas concerning life and death were linked symbolically to the earth, sky and sea in a grand cosmic scheme. As civilization developed, ancient spirits became powerful deities, controlling every aspect of sacred and secular life.

In Mesoamerican worldview, the earth was sacred, the sea the 'mother of fertility' and the sky an untouchable realm of gods and spirits whose influence reached down to affect all earthly life. This was a universe ruled by cyclical time, where myth was a living reality and everyday life punctuated by ceremonies which recapitulated the legendary events of the past. In pre-Columbian times, and still today, the rhythms of nature and human life-cycles were united with social, economic and political life, and every part of the natural world was infused with spiritual force. The shimmer of lakes and rivers, the lustrous sheen of jade and pearls, the iridescence of bird feathers and the crimson glow of human blood, were manifestations of the fertilizing cosmic power that permeated all existence. Throughout Mesoamerica, gods were deifications of natural phenomena – sun, moon, rain and wind – and intimately associated with human concerns of birth, death, fertility and war.

The Nature of Gods

At the heart of the Mesoamerican life was the symbolic equation of blood-for-water. Humans offered their blood to the gods and the gods reciprocated by forestalling drought, frost and, crucially, by sending rain to the earth to fertilize the crops. The daily worship of ambivalent but all-powerful deities was essential to keep the world in motion and the universe in balance. Exemplifying the uneasy relationship between Mesoamerican peoples and their deities was the supreme Aztec deity Tezcatlipoca, Lord of the Smoking Mirror. He was patron of royalty and warriors, master of human fate and inventor of human sacrifice through which he could be revered. Capricious by nature, cruel and generous by turns, he watched the world through his magical obsidian mirror, seeing into the very thoughts of his subjects. The Aztecs regarded themselves as his slaves, and their emperor as a living manifestation of the god. Equally bloodthirsty was Huitzilopochtli (Hummingbird of the South), the Aztec war and sun god, often depicted carrying his serpent-shaped spear-thrower. His association with war and death is reflected in his name, as hummingbirds were the souls of fallen warriors who accompanied their patron's solar image as it journeyed across the sky. Where these two gods sanctified the shedding of human blood, other Aztec deities were concerned with water and fertility.

Chief among these was Tlaloc, an ancient rain deity, worshipped throughout Mesoamerica under different names, such as Cociyo amongst the Zapotecs, and Chaak amongst the Maya. In Aztec belief, Tlaloc was associated with mountains where rain clouds gathered and mists lingered, and where young children were sacrificed to his cult – their tears an augury of the coming rains. So influential was Tlaloc that the lush and brilliantly coloured Aztec paradise or heaven was called Tlalocan. The god's consort was Chalchiuhtlicue (She of the Jade Skirt) who summoned hurricanes and was associated with the breaking waters which precede childbirth. Quetzalcoatl, Feathered Serpent, was also an ancient deity whose imagery is found in Olmec art and at Teotihuacán. During post-Classic times, the Maya knew Quetzalcoatl as Kukulkan (also Feathered Serpent), and the Aztec regarded him as a wind god, who announced the rains.

African Mythology

No real unified mythology exists in Africa – the migration of its peoples, the political fragmentation, and the sheer size of the continent have resulted in a huge diversity of lifestyles and traditions. Literally thousands of completely different languages are spoken, 2,000 in West Africa alone between the Senegal River and the headwaters of the Congo River. A complete collection of all myths of the African peoples would fill countless volumes, even if we were to ignore the fact that the collection is being added to all the time by modern-day enthusiasts.

To give a useful summary of the main characteristics of African mythology is therefore an extremely difficult task but, broadly speaking, a number of beliefs, ideas and themes are shared by African peoples, embellished by a creative spirit unique to a tribe, village or region. Nearly every tribe has its own set of cosmological myths – tales which attempt to explore the origin of the universe, the unseen forces of nature, the existence of God or a supreme being, the creation of mankind and the coming of mortality. Other stories, detailing the outrageous adventures and anti-social behaviour of one or another trickster figure are also common to nearly every tribe. Moral stories abound and animal fables, in particular, are some of the most popular of all African tales. But here we will outline a little about some key African mythological elements, gods, beings and monsters.

Supreme God

Despite its rich diversity, many African myths contain related themes, including gods and the origin of the world and humans. Most peoples in tropical and southern Africa share the hazy notion of a supreme sky god who originally lived on earth, but moved up to the sky by means of a spider's thread when humans started misbehaving. Earth and water are invariably goddesses. For the Yoruba, Ile is the goddess of earth and mother of all creatures; Yemoja is the goddess of water – her messengers are crocodile and hippopotamus and her daughter Aje is goddess of the Niger river from which Nigeria takes its name.

The Great Serpent

Given the prevalence of dangerous snakes in many parts of Africa, it is hardly surprising that several peoples talk of creation in terms of a huge serpent, usually a python, out of whose body the world and all creatures came. In northern areas, the sky god first made the cosmic serpent, whose head is in the sky and whose tail is in underground waters. In central and southern regions, the primordial serpent Chinawezi is identified with the rainbow. Whatever shape God's intermediary took, it is common for God to create sky and earth first, then fire and water, thunder and lightning. After these elements, the supreme being made the first living beings: a human, an elephant, a snake and a cow. In other legends, the supreme god first sent rain, lightning, locusts and then twins. Twins are often referred to as the 'children of heaven' and in some parts thought lucky, in others very unlucky and in the past have even been killed.

First Man and Woman

A widespread belief among the Zulus is that the first man and woman burst out of a reed; others say from a tree, yet others from a hole in the ground to the west of Lake Nyasa in Malawi. Many peoples do not speculate on the creation. The Masai of Kenya and Tanzania have a story about a time when meat hung down from the sky for people to eat. When it moved out of reach, people built a bamboo tower to the sky. To their surprise, sky messengers came down with three gifts: a bow to shoot the new wild animals in the bush, a plough with which to till the land in the new seasons of wind, rain and sun and a three-stringed fiddle to sing to in their leisure time. Other tales talk of earth and sky being connected by a rope by which gods sent down cattle.

In other creation stories, the world passed through three ages. First was an ideal or golden age when gods, humans and animals lived in harmony in a sort of celestial nirvana. Then came the age of creation in which the supreme god separated sky and earth, with the latter intended to mirror the harmony of the former age, and humans formed in the gods' image. But it did not work out, for humans were fallible and caused destruction, so introducing death: the Ashanti say humans set fire to the bush, so killing each other. The third age is the modern age where gods and humans live separately and people have lost their divine virtue of immortality completely. Through their myths and rituals, people are constantly trying to recreate the long-lost golden age.

African Monsters

In African legend, tales of monstrous beings other than those symbolic of the origins of the world, rarely involve epic battles and creatures like those of Classical mythology. They are more likely to take the form of shapeshifting witches and sorcerers, or demons and creatures raised by those same. Sorcerers and witches are often evil and perform black magic out of a hatred for people. Their tools are the spirits they control and they can enslave people by causing their death, before reviving them as the living dead – zombies (from the Congo word *zombi*, meaning 'enslaved spirit'). They also make fetishes possessed by servant spirits which fly through the air and attack victims. Often a victim dies of fright merely by seeing such a monster approaching.

Witches can change into animals at night or have animals as their familiars, especially baboons, hyenas, leopards or owls, and they can be seen flying through the air at night with fire coming out of their backsides. Their aim is to devour human bodies, dead or alive. But they can also change others into animals to be at their service. Mostly they brew poison, put it in the victim's food and enslave his or her spirit.

Other Central African peoples regard the forest as being the other or spirit world inhabited by dwarf-demons or imps, the *elokos*, who feed off human flesh. Anyone entering their world must perform certain rituals. Sorcerers carve a fetish or piece of wood taken from the spirit world (which therefore possesses magical properties) and use it to kill their enemies. Every tree has its spirit, which survives in the wood even after it has been chopped down and made into a hut, drum or boat. Without the spirit's goodwill, the carved item will bring only bad luck. Among the Ashanti of Ghana, the forest spirits are called the *mnoatia* and the forest ogre, Sasabonsam, is a hairy giant with large blood-red eyes and enormous feet that trip up unwary travellers.

Animal Myths

Animals – sometimes monstrous, often not – play a key role in mythology – and not only in Africa. African slaves took their stories around the world, often as fables, and adapted them to their new environments. The Uncle Remus stories of America's southern states (Brer Rabbit was originally the hare; Brer Terrapin was originally the tortoise) came from West Africa, as did the Aunt Nancy (Kwaku Anansi) spider tales of the Caribbean, originally told by the Ashanti, Yoruba, lbo and Dahomey. It is believed that the Greek slave Aesop originally came from Ethiopia.

In the oldest versions of African myths, the characters are mostly animals, such as the serpent involved in the world's creation. At this stage they are deities of supernatural size and strength. Anansi the spider can climb up to the heavens to commune with Nyame, the sky god (Ashanti); Simba the lion is a potent god from whom several African chiefs traced their ancestry (such as Haile Selassie, the Lion of Judah). Similarly, some Zulu chiefs have claimed descent from the python. Some clans bow before a python and address it as "Your Majesty", offering it sacrifices of goats. In Mozambique there are traces of the worship of

Sangu, the hippopotamus, a goddess who rules an underwater realm of lush, flowering meadows; she protects pregnant women and has to be sacrificed to by fishermen.

In the northwestern regions (Mali, Guinea), the sky god Faro sent down the antelope to teach the Bambara people farming skills; hence the many wooden carvings of the sacred antelope. According to the Bushmen of the Kalahari Desert, the mantis stole fire from the ostrich and passed it on to humans. The mantis is also credited among the Khosians of southwest Africa of inventing language through which animals and humans can converse.

As myths evolved, animals became half-human, half-animal characters who can be either good or evil, depending on their whim or veneration. They can take either form and foster human children, often coupling with human beings. Such children display both human and animal characteristics, so they can catch prey and speak animal languages. The human offspring of lions are particularly gifted: they can hunt at night and they know the bushlore and power of putting a spell on game (since no animal dies without the gods willing it). Ordinary mortals fear such half-human offspring, for they are brave, fierce warriors possessing magic and charms. Women love lion-men, who often become great rulers. As for lion-women, they grow up to be irresistibly attractive to men, who fall in love with them; the men, however, can end up being eaten by their wives. Lions are so potent that even a lion's eyelash can give a woman power over her husband, so that she can have children merely by instructing his mind to do so.

Native American Mythology

Demographic Diversity

The 'Native Americans' were no more a single people than the indigenous inhabitants of Africa or Asia were. North America alone represented a rich mosaic of different peoples with distinctive cultures: from the hunting, fishing, farming Ojibwe of the forest country to the north of the Great Lakes, all the way to the scorching deserts of the Southwest, whose 'Pueblo' peoples included the Navajo, the Zuni, the Zia and the Hopi. Further to the south, the tribes of the Iroquois Confederacy had extended their influence from what is now the northeast of the United States, taking territories – and subsuming peoples – as far south as Tennessee. Not till comparatively recently did the Sioux leave the woods definitively for the open Plains of the Midwest. That specialized bison-hunting lifestyle with which they were to enter the historical record had been made possible by the advent not only of the horse (introduced by the Spanish) but of the modern rifle.

High Spirits

Despite the many differences, certain continuities can still be found in Native Americans' traditional beliefs and myths. Most, for example – despite an essentially 'animist' belief that divinity resided in a great many different animals, plants and geographical features – attributed a special authority to a single supreme being. Characterized variously as Great Spirit, Great Ruler or 'Master of Life', the first Christian missionaries would find him tantalizingly analogous to their idea of God.

Like all such supreme beings, perhaps, he tended towards abstraction. Figures further down the spiritual hierarchy were more vividly imagined. Like Atahensic, the sky goddess of Iroquois lore, associated with marriage, childbirth, beauty and love – all things 'feminine', in short. In legend, it was her fall from heaven that brought our world into being. His hard shell piled with cushioning earth brought up by the muskrat from the very bottom of the earthly ocean, the great turtle arrested her descent.

Life-Sized

Not only did the turtle buoy Atahensic up safely on impact: he sustained her in the weeks and months that followed, even as she gradually grew in weight. For it turned out that Atahensic had been pregnant when she fell. Two sons resulted: Hahgwehdihyu ('Good Mind') and Hahgwehdaetgah ('Bad Mind'). They battled each other in creating the earth, the former shaping light and life; the latter retaliating with darkness and with death.

Also counterpoising the abstraction of the supreme being are an array of demigods – like mortal humans but with extraordinary insight or special strength. Hahgwehdihyu and Hahgwehdaetgah may very clearly represent rival principles, but they're also vividly real and quasi-human figures.

Another such demigod is Michabo, who, in Algonquin myth, murdered his brother Chokanipok and made geographical features from his flesh and fashioned forests and vegetation from his entrails. In some stories he's a man, in others a hare or rabbit. Either way, he's a trickster and a shape-shifter – a reminder that in North American mythology magic is not so much about monstrous forms as about a process of (and talent for) transformation.

Heroes and Monsters on a Human Scale

Mostly, the mythology of North America's First Nations does not employ the extravagant exaggeration of many 'Old World' traditions. We look in vain for any well-populated Olympus; or for the exotically-imagined Hydra or Minotaur of the classical tradition (the template, of course, for Western ideas of 'myth'). Hence, for the Ojibwe, Mudjikiwis, son of the West Wind, has a special significance. But the 'Great Bear' he defeats in battle seems monstrous only in his size (if that ... the mythical accounts are sketchy even about this aspect). When Mudjikiwis kills and cuts him up, new black bears spring from his scattered carcase. It's heroic, but it's all imagined on a human scale. So it is with the 'Serpent-Men' of the Sioux and the 'Man-Fish' of Wisconsin's Shawano.

Celtic Mythology

The Celts were polytheistic. The names of over 200 gods have been recorded. It is likely that individual deities went under several titles, so there were probably fewer than this. The scene remains complex, however, and attempts to reduce the Celtic pantheon to a coherent system have met with varying degrees of success.

The Celts had gods for all of the important aspects of their lives: warfare, hunting, fertility, healing, good harvests and so on. Much of the difficulty in classifying them arises from the fact that very few were recognized universally. In much greater numbers were local, tribal and possibly family deities. Our knowledge of the Celtic pantheon is based on the interpretations of contemporary observers, later vernacular literature (mainly from Ireland and Wales) and archaeological finds.

Very little iconography in the form of wood or stone sculptures has survived from before the Roman conquests, although a vast amount of perishable material must have existed. The earliest archaeological evidence from this period is from Provence and Central Europe. At Roquepertuse and Holtzerlingen, Celtic deities were represented in human form as early as the sixth and fifth centuries BC. Roman influence witnessed the production of many more permanent representations of the gods; dedicatory inscriptions reveal a huge array of native god names.

Caesar identified Celtic gods with what he saw as their Roman equivalents, probably to render them more comprehensible to a Roman readership. He said of the Gauls that the god they revered the most was Mercury and, next to him, Apollo, Mars, Jupiter and Minerva. Lucan (AD 39–65), a famous Roman poet, named three Celtic deities: Teutates (god of the tribe), Taranis (thunder) and Esus (multi-skilled). Other commentators identify Teutates with Mercury, Esus with Mars and Taranis with Dispater (the all father). Inscriptions on altars and monuments found across the Roman Empire, however, identify Teutates with Mars, Esus with Mercury and Taranis with Jupiter.

It is to Christian monks that we owe the survival of the ancient oral traditions of the pagan Celts and a more lucid insight into the nature of their deities. Very little was committed to paper before the monks began writing down Irish tales in the sixth century AD. The earliest written Welsh material dates from the twelfth century. Informative though they might be, however, the stories are influenced by Romano-Christian thinking and no doubt the monks censored the worst excesses of heathenism.

Earth-bound Heroes and Monsters

Indeed, across the board, they demoted what had been gods and goddesses to a status that, while still supernatural, was emphatically less than godly. What in Irish tradition came to be called the Tuatha Dé Danann didn't have divinity as such. (In the story of 'The Quest of the Children of Tuirenn', we actually find them a subject people, conquered by invaders from the sea.) Even so, they were 'larger than life' in either magical powers or monstrous aspects and contributed a richly varied cast of characters to Celtic myth. Bloodthirsty giants; lake-dwelling 'worms' and sinister serpents; man-eating water-horses; multi-headed beasts .... Celtic legend boasts an impressive menagerie of monsters.

The stories are collected in sequences which follow the exploits of heroes, legendary kings and mythical characters from their unusual forms of conception and birth to their remarkable deaths. Along the way we learn of their expeditions to the otherworld, their loves and their battles. Many of the Irish legends are contained in three such collections. The first, known as the *Mythological Cycle* or *Book of Invasions*, records the imagined early history of Ireland. The second, the *Ulster Cycle*, tells of Cúchulainn, a hero with superhuman strength and magical powers. The third is the story of another hero, Finn mac Cumaill, his son Ossian and their warriors, the Fianna. This is known as the *Fenian Cycle*.

The pagan character of the mythology found in Irish literature is very clear. The Welsh tales, collected mainly in the *Mabinogion*, are much later (fourteenth century) and are contaminated more by time and changing literary fashions.

Complex Indian Gods

The mythology of India is as vast and varied as her myriad cultures, languages and beliefs, as diverse as her philosophy and religion. Indeed, more than almost any other nation, India has intertwined her religion, literature and philosophy in a comprehensive mythology that encompasses most of her history in its breadth and vision. In India there are many languages spoken, and many religions observed, but the largest of these religions is Hindu.

In *Hinduism*, W. O'Flaherty wrote: 'If myths are stories about the gods, it is difficult to find a Hindu story that is not mythical. "Here there are more gods than men," a puzzled European remarked on India centuries ago, and the line between gods and men in Hinduism is as vague and ephemeral as the cloudy trail of a sky-writer.... Gods in India are no better than men, merely more powerful. Indeed, their extraordinary powers allow them to indulge in vices on an extraordinary scale: divine power corrupts divinely.'

Indian gods are given their identities by their heritage, and their history. They form an extensive pantheon which has included and occasionally dropped names across the centuries, as the religious beliefs are expounded and transformed.

Gods of Creation

Most of the myths contained within the *Rig-Veda*, the ancient collection of Vedic Sanskrit hymns composed about 1400 BC, deal with creation – heaven and earth and what intervenes. The hymns were addressed to the Vedic gods, who included: Agni (fire), Indra (thunder), Surya (sun), Vayu (wind), Aditi (firmament), Varuna (rain and sea), Ushas (dawn), Prithivi (earth), The Ashvins (Castor and Pollux), Dyaus-piter (the father of light), Yama (death), Vritra (drought), Rudra (storm) and Maruts (whirlwinds).

The *Vedas* describe a number of creation myths. One typical concept is that of the universe coming into existence as a result of divine incest in which an unnamed father begets a daughter – perhaps symbolic of the sky and the earth – and then proceeds to join with her and produce other gods and the various features of the natural world. Often the major gods, headed by Prajapati, are considered to be primordially existent. Thus, a variant of the previous myth attributes creation to an incestuous act between Prajapati and his daughter. After his seed flowed forth and formed a lake, the other gods blew upon it and formed the domesticated animals of the world. In an alternative version, Prajapati creates the god of fire, Agni, when he desires to create some offspring. Prajapati then made sacrificial offerings to Agni, a key feature of classical Indian religion, and as a result Prajapati successfully generated his own progeny. A similar combination of sacrificial offerings and incest is found in accounts of creation involving Brahma, who split himself into a male and female being, who proceeded to generate living beings from their union. Brahma then made offerings, using parts of his own body in the ritual, and produced fire, water and food.

Other forms of creation are mentioned in early Indian sacred texts, such as the primeval sacrifice of Purusha (man) who is dismembered and his parts distributed to form the gods, the universe and all the living creatures it contains. Equally well known is the myth of the Golden Egg (hiranya-garbha) which floated upon the waters of chaos at the beginning of time. From this egg were born the other gods and then the rest of creation. Still another version is recounted in connection with the god Indra who slays the demon of chaos and releases the wholesome elements of creation –this is one of the few Indian myths featured in this collection, since it deals with the battle of a god against a monstrous superhuman deity, a classic example of how 'monsters' in myth are often representative of epic and primeval concepts.

Shiva, Vishnu and Krishna

The two major divinities that are still worshipped today are the later gods Shiva and Vishnu. Many scholars argue that Vishnu and Shiva are essentially identical, and are indistinguishable from Prhama, or the creator. Shiva, a Sanskrit word meaning 'auspicious one', is a more remote god than Vishnu.

Though only mentioned occasionally in the *Rig-Veda*, Vishnu soon became one of the most important deities in the Indian pantheon. As the sustainer of the universe, Vishnu is generally portrayed in mythology as a benevolent, bountiful and all-pervading deity who intervenes on occasion to restore cosmic harmony when negative forces threaten the stability of the established order. Often when he does this, at the request of the other gods, he assumes a different form appropriate to the task. By early medieval times, ten of these manifestations were recognized, with groups of interconnected myths associated with each of them.

A vast range of popular myths are associated with one of Vishnu's manifestations in the world as Krishna. He is mentioned in the great epic, the *Mahabharata*, where he seems largely to be merely a human hero, although he does reveal himself as a god in the famous dialogue with his friend Arjuna on a day of the great battle included in the epic. Nevertheless, Krishna really comes into his own as a god in the early medieval *Bhagavata-Purana*, which recounts many episodes of his childhood, his love affair with Radha and his occasional battles with demons. As a form of Vishnu with many endearing human traits, Krishna has become one of the most revered gods in India.

Chinese Gods in Many Forms

Gods of Creation

A discussion of gods of China must surely begin with those of the creation. There are numerous creation myths in Chinese mythology, but several of these are worthy of note, each perhaps originating with one of the many different ethnic groups within ancient China.

A well-known creation myth concerns Pan Gu (Coiled Antiquity), who was viewed as a primal deity or semi-divine human being. He was born from a primordial egg and when the egg split, the hard, opaque parts sank to become the earth while the soft, transparent parts became the heavens. Like Atlas, the Titan from Greek mythology, Pan Gu stood up and held the heaven and earth apart until they solidified in their present state. Exhausted by his labour, Pan Gu lay down and died. Each part of his body then became something in the natural world: his breath the wind and clouds; his eyes the sun and moon; his hair the stars; his bones and teeth the rocks and minerals; and so on. The very insects crawling on his dead body became human beings.

One of the best known concerns Nu Wa, a strange reptilian goddess who came to earth after it had been separated from the heavens. Some myths say that she created all things, including living beings, by going through seventy transformations. Others relate that although the natural world existed at that time, there were no humans in it. Feeling lonely, she saw a reflection of herself and took some mud and made a small copy of herself. When it came to life, she was delighted and began to create many thousands more, who populated the world while she remained as their teacher and protector.

Other myths tell of the origin of the universe out of chaos, such as that of Hundun (Dense Chaos), who produced the world after he died after a misguided act of kindness, in which some fellow gods tried to carve him a face in return for his hospitality. The interplay of impersonal forces, such as the cosmic forces of the passive, dark, heavy feminine Yin and the active, sunny, light and masculine Yang, are also believed to have given rise to various elements in creation associated with their respective qualities.

Goddesses Shine Through

Unlike the mythologies of Mesopotamia, the Mediterranean and elsewhere, there is no structured pantheon of Chinese gods: literally hundreds are mentioned by name with brief myths associated with them in texts like the *Classic of Mountains and Seas*. Moreover, unlike other cultures, there are very few goddesses, perhaps reflecting the privileged status accorded to men in orthodox Chinese society.

The sun, moon and other heavenly bodies were of great significance to the ancient Chinese and their descendants and there are thus many gods associated with them. One of the best-known cycles of myths associated with the sun concerns the divine archer, Yi – originally a stellar god. Two goddesses are associated with the moon: Chang Xi (Constant Breath) and Chang E (Constant Sublime). Chang Xi gave birth to 12 moons, one for each month, while she dwelt in the wilderness of the west. It is said that she cared for her progeny by bathing them each night after their journey across the sky. Chang E, on the other hand, was the wife of the celestial archer Yi.

Though the later male writers who compiled collections of myths seem to have done their best to undervalue the significance of the female in tune with the orthodox Confucian views of society, other goddesses were important in ancient times as founders of early dynasties. Jian Di (Bamboo-slip Maiden) is mentioned as the progenitor of the first person of the Shang Dynasty, while Jiang the Originator was said to have been the mother of the first of the Zhou people. Like Hariti and other goddesses in India, disease and disaster is sometimes attributed to a female source in Chinese myth in the form of the Queen Mother of the West, a fierce and cruel being with tangled hair, tiger's fangs and a panther's tail, who was accompanied by other ferocious felines.

Japanese Gods and Supernatural Beings

Overall, Japanese mythology is rather monolithic in nature, since it largely represents the ideology of the early centralized state of Yamato, although traces of rival or earlier beliefs may still be discerned. Therefore, the account of the creation of Japan and the events that immediately ensued seem to be unconnected with later sun goddess beliefs.

The Japanese creation myth as recounted in the *Kojiki* and *Nihon Shoki* does not tell of a creation *ex nihilo* but speaks of an unbounded, amorphous, chaotic mass. This existed for many aeons until an area of light and transparency arose within it – Takama-gahara, the High Plains of Heaven. Three primordial gods materialized there, followed by a further two lesser gods who in turn engendered five generations of gods culminating in the primal couple, Izanagi and Izanami. Little is related about the divine beings who existed before Izanagi and Izanami beyond their names; these may just be remembered remnants of earlier, lost mythologies.

Izanagi and Izanami

Izanagi and Izanami were charged by the other divinities with bringing creation to completion and to this end they stood on the Floating Bridge of Heaven and together stirred the oily brine below with a jewelled spear. Drops falling from this spear fell to produce the first island where they took up residence. There they were joined together as the first couple, but their offspring was the deformed Hiruko (Leach Child), whom they abandoned in a reed boat. .

Among Izanami's children were the other islands that make up the Japanese archipelago, as well as the gods of the mountains, the plains, wind, trees and so on. While giving birth to her last child, Kagutsuchi, the god of fire, Izanami was so badly burnt that she died. As she lay dying, she gave birth to more divine beings, such as the god and goddess of metals and of earth, and finally Mizuhame-no-mikoto, the goddess of death.

Amaterasu, Sun Goddess

The sun goddess Amaterasu is of central significance to Japanese mythology, since the imperial family claimed descent from her until Japan's defeat in the Second World War. She is also unusual as a paramount female deity in a land where male pre-eminence has always been the norm, although there are stories connected with her that hint at male dissatisfaction with this state of affairs.

After his return from the underworld, Yomi (*see* page 18), Izanagi bathed to purify himself ritually from the pollution (*imi*) of contact with the dead. He then gave birth to a further sequence of gods and goddesses, culminating in the sun goddess Amaterasu, the moon god Tsuki-yomi and the storm god Susanoo. Before withdrawing from the world, Izanagi entrusted Amaterasu with rulership of the High Plains of Heaven, Tsuki-yomi with the realm of the night and Susanoo with the ocean. Susanoo was dissatisfied with his assignment and jealous of the ascendancy of his sister Amaterasu and so was banished by Izanagi.

Susanoo, Storm God and The Izumo Cycle

A small but important group of myths known as the Izumo Cycle, concerning the activities of Susanoo and of his descendants, seems to preserve traditions from another tribal group unconnected with those who transmitted the main Amaterasu myths. In contrast to the Amaterasu cult associated with eastern central Japan, the Izumo Cycle is intimately linked with the coastal regions of western central Japan.

Izumo was the place where the god Susanoo lived after he was exiled from heaven. After he had killed an eight-headed monster, Susanoo married the princess Kusanada-hime and settled in Izumo. Myths tell of his expanding the territory and developing the region for human habitation.

Jizo, the God of Children

Jizo, the God of little children and the God who makes calm the troubled sea, is certainly the most lovable of the Buddhist divinities, though Kwannon, the Goddess of Mercy, has somewhat similar attributes. The most popular Gods, be they of the East or West, are those Gods with the most human qualities. Jizo, though of Buddhist origin, is essentially Japanese, and we may best describe him as being the creation of innumerable Japanese women who have longed to project into the Infinite, into the shrouded Beyond, a deity who should be a divine Father and Mother to the souls of their little ones. And this is just what Jizo is, a God essentially of the feminine heart, and not a being to be tossed about in the hair-splitting debates of hoary theologians. Jizo has all the wisdom of the Lord Buddha himself, with this important difference, namely, that Jizo has waived aside Nirvana, and does not sit upon the Golden Lotus, but has become, through an exquisitely beautiful self-sacrifice, the divine playmate and protector of

Japanese children. He is the God of smiles and long sleeves, the enemy of evil spirits, and the one being who can heal the wound of a mother who has lost her child in death. We have a saying that all rivers find their way to the sea. To the Japanese woman who has laid her little one in the cemetery all rivers wind their silver courses into the place where the ever-waiting and ever-gentle Jizo is. That is why mothers who have lost their children in death write prayers on little slips of paper, and watch them float down the rivers on their way to the great spiritual Father and Mother who will answer all their petitions with a loving smile.

Kwannon, Goddess of Mercy

Kwannon, the Goddess of Mercy, resembles in many ways the no less merciful and gentle Jizo, for both renounced the joy of Nirvana that they might bring peace and happiness to others. Kwannon, however, is a much more complex divinity than Jizo, and though she is most frequently portrayed as a very beautiful and saintly Japanese woman, she nevertheless assumes a multitude of forms. We are familiar with certain Indian gods and goddesses with innumerable hands, and Kwannon is sometimes depicted as Senjiu-Kwannon, or Kwannon-of-the-Thousand-Hands. Each hand holds an object of some kind, as if to suggest that here indeed was a goddess ready in her love to give and to answer prayer to the uttermost.

Benten, Goddess of the Sea

Benten, the Goddess of the Sea, is also one of the Seven Divinities of Luck; and she is romantically referred to as the Goddess of Love, Beauty, and Eloquence. She is represented in Japanese art as riding on a dragon or serpent, which may account for the fact that in certain localities snakes are regarded as being sacred. Images of Benten depict her as having eight arms. Six hands are extended above her head and hold a bow, arrow, wheel, sword, key, and sacred jewel, while her two remaining hands are reverently crossed in prayer. She resembles Kwannon in many ways, and images of the two goddesses are frequently seen together, but the shrines of Benten are usually to be found on islands.

The Gods of Luck

Daikoku, the God of Wealth, Ebisu, his son, the God of Labour, and Hotei, the God of Laughter and Contentment, belong to that cycle of deities known as the Gods of Luck.

Thunder Beings

There are many quaint legends in regard to thunder, and in Bakin's *Kumono Tayema Ama Yo No Tsuki* ('The Moon, shining through a Cloud-rift, on a Rainy Night') the famous Japanese novelist, who was an ardent believer in many of the superstitions of his country, had much to say in regard to Raiden, the God of Thunder, and the supernatural beings associated with him.

Raiden is usually depicted as having red skin, the face of a demon, with two claws on each foot, and carrying on his back a great wheel or arc of drums. He is often found in company with Fugin, or with his son, Raitaro. When the Mongols attempted to invade Japan they were prevented from doing so by a great storm, and, according to legend, only three men escaped to tell the tale. Raiden's assistance in favour of Japan is often portrayed in Japanese art. He is depicted sitting on the clouds emitting lightnings and sending forth a shower of arrows upon the invaders. In

China the Thunder God is regarded as a being ever on the look-out for wicked people. When he finds them, the Goddess of Lightning flashes a mirror upon those whom the God wishes to strike.

Raiju, or Thunder Animal, appears to be more closely associated with lightning than with thunder. He is seen in forms resembling a weasel, badger, or monkey. In the *Shin-rai-ki* ('Thunder Record') we read the following: "On the twenty-second day of the sixth month of the second year of Meiwa [July 1766] a Thunder Animal fell at Oyama [Great Mountain], in the province of Sagami. It was captured by a farmer, who brought it to Edo, and exhibited it for money on the Riyo-goku Bridge. The creature was a little larger than a cat, and resembled a weasel: it had black hair, and five claws on each paw. During fine weather it was very tame and gentle; but, before and during a storm, exceedingly savage and unmanageable." In China the Thunder Animal is described as having "the head of a monkey, with crimson lips, eyes like mirrors, and two sharp claws on each paw." During a storm the Thunder Animal of Japan springs from tree to tree, and if any of the trees are found to have been struck by lightning it is believed to be the savage work of, the Thunder Animal's claws. This being, in common with the Thunder God himself, is said to have a weakness for human navels, so that for this reason many superstitious people endeavour, if possible, to lie flat on their stomachs during a thunderstorm. Bark torn by the Thunder Animal is carefully preserved, and is supposed to be an excellent remedy for toothache.

Raicho, Thunder Bird, resembles a rook, but it has spurs of flesh, which, when struck together, produce a horrible sound. These birds feed upon the tree-frog named *rai* (thunder), and are always seen flying about in the sky during a thunderstorm.

Little is known concerning Kaminari (Thunder Woman), except that on one occasion she is said to have appeared in the guise of a Chinese Empress.

The Kappa

The *Kappa* is a river goblin, a hairy creature with the body of a tortoise and scaly limbs. His head somewhat resembles that of an ape, in the top of which there is a cavity containing a mysterious fluid, said to be the source of the creature's power. The chief delight of the *Kappa* is to challenge human beings to single combat, and the unfortunate man who receives an invitation of this kind cannot refuse. Though the *Kappa* is fierce and quarrelsome, he is, nevertheless, extremely polite. The wayfarer who receives his peremptory summons gives the goblin a profound bow. The courteous *Kappa* acknowledges the obeisance, and in inclining his head the strength-giving liquid runs out from the hollow in his cranium, and becoming feeble, his warlike characteristics immediately disappear. To defeat the *Kappa*, however, is just as unfortunate as to receive a beating at his hands, for the momentary glory of the conquest is rapidly followed by a wasting away of the unfortunate wayfarer. The *Kappa* possesses the propensities of a vampire, for he strikes people in the water, as they bathe in lake or river, and sucks their blood. In a certain part of Japan the *Kappa* is said to claim two victims every year. When they emerge from the water their skin becomes blanched, and they gradually pine away as the result of a terrible disease.

The Tengu

Professor B.H. Chamberlain (1850–1935), a leading Japanologist of his time, described the *Tengu* as "a class of goblins or gnomes that haunt the mountains and woodlands, and play many pranks. They have an affinity to birds; for they are winged and beaked, sometimes clawed. But often the beak becomes a large and enormously long human nose, and the whole creature is conceived as human, nothing bird-like remaining but the fan of feathers with which it fans itself. It is often dressed in leaves, and wears on its head a tiny cap." In brief, the *Tengu* are minor divinities, and are supreme in the art of fencing, and, indeed, in the use of weapons generally. The ideographs with which the name is written signify "heavenly dog," which is misleading, for the creature bears no resemblance to a dog, and is, as we have already described, partly human and partly bird-like in appearance. There are other confusing traditions in regard to the word *Tengu*, for it is said that the Emperor Jomei gave the name to a certain meteor "which whirled from east to west with a loud detonation." Then, again, a still more ancient belief informs us that the *Tengu* were emanations from Susanoo, the Impetuous Male, and again, that they were female demons with heads of beasts and great ears and noses of such enormous length that they could carry men on them and fly with their suspended burden for thousands of miles without fatigue, and in addition their teeth were so strong and so sharp that these female demons could bite through swords and spears. The *Tengu* is still believed to inhabit certain forests and the recesses of high mountains. Generally speaking, the *Tengu* is not a malevolent being, for he possesses a keen sense of humour, and is fond of a practical joke. Sometimes, however, the *Tengu* mysteriously hides human beings, and when finally they return to their homes they do so in a demented condition. This strange occurrence is known as *Tengu-kakushi*, or hidden by a *Tengu*.

The Mountain Woman and the Mountain Man

The Mountain Woman's body is covered with long white hair. She is looked upon as an ogre (*kijo*), and, as such, figures in Japanese romance. She has cannibalistic tendencies, and is able to fly about like a moth and traverse pathless mountains with ease.

The Mountain Man is said to resemble a great darkhaired monkey. He is extremely strong, and thinks nothing of stealing food from the villages. He is, however, always ready to assist woodcutters, and will gladly carry their timber for them in exchange for a ball of rice. It is useless to capture or kill him, for an attack of any kind upon the Mountain Man brings misfortune, and sometimes death, upon the assailants.

The Dragon

The Dragon is undoubtedly the most famous of mythical beasts, but, though Chinese in origin, it has become intimately associated with Japanese mythology. The creature lives for the most part in the ocean, river, or lake, but it has the power of flight and rules over clouds and tempests. The Dragon of China and Japan resemble each other, with the exception that the Japanese variety has three claws, while that of the Celestial Kingdom has five. The Chinese Emperor Yao was said to be the son of a dragon, and many rulers of that country were metaphorically referred to as 'dragon-faced'. The Dragon has the head of a camel, horns of a deer, eyes of a hare, scales of a carp, paws of a tiger, and claws resembling those of an eagle. In addition it has whiskers, a bright jewel under its chin, and a measure on the top of its head which enables it to ascend to Heaven at will. This is merely a general description and does not apply to all dragons, some of which have heads of so extraordinary a kind that they cannot be compared with anything in the animal kingdom. The breath of the Dragon changes into clouds from which come either rain or fire. It is able to expand or contract its body, and in addition it has the power of transformation and invisibility. In both Chinese and Japanese mythology the watery principle is associated with the Dragon.

The Dragon (*Tatsu*) is one of the signs of the zodiac, and the four seas, which in the old Chinese conception limited the habitable earth, were ruled over by four Dragon Kings. The Celestial Dragon ruled over the Mansions of the Gods, the Spiritual Dragon presided over rain, the Earth Dragon marked the courses of rivers, and the Dragon or Hidden Treasure guarded precious metals and stones.

A white Dragon, which lived in a pond at Yamashiro, transformed itself every fifty years into a bird called *O-Goncho*, with a voice resembling the howling of a wolf. Whenever this bird appeared it brought with it a great famine. On one occasion, while Fuk Hi was standing by the Yellow River, the Yellow Dragon presented him with a scroll inscribed with mystic characters. This tradition is said to be the legendary origin of the Chinese system of writing.

Australian Aboriginal Mythology

The core of Aboriginal life is 'Dreamtime', or an individual's 'Dreaming', a rich body of mythology which explains the world, past and present, to the Aborigine. Dreamtime encompasses the Aboriginal cosmogony and history, maps out physical and metaphysical landscapes, and serves as a system of beliefs, controlling religion, rituals and social behaviour and customs. It intimately and inseparably links every Aborigine to their 'country' which, although localized in their perception and representation, is their very essence. As with any other mythologies, their tales feature heavenly gods – most significantly great creators – and entities such as monsters and spirits, sometimes in battle with each other.

Great Creator Gods

The great creator being of the Arrernte people of Central Australia is Altjira. He is said to have made the earth and then retired to the heavens. He still lives in the sky, indifferent to the lives of men and women. Altjira is usually represented as a man with the feet of an emu. The word is sometimes used more generally to refer to the Dreamtime.

Baiame is the great father and creator spirit of many Aborigines of the High Plains and south-east Australia. He made people and places and could summon up rain and floods.

According to the Kulin and Wurunjerri people of central Victoria, Bunjil shaped the landscape assisted by six wise men. He then fashioned the first man and woman from bark and clay, named them and breathed life into them through their mouths, nostrils and navels. He also taught mankind the arts of life. His work complete, he retired to the sky.

The Djanngawul (or Djanggau) are three siblings, one male and two female. The Yolngu people of Arnhem Land in north Australia say that long ago in the Dreamtime, they lived on an island, 'The Land of the Dead', far out at sea. One day, they decided to come to the mainland. They landed near Port Bradshaw and made their way through the land, creating everything in it and placing sacred objects in the ground. Song cycles and stories of the Djanggawul underlie many of the ceremonies performed by the Yolngu people. One tale tells how the sisters were both male and female until their brother cut off their male parts.

All the creatures of the world took shape inside Eingana, a snake goddess, but the great Ancestor had no hole by which to give birth. She grew and grew in size, suffering increasing agonies, until at last another Ancestor pierced a hole in her. Eingana is attached to every living being by a tendon. If she lets go, the creature will die.

Long ago, say the Aranda (Arrernte) people of Central Australia, some very rudimentary human beings known as Inapertwa lived beside the sea. These creatures had no limbs, eyes, ears or noses; they were just indistinct mounds. Two great Ancestral Spirits called Ungambikula ('out of nothing') came down from the sky and, wielding their large stone knives, they proceeded to cut these creatures open, turning them into men and women.

Long ago, say the Kuku-Yalanji people of the North Queensland rainforest, the great Ancestor Spirit, the Rainbow Serpent Kurriyala, appeared from the west. He formed Narabullga (Mount Mulligan), from his droppings and made a huge lake at the top. Next, he made another mountain; this one was in the shape of a snake and he called it Naradunga (Mount Mulgrave). Kurriyala continued shaping the landscape until at last he revealed himself to his people and showed them how to dance and paint their bodies.

According to the Nambutji people of Central Australia there was once a great flood. Afterwards, the kangaroo Ancestor Minawara emerged from the debris together with his brother Multutu. Together, they wandered the earth, shaping the landscape and introducing initiation rites.

The great Ancestor of the Tiwi people of Melville and Bathurst Islands off the north coast of Australia is Mudungkala (or Mudunungkarla), an old blind woman who emerged from beneath the ground. She crawled slowly northwards on her knees, carrying her three children with her, and the water that bubbled up behind her formed the Dundas Strait. Next, Mudungkala made the Tiwi islands, filled them with plants and animals and finally crawled away leaving her children behind to enjoy her creation.

According to the traditional teachings of the Aborigines of Southeast Australia, Pundjel made the first human beings, two men, from clay and bark. They were each given a wife by Pundjel's brother, Pallian. In due course the wives had children but the children were so wicked that Pundjel and Pallian cut them into pieces. It is from these pieces that the Aborigines are descended.

According to the Gunwinggu people of Arnhem Land, Waramurungundi was the first woman and the mother of all creation. She gave birth to the earth, fashioned every living creature and crossed the land sowing plants and making waterholes with her digging stick. Afterwards, she taught people how to speak and divided each language group from the next. Her work complete, she turned into a rock.

An important Ancestor Being for the Kuninjku people of Arnhem Land is Yingarna, who emerged from the sea at Malay Bay wearing a head ring from which hung 15 dillybags (traditional woven bags) full of babies. She dropped the babies off at different places throughout the region and taught them how to speak different languages, how to hunt and how to plant yams. When she had found the ideal home for each of her children, she left. Thus she was responsible for the creation of the Aboriginal people. At one point on her travels, Yingarna gave birth to a son, the Rainbow Serpent Ngalyod.

Gods of the Stars and Sky

The Aborigines of Central Australia say that there was once a man called Nullandi whom the great Ancestor Baiame looked on very kindly. When Nullandi grew old, Baiame raised him to the sky where he became Bahloo, the moon. Yhi, the sun, made advances towards Bahloo but the moon drew back, afraid of her ardour. To this day, Yhi can be seen chasing Bahloo across the sky.

A story from Arnhem Land in the north of Australia tells how the girl spirit, Barnumbir, the morning star, lives on Bralgu, the Island of the Dead. When people went fishing they would ask

Barnumbir to accompany them in order to light their way. Terrified of drowning, Barnumbir always refused. Eventually, two women tied a long string around Barnumbir so that, should she fall in to the water, they could pull her back to land. However, because she is tied to the string, Barnumbir cannot rise very high in the sky.

The Bandjin people of Hinchinbrook Island and Lucinda Point on the mainland of North Queensland tell a story about two boys called the Dhui Dhui. One day, these boys paddled out in their canoe and began to fish precisely where their elders had told them not to. The Elders were afraid the boys would be attacked by a huge shovelnose ray that lived there. Before long, the ray bit the boys' line and began to tow them around and around. The boys would not let go of the line and eventually they disappeared out of sight beyond the horizon. That night, they appeared in the sky as the constellation known as the Southern Cross.

According to the traditions of the Bullanji people of north-east Australia, Gidja is the moon spirit. People laughed at him for being round and fat but he courted the evening star so assiduously that she agreed to marry him. Another story tells how he castrated Yalungur in order to create the first woman.

The Mandjindja people of Western Australia say that Kidili was a moon man who tried to rape some of the first women. The two brothers known as the Wati-kutjara castrated Kidili with a boomerang and he died of his wounds in a waterhole. The women he attacked became the Kungkarangalpe (the Pleiades).

Monsters, Tricksters and Evil Spirits

In Arrernte tradition, Arunkulta is the spirit of evil. The great lizard Mangar-kunjer-kunja protected people from Arunkulta's influence.

According to the Murnging people of northern Australia, Bamapana is a trickster being who causes outrage by breaking taboos, in particular the taboo of tribal incest.

Then there is the more famous Bunyip. Long ago, there was an Aborigine who ignored his people's rules and ate his own totem animal. Baiame banished him whereupon the man became an evil water spirit called Bunyip. This Bunyip was a bellowing, monstrous creature about the size of a calf. He lived in waterholes and roamed around at night threatening to devour anyone he came across. Some young women once tried to spy on Bunyip, whereupon the monster enslaved them and turned them into water spirits. To this day, the women lure hunters into dark and dangerous waters where they drown.

The people of Mornington Island in the Gulf of Carpentaria say that there was once an old grasshopper woman, Ealgin, who came from the west with a giant dog called Gaiya. Both the dog and the woman hunted humans for food. One day, Gaiya set off in pursuit of two young men, the butcherbird brothers. However, these brothers proved far too clever for the dog and succeeded in killing the massive beast; afterwards, they invited all their people to come and eat him. The brothers sent Gaiya's spirit to the grasshopper woman, but by now the spirit was so angry that it jumped up and bit the grasshopper woman on the nose, leaving marks which can be seen to this day on the noses of all grasshoppers.

The Murinbata people of the Port Keats region of Northern Australia recall how once, long ago in the Dreamtime, the old woman Kalwadi was looking after her people's children when, fed up with the task, she swallowed ten of them whole. The children's parents returned and, realizing what had happened, they cut Kalwadi open and removed the children. To everyone's relief, they were still alive.

Luma Luma is a giant Ancestral Spirit from the Dreamtime and is said to have arrived in Arnhem Land from across the seas, perhaps from Indonesia or from Macassar. He transformed himself into a stingray so that he could travel through the sea more easily but, once on the mainland, he turned back into a giant. At first, the Gunwinggu people attacked Luma Luma but when they realized he meant them no harm, they lived together peacefully.

According to traditional Aboriginal belief, Marmoo is an evil spirit at war with the great Ancestor Baiame. Jealous of Baiame's power, Marmoo determined to prove himself by creating a swarm of insects. After breathing life into them, he sent them out from his cave as a vast black cloud that left a trail of misery behind it. To help men and women, Baiame created birds so that they might eat the insects. When the birds had done their job, Baiame rewarded them by giving them their beautiful voices.

According to the Tiwi people of Melville Island, the Mopaditis are the spirits of the dead. They look like humans but their bodies lack substance. The Mopaditis cannot be seen by day but at night they appear white, sometimes walking on the surface of water.

The Aborigines of Western Australia say that Najara is a wicked spirit whose whistling lures young boys away from their people and persuades them to forget their language and culture.

According to the Tiwi people of Melville Island, the Papinjuwaris are one-eyed giants who live in a hut at the end of the sky. They stride through the heavens wielding fire-sticks. From earth, they look like shooting stars. Papinjuwaris suck blood from the sick and climb in through their victims' mouths to drain the last drops.

Long ago in the Dreamtime, in the region of Uluru in the Northern Territory, there lived a race of giant cannibals called Pungalungas or Pungalunga Men. A fierce battle left only one Pungalunga alive. This solitary Pungalunga came across the mice women who had never set eyes on a man. When the Pungalunga attacked one of the women, the others all fell on him until he ran off.

According to Aboriginal tradition, the Yara-ma-yha-who is a small, red, toothless man with fingers and toes shaped like the suckers of an octopus. He lives in the tops of fig trees and waits for people to shelter underneath, then jumps down, clings onto the person with his suckers and drinks the victim's blood. The Yara-ma-yha-who then swallows his victim but later regurgitates him or her, still alive. If someone is caught and swallowed several times they begin to shrink. This story is told to young children to frighten them from wandering off from camp.

Last but not least, the Yowie-Whowie is a cross between a lizard and an ant. It crawls out of the ground at night and eats everything it comes across, including humans.

Polynesian Mythology

The Polynesians' pattern of stop–start settlement and migration cut them off to some extent from their own histories. With no continuous presence in any given place, their communal memory couldn't be expected to stretch back too far. By the tenth century, when the last islands of the South Pacific had been colonized, their ultimate origins had been more or less forgotten. A rich but imprecise mytho-history had taken the place of any real chronological record. Across Polynesia, people traced their origins back to a legendary homeland they called Hawaiki (or some variation on that name), but this just meant, tautologically, 'the place from which our ancestors came'.

And so there is a sense of infinite regression.... Where are we to find a starting point in this never-ending cycle of dwelling and departure (or, apparently as often, fight and flight)? Even where we do have a creation account, in a Maori tale recorded by Sir Edward Grey (1812–98), we are plunged immediately into what in the West we might call an oedipal drama, driven by the impulse to reject (often violently) the old and set off in search of something new. Hardly have the 'The Children of Heaven and Earth' been born than they're plotting what to do with their parents, Rangi (Heaven) and Papa (Earth): 'Let us now determine … whether it would be better to slay them or to rend them apart.' The resulting conflict all but destroys creation in its earliest moments of existence, though it finally gives us our world in all its beauty.

Like many other mythologies, that of Polynesia has a mercurial 'Trickster' figure. Maui (as he's most widely known) makes his own contribution to the world's creation – drawing the Hawaiian islands up from the ocean depths with his fishing line, for instance. The same line, snagging on the sun, slows its progress across the sky sufficiently to give humanity days of useful length. Maui also lights the night by bringing his peoples fire.

Diverse Deities

Maui's sister for the Maori, his mother in several other Polynesian traditions, Hina is an important goddess in just about all. An embodiment of femininity, she is closely associated with the moon. Her most celebrated shrine is in Hawaii, outside Hilo, on the Wailuku River, where she's said to have lived in a little cave behind the Rainbow Falls.

But many more gods and goddesses make their appearances. Like Fehuluni, who flew all the way to Samoa to bring the yam back to her native Tonga. Then there is Kauhuhu, the shark-god of Molokai, Hawaii, or Tonga's Tui Tofua. Versions of these gods were also to be found in the legends of Fiji and French Polynesia. Also from Molokai came Kalai-Pahua, god of sorcery and poison.

'When great clouds gather on the mountains and a rainbow spans the valley,' an old Hawaiian saying has it: 'look out for furious storms of wind and rain.' For all the joyous beauty of their shrines, and rituals associated with them, the gods in Polynesia were, often as not, figures of fear. Young boys, though proudly initiated into the secrets of Kauhuhu, the Shark-God's temple on Molokai, were still warned that 'certain things were sacred...and must not be touched'.

In Polynesian myth, the boundary between human, demigod and divine status is permeable, points out Westervelt: 'When the borders of mist-land are crossed, a rich store of folklore with a historical foundation is discovered. Chiefs and gods mingle together.' Kauhuhu is on the face of it exactly the kind of ravening, man-eating monster we might expect, but on closer acquaintance he's much more morally interesting.

Gods & Origins on a Grand Scale

Introduction

'IN THE BEGINNING...' A deity's first duty, both chronologically and cosmically, is as creator, bringing reality into being. Where, we asked in our first moments of self-consciousness as a species, did the world around us come from? The earth, its oceans and its continents; its landscapes, its animals, its plants, its peoples, its skies, its stars…all these things must at some point have been made.

Exactly how a universe is made has implications for the way it works, of course. Different civilizations have told the story in different ways. Since each account to some extent encodes the values of the culture that came up with it, the differences and similarities can be intriguing.

How did the gods themselves come into being? What do they stand for? What associations do they have? What qualities – and what weaknesses – do they exemplify? How do (or don't) they get on with one another? How are their duties demarcated? The answers to all these questions give important insights into how these civilizations understood themselves; where they felt they stood in relation to their world.

The creation didn't just bring the world into being: it set in motion the cycle of day and night; the succession of the seasons. It overlaid the features of physical geography with those of a mental one. It established structures of authority; inaugurated systems of law and order; marked out some things as pure and prized, others as taboo.'

As well as fundamental acts of creation and tales of origin, this section includes stories of further exploits and struggles of gods, divine beings and monsters on this very elemental and supernatural level.

Chaos and Nyx

AT FIRST, when all things lay in a great confused mass, the Earth did not exist. Land, sea, and air were mixed up together; so that the earth was not solid, the sea was not fluid, nor the air transparent.

Over this shapeless mass reigned a careless deity called Chaos, whose personal appearance could not be described, as there was no light by which he could be seen. He shared his throne with his wife, the dark goddess of Night, named Nyx or Nox, whose black robes, and still blacker countenance, did not tend to enliven the surrounding gloom.

These two divinities wearied of their power in the course of time, and called their son Erebus (Darkness) to their assistance. His first act was to dethrone and supplant Chaos; and then, thinking he would be happier with a helpmeet, he married his own mother, Nyx. Of course, with our present views, this marriage was a heinous sin; but the ancients, who at first had no fixed laws, did not consider this union unsuitable, and recounted how Erebus and Nyx ruled over the chaotic world together, until their two beautiful children, Aether (Light) and Hemera (Day), acting in concert, dethroned them, and seized the supreme power.

Space, illumined for the first time by their radiance, revealed itself in all its uncouthness. Aether and Hemera carefully examined the confusion, saw its innumerable possibilities, and decided to evolve from it a 'thing of beauty;' but quite conscious of the magnitude of such an undertaking, and feeling that some assistance would be desirable, they summoned Eros (Love), their own child, to their aid. By their combined efforts, Pontus (the Sea) and Gaea (Ge, Tellus, Terra), as the Earth was first called, were created.

In the beginning the Earth did not present the beautiful appearance that it does now. No trees waved their leafy branches on the hillsides; no flowers bloomed in the valleys; no grass grew on the plains; no birds flew through the air. All was silent, bare, and motionless. Eros, the first to perceive these deficiencies, seized his life-giving arrows and pierced the cold bosom of the Earth. Immediately the brown surface was covered with luxuriant verdure; birds of many colours flitted through the foliage of the new-born forest trees; animals of all kinds gamboled over the grassy plains; and swift-darting fishes swam in the limpid streams. All was now life, joy, and motion.

Gaea, roused from her apathy, admired all that had already been done for her embellishment, and, resolving to crown and complete the work so well begun, created Uranus (Heaven).

The Titans

CHAOS, EREBUS AND NYX were deprived of their power by Aether and Hemera, who did not long enjoy the possession of the sceptre; for Uranus and Gaea, more powerful than their progenitors, soon forced them to depart, and began to reign in their stead. They had not dwelt long on the summit of Mount Olympus, before they found themselves the parents of twelve gigantic children, the Titans, whose strength was such that their father, Uranus, greatly feared them. To prevent their ever making use of it against him, he seized them immediately after their birth, hurled them down into a dark abyss called Tartarus, and there chained them fast.

This chasm was situated far under the earth; and Uranus knew that his six sons (Oceanus, Coeus, Crius, Hyperion, Iapetus, and Cronus), as well as his six daughters, the Titanides (Ilia, Rhea, Themis, Thetis, Mnemosyne, and Phoebe), could not easily escape from its cavernous depths. The Titans did not long remain sole occupants of Tartarus, for one day the brazen doors were again thrown wide open to admit the Cyclopes – Brontes (Thunder), Steropes (Lightning), and Arges (Sheet-lightning) – three later-born children of Uranus and Gaea, who helped the Titans to make the darkness hideous with their incessant clamor for freedom. In due time their number was increased by the three terrible, giant Centimani (Hundred-handed), Cottus, Briareus, and Gyes, who were sent thither by Uranus to share their fate.

Greatly dissatisfied with the treatment her children had received at their father's hands, Gaea remonstrated, but all in vain. Uranus would not grant her request to set the giants free, and, whenever their muffled cries reached his ear, he trembled for his own safety. Angry beyond all expression, Gaea swore revenge, and descended into Tartarus, where she urged the Titans to conspire against their father, and attempt to wrest the sceptre from his grasp.

All listened attentively to the words of sedition; but none were courageous enough to carry out her plans, except Cronus, the youngest of the Titans, more familiarly known as Saturn or Time, who found confinement and chains peculiarly galling, and who hated his father for his cruelty. Gaea finally induced him to lay violent hands upon his sire, and, after releasing him from his bonds, gave him a scythe, and bade him be of good cheer and return victorious.

Thus armed and admonished, Cronus set forth, came upon his father unawares, defeated him, thanks to his extraordinary weapon, and, after binding him fast, took possession of the vacant throne, intending to rule the universe forever. Enraged at this insult, Uranus cursed his son, and prophesied that a day would come when he, too, would be supplanted by his children, and would suffer just punishment for his rebellion.

Cronus paid no heed to his father's imprecations, but calmly proceeded to release the Titans, his brothers and sisters, who, in their joy and gratitude to escape the dismal realm of Tartarus, expressed their willingness to be ruled by him. Their satisfaction was complete, however, when he chose his own sister Rhea (Cybele, Ops) for his consort, and assigned to each of the others some portion of the world to govern at will. To Oceanus and Thetis, for example, he gave charge over the ocean and all the rivers upon earth; while to Hyperion and Phoebe he entrusted the direction of the sun and moon, which the ancients supposed were daily driven across the sky in brilliant golden chariots.

The Birth of Zeus

PEACE AND SECURITY now reigned on and around Mount Olympus; and Cronus, with great satisfaction, congratulated himself on the result of his enterprise. One fine morning, however, his equanimity was disturbed by the announcement that a son was born to him. The memory of his father's curse then suddenly returned to his mind. Anxious to avert so great a calamity as the loss of his power, he hastened to his wife, determined to devour the child, and thus prevent him from causing further annoyance. Wholly unsuspicious, Rhea heard him enquire for his son. Gladly she placed him in his extended arms; but imagine her surprise and horror when she beheld her husband swallow the babe!

Time passed, and another child was born, but only to meet with the same cruel fate. One infant after another disappeared down the capacious throat of the voracious Cronus – a personification of Time, who creates only to destroy. In vain the bereaved mother besought the life of one little one: the selfish, hard-hearted father would not relent. As her prayers seemed unavailing, Rhea finally resolved to obtain by stratagem the boon her husband denied; and as soon as her youngest son, Zeus, was born, she concealed him.

Cronus, aware of his birth, soon made his appearance, determined to dispose of him in the usual summary manner. For some time Rhea pleaded with him, but at last pretended to yield to his commands. Hastily wrapping a large stone in swaddling clothes, she handed it to Cronus, simulating intense grief. Cronus was evidently not of a very inquiring turn of mind, for he swallowed the whole without investigating the real contents of the shapeless bundle.

Ignorant of the deception practiced upon him, Cronus then took leave, and the overjoyed mother clasped her rescued treasure to her breast. It was not sufficient, however, to have saved young Zeus from imminent death: it was also necessary that his father should remain unconscious of his existence.

To ensure this, Rhea entrusted her babe to the tender care of the Melian nymphs, who bore him off to a cave on Mount Ida. There a goat, Amalthea, was procured to act as nurse, and fulfilled her office so acceptably that she was eventually placed in the heavens as a constellation, a brilliant reward for her kind ministrations. To prevent Zeus' cries being heard in Olympus, the Curetes (Corybantes), Rhea's priests, uttered piercing screams, clashed their weapons, executed fierce dances, and chanted rude war songs.

The real significance of all this unwonted noise and commotion was not at all understood by Cronus, who, in the intervals of his numerous affairs, congratulated himself upon the cunning he had shown to prevent the accomplishment of his father's curse. But all his anxiety and fears were aroused when he suddenly became aware of the fraud practiced upon him, and of young Zeus' continued existence. He immediately tried to devise some plan to get rid of him; but, before he could put it into execution, he found himself attacked, and, after a short but terrible encounter, signally defeated.

Zeus, delighted to have triumphed so quickly, took possession of the supreme power, and aided by Rhea's counsels, and by a nauseous potion prepared by Metis, a daughter of Oceanus, compelled Cronus to produce the unfortunate children he had swallowed; i.e., Poseidon, Hades, Hestia, Demeter and Hera.

Following the example of his predecessor, Zeus gave his brothers and sisters a fair share of his new kingdom. The wisest among the Titans – Mnemosyne, Themis, Oceanus and Hyperion – submitted to the new sovereign without murmur, but the others refused their allegiance; which refusal, of course, occasioned a deadly conflict.

The Giants' War

ZEUS, FROM THE TOP of Mount Olympus, discerned the superior number of his foes, and, quite aware of their might, concluded that reinforcements to his party would not be superfluous. In haste, therefore, he released the Cyclopes from Tartarus, where they had languished so long, stipulating that in exchange for their freedom they should supply him with thunderbolts – weapons which only they knew how to forge. This new engine caused great terror and dismay in the ranks of the enemy, who, nevertheless, soon rallied, and struggled valiantly to overthrow the usurper and win back the sovereignty of the world.

During ten long years the war raged incessantly, neither party wishing to submit to the dominion of the other, but at the end of that time the rebellious Titans were obliged to yield. Some of them were hurled into Tartarus once more, where they were carefully secured by Poseidon, Zeus' brother, while the young conqueror joyfully proclaimed his victory.

The scene of this mighty conflict was supposed to have been in Thessaly, where the country bears the imprint of some great natural convulsion; for the ancients imagined that the gods, making the most of their gigantic strength and stature, hurled huge rocks at each other, and piled mountain upon mountain to reach the abode of Zeus, the Thunderer.

Cronus, the leader and instigator of the revolt, weary at last of bloodshed and strife, withdrew to Italy, or Hesperia, where he founded a prosperous kingdom, and reigned in peace for many long years.

Zeus, having disposed of all the Titans, now fancied he would enjoy the power so unlawfully obtained; but Gaea, to punish him for depriving her children of their birthright, created a terrible monster, called Typhoeus, or Typhon, which she sent to attack him. He was a giant, from whose trunk one hundred dragon heads arose; flames shot from his eyes, nostrils, and mouths; while he incessantly uttered such blood-curdling screams, that the gods, in terror, fled from Mount Olympus and sought refuge in Egypt. In mortal fear lest this terror-inspiring monster would pursue them, the gods there assumed the forms of different animals; and Zeus became a ram, while Hera, his sister and queen, changed herself into a cow.

The king of the gods, however, soon became ashamed of his cowardly flight, and resolved to return to Mount Olympus to slay Typhoeus with his terrible thunderbolts. A long and fierce struggle ensued, at the end of which, Zeus, again victorious, viewed his fallen foe with boundless pride; but his triumph was very short-lived.

Enceladus, another redoubtable giant, also created by Gaea, now appeared to avenge Typhoeus. He too was signally defeated, and bound with adamantine chains in a burning cave under Mount Etna. In early times, before he had become accustomed to his prison, he gave vent to his rage by outcries, imprecations, and groans: sometimes he even breathed forth fire and flames, in hopes of injuring his conqueror. But time, it is said, somewhat cooled his resentment; and now he is content with an occasional change of position, which, owing to his huge size, causes the earth to tremble over a space of many miles, producing what is called an earthquake.

Zeus had now conquered all his foes, asserted his right to the throne, and could at last reign over the world undisturbed; but he knew that it would be no small undertaking to rule well heaven, earth, and sea, and resolved to divide the power with his brothers. To avoid quarrels and recriminations, he portioned the world out into lots, allowing each of his brothers the privilege of drawing his own share.

Poseidon thus obtained control over the sea and all the rivers, and immediately expressed his resolve to wear a symbolic crown, composed exclusively of marine shells and aquatic plants, and to abide within the bounds of his watery realm.

Hades, the most taciturn of the brothers, received for his portion the sceptre of Tartarus and all the Lower World, where no beam of sunlight was ever allowed to find its way; while Zeus reserved for himself the general supervision of his brothers' estates, and the direct management of Heaven and Earth.

Peace now reigned throughout all the world. Not a murmur was heard, except from the Titans, who at length, seeing that further opposition would be useless, grew reconciled to their fate.

In the days of their prosperity, the Titans had intermarried. Cronus had taken Rhea 'for better or for worse;' and Iapetus had seen, loved, and wedded the fair Clymene, one of the ocean nymphs, or Oceanides, daughters of Oceanus. The latter pair became the proud parents of four gigantic sons – Atlas, Menetius, Prometheus (Forethought), and Epimetheus (Afterthought) – who were destined to play prominent parts in Grecian mythology.

The Creation of the Universe, the Earth, Night and Day

IN THE BEGINNING, before there was anything at all, there was a nothingness that stretched as far as there was space. There was no sand, nor sea, no waves nor earth nor heavens. And that space was a void that called to be filled, for its emptiness echoed with a deep and frozen silence. So it was that a land sprung up within that silence, and it took the place of half the universe. It was a land called Filheim, or land of fog, and where it ended sprung another land, where the air burned and blazed. This land was called Muspell. Where the regions met lay a great and profound void, called Ginnungagap, and here a peaceful river flowed, softly spreading into the frosty depths of the void where it froze, layer upon layer, until it formed a fundament. And it was here the heat from Muspell licked at the cold of Filheim until the energy they created spawned the great frost-giant Ymir. Ymir was the greatest and the first of all frost-giants, and his part in the creation of the universe led the frost-giants to believe that they should reign supreme on what he had made.

Filheim had existed for many ages, long before our own earth was created. In the centre was a mighty fountain and it was called Vergelmir, and from that great fountain all the rivers of the universe bubbled and stormed. There was another fountain called Elivagar (although some believe that it is the same fountain with a different name), and from this bubbled up a poisonous mass, which hardened into black ice. Elivagar is the beginning of evil, for goodness can never be black.

Muspell burned with eternal light and her heat was guarded by the flame giant, Surtr, who lashed at the air with his great sabre, filling it with glittering sparks of pure heat. Surtr was the fiercest of the fire giants who would one day make Muspell their home. The word Muspell means 'home of the destroyers of the world' and that description is both frightening and accurate because the fire giants were the most terrifying there were.

On the other side of the slowly filling chasm, Filheim lay in perpetual darkness, bathed in mists which circled and spun until all was masked. Here, between these stark contrasts, Ymir grew, the personification of the frozen ocean, the product of chaos. Fire and ice met here, and it was these profound contrasts that created a phenomenon like no other, and this was life itself. In the chasm another form was created by the frozen river, where the sparks of the Surtr's sabre caused the ice to drip, and to thaw, and then, when they rested, allowed it to freeze once again. This form was Audhumla, a cow who became known as the nourisher. Her udders were swollen with rich, pure milk, and Ymir drank greedily from the four rivers which formed from them.

Audhumla was a vast creature, spreading across the space where the fire met the ice. Her legs were columns, and they held up the corners of space.

Audhumla, the cow, also needed sustenance, and so she licked at the rime-stones which had formed from the crusted ice, and from these stones she drew salt from the depths of the earth. Audhumla licked continuously, and soon there appeared, under her thirsty tongue, the form of a god. On the first day there appeared hair, and on the second, a head. On the third day the whole god was freed from the ice and he stepped forth as Buri, also called the Producer. Buri was beautiful. He had taken the golden flames of the fire, which gave him a warm, gilded glow, and from the frost and ice he had drawn a purity, a freshness that could never be matched.

While Audhumla licked, Ymir slept, sated by the warmth of her milk. Under his arms the perspiration formed a son and a daughter, and his feet produced a giant called Thrudgemir, an evil frost-giant with six heads who went on to bear his own son, the giant Bergelmir. These were the first of the race of frost-giants.

Buri himself had produced a son, called Bor, which is another word for 'born', and as Buri and Bor became aware of the giants, an eternal battle was begun – one which is to this day waged on all parts of earth and heaven.

For giants represent evil in its many forms, and gods represent all that is good, and on that fateful day the fundamental conflict between them began – a cosmic battle which would create the world as we know it.

Buri and Bor fought against the giants, but by the close of each day a stalemate existed. And so it was that Bor married the giantess Bestla, who was the daughter of Bolthorn, or the thorn of evil. Bestla was to give him three fine, strong sons: Odin, Vili and Ve and with the combined forces of these brave boys, Bor was able to destroy the great Ymir. As they slayed him, a tremendous flood burst forth from his body, covering the earth and all the evil beings who inhabited it with his rich red blood.

The Creation of the Earth

Ymir's body was carried by Odin and his brothers to Ginnungagap, where it was placed in the centre. His flesh became the earth, and his skeleton the rocky crags which dipped and soared. From the soil sprang dwarfs, spontaneously, and they would soon be put to work. Ymir's teeth and shards of broken bones became the rocks and pits covering the earth and his blood was cleared to become the seas and waters that flowed across the land. The three men worked hard on the body of Ymir; his vast size meant that even a day's work would alter the corpse only slightly.

Ymir's skull became the sky and at each cardinal point of the compass was placed a dwarf whose supreme job it was to support it. These dwarfs were Nordri, Sudri, Austri and Westri and it was from these brave and sturdy dwarfs that the terms North, South, East and West were born. Ymir's hair created trees and bushes.

The brow of Ymir became walls which would protect the gods from all evil creatures, and in the very centre of these brows was Midgard, or 'middle garden', where humans could live safely.

Now almost all of the giants had fallen with the death of Ymir, drowned by his surging blood – all, that is, except Bergelmir, who escaped in a boat with his wife and sought asylum at the edge of the world. Here he created a new world, Jotunheim, or the home of the giants, where he set about the creation of a whole new breed of giants who would carry on his evil deeds.

Odin and his brothers had not yet completed their work. As the earth took on its present form, they slaved at Ymir's corpse to create greater and finer things. Ymir's brains were thrust into the skies to become clouds, and in order to light this new world, they secured the sparks from Surtr's sabre and dotted them among the clouds. The finest sparks were put to one side and they studded the heavenly vault with them; they became like glittering stars in the darkness. The stars were given positions; some were told to pass forward, and then back again in the heavens. This provided seasons, which were duly recorded.

The brightest of the remaining stars were joined together to become the sun and the moon, and they were sent out into the darkness in gleaming gold chariots. The chariots were drawn by Arvakr (the early waker) and Alsvin (the rapid goer), two magnificent white horses under whom were placed balls of cool air which had been trapped in great skins. A shield was placed before the sun so that her rays would not harm the milky hides of the steeds as they travelled into the darkness.

Although the moon and the sun had now been created, and they were sent out on their chariots, there was still no distinction between day and night, and that is a story of its own.

Night and Day

The chariots were ready, and the steeds were bursting at their harnesses to tend to the prestigious task of setting night and day in place. But who would guide them? The horses would need leadership of some sort, and so it was decided that the beautiful children of the giant Mundilfari – Mani (the moon) and Sol (the sun) would be given the direction of the steeds. And at once, they were launched into the heavens.

Next, Nott (night), who was daughter of one of the giants, Norvi, was provided with a rich black chariot which was drawn by a lustrous stallion called Hrim-faxi (frost mane). From his mane, the frost and dew were sent down to the earth in glimmering baubles. Nott was a goddess, and she had produced three children, each with a different father. From Naglfari, she had a son named Aud; Annar, her second husband, gave her Jord (earth), and with her third husband, the god Dellinger, a son was born and he was called Dag (day).

Dag was the most radiant of her children, and his beauty caused all who saw him to bend down in tears of rapture. He was given his own great chariot, drawn by a perfect white horse called Skin-faxi (shining mane), and as they travelled, wondrous beams of light shot out in every direction, brightening every dark corner of the world and providing much happiness to all.

Many believe that the chariots flew so quickly, and continued their journey round and round the world because they were pursued by wolves: Skoll (repulsion) and Hati (hatred). These evil wolves sought a way to create eternal darkness and like the perpetual battle of good and evil, there could be no end to their chase.

Mani brought along in his chariot Hiuki, who represented the waxing moon, and Bil, who was the waning moon. And so it was that Sun, Moon, Day and Night were in place, with Evening, Midnight, Morning, Forenoon, Noon and Afternoon sent to accompany them. Summer and Winter were rulers of all seasons: Summer was a popular and warm god, a descendant of Svasud. Winter, was an enemy for he represented all that contrasted with Summer, including the icy winds which blew cold and unhappiness over the earth. It was believed that the great frost-giant Hraesvelgr sat on the extreme north of the heavens and that he sent the frozen winds across the land, blighting all with their blasts of icy death.

Loki's Children

RED LOKI, the wickedest of all the Aesir, had done something of which he was very much ashamed. He had married a giantess, the ugliest, fiercest, most dreadful giantess that ever lived; and of course he wanted no one to find out what he had done, for he knew that Father Odin would be indignant with him for having wedded one of the enemies of the Aesir, and that none of his brothers would be grateful to him for giving them a sister-in-law so hideous.

But at last All-Father found out the secret that Loki had been hiding for years. Worst of all, he found that Loki and the giantess had three ugly children hidden away in the dark places of the earth, – three children of whom Loki was even more ashamed than of their mother, though he loved them too. For two of them were the most terrible monsters which time had ever seen. Hel his daughter was the least ugly of the three, though one could scarcely call her attractive. She was half black and half white, which must have looked very strange; and she was not easily mistaken by any one who chanced to see her, you can well understand. She was fierce and grim to see, and the very sight of her caused terror and death to him who gazed upon her.

But the other two! One was an enormous wolf, with long fierce teeth and flashing red eyes. And the other was a scaly, slimy, horrible serpent, huger than any serpent that ever lived, and a hundred times more ferocious. Can you wonder that Loki was ashamed of such children as these? The wonder is, how he could find anything about them to love. But Loki's heart loved evil in secret, and it was the evil in these three children of his which made them so ugly.

Now when Odin discovered that three such monsters had been living in the world without his knowledge, he was both angry and anxious, for he knew that these children of mischievous Loki and his wicked giantess-wife were dangerous to the peace of Asgard. He consulted the Norns, the three wise maidens who lived beside the Urdar-well, and who could see into the future to tell what things were to happen in coming years. And they bade him beware of Loki's children; they told him that the three monsters would bring great sorrow upon Asgard, for the giantess their mother would teach them all her hatred of Odin's race, while they would have their father's sly wisdom to help them in all mischief. So Odin knew that his fears had warned him truly. Something must be done to prevent the dangers which threatened Asgard. Something must be done to keep the three out of mischief.

Father Odin sent for all the gods, and bade them go forth over the world, find the children of Loki in the secret places where they were hidden, and bring them to him. Then the Aesir mounted their horses and set out on their difficult errand. They scoured Asgard, Midgard the world of men, Utgard and Jotunheim where the giants lived. And at last they found the three horrible creatures hiding in their mother's cave. They dragged them forth and took them up to Asgard, before Odin's high throne.

Now All-Father had been considering what should be done with the three monsters, and when they came, his mind was made up. Hel, the daughter, was less evil than the other two, but her face was dark and gloomy, and she brought death to those who looked upon her. She must be prisoned out of sight in some far place, where her sad eyes could not look sorrow into men's lives and death into their hearts. So he sent her down, down into the dark, cold land of Niflheim, which lay below one root of the great tree Yggdrasil. Here she must live forever and ever. And, because she was not wholly bad, Odin made her queen of that land, and for her subjects she was to have all the folk who died upon the earth, – except the heroes who perished in battle; for these the Valkyrs carried straight to Valhalla in Asgard. But all who died of sickness or of old age, all who met their deaths through accident or men's cruelty, were sent to Queen Hel, who gave them lodgings in her gloomy palace. Vast was her kingdom, huge as nine worlds, and it was surrounded by a high wall, so that no one who had once gone thither could ever return. And here thenceforth Loki's daughter reigned among the shadows, herself half shadow and half light, half good and half bad.

But the Midgard serpent was a more dangerous beast even than Death. Odin frowned when he looked upon this monster writhing before his throne. He seized the scaly length in his mighty arms and hurled it forth over the wall of Asgard. Down, down went the great serpent, twisting and twirling as he fell, while all the sky was black with the smoke from his nostrils, and the sound of his hissing made every creature tremble. Down, down he fell with a great splash into the deep ocean which surrounded the world. There he lay writhing and squirming, growing always larger and larger, until he was so huge that he stretched like a ring about the whole earth, with his tail in his mouth, and his wicked eyes glaring up through the water towards Asgard which he hated. Sometimes he heaved himself up, great body and all, trying to escape from the ocean which was his prison. At those times there were great waves in the sea, snow and stormy winds and rain upon the earth, and every one would be filled with fear lest he escape and bring horrors to pass. But he was never able to drag out his whole hideous length. For the evil in him had grown with his growth; and a weight of evil is the heaviest of all things to lift.

The third monster was the Fenris wolf, and this was the most dreadful of the three. He was so terrible that at first Father Odin decided not to let him out of his sight. He lived in Asgard then, among the Aesir. Only Tyr the brave had courage enough to give him food. Day by day he grew huger and huger, fiercer and fiercer, and finally, when All-Father saw how mighty he had become, and how he bid fair to bring destruction upon all Asgard if he were allowed to prowl and growl about as he saw fit, Odin resolved to have the beast chained up. The Aesir then went to their smithies and forged a long, strong chain which they thought no living creature could break. They took it to the wolf to try its strength, and he, looking sidewise, chuckled to himself and let them do what they would with him. But as soon as he stretched himself, the chain burst into a thousand pieces, as if it were made of twine. Then the Aesir hurried away and made another chain, far, far stronger than the first.

"If you can break this, O Fenrir," they said, "you will be famous indeed."

Again the wolf blinked at his chain; again he chuckled and let them fasten him without a struggle, for he knew that his own strength had been increased since he broke the other; but as soon as the chain was fastened, he shook his great shoulders, kicked his mighty legs, and – snap! – the links of the chain went whirling far and wide, and once more the fierce beast was free.

Then the Aesir were alarmed for fear that they would never be able to make a chain mighty enough to hold the wolf, who was growing stronger every minute; but they sent Skirnir, Frey's trusty messenger, to the land of the dwarfs for help. "Make us a chain," was the message he bore from the Aesir, – "make us a chain stronger than any chain that was ever forged; for the Fenris wolf must be captured and bound, or all the world must pay the penalty."

The dwarfs were the finest workmen in the world, as the Aesir knew; for it was they who made Thor's hammer, and Odin's spear, and Balder's famous ship, besides many other wondrous things that you remember. So when Skirnir gave them the message, they set to work with their little hammers and anvils, and before long they had welded a wonderful chain, such as no man had ever before seen. Strange things went to the making of it, – the sound of a cat's footsteps, the roots of a mountain, a bear's sinews, a fish's breath, and other magic materials that only the dwarfs knew how to put together; and the result was a chain as soft and twistable as a silken cord, but stronger than an iron cable. With this chain Skirnir galloped back to Asgard, and with it the gods were sure of chaining Fenrir; but they meant to go about the business slyly, so that the wolf should not suspect the danger which was so near.

"Ho, Fenrir!" they cried. "Here is a new chain for you. Do you think you can snap this as easily as you did the last? We warn you that it is stronger than it looks." They handed it about from one to another, each trying to break the links, but in vain. The wolf watched them disdainfully.

"Pooh! There is little honor in breaking a thread so slender!" he said. "I know that I could snap it with one bite of my big teeth. But there may be some trick about it; I will not let it bind my feet, – not I."

"Oho!" cried the Aesir. "He is afraid! He fears that we shall bind him in cords that he cannot loose. But see how slender the chain is. Surely, if you could burst the chain of iron, O Fenrir, you could break this far more easily." Still the wolf shook his head, and refused to let them fasten him, suspecting some trick. "But even if you find that you cannot break our chain," they said, "you need not be afraid. We shall set you free again."

"Set me free!" growled the wolf. "Yes, you will set me free at the end of the world, – not before! I know your ways, O Aesir; and if you are able to bind me so fast that I cannot free myself, I shall wait long to have the chain made loose. But no one shall call me coward. If one of you will place his hand in my mouth and hold it there while the others bind me, I will let the chain be fastened."

The gods looked at one another, their mouths drooping. Who would do this thing and bear the fury of the angry wolf when he should find himself tricked and captured? Yet this was their only chance to bind the monster and protect Asgard from danger. At last bold Tyr stepped forward, the bravest of all the Aesir. "Open your mouth, Fenrir," he cried, with a laugh. "I will pledge my hand to the trial."

Then the wolf yawned his great jaws, and Tyr thrust in his good right hand, knowing full well that he was to lose it in the game. The Aesir stepped up with the dwarfs' magic chain, and Fenrir let them fasten it about his feet. But when the bonds were drawn tight, he began to struggle; and the more he tugged, the tighter drew the chain, so that he soon saw himself to be entrapped. Then how he writhed and kicked, howled and growled, in his terrible rage! How the heavens trembled and the earth shook below! The Aesir set up a laugh to see him so helpless – all except Tyr; for at the first sound of laughter the wolf shut his great mouth with a click, and poor brave Tyr had lost the right hand which had done so many heroic deeds in battle, and which would never again wave sword before the warriors whom he loved and would help to win the victory. But great was the honor which he won that day, for without his generous deed the Fenris wolf could never have been captured.

And now the monster was safely secured by the strong chain which the dwarfs had made, and all his struggles to be free were in vain, for they only bound the silken rope all the tighter. The Aesir took one end of the chain and fastened it through a big rock which they planted far down in the earth, as far as they could drive it with a huge hammer of stone. Into the wolf's great mouth they thrust a sword crosswise, so that the hilt pierced his lower jaw while the point stuck through the upper one; and there in the heart of the world he lay howling and growling, but quite unable to move. Only the foam which dripped from his angry jaws trickled away and over the earth until it formed a mighty river; from his wicked mouth also came smoke and fire, and the sound of his horrible growls. And when men hear this and see this they run away as fast as they can, for they know that danger still lurks near where the Fenris wolf lies chained in the depths of the earth; and here he will lie until Ragnarok, – until the end of all things.

Thor's Fishing

ONCE UPON A TIME the Aesir went to take dinner with old Œgir, the king of the ocean. Down under the green waves they went to the coral palace where Œgir lived with his wife, Queen Ran, and his daughters, the Waves. But Œgir was not expecting so large a party to dinner, and he had not mead enough for them all to drink. "I must brew some more mead," he said to himself. But when he came to look for a kettle in which to make the brew, there was none in all the sea large enough for the purpose. At first Œgir did not know what to do; but at last he decided to consult the gods themselves, for he knew how wise and powerful his guests were, and he hoped that they might help him to a kettle.

Now when he told the Aesir his trouble they were much interested, for they were hungry and thirsty, and longed for some of Œgir's good mead. "Where can we find a kettle?" they said to one another. "Who has a kettle huge enough to hold mead for all the Aesir?"

Then Tyr the brave turned to Thor with a grand idea. "My father, the giant Hymir, has such a kettle," he said. "I have seen it often in his great palace near Elivagar, the river of ice. This famous kettle is a mile deep, and surely that is large enough to brew all the mead we may need."

"Surely, surely it is large enough," laughed Œgir. "But how are we to get the kettle, my distinguished guests? Who will go to Giant Land to fetch the kettle a mile deep?"

"That will I," said brave Thor. "I will go to Hymir's dwelling and bring thence the little kettle, if Tyr will go with me to show me the way." So Thor and Tyr set out together for the land of snow and ice, where the giant Hymir lived. They traveled long and they traveled fast, and finally they came to the huge house which had once been Tyr's home, before he went to live with the good folk in Asgard.

Well Tyr knew the way to enter, and it was not long before they found themselves in the hall of Hymir's dwelling, peering about for some sign of the kettle which they had come so far to seek; and sure enough, presently they discovered eight huge kettles hanging in a row from one of the beams in the ceiling. While the two were wondering which kettle might be the one they sought, there came in Tyr's grandmother, – and a terrible grandmother she was. No wonder that Tyr had run away from home when he was very little; for this dreadful creature was a giantess with nine hundred heads, each more ugly than the others, and her temper was as bad as were her looks. She began to roar and bellow; and no one knows what this evil old person would have done to her grandson and his friend had not there come into the hall at this moment another woman, fair and sweet, and glittering with golden ornaments. This was Tyr's good mother, who loved him dearly, and who had mourned his absence during long years.

With a cry of joy she threw herself upon her son's neck, bidding him welcome forty times over. She welcomed Thor also when she found out who he was; but she sent away the wicked old grandmother, that she might not hear, for Thor's name was not dear to the race of giants, to so many of whom he had brought dole and death.

"Why have you come, dear son, after so many years?" she cried. "I know that some great undertaking calls you and this noble fellow to your father's hall. Danger and death wait here for such as you and he; and only some quest with glory for its reward could have brought you to such risks. Tell me your secret, Tyr, and I will not betray it."

Then they told her how that they had come to carry away the giant kettle; and Tyr's mother promised that she would help them all she could. But she warned them that it would be dangerous indeed, for that Hymir had been in a terrible temper for many days, and that the very sight of a stranger made him wild with rage. Hastily she gave them meat and drink, for they were nearly famished after their long journey; and then she looked around to see where she should hide them against Hymir's return, who was now away at the hunt.

"Aha!" she cried. "The very thing! You shall hide in the great kettle itself; and if you escape Hymir's terrible eye, it may hap that you will find a way to make off with your hiding-place, which is what you want." So the kind creature helped them to climb into the great kettle where it hung from one of the rafters in a row with seven others; but this one was the biggest and the strongest of them all.

Hardly had they snuggled down out of sight when Tyr's mother began to tremble. "Hist!" she cried. "I hear him coming. Keep as still as ever you can, O Tyr and Thor!" The floor also began to tremble, and the eight kettles to clatter against one another, as Hymir's giant footsteps approached the house. Outside they could hear the icebergs shaking with a sound like thunder; indeed, the whole earth quivered as if with fear when the terrible giant Hymir strode home from the hunt. He came into the hall puffing and blowing, and immediately the air of the room grew chilly; for his beard was hung with icicles and his face was frosted hard, while his breath was a winter wind, – a freezing blast.

"Ho! wife," he growled, "what news, what news? For I see by the footprints in the snow outside that you have had visitors today."

Then indeed the poor woman trembled; but she tried not to look frightened as she answered, "Yes, you have a guest, O Hymir! – a guest whom you have long wished to see. Your son Tyr has returned to visit his father's hall."

"Humph!" growled Hymir, with a terrible frown. "Whom has he brought here with him, the rascal? There are prints of two persons' feet in the snow. Come, wife, tell me all; for I shall soon find out the truth, whether or no."

"He has brought a friend of his, – a dear friend, O Hymir!" faltered the mother. "Surely, our son's friends are welcome when he brings them to this our home, after so long an absence."

But Hymir howled with rage at the word 'friend.' "Where are they hidden?" he cried. "Friend, indeed! It is one of those bloody fellows from Asgard, I know, – one of those giant-killers whom my good mother taught me to hate with all my might. Let me get at him! Tell me instantly where he is hidden, or I will pull down the hall about your ears!"

Now when the wicked old giant spoke like this, his wife knew that he must be obeyed. Still she tried to put off the fateful moment of the discovery. "They are standing over there behind that pillar," she said. Instantly Hymir glared at the pillar towards which she pointed, and at his frosty glance – snick-snack! – the marble pillar cracked in two, and down crashed the great roof-beam which held the eight kettles. Smash! went the kettles; and there they lay shivered into little pieces at Hymir's feet, – all except one, the largest of them all, and that was the kettle in which Thor and Tyr lay hidden, scarcely daring to breathe lest the giant should guess where they were. Tyr's mother screamed when she saw the big kettle fall with the others: but when she found that this one, alone of them all, lay on its side unbroken, because it was so tough and strong, she held her breath to see what would happen next.

And what happened was this: out stepped Thor and Tyr, and making low bows to Hymir, they stood side by side, smiling and looking as unconcerned as if they really enjoyed all this hubbub; and I dare say that they did indeed, being Tyr the bold and Thor the thunderer, who had been in Giant Land many times ere this.

Hymir gave scarcely a glance at his son, but he eyed Thor with a frown of hatred and suspicion, for he knew that this was one of Father Odin's brave family, though he could not tell which one. However, he thought best to be civil, now that Thor was actually before him. So with gruff politeness he invited the two guests to supper.

Now Thor was a valiant fellow at the table as well as in war, as you remember; and at sight of the good things on the board his eyes sparkled. Three roast oxen there were upon the giant's table, and Thor fell to with a will and finished two of them himself! You should have seen the giant stare.

"Truly, friend, you have a goodly appetite," he said. "You have eaten all the meat that I have in my larder; and if you dine with us tomorrow, I must insist that you catch your own dinner of fish. I cannot undertake to provide food for such an appetite!"

Now this was not hospitable of Hymir, but Thor did not mind. "I like well to fish, good Hymir," he laughed; "and when you fare forth with your boat in the morning, I will go with you and see what I can find for my dinner at the bottom of the sea."

When the morning came, the giant made ready for the fishing, and Thor rose early to go with him.

"Ho, Hymir," exclaimed Thor, "have you bait enough for us both?"

Hymir answered gruffly, "You must dig your own bait when you go fishing with me. I have no time to waste on you, sirrah."

Then Thor looked about to see what he could use for bait; and presently he spied a herd of Hymir's oxen feeding in the meadow. "Aha! just the thing!" he cried; and seizing the hugest ox of all, he trotted down to the shore with it under his arm, as easily as you would carry a handful of clams for bait. When Hymir saw this, he was very angry. He pushed the boat off from shore and began to row away as fast as he could, so that Thor might not have a chance to come aboard. But Thor made one long step and planted himself snugly in the stern of the boat.

"No, no, brother Hymir," he said, laughing. "You invited me to go fishing, and a-fishing I will go; for I have my bait, and my hope is high that great luck I shall see this day." So he took an oar and rowed mightily in the stern, while Hymir the giant rowed mightily at the prow; and no one ever saw boat skip over the water so fast as this one did on the day when these two big fellows went fishing together.

Far and fast they rowed, until they came to a spot where Hymir cried, "Hold! Let us anchor here and fish; this is the place where I have best fortune."

"And what sort of little fish do you catch here, O Hymir?" asked Thor.

"Whales!" answered the giant proudly. "I fish for nothing smaller than whales."

"Pooh!" cried Thor. "Who would fish for such small fry! Whales, indeed; let us row out further, where we can find something really worth catching," and he began to pull even faster than before.

"Stop! stop!" roared the giant. "You do not know what you are doing. These are the haunts of the dreadful Midgard serpent, and it is not safe to fish in these waters."

"Oho! The Midgard serpent!" said Thor, delighted. "That is the very fish I am after. Let us drop in our lines here."

Thor baited his great hook with the whole head of the ox which he had brought, and cast his line, big round as a man's arm, over the side of the boat. Hymir also cast his line, for he did not wish Thor to think him a coward; but his hand trembled as he waited for a bite, and he glanced down into the blue depths with eyes rounded as big as dinner-plates through fear of the horrible creature who lived down below those waves.

"Look! You have a bite!" cried Thor, so suddenly that Hymir started and nearly tumbled out of the boat. Hand over hand he pulled in his line, and lo! he had caught two whales – two great flopping whales – on his one hook! That was a catch indeed.

Hymir smiled proudly, forgetting his fear as he said, "How is that, my friend? Let us see you beat this catch in your morning's fishing."

Lo, just at that moment Thor also had a bite – such a bite! The boat rocked to and fro, and seemed ready to capsize every minute. Then the waves began to roll high and to be lashed into foam for yards and yards about the boat, as if some huge creature were struggling hard below the water.

"I have him!" shouted Thor; "I have the old serpent, the brother of the Fenris wolf! Pull, pull, monster! But you shall not escape me now!"

Sure enough, the Midgard serpent had Thor's hook fixed in his jaw, and struggle as he might, there was no freeing himself from the line; for the harder he pulled the stronger grew Thor. In his Aesir-might Thor waxed so huge and so forceful that his legs went straight through the bottom of the boat and his feet stood on the bottom of the sea. With firm bottom as a brace for his strength, Thor pulled and pulled, and at last up came the head of the Midgard serpent, up to the side of the boat, where it thrust out of the water mountain high, dreadful to behold; his monstrous red eyes were rolling fiercely, his nostrils spouted fire, and from his terrible sharp teeth dripped poison, that sizzled as it fell into the sea. Angrily they glared at each other, Thor and the serpent, while the water streamed into the boat, and the giant turned pale with fear at the danger threatening him on all sides.

Thor seized his hammer, preparing to smite the creature's head; but even as he swung Miolnir high for the fatal blow, Hymir cut the fish-line with his knife, and down into the depths of ocean sank the Midgard serpent amid a whirlpool of eddies. But the hammer had sped from Thor's iron fingers. It crushed the serpent's head as he sank downward to his lair on the sandy bottom; it crushed, but did not kill him, thanks to the giant's treachery. Terrible was the disturbance it caused beneath the waves. It burst the rocks and made the caverns of the ocean shiver into bits. It wrecked the coral groves and tore loose the draperies of sea-weed. The fishes scurried about in every direction, and the sea-monsters wildly sought new places to hide themselves when they found their homes destroyed. The sea itself was stirred to its lowest depths, and the waves ran trembling into one another's arms. The earth, too, shrank and shivered. Hymir, cowering low in the boat, was glad of one thing, which was that the terrible Midgard serpent had vanished out of sight. And that was the last that was ever seen of him, though he still lived, wounded and sore from the shock of Thor's hammer.

Now it was time to return home. Silently and sulkily the giant swam back to land; Thor, bearing the boat upon his shoulders, filled with water and weighted as it was with the great whales which Hymir had caught, waded ashore, and brought his burden to the giant's hall. Here Hymir met him crossly enough, for he was ashamed of the whole morning's work, in which Thor had appeared so much more of a hero than he. Indeed, he was tired of even pretending hospitality towards this unwelcome guest, and was resolved to be rid of him; but first he would put Thor to shame.

"You are a strong fellow," he said, "good at the oar and at the fishing; most wondrously good at the hammer, by which I know that you are Thor. But there is one thing which you cannot do, I warrant, – you cannot break this little cup of mine, hard though you may try."

"That I shall see for myself," answered Thor; and he took the cup in his hand. Now this was a magic cup, and there was but one way of breaking it, but one thing hard enough to shatter its mightiness. Thor threw it with all his force against a stone of the flooring; but instead of breaking the cup, the stone itself was cracked into splinters. Then Thor grew angry, for the giant and all his servants were laughing as if this were the greatest joke ever played.

"Ho, ho! Try again, Thor!" cried Hymir, nearly bursting with delight; for he thought that now he should prove how much mightier he was than the visitor from Asgard. Thor clutched the cup more firmly and hurled it against one of the iron pillars of the hall; but like a rubber ball the magic cup merely bounded back straight into Hymir's hand. At this second failure the giants were full of merriment and danced about, making all manner of fun at the expense of Thor. You can fancy how well Thor the mighty enjoyed this! His brow grew black, and the glance of his eye was terrible. He knew there was some magic in the trick, but he knew not how to meet it. Just then he felt the soft touch of a woman's hand upon his arm, and the voice of Tyr's mother whispered in his ear:

"Cast the cup against Hymir's own forehead, which is the hardest substance in the world." No one except Thor heard the woman say these words, for all the giant folk were doubled up with mirth over their famous joke. But Thor dropped upon one knee, and seizing the cup fiercely, whirled it about his head, then dashed it with all his might straight at Hymir's forehead. Smash! Crash! What had happened? Thor looked eagerly to see. There stood the giant, looking surprised and a little dazed; but his forehead showed not even a scratch, while the strong cup was shivered into little pieces.

"Well done!" exclaimed Hymir hastily, when he had recovered a little from his surprise. But he was mortified at Thor's success, and set about to think up a new task to try his strength. "That was very well," he remarked patronizingly; "now you must perform a harder task. Let us see you carry the mead kettle out of the hall. Do that, my fine fellow, and I shall say you are strong indeed."

The mead kettle! The very thing Thor had come to get! He glanced at Tyr; he shot a look at Tyr's mother; and both of them caught the sparkle, which was very like a wink. To himself Thor muttered, "I must not fail in this! I must not, will not fail!"

"First let me try," cried Tyr; for he wanted to give Thor time for a resting-spell. Twice Tyr the mighty strained at the great kettle, but he could not so much as stir one leg of it from the floor where it rested. He tugged and heaved in vain, growing red in the face, till his mother begged him to give over, for it was quite useless.

Then Thor stepped forth upon the floor. He grasped the rim of the kettle, and stamped his feet through the stone of the flooring as he braced himself to lift. One, two, three! Thor straightened himself, and up swung the giant kettle to his head, while the iron handle clattered about his feet. It was a mighty burden, and Thor staggered as he started for the door; but Tyr was close beside him, and they had covered long leagues of ground on their way home before the astonished giants had recovered sufficiently to follow them. When Thor and Tyr looked back, however, they saw a vast crowd of horrible giants, some of them with a hundred heads, swarming out of the caverns in Hymir's land, howling and prowling upon their track.

"You must stop them, Thor, or they will never let us get away with their precious kettle, – they take such long strides!" cried Tyr. So Thor set down the kettle, and from his pocket drew out Miolnir, his wondrous hammer. Terribly it flashed in the air as he swung it over his head; then forth it flew towards Jotunheim; and before it returned to Thor's hand it had crushed all the heads of those many-headed giants, Hymir's ugly mother and Hymir himself among them. The only one who escaped was the good and beautiful mother of Tyr. And you may be sure she lived happily ever after in the palace which Hymir and his wicked old mother had formerly made so wretched a home for her.

Now Tyr and Thor had the giant kettle which they had gone so far and had met so many dangers to obtain. They took it to Œgir's sea-palace, where the banquet was still going on, and where the Aesir were still waiting patiently for their mead; for time does not go so fast below the quiet waves as on shore. Now that King Œgir had the great kettle, he could brew all the mead they needed. So every one thanked Tyr and congratulated Thor upon the success of their adventure.

"I was sure that Thor would bring the kettle," said fair Sif, smiling upon her brave husband.

"What Thor sets out to do, that he always accomplishes," said Father Odin gravely. And that was praise enough for any one.

Ragnarok

TOO LATE THE GODS REALISED how evil was this spirit that had found a home among them, and too late they banished Loki to earth, where men, following the gods' example, listened to his teachings, and were corrupted by his sinister influence.

Seeing that crime was rampant, and all good banished from the earth, the gods realised that the prophecies uttered of old were about to be fulfilled, and that the shadow of Ragnarok, the twilight or dusk of the gods, was already upon them. Sol and Mani grew pale with affright, and drove their chariots tremblingly along their appointed paths, looking back with fear at the pursuing wolves which would shortly overtake and devour them; and as their smiles disappeared the earth grew sad and cold, and the terrible Fimbul-winter began. Then snow fell from the four points of the compass at once, the biting winds swept down from the north, and all the earth was covered with a thick layer of ice.

This severe winter lasted during three whole seasons without a break, and was followed by three others, equally severe, during which all cheer departed from the earth, and the crimes of men increased with fearful rapidity, whilst, in the general struggle for life, the last feelings of humanity and compassion disappeared.

In the dim recesses of the Ironwood the giantess Iarnsaxa or Angur-boda diligently fed the wolves Hati, Skoll, and Managarm, the progeny of Fenris, with the marrow of murderers' and adulterers' bones; and such was the prevalence of these vile crimes, that the well-nigh insatiable monsters were never stinted for food. They daily gained strength to pursue Sol and Mani, and finally overtook and devoured them, deluging the earth with blood from their dripping jaws.

At this terrible calamity the whole earth trembled and shook, the stars, affrighted, fell from their places, and Loki, Fenris, and Garm, renewing their efforts, rent their chains asunder and rushed forth to take their revenge. At the same moment the dragon Nidhug gnawed through the root of the ash Yggdrasil, which quivered to its topmost bough; the red cock Fialar, perched above Valhalla, loudly crowed an alarm, which was immediately echoed by Gullin-kambi, the rooster in Midgard, and by Hel's dark-red bird in Niflheim.

Heimdall, noting these ominous portents and hearing the cock's shrill cry, immediately put the Giallar-horn to his lips and blew the long-expected blast, which was heard throughout the world. At the first sound of this rally Aesir and Einheriar sprang from their golden couches and sallied bravely out of the great hall, armed for the coming fray, and, mounting their impatient steeds, they galloped over the quivering rainbow bridge to the spacious field of Vigrid, where, as Vafthrudnir had predicted long before, the last battle was to take place.

The terrible Midgard snake Iormungandr had been aroused by the general disturbance, and with immense writhings and commotion, whereby the seas were lashed into huge waves such as had never before disturbed the deeps of ocean, he crawled out upon the land, and hastened to join the dread fray, in which he was to

One of the great waves, stirred up by Iormungandr's struggles, set afloat Nagilfar, the fatal ship, which was constructed entirely out of the nails of those dead folks whose relatives had failed, through the ages, in their duty, having neglected to pare the nails of the deceased, ere they were laid to rest. No sooner was this vessel afloat, than Loki boarded it with the fiery host from Muspellsheim, and steered it boldly over the stormy waters to the place of conflict.

This was not the only vessel bound for Vigrid, however, for out of a thick fog bank towards the north came another ship, steered by Hrym, in which were all the frost giants, armed to the teeth and eager for a conflict with the Aesir, whom they had always hated.

At the same time, Hel, the goddess of death, crept through a crevice in the earth out of her underground home, closely followed by the Hel-hound Garm, the malefactors of her cheerless realm, and the dragon Nidhug, which flew over the battlefield bearing corpses upon his wings.

As soon as he landed, Loki welcomed these reinforcements with joy, and placing himself at their head he marched with them to the fight.

Suddenly the skies were rent asunder, and through the fiery breach rode Surtr with his flaming sword, followed by his sons; and as they rode over the bridge Bifrost, with intent to storm Asgard, the glorious arch sank with a crash beneath their horses' tread.

The gods knew full well that their end was now near, and that their weakness and lack of foresight placed them under great disadvantages; for Odin had but one eye, Tyr but one hand, and Frey nothing but a stag's horn wherewith to defend himself, instead of his invincible sword. Nevertheless, the Aesir did not show any signs of despair, but, like true battle-gods of the North, they donned their richest attire, and gaily rode to the battlefield, determined to sell their lives as dearly as possible.

While they were mustering their forces, Odin once more rode down to the Urdar fountain, where, under the toppling Yggdrasil, the Norns sat with veiled faces and obstinately silent, their web lying torn at their feet. Once more the father of the gods whispered a mysterious communication to Mimir, after which he remounted Sleipnir and rejoined the waiting host.

The combatants were now assembled on Vigrid's broad plain. On one side were ranged the stern, calm faces of the Aesir, Vanas, and Einheriar; while on the other were gathered the motley host of Surtr, the grim frost giants, the pale army of Hel, and Loki and his dread followers, Garm, Fenris, and Iormungandr, the two latter belching forth fire and smoke, and exhaling clouds of noxious, deathly vapours, which filled all

All the pent-up antagonism of ages was now let loose in a torrent of hate, each member of the opposing hosts fighting with grim determination, as did our ancestors of old, hand to hand and face to face. With a mighty shock, heard above the roar of battle which filled the universe, Odin and the Fenris wolf came into impetuous contact, while Thor attacked the Midgard snake, and Tyr came to grips with the dog Garm. Frey closed with Surtr, Heimdall with Loki, whom he had defeated once before, and the remainder of the gods and all the Einheriar engaged foes equally worthy of their courage. But, in spite of their daily preparation in the heavenly city, Valhalla's host was doomed to succumb, and Odin was amongst the first of the shining ones to be slain. Not even the high courage and mighty attributes of Allfather could withstand the tide of evil as personified in the Fenris wolf. At each succeeding moment of the struggle its colossal size assumed greater proportions, until finally its wide-open jaws embraced all the space between heaven and earth, and the foul monster rushed furiously upon the father of gods and engulphed him bodily within its horrid maw.

None of the gods could lend Allfather a helping hand at that critical moment, for it was a time of sore trial to all. Frey put forth heroic efforts, but Surtr's flashing sword now dealt him a death-stroke. In his struggle with the arch-enemy, Loki, Heimdall fared better, but his final conquest was dearly bought, for he, too, fell dead. The struggle between Tyr and Garm had the same tragic end, and Thor, after a most terrible encounter with the Midgard snake, and after slaying him with a stroke from Miolnir, staggered back nine paces, and was drowned in the flood of venom which poured from the dying monster's jaws.

Vidar now came rushing from a distant part of the plain to avenge the death of his mighty sire, and the doom foretold fell upon Fenris, whose lower jaw now felt the impress of that shoe which had been reserved for this day. At the same moment Vidar seized the monster's upper jaw with his hands, and with one terrible wrench tore him asunder.

The other gods who took part in the fray, and all the Einheriar having now perished, Surtr suddenly flung his fiery brands over heaven, earth, and the nine kingdoms of Hel. The raging flames enveloped the massive stem of the world ash Yggdrasil, and reached the golden palaces of the gods, which were utterly consumed. The vegetation upon earth was likewise destroyed, and the fervent heat made all the waters seethe and boil.

The great conflagration raged fiercely until everything was consumed, when the earth, blackened and scarred, slowly sank beneath the boiling waves of the sea. Ragnarok had indeed come; the world tragedy was over, the divine actors were slain, and chaos seemed to have resumed its former sway. But as in a play, after the principals are slain and the curtain has fallen, the audience still looks for the favourites to appear and make their bow, so the ancient Northern races fancied that, all evil having perished in Surtr's flames, from the general ruin goodness would rise, to resume its sway over the earth, and that some of the gods would return to dwell in heaven for ever.

The Destruction of Mankind

THIS LEGEND WAS CUT IN HIEROGLYPHS on the walls of a small chamber in the tomb of Seti I, about 1350 BC.

When Ra, the self-begotten and self-formed god, had been ruling gods and men for some time, men began to complain about him, saying, "His Majesty has become old. His bones have turned into silver, his flesh into gold, and his hair into real lapis-lazuli." His Majesty heard these murmurings and commanded his followers to summon to his presence his Eye (i.e. the goddess Hathor), Shu, Tefnut, Keb, Nut, and the father and mother gods and goddesses who were with him in the watery abyss of Nu, and also the god of this water, Nu. They were to come to him with all their followers secretly, so that men should not suspect the reason for their coming, and take flight, and they were to assemble in the Great House in Heliopolis, where Ra would take counsel with them.

In due course all the gods assembled in the Great House, and they ranged themselves down the sides of the House, and they bowed down in homage before Ra until their heads touched the ground, and said, "Speak, for we are listening." Then Ra, addressing Nu, the father of the first-born gods, told him to give heed to what men were doing, for they whom he had created were murmuring against him. And he said, "Tell me what you would do. Consider the matter, invent a plan for me, and I will not slay them until I have heard what you shall say concerning this thing." Nu replied, "You, Oh my son Ra, are greater than the god who made you (i.e. Nu himself), you are the king of those who were created with you, your throne is established, and the fear of you is great. Let your Eye (Hathor) attack those who blaspheme you." And Ra said, "Lo, they have fled to the mountains, for their hearts are afraid because of what they have said." The gods replied, "Let your Eye go forth and destroy those who blasphemed you, for no eye can resist you when it goes forth in the form of Hathor." Thereupon the Eye of Ra, or Hathor, went in pursuit of the blasphemers in the mountains, and slew them all. On her return Ra welcomed her, and the goddess said that the work of vanquishing men was dear to her heart. Ra then said that he would be the master of men as their king, and that he would destroy them. For three nights the goddess Hathor-Sekhmet waded about in the blood of men, the slaughter beginning at Hensu (Herakleopolis Magna).

Then the Majesty of Ra ordered that messengers should be sent to Abu, a town at the foot of the First Cataract, to fetch mandrakes (?), and when they were brought he gave them to the god Sekti to crush. When the women slaves were bruising grain for making beer, the crushed mandrakes (?) were placed in the vessels that were to hold the beer, together with some of the blood of those who had been slain by Hathor. The beer was then made, and seven thousand vessels were filled with it. When Ra saw the beer he ordered it to be taken to the scene of slaughter, and poured out on the meadows of the four quarters of heaven. The object of putting mandrakes (?) in the beer was to make those who drank fall asleep quickly, and when the goddess Hathor came and drank the beer mixed with blood and mandrakes (?) she became very merry, and, the sleepy stage of drunkenness coming on her, she forgot all about men, and slew no more. At every festival of Hathor ever after 'sleepy beer' was made, and it was drunk by those who celebrated the feast.

Now, although the blasphemers of Ra had been put to death, the heart of the god was not satisfied, and he complained to the gods that he was smitten with the "pain of the fire of sickness". He said, "My heart is weary because I have to live with men; I have slain some of them, but worthless men still live, and I did not slay as many as I ought to have done considering my power." To this the gods replied, "Trouble not about your lack of action, for your power is in proportion to your will." Here the text becomes fragmentary, but it seems that the goddess Nut took the form of a cow, and that the other gods lifted Ra on to her back. When men saw that Ra was leaving the earth, they repented of their murmurings, and the next morning they went out with bows and arrows to fight the enemies of the Sun-god. As a reward for this Ra forgave those men their former blasphemies, but persisted in his intention of retiring from the earth. He ascended into the heights of heaven, being still on the back of the Cow-goddess Nut, and he created there Sekhet-hetep and Sekhet-Aaru as abodes for the blessed, and the flowers that blossomed therein he turned into stars. He also created the millions of beings who lived there in order that they might praise him. The height to which Ra had ascended was now so great that the legs of the Cow-goddess on which he was enthroned trembled, and to give her strength he ordained that Nut should be held up in her position by the godhead and upraised arms of the god Shu. This is why we see pictures of the body of Nut being supported by Shu. The legs of the Cow-goddess were supported by the various gods, and thus the seat of the throne of Ra became stable.

When this was done Ra caused the Earth-god Keb to be summoned to his presence, and when he came he spoke to him about the venomous reptiles that lived in the earth and were hostile to him. Then turning to Thoth, he bade him to prepare a series of spells and words of power, which would enable those who knew them to overcome snakes and serpents and deadly reptiles of all kinds. Thoth did so, and the spells which he wrote under the direction of Ra served as a protection of the servants of Ra ever after, and secured for them the help of Keb, who became sole lord of all the beings that lived and moved on and in his body, the earth. Before finally relinquishing his active rule on earth, Ra summoned Thoth and told him of his desire to create a Light-soul in the Tuat and in the Land of the Caves. Over this region he appointed Thoth to rule, and he ordered him to keep a register of those who were there, and to mete out just punishments to them. In fact, Thoth was to be ever after the representative of Ra in the Other World.

The Legend of Ra and Isis

THIS LEGEND IS FOUND WRITTEN in the hieratic character upon a papyrus preserved in Turin, and it illustrates a portion of the preceding legend. We have seen that Ra instructed Thoth to draw up a series of spells to be used against venomous reptiles of all kinds, and the reader will perceive from the following summary that Ra had good reason for doing this.

The legend opens with a list of the titles of Ra, the 'self-created god', creator of heaven, earth, breath of life, fire, gods, men, beasts, cattle, reptiles, feathered fowl, and fish, the King of gods and men, to whom cycles of 120 years are as years, whose manifold names are unknown even by the gods.

The text continues: Isis had the form of a woman, and knew words of power, but she was disgusted with men, and she yearned for the companionship of the gods and the spirits, and she meditated and asked herself whether, supposing she had the knowledge of the Name of Ra, it was not possible to make herself as great as Ra was in heaven and on the earth? Meanwhile Ra appeared in heaven each day upon his throne, but he had become old, and he dribbled at the mouth, and his spittle fell on the ground. One day Isis took some of the spittle and kneaded up dust in it, and made this paste into the form of a serpent with a forked tongue, so that if it struck anyone the person struck would find it impossible to escape death. This figure she placed on the path on which Ra walked as he came into heaven after his daily survey of the Two Lands (i.e. Egypt). Soon after this Ra rose up, and attended by his gods he came into heaven, but as he went along the serpent drove its fangs into him. As soon as he was bitten Ra felt the living fire leaving his body, and he cried out so loudly that his voice reached the uttermost parts of heaven. The gods rushed to him in great alarm, saying, "What is the matter?" At first Ra was speechless, and found himself unable to answer, for his jaws shook, his lips trembled, and the poison continued to run through every part of his body. When he was able to regain a little strength, he told the gods that some deadly creature had bitten him, something the like of which he had never seen, something which his hand had never made. He said, "Never before have I felt such pain; there is no pain worse than this." Ra then went on to describe his greatness and power, and told the listening gods that his father and mother had hidden his name in his body so that no one might be able to master him by means of any spell or word of power. In spite of this something had struck him, and he knew not what it was. "Is it fire?" he asked. "Is it water? My heart is full of burning fire, my limbs are shivering, shooting pains are in all my members." All the gods round about him uttered cries of lamentation, and at this moment Isis appeared. Going to Ra she said, "What is this, Oh divine father? What is this? Has a serpent bitten you? Has something made by you lifted up its head against you? Verily my words of power shall overthrow it; I will make it depart in the sight of your light." Ra then repeated to Isis the story of the incident, adding, "I am colder than water, I am hotter than fire. All my members sweat. My body quakes. My eye is unsteady. I cannot look on the sky, and my face is bedewed with water as in the time of the Inundation" (i.e. in the period of summer). Then Isis said, "Father, tell me your name, for he who can utter his own name lives."

Ra replied, "I am the maker of heaven and earth. I knit together the mountains and whatsoever lives on them. I made the waters. I made Mehturit (an ancient Cow-goddess of heaven) to come into being. I made Kamutef (a form of Amen-Ra). I made heaven, and the two hidden gods of the horizon, and put souls into the gods. I open my eyes, and there is light; I shut my eyes, and there is darkness. I speak the word[s], and the waters of the Nile appear. I am he whom the gods know not. I make the hours. I create the days. I open the year. I make the river [Nile]. I create the living fire whereby works in the foundries and workshops are carried out. I am Khepera in the morning, Ra at noon, and Temu in the evening." Meanwhile the poison of the serpent was coursing through the veins of Ra, and the enumeration of his works afforded the god no relief from it. Then Isis said to Ra, "Among all the things which you have named to me you have not named your name. Tell me your name, and the poison shall come forth from you." Ra still hesitated, but the poison was burning in his blood, and the heat thereof was stronger than that of a fierce fire. At length he said, "Isis shall search me through, and my name shall come forth from my body and pass into hers." Then Ra hid himself from the gods, and for a season his throne in the Boat of Millions of Years was empty. When the time came for the heart of the god to pass into Isis, the goddess said to Horus, her son, "The great god shall bind himself by an oath to give us his two eyes (i.e. the sun and the moon)." When the great god had yielded up his name Isis pronounced the following spell: "Flow poison, come out of Ra. Eye of Horus, come out of the god, and sparkle as you come through his mouth. I am the worker. I make the poison fall on the ground. The poison is conquered. Truly the name of the great god has been taken from him. Ra lives! The poison dies! If the poison live Ra shall die." These were the words which Isis spoke, Isis the great lady, the Queen of the gods, who knew Ra by his own name.

In late times magicians used to write the above legend on papyrus above figures of Temu and Heru-Hekenu, who gave Ra his secret name, and over figures of Isis and Horus, and sell the rolls as charms against snake bites.

The Birth of the Gods and the Battle Against Tiawath

AS IN SO MANY CREATION MYTHS we find chaotic darkness brooding over a waste of waters; heaven and earth were not as yet. Naught existed save the primeval ocean, Mommu Tiawath, from whose fertile depths came every living thing. Nor were the waters distributed, as in the days of man, into sea, river, or lake, but all were confined together in one vast and bottomless abyss. Neither did god or man exist: their names were unknown and their destinies undetermined. The future was as dark as the gloom which lay over the mighty gulf of chaos. Nothing had been designed or debated concerning it.

But there came a stirring in the darkness and the great gods arose. First came Lahmu and Lahame; and many epochs later, Ansar and Kisar, component parts of whose names signify 'Host of Heaven' and 'Host of Earth'. These latter names we may perhaps accept as symbolical of the spirits of heaven and of earth respectively. Many days afterward came forth their son Anu, god of the heavens.

At this point it should be explained that the name Tiawath affords a parallel to the expression *T'hom* or 'deep' of the Old Testament. Practically the same word is used in Assyrian in the form *Tamtu*, to signify the 'deep sea'. The reader will recall that it was upon the face of the deep that the spirit of God brooded, according to the first chapter of Genesis. The word and the idea which it contains are equally Semitic, but strangely enough it has an Akkadian origin. For the conception that the watery abyss was the source of all things originated with the worshippers of the sea-god Ea at Eridu. They termed the deep *apsu*, or a 'house of knowledge' wherein their tutelar god was supposed to have his dwelling, and this word was of Akkadian descent. This *apsu*, or 'abyss', in virtue of the animistic ideas prevailing in early Akkadian times, had become personalized as a female who was regarded as the mother of Ea. She was known by another name as well as that of Apsu, for she was also entitled Zigarun, the 'heaven', or the 'mother that has begotten heaven and earth'; and indeed she seems to have had a form or variant in which she was an earth-goddess as well. But it was not the existing earth or heaven that she represented in either of her forms, but the primeval abyss, out of which both of these were fashioned.

At this point the narrative exhibits numerous defects, and for a continuation of it we must apply to Damascius, the last of the Neoplatonists, who was born in Damascus about ad 480, and who is regarded by most Assyriologists as having had access to valuable written or traditional material. Damascius stated that Anu was followed by Bel (we retain the Babylonian form of the names rather than Damascius' Greek titles), and Ea the god of Eridu. "From Ea and Dawkina," he writes, "was born a son called Belos or Bel-Merodach, whom the Babylonians regarded as the creator of the world." From Damascius we can learn nothing further, and the defective character of the tablet does not permit us to proceed with any degree of certainty until we arrive at the name of Nudimmud, which appears to be simply a variant of the name of Ea. From obscure passages it may be generally gleaned that Tiawath and Apsu, once one, or rather originally representing the Babylonian and Akkadian forms of the deep, are now regarded as mates – Tiawath being the female and Apsu, once female, in this case the male. These have a son, Moumis or Mummu, a name which at one time seems to have been given to Tiawath, so that in these changes we may be able to trace the hand of the later mythographer, who, with less skill and greater levity than is to be found in most myths, has taken upon himself the responsibility of manufacturing three deities out of one. It may be that the scribe in question was well aware that his literary effort must square with and placate popular belief or popular prejudice, and in no era and at no time has priestly ingenuity been unequal to such a task, as is well evidenced by many myths which exhibit traces of late alteration. But in dwelling for a moment on this question, it is only just to the priesthood to admit that such changes did not always emanate from them, but were the work of poets and philosophers who, for aesthetic or rational reasons, took it upon themselves to recast the myths of their race according to the dictates of a nicer taste, or in the interests of 'reason'.

A Darksome Trinity

These three, then, Tiawath, Apsu, and Mummu, appear to have formed a trinity, which bore no good-will to the 'higher gods'. They themselves, as deities of a primeval epoch, were doubtless regarded by the theological opinion of a later day as dark, dubious, and unsatisfactory. It is notorious that in many lands the early, elemental gods came into bad odour in later times; and it may be that the Akkadian descent of this trio did not conduce to their popularity with the Babylonian people. Be that as it may, alien and aboriginal gods have in all times been looked upon by an invading and conquering race with distrust as the workers of magic and the sowers of evil, and even although a Babylonian name had been accorded one of them, it may not have been employed in a complimentary sense. Whereas the high gods regarded those of the abyss with distrust, the darker deities of chaos took up an attitude towards the divinities of light which can only be compared to the sarcastic tone which Milton's Satan adopts against the Power which thrust him into outer darkness. Apsu was the most ironical of all. There was no peace for him, he declared, so long as the new-comers dwelt on high: their way was not his way, neither was it that of Tiawath, who, if Apsu represented sarcasm deified, exhibited a fierce truculence much more overpowering than the irony of her mate. The trio discussed how they might rid themselves of those beings who desired a reign of light and happiness, and in these deliberations Mummu, the son, was the prime mover. Here again the Tablets fails us somewhat, but we learn sufficient further on to assure us that Mummu's project was one of open war against the gods of heaven.

In connection with this campaign, Tiawath made the most elaborate preparations along with her companions. She laboured without ceasing. From the waters of the great abyss over which she presided she called forth the most fearful monsters, who remind us strongly of those against which Horus, the Egyptian god of light, had to strive in his wars with Set. From the deep came gigantic serpents armed with stings, dripping with the most deadly poison; dragons of vast shape reared their heads above the flood, their huge jaws armed with row upon row of formidable teeth; giant dogs of indescribable savagery; men fashioned partly like scorpions; fish-men, and countless other horrible beings, were created and formed into battalions under the command of a god named Kingu, to whom Tiawath referred as her 'only husband' and to whom she promised the rule of heaven and of fate when once the detested gods of light are removed by his mighty arm.

The introduction of this being as the husband of Tiawath seems to point either to a fusion of legends or to the interpolation of some passage popular in Babylonian lore. At this juncture Apsu disappears, as does Mummu. Can it be that at this point a scribe or mythographer took up the tale who did not agree with his predecessor in describing Tiawath, Apsu, and Mummu, originally one, as three separate deities? This would explain the divergence, but the point is an obscure one, and hasty conclusions on slight evidence are usually doomed to failure. To resume our narrative, Tiawath, whoever her coadjutors, was resolved to retain in her own hands the source of all living things, that great deep over which she presided.

Merodach Battles Tiawath

But the gods of heaven were by no means lulled into peaceful security, for they were aware of the ill-will which Tiawath bore them. They learned of her plot, and great was their wrath. Ea, the god of water, was the first to hear of it, and related it to Ansar, his father, who filled heaven with his cries of anger. Ansar betook himself to his other son, Anu, god of the sky. "Speak to the great dragon," he urged him; "speak to her, my son, and her anger will be assuaged and her wrath vanish." Duly obedient, Anu betook himself to the realm of Tiawath to reason with her, but the monster snarled at him so fiercely that in dread he turned his back upon her and departed. Next came Nudimmud to her, but with no better success.

At length the gods decided that one of their number, called Merodach, should undertake the task of combating Tiawath the terrible. Merodach asked that it might be written that he should be victorious, and this was granted him. He was then given rule over the entire universe, and to test whether or not the greatest power had passed to him a garment was placed in the midst of the gods and Merodach spoke words commanding that it should disappear. Straightway it vanished and was not. Once more spoke the god, and the garment re-appeared before the eyes of the dwellers in heaven.

The portion of the epic which describes the newly acquired glories of Merodach is exceedingly eloquent. We are told that none among the gods can now surpass him in power, that the place of their gathering has become his home, that they have given him the supreme sovereignty, and they even beg that to them who put their trust in him he will be gracious. They pray that he may pour out the soul of the keeper of evil, and finally they place in his hands a marvellous weapon with which to cut off the life of Tiawath. "Let the winds carry her blood to secret places," they exclaimed in their desire that the waters of this fountain of wickedness should be scattered far and wide. Mighty was he to look upon when he set forth for the combat. His great bow he bore upon his back; he swung his massive club triumphantly. He set the lightning before him; he filled his body with swiftness; and he framed a great net to enclose the dragon of the sea. Then with a word he created terrible winds and tempests, whirlwinds, storms, seven in all, for the confounding of Tiawath. The hurricane was his weapon, and he rode in the chariot of destiny. His helm blazed with terror and awful was his aspect. The steeds which were yoked to his chariot rushed rapidly towards the abyss, their mouths frothing with venomous foam. Followed by all the good wishes of the gods, Merodach fared forth that day.

Soon he came to Tiawath's retreat, but at sight of the monster he halted, and with reason, for there crouched the great dragon, her scaly body still gleaming with the waters of the abyss, flame darting from her eyes and nostrils, and such terrific sounds issuing from her widely open mouth as would have terrified any but the bravest of the gods. Merodach reproached Tiawath for her rebellion and ended by challenging her to combat. Like the dragons of all time, Tiawath appears to have been versed in magic and hurled the most potent incantations against her adversary. She cast many a spell. But Merodach, unawed by this, threw over her his great net, and caused an evil wind which he had sent on before him to blow on her, so that she might not close her mouth. The tempest rushed between her jaws and held them open; it entered her body and racked her frame. Merodach swung his club on high, and with a mighty blow shattered her great flank and slew her. Down he cast her corpse and stood upon it; then he cut out her evil heart. Finally he overthrew the host of monsters which had followed her, so that at length they trembled, turned, and fled in headlong rout. These also he caught in his net and "kept them in bondage". Kingu he bound and took from him the tablets of destiny which had been granted to him by the slain Tiawath, which obviously means that the god of a later generation wrenches the power of fate from an earlier hierarchy, just as one earthly dynasty may overthrow and replace another. The north wind bore Tiawath's blood away to secret places, and at the sight Ea, sitting high in the heavens, rejoiced exceedingly. Then Merodach took rest and nourishment, and as he rested a plan arose in his mind. Rising, he flayed Tiawath of her scaly skin and cut her asunder.

We have already seen that the north wind bore her blood away, which probably symbolises the distribution of rivers over the earth. Then did Merodach take the two parts of her vast body, and with one of them he framed a covering for the heavens. Merodach next divided the upper from the lower waters, made dwellings for the gods, set lights in the heaven, and ordained their regular courses.

As the tablet poetically puts it, "he lit up the sky establishing the upper firmament, and caused Anu, Bel, and Ea to inhabit it." He then founded the constellations as stations for the great gods, and instituted the year, setting three constellations for each month, and placing his own star,

Nibiru, as the chief light in the firmament. Then he caused the new moon, Nannaru, to shine forth and gave him the rulership of the night, granting him a day of rest in the middle of the month. There is another mutilation at this point, and we gather that the net of Merodach, with which he had snared Tiawath, was placed in the heavens as a constellation along with his bow. The winds also appear to have been bound or tamed and placed in the several points of the compass; but the whole passage is very obscure, and doubtless information of surpassing interest has been lost through the mutilation of the tablet.

The tablets here allude to the creation of man; the gods, it is stated, so admired the handiwork of Merodach, that they desired to see him execute still further marvels. Now the gods had none to worship them or pay them homage, and Merodach suggested to his father, Ea, the creation of man out of his divine blood. Here once more the tablets fail us, and we must turn to the narrative of the Chaldean writer Berossus, as preserved by no less than three authors of the classical age. Berossus states that a certain woman Thalatth (that is, Tiawath) had many strange creatures at her bidding. Belus (that is, Bel-Merodach) attacked and cut her in twain, forming the earth out of one half and the heavens out of the other, and destroying all the creatures over which she ruled. Then did Merodach decapitate himself, and as his blood flowed forth the other gods mingled it with the earth and formed man from it. From this circumstance mankind is rational, and has a spark of the divine in it. Then did Merodach divide the darkness, separate the heavens from the earth, and order the details of the entire universe. But those animals which he had created were not able to bear the light, and died. A passage then occurs which states that the stars, the sun and moon, and the five planets were created, and it would seem from the repetition that there were two creations, that the first was a failure, in which Merodach had, as it were, essayed a first attempt, perfecting the process in the second creation. Of course it may be conjectured that Berossus may have drawn from two conflicting accounts, or that those who quote him have inserted the second passage.

The Sumerian incantation, which is provided with a Semitic translation, adds somewhat to our knowledge of this cosmogony. It states that in the beginning nothing as yet existed, none of the great cities of Babylonia had yet been built, indeed there was no land, nothing but sea. It was not until the veins of Tiawath had been cut through that paradise and the abyss appear to have been separated and the gods created by Merodach. Also did he create *annunaki* or gods of the earth, and established a wondrous city as a place in which they might dwell. Then men were formed with the aid of the goddess Aruru, and finally vegetation, trees, and animals. Then did Merodach raise the great temples of Erech and Nippur. From this account we see that instead of Merodach being alluded to as the son of the gods, he is regarded as their creator. In the library of Nineveh was also discovered a copy of a tablet written for the great temple of Nergal at Cuthah. Nergal himself is supposed to make the statement which it contains. He tells us how the hosts of chaos and confusion came into being. At first, as in the other accounts, nothingness reigned supreme, then did the great gods create warriors with the bodies of birds, and men with the faces of ravens. They founded them a city in the ground, and Tiawath, the great dragon, did suckle them. They were fostered in the midst of the mountains, and under the care of the 'mistress of the gods' they greatly increased and became heroes of might. Seven kings had they, who ruled over six thousand people. Their father was the god Benani, and their mother the queen, Melili. These beings, who might almost be called tame gods of evil, Nergal states that he destroyed. Thus all accounts agree concerning the original chaotic condition of the universe. They also agree that the powers of chaos and darkness were destroyed by a god of light.

The creation tablets are written in Semitic and allude to the great circle of the gods as already fully developed and having its full complement. Even the later deities are mentioned in them. This means that it must be assigned to a comparatively late date, but it possesses elements which go to show that it is a late edition of a much earlier composition – indeed the fundamental elements in it appear, as has been said, to be purely Akkadian in origin, and that would throw back the date of its original form to a very primitive period indeed. It has, as will readily be seen, a very involved cosmogony. Its characteristics show it to have been originally local, and of course Babylonian, in its secondary origin, but from time to time it was added to, so that such gods as were at a later date adopted into the Babylonian pantheon might be explained and accounted for by it; but the legend of the creation arising in the city of Babylon, the local folk-tale known and understood by the people, was never entirely shelved by the more consequential and polished epic, which was perhaps only known and appreciated in literary and aesthetic circles, and bore the same relation to the humbler folk-story that Milton's *Paradise Lost* bears to the medieval legends of the casting out of Satan from heaven.

Although it is quite easy to distinguish influences of extreme antiquity in the Babylonian creation myth, it is clear that in the shape in which it has come down to us it has been altered in such a manner as to make Merodach reap the entire credit of Tiawath's defeat instead of En-lil, or the deity who was his predecessor as monarch of the gods. Jastrow holds that the entire cosmological tale has been constructed from an account of a conflict with a primeval monster and a story of a rebellion against Ea; that these two tales have become fused, and that the first is again divisible into three versions, originating one at Uruk and the other two at Nippur at different epochs. The first celebrates the conquest of Anu over Tiawath, the second exalts Ninib as the conqueror, and the third replaces him by En-lil. We thus see how it was possible for the god of a conquering or popular dynasty to have a complete myth made over to him, and how at last it was competent for the mighty Merodach of Babylon to replace an entire line of deities as the central figure of a myth which must have been popular with untold generations of Akkadian and Babylonian people.

Zu

ZU (OR ANZU) WAS A STORM-GOD symbolized in the form of a bird (or sometimes half man and half bird). He may typify the advancing storm-cloud, which would have seemed to those of old as if hovering like a great bird above the land which it was about to strike. The North-American Indians possess such a mythological conception in the Thunder-bird, and it is probable that the great bird called roc, so well known to readers of the *Arabian Nights*, was a similar monster – perhaps the descendant of the Zu-bird. We remember how this enormous creature descended upon the ship in which Sindbad sailed and carried him off. Certain it is that we can trace the roc or rukh to the Persian simurgh, which is again referable to a more ancient Persian form, the amru or sinamru, the bird of immortality, and we may feel sure that what is found in ancient Persian lore has some foundation in Babylonian belief. The Zu-bird was evidently under the control of the sun, and his attempt to break away from the solar authority is related in the following legend.

It is told of the god Zu that on one occasion ambition awaking in his breast caused him to cast envious eyes on the power and sovereignty of Bel, so that he determined to purloin the Tablets of Destiny, which were the tangible symbols of Bel's greatness.

At this time, it may be recalled, the Tablets of Destiny had already an interesting history behind them. We are told in the creation legend how Apsu, the primeval, and Tiawath, chaos, the first parents of the gods, afterward conceived a hatred for their offspring, and how Tiawath, with her monster-brood of snakes and vipers, dragons and scorpion-men and raging hounds, made war on the hosts of heaven. Her son Kingu she made captain of her hideous army –

To march before the forces, to lead the host,
To give the battle-signal, to advance to the attack,
To direct the battle, to control the fight.

To him she gave the Tablets of Destiny, laying them on his breast with the words: "Thy command shall not be without avail, and the word of thy mouth shall be established." Through his possession of the divine tablets Kingu received the power of Anu, and was able to decree the fate of the gods. After several deities had refused the honour of becoming champion of heaven, Merodach was chosen. He succeeded at length in slaying Tiawath and destroying her evil host; and having vanquished Kingu, her captain, he took from him the Tablets of Destiny, which he sealed and laid on his own breast. It was this Merodach, or Marduk, who afterward became identified with Bel.

Now Zu, in his greed for power and dominion, was eager to obtain the potent symbols. He beheld the honour and majesty of Bel, and from contemplation of these he turned to look upon the Tablets of Destiny, saying within himself:

"Lo, I will possess the tablets of the gods, and all things shall be subject unto me. The spirits of heaven shall bow before me, the oracles of the gods shall be in my hands. I shall wear the crown, symbol of sovereignty, and the robe, symbol of godhead, and then shall I rule over all the hosts of heaven."

Thus inflamed, he sought the entrance to Bel's hall, where he awaited the dawn of day. The text goes on:

Now when Bel was pouring out the clear water, (i.e. the light of day?)
And his diadem was taken off and lay upon the throne,
(Zu) seized the Tablets of Destiny,
He took Bel's dominion, the power of giving commands.
Then Zu fled away and hid himself in his mountain.

Bel was greatly enraged at the theft, and all the gods with him. Anu, lord of heaven, summoned about him his divine sons, and asked for a champion to recover the tablets. But though the god Ramman was chosen, and after him several other deities, they all refused to advance against Zu.

The end of the legend is unfortunately missing, but from a passage in another tale, the legend of Etana, we gather that it was the sun-god, Shamash, who eventually stormed the mountain-stronghold of Zu, and with his net succeeded in capturing the presumptuous deity.

This legend is of the Prometheus type, but whereas Prometheus (once a bird-god) steals fire from heaven for the behoof of mankind, Zu steals the Tablets of Destiny for his own. These must, of course, be regained if the sovereignty of heaven is duly to continue, and to make the tale circumstantial the sun-god is provided with a fowler's net with which to capture the recalcitrant Zu-bird. Jastrow believes the myth to have been manufactured for the purpose of showing how the tablets of power were originally lost by the older Bel and gained by Merodach, but he has discounted the reference in the Etana legend relating to their recovery.

The Invasion of the Monsters

THOSE MONSTERS who had composed the host of Tiawath were supposed, after the defeat and destruction of their commandress, to have been hurled like Satan and his angels into the abyss beneath. We read of their confusion in four tablets of the creation epic. This legend seems to be the original source of the belief that those who rebelled against high heaven were thrust into outer darkness. In the Book of Enoch we read of a 'great abyss' regarding which an angel said to the prophet, "This is a place of the consummation of heaven and earth," and again, in a later chapter, "These are of the stars who have transgressed the command of God, the Highest, and are bound here till 10,000 worlds, the number of the days of their sins, shall have consummated ... this is the prison of the angels, and here they are held to eternity." Eleven great monsters are spoken of by Babylonian myth as comprising the host of Tiawath, besides many lesser forms having the heads of men and the bodies of birds. Strangely enough we find these monsters figuring in a legend concerning an early Babylonian king.

The tablets upon which this legend was impressed were at first known as 'the Cuthaean legend of creation' – a misnomer, for this legend does not give an account of the creation of the world at all, but deals with the invasion of Babylonia by a race of monsters who were descended from the gods, and who waged war against the legendary king of the period for three years. The King tells the story himself. Unfortunately the first portions of both tablets containing the story are missing, and we plunge right away into a description of the dread beings who came upon the people of Babylonia in their multitudes. We are told that they preferred muddy water to clear water. These creatures, says the King, were without moral sense, glorying in their power, and slaughtering those whom they took captives. They had the bodies of birds and some of them had the faces of ravens. They had evidently been fostered by the gods in some inaccessible region, and, multiplying greatly, they came like a storm-cloud on the land, 360,000 in number. Their king was called Benini, their mother Melili, and their leader Memangab, who had six subordinates. The King, perplexed, knew not what to do. He was afraid that if he gave them battle he might in some way offend the gods, but at last through his priests he addressed the divine beings and made offerings of lambs in sacrifice to them. He received a favourable answer and decided to give battle to the invaders, against whom he sent an army of 120,000 men, but not one of these returned alive. Again he sent 90,000 warriors to meet them, but the same fate overtook these, and in the third year he despatched an army of nearly 70,000 troops, all of whom perished to a man. Then the unfortunate monarch broke down, and, groaning aloud, cried out that he had brought misfortune and destruction upon his realm. Nevertheless, rising from his lethargy of despair, he stated his intention to go forth against the enemy in his own person, saying, "The pride of this people of the night I will curse with death and destruction, with fear, terror, and famine, and with misery of every kind."

Before setting out to meet the foe he made offerings to the gods. The manner in which he overcame the invaders is by no means clear from the text, but it would seem that he annihilated them by means of a deluge. In the last portion of the legend the King exhorts his successors not to lose heart when in great peril but to take courage from his example.

He inscribed a tablet with his advice, which he placed in the shrine of Nergal in the city of Cuthah. "Strengthen thy wall," he said, "fill thy cisterns with water, bring in thy treasure-chests and thy corn and thy silver and all thy possessions." He also advises those of his descendants who are faced by similar conditions not to expose themselves needlessly to the enemy.

It was thought at one time that this legend applied to the circumstances of the creation, and that the speaker was the god Nergal, who was waging war against the brood of Tiawath. It was believed that, according to local conditions at Cuthah, Nergal would have taken the place of Merodach, but it has now been made clear that although the tablet was intended to be placed in the shrine of Nergal, the speaker was in reality an early Babylonian king.

The Creation Story of the Four Suns

TONACATECUTLI AND TONACACIUATL dwelt from the beginning in the thirteenth heaven. To them were born, as to an elder generation, four gods – the ruddy Camaxtli (chief divinity of the Tlascalans); the black Tezcatlipoca, wizard of the night; Quetzalcoatl, the wind-god; and the grim Huitzilopochtli, of whom it was said that he was born without flesh, a skeleton.

For six hundred years these deities lived in idleness; then the four brethren assembled, creating first the fire (hearth of the universe) and afterward a half-sun. They formed also Oxomoco and Cipactonal, the first man and first woman, commanding that the former should till the ground, and the latter spin and weave; while to the woman they gave powers of divination and grains of maize that she might work cures. They also divided time into days and inaugurated a year of eighteen twenty-day periods, or three hundred and sixty days. Mictlantecutli and Mictlanciuatl they created to be Lord and Lady of Hell, and they formed the heavens that are below the thirteenth storey of the celestial regions, and the waters of the sea, making in the sea a monster Cipactli, from which they shaped the earth. The gods of the waters, Tlaloctecutli and his wife Chalchiuhtlicue, they created, giving them dominion over the Quarters.

The son of the first pair married a woman formed from a hair of the goddess Xochiquetzal; and the gods, noticing how little was the light given forth by the half-sun, resolved to make another half-sun, whereupon Tezcatlipoca became the sun-bearer – for what we behold traversing the daily heavens is not the sun itself, but only its brightness; the true sun is invisible. The other gods created huge giants, who could uproot trees by brute force, and whose food was acorns. For thirteen times fifty-two years, altogether six hundred and seventy-six, this period lasted – as long as its Sun endured; and it is from this first Sun that time began to be counted, for during the six hundred years of the idleness of the gods, while Huitzilopochtli was in his bones, time was not reckoned.

This Sun came to an end when Quetzalcoatl struck down Tezcatlipoca and became Sun in his place. Tezcatlipoca was metamorphosed into a jaguar (Ursa Major) which is seen by night in the skies wheeling down into the waters whither Quetzalcoatl cast him; and this jaguar devoured the giants of that period.

At the end of six hundred and seventy-six years Quetzalcoatl was treated by his brothers as he had treated Tezcatlipoca, and his Sun came to an end with a great wind which carried away most of the people of that time or transformed them into monkeys.

Then for seven times fifty-two years Tlaloc was Sun; but at the end of this three hundred and sixty-four years Quetzalcoatl rained fire from heaven and made Chalchiuhtlicue Sun in place of her husband, a dignity which she held for three hundred and twelve years (six times fifty-two); and it was in these days that maize began to be used.

Now two thousand six hundred and twenty-eight years had passed since the birth of the gods, and in this year it rained so heavily that the heavens themselves fell, while the people of that time were transformed into fish. When the gods saw this, they created four men, with whose aid Tezcatlipoca and Quetzalcoatl again upreared the heavens, even as they are today; and these two gods becoming lords of the heavens and of the stars, walked therein.

After the deluge and the restoration of the heavens, Tezcatlipoca discovered the art of making fire from sticks and of drawing it from the heart of flint. The first man, Piltzintecutli, and his wife, who had been made of a hair of Xochiquetzal, did not perish in the flood, because they were divine. A son was born to them, and the gods created other people just as they had formerly existed.

But since, except for the fires, all was in darkness, the gods resolved to create a new Sun. This was done by Quetzalcoatl, who cast his own son, by Chalchiuhtlicue, into a great fire, whence he issued as the Sun of our own time; Tlaloc hurled his son into the cinders of the fire, and thence rose the Moon, ever following after the Sun. This Sun, said the gods, should eat hearts and drink blood, and so they established wars that there might be sacrifices of captives to nourish the orbs of light.

The Creation of the Universe

BEFORE THE UNIVERSE WAS CREATED, there existed only a vast expanse of sky above and an endless stretch of water and uninhabited marshland below. Olorun, the wisest of the gods, was supreme ruler of the sky, while Olokun, the most powerful goddess, ruled the seas and marshes. Both kingdoms were quite separate at that time and there was never any conflict between the two deities. Olorun was more than satisfied with his domain in the sky and hardly noticed what took place below him. Olokun was content with the kingdom she occupied, even though it contained neither living creatures nor vegetation of any kind.

But the young god Obatala was not entirely satisfied with this state of affairs, and one day, as he looked down from the sky upon the dull, grey terrain ruled by Olokun, he thought to himself:

"The kingdom below is a pitiful, barren place. Something must be done to improve its murky appearance. Now if only there were mountains and forests to brighten it up, it would make a perfect home for all sorts of living creatures."

Obatala decided that he must visit Olorun, who was always prepared to listen to him.

"It is a good scheme, but also a very ambitious one," Olorun said to Obatala. "I have no doubt that the hills and valleys you describe would be far better than grey ocean, but who will create this new world, and how will they go about it?"

"If you will give me your blessing," Obatala replied, "I myself will undertake to do this work."

"Then it is settled," said Olorun. "I cannot help you myself, but I will arrange for you to visit my son Orunmila. He will be able to guide you."

Next day, Obatala called upon Orunmila, the eldest son of Olorun, who had been given the power to read the future and to understand the secret of existence. Orunmila produced his divining tray, and when he had placed sixteen palm nuts on it, he shook the tray and cast its contents high into the air. As the nuts dropped to the ground, he read their meaning aloud:

"First, Obatala," he announced, "you must find a chain of gold long enough for you to climb down from the sky to the watery wastes below. Then, as you descend, take with you a snail shell filled with sand, a white hen, a black cat and a palm nut. This is how you should begin your quest."

Obatala listened attentively to his friend's advice and immediately set off to find a goldsmith who would make him the chain he needed to descend from the sky to the surface of the water below.

"I would be happy to make you the chain you ask for," said the goldsmith, "provided you can give me all the gold I need. But I doubt that you will find enough here for me to complete my task."

Obatala would not be dissuaded, however, and having instructed the goldsmith to go ahead with his work, he approached the other sky gods and one by one explained to them his purpose, requesting that they contribute whatever gold they possessed. The response was generous. Some of the gods gave gold dust, others gave rings, bracelets or pendants, and before long a huge, glittering mound had been collected. The goldsmith examined all the gold that was brought before him, but still he complained that there was not enough.

"It is the best I can do," Obatala told him. "I have asked all of the other gods to help out and there is no more gold left in the sky. Make the chain as long as you possibly can and fix a hook to one end. Even if it fails to reach the water below, I am determined to climb down on it."

The goldsmith worked hard to complete the chain and when it was finished, the hook was fastened to the edge of the sky and the chain lowered far below. Orunmila appeared and handed Obatala a bag containing the sand-filled snail's shell, the white hen, the black cat and the palm nut, and as soon as he had slung it over his shoulder, the young god began climbing down the golden chain, lower and lower until he saw that he was leaving the world of light and entering a world of twilight.

Before long, Obatala could feel the damp mists rising up off the surface of the water, but at the same time, he realized that he had just about reached the end of his golden chain.

"I cannot jump from here," he thought. "If I let go of the chain I will fall into the sea and almost certainly drown."

And while he looked around him rather helplessly, he suddenly heard a familiar voice calling to him from up above.

"Make use of the sand I gave you," Orunmila instructed him, "toss it into the water below."

Obatala obeyed, and after he had poured out the sand, he heard Orunmila calling to him a second time:

"Release the white hen," Orunmila cried.

Obatala reached into his bag and pulled out the white hen, dropping her on to the waters beneath where he had sprinkled the sand. As soon as she had landed, the hen began to scratch in the sand, scattering it in all directions. Wherever the grains fell, dry land instantly appeared. The larger heaps of sand became hills, while the smaller heaps became valleys.

Obatala let go of his chain and jumped on to the solid earth. As he walked he smiled with pleasure, for the land now extended a great many miles in all directions. But he was proudest of the spot where his feet had first landed, and decided to name this place Ife. Stooping to the ground, he began digging a hole, and buried his palm nut in the soil. Immediately, a palm tree sprang up from the earth, shedding its seeds as it stretched to its full height so that other trees soon shot up around it. Obatala felled some of these trees and built for himself a sturdy house thatched with palm leaves. And here, in this place, he settled down, separated from the other sky gods, with only his black cat for company.

Obatala Creates Mankind

OBATALA LIVED QUITE CONTENTEDLY in his new home beneath the skies, quite forgetting that Olorun might wish to know how his plans were progressing. The supreme god soon grew impatient for news and ordered Agemo, the chameleon, to go down the golden chain to investigate. The chameleon descended and when he arrived at Ife, he knocked timidly on Obatala's door.

"Olorun has sent me here," he said, "to discover whether or not you have been successful in your quest."

"Certainly I have," replied Obatala, "look around you and you will see the land I have created and the plants I have raised from the soil. Tell Olorun that it is now a far more pleasant kingdom than it was before, and that I would be more than willing to spend the rest of my time here, except that I am growing increasingly weary of the twilight and long to see brightness once more."

Agemo returned home and reported to Olorun all that he had seen and heard. Olorun smiled, for it pleased him greatly that Obatala had achieved what he had set out to do. The young god, who was among his favourites, had earned a special reward, and so Olorun fashioned with his own hands a dazzling golden orb and tossed it into the sky.

"For you, Obatala, I have created the sun," said Olorun, "it will shed warmth and light on the new world you have brought to life below."

Obatala very gladly received this gift, and as soon as he felt the first rays of the sun shining down on him, his restless spirit grew calmer. He remained quite satisfied for a time, but then, as the weeks turned to months, he became unsettled once more and began to dream of spending time in the company of other beings, not unlike himself, who could move and speak and with whom he could share his thoughts and feelings.

Obatala sat down and began to claw at the soil as he attempted to picture the little creatures who would keep him company. He found that the clay was soft and pliable, so he began to shape tiny figures in his own image. He laid the first of them in the sun to dry and worked on with great enthusiasm until he had produced several more.

He had been sitting for a long time in the hot sunshine before he realized how tired and thirsty he felt.

"What I need is some palm wine to revive me," he thought to himself, and he stood up and headed off towards the nearest palm tree.

He placed his bowl underneath it and drew off the palm juice, leaving it to ferment in the heat until it had turned to wine. When the wine was ready, Obatala helped himself to a very long drink, and as he gulped down bowl after bowl of the refreshing liquid, he failed to realize that the wine was making him quite drunk.

Obatala had swallowed so much of the wine that his fingers grew clumsy, but he continued to work energetically, too drunk to notice that the clay figures he now produced were no longer perfectly formed. Some had crooked backs or crooked limbs, others had arms and legs of uneven length. Obatala was so pleased with himself he raised his head and called out jubilantly to the skies:

"I have created beings from the soil, but only you, Olorun, can breathe life into them. Grant me this request so that I will always have human beings to keep me company here in Ife."

Olorun heard Obatala's plea and did not hesitate to breathe life into the clay figures, watching with interest as they rose up from the ground and began to obey the commands of their creator. Soon they had built wooden shelters for themselves next to the god's own house, creating the first Yoruba village in Ife where before only one solitary house had stood. Obatala was filled with admiration and pride, but now, as the effects of the palm wine started to wear off, he began to notice that some of the humans he had created were contorted and misshapen. The sight of the little creatures struggling as they went about their chores filled him with sadness and remorse.

"My drunkenness has caused these people to suffer," he proclaimed solemnly, "and I swear that I will never drink palm wine again. From this day forward, I will be the special protector of all humans who are born with deformities."

Obatala remained faithful to his pledge and dedicated himself to the welfare of the human beings he had created, making sure that he always had a moment to spare for the lame and the blind. He saw to it that the people prospered and, before long, the Yoruba village of Ife had grown into an impressive city. Obatala also made certain that his people had all the tools they needed to clear and cultivate the land. He presented each man with a copper bush knife and a wooden hoe and taught them to grow millet, yams and a whole variety of other crops, ensuring that mankind had a plentiful supply of food for its survival.

Olokun's Revenge

AFTER HE HAD LIVED among the human race for a long period of time, Obatala came to the decision that he had done all he could for his people. The day had arrived for him to retire, he believed, and so he climbed up the golden chain and returned to his home in the sky once more, promising to visit the earth as frequently as possible. The other gods never tired of hearing Obatala describe the kingdom he had created below. Many were so captivated by the image he presented of the newly created human beings, that they decided to depart from the sky and go down to live among them. And as they prepared to leave, Olorun took them aside and counselled them:

"Each of you shall have a special role while you are down there, and I ask that you never forget your duty to the human race. Always listen to the prayers of the people and offer help when they are in need."

One deity, however, was not at all pleased with Obatala's work or the praise he had received from Olorun. The goddess Olokun, ruler of the sea, watched with increasing fury as, one by one, the other gods arrived in her domain and began dividing up the land amongst themselves.

"Obatala has never once consulted me about any of this," she announced angrily, "but he shall pay for the insult to my honour."

The goddess commanded the great waves of her ocean to rise up, for it was her intention to destroy the land Obatala had created and replace it with water once more. The terrible flood began, and soon the fields were completely submerged. Crops were destroyed and thousands of people were swept away by the roaring tide.

Those who survived the deluge fled to the hills and called to Obatala for help, but he could not hear them from his home high above in the sky.

In desperation, the people turned to Eshu, one of the gods recently descended to earth.

"Please return to the sky," they begged, "and tell the great gods of the flood that threatens to destroy everything."

"First you must show that you revere the gods," replied Eshu. "You must offer up a sacrifice and pray hard that you will be saved."

The people went away and returned with a goat which they sacrificed as food for Obatala. But still Eshu refused to carry the message.

"You ask me to perform this great service," he told them, "and yet you do not offer to reward me. If I am to be your messenger, I too deserve a gift."

The people offered up more sacrifices to Eshu and only when he was content that they had shown him appropriate respect did he begin to climb the golden chain back to the sky to deliver his message.

Obatala was deeply upset by the news and extremely anxious for the safety of his people, for he was uncertain how best to deal with so powerful a goddess as Olokun. Once more, he approached Orunmila and asked for advice. Orunmila consulted his divining nuts, and at last he said to Obatala:

"Rest here in the sky while I descend below. I will use my gifts to turn back the water and make the land rise again."

Orunmila went down and, using his special powers, brought the waves under control so that the marshes began to dry up and land became visible again. But although the people greeted the god as their saviour and pleaded with him to act as their protector, Orunmila confessed that he had no desire to remain among them. Before he departed, however, he passed on a great many of his gifts to the people, teaching them how to divine the future and to control the unseen forces of nature. What he taught the people was never lost and it was passed on like a precious heirloom from one generation to another.

Agemo Outwits Olokun

BUT EVEN AFTER ORUNMILA HAD RETURNED to his home in the sky, all was not yet settled between Olokun and the other sky gods. More embittered than ever before by her defeat, Olokun began to consider ways in which she might humiliate Olorun, the god who had allowed Obatala to usurp her kingdom.

Now the goddess was a highly skilled weaver, but she was also expert in dyeing the cloths she had woven. And knowing that no other sky god possessed greater knowledge of cloth making, she sent a message to Olorun challenging him to a weaving contest. Olorun received her message rather worriedly and said to himself:

"Olokun knows far more about making cloth that I will ever know, but I cannot allow her to think that she is superior to me in anything. Somehow I must appear to meet her challenge and yet avoid taking part in the contest. But how can I possibly do this?"

He pondered the problem a very long time until, at last, he was struck by a worthwhile thought. Smiling broadly, he summoned Agemo, the chameleon, to his side, and instructed him to carry an important message to Olokun.

Agemo climbed down the golden chain and went in search of Olokun's dwelling.

"The ruler of the sky, Olorun, greets you," he announced. "He says that if your cloth is as magnificent as you say it is, then the ruler of the sky will be happy to compete with you in the contest you have suggested. But he thinks it only fair to see some of your cloth in advance, and has asked me to examine it on his behalf so that I may report to him on its quality."

Olokun was happy to accommodate Olorun's request. She retired to a backroom and having put on a skirt of radiant green cloth, she stood confidently before the chameleon. But as the chameleon looked at the garment, his skin began to change colour until it was exactly the same brilliant shade as the skirt. Next Olokun put on an orange-hued cloth. But again, to her astonishment, the chameleon turned a beautiful shade of bright orange. One by one, the goddess put on skirts of various bright colours, but on each occasion the chameleon perfectly matched the colour of her robe. Finally the goddess thought to herself:

"This person is only a messenger, and if Olorun's servants can reproduce the exact colours of my very finest cloth, what hope will I have in a contest against the supreme god himself?"

The goddess conceded defeat and spoke earnestly to the chameleon:

"Tell your master that the ruler of the seas sends her greetings to the ruler of the sky. Say to him that I acknowledge his supremacy in weaving and in all other things as well."

And so it came to pass that Olorun and Olokun resumed their friendship and that peace was restored to the whole of the universe once more.

The Gods Descend from the Sky

NANA BALUKU, the mother of all creation, fell pregnant before she finally retired from the universe. Her offspring was androgynous, a being with one body and two faces. The face that resembled a woman was called Mawu and her eyes were the moon. She took control of the night and all territories to the west. The male face was called Lisa and his eyes were the sun. Lisa controlled the east and took charge of the daylight.

At the beginning of the present world, Mawu-Lisa was the only being in existence, but eventually the moon was eclipsed by the sun and many children were conceived. The first fruits of the union were a pair of twins, a male called Da Zodji and a female called Nyohwè Ananu. Another child followed shortly afterwards, a male and female form joined in one body, and this child was named Sogbo. The third birth again produced twins, a male, Agbè, and a female, Naètè. The fourth and fifth children were both male and were named Agè and Gu. Gu's torso was made of stone and a giant sword protruded from the hole in his neck where his head would otherwise have been. The sixth offspring was not made of flesh and blood. He was given the name Djo, meaning air, or atmosphere. Finally, the seventh child born was named Legba, and because he was the youngest, he became Mawu-Lisa's particular favourite.

When these children had grown to adulthood and the appropriate time had arrived to divide up the kingdoms of the universe among them, Mawu-Lisa gathered them together. To their first-born, the twins Da Zodji and Nyohwè Ananu, the parents gave the earth below and sent them, laden with heavenly riches, down from the sky to inhabit their new home. To Sogbo, who was both man and woman, they gave the sky, commanding him to rule over thunder and lightning. The twins Agbè and Naètè were sent to take command of the waters and the creatures of the deep, while Agè was ordered to live in the bush as a hunter where he could take control of all the birds and beasts of the earth.

To Gu, whom Mawu-Lisa considered their strength, they gave the forests and vast stretches of fertile soil, supplying him also with the tools and weapons mankind would need to cultivate the land. Mawu-Lisa ordered Djo to occupy the space between the earth and the sky and entrusted him with the life-span of human beings. It was also Djo's role to clothe the other sky gods, making them invisible to man.

To each of their offspring, Mawu-Lisa then gave a special language. These are the languages still spoken by the priests and mediums of the gods in their songs and oracles. To Da Zodji and Nyohwè Ananu, Mawu-Lisa gave the language of the earth and took from them all memory of the sky language. They gave to Sogbo, Agbè and Naètè, Agè and Gu the languages they would speak. But to Djo, they gave the language of men.

Then Mawu-Lisa said to Legba: "Because you are my youngest child, I will keep you with me always. Your work will be to visit all the kingdoms ruled over by your brothers and sisters and report to me on their progress."

And that is why Legba knows all the languages of his siblings, and he alone knows the language of Mawu-Lisa. You will find Legba everywhere, because all beings, human and gods, must first approach Legba before Mawu-Lisa, the supreme deity, will answer their prayers.

God Abandons the Earth

IN THE BEGINNING, God was very proud of the human beings he had created and wanted to live as close as possible to them. So he made certain that the sky was low enough for the people to touch and built for himself a home directly above their heads. God was so near that everyone on earth became familiar with his face and every day he would stop to make conversation with the people, offering a helping hand if they were ever in trouble.

This arrangement worked very well at first, but soon God observed that the people had started to take advantage of his closeness. Children began to wipe their greasy hands on the sky when they had finished their meals and often, if a woman was in search of an extra ingredient for dinner, she would simply reach up, tear a piece off the sky and add it to her cooking pot. God remained tolerant through all of this, but he knew his patience would not last forever and hoped that his people would not test its limit much further.

Then one afternoon, just as he had lain down to rest, a group of women gathered underneath the sky to pound the corn they had harvested. One old woman among them had a particularly large wooden bowl and a very long pestle, and as she thumped down on the grains, she knocked violently against the sky. God arose indignantly from his bed and descended below, but as he approached the woman to chastise her, she suddenly jerked back her arm and hit him in the eye with her very long pestle.

God gave a great shout, his voice booming like thunder through the air, and as he shouted, he raised his powerful arms above his head and pushed upwards against the sky with all his strength, flinging it far into the distance.

As soon as they realized that the earth and the sky were separated, the people became angry with the old woman who had injured God and pestered her day and night to bring him back to them. The woman went away and although she was not very clever, she thought long and hard about the problem until she believed she had found the solution. Returning to her village, she ordered her children to collect all the wooden mortars that they could find. These she piled one on top of the other until they had almost bridged the gap between the earth and the heavens. Only one more mortar was needed to complete the job, but although her children searched high and low, they could not find the missing object. In desperation, the old woman told them to remove the lowest mortar from the bottom of the pile and place it on the top. But as soon as they did this, all the mortars came crashing down, killing the old woman, her children and the crowd who had gathered to admire the towering structure.

Ever since that day, God has remained in the heavens where mankind can no longer approach him as easily as before. There are some, however, who say they have caught a glimpse of him and others who offer up sacrifices calling for his forgiveness and asking him to make his home among them once more.

The Coming of Darkness

WHEN GOD FIRST MADE THE WORLD, there was never any darkness or cold. The sun always shone brightly during the day, and at night, the moon bathed the earth in a softer light, ensuring that everything could still be seen quite clearly.

But one day God sent for the Bat and handed him a mysterious parcel to take to the moon. He told the Bat it contained darkness, but as he did not have the time to explain precisely what darkness was, the Bat went on his way without fully realizing the importance of his mission.

He flew at a leisurely pace with the parcel strapped on his back until he began to feel rather tired and hungry. He was in no great hurry he decided, and so he put down his load by the roadside and wandered off in search of something to eat.

But while he was away, a group of mischievous animals approached the spot where he had paused to rest and, seeing the parcel, began to open it, thinking there might be something of value inside of it. The Bat returned just as they were untying the last piece of string and rushed forward to stop them. But too late! The darkness forced its way through the opening and rose up into the sky before anyone had a chance to catch it.

Quickly the Bat gave chase, flying about everywhere, trying to grab hold of the darkness and return it to the parcel before God discovered what had happened. But the harder he tried, the more the darkness eluded him, so that eventually he fell into an exhausted sleep lasting several hours.

When the Bat awoke, he found himself in a strange twilight world and once again, he began chasing about in every direction, hoping he would succeed where he had failed before.

But the Bat has never managed to catch the darkness, although you will see him every evening just after the sun has set, trying to trap it and deliver it safely to the moon as God first commanded him.

How Death First Entered the World

MANY YEARS AGO, a great famine spread throughout the land, and at that time, the eldest son of every household was sent out in search of food and instructed not to return until he had found something for the family to eat and drink.

There was a certain young man among the Krachi whose responsibility it was to provide for the family, and so he wandered off in search of food, moving deeper and deeper into the bush every day until he finally came to a spot he did not recognize. Just up ahead of him, he noticed a large form lying on the ground. He approached it cautiously, hoping that if the creature were dead, it might be a good source of food, but he had taken only a few steps forward when the mound began to stir, revealing that it was not an animal at all, but a ferocious-looking giant with flowing white hair stretched out for miles on the ground around him, all the way from Krachi to Salaga.

The giant opened one eye and shouted at the young man to explain his presence. The boy stood absolutely terrified, yet after some minutes, he managed to blurt out that he had never intended to disturb the giant's rest, but had come a great distance in search of food.

"I am Owuo," said the giant, "but people also call me Death. You, my friend, have caught me in a good mood and so I will give you some food and water if you will fetch and carry for me in return."

The young man could scarcely believe his luck, and readily agreed to serve the giant in exchange for a few regular meals. Owuo arose and walked towards his cave where he began roasting some meat on a spit over the fire. Never before had the boy tasted such a fine meal, and after he had washed it down with a bowl of fresh water, he sat back and smiled, well pleased that he had made the acquaintance of the giant.

For a long time afterwards, the young man happily served Owuo, and every evening, in return for his work, he was presented with a plate of the most delicious meat for his supper.

But one day the boy awoke feeling terribly homesick and begged his master to allow him to visit his family, if only for a few days.

"You may visit your family for as long as you wish," said the giant, "on the condition that you bring another boy to replace you."

So the young man returned to his village where he told his family the whole story of his meeting with the giant. Eventually he managed to persuade his younger brother to go with him into the bush and here he handed him over to Owuo, promising that he would himself return before too long.

Several months had passed, and soon the young man grew hungry again and began to yearn for a taste of the meat the giant had cooked for him. Finally, he made up his mind to return to his master, and leaving his family behind, he returned to Owuo's hut and knocked boldly on the door.

The giant himself answered, and asked the young man what he wanted.

"I would like some more of the good meat you were once so generous to share with me," said the boy, hoping the giant would remember his face.

"Very well," replied Owuo, "you can have as much of it as you want, but you will have to work hard for me, as you did before."

The young man consented, and after he had eaten as much as he could, he went about his chores enthusiastically. The work lasted many weeks and every day the boy ate his fill of roasted meat. But to his surprise he never saw anything of his brother, and whenever he asked about him, the giant told him, rather aloofly, that the lad had simply gone away on business.

Once more, however, the young man grew homesick and asked Owuo for permission to visit his village. The giant agreed on condition that this time, he bring back a girl to carry out his duties while he was away. The young man hurried home and there he pleaded with his sister to go into the bush and keep the giant company for a few months. The girl agreed, and after she had waved goodbye to her brother, she entered the giant's cave quite merrily, accompanied by a slave companion her own age.

Only a short time had passed before the boy began to dream of the meat again, longing for even a small morsel of it. So he followed the familiar path through the bush until he found Owuo's cave. The giant did not seem particularly pleased to see him and grumbled loudly at the disturbance. But he pointed the way to a room at the back and told the boy to help himself to as much meat as he wanted.

The young man took up a juicy bone which he began to devour. But to his horror, he recognized it at once as his sister's thigh and as he looked more closely at all the rest of the meat, he was appalled to discover that he had been sitting there, happily chewing on the body of his sister and her slave girl.

As fast as his legs could carry him, he raced back to the village and immediately confessed to the elders what he had done and the awful things he had seen. At once, the alarm was sounded and all the people hurried out into the bush to investigate the giant's dwelling for themselves. But as they drew nearer, they became fearful of what he might do to them and scurried back to the village to consult among themselves what steps should be taken. Eventually, it was agreed to go to Salaga, where they knew the giant's long hair came to an end, and set it alight. The chief of the village carried the torch, and when they were certain that the giant's hair was burning well, they returned to the bush, hid themselves in the undergrowth, and awaited the giant's reaction.

Presently, Owuo began to sweat and toss about inside his cave. The closer the flames moved towards him, the more he thrashed about and grumbled until, at last, he rushed outside, his head on fire, and fell down screaming in agony.

The villagers approached him warily and only the young man had the courage to venture close enough to see whether the giant was still breathing. And as he bent over the huge form, he noticed a bundle of medicine concealed in the roots of Owuo's hair. Quickly he seized it and called to the others to come and see what he had found.

The chief of the village examined the bundle, but no one could say what power the peculiar medicine might have. Then one old man among the crowd suggested that no harm could be done if they took some of the medicine and sprinkled it on the bones and meat in the giant's hut. This was done, and to the delight of everyone gathered, the slave girl, her mistress and the boy's brother returned to life at once.

A small quantity of the medicine-dust remained, but when the young man proposed that he should put it on the giant and restore him to life, there was a great uproar among the people. Yet the boy insisted that he should help the giant who had once helped him, and so the chief, by way of compromise, allowed him to sprinkle the left-over dust into the eye of the dead giant.

The young man had no sooner done this when the giant's eye opened wide, causing the people to flee in great terror.

But it is from this eye that death comes. For every time that Owuo shuts that eye, a man dies, and unfortunately for mankind, he is forever blinking and winking, trying to clear the dust from his eye.

The Thunder's Bride

IN THIS STORY we find Imana associated with thunder and lightning, so that we may suppose him to be a sky-god, or, at any rate, to have been such in the beginning. In story which follows, the Thunder is treated as a distinct personage, but he is nowhere said to be identical with Imana.

There was a certain woman of Rwanda, the wife of Kwisaba. Her husband went away to the wars, and was absent for many months. One day while she was all alone in the hut she was taken ill, and found herself too weak and wretched to get up and make a fire, which would have been done for her at once had anyone been present. She cried out, talking wildly in her despair: "Oh, what shall I do? If only I had someone to split the kindling wood and build the fire! I shall die of cold if no one comes! Oh, if someone would but come – if it were the very Thunder of heaven himself!"

So the woman spoke, scarcely knowing what she said, and presently a little cloud appeared in the sky. She could not see it, but very soon it spread, other clouds collected, till the sky was quite overcast; it grew dark as night inside the hut, and she heard thunder rumbling in the distance. Then there came a flash of lightning close by, and she saw the Thunder standing before her, in the likeness of a man, with a little bright axe in his hand. He fell to, and had split all the wood in a twinkling; then he built it up and lit it, just with a touch of his hand, as if his fingers had been torches. When the blaze leapt up he turned to the woman and said, "Now, oh wife of Kwisaba, what will you give me?" She was quite paralysed with fright, and could not utter a word. He gave her a little time to recover, and then went on: "When your baby is born, if it is a girl, will you give her to me for a wife?" Trembling all over, the poor woman could only stammer out, "Yes!" and the Thunder vanished.

Not long after this a baby girl was born, who grew into a fine, healthy child, and was given the name of Miseke. When Kwisaba came home from the wars the women met him with the news that he had a little daughter, and he was delighted, partly, perhaps, with the thought of the cattle he would get as her bride-price when she was old enough to be married. But when his wife told him about the Thunder he looked very serious, and said, "When she grows older you must never on any account let her go outside the house, or we shall have the Thunder carrying her off."

So as long as Miseke was quite little she was allowed to play out of doors with the other children, but the time came all too soon when she had to be shut up inside the hut. One day some of the other girls came running to Miseke's mother in great excitement. "Miseke is dropping beads out of her mouth! We thought she had put them in on purpose, but they come dropping out every time she laughs." Sure enough the mother found that it was so, and not only did Miseke produce beads of the kinds most valued, but beautiful brass and copper bangles. Miseke's father was greatly troubled when they told him of this. He said it must be the Thunder, who sent the beads in this extraordinary way as the presents which a man always has to send to his betrothed while she is growing up. So Miseke had always to stay indoors and amuse herself as best she could – when she was not helping in the house work – by plaiting mats and making baskets. Sometimes her old playfellows came to see her, but they too did not care to be shut up for long in a dark, stuffy hut.

One day, when Miseke was about fifteen, a number of the girls made up a party to go and dig *inkwa* (white clay) and they thought it would be good fun to take Miseke along with them. They went to her mother's hut and called her, but of course her parents would not hear of her going, and she had to stay at home. They tried again another day, but with no better success. Some time after this, however, Kwisaba and his wife both went to see to their garden, which was situated a long way off, so that they had to start at daybreak, leaving Miseke alone in the hut. Somehow the girls got to hear of this, and as they had already planned to go for *inkwa* that day they went to fetch her. The temptation was too great, and she slipped out very quietly, and went with them to the watercourse where the white clay was to be found. So many people had gone there at different times for the same purpose that quite a large pit had been dug out. The girls got into it and fell to work, laughing and chattering, when, suddenly, they became aware that it was growing dark, and, looking up, saw a great black cloud gathering overhead. And then, suddenly, they saw the figure of a man standing before them, and he called out in a great voice, "Where is Miseke, daughter of Kwisaba?" One girl came out of the hole, and said, "I am not Miseke, daughter of Kwisaba. When Miseke laughs, beads and bangles drop from her lips." The Thunder said, "Well, then, laugh, and let me see." She laughed, and nothing happened. "No, I see you are not she." So one after another was questioned and sent on her way. Miseke herself came last, and tried to pass, repeating the same words that the others had said; but the Thunder insisted on her laughing, and a shower of beads fell on the ground. The Thunder caught her up and carried her off to the sky and married her.

Of course she was terribly frightened, but the Thunder proved a kind husband, and she settled down quite happily and, in due time, had three children, two boys and a girl. When the baby girl was a few weeks old Miseke told her husband that she would like to go home and see her parents. He not only consented, but provided her with cattle and beer (as provision for the journey and presents on arrival) and carriers for her hammock, and sent her down to earth with this parting advice: "Keep to the high road; do not turn aside into any unfrequented bypath." But, being unacquainted with the country, her carriers soon strayed from the main track. After they had gone for some distance along the wrong road they found the path barred by a strange monster called an *igikoko,* a sort of ogre, who demanded something to eat. Miseke told the servants to give him the beer they were carrying: he drank all the pots dry in no time. Then he seized one of the carriers and ate him, then a second – in short, he devoured them all, as well as the cattle, till no one was left but Miseke and her children. The ogre then demanded a child. Seeing no help for it, Miseke gave him the younger boy, and then, driven to extremity, the baby she was nursing, but while he was thus engaged she contrived to send off the elder boy, whispering to him to run till he came to a house. "If you see an old man sitting on the ash-heap in the front yard that will be your grandfather; if you see some young men shooting arrows at a mark they will be your uncles; the boys herding the cows are your cousins; and you will find your grandmother inside the hut. Tell them to come and help us."

The boy set off, while his mother kept off the ogre as best she could. He arrived at his grandfather's homestead, and told them what had happened, and they started at once, having first tied the bells on their hunting dogs. The boy showed them the way as well as he could, but they nearly missed Miseke just at last; only she heard the dogs' bells and called out. Then the young men rushed in and killed the ogre with their spears. Before he died he said, "If you cut off my big toe you will get back everything belonging to you." They did so, and, behold! out came the carriers and the cattle, the servants and the children, none of them any the worse. Then, first making sure that the ogre was really dead, they set off for Miseke's old home. Her parents were overjoyed to see her and the children, and the time passed all too quickly. At the end of a month she began to think she ought to return, and the old people sent out for cattle and all sorts of presents, as is the custom when a guest is going to leave. Everything was got together outside the village, and her brothers were ready to escort her, when they saw the clouds gathering, and, behold! all of a sudden Miseke, her children, her servants, her cattle, and her porters, with their loads, were all caught up into the air and disappeared. The family were struck dumb with amazement, and they never saw Miseke on earth again. It is to be presumed that she lived happily ever after.

Anansi Obtains the Sky-God's Stories

KWAKU ANANSI had one great wish. He longed to be the owner of all the stories known in the world, but these were kept by the Sky-God, Nyame [The Ashanti refer to God as 'Nyame'. The Dagomba call him 'Wuni', while the Krachi refer to him as 'Wulbari'.], in a safe hiding-place high above the clouds.

One day, Anansi decided to pay the Sky-God a visit to see if he could persuade Nyame to sell him the stories.

"I am flattered you have come so far, little creature," the Sky-God told Anansi, "but many rich and powerful men have preceded you and none has been able to purchase what they came here for. I am willing to part with my stories, but the price is very high. What makes you think that you can succeed where they have all failed?"

"I feel sure I will be able to buy them," answered Anansi bravely, "if you will only tell me what the price is."

"You are very determined, I see," replied Nyame, "but I must warn you that the price is no ordinary one. Listen carefully now to what I demand of you.

"First of all, you must capture Onini, the wise old python, and present him to me. When you have done this, you must go in search of the Mmoboro, the largest nest of hornets in the forest, and bring them here also. Finally, look for Osebo, the fastest of all leopards and set a suitable trap for him. Bring him to me either dead or alive.

"When you have delivered me these three things, all the stories of the world will be handed over to you."

"I shall bring you everything you ask for," Anansi declared firmly, and he hastened towards his home where he began making plans for the tasks ahead.

That afternoon, he sat down with his wife, Aso, and told her all about his visit to the Sky-God.

"How will I go about trapping the great python, Onini?" he asked her.

His wife, who was a very clever woman, instructed her husband to make a special trip to the centre of the woods:

"Go and cut yourself a long bamboo pole," she ordered him, "and gather some strong creeper-vines as well. As soon as you have done this, return here to me and I will tell you what to do with these things."

Anansi gathered these objects as his wife had commanded and after they had spent some hours consulting further, he set off enthusiastically towards the house of Onini.

As he approached closer, he suddenly began arguing with himself in a loud and angry voice:

"My wife is a stupid woman," he pronounced, "she says it is longer and stronger. I say it is shorter and weaker. She has no respect. I have a great deal. She is stupid. I am right."

"What's all this about?" asked the python, suddenly appearing at the door of his hut. "Why are you having this angry conversation with yourself?"

"Oh! Please ignore me," answered the spider. "It's just that my wife has put me in such a bad mood. For she says this bamboo pole is longer and stronger than you are, and I say she is a liar."

"There is no need for the two of you to argue so bitterly on my account," replied the python, "bring that pole over here and we will soon find out who is right."

So Anansi laid the bamboo pole on the earth and the python stretched himself out alongside it.

"I'm still not certain about this," said Anansi after a few moments. "When you stretch at one end, you appear to shrink at the other end. Perhaps if I tied you to the pole I would have a clearer idea of your size."

"Very well," answered the python, "just so long as we can sort this out properly."

Anansi then took the creeper-vine and wrapped it round and round the length of the python's body until the great creature was unable to move.

"Onini," said Anansi, "it appears my wife was right. You are shorter and weaker than this pole and more foolish into the bargain. Now you are my prisoner and I must take you to the Sky-God, as I have promised."

The great python lowered his head in defeat as Anansi tugged on the pole, dragging him along towards the home of Nyame.

"You have done well, spider," said the god, "but remember, there are two more, equally difficult quests ahead. You have much to accomplish yet, and it would not be wise to delay here any longer."

So Anansi returned home once more and sat down to discuss the next task with his wife.

"There are still hornets to catch," he told her, "and I cannot think of a way to capture an entire swarm all at once."

"Look for a gourd," his wife suggested, "and after you have filled it with water, go out in search of the hornets."

Anansi found a suitable gourd and filled it to the brim. Fortunately, he knew exactly the tree where the hornets had built their nest. But before he approached too close, he poured some of the water from the gourd over himself so that his clothes were dripping wet. Then, he began sprinkling the nest with the remaining water while shouting out to the hornets:

"Why do you remain in such a flimsy shelter Mmoboro, when the great rains have already begun? You will soon be swept away, you foolish people. Here, take cover in this dry gourd of mine and it will protect you from the storms."

The hornets thanked the spider for this most timely warning and disappeared one by one into the gourd. As soon as the last of them had entered, Anansi plugged the mouth of the vessel with some grass and chuckled to himself:

"Fools! I have outwitted you as well. Now you can join Onini, the python. I'm certain Nyame will be very pleased to see you."

Anansi was delighted with himself. It had not escaped his notice that even the Sky-God appeared rather astonished by his success and it filled him with great excitement to think that very soon he would own all the stories of the world.

Only Osebo, the leopard, stood between the spider and his great wish, but Anansi was confident that with the help of his wife he could easily ensnare the creature as he had done all the others.

"You must go and look for the leopard's tracks," his wife told him, "and then dig a hole where you know he is certain to walk."

Anansi went away and dug a very deep pit in the earth, covering it with branches and leaves so that it was well-hidden from the naked eye. Night-time closed in around him and soon afterwards, Osebo came prowling as usual and fell right into the deep hole, snarling furiously as he hit the bottom.

At dawn on the following morning, Anansi approached the giant pit and called to the leopard:

"What has happened here? Have you been drinking, leopard? How on earth will you manage to escape from this great hole?"

"I have fallen into a silly man-trap," said the leopard impatiently. "Help me out at once. I am almost starving to death in this wretched place."

"And if I help you out, how can I be sure you won't eat me?" asked Anansi. "You say you are very hungry, after all."

"I wouldn't do a thing like that," Osebo reassured him. "I beg you, just this once, to trust me. Nothing bad will happen to you, I promise."

Anansi hurried away from the opening of the pit and soon returned with a long, thick rope. Glancing around him, he spotted a tall green tree and bent it towards the ground, securing it with a length of the rope so that the top branches hung over the pit. Then he tied another piece of rope to these branches, dropping the loose end into the pit for the leopard to tie to his tail.

"As soon as you have tied a large knot, let me know and I will haul you up," shouted Anansi.

Osebo obeyed the spider's every word, and as soon as he gave the signal that he was ready, Anansi cut the rope pinning the tree to the ground. It sprung upright at once, pulling the leopard out of the hole in one swift motion. Osebo hung upside down, wriggling and twisting helplessly, trying with every ounce of his strength to loosen his tail from the rope. But Anansi was not about to take any chances and he plunged his knife deep into the leopard's chest, killing him instantly. Then he lifted the leopard's body from the earth and carried it all the way to the Sky-God.

Nyame now called together all the elders of the skies, among them the Adonten, the Oyoko, the Kontire and Akwam chiefs, and informed them of the great exploits of Anansi, the spider:

"Many great warriors and chiefs have tried before," the Sky-God told the congregation, "but none has been able to pay the price I have asked of them. Kwaku Anansi has brought me Onini the python, the Mmoboro nest and the body of the mighty Osebo. The time has come to repay him as he deserves. He has won the right to tell my stories. From today, they will no longer be called stories of the Sky-God, but stories of Anansi, the spider."

And so, with Nyame's blessing, Anansi became the treasurer of all the stories that have ever been told. And even now, whenever a man wishes to tell a story for the entertainment of his people, he must acknowledge first of all that the tale is a great gift, given to him by Anansi, the spider.

Sudika-Mbambi the Invincible

SUDIKA-MBAMBI was the son of Nzua dia Kimanaweze, who married the daughter of the Sun and Moon. The young couple were living with Nzua's parents, when one day Kimanaweze sent his son away to Loanda to trade. The son demurred, but the father insisted, so he went. While he was gone certain cannibal monsters, called *makishi*, descended on the village and sacked it – all the people who were not killed fled. Nzua, when he returned, found no houses and no people; searching over the cultivated ground, he at last came across his wife, but she was so changed that he did not recognize her at first. "The *makishi* have destroyed us," was her explanation of what had happened.

They seem to have camped and cultivated as best they could; and in due course Sudika-Mbambi ('the Thunderbolt') was born. He was a wonder-child, who spoke before his entrance into the world, and came forth equipped with knife, stick, and his *kilembe* (a 'mythic plant', explained as 'life-tree'), which he requested his mother to plant at the back of the house. Scarcely had he made his appearance when another voice was heard, and his twin brother Kabundungulu was born. The first thing they did was to cut down poles and build a house for their parents. Soon after this, Sudika-Mbambi announced that he was going to fight the *makishi*. He told Kabundungulu to stay at home and to keep an eye on the *kilembe*: if it withered he would know that his brother was dead; he then set out. On his way he was joined by four beings who called themselves *kipalendes* and boasted various accomplishments – building a house on the bare rock (a sheer impossibility under local conditions), carving ten clubs a day, and other more recondite operations, none of which, however, as the event proved, they could accomplish successfully. When they had gone a certain distance through the bush Sudika-Mbambi directed them to halt and build a house, in order to fight the *makishi*. As soon as he had cut one pole all the others needed cut themselves. He ordered the *kipalende* who had said he could erect a house on a rock to begin building, but as fast as a pole was set up it fell down again. The leader then took the work in hand, and it was speedily finished.

Next day he set out to fight the *makishi*, with three *kipalendes*, leaving the fourth in the house. To him soon after appeared an old woman, who told him that he might marry her granddaughter if he would fight her (the grandmother) and overcome her. They wrestled, but the old woman soon threw the *kipalende*, placed a large stone on top of him as he lay on the ground, and left him there, unable to move.

Sudika-Mbambi, who had the gift of second-sight, at once knew what had happened, returned with the other three, and released the *kipalende*. He told his story, and the others derided him for being beaten by a woman. Next day he accompanied the rest, the second *kipalende* remaining in the house. No details are given of the fighting with the *makishi*, beyond the statement that "they are firing." The second *kipalende* met with the same fate as his brother, and again Sudika-Mbambi was immediately aware of it. The incident was repeated on the third and on the fourth day. On the fifth Sudika-Mbambi sent the *kipalendes* to the war, and stayed behind himself. The old woman challenged him; he fought her and killed her – she seems to have been a peculiarly malignant kind of witch, who had kept her granddaughter shut up in a stone house, presumably as a lure for unwary strangers. It is not stated what she intended to do with the captives whom she secured under heavy stones, but, judging from what takes place in other stories of this kind, one may conclude that they were kept to be eaten in due course.

Sudika-Mbambi married the old witch's granddaughter, and they settled down in the stone house. The *kipalendes* returned with the news that the *makishi* were completely defeated, and all went well for a time.

Treachery of the Kipalendes

The *kipalendes*, however, became envious of their leader's good fortune, and plotted to kill him. They dug a hole in the place where he usually rested and covered it with mats; when he came in tired they pressed him to sit down, which he did, and immediately fell into the hole. They covered it up, and thought they had made an end of him. His younger brother, at home, went to look at the 'life-tree', and found that it had withered. Thinking that, perhaps, there was still some hope, he poured water on it, and it grew green again.

Sudika-Mbambi was not killed by the fall; when he reached the bottom of the pit he looked round and saw an opening. Entering this, he found himself in a road – the road, in fact, which leads to the country of the dead. When he had gone some distance he came upon an old woman, or, rather, the upper half of one (half-beings are very common in African folklore, but they are usually split lengthways, having one eye, one arm, one leg, and so on), hoeing her garden by the wayside. He greeted her, and she returned his greeting. He then asked her to show him the way, and she said she would do so if he would hoe a little for her, which he did. She set him on the road, and told him to take the narrow path, not the broad one, and before arriving at Kalunga-ngombe's house he must carry a jug of red pepper and a jug of wisdom. It is not explained how he was to procure these, though it is evident from the sequel that he did so, nor how they were to be used, except that Kalunga-ngombe makes it a condition that anyone who wants to marry his daughter must bring them with him. We have not previously been told that this was Sudika-Mbambi's intention. On arriving at the house a fierce dog barked at him; he scolded it, and it let him pass. He entered, and was courteously welcomed by people who showed him into the guest house and spread a mat for him. He then announced that he had come to marry the daughter of Kalunga-ngombe. Kalunga answered that he consented if Sudika-Mbambi had fulfilled the conditions. He then retired for the night, and a meal was sent in to him-a live cock and a bowl of the local porridge (*Junji*). He ate the porridge, with some meat which he had brought with him; instead of killing the cock he kept him under his bed. Evidently it was thought he would assume that the fowl was meant for him to eat (perhaps we have here a remnant of the belief, not known to or not understood by the narrator of the story, that the living must not eat of the food of the dead), and a trick was intended, to prevent his return to the upper world. In the middle of the night he heard people inquiring who had killed Kalunga's cock; but the cock crowed from under the bed, and Sudika-Mbambi was not trapped. Next morning, when he reminded Kalunga of his promise, he was told that the daughter had been carried off by the huge serpent called Kinyoka kya Tumba, and that if he wanted to marry her he must rescue her.

Sudika-Mbambi started for Kinyoka's abode, and asked for him. Kinyoka's wife said, "He has gone shooting." Sudika-Mbambi waited awhile, and presently saw driver ants approaching – the dreaded ants which would consume any living thing left helpless in their path. He stood his ground and beat them off; they were followed by red ants, these by a swarm of bees, and these by wasps, but none of them harmed him. Then Kinyoka's five heads appeared, one after the other. Sudika-Mbambi cut off each as it came, and when the fifth fell the snake was dead. He went into the house, found Kalunga's daughter there, and took her home to her father.

But Kalunga was not yet satisfied. There was a giant fish, Kimbiji, which kept catching his goats and pigs. Sudika-Mbambi baited a large hook with a sucking-pig and caught Kimbiji, but even he was not strong enough to pull the monster to land. He fell into the water, and Kimbiji swallowed him.

Kabundungulu, far away at their home, saw that his brother's life-tree had withered once more, and set out to find him. He reached the house where the *kipalendes* were keeping Sudika-Mbambi's wife captive, and asked where he was. They denied all knowledge of him, but he felt certain there had been foul play. "You have killed him. Uncover the grave." They opened up the pit, and Kabundungulu descended into it. He met with the old woman, and was directed to Kalunga-ngombe's dwelling. On inquiring for his brother he was told, "Kimbiji has swallowed him." Kabundungulu asked for a pig, baited his hook, and called the people to his help. Between them they landed the fish, and Kabundungulu cut it open. He found his brother's bones inside it, and took them out. Then he said, "My elder, arise!" and the bones came to life. Sudika-Mbambi married Kalunga-ngombe's daughter, and set out for home with her and his brother. They reached the pit, which had been filled in, and the ground cracked and they got out. They drove away the four *kipalendes* and, having got rid of them, settled down to a happy life.

Kabundungulu felt that he was being unfairly treated, since his brother had two wives, while he had none, and asked for one of them to be handed over to him. Sudika-Mbambi pointed out that this was impossible, as he was already married to both of them, and no more was said for the time being. But some time later, when Sudika-Mbambi returned from hunting, his wife complained to him that Kabundungulu was persecuting them both with his attentions. This led to a desperate quarrel between the brothers, and they fought with swords, but could not kill each other. Both were endowed with some magical power, so that the swords would not cut, and neither could be wounded. At last they got tired of fighting and separated, the elder going east and the younger west.

The Creation of the World

IN THE BEGINNING there was nothing at all except darkness. All was darkness and emptiness. For a long, long while, the darkness gathered until it became a great mass. Over this the spirit of Earth Doctor drifted to and fro like a fluffy bit of cotton in the breeze. Then Earth Doctor decided to make for himself an abiding place. So he thought within himself, "Come forth, some kind of plant," and there appeared the creosote bush. He placed this before him and set it upright. But it at once fell over. He set it upright again; again it fell. So it fell until the fourth time it remained upright. Then Earth Doctor took from his breast a little dust and flattened it into a cake. When the dust cake was still, he danced upon it, singing a magic song.

Next he created some black insects which made black gum on the creosote bush. Then he made a termite which worked with the small earth cake until it grew very large. As he sang and danced upon it, the flat World stretched out on all sides until it was as large as it is now. Then he made a round sky-cover to fit over it, round like the houses of the Pimas. But the earth shook and stretched, so that it was unsafe. So Earth Doctor made a gray spider which was to spin a web around the edges of the earth and sky, fastening them together. When this was done, the earth grew firm and solid.

Earth Doctor made water, mountains, trees, grass, and weeds – made everything as we see it now. But all was still inky blackness. Then he made a dish, poured water into it, and it became ice. He threw this round block of ice far to the north, and it fell at the place where the earth and sky were woven together. At once the ice began to gleam and shine. We call it now the sun. It rose from the ground in the north up into the sky and then fell back. Earth Doctor took it and threw it to the west where the earth and sky were sewn together. It rose into the sky and again slid back to the earth. Then he threw it to the far south, but it slid back again to the flat earth. Then at last he threw it to the east. It rose higher and higher in the sky until it reached the highest point in the round blue cover and began to slide down on the other side. And so the sun does even yet.

Then Earth Doctor poured more water into the dish and it became ice. He sang a magic song, and threw the round ball of ice to the north where the earth and sky are woven together. It gleamed and shone, but not so brightly as the sun. It became the moon, and it rose in the sky, but fell back again, just as the sun had done. So he threw the ball to the west, and then to the south, but it slid back each time to the earth. Then he threw it to the east, and it rose to the highest point in the sky-cover and began to slide down on the other side. And so it does even to-day, following the sun.

But Earth Doctor saw that when the sun and moon were not in the sky, all was inky darkness. So he sang a magic song, and took some water into his mouth and blew it into the sky, in a spray, to make little stars. Then he took his magic crystal and broke it into pieces and threw them into the sky, to make the larger stars. Next he took his walking stick and placed ashes on the end of it. Then he drew it across the sky to form the Milky Way. So Earth Doctor made all the stars.

The Story of the Creation

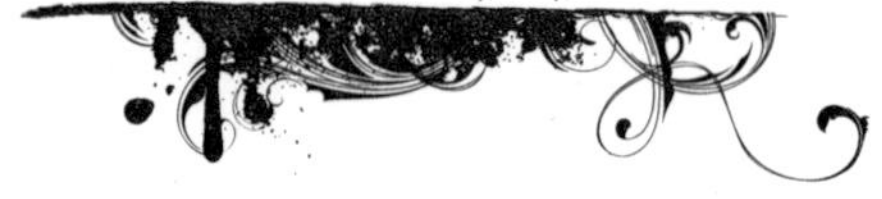

WHEN TU-CHAI-PAI MADE THE WORLD, the earth is the woman, the sky is the man. The sky came down upon the earth. The world in the beginning was pure lake covered with tules. Tu-chai-pai and Yo-ko-mat-is, the brother, sat together, stooping far over, bowed down under the weight of the sky. The Maker said to the brother, "What am I going to do?"

"I do not know," said Yo-ko-mat-is.

"Let us go a little farther," said the Maker.

Then they went a little farther and sat down again. "Now, what am I going to do? " said Tu-chai-pai.

"I do not know."

All this time Tu-chai-pai knew what he would do, but he was asking the brother.

Then he said, "We-hicht, we-hicht, we-hicht," three times; and he took tobacco in his hand, and rubbed it fine, and blew upon it three times, and every time he blew the heavens rose higher above their heads. Then the boy did the very same thing, because the Maker told him to do it. The heavens went high, and there was the sky. Then they did it both together, "We-hicht, we-hicht, we-hicht;" and both took the tobacco, and rubbed it, and puffed upon it, and sent the sky up, so – (into a concave arch).

Then they placed the North, South, East and West. Tu-chai-pai made a line upon the ground.

"Why do you make that line?"

"I am making the line from East to West, and I name them thus, Y-nak, East; A-uk, West. Now you may make it from North to South."

Then Yo-ko-mat-is was thinking very much.

"Why are you thinking?"

"Oh, I must think; but now I have arranged it. I draw a line thus (a crossline), and I name it Ya-wak, South; Ka-tulk, North."

"Why have we done this?"

"I do not know."

"Then I will tell you. Three or four men are coming from the East, and from the West three or four Indians are coming."

The boy asked, "And do four men come from the North, and two or three men come also from the South?"

Then Tu-chai-pai said, "Now I am going to make hills and valleys, and little hollows of water."

"Why are you making all these things?

The Maker said, "After a while, when men come and are walking back and forth in the world, they will need to drink water, or they will die." He had already put the ocean down in its bed, but he made these little waters for the people.

Then he made the forests, and said, "After a while men will die of cold unless I make wood for them to use. What are we going to do now?"

"I do not know."

"We are going to dig in the ground, and take mud, and make the Indians first." And he dug in the ground, and took mud, and made of it first the men, and after that the women. He made the men very well, but he did not make the women very well. It was much trouble to make them, and it took a longtime. He made a beard for the men and boys, but not for the women. After the Indians he made the Mexicans, and he finished all his making. Then he called out very loud, "You can never die, and you can never be tired, but you shall walk all the time." After that he made them so that they could sleep at night, and need not walk around all the time in the darkness. At last he told them that they must travel towards the East, towards the light.

The people walked in darkness till he made the light. Then they came out and searched for the light, and when they found it they were glad. Then be called out to make the moon, and he said to the other, "You may make the moon as I have made the sun. Some time it is going to die. When it grows very small, men may know that it is going to die, and at that time all men, young and old, must run races."

All the pueblos talked about the matter, and they understood that they must run these races, and that Tu-chai-pai was looking at them to see that they did this. After the Maker did all this he did nothing more, but he was thinking many days.

The Mother of the World

IN THE FROZEN REGIONS of the North, beyond the lands which are now the hunting-grounds of the Snakes and Coppermines, there lived, when no other being but herself was, a woman who became the mother of the world. She was a little woman, our fathers told us, not taller than the shoulders of a young maiden of our nation, but she was very beautiful and very wise. Whether she was good-tempered or cross, I cannot tell, for she had no husband, and so there was nothing to vex her, or to try her patience. She had not, as the women of our nation now have, to pound corn, or to fetch home heavy loads of buffalo flesh, or to make snow-sledges, or to wade into the icy rivers to spear salmon, or basket kepling, or to lie concealed among the wet marsh grass and wild rice to snare pelicans, and cranes, and goosanders, while her lazy, good-for-nothing husband lay at home, smoking his pipe, and drinking the pleasant juice of the Nishcaminnick by the warm fire in his cabin. She had only to procure her own food, and this was the berries, and hips, and sorrel, and rock-moss, which, being found plentifully near her cave, were plucked with little trouble. Of these she gathered, in their season, when the sun beamed on the earth like a maiden that loves and is beloved, a great deal to serve her for food when the snows hid the earth from her sight, and the cold winds from the fields of eternal frost obliged her to remain in her rude cavern. Though alone, she was happy. In the summer it was her amusement to watch the juniper and the alders, as they put forth, first their leaves, and then their buds, and when the latter became blossoms, promising to supply the fruit she loved, her observation became more curious and her feelings more interested; then would her heart beat with the rapture of a young mother, whose gaze is fixed on her sleeping child, and her eyes glisten with the dew of joy which wets the cheeks of those who meet long parted friends. Then she would wander forth to search for the little berry whose flower is yellow, and which requires keen eyes to find it in its hiding-place in the grass, and the larger which our white brother eats with his buffalo-meat; and their progress, from the putting forth of the leaf to the ripening of the fruit, was watched by her with eager joy. When tired of gazing upon the pine and stunted poplar, she would lie down in the shade of the creeping birch and dwarf willow, and sink to rest, and dream dreams which were not tinged with the darkness of evil. The sighing of the wind through the branches of the trees, and the murmur of little streams through the thicket, were her music. Throughout the land there was nothing to hurt her, or make her afraid, for there was nothing in it that had life, save herself and the little flower which blooms among thorns. And these two dwelt together like sisters.

One day, when the mother of the world was out gathering berries, and watching the growth of a young pine, which had sprung up near her friend the flower, and threatened, as the flower said, "to take away the beams of the sun from it," she was scared by the sight of a strange creature, which ran upon four legs, and to all her questions answered nothing but "Bow, wow, wow." To every question our mother asked, the creature made the same answer, "bow, wow, wow." So she left off asking him questions, for they were sure to be replied to in three words of a language she could not understand. Did he ask for berries? No, for she offered him a handful of the largest and juiciest which grew in the valley, and he neither took them nor thanked her, unless 'bow' meant 'thank you.' Was he admiring the tall young pines, or the beautiful blossoms of the cranberry, or the graceful bend of the willow, and asking her to join him in his admiration? She knew not, and leaving him to his thoughts, and to utter his strange words with none to reply, she returned to her cave.

Scarcely was she seated on her bed of dried leaves when he came in, and, wagging his tail, and muttering as before, lay down at her feet. Occasionally he would look up into her face very kindly, and then drop his head upon his paws. By and by he was fast asleep, and our mother, who had done no evil action, the remembrance of which should keep her awake, who never stole a beaver-trap, or told a lie, or laughed at a priest, was very soon in the same condition. Then the Manitou of Dreams came to her, and she saw strange things in her sleep. She dreamed that it was night, and the sun had sunk behind the high and broken hills which lay beyond the valley of her dwelling, that the dwarf willow bowed its graceful head still lower with the weight of its tears, which are the evening dew, and the dandelion again imprisoned its leaves within its veil of brown. So far her dreams so closely resembled the reality, that for a time she thought she was awake, and that it was her own world – her cave, her berries, and her flowers, which were before her vision. But an object speedily came to inform her that she dwelt in the paradise of dreams – in the land of departed ideas. At the foot of her couch of leaves, in the place of the dog which she had left there when she slept, stood a being somewhat resembling that she had beheld in the warm season, when bending over the river to lave her bosom with the cooling fluid. It was taller than herself, and there was something on its brow which proclaimed it to be fiercer and bolder, formed to wrestle with rough winds, and to laugh at the coming tempests. For the first time since she was, she turned away to tremble, her soul filled with a new and undefinable feeling, for which she could not account. After shading her eyes a moment from the vision, she looked again, and though her trembling increased, and her brain became giddy, she did not wish the being away, nor did she motion it to go. Why should she? There was a smile upon its lip and brow, and a softness diffused over every feature, which gradually restored her confidence, and gave her the assurance that it would not harm her. She dreamed that the creature came to her arms, and she thought that it passed the season of darkness with its cheek laid on her bosom. To her imagination, the breath which it breathed on her lips was balmy as the juice of the Sweet Gum Tree, or the dew from her little neighbour, the flower. When it spoke, though she could not understand its language, her heart heaved more tumultuously, she knew not why, and when it ceased speaking, her sighs came thick till it spoke again. When she awoke it was gone, the beams of the star of day shone through the fissures of her cavern, and, in the place of the beautiful and loved being lay the strange creature, with the four legs and the old 'bow, wow, wow.'

Four moons passed, and brought no change of scene to the mother of the world. By night, her dreams were ever the same: there was always the same dear and beloved being, each day dearer and more beloved, coming with the shades, and departing with the sun, folding her in its arms, breathing balm on her lips, and pressing her bosom with its downy cheek. By day, the dog was always at her side, whether she went to gather berries or cresses, or to lave her limbs in the stream. Whenever the dog was there, the more beloved being was not; when night came, the dog as surely disappeared, and the other, seen in dreams, supplied his place. But she herself became changed. She took no more joy in the scenes which once pleased her. The pines she had planted throve unnoticed; the creeping birch stifled the willow and the juniper, and she heeded it not; the sweetest berries grew tasteless – she even forgot to visit her pretty sister, the rose. Yet she knew not the cause of her sudden change, nor of the anxiety and apprehension which filled her mind. Why tears bedewed her cheeks till her eyes became blind, why she trembled at times, and grew sick, and feinted, and fell to the earth, she knew not. Her feelings told her of a change, but the relation of its cause, the naming to her startled ear of the mystery of 'the dog by day, and the man by night,' was reserved for a being, who was to prepare the world for the reception of the mighty numbers which were to be the progeny of its mother.

She had wandered forth to a lonely valley – lonely where all was lonely – to weep and sigh over her lost peace, and to think of the dear being with which that loss seemed to her to be in some way connected, when suddenly the sky became darkened, and she saw the form of a being shaped like that which visited her in her sleep, but of immense proportions, coming towards her from the east. The clouds wreathed themselves around his head, his hair swept the mists from the mountain-tops, his eyes were larger than the rising sun when he wears the red flush of anger in the Frog-Moon, and his voice, when he gave it full tone, was louder than the thunder of the Spirit's Bay of Lake Huron. But to the woman he spoke in soft whispers; his terrific accents were reserved for the dog, who quailed beneath them in evident terror, not daring even to utter his only words, 'bow, wow.' The mother of the world related to him her dreams, and asked him why, since she had had them, she was so changed – why she now found no joy in the scenes which once pleased her, but rather wished that she no longer was, her dreams being now all that she loved. The mighty being told her that they were not dreams, but a reality; that the dog which now stood by her side was invested by the Master of Life with power to quit, at the coming in of the shades, the shape of a dog, and to take that of Man, a being who was the counterpart of herself, but formed with strength and resolution, to counteract, by wisdom and sagacity, and to overcome, by strength and valour, the rough difficulties and embarrassments which were to spring up in the path of human life; that he was to be fierce and bold, and she gentle and afraid. He told her that the change she complained of, and which had given her so much grief, wetted her cheek with tears, and filled her bosom with sighs, was the natural result of the intimate connection of two such beings, and was the mode of perpetuating the human race, which had been decreed by the Master of Life; that before the buds now forming should be matured to fruit, she would give birth to two helpless little beings, whom she must feed with her milk, and rear with tender care, for from them would the world be peopled. He had been sent, he said, by the Good Spirit to level and prepare the earth for the reception of the race who were to inhabit it.

Hitherto the world had lain a rude and shapeless mass – the great, man now reduced it to order. He threw the rough and stony crags into the deep valleys – he moved the frozen mountain to fill up the boiling chasm. When he had levelled the earth, which before was a thing without form, he marked out with his great walking-staff the lakes, ponds, and rivers, and caused them to be filled with water from the interior of the earth, bidding them to be replenished from the rains and melted snows which should fall from the skies, till they should be no more.

When he had prepared the earth for the residence of the beings who were to people it, he caught the dog, and, notwithstanding the cries of the mother of the world, and her entreaties to him to spare its life, he tore it in pieces, and distributed it over the earth, and the water, and into air. The entrails he threw into the lakes, ponds, and rivers, commanding them to become fish, and they became fish. These waters, in which no living creature before moved, were now filled with salmon, trout, pike, tittymeg, methy, barble, turbot, and tench, while along the curling waves of the Great Lake the mighty black and white whale, the more sluggish porpoise, and many other finny creatures, sported their gambols. The flesh he dispersed over the land, commanding it to become different kinds of beasts and land-animals, and it obeyed his commands. The heavy moose, and the stupid we-was-kish, came to drink in the Coppermine with the musk-ox, and the deer, and the buffalo. The quiquehatch, and his younger brother, the black bear, and the wolf, that cooks his meat without fire, and the cunning fox, and the wild cat, and the wolverine, were all from the flesh of the dog. The otter was the tail of the dog, the wejack was one of his fore-paws, and the horned horse, and the walrus, were his nose.

Nor did the great man omit to make the skin furnish its proportion of the tribes of living beings. He tore it into many small pieces, and threw it into the air, commanding it to become the different tribes of fowls and birds, and it became the different tribes of fowls and birds. Then first was seen the mighty bird which builds its nest on trees which none can climb, and in the crevices of inaccessible rocks – the eagle, which furnishes the Indians with feathers to their arrows, and steals away the musk-rat and the young beaver as his recompense. Then was the sacred falcon first seen winging his way to the land of long winters; and the bird of alarm, the cunning old owl, and his sister's little son, the cob-a-de-cooch, and the ho-ho. All the birds which skim through the air, or plunge into the water, were formed from the skin of the dog.

When the great man had thus filled the earth with living creatures, he called the mother of the world to him, and gave to her and her offspring the things which he had created, with full power to kill, eat, and never to spare, telling her that he had commanded them to multiply for her use in abundance. When he had finished speaking, he returned to the place whence he came, and has never been heard of since. In due time, the mother of the world was delivered of two children, a son and a daughter, both having the dark visage of the Indian race, and from them proceeded the Dog-ribs, and all the other nations of the earth. The white men were from the same source, but the father of them, having once upon a time been caught stealing a beaver-trap, he become so terrified that he lost his original colour and never regained it, and his children remain with the same pale cheeks to this day.

Brothers, I have told you no lie.

Creation Myth of the Iroquois

AT THE DAWN OF CREATION, before mankind ever existed, the universe comprised two separate worlds. The lower world was a place of eternal darkness, peopled only by creatures of the water, while the upper world, a kingdom of bright light, was inhabited by the Great Ruler and his family. The goddess Atahensic was daughter of the Great Ruler, and at this time she was heavy with child and very close to her time of confinement. As the hour drew near, her relatives persuaded her to lie down on a soft mattress, wrapping her in a ray of light, so that her weary body would gather strength and refreshment for the task ahead. But as soon as she had closed her eyes, the bed on which she lay began to sink without warning through the thick clouds, plunging rapidly towards the lower world beneath her.

Dazzled and alarmed by the descending light, the monsters and creatures of the great water held an emergency council to decide what should be done.

"If the being from above falls on us," said the Water-hen, "it will surely destroy us. We must quickly find a place where it can rest."

"Only the oeh-da, the earth which lies at the very bottom of the water, will be strong enough to hold it," said the Beaver. "I will swim down and bring some back with me.' But the Beaver never returned from his search.

Then the Duck volunteered himself for the same duty, but soon his dead body floated up to the surface. Finally, however, the Muskrat came forward:

"I know the way better than anyone," he told the others, "but the oeh-da is extremely heavy and will grow very fast. Who is prepared to bear its weight when I appear with it?"

The Turtle, who was by far the most capable among them, readily agreed to suffer the load. Shortly afterwards, the Muskrat returned with a small quantity of the oeh-da in his paw which he smoothed on to the turtle's back. It began to spread rapidly, and as soon as it had reached a satisfactory size for the light to rest on, two birds soared into the air and bore the goddess on their outstretched wings down towards the water and safely on to the turtle's back. From that day onwards, the Turtle became known as the Earth Bearer, and whenever the seas rise up in great waves, the people know that it is the Turtle stirring in his bed.

A considerable island of earth now floated on the waves, providing a timely shelter, for soon Atahensic began to hear two voices within her womb, one soft and soothing, the other loud and aggressive, and she knew that her mission to people the island was close at hand. The conflict continued within, as one of her twin infants sought to pass out under the side of his mother's arm, while the other held him back, attempting to spare his mother this unnecessary pain. Both entered into the world in their own individual way, the first bringing trouble and strife, the second bringing freedom and peace. The goddess wisely accepted that it must be so, and named her children Hahgwehdiyu, meaning Good Mind, and Hahgwehdaetgah, meaning Bad Mind. Each went his way, Hahgwehdiyu anxious to bring beauty to the island, Hahgwehdaetgah determined that darkness and evil should prevail.

Not long after she had given birth, Atahensic passed away and the island grew dim in the dawn of its new life. Knowing the goddess would not have wished it this way, Hahgwehdiyu lifted his palm high into the air and began moulding the sky with his fingers. After he had done this, he took his mother's head from her body and placed it firmly in the centre of the firmament:

"You shall be known as the Sun," he announced, "and your face shall light up this new world where you shall rule forever."

But his brother saw all of this good work and set darkness in the west sky, forcing the Sun down behind it. Hahgwehdiyu would not be beaten, however, and removing a portion of his mother's breast, he cast it upwards, creating an orb, inferior to the sun, yet capable of illuminating the darkness. Then he surrounded the orb with numerous spots of light, giving them the name of stars and ordering them to regulate the days, nights, seasons and years. When he had completed this work above, he turned his attention to the soil beneath his feet. To the barren earth he gave the rest of his mother's body from which the seeds of all future life were destined to spring forth.

The Good Mind continued the works of creation, refusing all rest until he had accomplished everything he had set out to do. All over the land he formed creeks and rivers, valleys and hills, luscious pastures and evergreen forests. He created numerous species of animals to inhabit the forests, from the smallest to the greatest, and filled the seas and lakes with fishes and mammals of every variety and colour. He appointed thunder to water the earth and winds to scatter pollen so that, in time, the island became fruitful and productive. But all was not yet complete, for Hahgwehdiyu wisely observed that a greater being was needed to take possession of the Great Island. And so, he began forming two images from the dust of the ground in his own likeness. To these he gave the name of Eagwehowe, meaning the Real People, and by breathing into their nostrils he gave them living souls.

When the earth was created and Hahgwehdiyu had bestowed a protective spirit upon every object of his creation, he went out in search of his brother, hoping to persuade him to abandon his evil and vicious existence. But the Bad Mind was already hard at work, intent on destroying all evidence of Hahgwehdiyu's remarkable labour. Without much effort, he overcame the guardian spirits he encountered and marched throughout the island, bending the rivers, sundering the mountains, gnarling the forests and destroying food crops. He created lethal reptiles to injure mankind, led ferocious monsters into the sea and gathered great hurricanes in the sky. Still dissatisfied with the devastation, however, he began making two images of clay in the form of humans, aiming to create a more superior and destructive race. But he was quickly made to realize that he had not been blessed with the same creative powers as the Good Mind, for as he breathed life into them, his clay figures turned into hideous apes. Infuriated by this discovery, the Bad Mind thundered through the island like a terrible whirlwind, uprooting fruit-trees and wringing the necks of animals and birds. Only one thing would now satisfy his anger, a bloody and ruthless combat to the death, and with this purpose in mind, he hastened towards his twin-brother's dwelling.

Weary of the destruction he had witnessed, the Good Mind willingly submitted himself to the contest that would decide the ruler of the earth. The Bad Mind was keen to discover anything that might help to destroy his brother's temporal life and began to question him rather slyly on the type of weapons they should use.

"Tell me," he said, "what particular instrument would cause you the most injury, so that I may avoid its use, as a gesture of goodwill."

Hahgwehdiyu could see through this evil strategy, however, and falsely informed him that he would certainly be struck down by a lotus arrow.

"There is nothing I fear," the Bad Mind boasted, but Hahgwehdiyu knew this to be untrue, and wisely remembered that ever since childhood the horns of a stag had always induced feelings of terror in his brother.

The battle began and lasted for two days and two nights, causing panic and disruption throughout the earth as mountains shook violently under the strain of the combat and rivers overflowed with the blood of both brothers. At last, however, the Bad Mind could no longer ignore the temptation to shoot the lotus arrow in his brother's direction. The Good Mind responded by charging at him with the stag-horns, impaling him on their sharp points until he screamed in pain and fell to the ground begging for mercy.

Hahgwehdiyu, the supreme ruler of the earth, immediately banished his evil brother to a dark pit beneath the surface of the world, ordering him never to return. Gathering together as many hideous beasts and monsters as he could find, he flung them below so that they might share with their creator a life of eternal doom. Some escaped his grasp, however, and remained on the earth as Servers, half-human and half-beasts, eager to continue the destructive work of the Bad Mind who had now become known as the Evil Spirit.

Hahgwehdiyu, faithful to the wishes of his grandfather, the Great Ruler, carried on with his good work on the floating island, filling the woodlands with game, slaying the monsters, teaching the Indians to make fires and to raise crops, and instructing them in many of the other arts of life until the time had come for him to retire from the earth to his celestial home.

Spider's Creation

IN THE BEGINNING, long, long ago, there was but one being in the lower world. This was the spider, Sussistinnako. At that time there were no other insects, no birds, animals, or any other living creature.

The spider drew a line of meal from north to south and then crossed it with another line running east and west. On each side of the first line, north of the second, he placed two small parcels. They were precious but no one knows what was in them except Spider. Then he sat down near the parcels and began to sing. The music was low and sweet and the two parcels accompanied him, by shaking like rattles. Then two women appeared, one from each parcel. In a short time people appeared and began walking around. Then animals, birds, and insects appeared, and the spider continued to sing until his creation was complete.

But there was no light, and as there were many people, they did not pass about much for fear of treading upon each other. The two women first created were the mothers of all. One was named Utset and she as the mother of all Indians. The other was Now-utset, and she was the mother of all other nations. While it was still dark, the spider divided the people into clans, saying to some, "You are of the Corn clan, and you are the first of all." To others he said, "You belong to the Coyote clan." So he divided them into their clans, the clans of the Bear, the Eagle, and other clans.

After Spider had nearly created the earth, Ha-arts, he thought it would be well to have rain to water it, so he created the Cloud People, the Lightning People, the Thunder People, and the Rainbow People, to work for the people of Ha-arts, the earth. He divided this creation into six parts, and each had its home in a spring in the heart of a great mountain upon whose summit was a giant tree. One was in the spruce tree on the Mountain of the North; another in the pine tree on the Mountain of the West; another in the oak tree on the Mountain of the South; and another in the aspen tree on the Mountain of the East; the fifth was on the cedar tree on the Mountain of the Zenith; and the last in an oak on the Mountain of the Nadir.

The spider divided the world into three parts: Ha-arts, the earth; Tinia, the middle plain; and Hu-wa-ka, the upper plain. Then the spider gave to these People of the Clouds and to the rainbow, Tinia, the middle plain.

Now it was still dark, but the people of Ha-arts made houses for themselves by digging in the rocks and the earth. They could not build houses as they do now, because they could not see. In a short time Utset and Now-utset talked much to each other, saying, "We will make light, that our people may see. We cannot tell the people

now, but to-morrow will be a good day and the day after to-morrow will be a good day," meaning that their thoughts were good. So they spoke with one tongue. They said, "Now all is covered with darkness, but after a while we will have light."

Then these two mothers, being inspired by Sussistinnako, the spider, made the sun from white shell, turkis, red stone, and abalone shell. After making the sun, they carried him to the east and camped there, since there were no houses. The next morning they climbed to the top of a high mountain and dropped the sun down behind it. After a time he began to ascend. When the people saw the light they were happy.

When the sun was far off, his face was blue; as he came nearer, the face grew brighter. Yet they did not see the sun himself, but only a large mask which covered his whole body.

The people saw that the world was large and the country beautiful. When the two mothers returned to the village, they said to the people, "We are the mothers of all."

The sun lighted the world during the day, but there was no light at night. So the two mothers created the moon from a slightly black stone, many kinds of yellow stone, turkis, and a red stone, that the world might be lighted at night. But the moon travelled slowly and did not always give light. Then the two mothers created the Star People and made their eyes of sparkling white crystal that they might twinkle and brighten the world at night. When the Star People lived in the lower world they were gathered into beautiful groups; they were not scattered about as they are in the upper world.

The Great Deeds of Michabo

A VERY POWERFUL MANITTO once visited the earth and, falling in love with its only inhabitant, a beautiful young maiden, he made her his wife. From this union were born four healthy sons, but in giving birth the mother sadly passed away. The first son was named Michabo and he was destined to become the friend of the human race. Michabo, supreme deity of the Algonquin Indians, is very often represented as an invincible god, endowed with marvellous powers. Sometimes, however, he is given a far more human treatment, and is depicted as a trickster, or troublemaker, as in the story to follow. The second, Chibiabos, took charge of the dead and ruled the Land of Souls. The third, Wabassa, immediately fled to the north, transforming himself into a rabbit-spirit, while the fourth, Chokanipok, who was of a fiery temperament, spent his time arguing, especially with his eldest brother.

Michabo, the strongest and most courageous of the four brothers, had always attributed the death of his mother to Chokanipok, and the repeated combats between the two were often fiercely savage. During one particularly brutal confrontation, Michabo carved huge fragments of flesh from the body of his brother which, as soon as they fell to the ground, were transformed into flintstones. In time, the children of men found a use for these stones and used them to create fire, giving Chokanipok the name of Firestone, or Man of Flint.

After a long and tortuous battle, Chokanipok was finally slain by Michabo who tore out his bowels and changed them into long twining vines from which the earth's vegetation sprung forth. After this, Michabo journeyed far and wide, carrying with him all manner of tools and equipment which he distributed among men. He gave them lances and arrow-points; he taught them how to make axes or agukwats, he devised the art of knitting nets to catch fish; he furnished the hunter with charms and signs to use in his chase, and he taught mankind to lay traps and snares. In the course of his journeys he also killed the ferocious beasts and monsters threatening the human race and cleared the rivers and streams of many of the obstructions which the Evil Spirit had placed there.

When he saw that all this was done, Michabo placed four good spirits at the four cardinal points of the earth, instructing mankind that he should always blow the smoke from his calumet in each of these four directions as a mark of respect during the sacred feasts. The Spirit of the North, he told them, would always provide snow and ice, enabling man to hunt game. The Spirit of the South would give them melons, maize and tobacco. The Spirit he had placed in the West would ensure that rain fell upon the crops, and the Spirit of the East would never fail to bring light in place of darkness.

Then, retreating to an immense slab of ice in the Northern Ocean, Michabo kept a watchful eye on mankind, informing them that if ever the day should arrive when their wickedness forced him to depart the earth, his footprints would catch fire and the end of the world would come; for it was he who directed the sun in his daily walks around the earth.

A Legend of Manabozho

MANABOZHO MADE THE LAND. The occasion of his doing so was this.

One day he went out hunting with two wolves. After the first day's hunt one of the wolves left him and went to the left, but the other continuing with Manabozho he adopted him for his son. The lakes were in those days peopled by spirits with whom Manabozho and his son went to war. They destroyed all the spirits in one lake, and then went on hunting. They were not, however, very successful, for every deer the wolf chased fled to another of the lakes and escaped from them. It chanced that one day Manabozho started a deer, and the wolf gave chase. The animal fled to the lake, which was covered with ice, and the wolf pursued it. At the moment when the wolf had come up to the prey the ice broke, and both fell in, when the spirits, catching them, at once devoured them.

Manabozho went up and down the lake-shore weeping and lamenting. While he was thus distressed he heard a voice proceeding from the depths of the lake.

"Manabozho," cried the voice, "why do you weep?"

Manabozho answered, "Have I not cause to do so? I have lost my son, who has sunk in the waters of the lake."

"You will never see him more," replied the voice; "the spirits have eaten him."

Then Manabozho wept the more when he heard this sad news.

"Would," said he, "I might meet those who have thus cruelly treated me in eating my son. They should feel the power of Manabozho, who would be revenged."

The voice informed him that he might meet the spirits by repairing to a certain place, to which the spirits would come to sun themselves. Manabozho went there accordingly, and, concealing himself, saw the spirits, who appeared in all manner of forms, as snakes, bears, and other things. Manabozho, however, did not escape the notice of one of the two chiefs of the spirits, and one of the band who wore the shape of a very large snake was sent by them to examine what the strange object was.

Manabozho saw the spirit coming, and assumed the appearance of a stump. The snake coming up wrapped itself around the trunk and squeezed it with all its strength, so that Manabozho was on the point of crying out when the snake uncoiled itself. The relief was, however, only for a moment. Again the snake wound itself around him and gave him this time even a more severe hug than before. Manabozho restrained himself and did not suffer a cry to escape him, and the snake, now satisfied that the stump was what it appeared to be, glided off to its companions. The chiefs of the spirits were not, however, satisfied, so they sent a bear to try what he could make of the stump. The bear came up to Manabozho and hugged, and bit, and clawed him till he could hardly forbear screaming with the pain it caused him. The thought of his son and of the vengeance he wished to take on the spirits, however, restrained him, and the bear at last retreated to its fellows.

"It is nothing," it said; "it is really a stump."

Then the spirits were reassured, and, having sunned themselves, lay down and went to sleep. Seeing this, Manabozho assumed his natural shape, and stealing upon them with his bow and arrows, slew the chiefs of the spirits. In doing this he awoke the others, who, seeing their chiefs dead, turned upon Manabozho, who fled. Then the spirits pursued him in the shape of a vast flood of water. Hearing it behind him the fugitive ran as fast as he could to the hills, but each one became gradually submerged, so that Manabozho was at last driven to the top of the highest mountain. Here the waters still surrounding him and gathering in height, Manabozho climbed the highest pine-tree he could find. The waters still rose. Then Manabozho prayed that the tree would grow, and it did so. Still the waters rose. Manabozho prayed again that the tree would grow, and it did so, but not so much as before.

Still the waters rose, and Manabozho was up to his chin in the flood, when he prayed again, and the tree grew, but less than on either of the former occasions. Manabozho looked round on the waters, and saw many animals swimming about seeking land. Amongst them he saw a beaver, an otter, and a musk-rat. Then he cried to them, saying –

"My brothers, come to me. We must have some earth, or we shall all die."

So they came to him and consulted as to what had best be done, and it was agreed that they should dive down and see if they could not bring up some of the earth from below.

The beaver dived first, but was drowned before he reached the bottom. Then the otter went. He came within sight of the earth, but then his senses failed him before he could get a bite of it. The musk-rat followed. He sank to the bottom, and bit the earth. Then he lost his senses and came floating up to the top of the water. Manabozho awaited the reappearance of the three, and as they came up to the surface he drew them to him. He examined their claws, but found nothing. Then he looked in their mouths and found the beaver's and the otter's empty. In the musk-rat's, however, he found a little earth. This Manabozho took in his hands and rubbed till it was a fine dust. Then he dried it in the sun, and, when it was quite light, he blew it all round him over the water, and the dry land appeared.

Thus Manabozho made the land.

Machinitou, the Evil Spirit

CHEMANITOU, BEING THE MASTER OF LIFE, at one time became the origin of a spirit that has ever since caused him and all others of his creation a great deal of disquiet. His birth was owing to an accident. It was in this wise:

Metowac, or as the white people now call it, Long Island, was originally a vast plain, so level and free from any kind of growth that it looked like a portion of the great sea that had suddenly been made to move back and let the sand below appear, which was, in fact, the case.

Here it was that Chemanitou used to come and sit when he wished to bring any new creation to life. The place being spacious and solitary, the water upon every side, he had not only room enough, but was free from interruption.

It is well known that some of these early creations were of very great size, so that very few could live in the same place, and their strength made it difficult for even Chemanitou to control them, for when he has given them certain powers they have the use of the laws that govern those powers, till it is his will to take them back to himself. Accordingly it was the custom of Chemanitou, when he wished to try the effect of these creatures, to set them in motion upon the island of Metowac, and if they did not please him, he took the life away from them again. He would set up a mammoth, or other large animal, in the centre of the island, and build it up with great care, somewhat in the manner that a cabin or a canoe is made.

Even to this day may be found traces of what had been done here in former years, and the manner in which the earth sometimes sinks down shows that this island is nothing more than a great cake of earth, a sort of platter laid upon the sea for the convenience of Chemanitou, who used it as a table upon which he might work, never having designed it for anything else, the margin of the Chatiemac (the stately swan), or Hudson river, being better adapted to the purposes of habitation.

When the Master of Life wished to build up an elephant or mammoth, he placed four cakes of clay upon the ground, at proper distances, which were moulded into shape, and became the feet of the animal.

Now sometimes these were left unfinished, and to this day the green tussocks to be seen like little islands about the marshes show where these cakes of clay were placed.

As Chemanitou went on with his work, the Neebanawbaigs (or water-spirits), the Puck-wud-jinnies (little men who vanish), and, indeed, all the lesser manitoes, used to come and look on, and wonder what it would be, and how it would act.

When the animal was completed, and had dried a long time in the sun, Chemanitou opened a place in the side, and, entering in, remained there many days.

When he came forth the creature began to shiver and sway from side to side, in such a manner as shook the whole island for leagues. If its appearance pleased the Master of Life it was suffered to depart, and it was generally found that these animals plunged into the open sea upon the north side of the island, and disappeared in the great forests beyond.

Now at one time Chemanitou was a very long time building an animal of such great bulk that it looked like a mountain upon the centre of the island, and all the manitoes from all parts came to see what it was. The Puck-wud-jinnies especially made themselves very merry, capering behind its great ears, sitting within its mouth, each perched upon a tooth, and running in and out of the sockets of the eyes, thinking Chemanitou, who was finishing off other parts of the animal, would not see them.

But he can see right through everything he has made. He was glad to see the Puck-wud-jinnies so lively, and he bethought him of many new creations while he watched their motions.

When the Master of Life had completed this large animal, he was fearful to give it life, and so it was left upon the island, or work-table of Chemanitou, till its great weight caused it to break through, and, sinking partly down, it stuck fast, the head and tail holding it in such a manner as to prevent it slipping further down.

Chemanitou then lifted up a piece of the back, and found it made a very good cavity, into which the old creations which failed to please him might be thrown.

He sometimes amused himself by making creatures very small and active, with which he disported awhile, and finding them of very little use in the world, and not so attractive as the little vanishers, he would take out the life, taking it to himself, and then cast them into the cave made in the body of the unfinished animal.

In this way great quantities of very odd shapes were heaped together in this Roncomcomon, or Place of Fragments.

He was always careful before casting a thing he had created aside to take out the life.

One day the Master of Life took two pieces of clay and moulded them into two large feet, like those of a panther. He did not make four – there were two only.

He put his own feet into them, and found the tread very light and springy, so that he might go with great speed and yet make no noise.

Next he built up a pair of very tall legs, in the shape of his own, and made them walk about a while. He was pleased with the motion. Then followed a round body covered with large scales, like those of the alligator.

He now found the figure doubling forward, and he fastened a long black snake, that was gliding by, to the back part of the body, and wound the other end round a sapling which grew near, and this held the body upright, and made a very good tail.

The shoulders were broad and strong, like those of the buffalo, and covered with hair. The neck thick and short, and full at the back.

Thus far Chemanitou had worked with little thought, but when he came to the head he thought a long while.

He took a round ball of clay into his lap, and worked it over with great care. While he thought, he patted the ball of clay upon the top, which made it very broad and low, for Chemanitou was thinking of the panther feet and the buffalo neck. He remembered the Puck-wud-jinnies playing in the eye sockets of the great unfinished animal, and he bethought him to set the eyes out, like those of a lobster, so that the animal might see on every side.

He made the forehead broad and full, but low, for here was to be the wisdom of the forked tongue, like that of the serpent, which should be in its mouth. It should see all things and know all things. Here Chemanitou stopped, for he saw that he had never thought of such a creation before, one with two feet – a creature that should stand upright, and see upon every side.

The jaws were very strong, with ivory teeth and gills upon either side, which rose and fell whenever breath passed through them. The nose was like the beak of the vulture. A tuft of porcupine-quills made the scalp lock.

Chemanitou held the head out the length of his arm, and turned it first upon one side and then upon the other. He passed it rapidly through the air, and saw the gills rise and fall, the lobster eyes whirl round, and the vulture nose look keen.

Chemanitou became very sad, yet he put the head upon the shoulders. It was the first time he had made an upright figure. It seemed to be the first idea of a man.

It was now nearly right. The bats were flying through the air, and the roar of wild beasts began to be heard. A gusty wind swept in from the ocean and passed over the island of Metowac, casting the light sand to and fro. A wavy scud was skimming along the horizon, while higher up in the sky was a dark thick cloud, upon the verge of which the moon hung for a moment and was then shut in.

A panther came by and stayed a moment, with one foot raised and bent inward, while it looked up at the image and smelt the feet that were like its own.

A vulture swooped down with a great noise of its wings, and made a dash at the beak, but Chemanitou held it back.

Then came the porcupine, the lizard, and the snake, each drawn by its kind in the image.

Chemanitou veiled his face for many hours, and the gusty wind swept by, but he did not stir.

He saw that every beast of the earth seeks its kind, and that which is like draws its likeness to itself.

The Master of Life thought and thought. The idea grew into his mind that at some time he would create a creature who should be made, not after the things of the earth, but after himself.

The being should link this world to the spirit world, being made in the likeness of the Great Spirit, he should be drawn unto his likeness.

Many days and nights – whole seasons – passed while Chemanitou thought upon these things. He saw all things.

Then the Master of Life lifted up his head. The stars were looking down upon the image, and a bat had alighted upon the forehead, spreading its great wings upon each side. Chemanitou took the bat and held out its whole leathery wings (and ever since the bat, when he rests, lets his body hang down), so that he could try them over the head of the image. He then took the life of the bat away, and twisted off the body, by which means the whole thin part fell down over the head of the image and upon each side, making the ears, and a covering for the forehead like that of the hooded serpent.

Chemanitou did not cut off the face of the image below, but went on and made a chin and lips that were firm and round, that they might shut in the forked tongue and ivory teeth, and he knew that with the lips the image would smile when life should be given to it.

The image was now complete save for the arms, and Chemanitou saw that it was necessary it should have hands. He grew more grave.

He had never given hands to any creature. He made the arms and the hands very beautiful, after the manner of his own.

Chemanitou now took no pleasure in the work he had done. It was not good in his sight.

He wished he had not given it hands. Might it not, when trusted with life, create? Might it not thwart the plans of the Master of Life himself?

He looked long at the image. He saw what it would do when life should be given it. He knew all things.

He now put fire in the image, but fire is not life.

He put fire within and a red glow passed through and through it. The fire dried the clay of which the image was made, and gave the image an exceedingly fierce aspect. It shone through the scales upon the breast, through the gills, and the bat-winged ears. The lobster eyes were like a living coal.

Chemanitou opened the side of the image, but he did not enter. He had given it hands and a chin.

It could smile like the manitoes themselves.

He made it walk all about the island of Metowac, that he might see how it would act. This he did by means of his will.

He now put a little life into it, but he did not take out the fire. Chemanitou saw the aspect of the creature would be very terrible, and yet that it could smile in such a manner that it ceased to be ugly. He thought much upon these things. He felt that it would not be best to let such a creature live – a creature made up mostly from the beasts of the field, but with hands of power, a chin lifting the head upward, and lips holding all things within themselves.

While he thought upon these things he took the image in his hands and cast it into the cave. But Chemanitou forgot to take out the life.

The creature lay a long time in the cave and did not stir, for its fall was very great. It lay amongst the old creations that had been thrown in there without life.

Now when a long time had passed Chemanitou heard a great noise in the cave. He looked in and saw the image sitting there, and it was trying to put together the old broken things that had been cast in as of no value.

Chemanitou gathered together a vast heap of stones and sand, for large rocks are not to be had upon the island, and stopped the mouth of the cave. Many days passed and the noise within the cave grew louder. The earth shook, and hot smoke came from the ground. The manitoes crowded to Metowac to see what was the matter.

Chemanitou came also, for he remembered the image he had cast in there of which he had forgotten to take away the life.

Suddenly there was a great rising of the stones and sand, the sky grew black with wind and dust. Fire played about on the ground, and water gushed high into the air.

All the manitoes fled with fear, and the image came forth with a great noise and most terrible to behold. Its life had grown strong within it, for the fire had made it very fierce.

Everything fled before it and cried:

"Machinitou! machinitou," which means a god, but an evil god.

O-wel'-lin the Rock Giant

THERE WAS A GREAT GIANT who lived in the north. His name was Oo-wel'-lin, and he was as big as a pine tree. When he saw the country full of people he said they looked good to eat, and came and carried them off and ate them. He could catch ten men at a time and hold them between his fingers, and put more in a net on his back, and carry them off. He would visit a village and after eating all the people would move on to another, going southward from his home in the north. When he had gone to the south end of the world and had visited all the villages and eaten nearly all the people – not quite all, for a few had escaped – he turned back toward the north. He crossed the Wah-kal'-mut-ta (Merced River) at a narrow place in the canyon about six miles above Op'-lah (Merced Falls, where his huge footprints may still be seen in the rocks) showing the exact place where he stepped from Ang-e'-sa-w '-pah on the south side to Hik-ka'-nah on the north side. When night came he went into a cave in the side of a round-topped hill over the ridge from Se-saw-che (a little south of the present town of Coulterville).

The people who had escaped found his sleeping place in the cave and shot their arrows at him but were not able to hurt him, for he was a rock giant.

When he awoke he was hungry and took the trail to go hunting. Then the people said to Oo'-choom the Fly: "Go follow Oo-wel'-lin and when he is hot bite him all over, on his head, on his eyes and ears, and all over his body, everywhere, all the way down to the bottoms of his feet, and find out where he can be hurt.

"All right," answered Oo'-choom the Fly, and he did as he was told. He followed Oo-wel'-lin and bit him everywhere from the top of his head, all the way down to his feet without hurting him, till finally he bit him under the heel. This made Oo-wel'-lin kick. Oo'-choom waited, and when the giant had fallen asleep bit him under the heel of the other foot, and he kicked again. Then Oo'-choom told the people.

When the people heard this they took sharp sticks and long sharp splinters of stone and set them up firmly in the trail, and hid nearby and watched. After a while Oo-wel'-lin came back and stepped on the sharp points till the bottoms of his feet were stuck full of them. This hurt him dreadfully, and he fell down and died.

When he was dead the people asked, "Now he is dead, what are we to do with him?"

And they all answered that they did not know.

But a wise man said, "We will pack wood and make a big fire and burn him."

Then everyone said, "All right, let's burn him," and they brought a great quantity of dry wood and made a big fire and burned Oo-wel'-lin the Giant. When he began to burn, the wise man told everybody to watch closely all the time to see if any part should fly off to live again, and particularly to watch the whites of his eyes. So all the people watched closely all the time he was burning. His flesh did not fly off; his feet did not fly off; his hands did not fly off; but by and by the whites of his eyes flew off quickly – so quickly indeed that no one but Chik'-chik saw them go. Chik'-chik was a small bird whose eyes looked sore, but his sight was keen and quick. He was watching from a branch about twenty feet above the Giant's head and saw the whites of the eyes fly out. He saw them fly out and saw where they went and quickly darted after them and brought them back and put them in the fire again, and put on more wood and burnt them until they were completely consumed.

The people now made a hole and put Oo-wel'lin's ashes in it and piled rocks on the place and watched for two or three days. But Oo-wel'-lin was dead and never came out.

Then the wise man asked each person what he would like to be, and called their names. Each answered what animal he would be, and forthwith turned into that animal and has remained the same to this day.

This was the beginning of the animals as they are now – the deer, the ground squirrel, the bear, and other furry animals; the bluejay, the quail, and other birds of all kinds, and snakes and frogs and the yellowjacket wasp and so on.

Before that they were Hoi-ah'-ko – the first people.

Ganusquah, Last of the Stone Giants

AS A FINAL DESPERATE MEASURE in the bloody battle to rid themselves of the Stone Giants, the Iroquois called upon the Upholder of the Heavens, Tahahiawagon, to come to their aid. For generations, they had bravely suffered the carnage and destruction alone, but were now so depleted in numbers they agreed they had nowhere else to turn. Tahahiawagon, who had generously provided them with their hunting grounds and fisheries, was already aware of their distress and had waited patiently for the day when he could again demonstrate his loyalty and devotion.

Determined to relieve the Iroquois of these merciless invaders, the great god transformed himself into a stone giant and descended to earth where he placed himself among the most influential of their tribes. Before long, the giants began to marvel at his miraculous strength and fearlessness in battle and soon they reached the unanimous decision that Tahahiawagon should act as their new chief. The great god brandished his club high in the air:

"Now we will destroy the Iroquois," he roared. "Come, let us make a feast of these puny warriors and invite all the Stone Giants throughout the earth to celebrate it with us."

Carrying on with his façade, the new chief marched all the Stone Giants towards a strong fort of the Onondagas where he commanded them to lie low in a deep hollow in the valley until sunrise. At dawn, he told them, they would slaughter and destroy all the unsuspecting Indians while they still lay in their beds.

But during the night, Tahahiawagon scaled a great mountain nearby and began hewing the rock-face with an enormous chisel. When he had produced a great mass of boulders he raised his foot and kicked them over the land below. Only one Stone Giant managed to escape the horrifying avalanche. His name was Ganusquah, and he fled as fast as his legs would carry him through the darkness, all the way to the Allegheny Mountains.

As soon as he had reached this spot, he secreted himself in a cave where he remained until he had grown to a huge size and strength. No human being had ever set eyes on him, for to look upon his face meant instant death. He was vulnerable to attack only at the base of his foot, but it was not within the power of any mortal to wound him. And so, Ganusquah used the whole earth as his path, carving out a massive trail through the forests and mountains where his footprints formed huge caverns that filled with water to make the lakes.

If a river obstructed his path, he would swoop it up in his huge hands and turn it from its course. If a mountain stood in his way, he would push his fists through it to create a great tunnel. If ever he were hungry, he would devour a whole herd of buffalo. If ever he were thirsty, he would drink the ocean dry. Even in the tumult of the storms, he made his presence felt, as his voice rose high above the booming of the clouds, warning the Thunderess to keep away from his cave.

It was during one of these terrific storms that Ganusquah came closer than ever before to one of the human species. A young hunter, blinded and bruised by the hail which hurled itself like sharp pebbles upon him, soon lost his trail and took refuge within the hollow of an enormous rock. Nightfall approached, casting deep shadows on the walls of his temporary shelter and soon the young warrior began to drift off to sleep, pleased to have found a place of warmth and safety. He had no sooner indulged this comforting thought, however, when the rock which housed him began to move, but in the queerest manner, almost as if it was being tilted from side to side with the weight of some vast and heavy burden. The swaying motion intensified and was soon accompanied by the most perplexing jumble of sounds, at one moment as sweet and relaxed as a babbling brook, and the next, as eerie and tormented as a death-cry.

The young warrior stood up in alarm, straining his eyes to find the opening of the cave. But too late, for suddenly he felt a gigantic hand on his shoulder and heard a loud voice rumbling in his ear:

"Young warrior, beware! You are in the cave of the stone giant, Ganusquah. Close your eyes and do not look at me, for no human has yet survived who has gazed upon my face. Many have wandered into this cave, but they have come to hunt me. You alone have come here for shelter and I will not, therefore, turn you away.

"I shall spare your life if you agree to obey my commands for as long as I consider necessary. Although I will remain unseen, you will hear my voice whenever I wish to speak to you, and I will always be there to help you as you roam the earth. From here you must go forth and live freely among the animals, the birds and the fish. All these are your ancestors and it will be your task hereafter to dedicate your life to them.

"You will encounter many of them along your way. Do not pass until you have felled a strong tree and carved their image in the wood grain. When you first strike a tree, if it speaks, know that it is my voice urging you on with your task. Each tree has a voice and you must learn the language of the entire forest.

"Now, go on your way. I will be watching you and guiding you. Teach mankind kindness, the unspoken kindness of nature, and so win your way in life forever."

The young hunter walked out into the darkness and when he awoke next morning he found himself seated at the base of a basswood tree which gradually transformed itself into a mask and began relating to him the great breadth of its power.

The mask was the supreme being of the forest. It could see behind the stars. It could conjure up storms and summon the sunshine. It knew the remedy for each disease and could overpower death. The venomous reptiles knew its threat and avoided its path. It knew every poisonous root and could repel their evil influence.

"I am Gogonsa," said the mask. "My tree is basswood and there is nothing like it in the forest. My wood is soft and will make your task easier. My timber is porous and the sunlight can enter its darkness. Even the wind can whisper to it and it will hear. Ganusquah has called upon me to help you and when he is satisfied with your work, I will lead you back to your people."

The young hunter listened carefully to every word of advice Gogonsa offered him and then, forearmed with this knowledge, he set about the task of carving the gogonsasooh, the 'false faces' of the forest. On his travels he met many curious animals, birds, reptiles and insects, which he detained until he had carved them in the basswood, inviting them to stay with him until he had learned their language and customs. Guided by the voice of Ganusquah, he moved deeper into the forest and soon he had learned to interpret its many different voices, including the voices of the trees and grasses, mosses and flowers. He learned to love his surroundings and every last creature he encountered, and he knew he would be loathe to leave this world of his ancestors when the time eventually came for him to return to his own home.

A great many years were passed in this way until the hunter, who had entered the cave as a youth, had become an old man, bent in two with the burden of the gogonsasooh he carried with him from place to place. At last, he heard the voice of Ganusquah pronouncing an end to his labour and soon the mask appeared to guide him back to his own people. He wondered if he had the strength to make the journey, but he refused to abandon what he now considered his most precious possessions, the hundreds of gogonsasooh he had carved in basswood.

Wearily, he set off on the track, almost crushed by his heavy load, but after only a short time, he felt a sudden surge of energy. Slowly, his spine began to uncurl, his back began to broaden and strengthen and he felt himself growing taller until he had become a giant in stature, rising high above the trees. He stood up tall and proud and smiled, unaware that in the distance, a great cave had begun to crumble.

Michabo Defeats the King of Fishes

ONE MORNING, Michabo went out upon the lake in his canoe to fish. Casting his line into the middle of the water, he began to shout: "Meshenahmahgwai, King of Fishes, grab hold of my bait, you cannot escape me forever."

For a full hour he continued to call out these words until, at last, the King of Fishes, who had been attempting to rest at the bottom of the lake, could bear the dreadful commotion no longer.

"Michabo is beginning to irritate me," he complained. "Here, trout, take hold of the bait and keep this fellow silent."

The trout obeyed the request and sunk its jaws into the hook as Michabo commenced drawing in his catch. The line, which was very heavy, caused his canoe to stand almost perpendicular in the water, but he persevered bravely until the fish appeared above the surface. As soon as he saw the trout, however, he began to roar angrily: "Esa, Esa! Shame! Shame! Why did you take hold of my hook, you ugly creature?"

The trout let go at once and swam back down to the bottom of the lake. Michabo then cast his line into the water once more saying: "King of Fishes, I am still waiting and I will remain here for as long as it takes."

This time the King of Fishes caught hold of a giant sunfish and commanded him to do exactly as the trout had done before him. The sunfish obeyed and Michabo again drew up his line, his canoe turning in swift circles with the weight of the monstrous creature. Michabo felt certain he had succeeded and began crying out in excitement:

"Wha-wee-he! Wha-wee-he!" But he was quickly made to realize that he had been deceived once more and his face turned a bright shade of crimson as he screamed into the water:

"Esa! Esa! You hideous fish. You have contaminated my hook by placing it in your big mouth. Let go of it, you filthy brute." The sunfish dropped the hook and disappeared below the surface of the lake.

"Meshenahmahgwai! I have reached the end of my patience," Michabo bellowed with increasing fury. "Do as I have bid you and take hold of my hook."

By now, the King of Fishes was himself seething with anger and he grabbed hold of the bait, allowing himself to be tugged upwards through the water. He had no sooner reached the surface, however, when he opened his mouth wide, and in one gulp, swallowed Michabo, his fishing rod and his little wooden canoe.

Michabo stumbled about in the belly of the fish wondering, for an instant, who had turned the lights out in the sky. But then, he felt a sudden motion and a tremendous rumbling noise and it dawned on him that the King of Fishes had helped himself to an early supper. Michabo glanced around him and seeing his war-club lying in his canoe, lifted it above his shoulders and brought it down mercilessly wherever he could find a solid wall. He was hurled to and fro as the King of Fishes responded to these blows and complained to those around him:

"I am sick in my stomach for having swallowed that troublemaker, Michabo. He has not provided a satisfying meal." And as he spoke, Michabo continued with his attack, delivering a number of very severe blows to the fish's heart.

The King of Fishes began to heave violently and, fearing that he would be thrown up into the lake to drown, Michabo quickly rammed his canoe lengthways into the fish's throat. The pain induced by the obstruction, combined with the repeated beating he suffered internally, caused the King's heart to stop beating, and soon his great body, battered and lifeless, was tossed up by the waves upon the shore.

Michabo sat down in the darkness, faced now with an even greater problem, for he had not paused to consider how he would manage to free himself from the bowels of the King of Fishes once his victim lay dead. Had he been ejected, he might have stood some small chance of survival in spite of the fact that he could not swim, but now, there seemed little or no hope.

He chastized himself for his own folly and had begun to come to terms with his sorry fate when, all of a sudden, his ears were filled with the sound of tapping noises above his head. Certain that the King of Fishes lay dead, he was puzzled by the rhythm, but its source was soon revealed to him, as light began to filter in through an opening in the fleshy roof and the heads of gulls peered into the darkness below.

"What a good thing that you have come, my friends," cried Michabo. "Quickly, make the opening larger so that I can get out." The birds, utterly astonished to discover Michabo in the belly of a fish, chattered excitedly as they obeyed the god's command. In no time at all Michabo found himself at liberty and smiled broadly to find his feet touching firm soil once more.

"I have been foolish," he told the gulls, "and you have shown great kindness in releasing me from my confinement. From this day forth, you shall not be looked upon as scavengers, but shall be known as Kayosk, Noble Scratchers, and receive my special blessing."

Then, walking towards the shores of the lake, Michabo breathed life into the King of Fishes, restoring him to his former glory. The King took up his usual place at the bottom of the water and in this silent world, undisturbed by the cries of a keen fisherman, he carried on with his rest.

The Sun Ensnared

AT THE VERY BEGINNING OF TIME, when chaos and darkness reigned and hordes of bloodthirsty animals roamed the earth devouring mankind, there remained only two survivors of the human race. A young brother and sister, who managed to flee from the jaws of the ferocious beasts, took refuge in a secluded part of the forest where they built for themselves a little wooden lodge. Here, they carved out a meagre existence, relying on nature's kindness for their survival. The young girl, who was strong and hardworking, bravely accepted the responsibility of keeping the household together, for her younger brother had never grown beyond the size of an infant and demanded her constant care. Every morning she would go out in search of firewood, taking her brother with her and seating him on a comfortable bed of leaves while she chopped and stacked the logs they needed to keep a warm fire burning. Then, before heading homeward, she would gather the ripest berries from the surrounding hedgerows and both would sit down together to enjoy their first meal of the day.

They had passed many pleasant years in this way before the young girl began to grow anxious for her brother's future, fearing that she might not always be able to care for him. She had never considered it wise in the past to leave him alone while she went about her chores, but now she felt she must take that risk for his own good.

"Little brother," she said to him, "I will leave you behind today while I go out to gather wood, but you need not be afraid and I promise to return shortly."

And saying this, she handed him a bow and several small arrows.

"Hide yourself behind that bush," she added, "and soon you will see a snowbird coming to pick worms from the newly cut logs. When the bird appears, try your skill and see if you can shoot it."

Delighted at the opportunity to prove himself, the young boy sat down excitedly, ready to draw his bow as soon as the bird alighted on the logs. But the first arrow he shot went astray and before he was able to launch a second, the creature had risen again into the air. The little brother felt defeated and discouraged and bowed his head in shame, fully expecting that his sister would mock his failure. As soon as she returned, however, she began to reassure him, offering him encouragement and insisting that he try again on the following day.

Next morning, the little brother crouched down once more behind the bush and waited for the snowbird to appear. He was now more determined than ever to prove his skill and, on this occasion, his arrow shot swiftly through the air, piercing the bird's breast. Seeing his sister approach in the distance, he ran forward to meet her, his face beaming with pride and joy.

"I have killed a fine, large bird," he announced triumphantly. "Please will you skin it for me and stretch the skin out to dry in the sunshine. When I have killed more birds, there will be enough skins to make me a fine, long coat."

"I would be very happy to do this for you," his sister smiled. "But what shall I do with the body when I have skinned it?"

The young boy searched for an answer, and as he stood thinking his stomach groaned with hunger. It seemed wasteful to burn such a plump bird and he now began to wonder what it would be like to taste something other than wild berries and greens: "We have never before eaten flesh," he said, "but let us cut the body in two and cook one half of it in a pot over the fire. Then, if the food is good, we can savour the remaining half later."

His sister agreed that this was a wise decision and prepared for them their very first dish of game which they both ate with great relish that same evening.

The little brother had passed his very first test of manhood and with each passing day he grew more confident of his ability to survive in the wilderness. Soon he had killed ten birds whose skins were sewn into the coat he had been promised. Fiercely proud of his hunting skills, he wore this new garment both day and night and felt himself ready to meet any challenge life might throw at him.

"Are we really all alone in the world, sister?" he asked one day as he paraded up and down the lodge in his bird-skin coat, "since I cannot believe that this great broad earth with its fine blue sky was created simply for the pair of us."

"There may be other people living," answered his sister, "but they can only be terrible beings, very unlike us. It would be most unwise to go in search of these people, little brother, and you must never be tempted to stray too far from home."

But his sister's words only added to the young boy's curiosity, and he grew more impatient than ever to slip away quietly and explore the surrounding forests and countryside for himself.

Before the sun had risen on the following morning, he grabbed his bow and arrows and set off enthusiastically in the direction of the open hills. By midday, he had walked a very great distance, but still he hadn't discovered any other human beings. At length, he decided to rest for a while and lay down on the grass in the warmth of the sun's golden rays. He had happened upon a very beautiful spot, and was soon lulled gently to sleep by the tinkling sound of the waters dancing over the pebbles of a nearby stream. He slept for many hours in the heat of the brilliant sunshine and would have remained in this position a good while longer had he not been disturbed by the sensation that something close to him had begun to shrink and shrivel. At first, he thought he had been dreaming, but as he opened his eyes wider and gazed upon his bird-skin coat, he soon realized that it had tightened itself upon his body, so much so that he was scarcely able to breathe.

The young boy stood up in horror and began to examine his seared and singed coat more closely. The garment he had been so proud of was now totally ruined and he flew into a great passion, vowing to take vengeance on the sun for what it had done.

"Do not imagine that you can escape me because you are so high up in the sky," he shouted angrily. "What you have done will not go unpunished. I will pay you back before long." And after he had sworn this oath, he trudged back home wearily to tell his sister of the dreadful misfortune that had befallen his new coat.

The young girl was now more worried than ever for her little brother. Ever since his return, he had fallen into a deep depression, refusing all food and laying down on his side, as still as a corpse, for a full ten days, at the end of which he turned over and lay on his other side for a further ten days. When he eventually arose, he was pale and drawn, but his voice was firm and resolute as he informed his sister that she must make a snare for him with which he intended to catch the sun.

"Find me some material suitable for making a noose," he told her, but when his sister returned with a piece of dried deer sinew, he shook his head and said it would not do. Racking her brains, she searched again through their belongings, and came forward with a bird skin, left over from the coat she had made.

"This won't do either," her brother declared agitatedly, "the sun has had enough of my bird skins already. Go and find me something else."

Finally, his sister thought of her own beautiful long hair, and pulling several glossy strands from her head, she began to weave a thick black cord which she handed to her brother.

"This is exactly what I need," he said delightedly and began to draw it back and forth through his fingers until it grew rigid and strong. Then, having coiled it round his shoulders, he kissed his sister goodbye and set off to catch the sun, just as the last light began to fade in the sky.

Under cover of darkness, the little brother set his trap, fixing the snare on a spot where he knew the sun would first strike the land as it rose above the earth. He waited patiently, offering up many prayers. These were answered as soon as the sun attempted to rise from its sleepy bed, for it became fastened to the ground by the cord and could not ascend any higher. No light twinkled on the horizon and the land remained in deep shadow, deprived of the sun's warm rays.

Fear and panic erupted among the animals who ruled the earth as they awoke to discover a world totally submerged in darkness. They ran about blindly, calling to each other, desperate to find some explanation for what had happened. The most powerful among them immediately formed a council and it was agreed that someone would have to go forward to the edge of the horizon to investigate why the sun had not risen. This was a very dangerous undertaking, since whoever ventured so close to the sun risked severe burning and possible death. Only the dormouse, at that time the largest animal in the world, taller than any mountain, stood up bravely, offering to risk her life so that the others might be saved.

Hurriedly, she made her way to the place where the sun lay captive and quickly spotted the cord pinning it to the ground. Even now, though the dormouse was not yet close enough to begin gnawing the cord, her back began to smoke and the intense heat was almost overwhelming. Still she persevered, chewing the cord with her two front teeth while at the same time her huge bulk was turned into an enormous heap of ashes. When, at last, the sun was freed, it shot up into the sky as dazzling as it had ever been. But the dormouse, now shrunken to become one of the tiniest creatures in the world, fled in terror from its light and from that day forward she became known as Kug-e-been-gwa-kwa, or Blind Woman.

As soon as he discovered that the sun had escaped his snare, the little brother returned home once more to his sister. But he was now no longer anxious to take revenge, since his adventure had brought him greater wisdom and the knowledge that he had not been born to interfere with the ways of nature. For the rest of his life, he devoted himself to hunting, and within a very short time had shot enough snowbirds to make himself a new coat, even finer than the one which had led him to challenge the sun.

Eroneniera, or An Indian Visit to the Great Spirit

A DELAWARE INDIAN, called Eroneniera, anxious to know the Master of Life, resolved, without mentioning his design to any one, to undertake a journey to Paradise, which he knew to be God's residence. But, to succeed in his project, it was necessary for him to know the way to the celestial regions. Not knowing any person who, having been there himself, might aid him in finding the road, he commenced juggling, in the hope of drawing a good augury from his dream.

The Indian, in his dream, imagined that he had only to commence his journey, and that a continued walk would take him to the celestial abode. The next morning very early, he equipped himself as a hunter, taking a gun, powder-horn, ammunition, and a boiler to cook his provisions. The first part of his journey was pretty favorable; he walked a long time without being discouraged, having always a firm conviction that he should attain his aim. Eight days had already elapsed without his meeting with any one to oppose his desire. On the evening of the eighth day, at sunset, he stopped as usual on the bank of a brook, at the entrance of a little prairie, a place which he thought favorable for his night's encampment. As he was preparing his lodging, he perceived at the other end of the prairie three very wide and well-beaten paths; he thought this somewhat singular; he, however, continued to prepare his wigwam, that he might shelter himself from the weather. He also lighted a fire. While cooking, he found that, the darker it grew, the more distinct were those paths. This surprised, nay, even frightened him; he hesitated a few moments. Was it better for him to remain in his camp, or seek another at some distance? While in this incertitude, he remembered his juggling, or rather his dream. He thought that his only aim in undertaking his journey was to see the Master of Life. This restored him to his senses. He thought it probable that one of those three roads led to the place which he wished to visit. He therefore resolved upon remaining in his camp until the morrow, when he would, at random, take one of them. His curiosity, however, scarcely allowed him time to take his meal; he left his encampment and fire, and took the widest of the paths. He followed it until the middle of the day without seeing anything to impede his progress; but, as he was resting a little to take breath, he suddenly perceived a large fire coming from under ground. It excited his curiosity; he went towards it to see what it might be; but, as the fire appeared to increase as he drew nearer, he was so overcome with fear, that he turned back and took the widest of the other two paths. Having followed it for the same space of time as he had the first, he perceived a similar spectacle. His fright, which had been lulled by the change of road, awoke him, and he was obliged to take the third path, in which he walked a whole day without seeing anything. All at once, a mountain of a marvellous whiteness burst upon his sight. This filled him with astonishment; nevertheless, he took courage and advanced to examine it. Having arrived at the foot, he saw no signs of a road. He became very sad, not knowing how to continue his journey. In this conjuncture, he looked on all sides and perceived a female seated upon the mountain; her beauty was dazzling, and the whiteness of her garments surpassed that of snow. The woman said to him in his own language, "You appear surprised to find no longer a path to reach your wishes. I know that you have for a long time longed to see and speak to the Master of Life; and that you have undertaken this journey purposely to see him. The way which leads to his abode is upon this mountain. To ascend it, you must undress yourself completely, and leave all your accoutrements and clothing at the foot. No person shall injure them. You will then go and wash yourself in the river which I am now showing you, and afterward ascend the mountain."

The Indian obeyed punctually the woman's words; but one difficulty remained. How could he arrive at the top of the mountain, which was steep, without a path, and as smooth as glass? He asked the woman how he was to accomplish it. She replied, that if he really wished to see the Master of Life, he must, in mounting, only use his left hand and foot. This appeared almost impossible to the Indian. Encouraged, however, by the female, he commenced ascending, and succeeded after much trouble. When at the top, he was astonished to see no person, the woman having disappeared. He found himself alone, and without a guide. Three unknown villages were in sight; they were constructed on a different plan from his own, much handsomer, and more regular. After a few moments' reflection, he took his way towards the handsomest. When about half way from the top of the mountain, he recollected that he was naked, and was afraid to proceed; but a voice told him to advance, and have no apprehensions; that, as he had washed himself, he might walk in confidence. He proceeded without hesitation to a place which appeared to be the gate of the village, and stopped until some one came to open it. While he was considering the exterior of the village, the gate opened, and the Indian saw coming towards him a handsome man dressed all in white, who took him by the hand, and said he was going to satisfy his wishes by leading him to the presence of the Master of Life.

The Indian suffered himself to be conducted, and they arrived at a place of unequalled beauty. The Indian was lost in admiration. He there saw the Master of Life, who took him by the hand, and gave him for a seat a hat bordered with gold. The Indian, afraid of spoiling the hat, hesitated to sit down; but, being again ordered to do so, he obeyed without reply.

The Indian being seated, God said to him, "I am the Master of Life, whom thou wishest to see, and to whom thou wishest to speak. Listen to that which I will tell thee for thyself and for all the Indians. I am the Maker of Heaven and earth, the trees, lakes, rivers, men, and all that thou seest or hast seen on the earth or in the heavens; and because I love you, you must do my will; you must also avoid that which I hate; I hate you to drink as you do, until you lose your reason; I wish you not to fight one another; you take two wives, or run after other people's wives; you do wrong; I hate such conduct; you should have but one wife, and keep her until death. When you go to war, you juggle, you sing the medicine song, thinking you speak to me; you deceive yourselves; it is to the Manito that you speak; he is a wicked spirit who induces you to evil, and for want of knowing me, you listen to him.

"The land on which you are, I have made for you, not for others: wherefore do you suffer the whites to dwell upon your lands? Can you not do without them? I know that those whom you call the children of your great Father supply your wants. But, were you not wicked as you are, you would not need them. You might live as you did before you knew them. Before those whom you call your brothers had arrived, did not your bow and arrow maintain you? You needed neither gun, powder, nor any other object. The flesh of animals was your food, their skins your raiment. But when I saw you inclined to evil, I removed the animals into the depths of the forests, that you might depend on your brothers for your necessaries for your clothing. Again become good and do my will, and I will send animals for your sustenance. I do not, however, forbid suffering among you your Father's children; I love them, they know me, they pray to me; I supply their own wants, and give them that which they bring to you. Not so with those who are come to trouble your possessions. Drive them away; wage war against them. I love them not. They know me not. They are my enemies, they are your brothers' enemies. Send them back to the lands I have made for them. Let them remain there.

"Here is a written prayer which I give thee; learn it by heart, and teach it to all the Indians and children." (The Indian, observing here that he could not read, the Master of Life told him that, on his return upon earth, he should give it to the chief of his village, who would read it, and also teach it to him, as also to all the Indians). "It must be repeated," said the Master of Life, "morning and evening. Do all that I have told thee, and announce it to all the Indians as coming from the Master of Life. Let them drink but one draught, or two at most, in one day. Let them have but one wife, and discontinue running after other people's wives and daughters. Let them not fight one another. Let them not sing the medicine song, for in singing the medicine song they speak to the evil spirit. Drive from your lands," added the Master of Life, "those dogs in red clothing; they are only an injury to you. When you want anything, apply to me, as your brothers do, and I will give to both. Do not sell to your brothers that which I have placed on the earth as food. In short, become good, and you shall want nothing. When you meet one another, bow, and give one another the ... hand of the heart. Above all, I command thee to repeat, morning and evening, the prayer which I have given thee."

The Indian promised to do the will of the Master of Life, and also to recommend it strongly to the Indians; adding that the Master of Life should be satisfied with them.

His conductor then came, and leading him to the foot of the mountain, told him to take his garments and return to his village; which was immediately done by the Indian.

His return much surprised the inhabitants of the village, who did not know what had become of him. They asked him whence he came; but, as he had been enjoined to speak to no one until he saw the chief of the village, he motioned to them with his hand that he came from above. Having entered the village, he went immediately to the chief's wigwam, and delivered to him the prayer and laws intrusted to his care by the Master of Life.

The Quest of the Children of Tuirenn

NUADA OF THE SILVER HAND rose to become King of the Tuatha Dé Danann during the most savage days of the early invasions. The Fomorians, a repulsive band of sea-pirates, were the fiercest of opponents who swept through the country destroying cattle and property and imposing tribute on the people of the land. Every man of the Tuatha Dé Danann, no matter how rich or poor, was required to pay one ounce of gold to the Fomorians and those who neglected to pay this tax at the annual assembly on the Hill of Uisneach were maimed or murdered without compassion. Balor of the Evil Eye was leader of these brutal invaders, and it was well known that when he turned his one glaring eyeball on his foes they immediately fell dead as if struck by a thunderbolt. Everyone lived in mortal fear of Balor, for no weapon had yet been discovered that could slay or even injure him. Times were bleak for the Tuatha Dé Danann and the people had little faith in King Nuada who appeared powerless to resist Balor's tyranny and oppression. As the days passed by, they yearned for a courageous leader who would rescue them from their life of wretched servitude.

The appalling misery of the Tuatha Dé Danann became known far and wide and, after a time, it reached the ears of Lugh of the Long Arm of the fairymounds, whose father was Cian, son of Cainte. As soon as he had grown to manhood, Lugh had proven his reputation as one of the most fearless warriors and was so revered by the elders of Fairyland that they had placed in his charge the wondrous magical gifts of Manannan the sea-god which had protected their people for countless generations. Lugh rode the magnificent white steed of Manannan, known as Aenbarr, a horse as fleet of foot as the wailing gusts of winter whose charm was such that no rider was ever wounded while seated astride her. He had the boat of Manannan, which could read a man's thoughts and travel in whatever direction its keeper demanded. He also wore Manannan's breast-plate and body armour which no weapon could ever pierce, and he carried the mighty sword known as 'The Retaliator' that could cut through any battle shield.

The day approached once more for the People of Dana to pay their annual taxes to the Fomorians and they gathered together, as was customary, on the Hill of Uisneach to await the arrival of Balor's men. As they stood fearful and terrified in the chill morning air, several among them noticed a strange cavalry coming over the plain from the east towards them. At the head of this impressive group, seated high in command above the rest, was Lugh of the Long Arm, whose proud and noble countenance mirrored the splendour of the rising sun. The King was summoned to witness the spectacle and he rode forth to salute the leader of the strange army. The two had just begun to converse amiably when they were interrupted by the approach of a grimy-looking band of men, instantly known to all as Fomorian tax-collectors. King Nuada bowed respectfully towards them and instructed his subjects to deliver their tributes without delay. Such a sad sight angered and humiliated Lugh of the Long Arm and he drew the King aside and began to reproach him:

"Why do your subjects bow before such an evil-eyed brood," he demanded, "when they do not show you any mark of respect in return?"

"We are obliged to do this," replied Nuada. "If we refuse we would be killed instantly and our land has witnessed more than enough bloodshed at the hands of the Fomorians."

"Then it is time for the Tuatha Dé Danann to avenge this great injustice," replied Lugh, and with that, he began slaughtering Balor's emissaries single-handedly until all but one lay dead at his feet. Dragging the surviving creature before him, Lugh ordered him to deliver a stern warning to Balor:

"Return to your leader," he thundered, "and inform him that he no longer has any power over the People of Dana. Lugh of the Long Arm, the greatest of warriors, is more than eager to enter into combat with him if he possesses enough courage to meet the challenge."

Knowing that these words would not fail to enrage Balor, Lugh lost little time preparing himself for battle. He enlisted the King's help in assembling the strongest men in the kingdom to add to his own powerful army. Shining new weapons of steel were provided and three thousand of the swiftest white horses were made ready for his men. A magnificent fleet of ships, designed to withstand the most venomous ocean waves, remained moored at port, awaiting the moment when Balor and his malicious crew would appear on the horizon.

The time finally arrived when the King received word that Balor's fierce army had landed at Eas Dara on the northwest coast of Connacht. Within hours, the Fomorians had pillaged the lands of Bodb the Red and plundered the homes of noblemen throughout the province. Hearing of this wanton destruction, Lugh of the Long Arm was more determined than ever to secure victory for the Tuatha Dé Danann. He rode across the plains of Erin back to his home to enlist the help of Cian, his father, who controlled all the armies of the fairymounds. His two uncles, Cu and Cethen, also offered their support and the three brothers set off in different directions to round up the remaining warriors of Fairyland.

Cian journeyed northwards and he did not rest until he reached Mag Muirthemne on the outskirts of Dundalk. As he crossed the plain, he observed three men, armed and mailed, riding towards him. At first he did not recognize them, but as they drew closer, he knew them to be the sons of Tuirenn whose names were Brian, Iucharba and Iuchar. A long-standing feud had existed for years between the sons of Cainte and the sons of Tuirenn and the hatred and enmity they felt towards each other was certain to provoke a deadly contest. Wishing to avoid an unequal clash of arms, Cian glanced around him for a place to hide and noticed a large herd of swine grazing nearby. He struck himself with a druidic wand and changed himself into a pig. Then he trotted off to join the herd and began to root up the ground like the rest of them.

The sons of Tuirenn were not slow to notice that the warrior who had been riding towards them had suddenly vanished into thin air. At first, they all appeared puzzled by his disappearance, but then Brian, the eldest of the three, began to question his younger brothers knowingly:

"Surely brothers you also saw the warrior on horseback," he said to them. "Have you no idea what became of him?"

"We do not know," they replied.

"Then you are not fit to call yourselves warriors," chided Brian, "for that horseman can be no friend of ours if he is cowardly enough to change himself into one of these swine. The instruction you received in the City of Learning has been wasted on you if you cannot even tell an enchanted beast from a natural one."

And as he was saying this, he struck Iucharba and Iuchar with his own druidic wand, transforming them into two sprightly hounds that howled and yelped impatiently to follow the trail of the enchanted pig.

Before long, the pig had been hunted down and driven into a small wood where Brian cast his spear at it, driving it clean through the animal's chest. Screaming in pain, the injured pig began to speak in a human voice and begged his captors for mercy:

"Allow me a dignified death," the animal pleaded. "I am originally a human being, so grant me permission to pass into my own shape before I die."

"I will allow this," answered Brian, "since I am often less reluctant to kill a man than a pig."

Then Cian, son of Cainte, stood before them with blood trickling down his cloak from the gaping wound in his chest.

"I have outwitted you," he cried, "for if you had killed me as a pig you would only be sentenced for killing an animal, but now you must kill me in my own human shape. And I must warn you that the penalty you will pay for this crime is far greater than any ever paid before on the death of a nobleman, for the weapons you shall use will cry out in anguish, proclaiming your wicked deed to my son, Lugh of the Long Arm".

"We will not slay you with any weapons in that case," replied Brian triumphantly, "but with the stones that lie on the ground around us." And the three brothers began to pelt Cian with jagged rocks and stones until his body was a mass of wounds and he fell to the earth battered and lifeless. The sons of Tuirenn then buried him where he had fallen in an unmarked grave and hurried off to join the war against the Fomorians.

With the great armies of Fairyland and the noble cavalcade of King Nuada at his side, Lugh of the Long Arm won battle after battle against Balor and his men. Spears shot savagely through the air and scabbards clashed furiously until at last, the Fomorians could hold out no longer. Retreating to the coast, the terrified survivors and their leader boarded their vessels and sailed as fast as the winds could carry them back through the northern mists towards their own depraved land. Lugh of the Long Arm became the hero of his people and they presented him with the finest trophies of valour the kingdom had to offer, including a golden war chariot, studded with precious jewels which was driven by four of the brawniest milk-white steeds.

When the festivities had died down somewhat, and the Tuatha Dé Danann had begun to lead normal lives once more, Lugh began to grow anxious for news of his father. He called several of his companions to him and appealed to them for information, but none among them had received tidings of Cian since the morning he had set off towards the north to muster the armies of the fairymounds.

"I know that he is no longer alive," said Lugh, "and I give you my word that I will not rest again, or allow food or drink to pass my lips, until I have knowledge of what happened to him."

And so Lugh, together with a number of his kinsmen, rode forth to the place where he and his father had parted company. From here, the horse of Manannan guided him to the Plain of Muirthemne where Cian had met his tragic death. As soon as he entered the shaded wood, the stones of the ground began to cry out in despair and they told Lugh of how the sons of Tuirenn had murdered his father and buried him in the earth. Lugh wept bitterly when he heard this tale and implored his men to help him dig up the grave so that he might discover in what cruel manner Cian had been slain. The body was raised from the ground and the litter of wounds on his father's cold flesh was revealed to him. Lugh rose gravely to his feet and swore angry vengeance on the sons of Tuirenn:

"This death has so exhausted my spirit that I cannot hear through my ears, and I cannot see anything with my eyes, and there is not one pulse beating in my heart for grief of my father. Sorrow and destruction will fall on those that committed this crime and they shall suffer long when they are brought to justice."

The body was returned to the ground and Lugh carved a headstone and placed it on the grave. Then, after a long period of mournful silence, he mounted his horse and headed back towards Tara where the last of the victory celebrations were taking place at the palace.

Lugh of the Long Arm sat calmly and nobly next to King Nuada at the banqueting table and looked around him until he caught sight of the three sons of Tuirenn. As soon as he had fixed his eye on them, he stood up and ordered the Chain of Attention of the Court to be shaken so that everyone present would fall silent and listen to what he had to say.

"I put to you all a question," said Lugh. "I ask each of you what punishment you would inflict upon the man that had murdered your father?"

The King and his warriors were astonished at these words, but finally Nuada spoke up and enquired whether it was Lugh's own father that had been killed.

"It is indeed my own father who lies slain," replied Lugh "and I see before me in this very room the men who carried out the foul deed."

"Then it would be far too lenient a punishment to strike them down directly," said the King. "I myself would ensure that they died a lingering death and I would cut off a single limb each day until they fell down before me writhing in agony."

Those who were assembled agreed with the King's verdict and even the sons of Tuirenn nodded their heads in approval. But Lugh declared that he did not wish to kill any of the Tuatha Dé Danann, since they were his own people. Instead, he would insist that the perpetrators pay a heavy fine, and as he spoke he stared accusingly towards Brian, Iuchar and Iucharba, so that the identity of the murderers was clearly exposed to all. Overcome with guilt and shame, the sons of Tuirenn could not bring themselves to deny their crime, but bowed their heads and stood prepared for the sentence Lugh was about to deliver.

"This is what I demand of you," he announced.

"Three ripened apples
The skin of a pig
A pointed spear
Two steeds and a chariot
Seven pigs
A whelping pup
A cooking spit
Three shouts on a hill.

"And," Lugh added, "if you think this fine too harsh, I will now reduce part of it. But if you think it acceptable, you must pay it in full, without variation, and pledge your loyalty to me before the royal guests gathered here."

"We do not think it too great a fine," said Brian, "nor would it be too large a compensation if you multiplied it a hundredfold. Therefore, we will go out in search of all these things you have described and remain faithful to you until we have brought back every last one of these objects."

"Well, now," said Lugh, "since you have bound yourselves before the court to the quest assigned you, perhaps you would like to learn more detail of what lies in store," And he began to elaborate on the tasks that lay before the sons of Tuirenn.

"The apples I have requested of you," Lugh continued, "are the three apples of the Hesperides growing in the gardens of the Eastern World. They are the colour of burnished gold and have the power to cure the bloodiest wound or the most horrifying illness. To retrieve these apples, you will need great courage, for the people of the east have been forewarned that three young warriors will one day attempt to deprive them of their most cherished possessions.

"And the pig's skin I have asked you to bring me will not be easy to obtain either, for it belongs to the King of Greece who values it above everything else. It too has the power to heal all wounds and diseases.

"The spear I have demanded of you is the poisoned spear kept by Pisar, King of Persia. This spear is so keen to do battle that its blade must always be kept in a cauldron of freezing water to prevent its fiery heat melting the city in which it is kept.

"And do you know who keeps the chariot and the two steeds I wish to receive from you?" Lugh continued.

"We do not know," answered the sons of Tuirenn.

"They belong to Dobar, King of Sicily," said Lugh, "and such is their unique charm that they are equally happy to ride over sea or land, and the chariot they pull is unrivalled in beauty and strength.

"And the seven pigs you must gather together are the pigs of Asal, King of the Golden Pillars. Every night they are slaughtered, but every morning they are found alive again, and any person who eats part of them is protected from ill-health for the rest of his life.

"Three further things I have demanded of you," Lugh went on. "The whelping hound you must bring me guards the palace of the King of Iruad. Failinis is her name and all the wild beasts of the world fall down in terror before her, for she is stronger and more splendid than any other creature known to man.

"The cooking-spit I have called for is housed in the kitchen of the fairywomen on Inis Findcuire, an island surrounded by the most perilous waters that no man has ever safely reached.

"Finally, you must give the three shouts requested of you on the Hill of Midcain where it is prohibited for any man other than the sons of Midcain to cry aloud. It was here that my father received his warrior training and here that his death will be hardest felt. Even if I should one day forgive you of my father's murder, it is certain that the sons of Midcain will not."

As Lugh finished speaking, the children of Tuirenn were struck dumb by the terrifying prospect of all that had to be achieved by them and they went at once to where their father lived and told him of the dreadful sentence that had been pronounced on them.

"It is indeed a harsh fine," said Tuirenn, "but one that must be paid if you are guilty, though it may end tragically for all three of you." Then he advised his sons to return to Lugh to beg the loan of the boat of Manannan that would carry them swiftly over the seas on their difficult quest. Lugh kindly agreed to give them the boat and they made their way towards the port accompanied by their father. With heavy hearts, they exchanged a sad farewell and wearily set sail on the first of many arduous journeys.

"We shall go in search of the apples to begin with," said Brian, and his command was answered immediately by the boat of Manannan which steered a course towards the Eastern World and sailed without stopping until it came to rest in a sheltered harbour in the lands of the Hesperides. The brothers then considered how best they might remove the apples from the garden in which they were growing, and it was eventually decided among them that they should transform themselves into three screeching hawks.

"The tree is well guarded," Brian declared, "but we shall circle it, carefully avoiding the arrows that will be hurled at us until they have all been spent. Then we will swoop on the apples and carry them off in our beaks."

The three performed this task without suffering the slightest injury and headed back towards the boat with the stolen fruit. The news of the theft had soon spread throughout the kingdom, however, and the king's three daughters quickly changed themselves into three-taloned ospreys and pursued the hawks over the sea. Shafts of lightning lit up the skies around them and struck the wings of the hawks, scorching their feathers and causing them to plummet towards the waters below. But Brian managed to take hold of his druidic wand and he transformed himself and his brothers into swans that darted below the waves until the ospreys had given up the chase and it was safe for them to return to the boat.

After they had rested awhile, it was decided that they should travel on to Greece in search of the skin of the pig.

"Let us visit this land in the shape of three bards of Erin," said Brian, "for if we appear as such, we will be honoured and respected as men of wit and wisdom."

They dressed themselves appropriately and set sail for Greece composing some flattering verses in honour of King Tuis as they journeyed along. As soon as they had landed, they made their way to the palace and were enthusiastically welcomed as dedicated men of poetry who had travelled far in search of a worthy patron. An evening of drinking and merry-making followed; verses were read aloud by the King's poets and many ballads were sung by the court musicians. At length, Brian rose to his feet and began to recite the poem he had written for King Tuis. The King smiled rapturously to hear himself described as 'the oak among kings' and encouraged Brian to accept some reward for his pleasing composition.

"I will happily accept from you the pig's skin you possess," said Brian, "for I have heard that it can cure all wounds."

"I would not give this most precious object to the finest poet in the world," replied the King, "but I shall fill the skin three times over with red gold, one skin for each of you, which you may take away with you as the price of your poem."

The brothers agreed to this and the King's attendants escorted them to the treasure-house where the gold was to be measured out. They were about to weigh the very last share when Brian suddenly snatched the pig's skin and raced from the room, striking down several of the guards as he ran. He had just found his way to the outer courtyard when King Tuis appeared before him, his sword drawn in readiness to win back his most prized possession. Many bitter blows were exchanged and many deep wounds were inflicted by each man on the other until, at last, Brian dealt the King a fatal stroke and he fell to the ground never to rise again.

Armed with the pig's skin that could cure their battle wounds, and the apples that could restore them to health, the sons of Tuirenn grew more confident that they would succeed in their quest. They were determined to move on as quickly as possible to the next task Lugh had set them and instructed the boat of Manannan to take them to the land of Persia, to the court of King Pisar, where they appeared once more in the guise of poets. Here they were also made welcome and were treated with honour and distinction. After a time, Brian was called upon to deliver his poem and, as before, he recited some verses in praise of the King which won the approval of all who were gathered. Again, he was persuaded to accept some small reward for his poem and, on this occasion, he requested the magic spear of Persia. But the King grew very angry at this request and the benevolent attitude he had previously displayed soon turned to open hostility:

"It was most unwise of you to demand my beloved spear as a gift," bellowed the King, "the only reward you may expect now is to escape death for having made so insolent a request."

When Brian heard these words he too was incensed and grabbing one of the three golden apples, he flung it at the King's head, dashing out his brains. Then the three brothers rushed from the court, slaughtering all they encountered along the way, and hurried towards the stables where the spear of Pisar lay resting in a cauldron of water. They quickly seized the spear and headed for the boat of Manannan, shouting out their next destination as they ran, so that the boat made itself ready and turned around in the direction of Sicily and the kingdom of Dobar.

"Let us strike up a friendship with the King," said Brian, "by offering him our services as soldiers of Erin."

And when they arrived at Dobar's court they were well received and admitted at once to the King's great army where they won the admiration of all as the most valiant defenders of the realm. The brothers remained in the King's service for a month and two weeks, but during all this time they never once caught a glimpse of the two steeds and the chariot Lugh of the Long Arm had spoken of.

"We have waited long enough," Brian announced impatiently. "Let us go to the King and inform him that we will quit his service unless he shows us his famous steeds and his chariot."

So they went before King Dobar who was not pleased to receive news of their departure, for he had grown to rely on the three brave warriors. He immediately sent for his steeds and ordered the chariot to be yoked to them and they were paraded before the sons of Tuirenn. Brian watched carefully as the charioteer drove the steeds around in a circle and as they came towards him a second time he sprung onto the nearest saddle and seized the reins. His two brothers fought a fierce battle against those who tried to prevent them escaping, but it was not long before they were at Brian's side, riding furiously through the palace gates, eager to pursue their fifth quest.

They sailed onwards without incident until they reached the land of King Asal of the Pillars of Gold. But their high spirits were quickly vanquished by the sight of a large army guarding the harbour in anticipation of their arrival. For the fame of the sons of Tuirenn was widespread by this time, and their success in carrying away with them the most coveted treasures of the world was well known to all. King Asal himself now came forward to greet them and demanded to know why they had pillaged the lands of other kings and murdered so many in their travels. Then Brian told King Asal of the sentence Lugh of the Long Arm had pronounced upon them and of the many hardships they had already suffered as a result.

"And what have you come here for?" the King enquired.

"We have come for the seven pigs which Lugh has also demanded as part of that compensation," answered Brian, "and it would be far better for all of us if you deliver them to us in good will."

When the King heard these words, he took counsel with his people, and it was wisely decided that the seven pigs should be handed over peacefully, without bloodshed. The sons of Tuirenn expressed their gratitude to King Asal and pledged their services to him in all future battles. Then Asal questioned them on their next adventure, and when he discovered that they were journeying onwards to the land of Iruad in search of a puppy hound, he made the following request of them:

"Take me along with you," he said "for my daughter is married to the King of Iruad and I am desperate, for love of her, to persuade him to surrender what you desire of him without a show of arms."

Brian and his brothers readily agreed to this and the boats were made ready for them to sail together for the land of Iruad.

When they reached the shores of the kingdom, Asal went ahead in search of his son-in-law and told him the tale of the sons of Tuirenn from beginning to end and of how he had rescued his people from a potentially bloody war. But Iruad was not disposed to listen to the King's advice and adamantly refused to give up his hound without a fight. Seizing his weapon, he gave the order for his men to begin their attack and went himself in search of Brian in order to challenge him to single combat. A furious contest ensued between the two and they struck each other viciously and angrily. Eventually, however, Brian succeeded in overpowering King Iruad and he hauled him before Asal, bound and gagged like a criminal.

"I have spared his life," said Brian, "perhaps he will now hand over the hound in recognition of my clemency."

The King was untied and the hound was duly presented to the sons of Tuirenn who were more than pleased that the battle had come to a swift end. And there was no longer any bitterness between Iruad and the three brothers, for Iruad had been honestly defeated and had come to admire his opponents. They bid each other a friendly farewell and the sons of Tuirenn took their leave of the land of the Golden Pillars and set out to sea once again.

Far across the ocean in the land of Erin, Lugh of the Long Arm had made certain that news of every success achieved by the sons of Tuirenn had been brought to his attention. He was fully aware that the quest he had set them was almost drawing to a close and became increasingly anxious at the thought. But he desired above everything else to take possession of the valuable objects that had already been recovered, for Balor of the Evil Eye had again reared his ugly head and the threat of another Fomorian invasion was imminent. Seeking to lure the sons of Tuirenn back to Erin, Lugh sent a druidical spell after the brothers, causing them to forget that their sentence had not yet been fully completed. Under its influence, the sons of Tuirenn entertained visions of the heroic reception that awaited them on the shores of the Boyne and their hearts were filled with joy to think that they would soon be reunited with their father.

Within days, their feet had touched on Erin's soil again and they hastened to Tara to the Annual Assembly, presided over by the High King of Erin. Here, they were heartily welcomed by the royal family and the Tuatha Dé Danann who rejoiced alongside them and praised them for their great courage and valour. And it was agreed that they should submit the tokens of their quest to the High King himself who undertook to examine them and to inform Lugh of the triumphant return of the sons of Tuirenn. A messenger was despatched to Lugh's household and within an hour he had arrived at the palace of Tara, anxious to confront the men he still regarded as his enemies.

"We have paid the fine on your father's life," said Brian, as he pointed towards the array of objects awaiting Lugh's inspection.

"This is indeed an impressive sight," replied Lugh of the Long Arm, "and would suffice as payment for any other murder. But you bound yourselves before the court to deliver everything asked for and I see that you have not done so. Where is the cooking-spit I was promised? And what is to be done about the three shouts on the hill which you have not yet given?"

When the sons of Tuirenn heard this, they realized that they had been deceived and they collapsed exhausted to the floor. Gloom and despair fell upon them as they faced once more the reality of long years of searching and wandering. Leaving behind the treasures that had hitherto protected them, they made their way wearily towards their ship which carried them swiftly away over the storm-tossed seas.

They had spent three months at sea and still they could not discover the smallest trace of the island known as Inis Findcurie. But when their hopes had almost faded, Brian suggested that they make one final search beneath the ocean waves and he put on his magical water-dress and dived over the side of the boat. After two long weeks of swimming in the salt water, he at last happened upon the island, tucked away in a dark hollow of the ocean bed. He immediately went in search of the court and found it occupied by a large group of women, their heads bent in concentration, as they each embroidered a cloth of gold. The women appeared not to notice Brian and he seized this opportunity to move forward to where the cooking-spit rested in a corner of the room. He had just lifted it from the hearth when the women broke into peals of laughter and they laughed long and heartily until finally the eldest of them condescended to address him:

"Take the spit with you, as a reward for your heroism," she said mockingly, "but even if your two brothers had attended you here, the weakest of us would have had little trouble preventing you from removing what you came for."

And Brian took his leave of them knowing they had succeeded in humiliating him, yet he was grateful, nonetheless, that only one task remained to be completed.

They lost no time in directing the boat of Manannan towards their final destination and had reached the Hill of Midcain shortly afterwards, on whose summit they had pledged themselves to give three shouts. But as soon as they had begun to ascend to the top, the guardian of the hill, none other than Midcain himself, came forward to challenge the sons of Tuirenn:

"What is your business in my territory," demanded Midcain.

"We have come to give three shouts on this hill," said Brian, "in fulfilment of the quest we have been forced to pursue in the name of Lugh of the Long Arm."

"I knew his father well," replied Midcain, "and I am under oath not to permit anyone to cry aloud on my hill."

"Then we have no option but to fight for that permission," declared Brian, and he rushed at his opponent with his sword before Midcain had the opportunity to draw his own, killing him with a single thrust of his blade through the heart.

Then the three sons of Midcain came out to fight the sons of Tuirenn and the conflict that followed was one of the bitterest and bloodiest ever before fought by any group of warriors. They battled with the strength of wild bears and the ruthlessness of starving lions until they had carved each other to pieces and the grass beneath their feet ran crimson with blood. In the end, however, it was the sons of Tuirenn who were victorious, but their wounds were so deep that they fell to the ground one after the other and waited forlornly for death to come, wishing in vain that they still had the pig skin to cure them.

They had rested a long time before Brian had the strength to speak, and he reminded his brothers that they had not yet given the three shouts on the Hill of Midcain that Lugh had demanded of them. Then slowly they raised themselves up off the ground and did as they had been requested, satisfied at last that they had entirely fulfilled their quest. And after this, Brian lifted his wounded brothers into the boat, promising them a final glimpse of Erin if they would only struggle against death a brief while longer.

And on this occasion the boat of Manannan did not come to a halt on the shores of the Boyne, but moved speedily overland until it reached Dun Tuirenn where the dying brothers were delivered into their father's care. Then Brian, who knew that the end of his life was fast approaching, pleaded fretfully with Tuirenn:

"Go, beloved father," he urged, "and deliver this cooking-spit to Lugh, informing him that we have completed all the tasks assigned us. And beg him to allow us to cure our wounds with the pig skin he possesses, for we have suffered long and hard in the struggle to pay the fine on Cian's murder."

Then Tuirenn rode towards Tara in all haste, fearful that his sons might pass away before his return. And he demanded an audience with Lugh of the Long Arm who came out to meet him at once and graciously received the cooking-spit presented to him.

"My sons are gravely ill and close to death," Tuirenn exclaimed piteously. "I beg you to part with the healing pig skin they brought you for one single night, so that I may place it upon their battle wounds and witness it restore them to full health."

But Lugh of the Long Arm fell silent at this request and stared coldly into the distance towards the Plain of Muirthemne where his father had fallen. When at length he was ready to give Tuirenn his answer, the expression he wore was cruel and menacing and the tone of his voice was severe and merciless:

"I would rather give you the expanse of the earth in gold," said Lugh, "than hand over any object that would save the lives of your sons. Let them die in the knowledge that they have achieved something good because of me, and let them thank me for bringing them renown and glory through such a valorous death."

On hearing these words, Tuirenn hung his head in defeat and accepted that it was useless to bargain with Lugh of the Long Arm. He made his way back despondently to where his sons lay dying and gave them his sad news. The brothers were overcome with grief and despair and were so utterly devastated by Lugh's decision that not one of them lived to see the sun set in the evening sky. Tuirenn's heart was broken in two and after he had placed the last of his sons in the earth, all life departed from him and he fell dead over the bodies of Brian, Iucharba and Iuchar. The Tuatha Dé Danann witnessed the souls of all four rise towards the heavens and the tragic tale of the sons of Tuirenn was recounted from that day onwards throughout the land, becoming known as one of the Three Sorrows of Story-Telling.

Indra Defeats Vitra, Demon of Drought

INDRA'S COMBATS ARE REFLECTIONS of the natural phenomena of India. When the hot Indian summer draws to a close, the whole land is parched and thirsty for rain; rivers are low and many hill streams have dried up; man and beast are weary and wait release from the breathless atmosphere; they are even threatened by famine. Then dense masses of cloud gather in the sky; the tempest bellows, lightnings flash and thunder peals loudly; rain descends in a deluge; once again torrents pour down from the hills and rivers become swollen. Indra has waged his battle with the Drought Demons, broken down their fortress walls, and released the imprisoned cow-clouds which give nourishment to his human friends; the withered pastures become green with generous and rapid growth, and the rice harvest follows.

According to Vedic myth, Indra achieved his first great victory immediately after birth. Vritra, 'the encompasser', the Demon of Drought, was holding the cloud-cattle captive in his mountain fortress. Mankind begged for help from the gods, the shining ones, the world guardians.

Who will take pity? Who will bring refreshment?
Who will come nigh to help us in distress?
Counsels the thoughts within our hearts are counselling,
Wishes are wished and soar towards the highest –
O none but them, the shining ones, are merciful,
My longing wings itself towards the Eternals.

Indra heroically rose up to do battle for the sacrificers. Impulsively he seized the nectar of the gods, called Soma, and he drank that intoxicating juice. Then he snatched up his thunderstone which had been fashioned by the divine artisan Twashtri. His favourite horses, named the Bold and the Brown, were yoked in his golden chariot by his attendants and followers, the youthful Maruts.

Now, at the very beginning, Indra, the golden child, became the king of the three worlds. It was he who gave the air of life; he also gave strength. All the shining gods revered him and obeyed his commands. "His shadow is immortality; his shadow is death."

The Maruts, the sons of red Rudra, were the spirits of tempest and thunder. Their chariots were pulled by two spotted deer and one swift-footed, never-wearying red deer as leader. They were loyal and courageous youths; on their heads were golden helmets and they had golden breastplates, and wore bright skins on their shoulders; their ankles and arms were decked with golden bracelets. The Maruts were always strongly armed with bows and arrows and axes, and especially with gleaming spears. All beings feared those 'cloud shakers' when they charged forward with their lightning spears which 'shattered cattle like the thunderstone'; they were known to cleave cloud-rocks and drench the earth with quickening showers.

When Indra set off to attack the Drought Demon, the Maruts followed him, shouting with loud voices. They dashed towards the imprisoned cows of the clouds and chased them up into the air.

The dragon Vritra roared when Indra came near; at which heaven shook and the gods retreated. Mother Earth, the goddess Prithivi, was troubled regarding her golden son. But Indra advanced boldly with the roaring Maruts; he was inspired by the hymns of the priests; he had drank the Soma; he was strengthened by the sacrifices offered on earth's altars; and he wielded the thunderstone.

The Drought Demon deemed itself invulnerable, but Indra cast his weapon and soon discovered the vulnerable parts of its writhing body. He killed the monster and, as it lay face down in front of him, the torrents burst and carried it away to the sea of eternal darkness. Then Indra rejoiced and cried out:

I have slain Vritra, O ye hastening Maruts;
I have grown mighty through my own great vigour;
I am the hurler of the bolt of Thunder –
For man flow freely now the gleaming waters.

On earth the worshippers of the god were happy and the Rishi hymned his praises.

A post-Vedic version of the encounter between Indra and Vritra is found in the *Mahabharata*. Although it is coloured by the change which, in the process of time, passed over the religious beliefs of the Aryans, it retains some features of the original myth.

The story goes that in the first Age of the Universe a host of Danavas, or giants and demons, were so strongly armed that they were invincible in battle. They selected the dragon Vritra as their leader, and waged war against the gods, whom they scattered in all directions.

Realizing that they could not regain their power until they accomplished the death of Vritra, the celestials appeared before the Supreme Being, Brahma, the incarnation of the Soul of the Universe. Brahma instructed them to obtain the bones of a Rishi named Dadhicha, from which to construct a demon-slaying weapon. So the gods visited the Rishi and bowed down before him, and begged the request according to Brahma's advice.

Dadhicha agreed to renounce his body for the benefit of the gods. So the Rishi gave up his life, and from his bones Twashtri, the artisan god, shaped Indra's great weapon, which is called Vajra.

Twashtri spoke to Indra and said: "Oh chief of the celestials, with this, the best of weapons, reduce that fierce enemy of the gods to ashes! And, having slain him, happily rule the entire domain of heaven with those who follow you."

Then Indra led the gods against the mighty army. They found that Vritra was surrounded by dreaded Danavas, who resembled mountain peaks. A terrible battle was waged, but once again the gods were put to flight. Then Indra saw Vritra growing bolder, and he became dejected. But the Supreme Being protected him and the gods endowed him with their strength, so that he became mightier than before. Vritra was enraged, and roared loudly and fiercely, so that the heavens shook and the earth trembled with fear. Deeply agitated, Indra flung his divine weapon, which killed the leader of the Danavas. But Indra, thinking the demon was still alive, fled from the field in terror to seek shelter in a lake. The celestials, however, saw that Vritra had been slain, and they rejoiced and shouted the praises of Indra. Then, rallying once more, the gods attacked the panic-stricken Danavas, who turned and fled to the depths of ocean. There in the fathomless darkness they assembled together, and began to plot how they would accomplish the destruction of the three worlds.

Eventually the conspirators resolved to destroy all the Rishis who were possessed of knowledge and ascetic virtue, because the world was supported by them. So they made the ocean their home, raising waves high as hills for their protection, and they began to come out from their fortress to attack the mighty saints.

Krishna and Kaliya

ONE DAY, the cow-herds set out early, wandering through the woods and along the banks of the river until they came to a place called Kaliya. There they drank of the river waters, and allowed their cows to drink as well. Suddenly there was blackness and each of the cow-herds and cows laid down, the rich and instant poison of the naga or water snake called Kaliya entering their veins and causing them to die a painful death. Kaliya had come there from Ramanaka Dwipa, where he had once made his home. Garuda, who was the enemy of all serpents, had gone to live at Ramanaka Dwipa and Kaliya had fled immediately, taking refuge in the only place that Garuda was unable to visit, due to an ancient curse. Kaliya was an evil, frothing snake, and for miles around his shimmering form, the river bubbled with the heat of his poison.

Now on this day, Krishna set out to seek the company of the cow-herds and their cows, and he came upon their lifeless forms by the banks of the Jamna with some surprise. Krishna's powers were such that it took only a glance to restore the life to their bodies once more, and this he did at once. But Krishna was unhappy about his friends being plagued and he leapt into the water. Now the great Kaliya rose with all one hundred and ten hoods spluttering his poison, and the cowherds wept and wrung their hands at his certain death in that water. But Balarama was calm.

"Krishna will not die," he said calmly. "He cannot be slain."

Now Kaliya had wrapped himself around the body of Krishna, and he tightened his grip with all of his force. But Krishna outwitted him, and making himself so large, he caused the serpent to set him free. Again, Kaliya squeezed his bulk around the youth, but once again Krishna cast him aside by growing in size.

Then, Krishna suddenly leapt onto Kaliya's heads, and taking on the weight of the entire universe, he danced on the serpent's heads until Kaliya began to splutter, and then die. But there was silence and weeping, and the serpent's many wives came forward and begged Krishna to set their husband free. They laid themselves at his feet, and pledged eternal worship.

"Please release him," they asked, "or slay us with him. Please, Krishna, know that a serpent is venomous through nature not through will. Please pardon him."

And so it was that Krishna stepped from Kaliya's head and set the serpent free. Kaliya gasped his gratefulness, and prayed forgiveness for failing to recognize the great Krishna, the Lord, earlier. Krishna commanded Kaliya to return to Ramanaka Dwipa, but Kaliya lowered his head and explained that he could not return there for Garuda would make a meal of him at first sight. Krishna laughed, and pointed to the mark on Kaliya's head.

"Show him my mark, my friend," he said to the serpent, "for when Garuda sees that he will not touch you."

From that day, the waters were cleared of poisons and the people rejoiced. Krishna was Lord.

Pan Gu and the Creation of the Universe

AT THE VERY BEGINNING of time, when only darkness and chaos existed and the heavens and the earth had not yet been properly divided up, the universe resembled the shape of a large egg. And at the centre of this egg, the first living creature one day came into being. After many thousands of years, when he had gathered sufficient strength and energy and had grown to the size of a giant, the creature, who gave himself the name of Pan Gu, awoke fully refreshed from his long rest and stood upright within his shell. He began to yawn very loudly and to stretch his enormous limbs, and as he did so, the walls of the egg were cracked open and separated into two even portions. The lighter, more fragile, part of the egg floated delicately upwards to form the white silken sheet of the sky, while the heavier, more substantial part, dropped downwards to form the earth's crusty surface.

Now when Pan Gu observed this, he was happy and proud to have created some light in place of the darkness and chaos out of which he had emerged. But at the same time, he began to fear that the skies and the earth might fuse once more, and he stood and scratched his huge head, pondering a solution to the problem. And after he had thought things through for quite a while, he decided that the only way to keep the two elements at a safe distance from each other was to place his own great bulk between them. So he took up his position, heaving and pushing upwards against the sky with his hands and pressing downwards into the earth with all the weight of his massive feet until a reasonable gap had been formed.

For the next eighteen thousand years, Pan Gu continued to push the earth and the sky apart, growing taller and taller every day until the gap measured some thirty thousand miles. And when this distance between them had been established, the sky grew firm and solid and the earth became securely fixed far beneath it. Pan Gu then looked around him and seeing that there was no longer any danger of darkness returning to the universe, he felt at last that he could lay down and rest, for his bones ached and he had grown old and frail over the years. Breathing a heavy sigh, he fell into an exhausted sleep from which he never awoke. But as he lay dying, the various parts of his vast body were miraculously transformed to create the world as we mortals know it today.

Pan Gu's head became the mountain ranges; his blood became the rivers and streams; the hairs on his head were changed into colourful and fragrant blossoms and his flesh was restored to become the trees and soil. His left eye was transformed into the sun and his right eye became the moon; his breath was revived in the winds and the clouds and his voice resounded anew as thunder and lightning. Even his sweat and tears were put to good use and were transformed into delicate droplets of rain and sweet-smelling morning dew.

And when people later came to inhabit the earth, they worshipped Pan Gu as a great creator and displayed the utmost respect for all the natural elements, believing them to be his sacred body spread out like a carpet before them beneath the blue arch of the heavens.

Nu Wa Peoples the Earth

WHEN THE UNIVERSE first emerged from chaos, mankind had not yet been created and the firmament and all the territories beneath it were inhabited by Gods or giants who had sprung forth from the body of Pan Gu. At that time, one particularly powerful Goddess appeared on earth in the company of her chosen heavenly companion. The Goddess's name was Nu Wa and her companion's name was Fu Xi. Together these deities set out to bring an even greater sense of order and regulation to the world.

And of all the other Gods residing in the heavens, Nu Wa was the strangest and most unusual in appearance, for the upper half of her body was shaped like a human being, while the lower part took the form of a snake. Nu Wa also possessed the unique ability to change her shape up to seventy times a day and she frequently appeared on earth in several different guises.

Although Nu Wa took great pleasure in the wondrous beauty of the new-born world she occupied, deep within she felt it to be a little too silent and she yearned to create something that would fill the empty stillness. One day shortly afterwards, as she walked along the banks of the great Yellow River, she began to imagine spending time in the company of other beings not unlike herself, animated creatures who might talk and laugh with her and with whom she could share her thoughts and feelings. Sitting herself down on the earth, she allowed her fingers to explore its sandy texture and without quite realizing it, began to mould the surrounding clay into tiny figures. But instead of giving them the lower bodies of reptiles, the Goddess furnished her creatures with little legs so they would stand upright. Pleased with the result, she placed the first of them beside her on the earth and was most surprised and overjoyed to see it suddenly come to life, dancing around her and laughing excitedly. She placed another beside it and again the same thing happened. Nu Wa was delighted with herself and with her own bare hands she continued to make more and more of her little people as she rested by the river bank.

But as the day wore on, the Goddess grew tired and it was then that she decided to make use of her supernatural powers to complete the task she had begun. So breaking off a length of wood from a nearby mulberry tree, she dredged it through the water until it was coated in mud. Then she shook the branch furiously until several hundred drops of mud landed on the ground and as each drop landed it was instantly transformed into a human being. Then Nu Wa pronounced that the beings she had shaped with her own hands should live to become the rich and fortunate people of the world, while those created out of the drops of mud should lead ordinary and humble lives. And realizing that her little creatures should themselves be masters of their own survival, Nu Wa separated them into sons and daughters and declared that they should marry and multiply until the whole wide world had become their home and they were free once and for all from the threat of extinction.

The War Between the Gods of Fire and Water

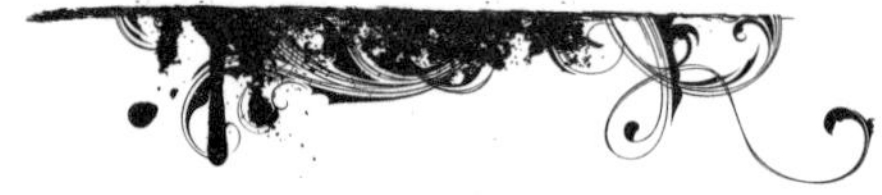

FOR A GREAT MANY YEARS after Nu Wa had created human beings, the earth remained a peaceful and joyous place and it was not until the final years of the Goddess's reign that mankind first encountered pain and suffering. For Nu Wa was extremely protective of the race she had created and considered it her supreme duty to shelter it from all harm and evil. People depended on Nu Wa for her guardianship and she, in turn, enabled them to live in comfort and security.

One day, however, two of the Gods who dwelt in the heavens, known as Gong Gong and Zhurong, became entangled in a fierce and bitter dispute. No one knew precisely why the two Gods began to shout and threaten one another, but before long they were resolved to do battle against each other and to remain fighting to the bitter end. Gong Gong, who was the God of Water, was well known as a violent and ambitious character and his bright red wavy hair perfectly mirrored his fiery and riotous spirit. Zhurong, the God of Fire, was equally belligerent when provoked and his great height and bulk rendered him no less terrifying in appearance.

Several days of fierce fighting ensued between the two of them during which the skies buckled and shifted under the strain of the combat. An end to this savage battle seemed to be nowhere in sight, as each God thrust and lunged with increasing fury and rage, determined to prove himself more powerful than the other. But on the fourth day, Gong Gong began to weary and Zhurong gained the upper hand, felling his opponent to the ground and causing him to tumble right out of the heavens.

Crashing to the earth with a loud bang, Gong Gong soon became acutely aware of the shame and disgrace of his defeat and decided that he would never again have the courage to face any of his fellow Gods. He was now resolved to end his own life and looked around him for some means by which he might perform this task honourably and successfully. And seeing a large mountain range in the distance rising in the shape of a giant pillar to the skies, Gong Gong ran towards it with all the speed he could muster and rammed his head violently against its base.

As soon as he had done this, a terrifying noise erupted from within the mountain, and gazing upwards, Gong Gong saw that a great wedge of rock had broken away from the peak, leaving behind a large gaping hole in the sky. Without the support of the mountain, the sky began to collapse and plummet towards the earth's surface, causing great crevasses to appear on impact. Many of these crevasses released intensely hot flames which instantly engulfed the earth's vegetation, while others spouted streams of filthy water which merged to form a great ocean. And as the flood and destruction spread throughout the entire world, Nu Wa's people no longer knew where to turn to for help. Thousands of them drowned, while others wandered the earth in terror and fear, their homes consumed by the raging flames and their crops destroyed by the swift-flowing water.

Nu Wa witnessed all of this in great distress and could not bear to see the race she had created suffer such appalling misery and deprivation. Though she was now old and looking forward to her time of rest, she decided that she must quickly take action to save her people, and it seemed that the only way for her to do this was to repair the heavens as soon as she possibly could with her very own hands.

Nu Wa Repairs the Sky

Nu Wa rapidly set about gathering the materials she needed to mend the great hole in the sky. One of the first places she visited in her search was the river Yangtze where she stooped down and gathered up as many pebbles as she could hold in both arms. These were carefully chosen in a variety of colours and carried to a forge in the heavens where they were melted down into a thick, gravel-like paste. Once she had returned to earth, Nu Wa began to repair the damage, anxiously filling the gaping hole with the paste and smoothing whatever remained of it into the surrounding cracks in the firmament. Then she hurried once more to the river bank and, collecting together the tallest reeds, she built a large, smouldering fire and burnt the reeds until they formed a huge mound of ashes. With these ashes Nu Wa sealed the crevasses of the earth, so that water no longer gushed out from beneath its surface and the swollen rivers gradually began to subside.

After she had done this, Nu Wa surveyed her work, yet she was still not convinced that she had done enough to prevent the heavens collapsing again in the future. So she went out and captured one of the giant immortal tortoises which were known to swim among the jagged rocks at the deepest point of the ocean and brought it ashore to slaughter it. And when she had killed the creature, she chopped off its four sturdy legs and stood them upright at the four points of the compass as extra support for the heavens. Only now was the Goddess satisfied and she began to gather round her some of her frightened people in an attempt to reassure them that order had finally been restored.

To help them forget the terrible experiences they had been put through, Nu Wa made a flute for them out of thirteen sticks of bamboo and with it she began to play the sweetest, most soothing music. All who heard it grew calmer almost at once and the earth slowly began to emerge from the chaos and destruction to which it had been subjected. From that day forth, Nu Wa's people honoured her by calling her 'Goddess of music' and many among them took great pride in learning the instrument she had introduced them to.

But even though the heavens had been repaired, the earth was never quite the same again. Gong Gong's damage to the mountain had caused the skies to tilt permanently towards the north-west so that the Pole Star, around which the heavens revolved, was dislodged from its position directly overhead. The sun and the moon were also tilted, this time in the direction of the west, leaving a great depression in the south-east. And not only that, but the peak of the mountain which had crashed to the earth had left a huge hollow where it landed in the east into which the rivers and streams of the world flowed incessantly.

Nu Wa had done all she could to salvage the earth and shortly afterwards, she died. Her body was transformed into a thousand fairies who watched over the human race on her behalf. Her people believe that the reason China's rivers flow eastwards was because of Gong Gong's foolish collision with the mountain, a belief that is still shared by their ancestors today.

Xing Tian, the Headless Giant

ONCE THERE WAS A GIANT named Xing Tian who was full of ambition and great plans for his future. At one time, he had been an official of the Fiery Emperor, but when Chiyou had conquered the region, he had quickly switched loyalties and offered his services to the new, corrupt usurper of the south. It greatly disturbed the giant to hear reports of the bloody deaths of Chiyou's men at the hands of the Yellow Emperor and he wanted nothing less than to meet the Emperor face to face and challenge him to single combat until one of them lay dead.

So Xing Tian took up his axe and his shield and set off for the divine palace at the top of Mount Kunlun, seething with anger and rage as he thundered along. But the Yellow Emperor had received word of the giant's approach and seized his most precious sword ready to meet him head on. For days the two battled furiously, lashing out savagely with their weapons as they fought into the clouds and down the side of the mountain. They fought along all the great mountain ranges of northern China until eventually they reached the place known as the Long Sheep range in the north-east.

And it was here that the Yellow Emperor caught the giant off-guard and, raising his sword high into the air just at the level of the giant's shoulder, he slashed sideways with his blade until he had sliced off Xing Tian's head. A terrifying scream escaped the gaping, bloody mouth of the giant as his head began to topple forward, crashing with a loud thud to the ground and rolling down the hill like a massive boulder.

The giant stood frozen in absolute horror, and then he began feeling desperately with his hands around the hole above his shoulders where his head ought to have been. Soon panic had taken control of him and he thrashed about wildly with his weapon, carving up trees and tossing huge rocks into the air until the valleys began to shake and the sky began to cloud over with dust from the debris.

Seeing the giant's great fury, the Yellow Emperor grew fearful that Xing Tian might actually find his head and put it back on his shoulders again. So he swiftly drew his sword and sliced open the mountain underneath which the head had finally come to rest. Then he kicked the head into the chasm and sealed up the gap once more.

For ten thousand years afterwards the giant roamed the mountainside searching for his head. But in all that time he never found what he was looking for although he remained defiant that he would one day face the Yellow Emperor again. Some people say that the giant grew to be very resourceful, and to help him in his long search he used his two breasts for eyes and his navel for a mouth.

The Ten Suns of Dijun and Xihe

THE GOD OF THE EAST, Dijun, had married the Goddess of the Sun, Xihe, and they lived together on the far eastern side of the world just at the edge of the great Eastern Ocean. Shortly after their marriage, the Goddess gave birth to ten suns, each of them a fiery, energetic, golden globe, and she placed the children lovingly in the giant Fusang tree close to the sea where they could frolic and bathe whenever they became overheated.

Each morning before breakfast, the suns took it in turns to spring from the enormous tree into the ocean below in preparation for their mother's visit when one of them would be lifted into her chariot and driven across the sky to bring light and warmth to the world. Usually the two remained together all day until they had travelled as far as the western abyss known as the Yuyuan. Then, when her sun had grown weary and the light had begun to fade from his body, Xihe returned him to the Fusang tree where he slept the night peacefully with his nine brothers. On the following morning, the Goddess would collect another of her suns, sit him beside her in her chariot, and follow exactly the same route across the sky. In this way, the earth was evenly and regularly heated, crops grew tall and healthy, and the people rarely suffered from the cold.

But one night, the ten suns began to complain among themselves that they had not yet been allowed to spend an entire day playing together without at least one of them being absent. And realizing how unhappy this situation made them feel, they decided to rebel against their mother and to break free of the tedious routine she insisted they follow. So the next morning, before the Goddess had arrived, all ten of them leapt into the skies at once, dancing joyfully above the earth, intent on making the most of their forbidden freedom. They were more than pleased to see the great dazzling light they were able to generate as they shone together, and made a solemn vow that they would never again allow themselves to become separated during the daytime.

The ten suns had not once paused to consider the disastrous consequences of their rebellion on the world below. For with ten powerful beams directed at the earth, crops began to wilt, rivers began to dry up, food became scarce and people began to suffer burns and wretched hunger pangs. They prayed for rains to drive away the suns, but none appeared. They called upon the great sorceress Nu Chou to perform her acts of magic, but her spells had no effect. They hid beneath the great trees of the forests for shade, but these were stripped of leaves and offered little or no protection. And now great hungry beasts of prey and dreaded monsters emerged from the wilderness and began to devour the human beings they encountered, unable to satisfy their huge appetites any longer. The destruction spread to every corner of the earth and the people were utterly miserable and filled with despair. They turned to their Emperor for help, knowing he was at a loss to know what to do, but he was their only hope, and they prayed that he would soon be visited by the God of Wisdom.

Yi, the Archer, is Summoned

Dijun and Xihe were horrified to see the effect their unruly children were having upon the earth and pleaded with them to return to their home in the Fusang tree. But in spite of their entreaties, the ten suns continued on as before, adamant that they would not return to their former lifestyle.

Emperor Yao now grew very impatient, and summoning Dijun to appear before him, he demanded that the God teach his suns to behave. Dijun heard the Emperor's plea but still he could not bring himself to raise a hand against the suns he loved so dearly. It was eventually settled between them, however, that one of Yao's officials in the heavens, known as Yi, should quickly descend to earth and do whatever he must to prevent any further catastrophe.

Yi was not a God of very impressive stature, but his fame as one of the most gifted archers in the heavens was widespread, for it was well known that he could shoot a sparrow down in full flight from a distance of fifty miles. Now Dijun went to meet with Yi to explain the problem his suns had created, and he handed the archer a new red bow and a quiver of white arrows and advised him what he must do.

"Try not to hurt my suns any more than you need to," he told Yi, "but take this bow and ensure that you bring them under control. See to it that the wicked beasts devouring mankind are also slain and that order and calm are restored once more to the earth."

Yi readily accepted this challenge and, taking with him his wife Chang E, he departed the Heavenly Palace and made his descent to the world below. Emperor Yao was overjoyed to see the couple approach and immediately organized a tour of the land for them, where Yi witnessed for himself the devastation brought about by Dijun's children, as he came face to face with half-burnt, starving people roaming aimlessly over the scorched, cracked earth.

And witnessing all of this terrible suffering, Yi grew more and more furious with the suns of Dijun and it slipped his mind entirely that he had promised to treat them leniently. "The time is now past for reasoning or persuasion," Yi thought to himself, and he strode to the highest mountain, tightened the string of his powerful bow and took aim with the first of his arrows. The weapon shot up into the sky and travelled straight through the centre of one of the suns, causing it to erupt into a thousand sparks as it split open and spun out of control to the ground, transforming itself on impact into a strange three-legged raven.

Now there were only nine suns left in the sky and Yi fitted the next arrow to his bow. One after another the arrows flew through the air, expertly hitting their targets, until the earth slowly began to cool down. But when the Emperor saw that there were only two suns left in the sky and that Yi had already taken aim, he wisely remembered that at least one sun should survive to brighten the earth and so he crept up behind the archer and stole the last of the white arrows from his quiver.

Having fulfilled his undertaking to rid Emperor Yao of the nine suns, Yi turned his attention to the task of hunting down the various hideous monsters threatening the earth. Gathering a fresh supply of arrows, he made his way southwards to fight the man-eating monster of the marsh with six feet and a human head, known as Zao Chi. And with the help of his divine bow, he quickly overcame the creature, piercing his huge heart with an arrow of steel. Travelling northwards, he tackled a great many other ferocious beasts, including the nine-headed monster, Jiu Ying, wading into a deep, black pool and throttling the fiend with his own bare hands. After that, he moved onwards to the Quingqiu marshes of the east where he came upon the terrible vulture Dafeng, a gigantic bird of unnatural strength with a wing span so enormous that whenever the bird took to the air, a great typhoon blew up around it. And on this occasion, Yi knew that his single remaining arrow would only wound the bird, so he tied a long black cord to the shaft of the arrow before taking aim. Then as the creature flew past, Yi shot him in the chest and even though the vulture pulled strongly on the cord as it attempted to make towards a place of safety, Yi dragged it to the ground, plunging his knife repeatedly into its breast until all life had gone from it.

All over the earth, people looked upon Yi as a great hero, the God who had single-handedly rescued them from destruction. Numerous banquets and ceremonial feasts were held in his honour, all of them attended by the Emperor himself, who could not do enough to thank Yi for his assistance. Emperor Yao invited Yi to make his home on earth, promising to build him the a very fine palace overlooking Jade Mountain, but Yi was anxious to return to the heavens in triumph where he felt he rightly belonged and where, in any event, Dijun eagerly awaited an account of his exploits.

Feng Po, God of the Wind

FENG PO, the God of the Wind, is represented as an old man with a white beard, yellow cloak, and blue and red cap. He holds a large sack, and directs the wind which comes from its mouth in any direction he pleases.

He is regarded as a stellar divinity under the control of the star Ch'i, because the wind blows at the time when the moon leaves that celestial mansion. He is also said to be a dragon called Fei Lien, at first one of the supporters of the rebel Ch'ih Yu, who was defeated by Huang Ti. Having been transformed into a spiritual monster, he stirred up tremendous winds in the southern regions. The Emperor Yao sent Shen I with three hundred soldiers to quiet the storms and appease Ch'ih Yu's relatives, who were wreaking their vengeance on the people. Shen I ordered the people to spread a long cloth in front of their houses, fixing it with stones. The wind, blowing against this, had to change its direction. Shen I then flew on the wind to the top of a high mountain, where he saw a monster at the base. It had the shape of a huge yellow and white sack and kept inhaling and exhaling in great gusts. Shen I, concluding that this was the cause of all these storms, shot an arrow and hit the monster, whereupon it took refuge in a deep cave. Here it turned on Shen I and, drawing a sword, dared him to attack the Mother of the Winds. Shen I, however, bravely faced the monster and discharged another arrow, this time hitting it in the knee. The monster immediately threw down its sword and begged that its life might be spared.

Lo Hsuan and the Ministry of Fire

IT IS BELIEVED that Lo Hsuan was originally a Taoist priest known as Yen-chung Hsien, of the island Huo-lung, meaning 'Fire-dragon'. His face was the colour of ripe fruit of the jujube-tree, his hair and beard red, the former done up in the shape of a fish-tail. He is also said to have had three eyes. He wore a red cloak ornamented with the pa kua; his horse snorted flames from its nostrils and fire darted from its hoofs.

While fighting in the service of the son of the tyrant emperor, Lo Hsuan suddenly changed himself into a giant with three heads and six arms. In each of his hands he held a magic weapon. These were a seal which reflected the heavens and the earth, a wheel of the five fire-dragons, a gourd containing ten thousand fire-crows, and, in the other hands, two swords which floated like smoke and a tall column of smoke enclosing swords of fire.

Having arrived at the city of Hsi Ch'i, Lo Hsuan sent forth his smoke-column and the air was filled with swords of fire. The ten thousand fire-crows, emerging from the gourd, spread themselves over the town and a terrible fire broke out, the whole place being ablaze in just a few minutes.

It was then that Princess Lung Chi, daughter of Wang-mu Niang-niang appeared in the sky. She spread her shroud of mist and dew over the city and the fire was extinguished by a heavy downpour of rain. All the mysterious mechanisms of Lo Hsuan lost their power and the magician took to his heels down the side of the mountain. There he was met by Li, the Pagoda-bearer, who threw his golden pagoda into the air. The pagoda fell on Lo Hsuan's head and broke his skull.

A Battle of the Gods

IT IS THOUGHT that during the wars that preceded the accession of the Chou dynasty in 1122 BC, a multitude of demigods, Buddhas and Immortals took part on one side or the other, some fighting for the old dynasty, some for the new. They were wonderful creatures, gifted with marvellous powers. They could change their form at will, multiply their heads and limbs, become invisible, and create – by simply uttering a word – terrible monsters who bit and destroyed, or sent forth poisonous gases, or emitted flames from their nostrils. In these battles there is much lightning, thunder, flight of fire dragons, dark clouds that vomit burning hails of murderous weapons; swords, spears, and arrows fall from the sky on to the heads of the combatants; the earth trembles and the pillars of Heaven shake.

One of these gifted warriors was Chun T'i, a Taoist of the Western Paradise, who appeared on the scene when the armies of the rival dynasties were facing each other. K'ung Hsuan was gallantly holding the pass of the Chin-chi Ling; Chiang Tzu-ya was trying to take it by assault – so far without success.

Chun T'i's mission was to take K'ung Hsuan to the abode of the blessed, his wisdom and general progress having now reached the required degree of perfection. This was a means of breaking down the invincible resistance of this powerful enemy and at the same time of rewarding his brilliant talents.

But K'ung Hsuan did not approve of this plan and a fight took place between the two champions. At one moment Chun T'i was seized by a luminous bow and carried into the air. While enveloped in a cloud of fire he appeared with eighteen arms and twenty-four heads, holding in each hand a powerful talisman.

He put a silk cord round K'ung Hsuan's neck, touched him with his wand and forced him to reassume his original form of a red one-eyed peacock. Chun T'i sat himself on the peacock's back and it flew across the sky, carrying its saviour and master to the Western Paradise. Brilliantly variegated clouds marked its track through space.

On the disappearance of its defender, the pass of Chin-chi Ling was captured and the village of Chieh-p'ai Kuan was reached. This place was the fort of the enemy's forces. It was defended by a host of genii and Immortals, the most distinguished among them being the Taoist T'ung-t'ien Chiao-chu, whose especially effective charms had so far kept the fort secure against every attempt on it.

Lao Tzu himself had descended from dwelling in happiness, together with Yuan-shih T'ien-tsun and Chieh-yin Tao-jen, to take part in the siege. But the town had four gates and these heavenly rulers were only three in number. So Chun T'i was recalled, and each member of the quartet was given the task of capturing one of the gates.

Chun T'i's duty was to take the Chueh-hsien Men, defended by T'ung-t'ien Chiao-chu. The warriors who had tried to enter the town by this gate had all paid for their temerity with their lives. The moment each had crossed the threshold a clap of thunder had resounded, and a mysterious sword, moving with lightning speed, had slain him.

As Chun T'i advanced at the head of his warriors terrible lightning filled the air and the mysterious sword descended like a thunderbolt on his head. But Chun T'i held up his Seven-Precious Branch. Thousands of lotus flowers emerged from it, which formed an impenetrable barrier and stopped the sword in its fall. This and the other gates were then forced, and a grand assault was now directed against the chief defender of the town.

T'ung-t'ien Chiao-chu, riding his ox and surrounded by his warriors, for the last time risked the chance of war and bravely faced his four terrible adversaries. With his sword held high, he threw himself on Chieh-yin Tao-jen, whose only weapon was his fly whisk. But there emerged from this a five-coloured lotus flower, which stopped the sword thrust. While Lao Tzu struck the hero with his staff, Yuan-shih T'ien-tsun warded off the terrible sword.

Chun T'i now called for the spiritual peacock to help. He took the form of a warrior with twenty-four heads and eighteen arms. His mysterious weapons surrounded T'ung-t'ien Chiao-chu, and Lao Tzu struck the hero so hard that fire came out from his eyes, nose and mouth. Unable to ward off the assaults of his adversaries, he next received a blow from Chun T'i's magic wand, which felled him. He took flight in a whirlwind of dust.

The defenders now offered no further resistance. Yuan-shih T'ien-tsun thanked Chun T'i for the valuable assistance he had given in the capture of the village. Afterwards the gods returned to their palace in the Western Heaven.

But T'ung-t'ien Chiao-chu swore to have his revenge. He called to the spirits of the twenty-eight constellations for help, and marched to attack Wu Wang's army. The honour of the victory that followed belonged to Chun T'i, who disarmed both the Immortal Wu Yun and T'ung-t'ien Chiao-chu.

Wu Yun, armed with his magic sword, attacked Chun T'i; but the latter opened his mouth and a blue lotus flower came out and stopped the blows aimed at him. Other thrusts were met by similar miracles.

"Why continue so useless a fight?" said Chun T'i at last. "Abandon the cause of the Shang and come with me to the Western Paradise. I came to save you, and you must not compel me to make you resume your original form."

An insulting flow of words was the reply; again the magic sword descended like lightning, and again the stroke was averted by a timely lotus flower. Chun T'i now waved his wand and the magic sword was broken to bits, with only the handle remaining in Wu Yun's hand.

Mad with rage, Wu Yun seized his club and tried to fell his enemy. But Chun T'i summoned a disciple, who appeared with a bamboo pole. This he thrust out like a fishing rod, and on a hook at the end of the line attached to the pole dangled a large golden-bearded turtle. This was the Immortal Wu Yun, now in his original form of a spiritual turtle. The disciple sat himself on its back, and both disappeared into space, returning to the Western Heavens.

To conquer T'ung-t'ien Chiao-chu was more difficult, but after a long fight Chun T'i waved his Wand of the Seven Treasures and broke his adversary's sword. The latter, disarmed and vanquished, disappeared in a cloud of dust. Chun T'i did not trouble to pursue him. The battle was won.

A disciple of T'ung-t'ien Chiao-chu, P'i-lu Hsien, 'the Immortal P'i-lu', seeing his master beaten in two successive engagements, left the battlefield and followed Chun T'i to the Western Paradise, to become a Buddha. He is known as P'i-lu Fo, one of the principal gods of Buddhism.

Chun T'i's festival is celebrated on the sixth day of the third moon. He is generally shown with eight hands and three faces, one of the latter being that of a pig.

The Guardian of the Gate of Heaven

IN BUDDHIST TEMPLES you will find a figure of a man holding a model of a pagoda in his hand. He is Li, the Prime Minister of Heaven and father of No-cha. He was a general under the tyrant Chou and commander of Ch'en-t'ang Kuan at the time when the bloody war was being waged that resulted in the extinction of the Yin dynasty.

No-cha is one of the most frequently mentioned heroes in Chinese romance; he is represented in one account as being Yu Huang's shield bearer, sixty feet in height, his three heads with nine eyes crowned by a golden wheel, his eight hands each holding a magic weapon and his mouth vomiting blue clouds. At the sound of his voice, we are told, the heavens shook and the foundations of the earth trembled. His duty was to bring into submission all the demons which desolated the world.

Li Ching's wife, Yin Shih, bore him three sons, the eldest Chin-cha, the second Mu-cha, and the third No-cha, generally known as 'the Third Prince'.

One night, Yin Shih dreamed that a Taoist priest entered her room. She indignantly exclaimed: "How dare you come into my room in this indiscreet manner?" The priest replied: "Woman, receive the child of the unicorn!" Before she could reply the Taoist pushed an object to her bosom.

Yin Shih awoke in a fright, a cold sweat all over her body. Having woken her husband, she told him of her dream. At that moment she was seized with the pains of childbirth. Li Ching left the room, uneasy at what seemed to be inauspicious omens. A little later two servants ran to him, crying out: "Your wife has given birth to a monstrous freak!"

Li Ching seized his sword and went into his wife's room, which he found filled with a red light and a most extraordinary odour. A ball of flesh was rolling on the floor like a wheel; with a blow of his sword he cut it open and a baby emerged, surrounded by a halo of red light. Its face was very white, a gold bracelet was on its right wrist and it wore a pair of red silk trousers, from which came rays of dazzling golden light. The bracelet was 'the horizon of Heaven and earth', and the two precious objects belonged to the cave Chin-kuang Tung of T'ai-i Chen-jen, the priest who had bestowed them upon him when he appeared to his mother during her sleep. The child itself was an avatar of Ling Chu-tzu, 'the Intelligent Pearl'.

Then next day T'ai-i Chen-jen returned and asked Li Ching's permission to see the newborn baby. "He shall be called No-cha," he said, "and will become my disciple."

At seven years of age No-cha was already six feet in height. One day he asked his mother if he might go for a walk outside the town. His mother granted him permission on condition that he was accompanied by a servant. She also told him not to remain too long outside the wall, for his father should become anxious.

It was in the fifth moon: the heat was excessive. No-cha had not gone far before he was sweating profusely. Some way ahead he saw a clump of trees. He decided to go there and, settling himself in the shade, opened his coat and breathed the fresher air with relief. In front of him he saw a stream of limpid green water running between two rows of willows – the water gently flowing round a rock. The child ran to the banks of the stream and said to his guardian: "I am covered with perspiration, and will bathe from the rock." "Be quick," said the servant; "if your father returns home before you he will be anxious." No-cha stripped himself, took his red silk trousers and dipped them in the water, intending to use them as a towel. No sooner were the magic trousers immersed in the stream than the water began to boil and Heaven and earth trembled. The water of the Chiu-wan Ho river ('Nine-bends River') turned completely red and Lung Wang's palace shook to its foundations. The Dragon king, surprised at seeing the walls of his crystal palace shaking, called his officers and asked: "How is it that the palace threatens to collapse? There should not be an earthquake at this time." He ordered one of his attendants to go at once and find out what evil was causing the commotion. When the officer reached the river he saw that the water was red but noticed nothing else except a boy dipping a band of silk in the stream. He called out angrily: "That child should be thrown into the water for making the river red and causing Lung Wang's palace to shake." No-cha replied, "Who is that who speaks so brutally?"

Then he jumped aside, realizing that the man intended to seize him. He took his gold bracelet and hurled it in the air. It fell on the head of the officer and No-cha left him dead on the rock. Then he picked up his bracelet and said smiling: "His blood has stained my precious horizon of Heaven and earth." He then washed it in the water.

"How is it that the officer does not return?" inquired Lung Wang. At that moment attendants came to inform him that the messenger had been murdered by a boy.

Ao Ping, the third son of Lung Wang, immediately placed himself at the head of a troop of marines, and with his trident in his hand he left the palace precincts. The warriors dashed into the river, raising on every side waves mountains high. Seeing the water rising, No-cha stood up on the rock and was confronted by Ao Ping mounted on a sea monster. "Who slew my messenger?" cried the warrior. "I did," answered No-cha. "Who are you?" demanded Ao Ping.

"I am No-cha, the third son of Li Ching of Ch'en-t'ang Kuan. I came here to bathe and refresh myself. Your messenger cursed me, and I killed him."

"Rascal! Do you not know that your victim was a deputy of the King of Heaven? How dare you kill him and then boast of your crime?" Ao Ping then thrust at the boy with his trident, but No-cha evaded the thrust.

"Who are you?" No-cha asked in turn.

"I am Ao Ping, the third son of Lung Wang."

"Ah, you are a blusterer," jeered the boy. "If you dare to touch me I will skin you alive, you and your mud eels!"

"You make me choke with rage," shouted Ao Ping, at the same time thrusting again with his trident.

Furious at this renewed attack, No-cha spread his silk trousers in the air. Thousands of balls of fire flew out of them, felling Lung Wang's son. No-cha put his foot on Ao Ping's head and struck it with his magic bracelet, causing Ao Ping to turn into his true form of a dragon.

"I am now going to pull out your sinews," he said, "in order to make a belt for my father."

No-cha was as good as his word, and Ao Ping's escort ran and informed Lung Wang of the fate of his son. The Dragon king went to Li Ching and demanded an explanation.

Being entirely ignorant of what had taken place, Li Ching went to No-cha to question him.

Li Ching found No-cha in the garden, busily weaving the belt of dragon sinew. "You have brought the most awful misfortunes upon us," he exclaimed. "Come and give an account of your conduct." "Have no fear," No-cha replied; "his son's sinews are still intact. I will give them back to him if he wishes."

When they entered the house he saluted the Dragon king, made a curt apology, and offered to return his son's sinews. The father, moved with grief at the sight of the proofs of the tragedy, said bitterly to Li Ching: "You have such a son and yet dare to deny his guilt, though you heard him admitting it! Tomorrow I shall report the matter to Yu Huang." Having said this, he departed.

Li Ching was overwhelmed at the enormity of his son's crime. His wife, hearing his cries of grief, went to her husband. "What obnoxious creature is this that you have brought into the world?" he said to her angrily. "He has slain two spirits, the son of Lung Wang and a steward sent by the King of Heaven. Tomorrow the Dragon king is to lodge a complaint with Yu Huang, and two or three days from now will see the end of our existence."

The poor mother began to weep. "What!" she sobbed, "you whom I suffered so much for, you are to be the cause of our ruin and death!"

No-cha, seeing his parents so distracted, fell on his knees. "Let me tell you once for all," he said, "that I am no ordinary mortal. I am the disciple of T'ai-i Chen-jen. The magic weapons I received from him – it is they that brought on me the undying hatred of Lung Wang. But he cannot prevail. Today I will go and ask my master's advice. The guilty alone should suffer the penalty; it is unjust that his parents should suffer."

No-cha then left for Ch'ien-yuan Shan. He entered the cave of his master T'ai-i Chen-jen, to whom he told of his adventures. The master considered the grave consequences of the murders. He then ordered No-cha to bare his breast. With his finger he drew on the skin a magic formula, after which he gave him some secret instructions. "Now," he said, "go to the gate of Heaven and await the arrival of Lung Wang, who plans to accuse you before Yu Huang. Then you must come again to consult me, so that your parents may not be molested because of your misdeeds."

When No-cha reached the gate of Heaven it was closed. He searched in vain for Lung Wang, but after a while he saw him approaching. Lung Wang did not see No-cha, as the formula written by T'ai-i Chen-jen rendered him invisible. As Lung Wang approached the gate, No-cha ran up to him and struck him so hard with his golden bracelet that he fell to the ground. Then No-cha stamped on him, cursing him.

The Dragon-king now recognized his assailant and sharply reproached him with his crimes, but the only reparation he got was a renewal of kicks and blows. Then, partially lifting Lung Wang's cloak and raising his shield, No-cha tore off about forty scales from his body. Blood flowed copiously and under stress of the pain the Dragon king begged his foe to spare his life. To this No-cha consented on condition that he relinquished his purpose of accusing him before Yu Huang.

"Now," went on No-cha, "change yourself into a small serpent so that I may take you back without fear of your escaping."

Lung Wang took the form of a small blue dragon and followed No-cha to his father's house. After entering the house Lung Wang resumed his normal form and accused No-cha of attacking him. "I will go with all the Dragon kings and lay an accusation before Yu Huang," he said. Then he transformed himself into a gust of wind and disappeared.

"Things are going from bad to worse," sighed Li Ching, His son, however, consoled him: "I beg you, my father, not to let the future trouble you. I am the chosen one of the gods. My master is T'ai-i Chen-jen. He has assured me that he can easily protect us."

Next No-cha went out and climbed a tower that overlooked the entrance of the fort. There he found a wonderful bow and three magic arrows. No-cha did not know that this was the spiritual weapon belonging to the fort. "My master informed me that I am destined to fight to establish the coming Chou dynasty; I ought therefore to perfect myself in the use of weapons. This is a good opportunity." So he seized the bow and shot an arrow toward the south west. A red trail indicated the path of the arrow, which hissed as it flew. At that moment Pi Yun, a servant of Shih-chi Niang-niang, happened to be at the foot of K'u-lou Shan (Skeleton Hill), in front of the cave of his mistress. The arrow pierced his throat and he fell dead, bathed in his blood. Shih-chi Niang-niang came out of her cave, and examining the arrow found that it bore the inscription: "Arrow which shakes the heavens." She knew that it must have come from Ch'en-t'ang Kuan, where the magic bow was kept.

The goddess mounted her blue phoenix, flew over the fort, seized Li Ching and carried him to her cave. There she made him kneel before her. She reminded him how she had protected him so that he might gain honour and glory on earth before he attained to immortality.

"And this is how you show your gratitude – by killing my servant!"

Li Ching swore that he was innocent; but the tell-tale arrow was there, and it could only have come from the fortress. Li Ching begged the goddess to set him free so that he might find the culprit and bring him to her. "If I cannot find him," he added, "you may take my life."

Once again No-cha frankly admitted his deed to his father and followed him to the cave of Shih-chi Niang-niang. When he reached the entrance the second servant reproached him with the crime, immediately after which No-cha struck him with a heavy blow. Shih-chi Niang-niang, infuriated, threw herself at No-cha, sword in hand; one after the other she wrenched from him his bracelet and magic trousers.

Deprived of his magic weapons, No-cha fled to his master, T'ai-i Chen-jen. The goddess followed and demanded that he be put to death. A terrible conflict ensued between the two champions, until T'ai-i Chen-jen hurled his globe of nine fire-dragons into the air. This fell on Shih-chi Niang-niang, enveloping her in a whirlwind of flame. When it had passed they saw that she had changed into stone.

"Now you are safe," said T'ai-i Chen-jen to No-cha, "but return quickly, for the Four Dragon kings have laid their accusation before Yu Huang, and they are going to carry off your parents. Follow my advice, and you will rescue your parents from their misfortune."

On his return No-cha found the Four Dragon-kings on the point of carrying off his parents. "It is I," he said, "who killed Ao Ping and I who should pay the penalty. Why are you molesting my parents? I am about to return to them what I received from them. Will it satisfy you?"

Lung Wang agreed, so No-cha took a sword and before their eyes cut off an arm, sliced open his stomach and fell unconscious. His soul, carried on the wind, went straight to the cave of T'ai-i Chen-jen, while his mother busied herself with burying his body.

"Your home is not here," said his master to him; "return to Ch'en-t'ang Kuan, and beg your mother to build a temple on Ts'ui-p'ing Shan. Incense will be burned to you for three years, at the end of which time you will be reincarnated."

During the night, while his mother was in a deep sleep, No-cha appeared to her in a dream and said: "My mother, pity me; since my death, my soul, separated from my body, wanders about without a home. Build me, I pray you, a temple on Ts'ui-p'ing Shan, that I may be reincarnated." His mother awoke in tears and related her vision to Li Ching, who reproached her for her blind attachment to her unnatural son – the cause of so much disaster.

For five or six nights the son appeared to his mother, each time repeating his request. The last time he added: "Do not forget that by nature I am ferocious; if you refuse my request evil will befall you."

His mother then sent builders to the mountain to construct a temple to No-cha, and his image was set up in it. Miracles were not wanting, and the number of pilgrims who visited the shrine increased daily.

One day Li Ching was passing this mountain with a troop of his soldiers. He saw the roads crowded with pilgrims of both sexes. "Where are these people going?" he asked. "For six months past," he was told, "the spirit of the temple on this mountain has continued to perform miracles. People come from far and near to worship him."

"What is the name of this spirit?" inquired Li Ching. "No-cha," they replied. "No-cha!" exclaimed the father. "I will go and see him myself." In a rage Li Ching entered the temple and examined the statue, which was the image of his son. By its side were images of two of his servants. He took his whip and began to beat the statue, cursing it all the while. "It is not enough, apparently, for you to have been a source of disaster to us," he said; "but even after your death you must deceive the multitude." He whipped the statue until it fell to pieces; he then kicked over the images of the servants, and went back, telling the people not to worship so wicked a man, the shame and ruin of his family. By his orders the temple was burnt to the ground.

When he reached Ch'en-t'ang Kuan his wife came to him but he received her coldly. "You gave birth to that cursed son," he said, "who has been the plague of our lives, and after his death you build him a temple in which he deceives the people. Do you wish to have me disgraced? If I were to be accused at Court of having instituted the worship of false gods, would not my destruction be certain? I have burned the temple, and intend that that shall settle the matter once and for all; if ever you think of rebuilding it I will break off all relations with you."

At the time of his father's visit No-cha was absent from the temple. On his return he found only its smoking remnants. "Who has demolished my temple?" he asked. "Li Ching," the spirits of his servants replied. "In doing this he has exceeded his powers," said No-cha. "I gave him back the substance I received from him; why did he come with violence to break up my image? I will have nothing more to do with him."

No-cha's soul had already begun to be spiritualized. So he decided to go to T'ai-i Chen-jen and beg for his help. "The worship given to you there," replied the Taoist, "had nothing in it that should have offended your father; it did not concern him. He was in the wrong. Before long Chiang Tzu-ya will descend to inaugurate the new dynasty, and since you must throw in your lot with him I will find a way to help you."

T'ai-i Chen-jen had two water lily stalks and three lotus leaves brought to him. He spread these on the ground in the form of a human being and placed the soul of No-cha in this lotus skeleton, uttering a magic spell as he worked. There emerged a new No-cha full of life, with a fresh complexion, purple lips and keen glance, who was sixteen feet tall. "Follow me to my peach garden," said T'ai-i Chen-jen, "and I will give you your weapons." He handed him a sharp fiery spear and two wind-and-fire wheels which, placed under his feet, served as a vehicle. A brick of gold in a panther-skin bag completed his magic armament. The new warrior, after thanking his master, mounted his wind-and-fire wheels and returned to Ch'en-t'ang Kuan.

Li Ching was informed that his son No-cha had returned and was threatening vengeance. So he took his weapons, mounted his horse and went to meet him. They joined in battle, but Li Ching was soon overcome and compelled to flee. No-cha pursued his father, but as he was on the point of overtaking him Li Ching's second son, Mu-cha, came on the scene. Mu-cha criticized his brother for his unfilial conduct.

"Li Ching is no longer my father," replied No-cha. "I gave him back my substance; why did he burn my temple and smash up my image?"

Mu-cha prepared to defend his father, but took a blow to his back from the golden brick. He fell, unconscious. No-cha then resumed his pursuit of Li Ching.

His strength exhausted and in danger of falling into the hands of his enemy, Li Ching drew his sword and was about to kill himself. "Stop!" cried a Taoist priest. "Come into my cave, and I will protect you."

When No-cha arrived he could not see Li Ching. He demanded his surrender from the Taoist. But he had to do with one stronger than himself, no less a being than Wen-chu T'ien-tsun, whom T'ai-i Chen-jen had sent in order that No-cha might receive a lesson. The Taoist, with the aid of his magic weapon, seized No-cha, and in a moment he found a gold ring fastened round his neck, two chains on his feet, and he was bound to a pillar of gold.

At this moment, as if by accident, T'ai-i Chen-jen appeared on the scene. His master had No-cha brought before Wen-chu T'ien-tsun and Li Ching, and advised him to live at peace with his father. But he also rebuked the father for having burned the temple on Ts'ui-p'ing Shan. This done, he ordered Li Ching to go home and No-cha to return to his cave. The latter, overflowing with anger and with his heart full of vengeance, started again in pursuit of Li Ching, swearing that he would punish him. But the Taoist reappeared and prepared to protect Li Ching.

No-cha, bristling like a savage cat, threw himself at his enemy and tried to pierce him with his spear. At that moment a white lotus flower emerged from the Taoist's mouth and arrested the course of the weapon. As No-cha continued to threaten him, the Taoist drew a mysterious object from his sleeve which rose in the air and, falling at the feet of No-cha, enveloped him in flames. Then No-cha prayed for mercy. The Taoist exacted from him three separate promises: to live in harmony with his father, to recognize and address him as his father, and to throw himself at his (the Taoist's) feet, to indicate his reconciliation with himself.

After this act of reconciliation had been performed, Wen-chu T'ien-tsun told Li Ching that he should leave his official post to become an Immortal. That he should place his services at the disposal of the new Chou dynasty, shortly to come into power. In order to ensure that their reconciliation should last forever, and to place it beyond No-cha's power to seek revenge, he gave Li Ching the wonderful object that had caused No-cha's feet to have been burned, and which had been the means of bringing him into subjection. It was a golden pagoda, which became the characteristic weapon of Li Ching, and gave rise to his nickname, Li the Pagoda-bearer. Finally, Yu Huang appointed him Generalissimo of the Twenty-Six Celestial Officers, Grand Marshal of the Skies, and Guardian of the Gate of Heaven.

Izanagi and Izanami

IZANAGI AND IZANAMI stood on the Floating Bridge of Heaven and looked down into the abyss. They inquired of each other if there were a country far, far below the great Floating Bridge. They were determined to find out. In order to do so they thrust down a jewel-spear, and found the ocean. Raising the spear a little, water dripped from it, coagulated, and became the island of Onogoro-jima ('Spontaneously-congeal-island').

Upon this island the two deities descended. Shortly afterwards they desired to become husband and wife, though as a matter of fact they were brother and sister; but such a relationship in the East has never precluded marriage. These deities accordingly set up a pillar on the island. Izanagi walked round one way, and Izanami the other. When they met, Izanami said: "How delightful! I have met with a lovely youth." One would have thought that this naive remark would have pleased Izanagi; but it made him, extremely angry, and he retorted: "I am a man, and by that right should have spoken first. How is it that on the contrary thou, a woman, shouldst have been the first to speak? This is unlucky. Let us go round again." So it happened that the two deities started afresh. Once again they met, and this time Izanagi remarked: "How delightful! I have met a lovely maiden." Shortly after this very ingenuous proposal Izanagi and Izanami were married.

When Izanami had given birth to islands, seas, rivers, herbs, and trees, she and her lord consulted together, saying: "We have now produced the Great-Eight-Island country, with the mountains, rivers, herbs, and trees. Why should we not produce someone who shall be the Lord of the Universe?"

The wish of these deities was fulfilled, for in due season Amaterasu, the Sun Goddess, was born. She was known as 'Heaven-Illumine-of-Great-Deity', and was so extremely beautiful that her parents determined to send her up the Ladder of Heaven, and in the high sky above to cast for ever her glorious sunshine upon the earth.

Their next child was the Moon God, Tsuki-yumi. His silver radiance was not so fair as the golden effulgence of his sister, the Sun Goddess, but he was, nevertheless, deemed worthy to be her consort. So up the Ladder of Heaven climbed the Moon God. They soon quarrelled, and Amaterasu said: "Thou art a wicked deity. I must not see thee face to face." They were therefore separated by a day and night, and dwelt apart.

The next child of Izanagi and Izanami was Susanoo ('The Impetuous Male'). We shall return to Susanoo and his doings later on, and content ourselves for the present with confining our attention to his parents.

Izanami gave birth to the Fire God, Kagutsuchi. The birth of this child made her extremely ill. Izanagi knelt on the ground, bitterly weeping and lamenting. But his sorrow availed nothing, and Izanami crept away into the Land of Yomi (Hades).

Her lord, however, could not live without her, and he too went into the Land of Yomi. When he discovered her, she said regretfully: "My lord and husband, why is thy coming so late? I have already eaten of the cooking-furnace of Yomi. Nevertheless, I am about to lie down to rest. I pray thee do not look at me."

Izanagi, moved by curiosity, refused to fulfil her wish. It was dark in the Land of Yomi, so he secretly took out his many-toothed comb, broke off a piece, and lighted it. The sight that greeted him was ghastly and horrible in the extreme. His once beautiful wife had now become a swollen and festering creature. Eight varieties of Thunder Gods rested upon her. The Thunder of the Fire, Earth, and Mountain were all there leering upon him, and roaring with their great voices.

Izanagi grew frightened and disgusted, saying: "I have come unawares to a hideous and polluted land." His wife retorted: "Why didst thou not observe that which I charged thee? Now am I put to shame."

Izanami was so angry with her lord for ignoring her wish and breaking in upon her privacy that she sent the Eight Ugly Females of Yomi to pursue him. Izanagi drew his sword and fled down the dark regions of the Underworld. As he ran he took off his headdress, and flung it to the ground. It immediately became a bunch of grapes. When the Ugly Females saw it, they bent down and ate the luscious fruit. Izanami saw them pause, and deemed it wise to pursue her lord herself.

By this time Izanagi had reached the Even Pass of Yomi. Here he placed a huge rock, and eventually came face to face with Izanami. One would scarcely have thought that amid such exciting adventures Izanagi would have solemnly declared a divorce. But this is just what he did do. To this proposal his wife replied: "My dear lord and husband, if thou sayest so, I will strangle to death the people in one day." This plaintive and threatening speech in no way influenced Izanagi, who readily replied that he would cause to be born in one day no less than fifteen hundred.

The above remark must have proved conclusive, for when we next hear of Izanagi he had escaped from the Land of Yomi, from an angry wife, and from the Eight Ugly Females. After his escape he was engaged in copious ablutions, by way of purification, from which numerous deities were born. We read in the *Nihon Shoki*: "After this, Izanagi, his divine task having been accomplished, and his spirit-career about to suffer a change, built himself an abode of gloom in the island of Ahaji, where he dwelt for ever in silence and concealment."

Amaterasu and Susanoo

SUSANOO, OR 'THE IMPETUOUS MALE', was the brother of Amaterasu, the Sun Goddess. Now Susanoo was a very undesirable deity indeed, and he figured in the Realm of the Japanese Gods as a decidedly disturbing element. His character has been clearly drawn in the *Nihon Shoki*, more clearly perhaps than that of any other deity mentioned in these ancient records. Susanoo had a very bad temper, which often resulted in many cruel and ungenerous acts. Moreover, in spite of his long beard, he had a habit of continually weeping and wailing. Where a child in a tantrum would crush a toy to pieces, the Impetuous Male, when in a towering rage, and without a moment's warning, would wither the once fair greenery of mountains, and in addition bring many people to an untimely end.

His parents, Izanagi and Izanami, were much troubled by his doings, and, after consulting together, they decided to banish their unruly son to the Land of Yomi. Susa, however, had a word to say in the matter. He made the following petition, saying: "I will now obey thy instructions and proceed to the Nether-Land (Yomi). Therefore I wish for a short time to go to the Plain of High Heaven and meet with my elder sister (Amaterasu), after which I will go away for ever." This apparently harmless request was granted, and Susanoo ascended to Heaven. His departure occasioned a great commotion of the sea, and the hills and mountains groaned aloud.

Now Amaterasu heard these noises, and perceiving that they denoted the near approach of her wicked brother Susanoo, she said to herself: "Is my younger brother coming with good intentions? I think it must be his purpose to rob me of my kingdom. By the charge which our parents gave to their children, each of us has his own allotted limits. Why, therefore, does he reject the kingdom to which he should proceed, and make bold to come spying here?"

Amaterasu then prepared for warfare. She tied her hair into knots and hung jewels upon it, and round her wrists "an august string of five hundred Yasaka jewels." She presented a very formidable appearance when in addition she slung over her back "a thousand-arrow quiver and a five-hundred-arrow quiver," and protected her arms with pads to deaden the recoil of the bowstring. Having arrayed herself for deadly combat, she brandished her bow, grasped her sword-hilt, and stamped on the ground till she had made a hole sufficiently large to serve as a fortification.

All this elaborate and ingenious preparation was in vain. The Impetuous Male adopted the manner of a penitent. "From the beginning," he said, "my heart has not been black. But as, in obedience to the stern behest of our parents, I am about to depart for ever to the Nether-Land, how could I bear to depart without having seen face to face thee my elder sister? It is for this reason that I have traversed on foot the clouds and mists and have come hither from afar. I am surprised that my elder sister should, on the contrary, put on so stern a countenance."

Amaterasu regarded these remarks with a certain amount of suspicion. Susanoo's filial piety and Susanoo's cruelty were not easily to be reconciled. She thereupon resolved to test his sincerity by a remarkable proceeding we need not describe. Suffice it to say that for the time being the test proved the Impetuous Male's purity of heart and general sincerity towards his sister.

But Susanoo's good behaviour was a very short-lived affair indeed. It happened that Amaterasu had made a number of excellent rice-fields in Heaven. Some were narrow and some were long, and Amaterasu was justly proud of these rice-fields. No sooner had she sown the seed in the spring than Susanoo broke down the divisions between the plots, and in the autumn let loose a number of piebald colts.

One day when he saw his sister in the sacred Weaving Hall, weaving the garments of the Gods, he made a hole through the roof and flung down a flayed horse. Amaterasu was so frightened that she accidentally wounded herself with the shuttle. Extremely angry, she determined to leave her abode; so, gathering her shining robes about her, she crept down the blue sky, entered a cave, fastened it securely, and there dwelt in seclusion.

Now the world was in darkness, and the alternation of night and day was unknown. When this dreadful catastrophe had taken place the Eighty Myriads of Gods assembled together on the bank of the River of Heaven and discussed how they might best persuade Amaterasu to grace Heaven once more with her shining glory. No less a God than

'Thought-combining', after much profound reasoning, gathered together a number of singing-birds from the Eternal Land. After sundry divinations with a deer's leg-bone, over a fire of cherry-bark, the Gods made a number of tools, bellows, and forges. Stars were welded together to form a mirror, and jewellery and musical instruments were eventually fashioned.

When all these things had been duly accomplished the Eighty Myriads of Gods came down to the rock-cavern where the Sun Goddess lay concealed, and gave an elaborate entertainment. On the upper branches of the True Sakaki Tree they hung the precious jewels, and on the middle branches the mirror. From every side there was a great singing of birds, which was only the prelude to what followed. Now Uzume ('Heavenly-alarming-female') took in her hand a spear wreathed with Eulalia grass, and made a headdress of the True Sakaki Tree. Then she placed a tub upside down, and proceeded to dance in a very immodest manner, till the Eighty Myriad Gods began to roar with laughter.

Such extraordinary proceedings naturally awakened the curiosity of Amaterasu, and she peeped forth. Once more the world became golden with her presence. Once more she dwelt in the Plain of High Heaven, and Susanoo was duly chastised and banished to the Yomi Land.

Susanoo and the Serpent

SUSANOO, HAVING DESCENDED from Heaven, arrived at the river Hi, in the province of Idzumo. Here he was disturbed by a sound of weeping. It was so unusual to hear any other than himself weep that he went in search of the cause of the sorrow. He discovered an old man and an old woman. Between them was a young girl, whom they fondly caressed and gazed at with pitiful eyes, as if they were reluctantly bidding her a last farewell. When Susanoo asked the old couple who they were and why they lamented, the old man replied: "I am an Earthly Deity, and my name is Ashinadzuchi ('Foot-stroke-elder'). My wife's name is Tenadzuchi ('Hand-stroke-elder'). This girl is our daughter, and her name is Kushinadahime ('Wondrous-Inada-Princess'). The reason of our weeping is that formerly we had eight children, daughters; but they have been devoured year by year by an eight-forked serpent, and now the time approaches for this girl to be devoured. There is no means of escape for her, and therefore do we grieve exceedingly."

The Impetuous Male listened to this painful recital with profound attention, and, perceiving that the maiden was extremely beautiful, he offered to slay the eight-forked serpent if her parents would give her to him in marriage as a fitting reward for his services. This request was readily granted.

Susanoo now changed Kushinadahime into a many-toothed comb and stuck it in his hair. Then he bade the old couple brew a quantity of *sake*. When the *sake* was ready, he poured it into eight tubs, and awaited the coming of the dreadful monster.

Eventually the serpent came. It had eight heads, and the eyes were red, "like winter-cherry." Moreover it had eight tails, and firs and cypress-trees grew on its back. It was in length the space of eight hills and eight valleys. Its lumbering progress was necessarily slow, but finding the *sake*, each head eagerly drank the tempting beverage till the serpent became extremely drunk, and fell asleep. Then Susanoo, having little to fear, drew his ten-span sword and chopped the great monster into little pieces. When he struck one of the tails his weapon became notched, and bending down he discovered a sword called the Murakumo-no-Tsurugi. Perceiving it to be a divine sword, he gave it to the Gods of Heaven.

Having successfully accomplished his task, Susanoo converted the many-toothed comb into Kushinadahime again, and at length came to Suga, in the province of Idzumo, in order that he might celebrate his marriage. Here he composed the following verse:

"Many clouds arise,
On all sides a manifold fence,
To receive within it the spouses,
They form a manifold fence:
Ah! that manifold fence!"

The Great Father

ONE DAY, BAIAME, the great Ancestor Spirit, was walking through the land he had created, surveying all the plants and animals. Realizing something was missing, he made a man and a woman from dust and, setting them upright, told them that they might eat the plants but not the animals. In due course, the first man and woman had children and slowly but surely they began to populate the world. Everyone thanked Baiame and praised him for what he had done.

In time, the rain ceased to fall and the plants began to die. Horrified, more and more people fell sick with hunger.

In desperation, one of the men broke Baiame's command and killed and ate a kangaroo rat, sharing it with his wife.

When the couple had eaten their fill, they offered some of the meat to a friend. Faint with hunger, the friend refused it and staggered away.

Death Enters the World

The man and woman decided to follow their friend's trail. At last, far in the distance, they spied him resting beneath a tree. As the couple stood there, they saw a black creature descend from the tree, snatch up their friend's body, and disappear back into the branches. Clutching each other in terror, they watched as the tree rose into the air and disappeared. And so it was that death entered the world.

Tales of the Rainbow Serpent

WE HAVE ALREADY SEEN how the great Ancestor Spirit, the Rainbow Serpent Kurriyala of the Kuku-Yalanji people of the North Queensland rainforest is said to have formed features of the land. Other rainbow serpent legends are as follows.

The Serpent Creates the Land and Waters

Long ago in the Dreamtime, the Rainbow Serpent emerged from beneath the ground and moved across the empty landscape, giving it form and shape. Some say that, after completing her travels, she went back to the place where she first emerged and called on the frogs to come out from underground. The frogs duly appeared, their bellies distended with water. When the Rainbow Serpent tickled them, they filled the tracks the great being had made with water, creating rivers and streams.

The Law of the Serpent

The Rainbow Serpent also introduced laws, as well as punishments for those who broke them. Many of the boulders scattered across Australia are said to be people whom the Rainbow Serpent turned to stone for ignoring her commands.

The Wawilak Sisters

The story of the Wawilak sisters is the inspiration for an important cycle of ceremonies in north-east Arnhem Land. The story is re-enacted during the initiation ceremony of Yolngu boys.

Long ago in the Dreamtime the two Wawilak sisters set off on a long journey through the land. As they walked, they sustained themselves with creatures and plants and gave names to everything they saw, bringing the landscape into existence. They began their travels somewhere in the interior and travelled northwards, towards Arnhem Land. One day, the two sisters met two men and lay with them, though to do so was taboo because it was incest as they were of the same moieties. Both women conceived and, in due course, the older of the sisters gave birth to a child. When the younger sister's time drew near, the women stopped by a waterhole and built a shelter in preparation for the birth.

Unknown to the sisters, the mighty Rainbow Serpent lived in the pool. When the baby was born, blood from the birth seeped into the waterhole, polluting it and rousing the great snake. The creature rose high into the sky and, towering above the sisters, summoned up thunder, lightning and rain.

Terrified, the sisters began to dance, hoping thereby to appease the monster. The Rainbow Serpent grew even angrier, however, so much so that the waterhole began to overflow causing a huge flood. At last the serpent bent down and swallowed the sisters in one gulp.

The Rainbow Serpent eventually regurgitated the sisters, who then instituted the initiation ceremonies of the Yolngu people of north-east Arnhem Land.

Totyerguil and Otchout

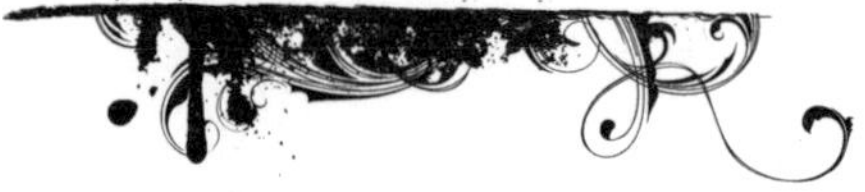

ACCORDING TO THE WOTOJOBALUK PEOPLE of Victoria, there was once a hunter called Totyerguil who was camping near Swan Hill when his two sons found a massive fish called Otchout in a nearby waterhole.

The boys ran to tell their father of their discovery whereupon Totyerguil paddled out to the fish, and threw his spear at it. The spear lodged in the fish's back and stayed there, sticking upwards. Attempting to escape, Otchout swam furiously to the edge ofthe waterhole and began to tear through the ground creating a channel. Indeed, the fish moved so quickly that Totyerguil could scarcely keep up with it.

That evening, Otchout made a huge billabong and rested there for the night. However, Totyerguil had not given up and threw another spear at the monster. This spear also stayed sticking up out of the fish's back. And so it went on for several days, the fish creating a vast channel by burrowing through the land with Totyerguil following in hot pursuit, throwing one spear after another at the creature. Eventually Totyerguil had no spears left and so, reluctantly, he gave up the chase. These spears are now the spines that can be seen sticking out of the back of the codfish. The channel Otchout created became the Murray River.

The Children of Heaven and Earth

Ko Nga Tama A Rangi – A Tradition Relating to the Origin of the Human Race

MEN HAD BUT ONE pair of primitive ancestors; they sprang from the vast heaven that exists above us, and from the earth which lies beneath us. According to the traditions of our race, Rangi and Papa, or Heaven and Earth, were the source from which, in the beginning, all things originated. Darkness then rested upon the heaven and upon the earth, and they still both clave together, for they had not yet been rent apart; and the children they had begotten were ever thinking amongst themselves what might be the difference between darkness and light; they knew that beings had multiplied and increased, and yet light had never broken upon them, but it ever continued dark. Hence these sayings are found in our ancient religious services: 'There was darkness from the first division of time, unto the tenth, to the hundredth, to the thousandth', that is, for a vast space of time; and these divisions of times were considered as beings, and were each termed a Po; and on their account there was as yet no world with its bright light, but darkness only for the beings which existed.

At last the beings who had been begotten by Heaven and Earth, worn out by the continued darkness, consulted amongst themselves, saying: 'Let us now determine what we should do with Rangi and Papa, whether it would be better to slay them or to rend them apart.' Then spoke Tu-matauenga, the fiercest of the children of Heaven and Earth: 'It is well, let us slay them.'

Then spake Tane-mahuta, the father of forests and of all things that inhabit them, or that are constructed from trees: 'Nay, not so. It is better to rend them apart, and to let the heaven stand far above us, and the earth lie under out feet. Let the sky become as a stranger to us, but the earth remain close to us as our nursing mother.'

The brothers all consented to this proposal, with the exception of Tawhiri-ma-tea, the father of winds and storms, and he, fearing that his kingdom was about to be overthrown, grieved greatly at the thought of his parents being torn apart. Five of the brothers willingly consented to the separation of their parents, but one of them would not agree to it.

Hence, also, these sayings of old are found in our prayers: 'Darkness, darkness, light, light, the seeking, the searching, in chaos, in chaos'; these sig-nified the way in which the offspring of heaven and earth sought for some mode of dealing with their parents, so that human beings might increase and live.

So, also, these sayings of old time. 'The multitude, the length', signified the multitude of the thoughts of the children of Heaven and Earth, and the length of time they considered whether they should slay their parents, that human beings might be called into existence; for it was in this manner that they talked and consulted amongst themselves.

But at length their plans having been agreed on, lo, Rongo-ma-tane, the god and father of the cultivated food of man, rises up, that he may rend apart the heavens and the earth; he struggles, but he rends them not apart. Lo, next, Tangaroa, the god and father of fish and reptiles, rises up, that he may rend apart the heavens and the earth; he also struggles, but he rends them not apart. Lo, next, Haumia-tikitiki, the god and father of the food of man which springs without cultivation, rises up and struggles, but ineffectually. Lo, then, Tu-matauenga, the god and father of fierce human beings, rises up and struggles, but he, too, fails in his efforts. Then, at last, slowly uprises Tane-mahuta, the god and father of forests, of birds, and of insects, and he struggles with his parents; in vain he strives to rend them apart with his hands and arms. Lo, he pauses; his head is now firmly planted on his mother the earth, his feet he raises up and rests against his father the skies, he strains his back and limbs with mighty effort. Now are rent apart Rangi and Papa, and with cries and groans of woe they shriek aloud: 'Wherefore slay you thus your parents? Why commit you so dreadful a crime as to slay us, as to rend your parents apart?' But Tane-mahuta pauses not, he regards not their shrieks and cries; far, far beneath him he presses down the earth; far, far above him he thrusts up the sky.

Hence these sayings of olden time: 'It was the fierce thrusting of Tane which tore the heaven from the earth, so that they were rent apart, and darkness was made manifest, and so was the light.'

No sooner was heaven rent from earth than the multitude of human beings were discovered whom they had begotten, and who had hitherto lain concealed between the bodies of Rangi and Papa.

Then, also, there arose in the breast of Tawhiri-ma-tea, the god and father of winds and storms, a fierce desire to wage war with his brothers, because they had rent apart their common parents. He from the first had refused to consent to his mother being torn from her lord and children; it was his brothers alone that wished for this separation, and desired that Papa-tu-a-nuku, or the Earth alone, should be left as a parent for them.

The god of hurricanes and storms dreads also that the world should become too fair and beautiful, so he rises, follows his father to the realm above, and hurries to the sheltered hollows in the boundless skies; there he liides and clings, and nestling in this place of rest he consults long with his parent, and as the vast Heaven listens to the suggestions of Tawhiri-ma-tea, thoughts and plans are formed in his breast, and Tawhiri-ma-tea also understands what he should do. Then by himself and the vast Heaven were begotten his numerous brood, and they rapidly increased and grew. Ta-whiri-ma-tea despatches one of them to the westward, and one to the southward, and one to the eastward, and one to the northward; and he gives corresponding names to himself and to his progeny the mighty winds.

He next sends forth fierce squalls, whirlwinds, dense clouds, massy clouds, dark clouds, gloomy thick clouds, fiery clouds, clouds which precede hurricanes, clouds of fiery black, clouds reflecting glowing red light, clouds wildly drifting from all quarters and wildly bursting, clouds of thunder storms, and clouds hurriedly flying. In the midst of these Tawhiri-ma-tea himself sweeps wildly on. Alas! alas! then rages the fierce hurricane; and whilst Tane-mahuta and his gigantic forests still stand, unconscious and unsuspecting, the blast of the breath of the mouth of Tawhiri-ma-tea smites them, the gigantic trees are snapt off right in the middle; alas! alas! they are rent to atoms, dashed to the earth, with boughs and branches torn and scattered, and lying on the earth, trees and branches all alike left for the insect, for the grub, and for loathsome rottenness.

From the forests and their inhabitants Tawhiri-ma-tea next swoops down upon the seas, and lashes in his wrath the ocean. Ah! ah! waves steep as cliffs arise, whose summits are so lofty that to look from them would make the beholder giddy; these soon eddy in whirlpools, and Tangaroa, the god of ocean, and father of all that dwell therein, flies affrighted through his seas; but before he fled, his children consulted together how they might secure their safety, for Tangaroa had begotten Punga, and he had begotten two children, Ika-tere, the father of fish, and Tu-te-wehiwehi, or Tu-te-wanawana, the father of reptiles.

When Tangaroa fled for safety to the ocean, then Tu-te-wehiwehi and Ika-tere, and their children, disputed together as to what they should do to escape from the storms, and Tu-te-wehiwehi and his party cried aloud: 'Let us fly inland'; but Ika-tere and his party cried aloud: 'Let us fly to the sea.' Some would not obey one order, some would not obey the other, and they escaped in two parties: the party of Tu-te-wehiwehi, or the rep–tiles, hid themselves ashore; the party of Punga rushed to the sea. This is what, in our ancient religious services, is called the separation of Ta–whiri-ma-tea.

Hence these traditions have been handed down:

'Ika-tere, the father of things which inhabit water, cried aloud to Tu-te-wehiwehi: 'Ho, ho, let us all escape to the sea.'

' But Tu-te-wehiwehi shouted in answer: 'Nay, nay, let us rather fly inland.'

Then Ika-tere warned him, saying: 'Fly inland, then; and the fate of you and your race will be, that when they catch you, before you are cooked, they will 6inge off your scales over a lighted wisp of dry fern.'

'But Tu-te-wehiwehi answered him, saying: 'Seek safety, then, in the sea; and the future fate of your race will be, that when they serve out little baskets of cooked vegetable food to each person you will be laid upon the top of the food to give a relish to it.'

Then without delay these two races of beings separated. The fish fled in confusion to the sea, the reptiles sought safety in the forests and scrubs.'

Tangaroa, enraged at some of his children deserting him, and, being sheltered by the god of the forests on dry land, has ever since waged war on his brother Tane, who, in return, has waged war against him.

Hence Tane supplies the offspring of his brother Tu-matauenga with canoes, with spears and with fish-hooks made from his trees, and with nets woven from his fibrous plants, that they may destroy the offspring of Tangaroa; whilst Tangaroa, in return, swallows up the offspring of Tane, overwhelming canoes with the surges of his sea, swallowing up the lands, trees, and houses that are swept off by floods, and ever wastes away, with his lapping waves, the shores that confine him, that the giants of the forests may be washed down and swept out into his boundless ocean, that he may then swallow up the insects, the young birds, and the various animals which inhabit them – all which things are recorded in the prayers which were offered to these gods.

Tawhiri-ma-tea next rushed on to attack his brothers Rongo-ma-tane and Haumia-tikitiki, the gods and progenitors of cultivated and uncultivated food; but Papa, to save these for her other children, caught them up, and hid them in a place of safety; and so well were these children of hers concealed by their mother Earth, that Tawhiri-ma-tea sought for them in vain.

Tawhiri-ma-tea having thus vanquished all his other brothers, next rushed against Tu-matauenga, to try his strength against his; he exerted all his force against him, but he could neither shake him nor prevail against him. What did Tu-matauenga care for his brother's wrath? he was the only one of the whole party of brothers who had planned the destruction of their parents, and had shown himself brave and fierce in war; his brothers had yielded at once before the tremendous assaults of Tawhiri-ma-tea and his progeny – Tane-mahuta and his offspring had been broken and torn in pieces – Tangaroa and his children had fled to the depths of the ocean or the recesses of the shore – Rongo-ma-tane and Haumia-tikitiki had been hidden from him in the earth – but Tu-matauenga, or man, still stood erect and unshaken upon the breast of his mother Earth; and now at length the hearts of Heaven and of the god of storms became tranquil, and their passions were assuaged.

Tu-matauenga, or fierce man, having thus successfully resisted his brother, the god of hurricanes and storms, next took thought how he could turn upon his brothers and slay them, because they had not assisted him or fought bravely when Tawhiri-ma-tea had attacked them to avenge the separation of their parents, and because they had left him alone to show his prowess in the fight. As yet death had no power over man. It was not until the birth of the children of Taranga and of Makea-tu-tara, of Maui-taha, of Maui-roto, of Maui-pae, of Maui-waho, and of Maui-tikitiki-o-Taranga, the demi-god who tried to drain Hine-nui-te-po, that death had power over men. If that goddess had not been deceived by Maui-tikitiki, men would not have died, but would in that case have lived for ever; it was from his deceiving Hine-nui-te-po that death obtained power over mankind, and penetrated to every part of the earth.

Tu-matauenga continued to reflect upon the cowardly manner in which his brothers had acted, in leaving him to show his courage alone, and he first sought some means of injuring Tane-mahuta, because he had not come to aid him in his combat with Tawhiri-ma-tea, and partly because he was aware that Tane had had a numerous progeny, who were rapidly increasing, and might at last prove hostile to him, and injure him, so he began to collect leaves of the whanake tree, and twisted them into nooses, and when his work was ended, he went to the forest to put up his snares, and hung them up – ha! ha! the children of Tane fell before him, none of them could any longer fly or move in safety.

Then he next determined to take revenge on his brother Tangaroa, who had also deserted him in the combat; so he sought for his offspring, and found them leaping or swimming in the water; then he cut many leaves from the flax-plant, and netted nets with the flax, and dragged these, and hauled the children of Tangaroa ashore.

After that, he determined also to be revenged upon his brothers Rongo-ma-tane and Haumia-tiki–tiki; he soon found them by their peculiar leaves, and he scraped into shape a wooden hoe, and plaited a basket, and dug in the earth and pulled up all kinds of plants with edible roots, and the plants which had been dug up withered in the sun.

Thus Tu-matauenga devoured all his brothers, and consumed the whole of them, in revenge for their having deserted him and left him to fight alone against Tawhiri-ma-tea and Rangi.

When his brothers had all thus been overcome by Tu, he assumed several names, namely, Tu-ka-riri, Tu-ka-nguha, Tu-ka-taua, Tu-whaka-heke–tan-gata, Tu-mata-wha-iti, and Tu-matauenga; he assumed one name for each of his attributes displayed in the victories over his brothers. Four of his brothers were entirely deposed by him, and became his food; but one of them, Tawhiri-ma-tea, he could not vanquish or make common, by eating him for food, so he, the last born child of Heaven and Earth, was left as an enemy for man, and still, with a rage equal to that of Man, this elder brother ever attacks him in storms and hurricanes, endeavouring to destroy him alike by sea and land.

Now, the meanings of these names of the children of the Heaven and Earth are as follows:

Tangaroa signifies fish of every kind; Rongo-ma-tane signifies the sweet potato, and all vegetables cultivated as food; Haumia-tikitiki signifies fern root, and all kinds of food which grow wild; Tane-mahuta signifies forests, the birds and insects which inhabit them, and all things fashioned from wood; Tawhiri-ma-tea signifies winds and storms; and Tu-matauenga signifies man.

Four of his brothers having, as before stated, been made common, or articles of food, by Tu-matauenga, he assigned for each of them fitting incanta–tions, that they might be abundant, and that he might easily obtain them.

Some incantations were proper to Tane-mahuta, they were called Tane.

Some incantations were for Tangaroa, they were called Tangaroa.

Some were for Rongo-ma-tane, they were called Rongo-ma-tane.

Some were for Haumia-tikitiki, they were called Haumia.

The reason that he sought out these incantations was, that his brothers might be made common by him, and serve for his food. There were also in–cantations for Tawhiri-ma-tea to cause favourable winds, and prayers to the vast Heaven for fair weather, as also for mother Earth that she might produce all things abundantly. But it was the great God that taught these prayers to man. There were also many prayers and incantations composed for man, suited to the different times and circumstances of his life – prayers at the baptism of an infant; prayers for abundance of food, for wealth; prayers in illness; prayers to spirits, and for many other things.

The bursting forth of the wrathful fury of Ta-whiri-ma-tea against his brothers, was the cause of the disappearance of a great part of the dry land; during that contest a great part of mother Earth was submerged. The names of those beings of ancient days who submerged so large a portion of the earth were – Terrible-rain, Long-continued-rain, Fierce-hail-storms; and their progeny were, Mist, Heavy-dew, and Light-dew, and these together submerged the greater part of the earth, so that only a small portion of dry land projected above the sea.

From that time clear light increased upon the earth, and all the beings which were hidden between Rangi and Papa before they were separated, now multiplied upon the earth. The first beings begotten by Rangi and Papa were not like human beings; but Tu-matauenga bore the likeness of a man, as did all his brothers, as also did a Po, a Ao, a Kore, te Kimihanga and Runuku, and thus it continued until the times of Ngainui and his generation, and of Whiro-te-tupua and his generation, and of Tiki-tawhito-ariki and his generation, and it has so continued to this day.

The children of Tu-matauenga were begotten on this earth, and they increased, and continued to multiply, until we reach at last the generation of Maui-taha, and of his brothers Maui-roto, Maui–waho, Maui-pae, and Maui-tikitiki-o-Taranga.

Up to this time the vast Heaven has still ever remained separated from his spouse the Earth. Yet their mutual love still continues – the soft warm sighs of her loving bosom still ever rise up to him, ascending from the woody mountains and valleys, and men call these mists; and the vast Heaven, as he mourns through the long nights his separation from his beloved, drops frequent teara upon her bosom, and men seeing these, term them dew-drops.

The Battle of the Giants

ONCE THE VOLCANOES Taranaki, Ruapehu, and Tongariro dwelled together. That was the time when Tongariro in her wonderful beauty had captured the fiery hearts of the two giants, so that their joy filled the heavens with majestic outbursts and covered the earth with their dark-glowing heart-blood of fiery lava and molten stones.

Softly then answered the gently ascending Steam-column of Tongariro, smiling and swaying, gold-bordered by the setting sun; smiling at both her suitors.

Ah, Tongariro was a woman!

Both, the straight and simple Taranaki and the rugged and strong Ruapehu, their cloud-piercing heads covered with spotless snow, or adorned in their passion-glowing lava-streams, were beloved by Tongariro; but the snows of the winter and the suns of the summer came and went from the first time, to the hundredth time, to the thousandth time, and still Tongariro was undecided whom she would prefer for a husband.

She became the sacred mountain of the Maori people; her beauty captured the hearts of all, so that she became the possessor of the highest tapu, and no foot dared walk upon her, and only the eyes of the new-born were directed towards her; and the eyes of the departing rested full love upon her beauty, whilst they wandered to the Reinga.

The eyes of generations upon generations of man.

Beautiful to behold from all the lands was the great love of the giants; now all covered with glittering snow, now hiding in the clouds and bursting forth, covered with strange and wonderful beauty; now girdling their bodies with clouds and lifting their endless heads into the golden heavens; and now again breaking forth into terrible passions, covering the earth with blackness.

Ah, Tongariro roused the passions of the giants: she made the volcanoes tremble! Their blood of fire and boiling stones shook them, the thundering of their voices, roaring insults at each other, made the earth tremble. Streams of lightning pierced the nights, and black smoke of deadly hate darkened the days, and the ears of man were filled with the roaring hate of the giants, and their wondering eyes beheld the beauty of Tongariro, smiling at both!

At last the two rivals decided to fight for Tongariro!

Now followed days of silence. The giants stood there grim and silent to the world, but they were gathering strength, and were melting stones in their insides, and lit terrible fires, their powerful weapons. So they stood silent and grim; the sun gilding their beautiful garments of snow, and Tongariro smiled at them with her graceful swaying column of steam; and the Maori people looked wonderingly upon the peaceful landscape.

Then a rolling grew into the nights, and rolling filled the days; louder and louder, night after night, day after day – a terrible groaning, damp and deep. Suddenly a crashing thunder shook the earth, and bursting forth from the mouth of Ruapehu a fiery mass of molten stones and black hate and fury fell upon Taranaki, covering him with a terrible coat of fire, whilst the flying winds howled and the melted snow-waters fled thundering down into the valleys.

A beautiful straight form gave the mass of fire and ashes to Taranaki – but he shook in terrible rage! He tore himself out of the ground, shaking the earth and breaking the lands asunder; he tried to fly at Ruapehu, to kill him with his weight. But Ruapehu made the water of his lake, high up in the snows, boil, and, hurling it down, it filled all the rends Taranaki had made in the earth, and burned all the inside of the earth and of Taranaki himself. He now, tearing the air with his roaring cries of pain and thundering howling of rage, threw a tremendous mass of stones at his enemy, and broke the highest cone, the loftiest peak of Ruapehu, so that his looks were not so majestic, and his reach not so far into the skies.

Ruapehu now, in deadly hate, swallowed his broken cone and melted it; he lit terrible fires in his inside, which spread to the lake Roto-aira, so that it rose and boiled, the steam covering all the world and blinding Taranaki. Then Ruapehu filled himself with the boiling water, and, throwing it out of his mouth down upon Taranaki, it filled all the crevices, and it lifted him, for he himself had loosened his bonds with the earth; and now, darkening day into night, he sent the molten mass of his swallowed cone against his enemy, so that he was compelled to retreat: blinded by steam, burned in his inside by the boiling water, and covered with the molten mass of the cone of Ruapehu he himself had broken.

He groaned, and rose, and tumbled, and shook himself; and he felt for a way to the sea to cool his burning pain; howling in unbearable pain he had to run, in order to get out of reach of Ruapehu, deeply hollowing his path through the lands. But his conqueror, Ruapehu, melting all his ice and snow, sent it as boiling water into this deep path, that his enemy might not come back again, for his strength also was exhausted.

On to the sea went Taranaki, and, when his pain had left him a little, he looked back at his conqueror, and saw how his three peaks were again covered with fresh snow, and how he was now the supreme lord over all the lands and the husband of Tongariro. They two were now the arikis over all the land; but it was waste now, and dead, for the terrible fight had killed all the people and the living beings all around. Once more a burst of black anger broke forth from Taranaki, and again it was answered by a wonderful swaying and smiling steam-column from Tongariro; and then he went and wandered along the coast till he had found a place for his sorrow. There he stands now, brooding on revenge.

'And my people know that one day he will come back in a straight line, to fight Ruapehu again; and none of my people will ever live or be buried in that lime; for one day he will come back to fight for Tongariro – who knows?'

But the path of Taranaki to the sea is now the Wanganui River.

Maui and Tuna

WHEN MAUI RETURNED from the voyages in which he discovered or 'fished up' from the ocean depths new islands, he gave deep thought to the things he had found. As the islands appeared to come out of the water he saw they were inhabited. There were houses and stages for drying and preserving food. He was greeted by barking dogs. Fires were burning, food cooking and people working. He evidently had gone so far away from home that a strange people was found. The legend which speaks of the death of his brothers, 'eaten' by the great fish drawn up from the floor of the sea, may very easily mean that the new people killed and ate the brothers.

Maui apparently learned some new lessons, for on his return he quickly established a home of his own, and determined to live after the fashion of the families in the new islands.

Maui sought Hina-a-te-lepo, 'daughter of the swamp,' and secured her as his wife. The New Zealand tribes tell legends which vary in different localities about this woman Hina. She sometimes bore the name Rau-kura – 'The red plume.'

She cared for his thatched house as any other Polynesian woman was in the habit of doing. She attempted the hurried task of cooking his food before he snared the sun and gave her sufficient daylight for her labors.

They lived near the bank of a river from which Hina was in the habit of bringing water for the household needs.

One day she went down to the stream with her calabash. She was entwined with wreaths of leaves and flowers, as was the custom among Polynesian women. While she was standing on the bank, Tuna-roa, 'the long eel,' saw her. He swam up to the bank and suddenly struck her and knocked her into the water and covered her with slime from the blow given by his tail.

Hina escaped and returned to her home, saying nothing to Maui about the trouble. But the next day, while getting water, she was again overthrown and befouled by the slime of Tuna-roa.

Then Hina became angry and reported the trouble to Maui.

Maui decided to punish the long eel and started out to find his hiding place. Some of the New Zealand legends as collected by White, state that Tuna-roa was a very smooth skinned chief, who lived on the opposite bank of the stream, and, seeing Hina, had insulted her.

When Maui saw this chief, he caught two pieces of wood over which he was accustomed to slide his canoe into the sea. These he carried to the stream and laid them from bank to bank as a bridge over which he might entice Tuna-roa to cross.

Maui took his stone axe, Ma-Tori-Tori, 'the severer,' and concealed himself near the bank of the river.

When 'the long eel' had crossed the stream, Maui rushed out and killed him with a mighty blow of the stone axe, cutting the head from the body.

Other legends say that Maui found Tuna-roa living as an eel in a deep water hole, in a swamp on the sea-coast of Tata-a, part of the island Ao-tea-roa. Other stories located Tuna-roa in the river near Maui's home.

Maui saw that he could not get at his enemy without letting off the water which protected him.

Therefore into the forest went Maui, and with sacred ceremonies, selected trees from the wood of which he prepared tools and weapons.

Meanwhile, in addition to the insult given to Hina, Tuna-roa had caught and devoured two of Maui's children, which made Maui more determined to kill him.

Maui made the narrow spade (named by the Maoris of New Zealand the 'ko,' and by the Hawaiians 'o-o') and the sharp spears, with which to pierce either the earth or his enemy. These spears and spades were consecrated to the work of preparing a ditch by which to draw off the water protecting 'the long eel.'

The work of trench-making was accomplished with many incantations and prayers. The ditch was named 'The sacred digging,' and was tabooed to all other purposes except that of catching Tuna-roa.

Across this ditch Maui stretched a strong net, and then began a new series of chants and ceremonies to bring down an abundance of rain. Soon the flood came and the overflowing waters rushed down the sacred ditch. The walls of the deep pool gave way and 'the long eel' was carried down the trench into the waiting net. Then there was commotion. Tuna-roa was struggling for freedom.

Maui saw him and hastened to grasp his stone axe, 'the severer.' Hurrying to the net, he struck Tuna-roa a terrible blow, and cut off the head. With a few more blows, he cut the body in pieces. The head and tail were carried out into the sea. The head became fish and the tail became the great conger-eel. Other parts of the body became sea monsters. But some parts which fell in fresh water became the common eels. From the hairs of the head came certain vines and creepers among the plants.

After the death of Tuna-roa the offspring of Maui were in no danger of being killed and soon multiplied into a large family.

Another New Zealand legend related by White says that Maui built a sliding place of logs, over which Tuna-roa must pass when coming from the river.

Maui also made a screen behind which he could secrete himself while watching for Tuna-roa.

He commanded Hina to come down to the river and wait on the bank to attract Tuna-roa. Soon the long eel was seen in the water swimming near to Hina. Hina went to a place back of the logs which Maui had laid down.

Tuna-roa came towards her, and began to slide down the skids.

Maui sprang out from his hiding place and killed Tuna-roa with his axe, and cut him in pieces.

The tail became the conger-eel. Parts of his body became fresh-water eels. Some of the blood fell upon birds and always after marked them with red spots. Some of the blood was thrown into certain trees, making this wood always red. The muscles became vines and creepers.

From this time the children of Maui caught and ate the eels of both salt and fresh water. Eel traps were made, and Maui taught the people the proper chants or incantations to use when catching eels.

This legend of Maui and the long eel was found by White in a number of forms among the different tribes of New Zealand, but does not seem to have had currency in many other island groups.

In Turner's 'Samoa' a legend is related which was probably derived from the Maui stories and yet differs in its romantic results. The Samoans say that among their ancient ones dwelt a woman named Sina. Sina among the Polynesians is the same as Hina – the 'h' is softened into 's'. She captured a small eel and kept it as a pet. It grew large and strong and finally attacked and bit her. She fled, but the eel followed her everywhere. Her father came to her assistance and raised high mountains between the eel and herself. But the eel passed over the barrier and pursued her. Her mother raised a new series of mountains. But again the eel surmounted the difficulties and attempted to seize Sina. She broke away from him and ran on and on. Finally she wearily passed through a village. The people asked her to stay and eat with them, but she said they could only help her by delivering her from the pursuing eel. The inhabitants of that village were afraid of the eel and refused to fight for her. So she ran on to another place. Here the chief offered her a drink of water and promised to kill the eel for her. He prepared awa, a stupefying drink, and put poison in it. When the eel came along the chief asked him to drink. He took the awa and prepared to follow Sina. When he came to the place where she was the pains of death had already seized him. While dying he begged her to bury his head by her home. This she did, and in time a plant new to the islands sprang up. It became a tree, and finally produced a cocoanut, whose two eyes could continually look into the face of Sina.

Tuna, in the legends of Fiji, was a demon of the sea. He lived in a deep sea cave, into which he sometimes shut himself behind closed doors of coral. When he was hungry, he swam through the ocean shadows, always watching the restless surface. When a canoe passed above him, he would throw himself swiftly through the waters, upset the canoe, and seize some of the boatmen and devour them. He was greatly feared by all the fishermen of the Fijian coasts.

Roko – a mo-o or dragon god – in his journey among the islands, stopped at a village by the sea and asked for a canoe and boatmen. The people said: 'We have nothing but a very old canoe out there by the water.' He went to it and found it in a very bad condition. He put it in the water, and decided that he could use it. Then he asked two men to go with him and paddle, but they refused because of fear, and explained this fear by telling the story of the water demon, who continually sought the destruction of this canoe, and also their own death. Roko encouraged them to take him to wage battle with Tuna, telling them he would destroy the monster. They paddled until they were directly over Tuna's cave. Roko told them to go off to one side and wait and watch, saying: 'I am going down to see this Tuna. If you see red blood boil up through the water, you may be sure that Tuna has been killed. If the blood is black, then you will know that he has the victory and I am dead.'

Roko leaped into the water and went down – down to the door of the cave. The coral doors were closed. He grasped them in his strong hands and tore them open, breaking them in pieces. Inside he found cave after cave of coral, and broke his way through until at last he awoke Tuna. The angry demon cried: 'Who is that?' Roko answered: 'It is I, Roko, alone. Who are you?'

Tuna aroused himself and demanded Roko's business and who guided him to that place. Roko replied: 'No one has guided me. I go from place to place, thinking that there is no one else in the world.'

Tuna shook himself angrily. 'Do you think I am nothing? This day is your last.'

Roko replied: 'Perhaps so. If the sky falls, I shall die.'

Tuna leaped upon Roko and bit him. Then came the mighty battle of the coral caves. Roko broke Tuna into several pieces – and the red blood poured in boiling bubbles upward through the clear ocean waters, and the boatmen cried: 'The blood is red – the blood is red – Tuna is dead by the hand of Roko.'

Roko lived for a time in Fiji, where his descendants still find their home. The people use this chant to aid them in difficulties:

'My load is a red one.
It points in front to Kawa (Roko's home).
Behind, it points to Dolomo – (a village on another island).'

In the Hawaiian legends, Hina was Maui's mother rather than his wife, and Kuna (Tuna) was a mo-o, a dragon or gigantic lizard possessing miraculous powers.

Hina's home was in the large cave under the beautiful Rainbow Falls near the city of Hilo. Above the falls the bed of the river is along the channel of an ancient lava flow. Sometimes the water pours in a torrent over the rugged lava, sometimes it passes through underground passages as well as along the black river bed, and sometimes it thrusts itself into boiling pools.

Maui lived on the northern side of the river, but a chief named Kuna-moo – a dragon – lived in the boiling pools. He attacked Hina and threw a dam across the river below Rainbow Falls, intending to drown Hina in her cave. The great ledge of rock filled the river bed high up the bank on the Hilo side of the river. Hina called on Maui for aid. Maui came quickly and with mighty blows cut out a new channel for the river – the path it follows to this day. The waters sank and Hina remained unharmed in her cave.

The place where Kuna dwelt was called Wai-kuna – the Kuna water. The river in which Hina and Kuna dwelt bears the name Wailuku – 'the destructive water.' Maui went above Kuna's home and poured hot water into the river. This part of the myth could easily have arisen from a lava outburst on the side of the volcano above the river. The hot water swept in a flood over Kuna's home. Kuna jumped from the boiling pools over a series of small falls near his home into the river below. Here the hot water again scalded him and in pain he leaped from the river to the bank, where Maui killed him by beating him with a club. His body was washed down the river over the falls under which Hina dwelt, into the ocean.

The story of Kuna or Tuna is a legend with a foundation in the enmity between two chiefs of the long ago, and also in a desire to explain the origin of the family of eels and the invention of nets and traps.

Heroic Encounters with Fearsome Beasts

Introduction

WHERE THE GODS EXEMPLIFY ALL THAT'S 'GOOD', mythic monsters are the opposite: the ugly, malevolent receptacles into which the evils of existence are distilled.

To a considerable extent, of course, those evils inhere in humanity itself: those nihilistic forces we haven't quite succeeded in controlling; those sinful desires we cannot quite contain. In this respect, the fight between the hero and the beast is really the struggle between our better and our worse self – in Freudian terms, the attempt of civilizing ego to overcome nihilistic id.

The good news is that the hero (or heroine, when she occasionally appears as the righteous actor rather than the 'monster') generally wins. One important function of the mythic monster is, paradoxically, to provide reassurance; to affirm the essential orderliness of the universe, the 'rightness' of the way things are. In its foulness and ferocity, it may horrify us, even seriously rock our confidence, but its defeat brings a heartening sense that all is well. In the hero who slays the ravening beast we get an inspiring glimpse of what we may be capable of as humans, as long as we go into battle with the gods' support.

Interesting as such symbolic oppositions may be, they're not the main 'point' of the monster. The stories in this section make that clear. The hideous menagerie we encounter here may illustrate the extraordinary range and resourcefulness of the human imagination, but they also show us something much more basic. However sophisticated we may think we are, we're simple souls who thrill to sensation- and suspense-packed narratives; to tales of epic courage and heroic drama.

The Beasts of Heracles' Labours

HERACLES IS BEST-KNOWN for the incredible daring and feats of strength he showed in achieving the twelve seemingly-impossible challenges set before him – most of which featured terrible beasts to overcome. And so we retell those tales here...

The Nemean Lion

His first task was to bring to Eurystheus the skin of the much-dreaded Nemean lion, which ravaged the territory between Cleone and Nemea, and whose hide was invulnerable against any mortal weapon.

Heracles proceeded to the forest of Nemea, where, having discovered the lion's lair, he attempted to pierce him with his arrows; but finding these of no avail he felled him to the ground with his club, and before the animal had time to recover from the terrible blow, Heracles seized him by the neck and, with a mighty effort, succeeded in strangling him. He then made himself a coat of mail of the skin, and a new helmet of the head of the animal. Thus attired, he so alarmed Eurystheus by appearing suddenly before him, that the king concealed himself in his palace, and henceforth forbade Heracles to enter his presence, but commanded him to receive his behests, for the future, through his messenger Copreus.

The Hydra

His second task was to slay the Hydra, a monster serpent (the offspring of Typhon and Echidna), bristling with nine heads, one of which was immortal. This monster infested the neighbourhood of Lerna, where she committed great depredations among the herds.

Heracles, accompanied by his nephew Iolaus, set out in a chariot for the marsh of Lerna, in the slimy waters of which he found her. He commenced the attack by assailing her with his fierce arrows, in order to force her to leave her lair, from which she at length emerged, and sought refuge in a wood on a neighbouring hill. Heracles now rushed forward and endeavoured to crush her heads by means of well-directed blows from his tremendous club; but no sooner was one head destroyed than it was immediately replaced by two others. He next seized the monster in his powerful grasp; but at this juncture a giant crab came to the assistance of the Hydra and commenced biting the feet of her assailant. Heracles destroyed this new adversary with his club, and now called upon his nephew to come to his aid. At his command Iolaus set fire to the neighbouring trees, and, with a burning branch, seared the necks of the monster as Heracles cut them off, thus effectually preventing the growth of more. Heracles next struck off the immortal head, which he buried by the road-side, and placed over it a heavy stone. Into the poisonous blood of the monster he then dipped his arrows, which ever afterwards rendered wounds inflicted by them incurable.

The Erymanthian Boar

The fourth task imposed upon Heracles by Eurystheus was to bring alive to Mycenae the Erymanthian boar, which had laid waste the region of Erymantia, and was the scourge of the surrounding neighbourhood.

On his way thither he craved food and shelter of a Centaur named Pholus, who received him with generous hospitality, setting before him a good and plentiful repast. When Heracles expressed his surprise that at such a well-furnished board wine should be wanting, his host explained that the wine cellar was the common property of all the Centaurs, and that it was against the rules for a cask to be broached, except all were present to partake of it. By dint of persuasion, however, Heracles prevailed on his kind host to make an exception in his favour; but the powerful, luscious odour of the good old wine soon spread over the mountains, and brought large numbers of Centaurs to the spot, all armed with huge rocks and fir-trees. Heracles drove them back with fire-brands, and then, following up his victory, pursued them with his arrows as far as Malea, where they took refuge in the cave of the kind old Centaur Chiron. Unfortunately, however, as Heracles was shooting at them with his poisoned darts, one of these pierced the knee of Chiron. When Heracles discovered that it was the friend of his early days that he had wounded, he was overcome with sorrow and regret. He at once extracted the arrow, and anointed the wound with a salve, the virtue of which had been taught him by Chiron himself. But all his efforts were unavailing. The wound, imbued with the deadly poison of the Hydra, was incurable, and so great was the agony of Chiron that, at the intercession of Heracles, death was sent him by the gods; for otherwise, being immortal, he would have been doomed to endless suffering.

Pholus, who had so kindly entertained Heracles, also perished by means of one of these arrows, which he had extracted from the body of a dead Centaur. While he was quietly examining it, astonished that so small and insignificant an object should be productive of such serious results, the arrow fell upon his foot and fatally wounded him. Full of grief at this untoward event, Heracles buried him with due honours, and then set out to chase the boar.

With loud shouts and terrible cries he first drove him out of the thickets into the deep snow-drifts which covered the summit of the mountain, and then, having at length wearied him with his incessant pursuit, he captured the exhausted animal, bound him with a rope, and brought him alive to Mycenae.

The Stymphalian Birds

The sixth task was to chase away the Stymphalides, which were immense birds of prey who, as we have seen (in the legend of the Argonauts), shot from their wings feathers sharp as arrows. The home of these birds was on the shore of the lake Stymphalis, in Arcadia (after which they were called), where they caused great destruction among men and cattle.

On approaching the lake, Heracles observed great numbers of them; and, while hesitating how to commence the attack, he suddenly felt a hand on his shoulder. Looking round he beheld the majestic form of Pallas-Athene, who held in her hand a gigantic pair of brazen clappers made by Hephaestus, with which she presented him; whereupon he ascended to the summit of a neighbouring hill, and commenced to rattle them violently. The shrill noise of these instruments was so intolerable to the birds that they rose into the air in terror, upon which he aimed at them with his arrows, destroying them in great numbers, whilst such as escaped his darts flew away, never to return.

The Cretan Bull

The seventh labour of Heracles was to capture the Cretan bull. Minos, king of Crete, having vowed to sacrifice to Poseidon any animal which should first appear out of the sea, the god caused a magnificent bull to emerge from the waves in order to test the sincerity of the Cretan king, who, in making this vow, had alleged that he possessed no animal, among his own herds, worthy the acceptance of the mighty sea-god. Charmed with the splendid animal sent by Poseidon, and eager to possess it, Minos placed it among his herds, and substituted as a sacrifice one of his own bulls. Hereupon Poseidon, in order to punish the cupidity of Minos, caused the animal to become mad, and commit such great havoc in the island as to endanger the safety of the inhabitants. When Heracles, therefore, arrived in Crete for the purpose of capturing the bull, Minos, far from opposing his design, gladly gave him permission to do so.

The hero not only succeeded in securing the animal, but tamed him so effectually that he rode on his back right across the sea as far as the Peloponnesus. He now delivered him up to Eurystheus, who at once set him at liberty, after which he became as ferocious and wild as before, roamed all over Greece into Arcadia, and was eventually killed by Theseus on the plains of Marathon.

The Mares of Diomedes

The eighth labour of Heracles was to bring to Eurystheus the mares of Diomedes, a son of Ares, and king of the Bistonians, a warlike Thracian tribe. This king possessed a breed of wild horses of tremendous size and strength, whose food consisted of human flesh, and all strangers who had the misfortune to enter the country were made prisoners and flung before the horses, who devoured them.

When Heracles arrived he first captured the cruel Diomedes himself, and then threw him before his own mares, who, after devouring their master, became perfectly tame and tractable. They were then led by Heracles to the sea-shore, when the Bistonians, enraged at the loss of their king, rushed after the hero and attacked him. He now gave the animals in charge of his friend Abderus, and made such a furious onslaught on his assailants that they turned and fled.

But on his return from this encounter he found, to his great grief, that the mares had torn his friend in pieces and devoured him. After celebrating due funereal rites to the unfortunate Abderus, Heracles built a city in his honour, which he named after him. He then returned to Tiryns, where he delivered up the mares to Eurystheus, who set them loose on Mount Olympus, where they became the prey of wild beasts.

It was after the performance of this task that Heracles joined the Argonauts in their expedition to gain possession of the Golden Fleece, and was left behind at Chios. During his wanderings he undertook his ninth labour, which was to bring to Eurystheus the girdle of Hippolyte, queen of the Amazons.

The Girdle of Hippolyte

The Amazons, who dwelt on the shores of the Black Sea, near the river Thermodon, were a nation of warlike women, renowned for their strength, courage, and great skill in horsemanship. Their queen, Hippolyte, had received from her father, Ares, a beautiful girdle, which she always wore as a sign of her royal power and authority, and it was this girdle which Heracles was required to place in the hands of Eurystheus, who designed it as a gift for his daughter Admete.

Foreseeing that this would be a task of no ordinary difficulty the hero called to his aid a select band of brave companions, with whom he embarked for the Amazonian town Themiscyra. Here they were met by queen Hippolyte, who was so impressed by the extraordinary stature and noble bearing of Heracles that, on learning his errand, she at once consented to present him with the coveted girdle. But Hera, his implacable enemy, assuming the form of an Amazon, spread the report in the town that a stranger was about to carry off their queen. The Amazons at once flew to arms and mounted their horses, whereupon a battle ensued, in which many of their bravest warriors were killed or wounded. Among the latter was their most skilful leader, Melanippe, whom Heracles afterwards restored to Hippolyte, receiving the girdle in exchange.

On his voyage home the hero stopped at Troy, where a new adventure awaited him.

During the time that Apollo and Poseidon were condemned by Zeus to a temporary servitude on earth, they built for king Laomedon the famous walls of Troy, afterwards so renowned in history; but when their work was completed the king treacherously refused to give them the reward due to them. The incensed deities now combined to punish the offender. Apollo sent a pestilence which decimated the people, and Poseidon a flood, which bore with it a marine monster, who swallowed in his huge jaws all that came within his reach.

In his distress Laomedon consulted an oracle, and was informed that only by the sacrifice of his own daughter Hesione could the anger of the gods be appeased. Yielding at length to the urgent appeals of his people he consented to make the sacrifice, and on the arrival of Heracles the maiden was already chained to a rock in readiness to be devoured by the monster.

When Laomedon beheld the renowned hero, whose marvellous feats of strength and courage had become the wonder and admiration of all mankind, he earnestly implored him to save his daughter from her impending fate, and to rid the country of the monster, holding out to him as a reward the horses which Zeus had presented to his grandfather Tros in compensation for robbing him of his son Ganymede.

Heracles unhesitatingly accepted the offer, and when the monster appeared, opening his terrible jaws to receive his prey, the hero, sword in hand, attacked and slew him. But the perfidious monarch once more broke faith, and Heracles, vowing future vengeance, departed for Mycenae, where he presented the girdle to Eurystheus.

The Oxen of Geryones

The tenth labour of Heracles was the capture of the magnificent oxen belonging to the giant Geryon or Geryones, who dwelt on the island of Erythia in the bay of Gadria (Cadiz). This giant, who was the son of Chrysaor, had three bodies with three heads, six hands, and six feet. He possessed a herd of splendid cattle, which were famous for their size, beauty, and rich red colour. They were guarded by another giant named Eurytion, and a two-headed dog called Orthrus, the offspring of Typhon and Echidna.

In choosing for him a task so replete with danger, Eurystheus was in hopes that he might rid himself for ever of his hated cousin. But the indomitable courage of the hero rose with the prospect of this difficult and dangerous undertaking.

After a long and wearisome journey he at last arrived at the western coast of Africa, where, as a monument of his perilous expedition, he erected the famous 'Pillars of Hercules,' one of which he placed on each side of the Straits of Gibraltar. Here he found the intense heat so insufferable that he angrily raised his bow towards heaven, and threatened to shoot the sun-god. But Helios, far from being incensed at his audacity, was so struck with admiration at his daring that he lent to him the golden boat with which he accomplished his nocturnal transit from West to East, and thus Heracles crossed over safely to the island of Erythia.

No sooner had he landed than Eurytion, accompanied by his savage dog Orthrus, fiercely attacked him; but Heracles, with a superhuman effort, slew the dog and then his master. Hereupon he collected the herd, and was proceeding to the sea-shore when Geryones himself met him, and a desperate encounter took place, in which the giant perished.

Heracles then drove the cattle into the sea, and seizing one of the oxen by the horns, swam with them over to the opposite coast of Iberia. Then driving his magnificent prize before him through Gaul, Italy, Illyria, and Thrace, he at length arrived, after many perilous adventures and hair-breadth escapes, at Mycenae, where he delivered them up to Eurystheus, who sacrificed them to Hera.

Heracles had now executed his ten tasks, which had been accomplished in the space of eight years; but Eurystheus refused to include the slaying of the Hydra and the cleansing of the stables of Augeas among the number, alleging as a reason that the one had been performed by the assistance of Iolaus, and that the other had been executed for hire. He therefore insisted on Heracles substituting two more labours in their place.

The Apples of the Hesperides

The eleventh task imposed by Eurystheus was to bring him the golden apples of the Hesperides, which grew on a tree presented by Gaea to Hera, on the occasion of her marriage with Zeus. This sacred tree was guarded by four maidens, daughters of Night, called the Hesperides, who were assisted in their task by a terrible hundred-headed dragon. This dragon never slept, and out of its hundred throats came a constant hissing sound, which effectually warned off all intruders. But what rendered the undertaking still more difficult was the complete ignorance of the hero as to the locality of the garden, and he was forced, in consequence, to make many fruitless journeys and to undergo many trials before he could find it.

He first travelled through Thessaly and arrived at the river Echedorus, where he met the giant Cycnus, the son of Ares and Pyrene, who challenged him to single combat. In this encounter Heracles completely vanquished his opponent, who was killed in the contest; but now a mightier adversary appeared on the scene, for the war-god himself came to avenge his son. A terrible struggle ensued, which had lasted some time, when Zeus interfered between the brothers, and put an end to the strife by hurling a thunderbolt between them. Heracles proceeded on his journey, and reached the banks of the river Eridanus, where dwelt the Nymphs, daughters of Zeus and Themis. On seeking advice from them as to his route, they directed him to the old sea-god Nereus, who alone knew the way to the Garden of the Hesperides. Heracles found him asleep, and seizing the opportunity, held him so firmly in his powerful grasp that he could not possibly escape, so that notwithstanding his various metamorphoses he was at last compelled to give the information required.

The hero then crossed over to Libya, where he engaged in a wrestling-match with king Antæus, son of Poseidon and Gaea. It was a fierce struggle, and, as the combatants were of equal size and strength, the victory seemed very uncertain. At last Heracles felt his great strength begin to fail, and noticed that every time his adversary touched the ground he seemed to renew his vigor. He therefore resolved to try and win by strategy, and, watching his opportunity, seized Antæus round the waist, raised him from the ground, and held him aloft in his powerful embrace. The giant struggled with all his might to get free; but Heracles held him fast, and felt him grow weaker and weaker, now that he was no longer sustained by his mother Earth, from whom he derived all his strength, until at last his struggles ceased, and he hung limp and lifeless in Heracles' crushing embrace.

From thence Heracles proceeded to Egypt, where reigned Busiris, another son of Poseidon, who (acting on the advice given by an oracle during a time of great scarcity) sacrificed all strangers to Zeus. When Heracles arrived he was seized and dragged to the altar; but the powerful demi-god burst asunder his bonds, and then slew Busiris and his son.

Resuming his journey he now wandered on through Arabia until he arrived at Mount Caucasus, where Prometheus groaned in unceasing agony. It was at this time that Heracles (as already related) shot the eagle which had so long tortured the noble and devoted friend of mankind. Full of gratitude for his deliverance, Prometheus instructed him how to find his way to that remote region in the far West where Atlas supported the heavens on his shoulders, near which lay the Garden of the Hesperides. He also warned Heracles not to attempt to secure the precious fruit himself, but to assume for a time the duties of Atlas, and to despatch him for the apples.

On arriving at his destination Heracles followed the advice of Prometheus. Atlas, who willingly entered into the arrangement, contrived to put the dragon to sleep, and then, having cunningly outwitted the Hesperides, carried off three of the golden apples, which he now brought to Heracles. But when the latter was prepared to relinquish his burden, Atlas, having once tasted the delights of freedom, declined to resume his post, and announced his intention of being himself the bearer of the apples to Eurystheus, leaving Heracles to fill his place. To this proposal the hero feigned assent, merely begging that Atlas would be kind enough to support the heavens for a few moments whilst he contrived a pad for his head. Atlas good-naturedly threw down the apples and once more resumed his load, upon which Heracles bade him adieu, and departed.

When Heracles conveyed the golden apples to Eurystheus the latter presented them to the hero, whereupon Heracles placed the sacred fruit on the altar of Pallas-Athene, who restored them to the garden of the Hesperides.

Cerberus

The twelfth and last labour which Eurystheus imposed on Heracles was to bring up Cerberus from the lower world, believing that all his heroic powers would be unavailing in the Realm of Shades, and that in this, his last and most perilous undertaking, the hero must at length succumb and perish.

Cerberus was a monster dog with three heads, out of whose awful jaws dripped poison; the hair of his head and back was formed of venomous snakes, and his body terminated in the tail of a dragon.

After being initiated into the Eleusinian Mysteries, and obtaining from the priests certain information necessary for the accomplishment of his task, Heracles set out for Taenarum in Lacolia, where there was an opening which led to the under-world. Conducted by Hermes, he commenced his descent into the awful gulf, where myriads of shades soon began to appear, all of whom fled in terror at his approach, Meleager and Medusa alone excepted. About to strike the latter with his sword, Hermes interfered and stayed his hand, reminding him that she was but a shadow, and that consequently no weapon could avail against her.

Arrived before the gates of Hades he found Theseus and Pirithöus, who had been fixed to an enchanted rock by Hades for their presumption in endeavouring to carry off Persephone. When they saw Heracles they implored him to set them free. The hero succeeded in delivering Theseus, but when he endeavoured to liberate Pirithöus, the earth shook so violently beneath him that he was compelled to relinquish his task.

Proceeding further Heracles recognized Ascalaphus, who, as we have seen in the history of Demeter, had revealed the fact that Persephone had swallowed the seeds of a pomegranate offered to her by her husband, which bound her to Hades for ever. Ascalaphus was groaning beneath a huge rock which Demeter in her anger had hurled upon him, and which Heracles now removed, releasing the sufferer.

Before the gates of his palace stood Hades the mighty ruler of the lower world, and barred his entrance; but Heracles, aiming at him with one of his unerring darts, shot him in the shoulder, so that for the first time the god experienced the agony of mortal suffering. Heracles then demanded of him permission to take Cerberus to the upper-world, and to this Hades consented on condition that he should secure him unarmed. Protected by his breastplate and lion's skin Heracles went in search of the monster, whom he found at the mouth of the river Acheron. Undismayed by the hideous barking which proceeded from his three heads, he seized the throat with one hand and the legs with the other, and although the dragon which served him as a tail bit him severely, he did not relinquish his grasp. In this manner he conducted him to the upper-world, through an opening near Troezen in Argolia.

When Eurystheus beheld Cerberus he stood aghast, and despairing of ever getting rid of his hated rival, he returned the hell-hound to the hero, who restored him to Hades, and with this last task the subjection of Heracles to Eurystheus terminated.

How Perseus Slew the Gorgon

SO PERSEUS STARTED on his journey, going dry-shod over land and sea; and his heart was high and joyful, for the winged sandals bore him each day a seven days' journey.

And he went by Cythnus, and by Ceos, and the pleasant Cyclades to Attica; and past Athens and Thebes, and the Copaic lake, and up the vale of Cephissus, and past the peaks of Oeta and Pindus, and over the rich Thessalian plains, till the sunny hills of Greece were behind him, and before him were the wilds of the north. Then he passed the Thracian mountains, and many a barbarous tribe, Paeons and Dardans and Triballi, till he came to the Ister stream, and the dreary Scythian plains. And he walked across the Ister dry-shod, and away through the moors and fens, day and night toward the bleak north-west, turning neither to the right hand nor the left, till he came to the Unshapen Land, and the place which has no name.

And seven days he walked through it, on a path which few can tell; for those who have trodden it like least to speak of it, and those who go there again in dreams are glad enough when they awake; till he came to the edge of the everlasting night, where the air was full of feathers, and the soil was hard with ice; and there at last he found the three Grey Sisters, by the shore of the freezing sea, nodding upon a white log of drift-wood, beneath the cold white winter moon; and they chanted a low song together, 'Why the old times were better than the new.'

There was no living thing around them, not a fly, not a moss upon the rocks. Neither seal nor sea-gull dare come near, lest the ice should clutch them in its claws. The surge broke up in foam, but it fell again in flakes of snow; and it frosted the hair of the three Grey Sisters, and the bones in the ice-cliff above their heads. They passed the eye from one to the other, but for all that they could not see; and they passed the tooth from one to the other, but for all that they could not eat; and they sat in the full glare of the moon, but they were none the warmer for her beams. And Perseus pitied the three Grey Sisters; but they did not pity themselves.

So he said, "Oh, venerable mothers, wisdom is the daughter of old age. You therefore should know many things. Tell me, if you can, the path to the Gorgon."

Then one cried, "Who is this who reproaches us with old age?" And another, "This is the voice of one of the children of men."

And he, "I do not reproach, but honour your old age, and I am one of the sons of men and of the heroes. The rulers of Olympus have sent me to you to ask the way to the Gorgon."

Then one, "There are new rulers in Olympus, and all new things are bad." And another, "We hate your rulers, and the heroes, and all the children of men. We are the kindred of the Titans, and the Giants, and the Gorgons, and the ancient monsters of the deep." And another, "Who is this rash and insolent man who pushes unbidden into our world?" And the first, "There never was such a world as ours, nor will be; if we let him see it, he will spoil it all."

Then one cried, "Give me the eye, that I may see him;" and another, "Give me the tooth, that I may bite him."

But Perseus, when he saw that they were foolish and proud, and did not love the children of men, left off pitying them, and said to himself, "Hungry men must needs be hasty; if I stay making many words here, I shall be starved." Then he stepped close to them, and watched till they passed the eye from hand to hand. And as they groped about between themselves, he held out his own hand gently, till one of them put the eye into it, fancying that it was the hand of her sister. Then he sprang back, and laughed, and cried:

"Cruel and proud old women, I have your eye; and I will throw it into the sea, unless you tell me the path to the Gorgon, and swear to me that you tell me right."

Then they wept, and chattered, and scolded; but in vain. They were forced to tell the truth, though, when they told it, Perseus could hardly make out the road.

"You must go," they said, "foolish boy, to the southward, into the ugly glare of the sun, till you come to Atlas the Giant, who holds the heaven and the earth apart. And you must ask his daughters, the Hesperides, who are young and foolish like yourself. And now give us back our eye, for we have forgotten all the rest."

So Perseus gave them back their eye; but instead of using it, they nodded and fell fast asleep, and were turned into blocks of ice, till the tide came up and washed them all away. And now they float up and down like icebergs for ever, weeping whenever they meet the sunshine, and the fruitful summer and the warm south wind, which fill young hearts with joy.

But Perseus leaped away to the southward, leaving the snow and the ice behind: past the isle of the Hyperboreans, and the tin isles, and the long Iberian shore, while the sun rose higher day by day upon a bright blue summer sea. And the terns and the sea-gulls swept laughing round his head, and called to him to stop and play, and the dolphins gambolled up as he passed, and offered to carry him on their backs. And all night long the sea-nymphs sang sweetly, and the Tritons blew upon their conchs, as they played round Galataea their queen, in her car of pearled shells. Day by day the sun rose higher, and leaped more swiftly into the sea at night, and more swiftly out of the sea at dawn; while Perseus skimmed over the billows like a sea-gull, and his feet were never wetted; and leapt on from wave to wave, and his limbs were never weary, till he saw far away a mighty mountain, all rose-red in the setting sun. Its feet were wrapped in forests, and its head in wreaths of cloud; and Perseus knew that it was Atlas, who holds the heavens and the earth apart.

He came to the mountain, and leapt on shore, and wandered upward, among pleasant valleys and waterfalls, and tall trees and strange ferns and flowers; but there was no smoke rising from any glen, nor house, nor sign of man.

At last he heard sweet voices singing; and he guessed that he was come to the garden of the Nymphs, the daughters of the Evening Star.

They sang like nightingales among the thickets, and Perseus stopped to hear their song; but the words which they spoke he could not understand; no, nor no man after him for many a hundred years. So he stepped forward and saw them dancing, hand in hand around the charmed tree, which bent under its golden fruit; and round the tree-foot was coiled the dragon, old Ladon the sleepless snake, who lies there for ever, listening to the song of the maidens, blinking and watching with dry bright eyes.

Then Perseus stopped, not because he feared the dragon, but because he was bashful before those fair maids; but when they saw him, they too stopped, and called to him with trembling voices:

"Who are you? Are you Heracles the mighty, who will come to rob our garden, and carry off our golden fruit?"

And he answered, "I am not Heracles the mighty, and I want none of your golden fruit. Tell me, fair Nymphs, the way which leads to the Gorgon, that I may go on my way and slay her."

"Not yet, not yet, fair boy; come dance with us around the tree in the garden which knows no winter, the home of the south wind and the sun. Come hither and play with us awhile; we have danced alone here for a thousand years, and our hearts are weary with longing for a playfellow. So come, come, come!"

"I cannot dance with you, fair maidens; for I must do the errand of the Immortals. So tell me the way to the Gorgon, lest I wander and perish in the waves."

Then they sighed and wept; and answered: "The Gorgon! She will freeze you into stone."

"It is better to die like a hero than to live like an ox in a stall. The Immortals have lent me weapons, and they will give me wit to use them."

Then they sighed again and answered, "Fair boy, if you are bent on your own ruin, be it so. We know not the way to the Gorgon; but we will ask the giant Atlas, above upon the mountain peak, the brother of our father, the silver Evening Star. He sits aloft and sees across the ocean, and far away into the Unshapen Land."

So they went up the mountain to Atlas their uncle, and Perseus went up with them. And they found the giant kneeling, as he held the heavens and the earth apart.

They asked him, and he answered mildly, pointing to the sea-board with his mighty hand, "I can see the Gorgons lying on an island far away, but this youth can never come near them, unless he has the hat of darkness, which whosoever wears cannot be seen."

Then cried Perseus, "Where is that hat, that I may find it?"

But the giant smiled. "No living mortal can find that hat, for it lies in the depths of Hades, in the regions of the dead. But my nieces are immortal, and they shall fetch it for you, if you will promise me one thing and keep your faith."

Then Perseus promised; and the giant said, "When you come back with the head of Medusa, you shall show me the beautiful horror, that I may lose my feeling and my breathing, and become a stone for ever; for it is weary labour for me to hold the heavens and the earth apart."

Then Perseus promised, and the eldest of the Nymphs went down, and into a dark cavern among the cliffs, out of which came smoke and thunder, for it was one of the mouths of Hell.

And Perseus and the Nymphs sat down seven days, and waited trembling, till the Nymph came up again; and her face was pale, and her eyes dazzled with the light, for she had been long in the dreary darkness; but in her hand was the magic hat.

Then all the Nymphs kissed Perseus, and wept over him a long while; but he was only impatient to be gone. And at last they put the hat upon his head, and he vanished out of their sight.

But Perseus went on boldly, past many an ugly sight, far away into the heart of the Unshapen Land, beyond the streams of Ocean, to the isles where no ship cruises, where is neither night nor day, where nothing is in its right place, and nothing has a name; till he heard the rustle of the

Gorgons' wings and saw the glitter of their brazen talons; and then he knew that it was time to halt, lest Medusa should freeze him into stone.

He thought awhile with himself, and remembered Athene's words. He rose aloft into the air, and held the mirror of the shield above his head, and looked up into it that he might see all that was below him.

And he saw the three Gorgons sleeping as huge as elephants. He knew that they could not see him, because the hat of darkness hid him; and yet he trembled as he sank down near them, so terrible were those brazen claws.

Two of the Gorgons were foul as swine, and lay sleeping heavily, as swine sleep, with their mighty wings outspread; but Medusa tossed to and fro restlessly, and as she tossed Perseus pitied her, she looked so fair and sad. Her plumage was like the rainbow, and her face was like the face of a nymph, only her eyebrows were knit, and her lips clenched, with everlasting care and pain; and her long neck gleamed so white in the mirror that Perseus had not the heart to strike, and said, "Ah, that it had been either of her sisters!"

But as he looked, from among her tresses the vipers' heads awoke, and peeped up with their bright dry eyes, and showed their fangs, and hissed; and Medusa, as she tossed, threw back her wings and showed her brazen claws; and Perseus saw that, for all her beauty, she was as foul and venomous as the rest.

Then he came down and stepped to her boldly, and looked steadfastly on his mirror, and struck with Herpé stoutly once; and he did not need to strike again.

Then he wrapped the head in the goat-skin, turning away his eyes, and sprang into the air aloft, faster than he ever sprang before.

For Medusa's wings and talons rattled as she sank dead upon the rocks; and her two foul sisters woke, and saw her lying dead.

Into the air they sprang yelling and looked for him who had done the deed. Thrice they swung round and round, like hawks who beat for a partridge; and thrice they snuffed round and round, like hounds who draw upon a deer. At last they struck upon the scent of the blood, and they checked for a moment to make sure; and then on they rushed with a fearful howl, while the wind rattled hoarse in their wings.

On they rushed, sweeping and flapping, like eagles after a hare; and Perseus' blood ran cold, for all his courage, as he saw them come howling on his track; and he cried, "Bear me well now, brave sandals, for the hounds of Death are at my heels!"

And well the brave sandals bore him, aloft through cloud and sunshine, across the shoreless sea; and fast followed the hounds of Death, as the roar of their wings came down the wind. But the roar came down fainter and fainter, and the howl of their voices died away; for the sandals were too swift, even for Gorgons, and by nightfall they were far behind, two black specks in the southern sky, till the sun sank and he saw them no more.

Then he came again to Atlas, and the garden of the Nymphs; and when the giant heard him coming he groaned, and said, "Fulfil thy promise to me."

Then Perseus held up to him the Gorgon's head, and he had rest from all his toil; for he became a crag of stone, which sleeps for ever far above the clouds.

Then he thanked the Nymphs, and asked them, "By what road shall I go homeward again, for I wandered far round in coming hither?"

And they wept and cried, "Go home no more, but stay and play with us, the lonely maidens, who dwell for ever far away from Gods and men."

But he refused, and they told him his road, and said, "Take with you this magic fruit, which, if you eat once, you will not hunger for seven days. For you must go eastward and eastward ever, over the doleful Lybian shore, which Poseidon gave to Father Zeus, when he burst open the Bosphorus and the Hellespont, and drowned the fair Lectonian land. And Zeus took that land in exchange, a fair bargain, much bad ground for a little good, and to this day it lies waste and desert with shingle, and rock, and sand."

Then they kissed Perseus, and wept over him, and he leapt down the mountain, and went on, lessening and lessening like a sea-gull, away and out to sea.

How Perseus Came to the Aethiops

SO PERSEUS flitted onward to the north-east, over many a league of sea, till he came to the rolling sand-hills and the dreary Lybian shore.

And he flitted on across the desert: over rock-ledges, and banks of shingle, and level wastes of sand, and shell-drifts bleaching in the sunshine, and the skeletons of great sea-monsters, and dead bones of ancient giants, strewn up and down upon the old sea-floor. And as he went the blood-drops fell to the earth from the Gorgon's head, and became poisonous asps and adders, which breed in the desert to this day.

Over the sands he went – he never knew how far or how long, feeding on the fruit which the Nymphs had given him, till he saw the hills of the Psylli, and the Dwarfs who fought with cranes. Their spears were of reeds and rushes, and their houses of the egg-shells of the cranes; and Perseus laughed, and went his way to the north-east, hoping all day long to see the blue Mediterranean sparkling, that he might fly across it to his home.

But now came down a mighty wind, and swept him back southward toward the desert. All day long he strove against it; but even the winged sandals could not prevail. So he was forced to float down the wind all night; and when the morning dawned there was nothing to be seen, save the same old hateful waste of sand.

And out of the north the sandstorms rushed upon him, blood-red pillars and wreaths, blotting out the noonday sun; and Perseus fled before them, lest he should be choked by the burning dust. At last the gale fell calm, and he tried to go northward again; but again came down the sandstorms, and swept him back into the waste, and then all was calm and cloudless as before. Seven days he strove against the storms, and seven days he was driven back, till he was spent with thirst and hunger, and his tongue clove to the roof of his mouth. Here and there he fancied that he saw a fair lake, and the sunbeams shining on the water; but when he came to it, it vanished at his feet, and there was nought but burning sand. And if he had not been of the race of the Immortals, he would have perished in the waste; but his life was strong within him, because it was more than man's.

Then he cried to Athene, and said:

"Oh, fair and pure, if thou hearest me, wilt thou leave me here to die of drought? I have brought thee the Gorgon's head at thy bidding, and hitherto thou hast prospered my journey; dost thou desert me at the last? Else why will not these immortal sandals prevail, even against the desert storms? Shall I never see my mother more, and the blue ripple round Seriphos, and the sunny hills of Hellas?"

So he prayed; and after he had prayed there was a great silence.

The heaven was still above his head, and the sand was still beneath his feet; and Perseus looked up, but there was nothing but the blinding sun in the blinding blue; and round him, but there was nothing but the blinding sand.

And Perseus stood still a while, and waited, and said, "Surely I am not here without the will of the Immortals, for Athene will not lie. Were not these sandals to lead me in the right road? Then the road in which I have tried to go must be a wrong road."

Then suddenly his ears were opened, and he heard the sound of running water.

And at that his heart was lifted up, though he scarcely dare believe his ears; and weary as he was, he hurried forward, though he could scarcely stand upright; and within a bowshot of him was a glen in the sand, and marble rocks, and date-trees, and a lawn of gay green grass. And through the lawn a streamlet sparkled and wandered out beyond the trees, and vanished in the sand.

The water trickled among the rocks, and a pleasant breeze rustled in the dry date-branches and Perseus laughed for joy, and leapt down the cliff, and drank of the cool water, and ate of the dates, and slept upon the turf, and leapt up and went forward again: but not toward the north this time; for he said, "Surely Athene hath sent me hither, and will not have me go homeward yet. What if there be another noble deed to be done, before I see the sunny hills of Hellas?"

So he went east, and east for ever, by fresh oases and fountains, date-palms, and lawns of grass, till he saw before him a mighty mountain-wall, all rose-red in the setting sun.

Then he towered in the air like an eagle, for his limbs were strong again; and he flew all night across the mountain till the day began to dawn, and rosy-fingered Eos came blushing up the sky. And then, behold, beneath him was the long green garden of Egypt and the shining stream of Nile.

And he saw cities walled up to heaven, and temples, and obelisks, and pyramids, and giant Gods of stone. And he came down amid fields of barley, and flax, and millet, and clambering gourds; and saw the people coming out of the gates of a great city, and setting to work, each in his place, among the water-courses, parting the streams among the plants cunningly with their feet, according to the wisdom of the Egyptians. But when they saw him they all stopped their work, and gathered round him, and cried:

"Who art thou, fair youth? And what bearest thou beneath thy goat-skin there? Surely thou art one of the Immortals; for thy skin is white like ivory, and ours is red like clay. Thy hair is like threads of gold, and ours is black and curled. Surely thou art one of the Immortals;" and they would have worshipped him then and there; but Perseus said:

"I am not one of the Immortals; but I am a hero of the Hellens. And I have slain the Gorgon in the wilderness, and bear her head with me. Give me food, therefore, that I may go forward and finish my work."

Then they gave him food, and fruit, and wine; but they would not let him go. And when the news came into the city that the Gorgon was slain, the priests came out to meet him, and the maidens, with songs and dances, and timbrels and harps; and they would have brought him to their temple and to their king; but Perseus put on the hat of darkness, and vanished away out of their sight.

Therefore the Egyptians looked long for his return, but in vain, and worshipped him as a hero, and made a statue of him in Chemmis, which stood for many a hundred years; and they said that he appeared to them at times, with sandals a cubit long; and that whenever he appeared the season was fruitful, and the Nile rose high that year.

Then Perseus went to the eastward, along the Red Sea shore; and then, because he was afraid to go into the Arabian deserts, he turned northward once more, and this time no storm hindered him.

He went past the Isthmus, and Mount Casius, and the vast Serbonian bog, and up the shore of Palestine, where the dark-faced Aethiops dwelt.

He flew on past pleasant hills and valleys, like Argos itself, or Lacedaemon, or the fair Vale of Tempe. But the lowlands were all drowned by floods, and the highlands blasted by fire, and the hills heaved like a babbling cauldron, before the wrath of King Poseidon, the shaker of the earth.

And Perseus feared to go inland, but flew along the shore above the sea; and he went on all the day, and the sky was black with smoke; and he went on all the night, and the sky was red with flame.

And at the dawn of day he looked toward the cliffs; and at the water's edge, under a black rock, he saw a white image stand.

"This," thought he, "must surely be the statue of some sea-God; I will go near and see what kind of Gods these barbarians worship."

So he came near; but when he came, it was no statue, but a maiden of flesh and blood; for he could see her tresses streaming in the breeze; and as he came closer still, he could see how she shrank and shivered when the waves sprinkled her with cold salt spray. Her arms were spread above her head, and fastened to the rock with chains of brass; and her head drooped on her bosom, either with sleep, or weariness, or grief. But now and then she looked up and wailed, and called her mother; yet she did not see Perseus, for the cap of darkness was on his head.

Full of pity and indignation, Perseus drew near and looked upon the maid. Her cheeks were darker than his were, and her hair was blue-black like a hyacinth; but Perseus thought, "I have never seen so beautiful a maiden; no, not in all our isles. Surely she is a king's daughter. Do barbarians treat their kings' daughters thus? She is too fair, at least, to have done any wrong I will speak to her."

And, lifting the hat from his head, he flashed into her sight. She shrieked with terror, and tried to hide her face with her hair, for she could not with her hands; but Perseus cried:

"Do not fear me, fair one; I am a Hellen, and no barbarian. What cruel men have bound you? But first I will set you free."

And he tore at the fetters, but they were too strong for him; while the maiden cried:

"Touch me not; I am accursed, devoted as a victim to the sea-Gods. They will slay you, if you dare to set me free."

"Let them try," said Perseus; and drawing Herpé from his thigh, he cut through the brass as if it had been flax.

"Now," he said, "you belong to me, and not to these sea-Gods, whosoever they may be!" But she only called the more on her mother.

"Why call on your mother? She can be no mother to have left you here. If a bird is dropped out of the nest, it belongs to the man who picks it up. If a jewel is cast by the wayside, it is his who dare win it and wear it, as I will win you and will wear you. I know now why Pallas-Athene sent me hither. She sent me to gain a prize worth all my toil and more."

And he clasped her in his arms, and cried, "Where are these sea-Gods, cruel and unjust, who doom fair maids to death? I carry the weapons of Immortals. Let them measure their strength against mine! But tell me, maiden, who you are, and what dark fate brought you here."

And she answered, weeping:

"I am the daughter of Cepheus, King of Iopa, and my mother is Cassiopoeia of the beautiful tresses, and they called me Andromeda, as long as life was mine. And I stand bound here, hapless that I am, for the sea-monster's food, to atone for my mother's sin. For she boasted of me once that I was fairer than Atergatis, Queen of the Fishes; so she in her wrath sent the sea-floods, and her brother the Fire King sent the earthquakes, and wasted all the land, and after the floods a monster bred of the slime, who devours all living things. And now he must devour me, guiltless though I am – me who never harmed a living thing, nor saw a fish upon the shore but I gave it life, and threw it back into the sea; for in our land we eat no fish, for fear of Atergatis their queen. Yet the priests say that nothing but my blood can atone for a sin which I never committed."

But Perseus laughed, and said, "A sea-monster? I have fought with worse than him: I would have faced Immortals for your sake; how much more a beast of the sea?"

Then Andromeda looked up at him, and new hope was kindled in her breast, so proud and fair did he stand, with one hand round her, and in the other the glittering sword. But she only sighed, and wept the more, and cried:

"Why will you die, young as you are? Is there not death and sorrow enough in the world already? It is noble for me to die, that I may save the lives of a whole people; but you, better than them all, why should I slay you too? Go you your way; I must go mine."

But Perseus cried, "Not so; for the Lords of Olympus, whom I serve, are the friends of the heroes, and help them on to noble deeds. Led by them, I slew the Gorgon, the beautiful horror; and not without them do I come hither, to slay this monster with that same Gorgon's head. Yet hide your eyes when I leave you, lest the sight of it freeze you too to stone."

But the maiden answered nothing, for she could not believe his words. And then, suddenly looking up, she pointed to the sea, and shrieked:

"There he comes, with the sunrise, as they promised. I must die now. How shall I endure it? Oh, go! Is it not dreadful enough to be torn piecemeal, without having you to look on?" And she tried to thrust him away.

But he said, "I go; yet promise me one thing ere I go: that if I slay this beast you will be my wife, and come back with me to my kingdom in fruitful Argos, for I am a king's heir. Promise me, and seal it with a kiss."

Then she lifted up her face, and kissed him; and Perseus laughed for joy, and flew upward, while Andromeda crouched trembling on the rock, waiting for what might befall.

On came the great sea-monster, coasting along like a huge black galley, lazily breasting the ripple, and stopping at times by creek or headland to watch for the laughter of girls at their bleaching, or cattle pawing on the sand-hills, or boys bathing on the beach. His great sides were fringed with clustering shells and sea-weeds, and the water gurgled in and out of his wide jaws, as he rolled along, dripping and glistening in the beams of the morning sun.

At last he saw Andromeda, and shot forward to take his prey, while the waves foamed white behind him, and before him the fish fled leaping.

Then down from the height of the air fell Perseus like a shooting star; down to the crests of the waves, while Andromeda hid her face as he shouted; and then there was silence for a while.

At last she looked up trembling, and saw Perseus springing toward her; and instead of the monster a long black rock, with the sea rippling quietly round it.

Who then so proud as Perseus, as he leapt back to the rock, and lifted his fair Andromeda in his arms, and flew with her to the cliff-top, as a falcon carries a dove?

Who so proud as Perseus, and who so joyful as all the Aethiop people? For they had stood watching the monster from the cliffs, wailing for the maiden's fate. And already a messenger had gone to Cepheus and Cassiopoeia, where they sat in sackcloth and ashes on the ground, in the innermost palace chambers, awaiting their daughter's end. And they came, and all the city with them, to see the wonder, with songs and with dances, with cymbals and harps, and received their daughter back again, as one alive from the dead.

Then Cepheus said, "Hero of the Hellens, stay here with me and be my son-in-law, and I will give you the half of my kingdom."

"I will be your son-in-law," said Perseus, "but of your kingdom I will have none, for I long after the pleasant land of Greece, and my mother who waits for me at home."

Then Cepheus said, "You must not take my daughter away at once, for she is to us like one alive from the dead. Stay with us here a year, and after that you shall return with honour." And Perseus consented; but before he went to the palace he bade the people bring stones and wood, and built three altars, one to Athene, and one to Hermes, and one to Father Zeus, and offered bullocks and rams.

And some said, "This is a pious man;" yet the priests said, "The Sea Queen will be yet more fierce against us, because her monster is slain." But they were afraid to speak aloud, for they feared the Gorgon's head. So they went up to the palace; and when they came in, there stood in the hall Phineus, the brother of Cepheus, chafing like a bear robbed of her whelps, and with him his sons, and his servants, and many an armed man; and he cried to Cepheus:

"You shall not marry your daughter to this stranger, of whom no one knows even the name. Was not Andromeda betrothed to my son? And now she is safe again, has he not a right to claim her?"

But Perseus laughed, and answered, "If your son is in want of a bride, let him save a maiden for himself. As yet he seems but a helpless bride-groom. He left this one to die, and dead she is to him. I saved her alive, and alive she is to me, but to no one else. Ungrateful man! Have I not saved your land, and the lives of your sons and daughters, and will you requite me thus? Go, or it will be worse for you." But all the men-at-arms drew their swords, and rushed on him like wild beasts.

Then he unveiled the Gorgon's head, and said, "This has delivered my bride from one wild beast: it shall deliver her from many." And as he spoke Phineus and all his men-at-arms stopped short, and stiffened each man as he stood; and before Perseus had drawn the goat-skin over the face again, they were all turned into stone.

Then Persons bade the people bring levers and roll them out; and what was done with them after that I cannot tell.

So they made a great wedding-feast, which lasted seven whole days, and who so happy as Perseus and Andromeda?

But on the eighth night Perseus dreamed a dream; and he saw standing beside him Pallas-Athene, as he had seen her in Seriphos, seven long years before; and she stood and called him by name, and said:

"Perseus, you have played the man, and see, you have your reward. Know now that the Gods are just, and help him who helps himself. Now give me here Herpé the sword, and the sandals, and the hat of darkness, that I may give them back to their owners; but the Gorgon's head you shall keep a while, for you will need it in your land of Greece. Then you shall lay it up in my temple at Seriphos, that I may wear it on my shield for ever, a terror to the Titans and the monsters, and the foes of Gods and men. And as for this land, I have appeased the sea and the fire, and there shall be no more floods nor earthquakes. But let the people build altars to Father Zeus, and to me, and worship the Immortals, the Lords of heaven and earth."

And Perseus rose to give her the sword, and the cap, and the sandals; but he woke, and his dream vanished away. And yet it was not altogether a dream; for the goat-skin with the head was in its place; but the sword, and the cap, and the sandals were gone, and Perseus never saw them more.

Then a great awe fell on Perseus; and he went out in the morning to the people, and told his dream, and bade them build altars to Zeus, the Father of Gods and men, and to Athene, who gives wisdom to heroes; and fear no more the earthquakes and the floods, but sow and build in peace. And they did so for a while, and prospered; but after Perseus was gone they forgot Zeus and Athene, and worshipped again Atergatis the queen, and the undying fish of the sacred lake, where Deucalion's deluge was swallowed up, and they burnt their children before the Fire King, till Zeus was angry with that foolish people, and brought a strange nation against them out of Egypt, who fought against them and wasted them utterly, and dwelt in their cities for many a hundred years.

The Slaying of the Minotaur

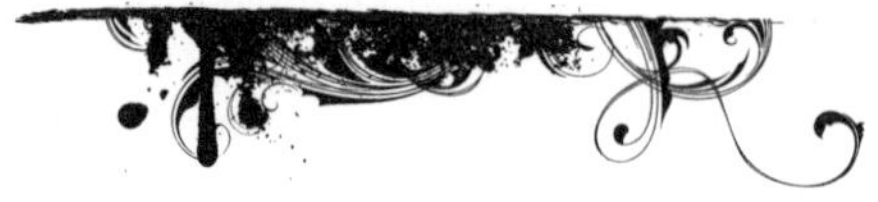

THESEUS FIRST FASTENED one end of his coil of string to a pointed rock, and then began to look about him. The labyrinth was dark, and he slowly walked, holding the string, down the broadest path, from which others turned off to right or left. He counted his steps, and he had taken near three thousand steps when he saw the pale sky showing in a small circle cut in the rocky roof, above his head, and he saw the fading stars. Sheer walls of rock went up on either hand of him, a roof of rock was above him, but in the roof was this one open place, across which were heavy bars. Soon the daylight would come.

Theseus set the lamp down on a rock behind a corner, and he waited, thinking, at a place where a narrow dark path turned at right angles to the left. Looking carefully round he saw a heap of bones, not human bones, but skulls of oxen and sheep, hoofs of oxen, and shank bones. "This," he thought, "must be the place where the food of the Minotaur is let down to him from above. They have not Athenian youths and maidens to give him every day! Beside his feeding place I will wait."

Saying this to himself, he rose and went round the corner of the dark narrow path cut in the rock to the left. He made his own breakfast, from the food that Ariadne had given him, and it occurred to his mind that probably the Minotaur might also be thinking of breakfast time.

He sat still, and from afar away within he heard a faint sound, like the end of the echo of a roar, and he stood up, drew his long sword, and listened keenly. The sound came nearer and louder, a strange sound, not deep like the roar of a bull, but more shrill and thin. Theseus laughed silently. A monster with the head and tongue of a bull, but with the chest of a man, could roar no better than that! The sounds came nearer and louder, but still with the thin sharp tone in them. Theseus now took from his bosom the phial of gold that Medea had given him in Athens when she told him about the Minotaur. He removed the stopper, and held his thumb over the mouth of the phial, and grasped his long sword with his left hand, after fastening the clue of thread to his belt.

The roars of the hungry Minotaur came nearer and nearer; now his feet could be heard padding along the echoing floor of the labyrinth. Theseus moved to the shadowy corner of the narrow path, where it opened into the broad light passage, and he crouched there; his heart was beating quickly. On came the Minotaur, up leaped Theseus, and dashed the contents of the open phial in the eyes of the monster; a white dust flew out, and Theseus leaped back into his hiding place. The Minotaur uttered strange shrieks of pain; he rubbed his eyes with his monstrous hands; he raised his head up towards the sky, bellowing and confused; he stood tossing his head up and down; he turned round and round about, feeling with his hands for the wall. He was quite blind. Theseus drew his short sword, crept up, on naked feet, behind the monster, and cut through the back sinews of his legs at the knees. Down fell the Minotaur, with a crash and a roar, biting at the rocky floor with his lion's teeth, and waving his hands, and clutching at the empty air. Theseus waited for his chance, when the clutching hands rested, and then, thrice he drove the long sharp blade of bronze through the heart of the Minotaur. The body leaped, and lay still.

Theseus kneeled down, and thanked all the gods, and promised rich sacrifices, and a new temple to Pallas-Athene, the Guardian of Athens. When he had finished his prayer, he drew the short sword, and hacked off the head of the Minotaur. He sheathed both his swords, took the head in his hand, and followed the string back out of the daylit place, to the rock where he had left his lamp. With the lamp and the guidance of the string he easily found his way to the door, which he unlocked. He noticed that the thick bronze plates of the door were dinted and scarred by the points of the horns of the Minotaur, trying to force his way out.

He went out into the fresh early morning; all the birds were singing merrily, and merry was the heart of Theseus. He locked the door, and crossed to the palace, which he entered, putting the key in the place which Ariadne had shown him. She was there, with fear and joy in her eyes.

"Touch me not," said Theseus, "for I am foul with the blood of the Minotaur." She brought him to the baths on the ground floor, and swiftly fled up a secret stair. In the bathroom Theseus made himself clean, and clad himself in fresh raiment which was lying ready for him. When he was clean and clad he tied a rope of byblus round the horns of the head of the Minotaur, and went round the back of the palace, trailing the head behind him, till he came to a sentinel. "I would see King Minos," he said, "I have the password, *Androgeos*!"

The sentinel, pale and wondering, let him pass, and so he went through the guards, and reached the great door of the palace, and there the servants wrapped the bleeding head in cloth, that it might not stain the floors. Theseus bade them lead him to King Minos, who was seated on his throne, judging the four guardsmen, that had been found asleep.

When Theseus entered, followed by the serving men with their burden, the king never stirred on his throne, but turned his grey eyes on Theseus.

"My lord," said Theseus, "that which was to be done is done."

The servants laid their burden at the feet of King Minos, and removed the top fold of the covering.

The king turned to the captain of his guard. "A week in the cells for each of these four men," said he, and the four guards, who had expected to die by a cruel death, were led away. "Let that head and the body also be burned to ashes and thrown into the sea, far from the shore," said Minos, and his servants silently covered the head of the Minotaur, and bore it from the throne room.

Then, at last, Minos rose from his throne, and took the hand of Theseus, and said, "Sir, I thank you, and I give you back your company safe and free; and I am no more in hatred with your people. Let there be peace between me and them. But will you not abide with us awhile, and be our guests?"

Theseus was glad enough, and he and his company tarried in the palace, and were kindly treated. Minos showed Theseus all the splendour and greatness of his kingdom and his ships, and great armouries, full of all manner of weapons: the names and numbers of them are yet known, for they are written on tablets of clay, that were found in the storehouse of the king. Later, in the twilight, Theseus and Ariadne would walk together in the fragrant gardens where the nightingales sang, and Minos knew it, and was glad. He thought that nowhere in the world could he find such a husband for his daughter, and he deemed it wise to have the alliance of so great a king as Theseus promised to be. But, loving his daughter, he kept Theseus with him long, till the prince was ashamed of his delay, knowing that his father, King Aegeus, and all the people of his country, were looking for him anxiously.

Therefore he told what was in his heart to Minos, who sighed, and said, "I knew what is in your heart, and I cannot say you nay. I give to you my daughter as gladly as a father may."

Then they spoke of things of state, and made firm alliance between Cnossos and Athens while they both lived; and the wedding was done with great splendour, and, at last, Theseus and Ariadne and all their company went aboard, and sailed from Crete. One misfortune they had: the captain of their ship died of a sickness while they were in Crete, but Minos gave them the best of his captains. Yet by reason of storms and tempests they had a long and terrible voyage, driven out of their course into strange seas. When at length they found their bearings, a grievous sickness fell on beautiful Ariadne. Day by day she was weaker, till Theseus, with a breaking heart, stayed the ship at an isle but two days' sail from Athens. There Ariadne was carried ashore, and laid in a bed in the house of the king of that island, and the physicians and the wise women did for her what they could. But she died with her hands in the hands of Theseus, and his lips on her lips. In that isle she was buried, and Theseus went on board his ship, and drew his cloak over his head, and so lay for two days, never moving nor speaking, and tasting neither meat nor drink. No man dared to speak to him, but when the vessel stopped in the harbour of Athens, he arose, and stared about him.

The shore was dark with people all dressed in mourning raiment, and the herald of the city came with the news that Aegeus the King was dead. For the Cretan captain did not know that he was to hoist the scarlet sail if Theseus came home in triumph, and Aegeus, as he watched the waters, had descried the dark sail from afar off, and, in his grief, had thrown himself down from the cliff, and was drowned. This was the end of the voyaging of Theseus.

Theseus wished to die, and be with Ariadne, in the land of Queen Persephone. But he was a strong man, and he lived to be the greatest of the Kings of Athens, for all the other towns came in, and were his subjects, and he ruled them well. His first care was to build a great fleet in secret harbours far from towns and the ways of men, for, though he and Minos were friends while they both lived, when Minos died the new Cretan king might oppress Athens.

Minos died, at last, and his son picked a quarrel with Theseus, who refused to give up a man that had fled to Athens because the new king desired to slay him, and news came to Theseus that a great navy was being made ready in Crete to attack him. Then he sent heralds to the king of a fierce people, called the Dorians, who were moving through the countries to the north-west of Greece, seizing lands, settling on them, and marching forward again in a few years. They were wild, strong, and brave, and they are said to have had swords of iron, which were better than the bronze weapons of the Greeks.

The heralds of Theseus said to them, "Come to our king, and he will take you across the sea, and show you plunder enough. But you shall swear not to harm his kingdom."

This pleased the Dorians well, and the ships of Theseus brought them round to Athens, where Theseus joined them with many of his own men, and they did the oath. They sailed swiftly to Crete, where, as they arrived in the dark, the Cretan captains thought that they were part of their own navy, coming in to join them in the attack on Athens; for that Theseus had a navy the Cretans knew not; he had built it so secretly. In the night he marched his men to Cnossos, and took the garrison by surprise, and burned the palace, and plundered it. Even now we can see that the palace has been partly burned, and hurriedly robbed by some sudden enemy.

The Dorians stayed in Crete, and were there in the time of Odysseus, holding part of the island, while the true Cretans held the greater part of it. But Theseus returned to Athens, and married Hippolyte, Queen of the Amazons. The story of their wedding festival is told in Shakespeare's play, *A Midsummer Night's Dream*. And Theseus had many new adventures, and many troubles, but he left Athens rich and strong, and in no more danger from the kings of Crete. Though the Dorians, after the time of Odysseus, swept all over the rest of Greece, and seized Mycenae and Lacedaemon, the towns of Agamemnon and Menelaus, they were true to their oath to Theseus, and left Athens to the Athenians.

How the Argonauts Sailed to Colchis

Jason and the many heroes who have joined him upon the Argo to become his Argonauts, have just launched their newly built ship and set out on their journey to search for the golden fleece.

AND WHAT HAPPENED NEXT, whether it be true or not, stands written in ancient songs. And grand old songs they are, written in grand old rolling verse; and they call them the Songs of Orpheus, or the Orphics, to this day. And they tell how the heroes came to Aphetai, across the bay, and waited for the south-west wind, and chose themselves a captain from their crew: and how all called for Heracles, because he was the strongest and most huge; but Heracles refused, and called for Jason, because he was the wisest of them all. So Jason was chosen captain; and Orpheus heaped a pile of wood, and slew a bull, and offered it to Hera, and called all the heroes to stand round, each man's head crowned with olive, and to strike their swords into the bull. Then he filled a golden goblet with the bull's blood, and with wheaten flour, and honey, and wine, and the bitter salt-sea water, and bade the heroes taste. So each tasted the goblet, and passed it round, and vowed an awful vow: and they vowed before the sun, and the night, and the blue-haired sea who shakes the land, to stand by Jason faithfully in the adventure of the golden fleece; and whosoever shrank back, or disobeyed, or turned traitor to his vow, then justice should minister against him, and the Erinnues who track guilty men.

Then Jason lighted the pile, and burnt the carcase of the bull; and they went to their ship and sailed eastward, like men who have a work to do; and the place from which they went was called Aphetai, the sailing-place, from that day forth. Three thousand years and more they sailed away, into the unknown Eastern seas; and great nations have come and gone since then, and many a storm has swept the earth; and many a mighty armament, to which *Argo* would be but one small boat; English and French, Turkish and Russian, have sailed those waters since; yet the fame of that small *Argo* lives for ever, and her name is become a proverb among men.

So they sailed past the Isle of Sciathos, with the Cape of Sepius on their left, and turned to the northward toward Pelion, up the long Magnesian shore. On their right hand was the open sea, and on their left old Pelion rose, while the clouds crawled round his dark pine-forests, and his caps of summer snow. And their hearts yearned for the dear old mountain, as they thought of pleasant days gone by, and of the sports of their boyhood, and their hunting, and their schooling in the cave beneath the cliff. And at last Peleus spoke, "Let us land here, friends, and climb the dear old hill once more. We are going on a fearful journey; who knows if we shall see Pelion again? Let us go up to Cheiron our master, and ask his blessing ere we start. And I have a boy, too, with him, whom he trains as he trained me once – the son whom Thetis brought me, the silver-footed lady of the sea, whom I caught in the cave, and tamed her, though she changed her shape seven times. For she changed, as I held her, into water, and to vapour, and to burning flame, and to a rock, and to a black-maned lion, and to a tall and stately tree. But I held her and held her ever, till she took her own shape again, and led her to my father's house, and won her for my bride. And all the rulers of Olympus came to our wedding, and the heavens and the earth rejoiced together, when an Immortal wedded mortal man. And now let me see my son; for it is not often I shall see him upon earth: famous he will be, but short-lived, and die in the flower of youth."

So Tiphys the helmsman steered them to the shore under the crags of Pelion; and they went up through the dark pine-forests towards the Centaur's cave.

And they came into the misty hall, beneath the snow-crowned crag; and saw the great Centaur lying, with his huge limbs spread upon the rock; and beside him stood Achilles, the child whom no steel could wound, and played upon his harp right sweetly, while Cheiron watched and smiled.

Then Cheiron leapt up and welcomed them, and kissed them every one, and set a feast before them of swine's flesh, and venison, and good wine; and young Achilles served them, and carried the golden goblet round. And after supper all the heroes clapped their hands, and called on Orpheus to sing; but he refused, and said, "How can I, who am the younger, sing before our ancient host?" So they called on Cheiron to sing, and Achilles brought him his harp; and he began a wondrous song; a famous story of old time, of the fight between the Centaurs and the Lapithai, which you may still see carved in stone. He sang how his brothers came to ruin by their folly, when they were mad with wine; and how they and the heroes fought, with fists, and teeth, and the goblets from which they drank; and how they tore up the pine-trees in their fury, and hurled great crags of stone, while the mountains thundered with the battle, and the land was wasted far and wide; till the Lapithai drove them from their home in the rich Thessalian plains to the lonely glens of Pindus, leaving Cheiron all alone. And the heroes praised his song right heartily; for some of them had helped in that great fight.

Then Orpheus took the lyre, and sang of Chaos, and the making of the wondrous World, and how all things sprang from Love, who could not live alone in the Abyss. And as he sang, his voice rose from the cave, above the crags, and through the tree-tops, and the glens of oak and pine. And the trees bowed their heads when they heard it, and the grey rocks cracked and rang, and the forest beasts crept near to listen, and the birds forsook their nests and hovered round. And old Cheiron claps his hands together, and beat his hoofs upon the ground, for wonder at that magic song.

Then Peleus kissed his boy, and wept over him, and they went down to the ship; and Cheiron came down with them, weeping, and kissed them one by one, and blest them, and promised to them great renown. And the heroes wept when they left him, till their great hearts could weep no more; for he was kind and just and pious, and wiser than all beasts and men. Then he went up to a cliff, and prayed for them, that they might come home safe and well; while the heroes rowed away, and watched him standing on his cliff above the sea, with his great hands raised toward heaven, and his white locks waving in the wind; and they strained their eyes to watch him to the last, for they felt that they should look on him no more.

So they rowed on over the long swell of the sea, past Olympus, the seat of the Immortals, and past the wooded bays of Athos, and Samothrace the sacred isle; and they came past Lemnos to the Hellespont, and through the narrow strait of Abydos, and so on into the Propontis, which we call Marmora now. And there they met with Cyzicus, ruling in Asia over the Dolions, who, the songs say, was the son of Aeneas, of whom you will hear many a tale some day. For Homer tells us how he fought at Troy, and Virgil how he sailed away and founded Rome; and men believed until late years that from him sprang our old British kings. Now Cyzicus, the songs say, welcomed the heroes, for his father had been one of Cheiron's scholars; so he welcomed them, and feasted them, and stored their ship with corn and wine, and cloaks and rugs, the songs say, and shirts, of which no doubt they stood in need.

But at night, while they lay sleeping, came down on them terrible men, who lived with the bears in the mountains, like Titans or giants in shape; for each of them had six arms, and they fought with young firs and pines. But Heracles killed them all before morn with his deadly poisoned arrows; but among them, in the darkness, he slew Cyzicus the kindly prince.

Then they got to their ship and to their oars, and Tiphys bade them cast off the hawsers and go to sea. But as he spoke a whirlwind came, and spun the *Argo* round, and twisted the hawsers together, so that no man could loose them. Then Tiphys dropped the rudder from his hand, and cried, "This comes from the Gods above." But Jason went forward, and asked counsel of the magic bough.

Then the magic bough spoke, and answered, "This is because you have slain Cyzicus your friend. You must appease his soul, or you will never leave this shore."

Jason went back sadly, and told the heroes what he had heard. And they leapt on shore, and searched till dawn; and at dawn they found the body, all rolled in dust and blood, among the corpses of those monstrous beasts. And they wept over their kind host, and laid him on a fair bed, and heaped a huge mound over him, and offered black sheep at his tomb, and Orpheus sang a magic song to him, that his spirit might have rest. And then they held games at the tomb, after the custom of those times, and Jason gave prizes to each winner. To Ancaeus he gave a golden cup, for he wrestled best of all; and to Heracles a silver one, for he was the strongest of all; and to Castor, who rode best, a golden crest; and Polydeuces the boxer had a rich carpet, and to Orpheus for his song a sandal with golden wings. But Jason himself was the best of all the archers, and the Minuai crowned him with an olive crown; and so, the songs say, the soul of good Cyzicus was appeased and the heroes went on their way in peace.

But when Cyzicus' wife heard that he was dead she died likewise of grief; and her tears became a fountain of clear water, which flows the whole year round.

Then they rowed away, the songs say, along the Mysian shore, and past the mouth of Rhindacus, till they found a pleasant bay, sheltered by the long ridges of Arganthus, and by high walls of basalt rock. And there they ran the ship ashore upon the yellow sand, and furled the sail, and took the mast down, and lashed it in its crutch. And next they let down the ladder, and went ashore to sport and rest.

And there Heracles went away into the woods, bow in hand, to hunt wild deer; and Hylas the fair boy slipt away after him, and followed him by stealth, until he lost himself among the glens, and sat down weary to rest himself by the side of a lake; and there the water nymphs came up to look at him, and loved him, and carried him down under the lake to be their playfellow, for ever happy and young. And Heracles sought for him in vain, shouting his name till all the mountains rang; but Hylas never heard him, far down under the sparkling lake. So while Heracles wandered searching for him, a fair breeze sprang up, and Heracles was nowhere to be found; and the *Argo* sailed away, and Heracles was left behind, and never saw the noble Phasian stream.

Then the Minuai came to a doleful land, where Amycus the giant ruled, and cared nothing for the laws of Zeus, but challenged all strangers to box with him, and those whom he conquered he slew. But Polydeuces the boxer struck him a harder blow than he ever felt before, and slew him; and the Minuai went on up the Bosphorus, till they came to the city of Phineus, the fierce Bithynian king; for Zetes and Calais bade Jason land there, because they had a work to do.

And they went up from the shore toward the city, through forests white with snow; and Phineus came out to meet them with a lean and woful face, and said, "Welcome, gallant heroes, to the land of bitter blasts, the land of cold and misery; yet I will feast you as best I can." And he led them in, and set meat before them; but before they could put their hands to their mouths, down came two fearful monsters, the like of whom man never saw; for they had the faces and the hair of fair maidens, but the wings and claws of hawks; and they snatched the meat from off the table, and flew shrieking out above the roofs.

Then Phineus beat his breast and cried, "These are the Harpies, whose names are the Whirlwind and the Swift, the daughters of Wonder and of the Amber-nymph, and they rob us night and day. They carried off the daughters of Pandareus, whom all the Gods had blest; for Aphrodite fed them on Olympus with honey and milk and wine; and Hera gave them beauty and wisdom, and Athene skill in all the arts; but when they came to their wedding, the Harpies snatched them both away, and gave them to be slaves to the Erinnues, and live in horror all their days. And now they haunt me, and my people, and the Bosphorus, with fearful storms; and sweep away our food from off our tables, so that we starve in spite of all our wealth."

Then up rose Zetes and Calais, the winged sons of the North-wind, and said, "Do you not know us, Phineus, and these wings which grow upon our backs?" And Phineus hid his face in terror; but he answered not a word.

"Because you have been a traitor, Phineus, the Harpies haunt you night and day. Where is Cleopatra our sister, your wife, whom you keep in prison? And where are her two children, whom you blinded in your rage, at the bidding of an evil woman, and cast them out upon the rocks? Swear to us that you will right our sister, and cast out that wicked woman; and then we will free you from your plague, and drive the whirlwind maidens to the south; but if not, we will put out your eyes, as you put out the eyes of your own sons."

Then Phineus swore an oath to them, and drove out the wicked woman; and Jason took those two poor children, and cured their eyes with magic herbs.

But Zetes and Calais rose up sadly and said, "Farewell now, heroes all; farewell, our dear companions, with whom we played on Pelion in old times; for a fate is laid upon us, and our day is come at last, in which we must hunt the whirlwinds over land and sea for ever; and if we catch them they die, and if not, we die ourselves."

At that all the heroes wept; but the two young men sprang up, and aloft into the air after the Harpies, and the battle of the winds began.

The heroes trembled in silence as they heard the shrieking of the blasts; while the palace rocked and all the city, and great stones were torn from the crags, and the forest pines were hurled earthward, north and south and east and west, and the Bosphorus boiled white with foam, and the clouds were dashed against the cliffs.

But at last the battle ended, and the Harpies fled screaming toward the south, and the sons of the North-wind rushed after them, and brought clear sunshine where they passed. For many a league they followed them, over all the isles of the Cyclades, and away to the south-west across Hellas, till they came to the Ionian Sea, and there they fell upon the Echinades, at the mouth of the Achelous; and those isles were called the Whirlwind Isles for many a hundred years. But what became of Zetes and Calais I know not, for the heroes never saw them again: and some say that Heracles met them, and quarrelled with them, and slew them with his arrows; and some say that they fell down from weariness and the heat of the summer sun, and that the Sun-god buried them among the Cyclades, in the pleasant Isle of Tenos; and for many hundred years their grave was shown there, and over it a pillar, which turned to every wind. But those dark storms and whirlwinds haunt the Bosphorus until this day.

But the Argonauts went eastward, and out into the open sea, which we now call the Black Sea, but it was called the Euxine then. No Hellen had ever crossed it, and all feared that dreadful sea, and its rocks, and shoals, and fogs, and bitter freezing storms; and they told strange stories of it, some false and some half-true, how it stretched northward to the ends of the earth, and the sluggish Putrid Sea, and the everlasting night, and the regions of the dead. So the heroes trembled, for all their courage, as they came into that wild Black Sea, and saw it stretching out before them, without a shore, as far as eye could see.

And first Orpheus spoke, and warned them, "We shall come now to the wandering blue rocks; my mother warned me of them, Calliope, the immortal muse."

And soon they saw the blue rocks shining like spires and castles of grey glass, while an ice-cold wind blew from them and chilled all the heroes' hearts. And as they neared they could see them heaving, as they rolled upon the long sea-waves, crashing and grinding together, till the roar went up to heaven. The sea sprang up in spouts between them, and swept round them in white sheets of foam; but their heads swung nodding high in air, while the wind whistled shrill among the crags.

The heroes' hearts sank within them, and they lay upon their oars in fear; but Orpheus called to Tiphys the helmsman, "Between them we must pass; so look ahead for an opening, and be brave, for Hera is with us."

But Tiphys the cunning helmsman stood silent, clenching his teeth, till he saw a heron come flying mast-high toward the rocks, and hover awhile before them, as if looking for a passage through. Then he cried, "Hera has sent us a pilot; let us follow the cunning bird."

Then the heron flapped to and fro a moment, till he saw a hidden gap, and into it he rushed like an arrow, while the heroes watched what would befall.

And the blue rocks clashed together as the bird fled swiftly through; but they struck but a feather from his tail, and then rebounded apart at the shock.

Then Tiphys cheered the heroes, and they shouted; and the oars bent like withes beneath their strokes as they rushed between those toppling ice-crags and the cold blue lips of death. And ere the rocks could meet again they had passed them, and were safe out in the open sea.

And after that they sailed on wearily along the Asian coast, by the Black Cape and Thyneis, where the hot stream of Thymbris falls into the sea, and Sangarius, whose waters float on the Euxine, till they came to Wolf the river, and to Wolf the kindly king. And there died two brave heroes, Idmon and Tiphys the wise helmsman: one died of an evil sickness, and one a wild boar slew. So the heroes heaped a mound above them, and set upon it an oar on high, and left them there to sleep together, on the far-off Lycian shore. But Idas killed the boar, and avenged Tiphys; and Ancaios took the rudder and was helmsman, and steered them on toward the east.

And they went on past Sinope, and many a mighty river's mouth, and past many a barbarous tribe, and the cities of the Amazons, the warlike women of the East, till all night they heard the clank of anvils and the roar of furnace-blasts, and the forge-fires shone like sparks through the darkness in the mountain glens aloft; for they were come to the shores of the Chalybes, the smiths who never tire, but serve Ares the cruel War-god, forging weapons day and night.

And at day-dawn they looked eastward, and midway between the sea and the sky they saw white snow-peaks hanging, glittering sharp and bright above the clouds. And they knew that they were come to Caucasus, at the end of all the earth: Caucasus the highest of all mountains, the father of the rivers of the East. On his peak lies chained the Titan, while a vulture tears his heart; and at his feet are piled dark forests round the magic Colchian land.

And they rowed three days to the eastward, while Caucasus rose higher hour by hour, till they saw the dark stream of Phasis rushing headlong to the sea, and, shining above the tree-tops, the golden roofs of King Aeetes, the child of the Sun.

Then out spoke Ancaios the helmsman, "We are come to our goal at last, for there are the roofs of Aeetes, and the woods where all poisons grow; but who can tell us where among them is hid the golden fleece? Many a toil must we bear ere we find it, and bring it home to Greece."

But Jason cheered the heroes, for his heart was high and bold; and he said, "I will go alone up to Aeetes, though he be the child of the Sun, and win him with soft words. Better so than to go altogether, and to come to blows at once."

But the Minuai would not stay behind, so they rowed boldly up the stream.

And a dream came to Aèetes, and filled his heart with fear. He thought he saw a shining star, which fell into his daughter's lap; and that Medea his daughter took it gladly, and carried it to the river-side, and cast it in, and there the whirling river bore it down, and out into the Euxine Sea.

Then he leapt up in fear, and bade his servants bring his chariot, that he might go down to the river-side and appease the nymphs, and the heroes whose spirits haunt the bank. So he went down in his golden chariot, and his daughters by his side, Medea the fair witch-maiden, and Chalciope, who had been Phrixus' wife, and behind him a crowd of servants and soldiers, for he was a rich and mighty prince.

And as he drove down by the reedy river he saw *Argo* sliding up beneath the bank, and many a hero in her, like Immortals for beauty and for strength, as their weapons glittered round them in the level morning sunlight, through the white mist of the stream. But Jason was the noblest of all; for Hera, who loved him, gave him beauty and tallness and terrible manhood.

And when they came near together and looked into each other's eyes the heroes were awed before Aeetes as he shone in his chariot, like his father the glorious Sun; for his robes were of rich gold tissue, and the rays of his diadem flashed fire; and in his hand he bore a jewelled sceptre, which glittered like the stars; and sternly he looked at them under his brows, and sternly he spoke and loud:

"Who are you, and what want you here, that you come to the shore of Cutaia? Do you take no account of my rule, nor of my people the Colchians who serve me, who never tired yet in the battle, and know well how to face an invader?"

And the heroes sat silent awhile before the face of that ancient king. But Hera the awful goddess put courage into Jason's heart, and he rose and shouted loudly in answer, "We are no pirates nor lawless men. We come not to plunder and to ravage, or carry away slaves from your land; but my uncle, the son of Poseidon, Pelias the Minuan king, he it is who has set me on a quest to bring home the golden fleece. And these too, my bold comrades, they are no nameless men; for some are the sons of Immortals, and some of heroes far renowned. And we too never tire in battle, and know well how to give blows and to take: yet we wish to be guests at your table: it will be better so for both."

Then Aeetes' race rushed up like a whirlwind, and his eyes flashed fire as he heard; but he crushed his anger down in his breast, and spoke mildly a cunning speech –

"If you will fight for the fleece with my Colchians, then many a man must die. But do you indeed expect to win from me the fleece in fight? So few you are that if you be worsted I can load your ship with your corpses. But if you will be ruled by me, you will find it better far to choose the best man among you, and let him fulfil the labours which I demand. Then I will give him the golden fleece for a prize and a glory to you all."

So saying, he turned his horses and drove back in silence to the town. And the Minuai sat silent with sorrow, and longed for Heracles and his strength; for there was no facing the thousands of the Colchians and the fearful chance of war.

But Chalciope, Phrixus' widow, went weeping to the town; for she remembered her Minuan husband, and all the pleasures of her youth, while she watched the fair faces of his kinsmen, and their long locks of golden hair. And she whispered to Medea her sister, "Why should all these brave men die? Why does not my father give them up the fleece, that my husband's spirit may have rest?"

And Medea's heart pitied the heroes, and Jason most of all; and she answered, "Our father is stern and terrible, and who can win the golden fleece?"

But Chalciope said, "These men are not like our men; there is nothing which they cannot dare nor do."

And Medea thought of Jason and his brave countenance, and said, "If there was one among them who knew no fear, I could show him how to win the fleece."

So in the dusk of evening they went down to the river-side, Chalciope and Medea the witch-maiden, and Argus, Phrixus' son. And Argus the boy crept forward, among the beds of reeds, till he came where the heroes were sleeping, on the thwarts of the ship, beneath the bank, while Jason kept ward on shore, and leant upon his lance full of thought. And the boy came to Jason, and said:

"I am the son of Phrixus, your Cousin; and Chalciope my mother waits for you, to talk about the golden fleece."

Then Jason went boldly with the boy, and found the two princesses standing; and when Chalciope saw him she wept, and took his hands, and cried: "O cousin of my beloved, go home before you die!"

"It would be base to go home now, fair princess, and to have sailed all these seas in vain." Then both the princesses besought him; but Jason said, "It is too late."

"But you know not," said Medea, "what he must do who would win the fleece. He must tame the two brazen-footed bulls, who breathe devouring flame; and with them he must plough ere nightfall four acres in the field of Ares; and he must sow them with serpents' teeth, of which each tooth springs up into an armed man. Then he must fight with all those warriors; and little will it profit him to conquer them, for the fleece is guarded by a serpent, more huge than any mountain pine; and over his body you must step if you would reach the golden fleece."

Then Jason laughed bitterly. "Unjustly is that fleece kept here, and by an unjust and lawless king; and unjustly shall I die in my youth, for I will attempt it ere another sun be set."

Then Medea trembled, and said, "No mortal man can reach that fleece unless I guide him through. For round it, beyond the river, is a wall full nine ells high, with lofty towers and buttresses, and mighty gates of threefold brass; and over the gates the wall is arched, with golden battlements above. And over the gateway sits Brimo, the wild witch-huntress of the woods, brandishing a pine-torch in her hands, while her mad hounds howl around. No man dare meet her or look on her, but only I her priestess, and she watches far and wide lest any stranger should come near."

"No wall so high but it may be climbed at last, and no wood so thick but it may be crawled through; no serpent so wary but he may be charmed, or witch-queen so fierce but spells may soothe her; and I may yet win the golden fleece, if a wise maiden help bold men."

And he looked at Medea cunningly, and held her with his glittering eye, till she blushed and trembled, and said:

"Who can face the fire of the bulls' breath, and fight ten thousand armed men?"

"He whom you help," said Jason, flattering her, "for your fame is spread over all the earth. Are you not the queen of all enchantresses, wiser even than your sister Circe, in her fairy island in the West?"

"Would that I were with my sister Circe in her fairy island in the West, far away from sore temptation and thoughts which tear the heart! But if it must be so – for why should you die? – I have an ointment here; I made it from the magic ice-flower which sprang from Prometheus' wound, above the clouds on Caucasus, in the dreary fields of snow. Anoint yourself with that, and you shall have in you seven men's strength; and anoint your shield with it, and neither fire nor sword can harm you. But what you begin you must end before sunset, for its virtue lasts only one day. And anoint your helmet with it before you sow the serpents' teeth; and when the sons of earth spring up, cast your helmet among their ranks, and the deadly crop of the War-god's field will mow itself, and perish."

Then Jason fell on his knees before her, and thanked her and kissed her hands; and she gave him the vase of ointment, and fled trembling through the reeds. And Jason told his comrades what had happened, and showed them the box of ointment; and all rejoiced but Idas, and he grew mad with envy.

And at sunrise Jason went and bathed, and anointed himself from head to foot, and his shield, and his helmet, and his weapons, and bade his comrades try the spell. So they tried to bend his lance, but it stood like an iron bar; and Idas in spite hewed at it with his sword, but the blade flew to splinters in his face. Then they hurled their lances at his shield, but the spear-points turned like lead; and Caineus tried to throw him, but he never stirred a foot; and Polydeuces struck him with his fist a blow which would have killed an ox, but Jason only smiled, and the heroes danced about him with delight; and he leapt, and ran, and shouted in the joy of that enormous strength, till the sun rose, and it was time to go and to claim Aeetes' promise.

So he sent up Telamon and Aithalides to tell Aeetes that he was ready for the fight; and they went up among the marble walls, and beneath the roofs of gold, and stood in Aeetes' hall, while he grew pale with rage.

"Fulfil your promise to us, child of the blazing Sun. Give us the serpents' teeth, and let loose the fiery bulls; for we have found a champion among us who can win the golden fleece."

And Aeetes bit his lips, for he fancied that they had fled away by night: but he could not go back from his promise; so he gave them the serpents' teeth.

Then he called for his chariot and his horses, and sent heralds through all the town; and all the people went out with him to the dreadful War-god's field.

And there Aeetes sat upon his throne, with his warriors on each hand, thousands and tens of thousands, clothed from head to foot in steel chain-mail. And the people and the women crowded to every window and bank and wall; while the Minuai stood together, a mere handful in the midst of that great host.

And Chalciope was there and Argus, trembling, and Medea, wrapped closely in her veil; but Aeetes did not know that she was muttering cunning spells between her lips.

Then Jason cried, "Fulfil your promise, and let your fiery bulls come forth."

Then Aeetes bade open the gates, and the magic bulls leapt out. Their brazen hoofs rang upon the ground, and their nostrils sent out sheets of flame, as they rushed with lowered heads upon Jason; but he never flinched a step. The flame of their breath swept round him, but it singed not a hair of his head; and the bulls stopped short and trembled when Medea began her spell.

Then Jason sprang upon the nearest and seized him by the horn; and up and down they wrestled, till the bull fell grovelling on his knees; for the heart of the brute died within him, and his mighty limbs were loosed, beneath the steadfast eye of that dark witch-maiden and the magic whisper of her lips.

So both the bulls were tamed and yoked; and Jason bound them to the plough, and goaded them onward with his lance till he had ploughed the sacred field.

And all the Minuai shouted; but Aeetes bit his lips with rage, for the half of Jason's work was over, and the sun was yet high in heaven.

Then he took the serpents' teeth and sowed them, and waited what would befall. But Medea looked at him and at his helmet, lest he should forget the lesson she had taught.

And every furrow heaved and bubbled, and out of every clod arose a man. Out of the earth they rose by thousands, each clad from head to foot in steel, and drew their swords and rushed on Jason, where he stood in the midst alone.

Then the Minuai grew pale with fear for him; but Aeetes laughed a bitter laugh. "See! If I had not warriors enough already round me, I could call them out of the bosom of the earth."

But Jason snatched off his helmet, and hurled it into the thickest of the throng. And blind madness came upon them, suspicion, hate, and fear; and one cried to his fellow, "Thou didst strike me!" and another, "Thou art Jason; thou shalt die!"

So fury seized those earth-born phantoms, and each turned his hand against the rest; and they fought and were never weary, till they all lay dead upon the ground. Then the magic furrows opened, and the kind earth took them home into her breast and the grass grew up all green again above them, and Jason's work was done.

Then the Minuai rose and shouted, till Prometheus heard them from his crag. And Jason cried, "Lead me to the fleece this moment, before the sun goes down."

But Aeetes thought, "He has conquered the bulls, and sown and reaped the deadly crop. Who is this who is proof against all magic? He may kill the serpent yet."

So he delayed, and sat taking counsel with his princes till the sun went down and all was dark. Then he bade a herald cry, "Every man to his home for tonight. Tomorrow we will meet these heroes, and speak about the golden fleece."

Then he turned and looked at Medea. "This is your doing, false witch-maid! You have helped these yellow-haired strangers, and brought shame upon your father and yourself!"

Medea shrank and trembled, and her face grew pale with fear; and Aeetes knew that she was guilty, and whispered, "If they win the fleece, you die!"

But the Minuai marched toward their ship, growling like lions cheated of their prey; for they saw that Aeetes meant to mock them, and to cheat them out of all their toil. And Oileus said, "Let us go to the grove together, and take the fleece by force."

And Idas the rash cried, "Let us draw lots who shall go in first; for, while the dragon is devouring one, the rest can slay him and carry off the fleece in peace." But Jason held them back, though he praised them; for he hoped for Medea's help.

And after awhile Medea came trembling, and wept a long while before she spoke. And at last –

"My end is come, and I must die; for my father has found out that I have helped you. You he would kill if he dared; but he will not harm you, because you have been his guests. Go then, go, and remember poor Medea when you are far away across the sea."

But all the heroes cried: "If you die, we die with you; for without you we cannot win the fleece, and home we will not go without it, but fall here fighting to the last man."

"You need not die," said Jason. "Flee home with us across the sea. Show us first how to win the fleece; for you can do it. Why else are you the priestess of the grove? Show us but how to win the fleece, and come with us, and you shall be my queen, and rule over the rich princes of the Minuai, in Iolcos by the sea."

And all the heroes pressed round, and vowed to her that she should be their queen.

Medea wept, and shuddered, and hid her face in her hands; for her heart yearned after her sisters and her playfellows, and the home where she was brought up as a child. But at last she looked up at Jason, and spoke between her sobs:

"Must I leave my home and my people, to wander with strangers across the sea? The lot is cast, and I must endure it. I will show you how to win the golden fleece. Bring up your ship to the wood-side, and moor her there against the bank; and let Jason come up at midnight, and one brave comrade with him, and meet me beneath the wall."

Then all the heroes cried together, "I will go!" "and I!" "and I!"

And Idas the rash grew mad with envy; for he longed to be foremost in all things. But Medea calmed them, and said, "Orpheus shall go with Jason, and bring his magic harp; for I hear of him that he is the king of all minstrels, and can charm all things on earth."

And Orpheus laughed for joy, and clapped his hands, because the choice had fallen on him; for in those days poets and singers were as bold warriors as the best.

So at midnight they went up the bank, and found Medea; and beside came Absyrtus her young brother, leading a yearling lamb.

Then Medea brought them to a thicket beside the War-god's gate; and there she bade Jason dig a ditch, and kill the lamb, and leave it there, and strew on it magic herbs and honey from the honeycomb.

Then sprang up through the earth, with the red fire flashing before her, Brimo the wild witch-huntress, while her mad hounds howled around. She had one head like a horse's, and another like a ravening hound's, and another like a hissing snake's, and a sword in either hand. And she leapt into the ditch with her hounds, and they ate and drank their fill, while Jason and Orpheus trembled, and Medea hid her eyes. And at last the witch-queen vanished, and fled with her hounds into the woods; and the bars of the gates fell down, and the brazen doors flew wide, and Medea and the heroes ran forward and hurried through the poison wood, among the dark stems of the mighty beeches, guided by the gleam of the golden fleece, until they saw it hanging on one vast tree in the midst. And Jason would have sprung to seize it; but Medea held him back, and pointed, shuddering, to the tree-foot, where the mighty serpent lay, coiled in and out among the roots, with a body like a mountain pine. His coils stretched many a fathom, spangled with bronze and gold; and half of him they could see, but no more, for the rest lay in the darkness far beyond.

And when he saw them coming he lifted up his head, and watched them with his small bright eyes, and flashed his forked tongue, and roared like the fire among the woodlands, till the forest tossed and groaned. For his cries shook the trees from leaf to root, and swept over the long reaches of the river, and over Aeetes' hall, and woke the sleepers in the city, till mothers clasped their children in their fear.

But Medea called gently to him, and he stretched out his long spotted neck, and licked her hand, and looked up in her face, as if to ask for food. Then she made a sign to Orpheus, and he began his magic song.

And as he sung, the forest grew calm again, and the leaves on every tree hung still; and the serpent's head sank down, and his brazen coils grew limp, and his glittering eyes closed lazily, till he breathed as gently as a child, while Orpheus called to pleasant Slumber, who gives peace to men, and beasts, and waves.

Then Jason leapt forward warily, and stepped across that mighty snake, and tore the fleece from off the tree-trunk; and the four rushed down the garden, to the bank where the *Argo* lay.

There was a silence for a moment, while Jason held the golden fleece on high. Then he cried, "Go now, good *Argo*, swift and steady, if ever you would see Pelion more."

And she went, as the heroes drove her, grim and silent all, with muffled oars, till the pine-wood bent like willow in their hands, and stout *Argo* groaned beneath their strokes.

On and on, beneath the dewy darkness, they fled swiftly down the swirling stream; underneath black walls, and temples, and the castles of the princes of the East; past sluice-mouths, and fragrant gardens, and groves of all strange fruits; past marshes where fat kine lay sleeping, and long beds of whispering reeds; till they heard the merry music of the surge upon the bar, as it tumbled in the moonlight all alone.

Into the surge they rushed, and *Argo* leapt the breakers like a horse; for she knew the time was come to show her mettle, and win honour for the heroes and herself.

Into the surge they rushed, and *Argo* leapt the breakers like a horse, till the heroes stopped all panting, each man upon his oar, as she slid into the still broad sea.

Then Orpheus took his harp and sang a paean, till the heroes' hearts rose high again; and they rowed on stoutly and steadfastly, away into the darkness of the West.

How the Argonauts Were Driven into the Unknown Sea

SO THEY FLED AWAY in haste to the westward; but Aeetes manned his fleet and followed them. And Lynceus the quick-eyed saw him coming, while he was still many a mile away, and cried, "I see a hundred ships, like a flock of white swans, far in the east." And at that they rowed hard, like heroes; but the ships came nearer every hour.

Then Medea, the dark witch-maiden, laid a cruel and a cunning plot; for she killed Absyrtus her young brother, and cast him into the sea, and said, "Ere my father can take up his corpse and bury it, he must wait long, and be left far behind."

And all the heroes shuddered, and looked one at the other for shame; yet they did not punish that dark witch-woman, because she had won for them the golden fleece.

And when Aeetes came to the place he saw the floating corpse; and he stopped a long while, and bewailed his son, and took him up, and went home. But he sent on his sailors toward the westward, and bound them by a mighty curse: "Bring back to me that dark witch-woman, that she may die a dreadful death. But if you return without her, you shall die by the same death yourselves."

So the Argonauts escaped for that time: but Father Zeus saw that foul crime; and out of the heavens he sent a storm, and swept the ship far from her course. Day after day the storm drove her, amid foam and blinding mist, till they knew no longer where they were, for the sun was blotted from the skies. And at last the ship struck on a shoal, amid low isles of mud and sand, and the waves rolled over her and through her, and the heroes lost all hope of life.

Then Jason cried to Hera, "Fair queen, who hast befriended us till now, why hast thou left us in our misery, to die here among unknown seas? It is hard to lose the honour which we have won with such toil and danger, and hard never to see Hellas again, and the pleasant bay of Pagasai."

Then out and spoke the magic bough which stood upon the *Argo's* beak, "Because Father Zeus is angry, all this has fallen on you; for a cruel crime has been done on board, and the sacred ship is foul with blood."

At that some of the heroes cried, "Medea is the murderess. Let the witch-woman bear her sin, and die!" And they seized Medea, to hurl her into the sea, and atone for the young boy's death; but the magic bough spoke again, "Let her live till her crimes are full. Vengeance waits for her, slow and sure; but she must live, for you need her still. She must show you the way to her sister Circe, who lives among the islands of the West. To her you must sail, a weary way, and she shall cleanse you from your guilt."

Then all the heroes wept aloud when they heard the sentence of the oak; for they knew that a dark journey lay before them, and years of bitter toil. And some upbraided the dark witch-woman, and some said, "Nay, we are her debtors still; without her we should never have won the fleece." But most of them bit their lips in silence, for they feared the witch's spells.

And now the sea grew calmer, and the sun shone out once more, and the heroes thrust the ship off the sand-bank, and rowed forward on their weary course under the guiding of the dark witch-maiden, into the wastes of the unknown sea.

Whither they went I cannot tell, nor how they came to Circe's isle. Some say that they went to the westward, and up the Ister stream, and so came into the Adriatic, dragging their ship over the snowy Alps. And others say that they went southward, into the Red Indian Sea, and past the sunny lands where spices grow, round Aethiopia toward the West; and that at last they came to Libya, and dragged their ship across the burning sands, and over the hills into the Syrtes, where the flats and quicksands spread for many a mile, between rich Cyrene and the Lotus-eaters' shore. But all these are but dreams and fables, and dim hints of unknown lands.

But all say that they came to a place where they had to drag their ship across the land nine days with ropes and rollers, till they came into an unknown sea. And the best of all the old songs tells us how they went away toward the North, till they came to the slope of Caucasus, where it sinks into the sea; and to the narrow Cimmerian Bosphorus, where the Titan swam across upon the bull; and thence into the lazy waters of the still Maeotid lake. And thence they went northward ever, up the Tanais, which we call Don, past the Geloni and Sauromatai, and many a wandering shepherd-tribe, and the one-eyed Arimaspi, of whom old Greek poets tell, who steal the gold from the Griffins, in the cold Riphaian hills.

And they passed the Scythian archers, and the Tauri who eat men, and the wandering Hyperboreai, who feed their flocks beneath the pole-star, until they came into the northern ocean, the dull dead Cronian Sea. And there *Argo* would move on no longer; and each man clasped his elbow, and leaned his head upon his hand, heart-broken with toil and hunger, and gave himself up to death. But brave Ancaios the helmsman cheered up their hearts once more, and bade them leap on land, and haul the ship with ropes and rollers for many a weary day, whether over land, or mud, or ice, I know not, for the song is mixed and broken like a dream. And it says next, how they came to the rich nation of the famous long-lived men; and to the coast of the Cimmerians, who never saw the sun, buried deep in the glens of the snow mountains; and to the fair land of Hermione, where dwelt the most righteous of all nations; and to the gates of the world below, and to the dwelling-place of dreams.

And at last Ancaios shouted, "Endure a little while, brave friends, the worst is surely past; for I can see the pure west wind ruffle the water, and hear the roar of ocean on the sands. So raise up the mast, and set the sail, and face what comes like men."

Then out spoke the magic bough, "Ah, would that I had perished long ago, and been whelmed by the dread blue rocks, beneath the fierce swell of the Euxine! Better so, than to wander for ever, disgraced by the guilt of my princes; for the blood of Absyrtus still tracks me, and woe follows hard upon woe. And now some dark horror will clutch me, if I come near the Isle of Ierne. Unless you will cling to the land, and sail southward and southward for ever, I shall wander beyond the Atlantic, to the ocean which has no shore."

Then they blest the magic bough, and sailed southward along the land. But ere they could pass Ierne, the land of mists and storms, the wild wind came down, dark and roaring, and caught the sail, and strained the ropes. And away they drove twelve nights, on the wide wild western sea, through the foam, and over the rollers, while they saw neither sun nor stars. And they cried again, "We shall perish, for we know not where we are. We are lost in the dreary damp darkness, and cannot tell north from south."

But Lynceus the long-sighted called gaily from the bows, "Take heart again, brave sailors; for I see a pine-clad isle, and the halls of the kind Earth-mother, with a crown of clouds around them."

But Orpheus said, "Turn from them, for no living man can land there: there is no harbour on the coast, but steep-walled cliffs all round."

So Ancaios turned the ship away; and for three days more they sailed on, till they came to Aiaia, Circe's home, and the fairy island of the West.

And there Jason bid them land, and seek about for any sign of living man. And as they went inland Circe met them, coming down toward the ship; and they trembled when they saw her, for her hair, and face, and robes shone like flame.

And she came and looked at Medea; and Medea hid her face beneath her veil.

And Circe cried, "Ah, wretched girl, have you forgotten all your sins, that you come hither to my island, where the flowers bloom all the year round? Where is your aged father, and the brother whom you killed? Little do I expect you to return in safety with these strangers whom you love. I will send you food and wine: but your ship must not stay here, for it is foul with sin, and foul with sin its crew."

And the heroes prayed her, but in vain, and cried, "Cleanse us from our guilt!" But she sent them away, and said, "Go on to Malea, and there you may be cleansed, and return home."

Then a fair wind rose, and they sailed eastward by Tartessus on the Iberian shore, till they came to the Pillars of Hercules, and the Mediterranean Sea. And thence they sailed on through the deeps of Sardinia, and past the Ausonian islands, and the capes of the Tyrrhenian shore, till they came to a flowery island, upon a still bright summer's eve. And as they neared it, slowly and wearily, they heard sweet songs upon the shore. But when Medea heard it, she started, and cried, "Beware, all heroes, for these are the rocks of the Sirens. You must pass close by them, for there is no other channel; but those who listen to that song are lost."

Then Orpheus spoke, the king of all minstrels, "Let them match their song against mine. I have charmed stones, and trees, and dragons, how much more the hearts of men!" So he caught up his lyre, and stood upon the poop, and began his magic song.

And now they could see the Sirens on Anthemousa, the flowery isle; three fair maidens sitting on the beach, beneath a red rock in the setting sun, among beds of crimson poppies and golden asphodel. Slowly they sung and sleepily, with silver voices, mild and clear, which stole over the golden waters, and into the hearts of all the heroes, in spite of Orpheus' song.

And all things stayed around and listened; the gulls sat in white lines along the rocks; on the beach great seals lay basking, and kept time with lazy heads; while silver shoals of fish came up to hearken, and whispered as they broke the shining calm. The Wind overhead hushed his whistling, as he shepherded his clouds toward the west; and the clouds stood in mid blue, and listened dreaming, like a flock of golden sheep.

And as the heroes listened, the oars fell from their hands, and their heads drooped on their breasts, and they closed their heavy eyes; and they dreamed of bright still gardens, and of slumbers under murmuring pines, till all their toil seemed foolishness, and they thought of their renown no more.

Then one lifted his head suddenly, and cried, "What use in wandering for ever? Let us stay here and rest awhile." And another, "Let us row to the shore, and hear the words they sing." And another, "I care not for the words, but for the music. They shall sing me to sleep, that I may rest."

And Butes, the son of Pandion, the fairest of all mortal men, leapt out and swam toward the shore, crying, "I come, I come, fair maidens, to live and die here, listening to your song."

Then Medea clapped her hands together, and cried, "Sing louder, Orpheus, sing a bolder strain; wake up these hapless sluggards, or none of them will see the land of Hellas more."

Then Orpheus lifted his harp, and crashed his cunning hand across the strings; and his music and his voice rose like a trumpet through the still evening air; into the air it rushed like thunder, till the rocks rang and the sea; and into their souls it rushed like wine, till all hearts beat fast within their breasts.

And he sung the song of Perseus, how the Gods led him over land and sea, and how he slew the loathly Gorgon, and won himself a peerless bride; and how he sits now with the Gods upon Olympus, a shining star in the sky, immortal with his immortal bride, and honoured by all men below.

So Orpheus sang, and the Sirens, answering each other across the golden sea, till Orpheus' voice drowned the Sirens', and the heroes caught their oars again.

And they cried, "We will be men like Perseus, and we will dare and suffer to the last. Sing us his song again, brave Orpheus, that we may forget the Sirens and their spell."

And as Orpheus sang, they dashed their oars into the sea, and kept time to his music, as they fled fast away; and the Sirens' voices died behind them, in the hissing of the foam along their wake.

But Butes swam to the shore, and knelt down before the Sirens, and cried, "Sing on! Sing on!"

But he could say no more, for a charmed sleep came over him, and a pleasant humming in his ears; and he sank all along upon the pebbles, and forgot all heaven and earth, and never looked at that sad beach around him, all strewn with the bones of men.

Then slowly rose up those three fair sisters, with a cruel smile upon their lips; and slowly they crept down towards him, like leopards who creep upon their prey; and their hands were like the talons of eagles as they stepped across the bones of their victims to enjoy their cruel feast.

But fairest Aphrodite saw him from the highest Idalian peak, and she pitied his youth and his beauty, and leapt up from her golden throne; and like a falling star she cleft the sky, and left a trail of glittering light, till she stooped to the Isle of the Sirens, and snatched their prey from their claws. And she lifted Butes as he lay sleeping, and wrapped him in golden mist; and she bore him to the peak of Lilybaeum, and he slept there many a pleasant year.

But when the Sirens saw that they were conquered, they shrieked for envy and rage, and leapt from the beach into the sea, and were changed into rocks until this day.

Then they came to the straits by Lilybaeum, and saw Sicily, the three-cornered island, under which Enceladus the giant lies groaning day and night, and when he turns the earth quakes, and his breath bursts out in roaring flames from the highest cone of Etna, above the chestnut woods. And there Charybdis caught them in its fearful coils of wave, and rolled mast-high about them, and spun them round and round; and they could go neither back nor forward, while the whirlpool sucked them in.

And while they struggled they saw near them, on the other side the strait, a rock stand in the water, with its peak wrapped round in clouds – a rock which no man could climb, though he had twenty hands and feet, for the stone was smooth and slippery, as if polished by man's hand; and halfway up a misty cave looked out toward the west.

And when Orpheus saw it he groaned, and struck his hands together. And "Little will it help us," he cried, "to escape the jaws of the whirlpool; for in that cave lives Scylla, the sea-hag with a young whelp's voice; my mother warned me of her ere we sailed away from Hellas; she has six heads, and six long necks, and hides in that dark cleft. And from her cave she fishes for all things which pass by – for sharks, and seals, and dolphins, and all the herds of Amphitrite. And never ship's crew boasted that they came safe by her rock, for she bends her long necks down to them, and every mouth takes up a man. And who will help us now? For Hera and Zeus hate us, and our ship is foul with guilt; so we must die, whatever befalls."

Then out of the depths came Thetis, Peleus' silver-footed bride, for love of her gallant husband, and all her nymphs around her; and they played like snow-white dolphins, diving on from wave to wave, before the ship, and in her wake, and beside her, as dolphins play. And they caught the ship, and guided her, and passed her on from hand to hand, and tossed her through the billows, as maidens toss the ball. And when Scylla stooped to seize her, they struck back her ravening heads, and foul Scylla whined, as a whelp whines, at the touch of their gentle hands. But she shrank into her cave affrighted – for all bad things shrink from good – and *Argo* leapt safe past her, while a fair breeze rose behind. Then Thetis and her nymphs sank down to their coral caves beneath the sea, and their gardens of green and purple, where live flowers bloom all the year round; while the heroes went on rejoicing, yet dreading what might come next.

After that they rowed on steadily for many a weary day, till they saw a long high island, and beyond it a mountain land. And they searched till they found a harbour, and there rowed boldly in. But after awhile they stopped, and wondered, for there stood a great city on the shore, and temples and walls and gardens, and castles high in air upon the cliffs. And on either side they saw a harbour, with a narrow mouth, but wide within; and black ships without number, high and dry upon the shore.

Then Ancaios, the wise helmsman, spoke, "What new wonder is this? I know all isles, and harbours, and the windings of all seas; and this should be Corcyra, where a few wild goat-herds dwell. But whence come these new harbours and vast works of polished stone?"

But Jason said, "They can be no savage people. We will go in and take our chance."

So they rowed into the harbour, among a thousand black-beaked ships, each larger far than *Argo*, toward a quay of polished stone. And they wondered at that mighty city, with its roofs of burnished brass, and long and lofty walls of marble, with strong palisades above. And the quays were full of people, merchants, and mariners, and slaves, going to and fro with merchandise among the crowd of ships. And the heroes' hearts were humbled, and they looked at each other and said, "We thought ourselves a gallant crew when we sailed from Iolcos by the sea; but how small we look before this city, like an ant before a hive of bees."

Then the sailors hailed them roughly from the quay, "What men are you? – We want no strangers here, nor pirates. We keep our business to ourselves."

But Jason answered gently, with many a flattering word, and praised their city and their harbour, and their fleet of gallant ships. "Surely you are the children of Poseidon, and the masters of the sea; and we are but poor wandering mariners, worn out with thirst and toil. Give us but food and water, and we will go on our voyage in peace."

Then the sailors laughed, and answered, "Stranger, you are no fool; you talk like an honest man, and you shall find us honest too. We are the children of Poseidon, and the masters of the sea; but come ashore to us, and you shall have the best that we can give."

So they limped ashore, all stiff and weary, with long ragged beards and sunburnt cheeks, and garments torn and weather-stained, and weapons rusted with the spray, while the sailors laughed at them (for they were rough-tongued, though their hearts were frank and kind). And one said, "These fellows are but raw sailors; they look as if they had been sea-sick all the day." And another, "Their legs have grown crooked with much rowing, till they waddle in their walk like ducks."

At that Idas the rash would have struck them; but Jason held him back, till one of the merchant kings spoke to them, a tall and stately man.

"Do not be angry, strangers; the sailor boys must have their jest. But we will treat you justly and kindly, for strangers and poor men come from God; and you seem no common sailors by your strength, and height, and weapons. Come up with me to the palace of Alcinous, the rich sea-going king, and we will feast you well and heartily; and after that you shall tell us your name."

But Medea hung back, and trembled, and whispered in Jason's ear, "We are betrayed, and are going to our ruin, for I see my countrymen among the crowd; dark-eyed Colchi in steel mail-shirts, such as they wear in my father's land."

"It is too late to turn," said Jason. And he spoke to the merchant king, "What country is this, good sir; and what is this new-built town?"

'This is the land of the Phaeaces, beloved by all the Immortals; for they come hither and feast like friends with us, and sit by our side in the hall. Hither we came from Liburnia to escape the unrighteous Cyclopes; for they robbed us, peaceful merchants, of our hard-earned wares and wealth. So Nausithous, the son of Poseidon, brought us hither, and died in peace; and now his son Alcinous rules us, and Arete the wisest of queens."

So they went up across the square, and wondered still more as they went; for along the quays lay in order great cables, and yards, and masts, before the fair temple of Poseidon, the blue-haired king of the seas. And round the square worked the ship-wrights, as many in number as ants, twining ropes, and hewing timber, and smoothing long yards and oars. And the Minuai went on in silence through clean white marble streets, till they came to the hall of Alcinous, and they wondered then still more. For the lofty palace shone aloft in the sun, with walls of plated brass, from the threshold to the innermost chamber, and the doors were of silver and gold. And on each side of the doorway sat living dogs of gold, who never grew old or died, so well Hephaestus had made them in his forges in smoking Lemnos, and gave them to Alcinous to guard his gates by night. And within, against the walls, stood thrones on either side, down the whole length of the hall, strewn with rich glossy shawls; and on them the merchant kings of those crafty sea-roving Phaeaces sat eating and drinking in pride, and feasting there all the year round. And boys of molten gold stood each on a polished altar, and held torches in their hands, to give light all night to the guests. And round the house sat fifty maid-servants, some grinding the meal in the mill, some turning the spindle, some weaving at the loom, while their hands twinkled as they passed the shuttle, like quivering aspen leaves.

And outside before the palace a great garden was walled round, filled full of stately fruit-trees, grey olives and sweet figs, and pomegranates, pears, and apples, which bore the whole year round. For the rich south-west wind fed them, till pear grew ripe on pear, fig on fig, and grape on grape, all the winter and the spring. And at the farther end gay flower-beds bloomed through all seasons of the year; and two fair fountains rose, and ran, one through the garden grounds, and one beneath the palace gate, to water all the town. Such noble gifts the heavens had given to Alcinous the wise.

So they went in, and saw him sitting, like Poseidon, on his throne, with his golden sceptre by him, in garments stiff with gold, and in his hand a sculptured goblet, as he pledged the merchant kings; and beside him stood Arete, his wise and lovely queen, and leaned against a pillar as she spun her golden threads.

Then Alcinous rose, and welcomed them, and bade them sit and eat; and the servants brought them tables, and bread, and meat, and wine.

But Medea went on trembling toward Arete the fair queen, and fell at her knees, and clasped them, and cried, weeping, as she knelt:

"I am your guest, fair queen, and I entreat you by Zeus, from whom prayers come. Do not send me back to my father to die some dreadful death; but let me go my way, and bear my burden. Have I not had enough of punishment and shame?"

"Who are you, strange maiden? And what is the meaning of your prayer?"

"I am Medea, daughter of Aeetes, and I saw my countrymen here today; and I know that they are come to find me, and take me home to die some dreadful death."

Then Arete frowned, and said, "Lead this girl in, my maidens; and let the kings decide, not I."

And Alcinous leapt up from his throne, and cried, "Speak, strangers, who are you? And who is this maiden?"

"We are the heroes of the Minuai," said Jason; "and this maiden has spoken truth. We are the men who took the golden fleece, the men whose fame has run round every shore. We came hither out of the ocean, after sorrows such as man never saw before. We went out many, and come back few, for many a noble comrade have we lost. So let us go, as you should let your guests go, in peace; that the world may say, 'Alcinous is a just king.'"

But Alcinous frowned, and stood deep in thought; and at last he spoke:

"Had not the deed been done which is done, I should have said this day to myself, 'It is an honour to Alcinous, and to his children after him, that the far-famed Argonauts are his guests.' But these Colchi are my guests, as you are; and for this month they have waited here with all their fleet, for they have hunted all the seas of Hellas, and could not find you, and dared neither go farther, nor go home."

"Let them choose out their champions, and we will fight them, man for man."

"No guests of ours shall fight upon our island, and if you go outside they will outnumber you. I will do justice between you, for I know and do what is right."

Then he turned to his kings, and said, "This may stand over till tomorrow. Tonight we will feast our guests, and hear the story of all their wanderings, and how they came hither out of the ocean."

So Alcinous bade the servants take the heroes in, and bathe them, and give them clothes. And they were glad when they saw the warm water, for it was long since they had bathed. And they washed off the sea-salt from their limbs, and anointed themselves from head to foot with oil, and combed out their golden hair. Then they came back again into the hall, while the merchant kings rose up to do them honour. And each man said to his neighbour, "No wonder that these men won fame. How they stand now like Giants, or Titans, or Immortals come down from Olympus, though many a winter has worn them, and many a fearful storm. What must they have been when they sailed from Iolcos, in the bloom of their youth, long ago?"

Then they went out to the garden; and the merchant princes said, "Heroes, run races with us. Let us see whose feet are nimblest."

"We cannot race against you, for our limbs are stiff from sea; and we have lost our two swift comrades, the sons of the north wind. But do not think us cowards: if you wish to try our strength, we will shoot, and box, and wrestle, against any men on earth."

And Alcinous smiled, and answered, "I believe you, gallant guests; with your long limbs and broad shoulders, we could never match you here. For we care nothing here for boxing, or for shooting with the bow; but for feasts, and songs, and harping, and dancing, and running races, to stretch our limbs on shore."

So they danced there and ran races, the jolly merchant kings, till the night fell, and all went in.

And then they ate and drank, and comforted their weary souls, till Alcinous called a herald, and bade him go and fetch the harper.

The herald went out, and fetched the harper, and led him in by the hand; and Alcinous cut him a piece of meat, from the fattest of the haunch, and sent it to him, and said, "Sing to us, noble harper, and rejoice the heroes' hearts."

So the harper played and sang, while the dancers danced strange figures; and after that the tumblers showed their tricks, till the heroes laughed again.

Then, "Tell me, heroes," asked Alcinous, "you who have sailed the ocean round, and seen the manners of all nations, have you seen such dancers as ours here, or heard such music and such singing? We hold ours to be the best on earth."

"Such dancing we have never seen," said Orpheus; "and your singer is a happy man, for Phoebus himself must have taught him, or else he is the son of a Muse, as I am also, and have sung once or twice, though not so well as he."

"Sing to us, then, noble stranger," said Alcinous; "and we will give you precious gifts."

So Orpheus took his magic harp, and sang to them a stirring song of their voyage from Iolcos, and their dangers, and how they won the golden fleece; and of Medea's love, and how she helped them, and went with them over land and sea; and of all their fearful dangers, from monsters, and rocks, and storms, till the heart of Arete was softened, and all the women wept. And the merchant kings rose up, each man from off his golden throne, and clapped their hands, and shouted, "Hail to the noble Argonauts, who sailed the unknown sea!"

Then he went on, and told their journey over the sluggish northern main, and through the shoreless outer ocean, to the fairy island of the west; and of the Sirens, and Scylla, and Charybdis, and all the wonders they had seen, till midnight passed and the day dawned; but the kings never thought of sleep. Each man sat still and listened, with his chin upon his hand.

And at last, when Orpheus had ended, they all went thoughtful out, and the heroes lay down to sleep, beneath the sounding porch outside, where Arete had strewn them rugs and carpets, in the sweet still summer night.

But Arete pleaded hard with her husband for Medea, for her heart was softened. And she said, "The Gods will punish her, not we. After all, she is our guest and my suppliant, and prayers are the daughters of Zeus. And who, too, dare part man and wife, after all they have endured together?"

And Alcinous smiled. "The minstrel's song has charmed you: but I must remember what is right, for songs cannot alter justice; and I must be faithful to my name. Alcinous I am called, the man of sturdy sense; and Alcinous I will be." But for all that Arete besought him, until she won him round.

So next morning he sent a herald, and called the kings into the square, and said, "This is a puzzling matter: remember but one thing. These Minuai live close by us, and we may meet them often on the seas; but Aeetes lives afar off, and we have only heard his name. Which, then, of the two is it safer to offend – the men near us, or the men far off?"

The princes laughed, and praised his wisdom; and Alcinous called the heroes to the square, and the Colchi also; and they came and stood opposite each other, but Medea stayed in the palace. Then Alcinous spoke, "Heroes of the Colchi, what is your errand about this lady?"

"To carry her home with us, that she may die a shameful death; but if we return without her, we must die the death she should have died."

"What say you to this, Jason the Aeolid?" said Alcinous, turning to the Minuai.

"I say," said the cunning Jason, "that they are come here on a bootless errand. Do you think that you can make her follow you, heroes of the Colchi – her, who knows all spells and charms? She will cast away your ships on quicksands, or call down on you Brimo the wild huntress; or the chains will fall from off her wrists, and she will escape in her dragon-car; or if not thus, some other way, for she has a thousand plans and wiles. And why return home at all, brave heroes, and face the long seas again, and the Bosphorus, and the stormy Euxine, and double all your toil? There is many a fair land round these coasts, which waits for gallant men like you. Better to settle there, and build a city, and let Aeetes and Colchis help themselves."

Then a murmur rose among the Colchi, and some cried "He has spoken well;" and some, "We have had enough of roving, we will sail the seas no more!" And the chief said at last, "Be it so, then; a plague she has been to us, and a plague to the house of her father, and a plague she will be to you. Take her, since you are no wiser; and we will sail away toward the north."

Then Alcinous gave them food, and water, and garments, and rich presents of all sorts; and he gave the same to the Minuai, and sent them all away in peace.

So Jason kept the dark witch-maiden to breed him woe and shame; and the Colchi went northward into the Adriatic, and settled, and built towns along the shore.

Then the heroes rowed away to the eastward, to reach Hellas, their beloved land; but a storm came down upon them, and swept them far away toward the south. And they rowed till they were spent with struggling, through the darkness and the blinding rain; but where they were they could not tell, and they gave up all hope of life. And at last touched the ground, and when daylight came waded to the shore; and saw nothing round but sand and desolate salt pools, for they had come to the quicksands of the Syrtis, and the dreary treeless flats which lie between Numidia and Cyrene, on the burning shore of Africa. And there they wandered starving for many a weary day, ere they could launch their ship again, and gain the open sea. And there Canthus was killed, while he was trying to drive off sheep, by a stone which a herdsman threw.

And there too Mopsus died, the seer who knew the voices of all birds; but he could not foretell his own end, for he was bitten in the foot by a snake, one of those which sprang from the Gorgon's head when Perseus carried it across the sands.

At last they rowed away toward the northward, for many a weary day, till their water was spent, and their food eaten; and they were worn out with hunger and thirst. But at last they saw a long steep island, and a blue peak high among the clouds; and they knew it for the peak of Ida, and the famous land of Crete. And they said, "We will land in Crete, and see Minos the just king, and all his glory and his wealth; at least he will treat us hospitably, and let us fill our water-casks upon the shore."

But when they came nearer to the island they saw a wondrous sight upon the cliffs. For on a cape to the westward stood a giant, taller than any mountain pine, who glittered aloft against the sky like a tower of burnished brass. He turned and looked on all sides round him, till he saw the *Argo* and her crew; and when he saw them he came toward them, more swiftly than the swiftest horse, leaping across the glens at a bound, and striding at one step from down to down. And when he came abreast of them he brandished his arms up and down, as a ship hoists and lowers her yards, and shouted with his brazen throat like a trumpet from off the hills, "You are pirates, you are robbers! If you dare land here, you die."

Then the heroes cried, "We are no pirates. We are all good men and true, and all we ask is food and water;" but the giant cried the more:

"You are robbers, you are pirates all; I know you; and if you land, you shall die the death."

Then he waved his arms again as a signal, and they saw the people flying inland, driving their flocks before them, while a great flame arose among the hills. Then the giant ran up a valley and vanished, and the heroes lay on their oars in fear.

But Medea stood watching all from under her steep black brows, with a cunning smile upon her lips, and a cunning plot within her heart. At last she spoke, "I know this giant. I heard of him in the East. Hephaestus the Fire King made him in his forge in Etna beneath the earth, and called him Talus, and gave him to Minos for a servant, to guard the coast of Crete. Thrice a day he walks round the island, and never stops to sleep; and if strangers land he leaps into his furnace, which flames there among the hills; and when he is red-hot he rushes on them, and burns them in his brazen hands."

Then all the heroes cried, "What shall we do, wise Medea? We must have water, or we die of thirst. Flesh and blood we can face fairly; but who can face this red-hot brass?"

"I can face red-hot brass, if the tale I hear be true. For they say that he has but one vein in all his body, filled with liquid fire; and that this vein is closed with a nail: but I know not where that nail is placed. But if I can get it once into these hands, you shall water your ship here in peace."

Then she bade them put her on shore, and row off again, and wait what would befall.

And the heroes obeyed her unwillingly, for they were ashamed to leave her so alone; but Jason said, "She is dearer to me than to any of you, yet I will trust her freely on shore; she has more plots than we can dream of in the windings of that fair and cunning head."

So they left the witch-maiden on the shore; and she stood there in her beauty all alone, till the giant strode back red-hot from head to heel, while the grass hissed and smoked beneath his tread.

And when he saw the maiden alone, he stopped; and she looked boldly up into his face without moving, and began her magic song:

"Life is short, though life is sweet; and even men of brass and fire must die. The brass must rust, the fire must cool, for time gnaws all things in their turn. Life is short, though life is sweet: but sweeter to live for ever; sweeter to live ever youthful like the Gods, who have ichor in their veins – ichor which gives life, and youth, and joy, and a bounding heart."

Then Talus said, "Who are you, strange maiden, and where is this ichor of youth?"

Then Medea held up a flask of crystal, and said, "Here is the ichor of youth. I am Medea the enchantress; my sister Circe gave me this, and said, 'Go and reward Talus, the faithful servant, for his fame is gone out into all lands.' So come, and I will pour this into your veins, that you may live for ever young."

And he listened to her false words, that simple Talus, and came near; and Medea said, "Dip yourself in the sea first, and cool yourself, lest you burn my tender hands; then show me where the nail in your vein is, that I may pour the ichor in."

Then that simple Talus dipped himself in the sea, till it hissed, and roared, and smoked; and came and knelt before Medea, and showed her the secret nail.

And she drew the nail out gently, but she poured no ichor in; and instead the liquid fire spouted forth, like a stream of red-hot iron. And Talus tried to leap up, crying, "You have betrayed me, false witch-maiden!" But she lifted up her hands before him, and sang, till he sank beneath her spell. And as he sank, his brazen limbs clanked heavily, and the earth groaned beneath his weight; and the liquid fire ran from his heel, like a stream of lava, to the sea; and Medea laughed, and called to the heroes, "Come ashore, and water your ship in peace."

So they came, and found the giant lying dead; and they fell down, and kissed Medea's feet; and watered their ship, and took sheep and oxen, and so left that inhospitable shore.

At last, after many more adventures, they came to the Cape of Malea, at the south-west point of the Peloponnese. And there they offered sacrifices, and Orpheus purged them from their guilt. Then they rode away again to the northward, past the Laconian shore, and came all worn and tired by Sunium, and up the long Euboean Strait, until they saw once more Pelion, and Aphetai, and Iolcos by the sea.

And they ran the ship ashore; but they had no strength left to haul her up the beach; and they crawled out on the pebbles, and sat down, and wept till they could weep no more. For the houses and the trees were all altered; and all the faces which they saw were strange; and their joy was swallowed up in sorrow, while they thought of their youth, and all their labour, and the gallant comrades they had lost.

And the people crowded round, and asked them "Who are you, that you sit weeping here?"

"We are the sons of your princes, who sailed out many a year ago. We went to fetch the golden fleece, and we have brought it, and grief therewith. Give us news of our fathers and our mothers, if any of them be left alive on earth."

Then there was shouting, and laughing, and weeping; and all the kings came to the shore, and they led away the heroes to their homes, and bewailed the valiant dead.

Then Jason went up with Medea to the palace of his uncle Pelias. And when he came in Pelias sat by the hearth, crippled and blind with age; while opposite him sat Aeson, Jason's father, crippled and blind likewise; and the two old men's heads shook together as they tried to warm themselves before the fire.

And Jason fell down at his father's knees, and wept, and called him by his name. And the old man stretched his hands out, and felt him, and said, "Do not mock me, young hero. My son Jason is dead long ago at sea."

"I am your own son Jason, whom you trusted to the Centaur upon Pelion; and I have brought home the golden fleece, and a princess of the Sun's race for my bride. So now give me up the kingdom, Pelias my uncle, and fulfil your promise as I have fulfilled mine."

Then his father clung to him like a child, and wept, and would not let him go; and cried, "Now I shall not go down lonely to my grave. Promise me never to leave me till I die."

Cadmus

THE FOLLOWING is the legendary account of the founding of Thebes. After the abduction of his daughter Europa by Zeus, Agenor, king of Phoenicia, unable to reconcile himself to her loss, dispatched his son Cadmus in search of her, desiring him not to return without his sister.

For many years Cadmus pursued his search through various countries, but without success. Not daring to return home without her, he consulted the oracle of Apollo at Delphi; and the reply was that he must desist from his task, and take upon himself a new duty, i.e. that of founding a city, the site of which would be indicated to him by a heifer which had never borne the yoke, and which would lie down on the spot whereon the city was to be built.

Scarcely had Cadmus left the sacred fane, when he observed a heifer who bore no marks of servitude on her neck, walking slowly in front of him. He followed the animal for a considerable distance, until at length, on the site where Thebes afterwards stood, she looked towards heaven and, gently lowing, lay down in the long grass. Grateful for this mark of divine favour, Cadmus resolved to offer up the animal as a sacrifice, and accordingly sent his followers to fetch water for the libation from a neighbouring spring. This spring, which was sacred to Ares, was situated in a wood, and guarded by a fierce dragon, who, at the approach of the retainers of Cadmus, suddenly pounced upon them and killed them.

After waiting some time for the return of his servants Cadmus grew impatient, and hastily arming himself with his lance and spear, set out to seek them. On reaching the spot, the mangled remains of his unfortunate followers met his view, and near them he beheld the frightful monster, dripping with the blood of his victims. Seizing a huge rock, the hero hurled it with all his might upon the dragon; but protected by his tough black skin and steely scales as by a coat of mail, he remained unhurt. Cadmus now tried his lance, and with more success, for it pierced the side of the beast, who, furious with pain, sprang at his adversary, when Cadmus, leaping aside, succeeded in fixing the point of his spear within his jaws, which final stroke put an end to the encounter.

While Cadmus stood surveying his vanquished foe Pallas-Athene appeared to him, and commanded him to sow the teeth of the dead dragon in the ground. He obeyed; and out of the furrows there arose a band of armed men, who at once commenced to fight with each other, until all except five were killed. These last surviving warriors made peace with each other, and it was with their assistance that Cadmus now built the famous city of Thebes. In later times the noblest Theban families proudly claimed their descent from these mighty earth-born warriors.

Ares was furious with rage when he discovered that Cadmus had slain his dragon, and would have killed him had not Zeus interfered, and induced him to mitigate his punishment to that of servitude for the term of eight years. At the end of that time the god of war became reconciled to Cadmus, and, in token of his forgiveness, bestowed upon him the hand of his daughter Harmonia in marriage. Their nuptials were almost as celebrated as those of Peleus and Thetis. All the gods honoured them with their presence, and offered rich gifts and congratulations. Cadmus himself presented his lovely bride with a splendid necklace fashioned by Hephaestus, which, however, after the death of Harmonia, always proved fatal to its possessor.

The children of Cadmus and Harmonia were one son, Polydorus, and four daughters, Autonoe, Ino, Semele, and Agave. For many years the founder of Thebes reigned happily, but at length a conspiracy was formed against him, and he was deprived of his throne by his grandson Pentheus. Accompanied by his faithful wife Harmonia, he retired into Illyria, and after death they were both changed by Zeus into serpents, and transferred to Elysium.

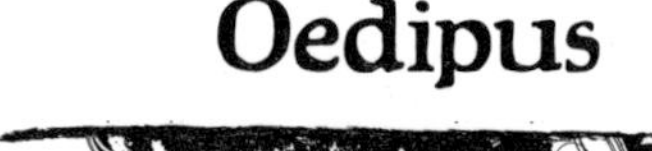

Oedipus

LAIUS AND JOCASTA, King and Queen of Thebes, in Boeotia, were greatly delighted at the birth of a little son. In their joy they sent for the priests of Apollo, and bade them foretell the glorious deeds their heir would perform; but all their joy was turned to grief when told that the child was destined to kill his father, marry his mother, and bring great misfortunes upon his native city.

To prevent the fulfillment of this dreadful prophecy, Laius bade a servant carry the new-born child out of the city, and end its feeble little life. The king's mandate was obeyed only in part; for the servant, instead of killing the child, hung it up by its ankles to a tree in a remote place, and left it there to perish from hunger and exposure if it were spared by the wild beasts.

When he returned, none questioned how he had performed the appointed task, but all sighed with relief to think that the prophecy could never be accomplished. The child, however, was not dead, as all supposed. A shepherd in quest of a stray lamb had heard his cries, delivered him from his painful position, and carried him to Polybus, King of Corinth, who, lacking an heir of his own, gladly adopted the little stranger. The Queen of Corinth and her handmaidens hastened with tender concern to bathe the swollen ankles, and called the babe Oedipus (swollen-footed).

Years passed by. The young prince grew up in total ignorance of the unfortunate circumstances under which he had made his first appearance at court, until one day at a banquet one of his companions, heated by drink, began to quarrel with him, and taunted him about his origin, declaring that those whom he had been accustomed to call parents were in no way related to him.

These words, coupled with a few meaning glances hastily exchanged by the guests, excited Oedipus' suspicions, and made him question the queen, who, afraid lest he might do himself an injury in the first moment of his despair if the truth were revealed to him, had recourse to prevarication, and quieted him by the assurance that he was her beloved son.

Something in her manner, however, left a lingering doubt in Oedipus' mind, and made him resolve to consult the oracle of Delphi, whose words he knew would reveal the exact truth. He therefore went to this shrine; but, as usual, the oracle answered somewhat ambiguously, and merely warned him that fate had decreed he should kill his father, marry his mother, and cause great woes to his native city.

What! Kill Polybus, who had ever been such an indulgent father, and marry the queen, whom he revered as his mother! Never! Rather than perpetrate these awful crimes, and bring destruction upon the people of Corinth, whom he loved, he would wander away over the face of the earth, and never see city or parents again.

But his heart was filled with intense bitterness, and as he journeyed he did not cease to curse the fate which drove him away from home. After some time, he came to three crossroads; and while he stood there, deliberating which direction to take, a chariot, wherein an aged man was seated, came rapidly toward him.

The herald who preceded it haughtily called to the youth to stand aside and make way for his master; but Oedipus, who, as Polybus' heir, was accustomed to be treated with deference, resented the commanding tone, and refused to obey. Incensed at what seemed unparalleled impudence, the herald struck the youth, who, retaliating, stretched his assailant lifeless at his feet.

This affray attracted the attention of the master and other servants. They immediately attacked the murderer, who slew them all, thus unconsciously accomplishing the first part of the prophecy; for the aged man was Laius, his father, journeying incognito from Thebes to Delphi, where he wished to consult the oracle.

Oedipus then leisurely pursued his way until he came to the gates of Thebes, where he found the whole city in an uproar, "because the king had been found lifeless by the roadside, with all his attendants slain beside him, presumably the work of a band of highway robbers or assassins."

Of course, Oedipus did not connect the murder of such a great personage as the King of Thebes by an unknown band of robbers, with the death he had dealt to an arrogant old man, and he therefore composedly inquired what the second calamity alluded to might be.

With lowered voices, as if afraid of being overheard, the Thebans described the woman's head, bird's wings and claws, and lion's body, which were the outward presentment of a terrible monster called the Sphinx, which had taken up its station without the city gates beside the highway, and would allow none to pass in or out without propounding a difficult riddle. Then, if any hesitated to give the required answer, or failed to give it correctly, they were mercilessly devoured by the terrible Sphinx, which no one dared attack or could drive away.

While listening to these tidings, Oedipus saw a herald pass along the street, proclaiming that the throne and the queen's hand would be the reward of any man who dared encounter the Sphinx, and was fortunate enough to free the country of its terrible presence.

As Oedipus attached no special value to the life made desolate by the oracle's predictions, he resolved to slay the dreaded monster, and, with that purpose in view, advanced slowly, sword in hand, along the road where lurked the Sphinx. He soon found the monster, which from afar propounded the following enigma, warning him, at the same time, that he forfeited his life if he failed to give the right answer:

Oedipus was not devoid of intelligence, by any manner of means, and soon concluded that the animal could only be man, who in infancy, when too weak to stand, creeps along on hands and knees, in manhood walks erect, and in old age supports his tottering steps with a staff.

This reply, evidently as correct as unexpected, was received by the Sphinx with a hoarse cry of disappointment and rage as it turned to fly; but ere it could effect its purpose, it was stayed by Oedipus, who drove it at his sword's point over the edge of a neighboring precipice, where it was killed. On his return to the city, Oedipus was received with cries of joy, placed on a chariot, crowned King of Thebes, and married to his own mother, Jocasta, unwittingly fulfilling the second fearful clause of the prophecy.

A number of happy and moderately uneventful years now passed by, and Oedipus became the father of two manly sons, Eteocles and Polynices, and two beautiful daughters, Ismene and Antigone; but prosperity was not doomed to favour him long.

Just when he fancied himself most happy, and looked forward to a peaceful old age, a terrible scourge visited Thebes, causing the death of many faithful subjects, and filling the hearts of all with great terror. The people now turned to him, beseeching him to aid them, as he had done once before when threatened by the Sphinx; and Oedipus sent messengers to consult the Delphic oracle, who declared the plague would cease only when the former king's murderers had been found and punished.

Messengers were sent in every direction to collect all possible information about the murder committed so long ago, and after a short time they brought unmistakable proofs which convicted Oedipus of the crime. At the same time the guilty servant confessed that he had not killed the child, but had exposed it on a mountain, whence it was carried to Corinth's king.

The chain of evidence was complete, and now Oedipus discovered that he had involuntarily been guilty of the three crimes to avoid which he had fled from Corinth. The rumor of these dreadful discoveries soon reached Jocasta, who, in her despair at finding herself an accomplice, committed suicide.

Oedipus, apprised of her intention, rushed into her apartment too late to prevent its being carried out, and found her lifeless. This sight was more than the poor monarch could bear, and in his despair he blinded himself with one of her ornaments.

Penniless, blind, and on foot, he then left the scene of his awful crimes, accompanied by his daughter Antigone, the only one who loved him still, and who was ready to guide his uncertain footsteps wherever he wished to go. After many days of weary wandering, father and daughter reached Colonus, where grew a mighty forest sacred to the avenging deities, the Furies, or Eumenides.

Here Oedipus expressed his desire to remain, and, after bidding his faithful daughter an affectionate farewell, he groped his way into the dark forest alone. The wind rose, the lightning flashed, the thunder pealed; but although, as soon as the storm was over, a search was made for Oedipus, no trace of him was ever found, and the ancients fancied that the Furies had dragged him down to Hades to receive the punishment of all his crimes.

Antigone, no longer needed by her unhappy father, slowly wended her way back to Thebes, where she found that the plague had ceased, but that her brothers had quarreled about the succession to the throne. A compromise was finally decided upon, whereby it was decreed that Eteocles, the elder son, should reign one year, and at the end of that period resign the throne to Polynices for an equal space of time, both brothers thus exercising the royal authority in turn. This arrangement seemed satisfactory to Eteocles; but when, at the end of the first year, Polynices returned from his travels in foreign lands to claim the sceptre, Eteocles refused to relinquish it, and, making use of his power, drove the claimant away.

Odysseus' Encounter with the Cyclops Polyphemus

Book 9 of The Odyssey

We join the narrative of Homer's epic poem The Odyssey *at Book 9. Odysseus has wept at hearing the bard Demodocus sing the story of the Trojan Horse, and Alcinous, king of the Phaiacians and host to Odysseus after he escaped from Calypso on Ogyia, has requested that Odysseus reveal his identity and tell them of his adventures:*

AND ODYSSEUS ANSWERED, "King Alcinous, it is a good thing to hear a bard with such a divine voice as this man has. There is nothing better or more delightful than when a whole people make merry together, with the guests sitting orderly to listen, while the table is loaded with bread and meats, and the cup-bearer draws wine and fills his cup for every man. This is indeed as fair a sight as a man can see. Now, however, since you are inclined to ask the story of my sorrows, and rekindle my own sad memories in respect of them, I do not know how to begin, nor yet how to continue and conclude my tale, for the hand of heaven has been laid heavily upon me.

"Firstly, then, I will tell you my name that you too may know it, and one day, if I outlive this time of sorrow, may become my guests though I live so far away from all of you. I am Odysseus son of Laertes, renowned among mankind for all manner of subtlety, so that my fame ascends to heaven. I live in Ithaca, where there is a high mountain called Neritum, covered with forests; and not far from it there is a group of islands very near to one another – Dulichium, Same, and the wooded island of Zacynthus. It lies squat on the horizon, all highest up in the sea towards the sunset, while the others lie away from it towards dawn. It is a rugged island, but it breeds brave men, and my eyes know none that they better love to look upon. The goddess Calypso kept me with her in her cave, and wanted me to marry her, as did also the cunning Aeaean goddess Circe; but they could neither of them persuade me, for there is nothing dearer to a man than his own country and his parents, and however splendid a home he may have in a foreign country, if it be far from father or mother, he does not care about it. Now, however, I will tell you of the many hazardous adventures which by Zeus's will I met with on my return from Troy.

* * *

"When I had set sail thence the wind took me first to Ismarus, which is the city of the Cicons. There I sacked the town and put the people to the sword. We took their wives and also much booty, which we divided equitably amongst us, so that none might have reason to complain. I then said that we had better make off at once, but my men very foolishly would not obey me, so they staid there drinking much wine and killing great numbers of sheep and oxen on the sea shore. Meanwhile the Cicons cried out for help to other Cicons who lived inland. These were more in number, and stronger, and they were more skilled in the art of war, for they could fight, either from chariots or on foot as the occasion served; in the morning, therefore, they came as thick as leaves and bloom in summer, and the hand of heaven was against us, so that we were hard pressed. They set the battle in array near the ships, and the hosts aimed their bronze-shod spears at one another. So long as the day waxed and it was still morning, we held our own against them, though they were more in number than we; but as the sun went down, towards the time when men loose their oxen, the Cicons got the better of us, and we lost half a dozen men from every ship we had; so we got away with those that were left.

"Thence we sailed onward with sorrow in our hearts, but glad to have escaped death though we had lost our comrades, nor did we leave till we had thrice invoked each one of the poor fellows who had perished by the hands of the Cicons. Then Zeus raised the North wind against us till it blew a hurricane, so that land and sky were hidden in thick clouds, and night sprang forth out of the heavens. We let the ships run before the gale, but the force of the wind tore our sails to tatters, so we took them down for fear of shipwreck, and rowed our hardest towards the land. There we lay two days and two nights suffering much alike from toil and distress of mind, but on the morning of the third day we again raised our masts, set sail, and took our places, letting the wind and steersmen direct our ship. I should have got home at that time unharmed had not the North wind and the currents been against me as I was doubling Cape Malea, and set me off my course hard by the island of Cythera.

"I was driven thence by foul winds for a space of nine days upon the sea, but on the tenth day we reached the land of the Lotus-eaters, who live on a food that comes from a kind of flower. Here we landed to take in fresh water, and our crews got their mid-day meal on the shore near the ships. When they had eaten and drunk I sent two of my company to see what manner of men the people of the place might be, and they had a third man under them. They started at once, and went about among the Lotus-eaters, who did them no hurt, but gave them to eat of the lotus, which was so delicious that those who ate of it left off caring about home, and did not even want to go back and say what had happened to them, but were for staying and munching lotus with the Lotus-eaters without thinking further of their return; nevertheless, though they wept bitterly I forced them back to the ships and made them fast under the benches. Then I told the rest to go on board at once, lest any of them should taste of the lotus and leave off wanting to get home, so they took their places and smote the grey sea with their oars.

"We sailed hence, always in much distress, till we came to the land of the lawless and inhuman Cyclopes. Now the Cyclopes neither plant nor plough, but trust in providence, and live on such wheat, barley, and grapes as grow wild without any kind of tillage, and their wild grapes yield them wine as the sun and the rain may grow them. They have no laws nor assemblies of the people, but live in caves on the tops of high mountains; each is lord and master in his family, and they take no account of their neighbours.

"Now off their harbour there lies a wooded and fertile island not quite close to the land of the Cyclopes, but still not far. It is over-run with wild goats, that breed there in great numbers and are never disturbed by foot of man; for sportsmen – who as a rule will suffer so much hardship in forest or among mountain precipices – do not go there, nor yet again is it ever ploughed or fed down, but it lies a wilderness untilled and unsown from year to year, and has no living thing upon it but only goats. For the Cyclopes have no ships, nor yet shipwrights who could make ships for them; they cannot therefore go from city to city, or sail over the sea to one another's country as people who have ships can do; if they had had these they would have colonised the island, for it is a very good one, and would yield everything in due season. There are meadows that in some places come right down to the sea shore, well watered and full of luscious grass; grapes would do there excellently; there is level land for ploughing, and it would always yield heavily at harvest time, for the soil is deep. There is a good harbour where no cables are wanted, nor yet anchors, nor need a ship be moored, but all one has to do is to beach one's vessel and stay there till the wind becomes fair for putting out to sea again. At the head of the harbour there is a spring of clear water coming out of a cave, and there are poplars growing all round it.

"Here we entered, but so dark was the night that some god must have brought us in, for there was nothing whatever to be seen. A thick mist hung all round our ships; the moon was hidden behind a mass of clouds so that no one could have seen the island if he had looked for it, nor were there any breakers to tell us we were close in shore before we found ourselves upon the land itself; when, however, we had beached the ships, we took down the sails, went ashore and camped upon the beach till daybreak.

"When the child of morning, rosy-fingered Dawn appeared, we admired the island and wandered all over it, while the nymphs Zeus's daughters roused the wild goats that we might get some meat for our dinner. On this we fetched our spears and bows and arrows from the ships, and dividing ourselves into three bands began to shoot the goats. Heaven sent us excellent sport; I had twelve ships with me, and each ship got nine goats, while my own ship had ten; thus through the livelong day to the going down of the sun we ate and drank our fill, and we had plenty of wine left, for each one of us had taken many jars full when we sacked the city of the Cicons, and this had not yet run out. While we were feasting we kept turning our eyes towards the land of the Cyclopes, which was hard by, and saw the smoke of their stubble fires. We could almost fancy we heard their voices and the bleating of their sheep and goats, but when the sun went down and it came on dark, we camped down upon the beach, and next morning I called a council.

"'Stay here, my brave fellows,' said I, 'all the rest of you, while I go with my ship and exploit these people myself: I want to see if they are uncivilised savages, or a hospitable and humane race.'

"I went on board, bidding my men to do so also and loose the hawsers; so they took their places and smote the grey sea with their oars. When we got to the land, which was not far, there, on the face of a cliff near the sea, we saw a great cave overhung with laurels. It was a station for a great many sheep and goats, and outside there was a large yard, with a high wall round it made of stones built into the ground and of trees both pine and oak. This was the abode of a huge monster who was then away from home shepherding his flocks. He would have nothing to do with other people, but led the life of an outlaw. He was a horrid creature, not like a human being at all, but resembling rather some crag that stands out boldly against the sky on the top of a high mountain.

"I told my men to draw the ship ashore, and stay where they were, all but the twelve best among them, who were to go along with myself. I also took a goatskin of sweet black wine which had been given me by Maron, son of Euanthes, who was priest of Apollo the patron god of Ismarus, and lived within the wooded precincts of the temple. When we were sacking the city we respected him, and spared his life, as also his wife and child; so he made me some presents of great value – seven talents of fine gold, and a bowl of silver, with twelve jars of sweet wine, unblended, and of the most exquisite flavour. Not a man nor maid in the house knew about it, but only himself, his wife, and one housekeeper: when he drank it he mixed twenty parts of water to one of wine, and yet the fragrance from the mixing-bowl was so exquisite that it was impossible to refrain from drinking. I filled a large skin with this wine, and took a wallet full of provisions with me, for my mind misgave me that I might have to deal with some savage who would be of great strength, and would respect neither right nor law.

"We soon reached his cave, but he was out shepherding, so we went inside and took stock of all that we could see. His cheese-racks were loaded with cheeses, and he had more lambs and kids than his pens could hold. They were kept in separate flocks; first there were the hoggets, then the oldest of the younger lambs and lastly the very young ones all kept apart from one another; as for his dairy, all the vessels, bowls, and milk pails into which he milked, were swimming with whey. When they saw all this, my men begged me to let them first steal some cheeses, and make off with them to the ship; they would then return, drive down the lambs and kids, put them on board and sail away with them. It would have been indeed better if we had done so but I would not listen to them, for I wanted to see the owner himself, in the hope that he might give me a present. When, however, we saw him my poor men found him ill to deal with.

"We lit a fire, offered some of the cheeses in sacrifice, ate others of them, and then sat waiting till the Cyclops should come in with his sheep. When he came, he brought in with him a huge load of dry firewood to light the fire for his supper, and this he flung with such a noise on to the floor of his cave that we hid ourselves for fear at the far end of the cavern. Meanwhile he drove all the ewes inside, as well as the she-goats that he was going to milk, leaving the males, both rams and he-goats, outside in the yards. Then he rolled a huge stone to the mouth of the cave – so huge that two and twenty strong four-wheeled waggons would not be enough to draw it from its place against the doorway. When he had so done he sat down and milked his ewes and goats, all in due course, and then let each of them have her own young. He curdled half the milk and set it aside in wicker strainers, but the other half he poured into bowls that he might drink it for his supper. When he had got through with all his work, he lit the fire, and then caught sight of us, whereon he said:

"'Strangers, who are you? Where do sail from? Are you traders, or do you sail the sea as rovers, with your hands against every man, and every man's hand against you?'

"We were frightened out of our senses by his loud voice and monstrous form, but I managed to say, 'We are Achaeans on our way home from Troy, but by the will of Zeus, and stress of weather, we have been driven far out of our course. We are the people of Agamemnon, son of Atreus, who has won infinite renown throughout the whole world, by sacking so great a city and killing so many people. We therefore humbly pray you to show us some hospitality, and otherwise make us such presents as visitors may reasonably expect. May your excellency fear the wrath of heaven, for we are your suppliants, and Zeus takes all respectable travellers under his protection, for he is the avenger of all suppliants and foreigners in distress.'

"To this he gave me but a pitiless answer, 'Stranger,' said he, 'you are a fool, or else you know nothing of this country. Talk to me, indeed, about fearing the gods or shunning their anger? We Cyclopes do not care about Zeus or any of your blessed gods, for we are ever so much stronger than they. I shall not spare either yourself or your companions out of any regard for Zeus, unless I am in the humour for doing so. And now tell me where you made your ship fast when you came on shore. Was it round the point, or is she lying straight off the land?'

"He said this to draw me out, but I was too cunning to be caught in that way, so I answered with a lie; 'Poseidon,' said I, 'sent my ship on to the rocks at the far end of your country, and wrecked it. We were driven on to them from the open sea, but I and those who are with me escaped the jaws of death.'

"The cruel wretch vouchsafed me not one word of answer, but with a sudden clutch he gripped up two of my men at once and dashed them down upon the ground as though they had been puppies. Their brains were shed upon the ground, and the earth was wet with their blood. Then he tore them limb from limb and supped upon them. He gobbled them up like a lion in the wilderness, flesh, bones, marrow, and entrails, without leaving anything uneaten. As for us, we wept and lifted up our hands to heaven on seeing such a horrid sight, for we did not know what else to do; but when the Cyclops had filled his huge paunch, and had washed down his meal of human flesh with a drink of neat milk, he stretched himself full length upon the ground among his sheep, and went to sleep. I was at first inclined to seize my sword, draw it, and drive it into his vitals, but I reflected that if I did we should all certainly be lost, for we should never be able to shift the stone which the monster had put in front of the door. So we stayed sobbing and sighing where we were till morning came.

"When the child of morning, rosy-fingered dawn, appeared, he again lit his fire, milked his goats and ewes, all quite rightly, and then let each have her own young one; as soon as he had got through with all his work, he clutched up two more of my men, and began eating them for his morning's meal. Presently, with the utmost ease, he rolled the stone away from the door and drove out his sheep, but he at once put it back again – as easily as though he were merely clapping the lid on to a quiver full of arrows. As soon as he had done so he shouted, and cried 'Shoo, shoo,' after his sheep to drive them on to the mountain; so I was left to scheme some way of taking my revenge and covering myself with glory.

"In the end I deemed it would be the best plan to do as follows: The Cyclops had a great club which was lying near one of the sheep pens; it was of green olive wood, and he had cut it intending to use it for a staff as soon as it should be dry. It was so huge that we could only compare it to the mast of a twenty-oared merchant vessel of large burden, and able to venture out into open sea. I went up to this club and cut off about six feet of it; I then gave this piece to the men and told them to fine it evenly off at one end, which they proceeded to do, and lastly I brought it to a point myself, charring the end in the fire to make it harder. When I had done this I hid it under dung, which was lying about all over the cave, and told the men to cast lots which of them should venture along with myself to lift it and bore it into the monster's eye while he was asleep. The lot fell upon the very four whom I should have chosen, and I myself made five. In the evening the wretch came back from shepherding, and drove his flocks into the cave – this time driving them all inside, and not leaving any in the yards; I suppose some fancy must have taken him, or a god must have prompted him to do so. As soon as he had put the stone back to its place against the door, he sat down, milked his ewes and his goats all quite rightly, and then let each have her own young one; when he had got through with all this work, he gripped up two more of my men, and made his supper off them. So I went up to him with an ivy-wood bowl of black wine in my hands:

"'Look here, Cyclops,' said I, you have been eating a great deal of man's flesh, so take this and drink some wine, that you may see what kind of liquor we had on board my ship. I was bringing it to you as a drink-offering, in the hope that you would take compassion upon me and further me on my way home, whereas all you do is to go on ramping and raving most intolerably. You ought to be ashamed of yourself; how can you expect people to come see you any more if you treat them in this way?'

"He then took the cup and drank. He was so delighted with the taste of the wine that he begged me for another bowl full. 'Be so kind,' he said, 'as to give me some more, and tell me your name at once. I want to make you a present that you will be glad to have. We have wine even in this country, for our soil grows grapes and the sun ripens them, but this drinks like Nectar and Ambrosia all in one.'

"I then gave him some more; three times did I fill the bowl for him, and three times did he drain it without thought or heed; then, when I saw that the wine had got into his head,

I said to him as plausibly as I could: 'Cyclops, you ask my name and I will tell it you; give me, therefore, the present you promised me; my name is Noman; this is what my father and mother and my friends have always called me.'

"But the cruel wretch said, 'Then I will eat all Noman's comrades before Noman himself, and will keep Noman for the last. This is the present that I will make him.'

"As he spoke he reeled, and fell sprawling face upwards on the ground. His great neck hung heavily backwards and a deep sleep took hold upon him. Presently he turned sick, and threw up both wine and the gobbets of human flesh on which he had been gorging, for he was very drunk. Then I thrust the beam of wood far into the embers to heat it, and encouraged my men lest any of them should turn faint-hearted. When the wood, green though it was, was about to blaze, I drew it out of the fire glowing with heat, and my men gathered round me, for heaven had filled their hearts with courage. We drove the sharp end of the beam into the monster's eye, and bearing upon it with all my weight I kept turning it round and round as though I were boring a hole in a ship's plank with an auger, which two men with a wheel and strap can keep on turning as long as they choose. Even thus did we bore the red hot beam into his eye, till the boiling blood bubbled all over it as we worked it round and round, so that the steam from the burning eyeball scalded his eyelids and eyebrows, and the roots of the eye sputtered in the fire. As a blacksmith plunges an axe or hatchet into cold water to temper it – for it is this that gives strength to the iron – and it makes a great hiss as he does so, even thus did the Cyclops' eye hiss round the beam of olive wood, and his hideous yells made the cave ring again. We ran away in a fright, but he plucked the beam all besmirched with gore from his eye, and hurled it from him in a frenzy of rage and pain, shouting as he did so to the other Cyclopes who lived on the bleak headlands near him; so they gathered from all quarters round his cave when they heard him crying, and asked what was the matter with him.

"'What ails you, Polyphemus,' said they, 'that you make such a noise, breaking the stillness of the night, and preventing us from being able to sleep? Surely no man is carrying off your sheep? Surely no man is trying to kill you either by fraud or by force?'

"But Polyphemus shouted to them from inside the cave, 'Noman is killing me by fraud; no man is killing me by force.'

"'Then,' said they, 'if no man is attacking you, you must be ill; when Zeus makes people ill, there is no help for it, and you had better pray to your father Poseidon.'

"Then they went away, and I laughed inwardly at the success of my clever stratagem, but the Cyclops, groaning and in an agony of pain, felt about with his hands till he found the stone and took it from the door; then he sat in the doorway and stretched his hands in front of it to catch anyone going out with the sheep, for he thought I might be foolish enough to attempt this.

"As for myself I kept on puzzling to think how I could best save my own life and those of my companions; I schemed and schemed, as one who knows that his life depends upon it, for the danger was very great. In the end I deemed that this plan would be the best; the male sheep were well grown, and carried a heavy black fleece, so I bound them noiselessly in threes together, with some of the withies on which the wicked monster used to sleep. There was to be a man under the middle sheep, and the two on either side were to cover him, so that there were three sheep to each man. As for myself there was a ram finer than any of the others, so I caught hold of him by the back, ensconced myself in the thick wool under his belly, and hung on patiently to his fleece, face upwards, keeping a firm hold on it all the time.

"Thus, then, did we wait in great fear of mind till morning came, but when the child of morning, rosy-fingered Dawn, appeared, the male sheep hurried out to feed, while the ewes remained bleating about the pens waiting to be milked, for their udders were full to bursting; but their master in spite of all his pain felt the backs of all the sheep as they stood upright, without being sharp enough to find out that the men were underneath their bellies. As the ram was going out, last of all, heavy with its fleece and with the weight of my crafty self, Polyphemus laid hold of it and said:

"'My good ram, what is it that makes you the last to leave my cave this morning? You are not wont to let the ewes go before you, but lead the mob with a run whether to flowery mead or bubbling fountain, and are the first to come home again at night; but now you lag last of all. Is it because you know your master has lost his eye, and are sorry because that wicked Noman and his horrid crew has got him down in his drink and blinded him? But I will have his life yet. If you could understand and talk, you would tell me where the wretch is hiding, and I would dash his brains upon the ground till they flew all over the cave. I should thus have some satisfaction for the harm this no-good Noman has done me.'

"As he spoke he drove the ram outside, but when we were a little way out from the cave and yards, I first got from under the ram's belly, and then freed my comrades; as for the sheep, which were very fat, by constantly heading them in the right direction we managed to drive them down to the ship. The crew rejoiced greatly at seeing those of us who had escaped death, but wept for the others whom the Cyclops had killed. However, I made signs to them by nodding and frowning that they were to hush their crying, and told them to get all the sheep on board at once and put out to sea; so they went aboard, took their places, and smote the grey sea with their oars. Then, when I had got as far out as my voice would reach, I began to jeer at the Cyclops.

"'Cyclops,' said I, 'you should have taken better measure of your man before eating up his comrades in your cave. You wretch, eat up your visitors in your own house? You might have known that your sin would find you out, and now Zeus and the other gods have punished you.'

"He got more and more furious as he heard me, so he tore the top from off a high mountain, and flung it just in front of my ship so that it was within a little of hitting the end of the rudder. The sea quaked as the rock fell into it, and the wash of the wave it raised carried us back towards the mainland, and forced us towards the shore. But I snatched up a long pole and kept the ship off, making signs to my men by nodding my head, that they must row for their lives, whereon they laid out with a will. When we had got twice as far as we were before, I was for jeering at the Cyclops again, but the men begged and prayed of me to hold my tongue.

"'Do not,' they exclaimed, 'be mad enough to provoke this savage creature further; he has thrown one rock at us already which drove us back again to the mainland, and we made sure it had been the death of us; if he had then heard any further sound of voices he would have pounded our heads and our ship's timbers into a jelly with the rugged rocks he would have heaved at us, for he can throw them a long way.'

"But I would not listen to them, and shouted out to him in my rage, 'Cyclops, if any one asks you who it was that put your eye out and spoiled your beauty, say it was the valiant warrior Odysseus, son of Laertes, who lives in Ithaca.'

"On this he groaned, and cried out, 'Alas, alas, then the old prophecy about me is coming true. There was a prophet here, at one time, a man both brave and of great stature, Telemus son of Eurymus, who was an excellent seer, and did all the prophesying for the Cyclopes till he grew old; he told me that all this would happen to me some day, and said I should lose my sight by the hand of Odysseus. I have been all along expecting some one of imposing presence and superhuman strength, whereas he turns out to be a little insignificant weakling, who has managed to blind my eye by taking advantage of me in my drink; come here, then, Odysseus, that I may make you presents to show my hospitality, and urge Poseidon to help you forward on your journey – for Poseidon and I are father and son. He, if he so will, shall heal me, which no one else neither god nor man can do.'

"Then I said, 'I wish I could be as sure of killing you outright and sending you down to the house of Hades, as I am that it will take more than Poseidon to cure that eye of yours.'

"On this he lifted up his hands to the firmament of heaven and prayed, saying, 'Hear me, great Poseidon; if I am indeed your own true begotten son, grant that Odysseus may never reach his home alive; or if he must get back to his friends at last, let him do so late and in sore plight after losing all his men let him reach his home in another man's ship and find trouble in his house.'

"Thus did he pray, and Poseidon heard his prayer. Then he picked up a rock much larger than the first, swung it aloft and hurled it with prodigious force. It fell just short of the ship, but was within a little of hitting the end of the rudder. The sea quaked as the rock fell into it, and the wash of the wave it raised drove us onwards on our way towards the shore of the island.

"When at last we got to the island where we had left the rest of our ships, we found our comrades lamenting us, and anxiously awaiting our return. We ran our vessel upon the sands and got out of her on to the sea shore; we also landed the Cyclops' sheep, and divided them equitably amongst us so that none might have reason to complain. As for the ram, my companions agreed that I should have it as an extra share; so I sacrificed it on the sea shore, and burned its thigh bones to Zeus, who is the lord of all. But he heeded not my sacrifice, and only thought how he might destroy both my ships and my comrades.

"Thus through the livelong day to the going down of the sun we feasted our fill on meat and drink, but when the sun went down and it came on dark, we camped upon the beach. When the child of morning rosy-fingered Dawn appeared, I bade my men on board and loose the hawsers. Then they took their places and smote the grey sea with their oars; so we sailed on with sorrow in our hearts, but glad to have escaped death though we had lost our comrades.

Odysseus and the Laestrygonians

Book 10 of The Odyssey

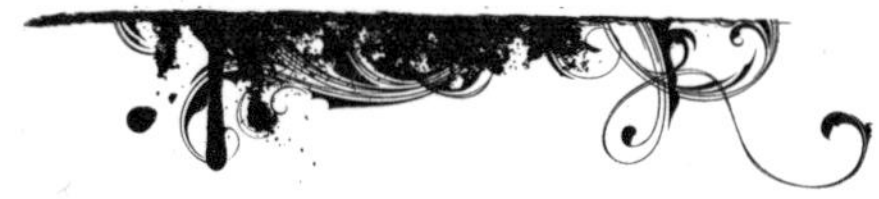

We continue with Book 10 of Homer's Odyssey, *wherein Odysseus tells of the disastrous encounter with the man-eating giants known as the Laestrygonians, and later suffering at the hands of the enchantress Circe:*

"THENCE WE WENT on to the Aeolian island where lives Aeolus son of Hippotas, dear to the immortal gods. It is an island that floats (as it were) upon the sea, iron bound with a wall that girds it. Now, Aeolus has six daughters and six lusty sons, so he made the sons marry the daughters, and they all live with their dear father and mother, feasting and enjoying every conceivable kind of luxury. All day long the atmosphere of the house is loaded with the savour of roasting meats till it groans again, yard and all; but by night they sleep on their well made bedsteads, each with his own wife between the blankets. These were the people among whom we had now come.

"Aeolus entertained me for a whole month asking me questions all the time about Troy, the Argive fleet, and the return of the Achaeans. I told him exactly how everything had happened, and when I said I must go, and asked him to further me on my way, he made no sort of difficulty, but set about doing so at once. Moreover, he flayed me a prime ox-hide to hold the ways of the roaring winds, which he shut up in the hide as in a sack – for Zeus had made him captain over the winds, and he could stir or still each one of them according to his own pleasure. He put the sack in the ship and bound the mouth so tightly with a silver thread that not even a breath of a side-wind could blow from any quarter. The West wind which was fair for us did he alone let blow as it chose; but it all came to nothing, for we were lost through our own folly.

"Nine days and nine nights did we sail, and on the tenth day our native land showed on the horizon. We got so close in that we could see the stubble fires burning, and I, being then dead beat, fell into a light sleep, for I had never let the rudder out of my own hands, that we might get home the faster. On this the men fell to talking among themselves, and said I was bringing back gold and silver in the sack that Aeolus had given me. 'Bless my heart,' would one turn to his neighbour, saying, 'how this man gets honoured and makes friends to whatever city or country he may go. See what fine prizes he is taking home from Troy, while we, who have travelled just as far as he has, come back with hands as empty as we set out with – and now Aeolus has given him ever so much more. Quick – let us see what it all is, and how much gold and silver there is in the sack he gave him.'

"Thus they talked and evil counsels prevailed. They loosed the sack, whereupon the wind flew howling forth and raised a storm that carried us weeping out to sea and away from our own country. Then I awoke, and knew not whether to throw myself into the sea or to live on and make the best of it; but I bore it, covered myself up, and lay down in the ship, while the men lamented bitterly as the fierce winds bore our fleet back to the Aeolian island.

"When we reached it we went ashore to take in water, and dined hard by the ships. Immediately after dinner I took a herald and one of my men and went straight to the house of Aeolus, where I found him feasting with his wife and family; so we sat down as suppliants on the threshold. They were astounded when they saw us and said, 'Odysseus, what brings you here? What god has been ill-treating you? We took great pains to further you on your way home to Ithaca, or wherever it was that you wanted to go to.'

"Thus did they speak, but I answered sorrowfully, 'My men have undone me; they, and cruel sleep, have ruined me. My friends, mend me this mischief, for you can if you will.'

"I spoke as movingly as I could, but they said nothing, till their father answered, 'Vilest of mankind, get you gone at once out of the island; him whom heaven hates will I in no wise help. Be off, for you come here as one abhorred of heaven.' And with these words he sent me sorrowing from his door.

"Thence we sailed sadly on till the men were worn out with long and fruitless rowing, for there was no longer any wind to help them. Six days, night and day did we toil, and on the seventh day we reached the rocky stronghold of Lamus – Telepylus, the city of the Laestrygonians, where the shepherd who is driving in his sheep and goats to be milked salutes him who is driving out his flock to feed and this last answers the salute. In that country a man who could do without sleep might earn double wages, one as a herdsman of cattle, and another as a shepherd, for they work much the same by night as they do by day.

"When we reached the harbour we found it land-locked under steep cliffs, with a narrow entrance between two headlands. My captains took all their ships inside, and made them fast close to one another, for there was never so much as a breath of wind inside, but it was always dead calm. I kept my own ship outside, and moored it to a rock at the very end of the point; then I climbed a high rock to reconnoitre, but could see no sign neither of man nor cattle, only some smoke rising from the ground. So I sent two of my company with an attendant to find out what sort of people the inhabitants were.

"The men when they got on shore followed a level road by which the people draw their firewood from the mountains into the town, till presently they met a young woman who had come outside to fetch water, and who was daughter to a Laestrygonian named Antiphates. She was going to the fountain Artacia from which the people bring in their water, and when my men had come close up to her, they asked her who the king of that country might be, and over what kind of people he ruled; so she directed them to her father's house, but when they got there they found his wife to be a giantess as huge as a mountain, and they were horrified at the sight of her.

"She at once called her husband Antiphates from the place of assembly, and forthwith he set about killing my men. He snatched up one of them, and began to make his dinner off him then and there, whereon the other two ran back to the ships as fast as ever they could. But Antiphates raised a hue-and-cry after them, and thousands of sturdy Laestrygonians sprang up from every quarter – ogres, not men. They threw vast rocks at us from the cliffs as though they had been mere stones, and I heard the horrid sound of the ships crunching up against one another, and the death cries of my men, as the Laestrygonians speared them like fishes and took them home to eat them. While they were thus killing my men within the harbour I drew my sword, cut the cable of my own ship, and told my men to row with all their might if they too would not fare like the rest; so they laid out for their lives, and we were thankful enough when we got into open water out of reach of the rocks they hurled at us. As for the others there was not one of them left.

"Thence we sailed sadly on, glad to have escaped death, though we had lost our comrades, and came to the Aeaean island, where Circe lives – a great and cunning goddess who is own sister to the magician Aeetes – for they are both children of the sun by Perse, who is daughter to Oceanus. We brought our ship into a safe harbour without a word, for some god guided us thither, and having landed we lay there for two days and two nights, worn out in body and mind. When the morning of the third day came I took my spear and my sword, and went away from the ship to reconnoitre, and see if I could discover signs of human handiwork, or hear the sound of voices. Climbing to the top of a high look-out I espied the smoke of Circe's house rising upwards amid a dense forest of trees, and when I saw this I doubted whether, having seen the smoke, I would not go on at once and find out more, but in the end I deemed it best to go back to the ship, give the men their dinners, and send some of them instead of going myself.

"When I had nearly got back to the ship some god took pity upon my solitude, and sent a fine antlered stag right into the middle of my path. He was coming down his pasture in the forest to drink of the river, for the heat of the sun drove him, and as he passed I struck him in the middle of the back; the bronze point of the spear went clean through him, and he lay groaning in the dust until the life went out of him. Then I set my foot upon him, drew my spear from the wound, and laid it down; I also gathered rough grass and rushes and twisted them into a fathom or so of good stout rope, with which I bound the four feet of the noble creature together; having so done I hung him round my neck and walked back to the ship leaning upon my spear, for the stag was much too big for me to be able to carry him on my shoulder, steadying him with one hand. As I threw him down in front of the ship, I called the men and spoke cheeringly man by man to each of them. 'Look here my friends,' said I, 'we are not going to die so much before our time after all, and at any rate we will not starve so long as we have got something to eat and drink on board.' On this they uncovered their heads upon the sea shore and admired the stag, for he was indeed a splendid fellow. Then, when they had feasted their eyes upon him sufficiently, they washed their hands and began to cook him for dinner.

"Thus through the livelong day to the going down of the sun we stayed there eating and drinking our fill, but when the sun went down and it came on dark, we camped upon the sea shore. When the child of morning, rosy-fingered Dawn, appeared, I called a council and said, 'My friends, we are in very great difficulties; listen therefore to me. We have no idea where the sun either sets or rises, so that we do not even know East from West. I see no way out of it; nevertheless, we must try and find one. We are certainly on an island, for I went as high as I could this morning, and saw the sea reaching all round it to the horizon; it lies low, but towards the middle I saw smoke rising from out of a thick forest of trees.'

"Their hearts sank as they heard me, for they remembered how they had been treated by the Laestrygonian Antiphates, and by the savage ogre Polyphemus. They wept bitterly in their dismay, but there was nothing to be got by crying, so I divided them into two companies and set a captain over each; I gave one company to Eurylochus, while I took command of the other myself. Then we cast lots in a helmet, and the lot fell upon Eurylochus; so he set out with his twenty-two men, and they wept, as also did we who were left behind.

"When they reached Circe's house they found it built of cut stones, on a site that could be seen from far, in the middle of the forest. There were wild mountain wolves and lions prowling all round it – poor bewitched creatures whom she had tamed by her enchantments and drugged into subjection. They did not attack my men, but wagged their great tails, fawned upon them, and rubbed their noses lovingly against them. As hounds crowd round their master when they see him coming from dinner – for they know he will bring them something – even so did these wolves and lions with their great claws fawn upon my men, but the men were terribly frightened at seeing such strange creatures. Presently they reached the gates of the goddess' house, and as they stood there they could hear Circe within, singing most beautifully as she worked at her loom, making a web so fine, so soft, and of such dazzling colours as no one but a goddess could weave. On this Polites, whom I valued and trusted more than any other of my men, said, 'There is some one inside working at a loom and singing most beautifully; the whole place resounds with it, let us call her and see whether she is woman or goddess.'

"They called her and she came down, unfastened the door, and bade them enter. They, thinking no evil, followed her, all except Eurylochus, who suspected mischief and staid outside. When she had got them into her house, she set them upon benches and seats and mixed them a mess with cheese, honey, meal, and Pramnian wine, but she drugged it with wicked poisons to make them forget their homes, and when they had drunk she turned them into pigs by a stroke of her wand, and shut them up in her pig-styes. They were like pigs – head, hair, and all, and they grunted just as pigs do; but their senses were the same as before, and they remembered everything.

"Thus then were they shut up squealing, and Circe threw them some acorns and beech masts such as pigs eat, but Eurylochus hurried back to tell me about the sad fate of our comrades. He was so overcome with dismay that though he tried to speak he could find no words to do so; his eyes filled with tears and he could only sob and sigh, till at last we forced his story out of him, and he told us what had happened to the others.

"'We went,' said he, 'as you told us, through the forest, and in the middle of it there was a fine house built with cut stones in a place that could be seen from far. There we found a woman, or else she was a goddess, working at her loom and singing sweetly; so the men shouted to her and called her, whereon she at once came down, opened the door, and invited us in. The others did not suspect any mischief so they followed her into the house, but I staid where I was, for I thought there might be some treachery. From that moment I saw them no more, for not one of them ever came out, though I sat a long time watching for them.'

"Then I took my sword of bronze and slung it over my shoulders; I also took my bow, and told Eurylochus to come back with me and shew me the way. But he laid hold of me with both his hands and spoke piteously, saying, 'Sir, do not force me to go with you, but let me stay here, for I know you will not bring one of them back with you, nor even return alive yourself; let us rather see if we cannot escape at any rate with the few that are left us, for we may still save our lives.'

"'Stay where you are, then,' answered I, 'eating and drinking at the ship, but I must go, for I am most urgently bound to do so.'

"With this I left the ship and went up inland. When I got through the charmed grove, and was near the great house of the enchantress Circe, I met Hermes with his golden wand, disguised as a young man in the hey-day of his youth and beauty with the down just coming upon his face. He came up to me and took my hand within his own, saying, 'My poor unhappy man, whither are you going over this mountain top, alone and without knowing the way? Your men are shut up in Circe's pigstyes, like so many wild boars in their lairs. You surely do not fancy that you can set them free? I can tell you that you will never get back and will have to stay there with the rest of them. But never mind, I will protect you and get you out of your difficulty. Take this herb, which is one of great virtue, and keep it about you when you go to Circe's house, it will be a talisman to you against every kind of mischief.

"'And I will tell you of all the wicked witchcraft that Circe will try to practice upon you. She will mix a mess for you to drink, and she will drug the meal with which she makes it, but she will not be able to charm you, for the virtue of the herb that I shall give you will prevent her spells from working. I will tell you all about it. When Circe strikes you with her wand, draw your sword and spring upon her as though you were going to kill her. She will then be frightened, and will desire you to go to bed with her; on this you must not point blank refuse her, for you want her to set your companions free, and to take good care also of yourself, but you must make her swear solemnly by all the blessed gods that she will plot no further mischief against you, or else when she has got you naked she will unman you and make you fit for nothing.'

"As he spoke he pulled the herb out of the ground and shewed me what it was like. The root was black, while the flower was as white as milk; the gods call it Moly, and mortal men cannot uproot it, but the gods can do whatever they like.

"Then Hermes went back to high Olympus passing over the wooded island; but I fared onward to the house of Circe, and my heart was clouded with care as I walked along. When I got to the gates I stood there and called the goddess, and as soon as she heard me she came down, opened the door, and asked me to come in; so I followed her – much troubled in my mind. She set me on a richly decorated seat inlaid with silver, there was a footstool also under my feet, and she mixed a mess in a golden goblet for me to drink; but she drugged it, for she meant me mischief. When she had given it me, and I had drunk it without its charming me, she struck me with her wand. 'There now,' she cried, 'be off to the pigstye, and make your lair with the rest of them.'

"But I rushed at her with my sword drawn as though I would kill her, whereon she fell with a loud scream, clasped my knees, and spoke piteously, saying, 'Who and whence are you? from what place and people have you come? How can it be that my drugs have no power to charm you? Never yet was any man able to stand so much as a taste of the herb I gave you; you must be spell-proof; surely you can be none other than the bold hero Odysseus, who Hermes always said would come here some day with his ship while on his way home from Troy; so be it then; sheathe your sword and let us go to bed, that we may make friends and learn to trust each other.'

"And I answered, 'Circe, how can you expect me to be friendly with you when you have just been turning all my men into pigs? And now that you have got me here myself, you mean me mischief when you ask me to go to bed with you, and will unman me and make me fit for nothing. I shall certainly not consent to go to bed with you unless you will first take your solemn oath to plot no further harm against me.'

"So she swore at once as I had told her, and when she had completed her oath then I went to bed with her.

"Meanwhile her four servants, who are her housemaids, set about their work. They are the children of the groves and fountains, and of the holy waters that run down into the sea. One of them spread a fair purple cloth over a seat, and laid a carpet underneath it. Another brought tables of silver up to the seats, and set them with baskets of gold. A third mixed some sweet wine with water in a silver bowl and put golden cups upon the tables, while the fourth brought in water and set it to boil in a large cauldron over a good fire which she had lighted. When the water in the cauldron was boiling, she poured cold into it till it was just as I liked it, and then she set me in a bath and began washing me from the cauldron about the head and shoulders, to take the tire and stiffness out of my limbs. As soon as she had done washing me and anointing me with oil, she arrayed me in a good cloak and shirt and led me to a richly decorated seat inlaid with silver; there was a footstool also under my feet. A maid servant then brought me water in a beautiful golden ewer and poured it into a silver basin for me to wash my hands, and she drew a clean table beside me; an upper servant brought me bread and offered me many things of what there was in the house, and then Circe bade me eat, but I would not, and sat without heeding what was before me, still moody and suspicious.

"When Circe saw me sitting there without eating, and in great grief, she came to me and said, 'Odysseus, why do you sit like that as though you were dumb, gnawing at your own heart, and refusing both meat and drink? Is it that you are still suspicious? You ought not to be, for I have already sworn solemnly that I will not hurt you.'

"And I said, 'Circe, no man with any sense of what is right can think of either eating or drinking in your house until you have set his friends free and let him see them. If you want me to eat and drink, you must free my men and bring them to me that I may see them with my own eyes.'

"When I had said this she went straight through the court with her wand in her hand and opened the pigstye doors. My men came out like so many prime hogs and stood looking at her, but she went about among them and anointed each with a second drug, whereon the bristles that the bad drug had given them fell off, and they became men again, younger than they were before, and much taller and better looking. They knew me at once, seized me each of them by the hand, and wept for joy till the whole house was filled with the sound of their halloa-ballooing, and Circe herself was so sorry for them that she came up to me and said, 'Odysseus, noble son of Laertes, go back at once to the sea where you have left your ship, and first draw it on to the land. Then, hide all your ship's gear and property in some cave, and come back here with your men.'

"I agreed to this, so I went back to the sea shore, and found the men at the ship weeping and wailing most piteously. When they saw me the silly blubbering fellows began frisking round me as calves break out and gambol round their mothers, when they see them coming home to be milked after they have been feeding all day, and the homestead resounds with their lowing. They seemed as glad to see me as though they had got back to their own rugged Ithaca, where they had been born and bred. 'Sir,' said the affectionate creatures, 'we are as glad to see you back as though we had got safe home to Ithaca; but tell us all about the fate of our comrades.'

"I spoke comfortingly to them and said, 'We must draw our ship on to the land, and hide the ship's gear with all our property in some cave; then come with me all of you as fast as you can to Circe's house, where you will find your comrades eating and drinking in the midst of great abundance.'

"On this the men would have come with me at once, but Eurylochus tried to hold them back and said, 'Alas, poor wretches that we are, what will become of us? Rush not on your ruin by going to the house of Circe, who will turn us all into pigs or wolves or lions, and we shall have to keep guard over her house. Remember how the Cyclops treated us when our comrades went inside his cave, and Odysseus with them. It was all through his sheer folly that those men lost their lives.'

"When I heard him I was in two minds whether or no to draw the keen blade that hung by my sturdy thigh and cut his head off in spite of his being a near relation of my own; but the men interceded for him and said, 'Sir, if it may so be, let this fellow stay here and mind the ship, but take the rest of us with you to Circe's house.'

"On this we all went inland, and Eurylochus was not left behind after all, but came on too, for he was frightened by the severe reprimand that I had given him.

"Meanwhile Circe had been seeing that the men who had been left behind were washed and anointed with olive oil; she had also given them woollen cloaks and shirts, and when we came we found them all comfortably at dinner in her house. As soon as the men saw each other face to face and knew one another, they wept for joy and cried aloud till the whole palace rang again. Thereon Circe came up to me and said, 'Odysseus, noble son of Laertes, tell your men to leave off crying; I know how much you have all of you suffered at sea, and how ill you have fared among cruel savages on the mainland, but that is over now, so stay here, and eat and drink till you are once more as strong and hearty as you were when you left Ithaca; for at present you are weakened both in body and mind; you keep all the time thinking of the hardships you have suffered during your travels, so that you have no more cheerfulness left in you.'

"Thus did she speak and we assented. We stayed with Circe for a whole twelvemonth feasting upon an untold quantity both of meat and wine. But when the year had passed in the waning of moons and the long days had come round, my men called me apart and said, 'Sir, it is time you began to think about going home, if so be you are to be spared to see your house and native country at all.'

"Thus did they speak and I assented. Thereon through the livelong day to the going down of the sun we feasted our fill on meat and wine, but when the sun went down and it came on dark the men laid themselves down to sleep in the covered cloisters. I, however, after I had got into bed with Circe, besought her by her knees, and the goddess listened to what I had got to say. 'Circe,' said I, 'please to keep the promise you made me about furthering me on my homeward voyage. I want to get back and so do my men, they are always pestering me with their complaints as soon as ever your back is turned.'

"And the goddess answered, 'Odysseus, noble son of Laertes, you shall none of you stay here any longer if you do not want to, but there is another journey which you have got to take before you can sail homewards. You must go to the house of Hades and of dread Persephone to consult the ghost of the blind Theban prophet Teiresias, whose reason is still unshaken. To him alone has Persephone left his understanding even in death, but the other ghosts flit about aimlessly.'

"I was dismayed when I heard this. I sat up in bed and wept, and would gladly have lived no longer to see the light of the sun, but presently when I was tired of weeping and tossing myself about, I said, 'And who shall guide me upon this voyage – for the house of Hades is a port that no ship can reach.'

"'You will want no guide,' she answered; 'raise your mast, set your white sails, sit quite still, and the North Wind will blow you there of itself. When your ship has traversed the waters of Oceanus, you will reach the fertile shore of Persephone's country with its groves of tall poplars and willows that shed their fruit untimely; here beach your ship upon the shore of Oceanus, and go straight on to the dark abode of Hades. You will find it near the place where the rivers Pyriphlegethon and Cocytus (which is a branch of the river Styx) flow into Acheron, and you will see a rock near it, just where the two roaring rivers run into one another.

"'When you have reached this spot, as I now tell you, dig a trench a cubit or so in length, breadth, and depth, and pour into it as a drink-offering to all the dead, first, honey mixed with milk, then wine, and in the third place water – sprinkling white barley meal over the whole. Moreover you must offer many prayers to the poor feeble ghosts, and promise them that when you get back to Ithaca you will sacrifice a barren heifer to them, the best you have, and will load the pyre with good things. More particularly you must promise that Teiresias shall have a black sheep all to himself, the finest in all your flocks.

"'When you shall have thus besought the ghosts with your prayers, offer them a ram and a black ewe, bending their heads towards Erebus; but yourself turn away from them as though you would make towards the river. On this, many dead men's ghosts will come to you, and you must tell your men to skin the two sheep that you have just killed, and offer them as a burnt sacrifice with prayers to Hades and to Persephone. Then draw your sword and sit there, so as to prevent any other poor ghost from coming near the spilt blood before Teiresias shall have answered your questions. The seer will presently come to you, and will tell you about your voyage – what stages you are to make, and how you are to sail the sea so as to reach your home.'

"It was day-break by the time she had done speaking, so she dressed me in my shirt and cloak. As for herself she threw a beautiful light gossamer fabric over her shoulders, fastening it with a golden girdle round her waist, and she covered her head with a mantle. Then I went about among the men everywhere all over the house, and spoke kindly to each of them man by man: 'You must not lie sleeping here any longer,' said I to them, 'we must be going, for Circe has told me all about it.' And on this they did as I bade them.

"Even so, however, I did not get them away without misadventure. We had with us a certain youth named Elpenor, not very remarkable for sense or courage, who had got drunk and was lying on the house-top away from the rest of the men, to sleep off his liquor in the cool. When he heard the noise of the men bustling about, he jumped up on a sudden and forgot all about coming down by the main staircase, so he tumbled right off the roof and broke his neck, and his soul went down to the house of Hades.

"When I had got the men together I said to them, 'You think you are about to start home again, but Circe has explained to me that instead of this, we have got to go to the house of Hades and Persephone to consult the ghost of the Theban prophet Teiresias.'

"The men were broken-hearted as they heard me, and threw themselves on the ground groaning and tearing their hair, but they did not mend matters by crying. When we reached the sea shore, weeping and lamenting our fate, Circe brought the ram and the ewe, and we made them fast hard by the ship. She passed through the midst of us without our knowing it, for who can see the comings and goings of a god, if the god does not wish to be seen?

Odysseus, the Sirens and Scylla and Charybdis

Book 12 of The Odyssey

We rejoin Homer's Odyssey *at Book 12. Odysseus is returning to Circe's island, Aeaea, from the underworld after consulting with the prophet Teiresias on how to make the journey home. There he also encountered the ghost of his young comrade Elpenor, who begged for a proper burial.*

"AFTER WE WERE CLEAR of the river Oceanus, and had got out into the open sea, we went on till we reached the Aeaean island where there is dawn and sun-rise as in other places. We then drew our ship on to the sands and got out of her on to the shore, where we went to sleep and waited till day should break.

"Then, when the child of morning, rosy-fingered Dawn, appeared, I sent some men to Circe's house to fetch the body of Elpenor. We cut firewood from a wood where the headland jutted out into the sea, and after we had wept over him and lamented him we performed his funeral rites. When his body and armour had been burned to ashes, we raised a cairn, set a stone over it, and at the top of the cairn we fixed the oar that he had been used to row with.

"While we were doing all this, Circe, who knew that we had got back from the house of Hades, dressed herself and came to us as fast as she could; and her maid servants came with her bringing us bread, meat, and wine. Then she stood in the midst of us and said, 'You have done a bold thing in going down alive to the house of Hades, and you will have died twice, to other people's once; now, then, stay here for the rest of the day, feast your fill, and go on with your voyage at daybreak tomorrow morning. In the meantime I will tell Odysseus about your course, and will explain everything to him so as to prevent your suffering from misadventure either by land or sea.'

"We agreed to do as she had said, and feasted through the livelong day to the going down of the sun, but when the sun had set and it came on dark, the men laid themselves down to sleep by the stern cables of the ship. Then Circe took me by the hand and bade me be seated away from the others, while she reclined by my side and asked me all about our adventures.

"'So far so good,' said she, when I had ended my story, 'and now pay attention to what I am about to tell you – heaven itself, indeed, will recall it to your recollection. First you will come to the Sirens who enchant all who come near them. If any one unwarily draws in too close and hears the singing of the Sirens, his wife and children will never welcome him home again, for they sit in a green field and warble him to death with the sweetness of their song. There is a great heap of dead men's bones lying all around, with the flesh still rotting off them. Therefore pass these Sirens by, and stop your men's ears with wax that none of them may hear; but if you like you can listen yourself, for you may get the men to bind you as you stand upright on a cross piece half way up the mast, and they must lash the rope's ends to the mast itself, that you may have the pleasure of listening. If you beg and pray the men to unloose you, then they must bind you faster.

"'When your crew have taken you past these Sirens, I cannot give you coherent directions as to which of two courses you are to take; I will lay the two alternatives before you, and you must consider them for yourself. On the one hand there are some overhanging rocks against which the deep blue waves of Amphitrite beat with terrific fury; the blessed gods call these rocks the Wanderers. Here not even a bird may pass, no, not even the timid doves that bring ambrosia to Father Zeus, but the sheer rock always carries off one of them, and Father Zeus has to send another to make up their number; no ship that ever yet came to these rocks has got away again, but the waves and whirlwinds of fire are freighted with wreckage and with the bodies of dead men. The only vessel that ever sailed and got through, was the famous *Argo* on her way from the house of Aeetes, and she too would have gone against these great rocks, only that Hera piloted her past them for the love she bore to Jason.

"'Of these two rocks the one reaches heaven and its peak is lost in a dark cloud. This never leaves it, so that the top is never clear not even in summer and early autumn. No man though he had twenty hands and twenty feet could get a foothold on it and climb it, for it runs sheer up, as smooth as though it had been polished. In the middle of it there is a large cavern, looking West and turned towards Erebus; you must take your ship this way, but the cave is so high up that not even the stoutest archer could send an arrow into it. Inside it Scylla sits and yelps with a voice that you might take to be that of a young hound, but in truth she is a dreadful monster and no one – not even a god – could face her without being terror-struck. She has twelve mis-shapen feet, and six necks of the most prodigious length; and at the end of each neck she has a frightful head with three rows of teeth in each, all set very close together, so that they would crunch any one to death in a moment, and she sits deep within her shady cell thrusting out her heads and peering all round the rock, fishing for dolphins or dogfish or any larger monster that she can catch, of the thousands with which Amphitrite teems. No ship ever yet got past her without losing some men, for she shoots out all her heads at once, and carries off a man in each mouth.

"'You will find the other rock lie lower, but they are so close together that there is not more than a bow-shot between them. A large fig tree in full leaf grows upon it, and under it lies the sucking whirlpool of Charybdis. Three times in the day does she vomit forth her waters, and three times she sucks them down again; see that you be not there when she is sucking, for if you are, Poseidon himself could not save you; you must hug the Scylla side and drive ship by as fast as you can, for you had better lose six men than your whole crew.'

"'Is there no way,' said I, 'of escaping Charybdis, and at the same time keeping Scylla off when she is trying to harm my men?'

"'You dare devil,' replied the goddess, 'you are always wanting to fight somebody or something; you will not let yourself be beaten even by the immortals. For Scylla is not mortal; moreover she is savage, extreme, rude, cruel and invincible. There is no help for it; your best chance will be to get by her as fast as ever you can, for if you dawdle about her rock while you are putting on your armour, she may catch you with a second cast of her six heads, and snap up another half dozen of your men; so drive your ship past her at full speed, and roar out lustily to Crataiis who is Scylla's dam, bad luck to her; she will then stop her from making a second raid upon you.'

"'You will now come to the Thrinacian island, and here you will see many herds of cattle and flocks of sheep belonging to the sun-god – seven herds of cattle and seven flocks of sheep, with fifty head in each flock. They do not breed, nor do they become fewer in number, and they are tended by the goddesses Phaethusa and Lampetie, who are children of the sun-god Hyperion by Neaera. Their mother when she had borne them and had done suckling them sent them to the Thrinacian island, which was a long way off, to live there and look after their father's flocks and herds. If you leave these flocks unharmed, and think of nothing but getting home, you may yet after much hardship reach Ithaca; but if you harm them, then I forewarn you of the destruction both of your ship and of your comrades; and even though you may yourself escape, you will return late, in bad plight, after losing all your men.'

"Here she ended, and dawn enthroned in gold began to show in heaven, whereon she returned inland. I then went on board and told my men to loose the ship from her moorings; so they at once got into her, took their places, and began to smite the grey sea with their oars. Presently the great and cunning goddess Circe befriended us with a fair wind that blew dead aft, and staid steadily with us, keeping our sails well filled, so we did whatever wanted doing to the ship's gear, and let her go as wind and helmsman headed her.

"Then, being much troubled in mind, I said to my men, 'My friends, it is not right that one or two of us alone should know the prophecies that Circe has made me, I will therefore tell you about them, so that whether we live or die we may do so with our eyes open. First she said we were to keep clear of the Sirens, who sit and sing most beautifully in a field of flowers; but she said I might hear them myself so long as no one else did. Therefore, take me and bind me to the crosspiece half way up the mast; bind me as I stand upright, with a bond so fast that I cannot possibly break away, and lash the rope's ends to the mast itself. If I beg and pray you to set me free, then bind me more tightly still.'

"I had hardly finished telling everything to the men before we reached the island of the two Sirens, for the wind had been very favourable. Then all of a sudden it fell dead calm; there was not a breath of wind nor a ripple upon the water, so the men furled the sails and stowed them; then taking to their oars they whitened the water with the foam they raised in rowing. Meanwhile I look a large wheel of wax and cut it up small with my sword. Then I kneaded the wax in my strong hands till it became soft, which it soon did between the kneading and the rays of the sun-god son of Hyperion. Then I stopped the ears of all my men, and they bound me hands and feet to the mast as I stood upright on the cross piece; but they went on rowing themselves. When we had got within earshot of the land, and the ship was going at a good rate, the Sirens saw that we were getting in shore and began with their singing.

"'Come here,' they sang, 'renowned Odysseus, honour to the Achaean name, and listen to our two voices. No one ever sailed past us without staying to hear the enchanting sweetness of our song – and he who listens will go on his way not only charmed, but wiser, for we know all the ills that the gods laid upon the Argives and Trojans before Troy, and can tell you everything that is going to happen over the whole world.'

"They sang these words most musically, and as I longed to hear them further I made signs by frowning to my men that they should set me free; but they quickened their stroke, and Eurylochus and Perimedes bound me with still stronger bonds till we had got out of hearing of the Sirens' voices. Then my men took the wax from their ears and unbound me.

"Immediately after we had got past the island I saw a great wave from which spray was rising, and I heard a loud roaring sound. The men were so frightened that they loosed hold of their oars, for the whole sea resounded with the rushing of the waters, but the ship stayed where it was, for the men had left off rowing. I went round, therefore, and exhorted them man by man not to lose heart.

"'My friends,' said I, 'this is not the first time that we have been in danger, and we are in nothing like so bad a case as when the Cyclops shut us up in his cave; nevertheless, my courage and wise counsel saved us then, and we shall live to look back on all this as well. Now, therefore, let us all do as I say, trust in Zeus and row on with might and main. As for you, coxswain, these are your orders; attend to them, for the ship is in your hands; turn her head away from these steaming rapids and hug the rock, or she will give you the slip and be over yonder before you know where you are, and you will be the death of us.'

"So they did as I told them; but I said nothing about the awful monster Scylla, for I knew the men would not go on rowing if I did, but would huddle together in the hold. In one thing only did I disobey Circe's strict instructions – I put on my armour. Then seizing two strong spears I took my stand on the ship's bows, for it was there that I expected first to see the monster of the rock, who was to do my men so much harm; but I could not make her out anywhere, though I strained my eyes with looking the gloomy rock all over and over.

"Then we entered the Straits in great fear of mind, for on the one hand was Scylla, and on the other dread Charybdis kept sucking up the salt water. As she vomited it up, it was like the water in a cauldron when it is boiling over upon a great fire, and the spray reached the top of the rocks on either side. When she began to suck again, we could see the water all inside whirling round and round, and it made a deafening sound as it broke against the rocks. We could see the bottom of the whirlpool all black with sand and mud, and the men were at their wits ends for fear. While we were taken up with this, and were expecting each moment to be our last, Scylla pounced down suddenly upon us and snatched up my six best men. I was looking at once after both ship and men, and in a moment I saw their hands and feet ever so high above me, struggling in the air as Scylla was carrying them off, and I heard them call out my name in one last despairing cry. As a fisherman, seated, spear in hand, upon some jutting rock throws bait into the water to deceive the poor little fishes, and spears them with the ox's horn with which his spear is shod, throwing them gasping on to the land as he catches them one by one – even so did Scylla land these panting creatures on her rock and munch them up at the mouth of her den, while they screamed and stretched out their hands to me in their mortal agony. This was the most sickening sight that I saw throughout all my voyages.

"When we had passed the Wandering rocks, with Scylla and terrible Charybdis, we reached the noble island of the sun-god, where were the goodly cattle and sheep belonging to the sun Hyperion. While still at sea in my ship I could bear the cattle lowing as they came home to the yards, and the sheep bleating. Then I remembered what the blind Theban prophet Teiresias had told me, and how carefully Aeaean Circe had warned me to shun the island of the blessed sun-god. So being much troubled I said to the men, 'My men, I know you are hard pressed, but listen while I tell you the prophecy that Teiresias made me, and how carefully Aeaean Circe warned me to shun the island of the blessed sun-god, for it was here, she said, that our worst danger would lie. Head the ship, therefore, away from the island.'

"The men were in despair at this, and Eurylochus at once gave me an insolent answer. 'Odysseus,' said he, 'you are cruel; you are very strong yourself and never get worn out; you seem to be made of iron, and now, though your men are exhausted with toil and want of sleep, you will not let them land and cook themselves a good supper upon this island, but bid them put out to sea and go faring fruitlessly on through the watches of the flying night. It is by night that the winds blow hardest and do so much damage; how can we escape should one of those sudden squalls spring up from South West or West, which so often wreck a vessel when our lords the gods are unpropitious? Now, therefore, let us obey the behests of night and prepare our supper here hard by the ship; tomorrow morning we will go on board again and put out to sea.'

"Thus spoke Eurylochus, and the men approved his words. I saw that heaven meant us a mischief and said, 'You force me to yield, for you are many against one, but at any rate each one of you must take his solemn oath that if he meet with a herd of cattle or a large flock of sheep, he will not be so mad as to kill a single head of either, but will be satisfied with the food that Circe has given us.'

"They all swore as I bade them, and when they had completed their oath we made the ship fast in a harbour that was near a stream of fresh water, and the men went ashore and cooked their suppers. As soon as they had had enough to eat and drink, they began talking about their poor comrades whom Scylla had snatched up and eaten; this set them weeping and they went on crying till they fell off into a sound sleep.

"In the third watch of the night when the stars had shifted their places, Zeus raised a great gale of wind that flew a hurricane so that land and sea were covered with thick clouds, and night sprang forth out of the heavens. When the child of morning, rosy-fingered Dawn, appeared, we brought the ship to land and drew her into a cave wherein the sea-nymphs hold their courts and dances, and I called the men together in council.

"'My friends,' said I, 'we have meat and drink in the ship, let us mind, therefore, and not touch the cattle, or we shall suffer for it; for these cattle and sheep belong to the mighty sun, who sees and gives ear to everything.' And again they promised that they would obey.

"For a whole month the wind blew steadily from the South, and there was no other wind, but only South and East. As long as corn and wine held out the men did not touch the cattle when they were hungry; when, however, they had eaten all there was in the ship, they were forced to go further afield, with hook and line, catching birds, and taking whatever they could lay their hands on; for they were starving. One day, therefore, I went up inland that I might pray heaven to show me some means of getting away. When I had gone far enough to be clear of all my men, and had found a place that was well sheltered from the wind, I washed my hands and prayed to all the gods in Olympus till by and by they sent me off into a sweet sleep.

"Meanwhile Eurylochus had been giving evil counsel to the men, 'Listen to me,' said he, 'my poor comrades. All deaths are bad enough but there is none so bad as famine. Why should not we drive in the best of these cows and offer them in sacrifice to the immortal gods? If we ever get back to Ithaca, we can build a fine temple to the sun-god and enrich it with every kind of ornament; if, however, he is determined to sink our ship out of revenge for these homed cattle, and the other gods are of the same mind, I for one would rather drink salt water once for all and have done with it, than be starved to death by inches in such a desert island as this is.'

"Thus spoke Eurylochus, and the men approved his words. Now the cattle, so fair and goodly, were feeding not far from the ship; the men, therefore, drove in the best of them, and they all stood round them saying their prayers, and using young oak-shoots instead of barley-meal, for there was no barley left. When they had done praying they killed the cows and dressed their carcasses; they cut out the thigh bones, wrapped them round in two layers of fat, and set some pieces of raw meat on top of them. They had no wine with which to make drink-offerings over the sacrifice while it was cooking, so they kept pouring on a little water from time to time while the inward meats were being grilled; then, when the thigh bones were burned and they had tasted the inward meats, they cut the rest up small and put the pieces upon the spits.

"By this time my deep sleep had left me, and I turned back to the ship and to the sea shore. As I drew near I began to smell hot roast meat, so I groaned out a prayer to the immortal gods. 'Father Zeus,' I exclaimed, 'and all you other gods who live in everlasting bliss, you have done me a cruel mischief by the sleep into which you have sent me; see what fine work these men of mine have been making in my absence.'

"Meanwhile Lampetie went straight off to the sun and told him we had been killing his cows, whereon he flew into a great rage, and said to the immortals, 'Father Zeus, and all you other gods who live in everlasting bliss, I must have vengeance on the crew of Odysseus' ship: they have had the insolence to kill my cows, which were the one thing I loved to look upon, whether I was going up heaven or down again. If they do not square accounts with me about my cows, I will go down to Hades and shine there among the dead.'

"'Sun,' said Zeus, 'go on shining upon us gods and upon mankind over the fruitful earth. I will shiver their ship into little pieces with a bolt of white lightning as soon as they get out to sea.'

"I was told all this by Calypso, who said she had heard it from the mouth of Hermes.

"As soon as I got down to my ship and to the sea shore I rebuked each one of the men separately, but we could see no way out of it, for the cows were dead already. And indeed the gods began at once to show signs and wonders among us, for the hides of the cattle crawled about, and the joints upon the spits began to low like cows, and the meat, whether cooked or raw, kept on making a noise just as cows do.

"For six days my men kept driving in the best cows and feasting upon them, but when Zeus the son of Cronus had added a seventh day, the fury of the gale abated; we therefore went on board, raised our masts, spread sail, and put out to sea. As soon as we were well away from the island, and could see nothing but sky and sea, the son of Cronus raised a black cloud over our ship, and the sea grew dark beneath it. We did not get on much further, for in another moment we were caught by a terrific squall from the West that snapped the forestays of the mast so that it fell aft, while all the ship's gear tumbled about at the bottom of the vessel. The mast fell upon the head of the helmsman in the ship's stern, so that the bones of his head were crushed to pieces, and he fell overboard as though he were diving, with no more life left in him.

"Then Zeus let fly with his thunderbolts, and the ship went round and round, and was filled with fire and brimstone as the lightning struck it. The men all fell into the sea; they were carried about in the water round the ship, looking like so many sea-gulls, but the god presently deprived them of all chance of getting home again.

"I stuck to the ship till the sea knocked her sides from her keel (which drifted about by itself) and struck the mast out of her in the direction of the keel; but there was a backstay of stout ox-thong still hanging about it, and with this I lashed the mast and keel together, and getting astride of them was carried wherever the winds chose to take me.

"The gale from the West had now spent its force, and the wind got into the South again, which frightened me lest I should be taken back to the terrible whirlpool of Charybdis. This indeed was what actually happened, for I was borne along by the waves all night, and by sunrise had reached the rock of Scylla, and the whirlpool. She was then sucking down the salt sea water, but I was carried aloft toward the fig tree, which I caught hold of and clung on to like a bat. I could not plant my feet anywhere so as to stand securely, for the roots were a long way off and the boughs that overshadowed the whole pool were too high, too vast, and too far apart for me to reach them; so I hung patiently on, waiting till the pool should discharge my mast and raft again – and a very long while it seemed. A jury-man is not more glad to get home to supper, after having been long detained in court by troublesome cases, than I was to see my raft beginning to work its way out of the whirlpool again. At last I let go with my hands and feet, and fell heavily into the sea, hard by my raft on to which I then got, and began to row with my hands. As for Scylla, the father of gods and men would not let her get further sight of me – otherwise I should have certainly been lost.

"Hence I was carried along for nine days till on the tenth night the gods stranded me on the Ogygian island, where dwells the great and powerful goddess Calypso. She took me in and was kind to me, but I need say no more about this, for I told you and your noble wife all about it yesterday, and I hate saying the same thing over and over again."

Bellerephon

BELLEREPHON, a brave young prince, the grandson of Sisyphus, King of Corinth, had the great misfortune to kill his own brother while hunting in the forest. His grief was, of course, intense; and the horror he felt for the place where the catastrophe had occurred, added to his fear lest he should incur judicial punishment for his involuntary crime, made him flee to the court of Argos, where he took refuge with Proetus, the king, who was also his kinsman.

He had not sojourned there very long, before Anteia, the queen, fell in love with him; and although her husband, Proetus, treated her with the utmost kindness, she made up her mind to desert him, and tried to induce Bellerophon to elope with her. Too honest to betray a man who had treated him as a friend, the young prince refused to listen to the queen's proposals. His refusal was to cost him dear, however; for, when Anteia saw that the youth would never yield to her wishes, she became very angry indeed, sought her husband, and accused the young stranger of crimes he had never even dreamed of committing.

Proetus, indignant at what he deemed deep treachery on the part of an honored guest, yet reluctant to punish him with his own hand as he deserved, sent Bellerophon to Iobates, King of Lycia, with a sealed message bidding him put the bearer to death.

Quite unconscious of the purport of this letter, Bellerophon traveled gayly onward, and presented himself before Iobates, who received him very hospitably, and, without inquiring his name or errand, entertained him royally for many days. After some time, Bellerophon suddenly remembered the sealed message intrusted to his care, and hastened to deliver it to Iobates, with many apologies for his forgetfulness.

With blanched cheeks and every outward sign of horror, the king read the missive, and then fell into a deep reverie. He did not like to take a stranger's life, and still could not refuse to comply with Proetus' urgent request: so, after much thought, he decided to send Bellerophon to attack the Chimera, a terrible monster with a lion's head, a goat's body, and a dragon's tail.

His principal motive in choosing this difficult task was, that, although many brave men had set forth to slay the monster, none had ever returned, for one and all had perished in the attempt.

Although very courageous, Bellerophon's heart beat fast with fear when told what great deed he must accomplish; and he left Iobates' palace very sorrowfully, for he dearly loved the king's fair daughter, Philonoe, and was afraid he would never see her again.

While thus inwardly bewailing the ill luck which had so persistently dogged his footsteps, Bellerophon suddenly saw Athene appear before him in all her splendor, and heard her inquire in gentle tones the cause of his too evident dejection. He had no sooner apprised her of the difficult task appointed him, than she promised him her aid, and before she vanished gave him a beautiful golden bridle, which she bade him use to control Pegasus.

Bridle in hand, Bellerophon stood pondering her words, and gradually remembered that Pegasus was a wonderful winged steed, born from the blood which fell into the foam of the sea from Medusa's severed head. This horse, as white as snow, and gifted with immortal life as well as incredible speed, was the favourite mount of Apollo and the Muses, who delighted in taking aerial flights on his broad back; and Bellerophon knew that from time to time he came down to earth to drink of the cool waters of the Hippocrene (a fountain which had bubbled forth where his hoofs first touched the earth), or to visit the equally limpid spring of Pirene, near Corinth.

Bellerophon now proceeded to the latter fountain, where, after lingering many days in the vain hope of catching even a glimpse of the winged steed, he finally beheld him sailing downward in wide curves, like a bird of prey. From his place of concealment in a neighboring thicket, Bellerophon watched his opportunity, and, while the winged steed was grazing, he boldly vaulted upon his back.

Pegasus, who had never before been ridden by a mortal, reared and pranced, and flew up to dizzy heights; but all his efforts failed to unseat the brave rider, who, biding his time, finally thrust Athene's golden bit between his teeth, and immediately he became gentle and tractable. Mounted upon this incomparable steed, Bellerophon now went in search of the winged monster Chimera, who had given birth to the Nemean lion and to the riddle-loving Sphinx.

From an unclouded sky Bellerophon and Pegasus swooped suddenly and unexpectedly down upon the terrible Chimera, whose fiery breath and great strength were of no avail; for after a protracted struggle Bellerophon and Pegasus were victorious, and the monster lay lifeless upon the blood-soaked ground.

This mighty deed of valor accomplished, Bellerophon returned to Iobates, to report the success of his undertaking; and, although the king was heartily glad to know the Chimera was no more, he was very sorry to see Bellerophon safe and sound, and tried to devise some other plan to get rid of him.

He therefore sent him to fight the Amazons; but the hero, aided by the gods, defeated these warlike women also, and returned to Lycia, where, after escaping from an ambush posted by the king for his destruction, he again appeared victorious at court.

These repeated and narrow escapes from certain death convinced Iobates that the youth was under the special protection of the gods; and this induced the king not only to forego further attempts to slay him, but also to bestow upon the young hero his daughter's hand in marriage.

Bellerophon, having now attained his dearest wishes, might have settled down in peace; but his head had been utterly turned by the many lofty flights he had taken upon Pegasus' back, and, encouraged by the fulsome flattery of his courtiers, he finally fancied himself the equal of the immortal gods, and wished to join them in their celestial abode.

Summoning his faithful Pegasus once more, he rose higher and higher, and would probably have reached Olympus' heights, had not Zeus sent a gadfly, which stung poor Pegasus so cruelly, that he shied viciously, and flung his too confident rider far down to the earth below.

This fall, which would doubtless have killed any one but a mythological hero, merely deprived Bellerophon of his eyesight; and ever after he groped his way disconsolately, thinking of the happy days when he rode along the paths of air, and gazed upon the beautiful earth at his feet.

Bellerophon, mounted upon Pegasus, winging his flight through the air or fighting the Chimera, is a favourite subject in sculpture and painting, which has frequently been treated by ancient artists, a few of whose most noted works are still extant in various museums.

This story, like many others, is merely a sun myth, in which Bellerophon, the orb of day, rides across the sky on Pegasus, the fleecy white clouds, and slays Chimera, the dread monster of darkness, which he alone can overcome. Driven from home early in life, Bellerophon wanders throughout the world like his brilliant prototype, and, like it, ends his career in total darkness.

The Calydonian Boar Hunt

ARTEMIS RESENTED any disregard or neglect of her worship; a remarkable instance of this is shown in the story of the Calydonian boar hunt, which is as follows:

Oeneus, king of Calydon in Aetolia, had incurred the displeasure of Artemis by neglecting to include her in a general sacrifice to the gods which he had offered up, out of gratitude for a bountiful harvest. The goddess, enraged at this neglect, sent a wild boar of extraordinary size and prodigious strength, which destroyed the sprouting grain, laid waste the fields, and threatened the inhabitants with famine and death. At this juncture, Meleager, the brave son of Oeneus, returned from the Argonautic expedition, and finding his country ravaged by this dreadful scourge, entreated the assistance of all the celebrated heroes of the age to join him in hunting the ferocious monster. Among the most famous of those who responded to his call were Jason, Castor and Polydeuces, Idas and Lynceus, Peleus, Telamon, Admetus, Perithous, and Theseus. The brothers of Althea, wife of Oeneus, joined the hunters, and Meleager also enlisted into his service the fleet-footed huntress Atalanta.

The father of this maiden was Schoeneus, an Arcadian, who, disappointed at the birth of a daughter when he had particularly desired a son, had exposed her on the Parthenian Hill, where he left her to perish. Here she was nursed by a she-bear, and at last found by some hunters, who reared her, and gave her the name of Atalanta. As the maiden grew up, she became an ardent lover of the chase, and was alike distinguished for her beauty and courage. Though often wooed, she led a life of strict celibacy, an oracle having predicted that inevitable misfortune awaited her, should she give herself in marriage to any of her numerous suitors.

Many of the heroes objected to hunt in company with a maiden; but Meleager, who loved Atalanta, overcame their opposition, and the valiant band set out on their expedition. Atalanta was the first to wound the boar with her spear, but not before two of the heroes had met their death from his fierce tusks. After a long and desperate encounter, Meleager succeeded in killing the monster, and presented the head and hide to Atalanta, as trophies of the victory. The uncles of Meleager, however, forcibly took the hide from the maiden, claiming their right to the spoil as next of kin, if Meleager resigned it. Artemis, whose anger was still unappeased, caused a violent quarrel to arise between uncles and nephew, and, in the struggle which ensued, Meleager killed his mother's brothers, and then restored the hide to Atalanta. When Althea beheld the dead bodies of the slain heroes, her grief and anger knew no bounds. She swore to revenge the death of her brothers on her own son, and unfortunately for him, the instrument of vengeance lay ready to her hand.

At the birth of Meleager, the Moirae, or Fates, entered the house of Oeneus, and pointing to a piece of wood then burning on the hearth, declared that as soon as it was consumed the babe would surely die. On hearing this, Althea seized the brand, laid it up carefully in a chest, and henceforth preserved it as her most precious possession. But now, love for her son giving place to the resentment she felt against the murderer of her brothers, she threw the fatal brand into the devouring flames. As it consumed, the vigour of Meleager wasted away, and when it was reduced to ashes, he expired. Repenting too late the terrible effects of her rash deed, Althea, in remorse and despair, took away her own life.

The news of the courage and intrepidity displayed by Atalanta in the famous boar hunt, being carried to the ears of her father, caused him to acknowledge his long-lost child. Urged by him to choose one of her numerous suitors, she consented to do so, but made it a condition that he alone, who could outstrip her in the race, should become her husband, whilst those she defeated should be put to death by her, with the lance which she bore in her hand. Thus many suitors had perished, for the maiden was unequalled for swiftness of foot, but at last a beautiful youth, named Hippomenes, who had vainly endeavoured to win her love by his assiduous attentions in the chase, ventured to enter the fatal lists. Knowing that only by stratagem could he hope to be successful, he obtained, by the help of Aphrodite, three golden apples from the garden of the Hesperides, which he threw down at intervals during his course. Atalanta, secure of victory, stooped to pick up the tempting fruit, and, in the meantime, Hippomenes arrived at the goal. He became the husband of the lovely Atalanta, but forgot, in his newly found happiness, the gratitude which he owed to Aphrodite, and the goddess withdrew her favour from the pair. Not long after, the prediction which foretold misfortune to Atalanta, in the event of her marriage, was verified, for she and her husband, having strayed unsanctioned into a sacred grove of Zeus, were both transformed into lions.

The trophies of the ever-memorable boar hunt had been carried by Atalanta into Arcadia, and, for many centuries, the identical hide and enormous tusks of the Calydonian boar hung in the temple of Athene at Tegea. The tusks were afterwards conveyed to Rome, and shown there among other curiosities.

A similar forcible instance of the manner in which Artemis resented any intrusion on her retirement, is seen in the fate which befell the famous hunter Actaeon, who happening one day to see Artemis and her attendants bathing, imprudently ventured to approach the spot. The goddess, incensed at his audacity, sprinkled him with water, and transformed him into a stag, whereupon he was torn in pieces and devoured by his own dogs.

Sigurd's Fight with the Dragon

SIGURD NOW WENT upon a farewell visit to Gripir, who, knowing the future, foretold every event in his coming career; after which he took leave of his mother, and accompanied by Regin set sail for the land of his fathers, vowing to slay the dragon when he had fulfilled his first duty, which was to avenge the death of Sigmund.

On his way to the land of the Volsungs a most marvellous sight was seen, for there came a man walking on the waters. Sigurd straightway took him on board his dragon ship, and the stranger, who gave his name as Feng or Fiollnir, promised favourable winds. Also he taught Sigurd how to distinguish auspicious omens. In reality the old man was Odin or Hnikar, the wave-stiller, but Sigurd did not suspect his identity.

Sigurd was entirely successful in his descent upon Lygni, whom he slew, together with many of his followers. He then departed from his reconquered kingdom and returned with Regin to slay Fafnir. Together they rode through the mountains, which ever rose higher and higher before them, until they came to a great tract of desert which Regin said was the haunt of Fafnir. Sigurd now rode on alone until he met a one-eyed stranger, who bade him dig trenches in the middle of the track along which the dragon daily dragged his slimy length to the river to quench his thirst, and to lie in wait in one of these until the monster passed over him, when he could thrust his sword straight into its heart.

Sigurd gratefully followed this counsel, and was rewarded with complete success, for as the monster's loathsome folds rolled overhead, he thrust his sword upward into its left breast, and as he sprang out of the trench the dragon lay gasping in the throes of death.

Regin had prudently remained at a distance until all danger was past, but seeing that his foe was slain, he now came up. He was fearful lest the young hero should claim a reward, so he began to accuse him of having murdered his kin, but, with feigned magnanimity, he declared that instead of requiring life for life, in accordance with the custom of the North, he would consider it sufficient atonement if Sigurd would cut out the monster's heart and roast it for him on a spit.

Sigurd was aware that a true warrior never refused satisfaction of some kind to the kindred of the slain, so he agreed to the seemingly small proposal, and immediately prepared to act as cook, while Regin dozed until the meat was ready. After an interval Sigurd touched the roast to ascertain whether it were tender, but burning his fingers severely, he instinctively thrust them into his mouth to allay the smart. No sooner had Fafnir's blood thus touched his lips than he discovered, to his utter surprise, that he could understand the songs of the birds, many of which were already gathering round the carrion. Listening attentively, he found that they were telling how Regin meditated mischief against him, and how he ought to slay the old man and take the gold, which was his by right of conquest, after which he ought to partake of the heart and blood of the dragon. As this coincided with his own wishes, he slew the evil old man with a thrust of his sword and proceeded to eat and drink as the birds had suggested, reserving a small portion of Fafnir's heart for future consumption. He then wandered off in search of the mighty hoard, and, after donning the Helmet of Dread, the hauberk of gold, and the ring Andvaranaut, and loading Greyfell with as much gold as he could carry, he sprang to the saddle and sat listening eagerly to the birds' songs to know what his future course should be.

When Grettir the Strong Slew Glam

This chapter from the Icelandic Grettis Saga describes what happens when the outlaw hero Grettir Ásmundarson meets the shepherd Glam (or Glámr), who has risen from the dead to become a 'graugr' (walking dead, or undead) and is causing havoc among the villages and farms.

Chapter 35
Grettir Goes to Thorhall-Stead, and Has to Do with Glam

GRETTIR rode to Thorhall-stead, and the bonder gave him good welcome; he asked whither Grettir was minded to fare, but Grettir said he would be there that night if the bonder would have it so.

Thorhall said that he thanked him therefor, "But few have thought it a treat to guest here for any time; thou must needs have heard what is going on here, and I fain would that thou shouldest have no trouble from me: but though thou shouldest come off whole thyself, that know I for sure, that thou wilt lose thy horse, for none keeps his horse whole who comes here."

Grettir said that horses were to be had in plenty whatsoever might hap to this. Then Thorhall was glad that Grettir was to be there, and gave him a hearty welcome.

Now Grettir's horse was locked up in a strong house, and they went to sleep; and so the night slipped by, and Glam came not home.

Then said Thorhall, "Things have gone well at thy coming, for every night is Glam wont to ride the house-roofs, or break open doors, as thou mayest well see."

Grettir said, "Then shall one of two things be, either he shall not hold himself back for long, or the hauntings will abate for more than one night; I will bide here another night and see how things fare."

Thereafter they went to Grettir's horse, and nought had been tried against it; then all seemed to the bonder to go one way.

Now is Grettir there another night, and neither came the thrall home; that the farmer deemed very hopeful; withal he fared to see after Grettir's horse. When the farmer came there, he found the house broken into, but the horse was dragged out to the door, and every bone in him broken to pieces. Thorhall told Grettir what had happed there, and bade him save himself, "For sure is thy death if thou abidest Glam."

Grettir answered, "I must not have less for my horse than a sight of the thrall."

The bonder said it was no boon to see him, for he was unlike any shape of man; "but good methinks is every hour that thou art here."

Now the day goes by, and when men should go to sleep Grettir would not put off his clothes, but lay down on the seat over against the bonder's lock-bed. He had a drugget cloak over him, and wrapped one skirt of it under his feet, and twined the other under his head, and looked out through the head-opening; a seat-beam was before the seat, a very strong one, and against this he set his feet. The door-fittings were all broken from the outer door, but a wrecked door was now bound thereby, and all was fitted up in the wretchedest wise. The panelling which had been before the seat athwart the hall, was all broken away both above and below the cross-beam; all beds had been torn out of place, and an uncouth place it was.

Light burned in the hall through the night; and when the third part of the night was passed, Grettir heard huge din without, and then one went up upon the houses and rode the hall, and drave his heels against the thatch so that every rafter cracked again.

That went on long, and then he came down from the house and went to the door; and as the door opened, Grettir saw that the thrall stretched in his head, which seemed to him monstrously big, and wondrous thick cut.

Glam fared slowly when he came into the door and stretched himself high up under the roof, and turned looking along the hall, and laid his arms on the tie-beam, and glared inwards over the place. The farmer would not let himself be heard, for he deemed he had had enough in hearing himself what had gone on outside. Grettir lay quiet, and moved no whit; then Glam saw that some bundle lay on the seat, and therewith he stalked up the hall and griped at the wrapper wondrous hard; but Grettir set his foot against the beam, and moved in no wise; Glam pulled again much harder, but still the wrapper moved not at all; the third time he pulled with both hands so hard, that he drew Grettir upright from the seat; and now they tore the wrapper asunder between them.

Glam gazed at the rag he held in his hand, and wondered much who might pull so hard against him; and therewithal Grettir ran under his hands and gripped him round the middle, and bent back his spine as hard as he might, and his mind it was that Glam should shrink thereat; but the thrall lay so hard on Grettir's arms, that he shrank all aback because of Glam's strength.

Then Grettir bore back before him into sundry seats; but the seat-beams were driven out of place, and all was broken that was before them. Glam was fain to get out, but Grettir set his feet against all things that he might; nathless Glam got him dragged from out the hall; there had they a wondrous hard wrestling, because the thrall had a mind to bring him out of the house; but Grettir saw that ill as it was to deal with Glam within doors, yet worse would it be without; therefore he struggled with all his might and main against going out-a-doors.

Now Glam gathered up his strength and knit Grettir towards him when they came to the outer door; but when Grettir saw that he might not set his feet against that, all of a sudden in one rush he drave his hardest against the thrall's breast, and spurned both feet against the half-sunken stone that stood in the threshold of the door; for this the thrall was not ready, for he had been tugging to draw Grettir to him, therefore he reeled aback and spun out against the door, so that his shoulders caught the upper door-case, and the roof burst asunder, both rafters and frozen thatch, and therewith he fell open-armed aback out of the house, and Grettir over him.

Bright moonlight was there without, and the drift was broken, now drawn over the moon, now driven from off her; and, even as Glam fell, a cloud was driven from the moon, and Glam glared up against her. And Grettir himself says that by that sight only was he dismayed amidst all that he ever saw.

Then his soul sank within him so, from all these things both from weariness, and because he had seen Glam turn his eyes so horribly, that he might not draw the short-sword, and lay well-nigh 'twixt home and hell.

But herein was there more fiendish craft in Glam than in most other ghosts, that he spake now in this wise:

"Exceeding eagerly hast thou wrought to meet me, Grettir, but no wonder will it be deemed, though thou gettest no good hap of me; and this must I tell thee, that thou now hast got half the strength and manhood, which was thy lot if thou hadst not met me: now I may not take from thee the strength which thou hast got before this; but that may I rule, that thou shalt never be mightier than now thou art; and nathless art thou mighty enow, and that shall many an one learn. Hitherto hast thou earned fame by thy deeds, but henceforth will wrongs and man-slayings fall on thee, and the most part of thy doings will turn to thy woe and ill-hap; an outlaw shalt thou be made, and ever shall it be thy lot to dwell alone abroad; therefore this weird I lay on thee, ever in those days to see these eyes with thine eyes, and thou wilt find it hard to be alone – and that shall drag thee unto death."

Now when the thrall had thus said, the astonishment fell from Grettir that had lain on him, and therewith he drew the short-sword and hewed the head from Glam, and laid it at his thigh.

Then came the farmer out; he had clad himself while Glam had his spell going, but he durst come nowhere nigh till Glam had fallen.

Thorhall praised God therefor, and thanked Grettir well for that he had won this unclean spirit. Then they set to work and burned Glam to cold coals, thereafter they gathered his ashes into the skin of a beast, and dug it down whereas sheep-pastures were fewest, or the ways of men. They walked home thereafter, and by then it had got far on towards day; Grettir laid him down, for he was very stiff: but Thorhall sent to the nearest farm for men, and both showed them and told them how all things had fared.

All men who heard thereof deemed this a deed of great worth, and in those days it was said by all that none in all the land was like to Grettir Asmundson for great heart and prowess.

Thorhall saw off Grettir handsomely, and gave him a good horse and seemly clothes, for those were all torn to pieces that he had worn before; so they parted in friendly wise. Grettir rode thence to the Ridge in Waterdale, and Thorvald received him well, and asked closely about the struggle with Glam. Grettir told him all, and said thereto that he had never had such a trial of strength, so long was their struggle.

Thorvald bade him keep quiet, "Then all will go well with thee, else wilt thou be a man of many troubles."

Grettir said that his temper had been nowise bettered by this, that he was worse to quiet than before, and that he deemed all trouble worse than it was; but that herein he found the greatest change, in that he was become so fearsome a man in the dark, that he durst go nowhither alone after nightfall, for then he seemed to see all kinds of horrors.

And that has fallen since into a proverb, that Glam lends eyes, or gives Glamsight to those who see things nowise as they are.

But Grettir rode home to Biarg when he had done his errands, and sat at home through the winter.

Gilgamesh's Encounters with Curious Creatures

The legendary Babylonian semi-divine hero Gilgamesh is famed for his exploits as related in the epic poem. Here we relate some sections of the Epic of Gilgamesh that are particularly pertinent to the theme of mythical beasts and monsters.

The Monster Khumbaba

THE FOURTH TABLET of the Standard Babylonian version of the Gilgamesh epic is concerned with a description of the monster with whom the heroes are about to do battle. Khumbaba, guardian of the abode of the goddess Irnina (a form of Ishtar), in the Forest of Cedars, whom Bel had appointed to guard the cedar (*i.e.*, one particular cedar which appears to be of greater height and sanctity than the others), is a creature of most terrifying aspect, the very presence of whom in the forest makes those who enter it grow weak and impotent.

As the heroes draw near, Eabani complains that his hands are feeble and his arms without strength, but Gilgamesh speaks words of encouragement to him.

The next fragments bring us into the fifth tablet. The heroes, having reached "a verdant mountain", paused to survey the Forest of Cedars. When they entered the forest the death of Khumbaba was foretold to one or other, or both of them, in a dream, and they hastened forward to the combat. Unfortunately the text of the actual encounter has not been preserved, but we learn from the context that the heroes were successful in slaying Khumbaba.

The Bull of Anu

In her wrath and humiliation (after Gilgamesh had spurned her advances) Ishtar appealed to her father and mother, Anu and Anatu, and begged the former to create a mighty bull and send it against Gilgamesh. Anu at first demurred, declaring that if he did so it would result in seven years' sterility on the earth; but finally he consented, and a great bull, Alu, was sent to do battle with Gilgamesh. The portion of the text which deals with the combat is much mutilated, but it appears that the conflict was hot and sustained, the celestial animal finally succumbing to a sword-thrust from Gilgamesh. Ishtar looks on in impotent anger. "Then Ishtar went up on to the wall of strong-walled Erech; she mounted to the top and she uttered a curse, (saying), 'Cursed be Gilgamesh, who has provoked me to anger, and has slain the bull from heaven.'" Then Eabani incurs the anger of the deity – "When Eabani heard these words of Ishtar, he tore out the entrails of the bull, and he cast them before her, saying, 'As for thee, I will conquer thee, and I will do to thee even as I have done to him.'" Ishtar was beside herself with rage. Gilgamesh and his companion dedicated the great horns of the bull to the sun-god, and having washed their hands in the river Euphrates, returned once more to Erech. As the triumphal procession passed through the city the people came out of their houses to do honour to the heroes. The remainder of the tablet is concerned with a great banquet given by Gilgamesh to celebrate his victory over the bull Alu, and with further visions of Eabani.

The seventh and eighth tablets are extremely fragmentary, and so much of the text as is preserved is open to various readings. It is possible that to the seventh tablet belongs a description of the underworld given to Eabani in a dream by the temple-maiden Ukhut, whom he had cursed in a previous tablet, and who had since died. The description answers to that given in another ancient text – the myth of Ishtar's descent into Hades – and evidently embodies the popular belief concerning the underworld. "Come, descend with me to the house of darkness, the abode of Irkalla, to the house whence the enterer goes not forth, to the path whose way has no return, to the house whose dwellers are deprived of light, where dust is their nourishment and earth their good. They are clothed, like the birds, in a garment of feathers; they see not the light, they dwell in darkness."

The Quest of Gilgamesh

On the heart of Gilgamesh, the fear of death had taken hold, and he determined to go in search of his ancestor, Ut-Napishtim, who might be able to show him a way of escape. Straightway putting his determination into effect, Gilgamesh set out for the abode of Ut-Napishtim. On the way he had to pass through mountain gorges, made terrible by the presence of wild beasts. From the power of these he was delivered by Sin, the moon-god, who enabled him to traverse the mountain passes in safety.

At length he came to a mountain higher than the rest, the entrance to which was guarded by scorpion-men. This was Mashu, the Mountain of the Sunset, which lies on the western horizon, between the earth and the underworld. "Then he came to the mountain of Mashu, the portals of which are guarded every day by monsters; their backs mount up to the ramparts of heaven, and their foreparts reach down beneath Aralu. Scorpion-men guard the gate (of Mashu); they strike terror into men, and it is death to behold them. Their splendour is great, for it overwhelms the mountains; from sunrise to sunset they guard the sun. Gilgamesh beheld them, and his face grew dark with fear and terror, and the wildness of their aspect robbed him of his senses." On approaching the entrance to the mountain Gilgamesh found his way barred by these scorpion-men, who, perceiving the strain of divinity in him, did not blast him with their glance, but questioned him regarding his purpose in drawing near the mountain of Mashu. When Gilgamesh had replied to their queries, telling them how he wished to reach the abode of his ancestor, Ut-Napishtim, and there learn the secret of perpetual life and youthfulness, the scorpion-men advised him to turn back. Before him, they said, lay the region of thick darkness; for twelve *kasbu* (twenty-four hours) he would have to journey through the thick darkness ere he again emerged into the light of day. And so they refused to let him pass. But Gilgamesh implored, "with tears," says the narrative, and at length the monsters consented to admit him. Having passed the gate of the Mountain of the Sunset (by virtue of his character as a solar deity) Gilgamesh traversed the region of thick darkness during the space of twelve *kasbu*. Toward the end of that period the darkness became ever less pronounced; finally it was broad day, and Gilgamesh found himself in a beautiful garden or park studded with trees, among which was the tree of the gods, thus charmingly depicted in the text – "Precious stones it bore as fruit, branches hung from it which were beautiful to behold. The top of the tree was lapis-lazuli, and it was laden with fruit which dazzled the eye of him that beheld." Having paused to admire the beauty of the scene, Gilgamesh bent his steps shoreward.

The tenth tablet describes the hero's encounter with the sea-goddess Sabitu, who, on the approach of one "who had the appearance of a god, in whose body was grief, and who looked as though he had made a long journey," retired into her palace and fastened the door. But Gilgamesh, knowing that her help was necessary to bring him to the dwelling of Ut-Napishtim, told her of his quest, and in despair threatened to break down the door unless she opened to him. At last Sabitu consented to listen to him whilst he asked the way to Ut-Napishtim. Like the scorpion-men, the sea-goddess perceived that Gilgamesh was not to be turned aside from his quest, so at last she bade him go to Adad-Ea, Ut-Napishtim's ferryman, without whose aid, she said, it would be futile to persist further in his mission. Adad-Ea, likewise, being consulted by Gilgamesh, advised him to desist, but the hero, pursuing his plan of intimidation, began to smash the ferryman's boat with his axe, whereupon Adad-Ea was obliged to yield. He sent his would-be passenger into the forest for a new rudder, and after that the two sailed away.

Hun-Apu and Xbalanque Chastise Vukub-Cakix and the Earth Giants

ERE THE EARTH WAS QUITE RECOVERED from the wrathful flood which had descended upon it there lived a being orgulous and full of pride, the great macaw called Vukub-Cakix (Seven-times-the-colour-of-fire – the Kiche name for the great macaw bird). His teeth were of emerald, and other parts of him shone with the brilliance of gold and silver. In short, it is evident that he was a sun-and-moon god of prehistoric times. He boasted dreadfully, and his conduct so irritated the other gods that they resolved upon his destruction. His two sons, Zipacna and Cabrakan

(Cockspur or Earth-heaper, and Earthquake), were earthquake-gods of the type of the Jötuns of Scandinavian myth or the Titans of Greek legend. These also were prideful and arrogant, and to cause their downfall the gods despatched the heavenly twins Hun-Apu and Xbalanque to earth, with instructions to chastise the trio.

Vukub-Cakix prided himself upon his possession of the wonderful nanze-tree, the tapal, bearing a fruit round, yellow, and aromatic, upon which he breakfasted every morning. One morning he mounted to its summit, whence he could best espy the choicest fruits, when he was surprised and infuriated to observe that two strangers had arrived there before him, and had almost denuded the tree of its produce. On seeing Vukub, Hun-Apu raised a blow-pipe to his mouth and blew a dart at the giant. It struck him on the mouth, and he fell from the top of the tree to the ground. Hun-Apu leapt down upon Vukub and grappled with him, but the giant in terrible anger seized the god by the arm and wrenched it from the body. He then returned to his house, where he was met by his wife, Chimalmat, who inquired for what reason he roared with pain. In reply he pointed to his mouth, and so full of anger was he against Hun-Apu that he took the arm he had wrenched from him and hung it over a blazing fire. He then threw himself down to bemoan his injuries, consoling himself, however, with the idea that he had avenged himself upon the disturbers of his peace.

Whilst Vukub-Cakix moaned and howled with the dreadful pain which he felt in his jaw and teeth (for the dart which had pierced him was probably poisoned) the arm of Hun-Apu hung over the fire, and was turned round and round and basted by Vukub's spouse, Chimalmat. The sun-god rained bitter imprecations upon the interlopers who had penetrated to his paradise and had caused him such woe, and he gave vent to dire threats of what would happen if he succeeded in getting them into his power.

But Hun-Apu and Xbalanque were not minded that Vukub-Cakix should escape so easily, and the recovery of Hun-Apu's arm must be made at all hazards. So they went to consult two great and wise magicians, Xpiyacoc and Xmucane, in whom we see two of the original Kiche creative deities, who advised them to proceed with them in disguise to the dwelling of Vukub, if they wished to recover the lost arm. The old magicians resolved to disguise themselves as doctors, and dressed Hun-Apu and Xbalanque in other garments to represent their sons.

Shortly they arrived at the mansion of Vukub, and while still some way off they could hear his groans and cries. Presenting themselves at the door, they accosted him. They told him that they had heard some one crying out in pain, and that as famous doctors they considered it their duty to ask who was suffering.

Vukub appeared quite satisfied, but closely questioned the old wizards concerning the two young men who accompanied them.

"They are our sons," they replied.

"Good," said Vukub. "Do you think you will be able to cure me?"

"We have no doubt whatever upon that head," answered Xpiyacoc. "You have sustained very bad injuries to your mouth and eyes."

"The demons who shot me with an arrow from their blow-pipe are the cause of my sufferings," said Vukub. "If you are able to cure me I shall reward you richly."

"Your Highness has many bad teeth, which must be removed," said the wily old magician. "Also the balls of your eyes appear to me to be diseased."

Vukub appeared highly alarmed, but the magicians speedily reassured him.

"It is necessary," said Xpiyacoc, "that we remove your teeth, but we will take care to replace them with grains of maize, which you will find much more agreeable in every way."

The unsuspicious giant agreed to the operation, and very quickly Xpiyacoc, with the help of Xmucane, removed his teeth of emerald, and replaced them by grains of white maize. A change quickly came over the Titan. His brilliancy speedily vanished, and when they removed the balls of his eyes he sank into insensibility and died.

All this time the wife of Vukub was turning Hun-Apu's arm over the fire, but Hun-Apu snatched the limb from above the brazier, and with the help of the magicians replaced it upon his shoulder. The discomfiture of Vukub was then complete. The party left his dwelling feeling that their mission had been accomplished.

The Earth-Giants

But in reality it was only partially accomplished, because Vukub's two sons, Zipacna and Cabrakan, still remained to be dealt with. Zipacna was daily employed in heaping up mountains, while Cabrakan, his brother, shook them in earthquake. The vengeance of Hun-Apu and Xbalanque was first directed against Zipacna, and they conspired with a band of young men to bring about his death.

The young men, four hundred in number, pretended to be engaged in building a house. They cut down a large tree, which they made believe was to be the roof-tree of their dwelling, and waited in a part of the forest through which they knew Zipacna must pass. After a while they could hear the giant crashing through the trees. He came into sight, and when he saw them standing round the giant tree-trunk, which they could not lift, he seemed very much amused.

"What have you there, O little ones?" he said laughing.

"Only a tree, your Highness, which we have felled for the roof-tree of a new house we are building."

"Cannot you carry it?" asked the giant disdainfully.

"No, your Highness," they made answer; "it is much too heavy to be lifted even by our united efforts."

With a good-natured laugh the Titan stooped and lifted the great trunk upon his shoulder. Then, bidding them lead the way, he trudged through the forest, evidently not disconcerted in the least by his great burden. Now the young men, incited by Hun-Apu and Xbalanque, had dug a great ditch, which they pretended was to serve for the foundation of their new house. Into this they requested Zipacna to descend, and, scenting no mischief, the giant readily complied. On his reaching the bottom his treacherous acquaintances cast huge trunks of trees upon him, but on hearing them coming down he quickly took refuge in a small side tunnel which the youths had constructed to serve as a cellar beneath their house.

Imagining the giant to be killed, they began at once to express their delight by singing and dancing, and to lend colour to his stratagem Zipacna despatched several friendly ants to the surface with strands of hair, which the young men concluded had been taken from his dead body. Assured by the seeming proof of his death, the youths proceeded to build their house upon the tree-trunks which they imagined covered Zipacna's body, and, producing a quantity of *pulque*, they began to make merry over the end of their enemy. For some hours their new dwelling rang with revelry.

All this time Zipacna, quietly hidden below, was listening to the hubbub and waiting his chance to revenge himself upon those who had entrapped him.

Suddenly arising in his giant might, he cast the house and all its inmates high in the air. The dwelling was utterly demolished, and the band of youths were hurled with such force into the sky that they remained there, and in the stars we call the Pleiades we can still discern them wearily waiting an opportunity to return to earth.

The Undoing of Zipacna

But Hun-Apu and Xbalanque, grieved that their comrades had so perished, resolved that Zipacna must not be permitted to escape so easily. He, carrying the mountains by night, sought his food by day on the shore of the river, where he wandered catching fish and crabs. The brothers made a large artificial crab, which they placed in a cavern at the bottom of a ravine. They then cunningly undermined a huge mountain, and awaited events. Very soon they saw Zipacna wandering along the side of the river, and asked him where he was going.

"Oh, I am only seeking my daily food," replied the giant.

"And what may that consist of?" asked the brothers.

"Only of fish and crabs," replied Zipacna.

"Oh, there is a crab down yonder," said the crafty brothers, pointing to the bottom of the ravine. "We espied it as we came along. Truly, it is a great crab, and will furnish you with a capital breakfast."

"Splendid!" cried Zipacna, with glistening eyes. "I must have it at once," and with one bound he leapt down to where the cunningly contrived crab lay in the cavern.

No sooner had he reached it than Hun-Apu and Xbalanque cast the mountain upon him; but so desperate were his efforts to get free that the brothers feared he might rid himself of the immense weight of earth under which he was buried, and to make sure of his fate they turned him into stone.

Thus at the foot of Mount Meah an, near Vera Paz, perished the proud Mountain-Maker.

The Discomfiture of Cabrakan

Now only the third of this family of boasters remained, and he was the most proud of any.

"I am the Overturner of Mountains!" said he.

But Hun-Apu and Xbalanque had made up their minds that not one of the race of Vukub should be left alive.

At the moment when they were plotting the overthrow of Cabrakan he was occupied in moving mountains. He seized the mountains by their bases and, exerting his mighty strength, cast them into the air; and of the smaller mountains he took no account at all. While he was so employed he met the brothers, who greeted him cordially.

"Good day, Cabrakan," said they. "What may you be doing?"

"Bah! nothing at all," replied the giant. "Cannot you see that I am throwing the mountains about, which is my usual occupation? And who may you be that ask such stupid questions? What are your names?"

"We have no names," replied they. "We are only hunters, and here we have our blow-pipes, with which we shoot the birds that live in these mountains. So you see that we do not require names, as we meet no one."

Cabrakan looked at the brothers disdainfully, and was about to depart when they said to him: "Stay; we should like to behold these mountain-throwing feats of yours."

This aroused the pride of Cabrakan.

"Well, since you wish it," said he, "I will show you how I can move a really great mountain. Now, choose the one you would like to see me destroy, and before you are aware of it I shall have reduced it to dust."

Hun-Apu looked around him, and espying a great peak pointed toward it. "Do you think you could overthrow that mountain?" he asked.

"Without the least difficulty," replied Cabrakan, with a great laugh. "Let us go toward it."

"But first you must eat," said Hun-Apu. "You have had no food since morning, and so great a feat can hardly be accomplished fasting."

The giant smacked his lips. "You are right," he said, with a hungry look. Cabrakan was one of those people who are always hungry. "But what have you to give me?"

"We have nothing with us," said Hun-Apu.

"Umph!" growled Cabrakan, "you are a pretty fellow. You ask me what I will have to eat, and then tell me you have nothing," and in his anger he seized one of the smaller mountains and threw it into the sea, so that the waves splashed up to the sky.

"Come," said Hun-Apu, "don't get angry. We have our blow-pipes with us, and will shoot a bird for your dinner."

On hearing this Cabrakan grew somewhat quieter.

"Why did you not say so at first?" he growled. "But be quick, because I am hungry."

Just at that moment a large bird passed overhead, and Hun-Apu and Xbalanque raised their blow-pipes to their mouths. The darts sped swiftly upward, and both of them struck the bird, which came tumbling down through the air, falling at the feet of Cabrakan.

"Wonderful, wonderful!" cried the giant. "You are clever fellows indeed," and, seizing the dead bird, he was going to eat it raw when Hun-Apu stopped him.

"Wait a moment," said he. "It will be much nicer when cooked," and, rubbing two sticks together, he ordered Xbalanque to gather some dry wood, so that a fire was soon blazing.

The bird was then suspended over the fire, and in a short time a savoury odour mounted to the nostrils of the giant, who stood watching the cooking with hungry eyes and watering lips.

Before placing the bird over the fire to cook, however, Hun-Apu had smeared its feathers with a thick coating of mud. The Indians in some parts of Central America still do this, so that when the mud dries with the heat of the fire the feathers will come off with it, leaving the flesh of the bird quite ready to eat. But Hun-Apu had done this with a purpose. The mud that he spread on the feathers was that of a poisoned earth, called *tizate*, the elements of which sank deeply into the flesh of the bird.

When the savoury mess was cooked, he handed it to Cabrakan, who speedily devoured it.

"Now," said Hun-Apu, "let us go toward that great mountain and see if you can lift it as you boast."

But already Cabrakan began to feel strange pangs.

"What is this?" said he, passing his hand across his brow. "I do not seem to see the mountain you mean."

"Nonsense," said Hun-Apu. "Yonder it is, see, to the east there."

"My eyes seem dim this morning," replied the giant.

"No, it is not that," said Hun-Apu. "You have boasted that you could lift this mountain, and now you are afraid to try."

"I tell you," said Cabrakan, "that I have difficulty in seeing. Will you lead me to the mountain?"

"Certainly," said Hun-Apu, giving him his hand, and with several strides they were at the foot of the eminence.

"Now," said Hun-Apu, "see what you can do, boaster."

Cabrakan gazed stupidly at the great mass in front of him. His knees shook together so that the sound was like the beating of a war-drum, and the sweat poured from his forehead and ran in a little stream down the side of the mountain.

"Come," cried Hun-Apu derisively, "are you going to lift the mountain or not?"

"He cannot," sneered Xbalanque. "I knew he could not."

Cabrakan shook himself into a final effort to regain his senses, but all to no purpose. The poison rushed through his blood, and with a groan he fell dead before the brothers.

Thus perished the last of the earth-giants of Guatemala, whom Hun-Apu and Xbalanque had been sent to destroy.

Hun-Apu and Xbalanque in Xibalba

THE CHILDHOOD OF THE MAYAN HERO TWINS HUN-APU AND XBALANQUE was full of such episodes as might be expected from these beings. We find in the Mayan mythological text the *Popol Vuh*, for example, that on attempting to clear a *milpa* (maize plantation) they employed magic tools which could be trusted to undertake a good day's work whilst they were absent at the chase. Returning at night, they smeared soil over their hands and faces, for the purpose of deluding Xmucane into the belief that they had been toiling all day in the fields.

But the wild beasts met in conclave during the night, and replaced all the roots and shrubs which the magic tools had cleared away. The twins recognized the work of the various animals, and placed a large net on the ground, so that if the creatures came to the spot on the following night they might be caught in its folds. They did come, but all made good their escape save the rat. The rabbit and deer lost their tails, however, and that is why these animals possess no caudal appendages! The rat, in gratitude for their sparing its life, told the brothers the history of their father and uncle, of their heroic efforts against the powers of Xibalba, and of the existence of a set of clubs and balls with which they might play *tlachtli* on the ball-ground at Ninxor-Carchah, where Hunhun-Apu and Vukub-Hunapu had played before them.

But the watchful Hun-Came and Vukub-Came soon heard that the sons and nephews of their first victims had adopted the game which had led these last into the clutches of the cunning Xibalbans, and they resolved to send a similar challenge to Hun-Apu and Xbalanque, thinking that the twins were unaware of the fate of Hunhun-Apu and Vukub-Hunapu. They therefore despatched messengers to the home of Xmucane with a challenge to play them at the ball-game, and Xmucane, alarmed by the nature of the message, sent a louse to warn her grandsons. The louse, unable to proceed as quickly as he wished, permitted himself to be swallowed by a toad, the toad by a serpent, and the serpent by the bird Voc, the messenger of Hurakan. At the end of the journey the other animals duly liberated each other, but the toad could not rid himself of the louse, who had in reality hidden himself in the toad's gums, and had not been swallowed at all. At last the message was delivered, and the twins returned to the abode of Xmucane, to bid farewell to their grandmother and mother. Before leaving they each planted a cane in the midst of the hut, saying that it would wither if any fatal accident befell them.

The Tricksters Tricked

They then proceeded to Xibalba, on the road trodden by Hunhun-Apu and Vukub-Hunapu, and passed the river of blood as the others had done. But they adopted the precaution of despatching ahead an animal called Xan as a sort of spy or scout. They commanded this animal to prick all the Xibalbans with a hair from Hun-Apu's leg, in order that they might discover which of them were made of wood, and incidentally learn the names of the others as they addressed one another when pricked by the hair. They were thus enabled to ignore the wooden images on their arrival at Xibalba, and they carefully avoided the red-hot stone. Nor did the ordeal of the House of Gloom affright them, and they passed through it scatheless. The inhabitants of the Underworld were both amazed and furious with disappointment. To add to their annoyance, they were badly beaten in the game of ball which followed. The Lords of Hell then requested the twins to bring them four bouquets of flowers from the royal garden of Xibalba, at the same time commanding the gardeners to keep good watch over the flowers so that none of them might be removed. But the brothers called to their aid a swarm of ants, who succeeded in returning with the flowers. The anger of the Xibalbans increased to a white fury, and they incarcerated Hun-Apu and Xbalanque in the House of Lances, a dread abode where demons armed with sharp spears thrust at them fiercely. But they bribed the lancers and escaped. The Xibalbans slit the beaks of the owls who guarded the royal gardens, and howled in fury.

The Houses of the Ordeals

They were next thrust into the House of Cold. Here they escaped a dreadful death from freezing by warming themselves with burning pine-cones. Into the House of Tigers and the House of Fire they were thrown for a night each, but escaped from both. But they were not so lucky in the House of Bats. As they threaded this place of terror, Camazotz, Ruler of the Bats, descended upon them with a whirring of leathern wings, and with one sweep of his sword-like claws cut off Hun-Apu's head. But a tortoise which chanced to pass the severed neck of the hero's prostrate body and came into contact with it was immediately turned into a head, and Hun-Apu arose from his terrible experience not a whit the worse.

With the object of proving their immortal nature to their adversaries, Hun-Apu and Xbalanque, first arranging for their resurrection with two sorcerers, Xulu and Pacaw, stretched themselves upon a bier and died. Their bones were ground to powder and thrown into the river. They then went through a kind of evolutionary process, appearing on the fifth day after their deaths as men-fishes and on the sixth as old men, ragged and tatterdemalion in appearance, killing and restoring each other to life. At the request of the princes of Xibalba, they burned the royal palace and restored it to its pristine splendour, killed and resuscitated the king's dog, and cut a man in pieces, bringing him to life again. The Lords of Hell were curious about the sensation of death, and asked to be killed and resuscitated. The first portion of their request the hero-brothers speedily granted, but did not deem it necessary to pay any regard to the second.

Throwing off all disguise, the brothers assembled the now thoroughly cowed princes of Xibalba, and announced their intention of punishing them for their animosity against themselves, their father and uncle. They were forbidden to partake in the noble and classic game of ball – a great indignity in the eyes of Maya of the higher caste – they were condemned to menial tasks, and they were to have sway over the beasts of the forest alone. After this their power rapidly waned. These princes of the Underworld are described as being owl-like, with faces painted black and white, as symbolical of their duplicity and faithless disposition.

As some reward for the dreadful indignities they had undergone, the souls of Hunhun-Apu and Vukub-Hunapu, the first adventurers into the darksome region of Xibalba, were translated to the skies, and became the sun and moon, and with this apotheosis the second book of the *Popol Vuh* ends.

The Boy Kinneneh and the Gorilla

IN THE EARLY DAYS of Uganda, there was a small village situate on the other side of the Katonga, in Buddu, and its people had planted bananas and plantains which in time grew to be quite a large grove, and produced abundant and very fine fruit. From a grove of bananas when its fruit is ripe there comes a very pleasant odour, and when a puff of wind blows over it, and bears the fragrance towards you, I know of nothing so well calculated to excite the appetite, unless it be the smell of roasted meat. Anyhow, such must have been the feeling of a mighty big gorilla, who one day, while roaming about alone in the woods searching for nuts to eat, stopped suddenly and stood up and sniffed for some time, with his nose well out in the direction of the village. After a while he shook his head and fell on all fours again to resume his search for food. Again there came with a whiff of wind a strong smell of ripe bananas, and he stood on his feet once more, and with his nose shot out thus he drew in a greedy breath and then struck himself over the stomach, and said:

"I thought it was so. There are bananas that way, and I must get some."

Down he fell on all fours, and put out his arms with long stretches, just as a fisherman draws in a heavy net, and is eager to prevent the escape of the fish.

In a little while he came to the edge of the grove, and stood and looked gloatingly on the beautiful fruit hanging in great bunches. Presently he saw something move. It was a woman bent double over a basket, and packing the fruit neatly in it, so that she could carry a large quantity at one journey.

The gorilla did not stay long thinking, but crawled up secretly to her; and then with open arms rushed forward and seized her. Before the woman could utter her alarm he had lifted her and her basket and trotted away with them into the deepest bush. On reaching his den he flung the woman on the ground, as you would fling dead meat, and bringing the banana basket close to him, his two legs hugging it close to his round paunch, he began to gorge himself, muttering while he peeled the fruit strange sounds. By-and-by the woman came to her senses, but instead of keeping quiet, she screamed and tried to run away. If it were not for that movement and noise, she perhaps might have been able to creep away unseen, but animals of all kinds never like to be disturbed while eating, so Gorilla gave one roar of rage, and gave her such a squeeze that the breath was clean driven out of her. When she was still he fell to again, and tore the peeling off the bananas, and tossed one after another down his wide throat, until there was not one of the fruit left in the basket, and the big paunch was swollen to twice its first size. Then, after laying his paw on the body to see if there was any life left in it, he climbed up to his nest above, and curled himself into a ball for a sleep.

When he woke he shook himself and yawned, and looking below he saw the body of the woman, and her empty basket, and he remembered what had happened. He descended the tree, lifted the body and let it fall, then took up the basket, looked inside and outside of it, raked over the peelings of the bananas, but could not find anything left to eat.

He began to think, scratching the fur on his head, on his sides, and his paunch, picking up one thing and then another in an absent-minded way. And then he appeared to have made up a plan.

Whatever it was, this is what he did. It was still early morning, and as there was no sign of a sun, it was cold, and human beings must have been finishing their last sleep. He got up and went straight for the plantation. On the edge of the banana-grove he heard a cock crow; he stopped and listened to it; he became angry.

"Someone," he said to himself, "is stealing my bananas," and with that he marched in the direction where the cock was crowing.

He came to the open place in front of the village, and saw several tall houses much larger than his own nest; and while he was looking at them, the door of one of them was opened, and a man came out. He crept towards him, and before he could cry out the gorilla had squeezed him until his ribs had cracked, and he was dead; he flung him down, and entered into the hut. He there saw a woman, who was blowing a fire on the hearth, and he took hold of her and squeezed her until there was no life left in her body. There were three children inside, and a bed on the floor. He treated them also in the same way, and they were all dead. Then he went into another house, and slew all the people in it, one with a squeeze, another with a squeeze and a bite with his great teeth, and there was not one left alive. In this way he entered into five houses and killed all the people in them, but in the sixth house lived the boy Kinneneh and his old mother.

Kinneneh had fancied that he heard an unusual sound, and he had stood inside with his eyes close to a chink in the reed door for some time when he saw something that resembled what might be said to be half animal and half man. He walked like a man, but had the fur of a beast. His arms were long, and his body was twice the breadth and thickness of a full-grown man. He did not know what it was, and when he saw it go into his neighbours' houses, and heard those strange sounds, he grew afraid, and turned and woke his mother, saying,

"Mother, wake up! there is a strange big beast in our village killing our people. So wake up quickly and follow me."

"But whither shall we fly, my son?" she whispered anxiously.

"Up to the loft, and lie low in the darkest place," replied Kinneneh, and he set her the example and assisted his mother.

Now those Uganda houses are not low-roofed like these of Congo-land, but are very high, as high as a tree, and they rise to a point, and near the top there is a loft where we stow our nets, and pots, and where our spear-shafts and bows are kept to season, and where our corn is kept to dry, and green bananas are stored to ripen. It was in this dark lofty place that Kinneneh hid himself and his mother, and waited in silence.

In a short time the gorilla put his head into their house and listened, and stepping inside he stood awhile, and looked searchingly around. He could see no one and heard nothing stir. He peered under the bed-grass, into the black pots and baskets, but there was no living being to be found.

"Ha, ha," he cried, thumping his chest like a man when he has got the big head. "I am the boss of this place now, and the tallest of these human nests shall be my own, and I shall feast every day on ripe bananas and plantains, and there is no one who can molest me – ha, ha!"

"Ha, ha!" echoed a shrill, piping voice after his great bass.

The gorilla looked around once more, among the pots, and the baskets, but finding nothing walked out. Kinneneh, after a while skipped down the ladder and watched between the open cane-work of the door, and saw him enter the banana-grove, and waited there until he returned with a mighty load of the fruit. He then saw him go out again into the grove, and bidding his mother lie still and patient, Kinneneh slipped out and ascended into the loft of the house chosen by the gorilla for his nest, where he hid himself and waited.

Presently the gorilla returned with another load of the fruit, and, squatting on his haunches, commenced to peel the fruit, and fill his throat and mouth with it, mumbling and chuckling, and saying,

"Ha, ha! This is grand! Plenty of bananas to eat, and all – all my own. None to say, 'Give me some,' but all my very own. Ho, ho! I shall feast every day. Ha, ha!"

"Ha, ha," echoed the piping voice again.

The gorilla stopped eating and made an ugly frown as he listened. Then he said:

"That is the second time I have heard a thin voice saying, 'Ha, ha!' If I only knew who he was that cried 'Ha, ha!' I would squeeze him, and squeeze him until he cried, 'Ugh, ugh!'"

"Ugh, ugh!" echoed the little voice again.

The gorilla leaped to his feet and rummaged around the pots and the baskets, took hold of the bodies one after another and dashed them against the floor, then went to every house and searched, but could not discover who it was that mocked him.

In a short time he returned and ate a pile of bananas that would have satisfied twenty men, and afterwards he went out, saying to himself that it would be a good thing to fill the nest with food, as it was a bore to leave the warm nest each time he felt a desire to eat.

No sooner had he departed than Kinneneh slipped down, and carried every bunch that had been left away to his own house, where they were stowed in the loft for his mother, and after enjoining his mother to remain still, he waited, peering through the chinks of the door.

He soon saw Gorilla bearing a pile of bunches that would have required ten men to carry, and after flinging them into the chief's house, return to the plantation for another supply. While Gorilla was tearing down the plants and plucking at the bunches, Kinneneh was actively engaged in transferring what he brought into the loft by his mother's side. Gorilla made many trips in this manner, and brought in great heaps, but somehow his stock appeared to be very small. At last his strength was exhausted, and feeling that he could do no more that day, he commenced to feed on what he had last brought, promising to himself that he would do better in the morning.

At dawn the gorilla hastened out to obtain a supply of fruit for his breakfast, and Kinneneh took advantage of his absence to hide himself overhead.

He was not long in his place before Gorilla came in with a huge lot of ripe fruit, and after making himself comfortable on his haunches with a great bunch before him he rocked himself to and fro, saying while he munched:

"Ha, ha! Now I have plenty again, and I shall eat it all myself. Ha, ha!"

"Ha, ha," echoed a thin voice again, so close and clear it seemed to him, that leaping up he made sure to catch it. As there appeared to be no one in the house, he rushed out raging, champing his teeth, and searched the other houses, but meantime Kinneneh carried the bananas to the loft of the gorilla's house, and covered them with bark-cloth.

In a short time Gorilla returned furious and disappointed, and sat down to finish the breakfast he had only begun, but on putting out his hands he found only the withered peelings of yesterday's bananas. He looked and rummaged about, but there was positively nothing left to eat. He was now terribly hungry and angry, and he bounded out to obtain another supply, which he brought in and flung on the floor, saying,

"Ha, ha! I will now eat the whole at once – all to myself, and that other thing which says, 'Ha, ha!' after me, I will hunt and mash him like this," and he seized a ripe banana and squeezed it with his paw with so much force that the pulp was squirted all over him. "Ha, ha!" he cried.

"Ha, ha!" mocked the shrill voice, so clear that it appeared to come from behind his ear.

This was too much to bear; Gorilla bounded up and vented a roar of rage. He tossed the pots, the baskets, the bodies, and bed-grass about – bellowing so loudly and funnily in his fury that Kinneneh, away up in the loft, could scarcely forbear imitating him. But the mocker could not be found, and Gorilla roared loudly in the open place before the village, and tore in and out of each house, looking for him.

Kinneneh descended swiftly from his hiding-place, and bore every banana into the loft as before.

Gorilla hastened to the plantation again, and so angry was he that he uprooted the banana-stalks by the root, and snapped off the clusters with one stroke of his great dog-teeth, and having got together a large stock, he bore it in his arms to the house.

"There," said he, "ha, ha! Now I shall eat in comfort and have a long sleep afterwards, and if that fellow who mocks me comes near – ah! I would" – and he crushed a big bunch in his arms and cried, "ha, ha!"

"Ha, ha! Ha, ha!" cried the mocking voice; and again it seemed to be at the back of his head. Whereupon Gorilla flung his arms behind in the hope of catching him, but there was nothing but his own back, which sounded like a damp drum with the stroke.

"Ha, ha! Ha, ha!" repeated the voice, at which Gorilla shot out of the door, and raced round the house, thinking that the owner was flying before him, but he never could overtake the flyer. Then he went around outside of the other houses, and flew round and round the village, but he could discover naught. But meanwhile Kinneneh had borne all the stock of bananas up into the loft above, and when Gorilla returned there was not one banana of all the great pile he had brought left on the floor.

When, after he was certain that there was not a single bit of a banana left for him to eat, he scratched his sides and his legs, and putting his hand on the top of his head, he uttered a great cry just like a great, stupid child, but the crying did not fill his tummy. No, he must have bananas for that – and he rose up after awhile and went to procure some more fruit.

But when he had brought a great pile of it and had sat down with his nice-smelling bunch before him, he would exclaim, "Ha, ha! Now – now I shall eat and be satisfied. I shall fill myself with the sweet fruit, and then lie down and sleep. Ha, ha!"

Then instantly the mocking voice would cry out after him, "Ha, ha!" and sometimes it sounded close to his ears, and then behind his head, sometimes it appeared to come from under the bananas and sometimes from the doorway: – that Gorilla would roar in fury, and he would grind his teeth just like two grinding-stones, and chatter to himself, and race about the village, trying to discover whence the voice came, but in his absence the fruit would be swept away by his invisible enemy, and when he would come in to finish his meal, lo! there were only blackened and stained banana peelings – the refuse of his first feast.

Gorilla would then cry like a whipped child, and would go again into the plantation, to bring some more fruit into the house, but when he returned with it he would always boast of what he was going to do, and cry out "Ha, ha!" and instantly his unseen enemy would mock him and cry "Ha, ha!" and he would start up raving and screaming in rage, and search for him, and in his absence his bananas would be whisked away. And Gorilla's hunger grew on him, until his paunch became like an empty sack, and what with his hunger and grief and rage, and furious raving and racing about, his strength was at last quite exhausted, and the end of him was that on the fifth day he fell from weakness across the threshold of the chief's house, which he had chosen to make his nest, and there died.

When the people of the next village heard of how Kinneneh, a little boy, had conquered the man-killing gorilla, they brought him and his mother away, and they gave him a fine new house and a plantation, and male and female slaves to tend it, and when their old king died, and the period of mourning for him was over, they elected wise Kinneneh to be king over them.

"Ah, friends," said Safeni to his companions, after Kadu had concluded his story, "there is no doubt that the cunning of a son of man prevails over the strongest brute, and it is well for us,

Mashallah! that it should be so; for if the elephant, or the lion, or the gorilla possessed but cunning equal to their strength, what would become of us!"

And each man retired to his hut, congratulating himself that he was born a man-child, and not a thick, muddle-headed beast.

Lelimo and the Magic Cap

ONCE LONG AGO, when giants dwelt upon the earth, there lived in a little village, far up in the mountains, a woman who had the power of making magic caps. When her daughter Siloane grew old enough to please the eyes of men, her mother made her a magic cap. "Keep this cap safely, my child, for it will protect you from the power of Lelimo (the giant). If you lose it, he will surely seize you and carry you away to his dwelling in the mountains, where he and his children will eat you."

Siloane promised to be very careful, and for a long time always carried the magic cap with her whenever she went beyond the village.

Now it was the custom each year for the maidens of the village to go to a certain spot, where the 'tuani' or long rushes grew, there to gather great bundles with which to make new mats for the floors of the houses. When the time came, Siloane and many more maidens set out for the place. The distance was great, and as they must reach their destination at the rising of the sun, they set off from the village at midnight.

Just as the sun rose from sleep, the maidens arrived at the graves on which the rushes grew. Soon all were busy cutting rushes and making mats. Siloane laid down her cap on one of the graves by which she was working. All day the maidens worked, and at sunset they started on their homeward journey. Soon the moon arose and lighted the land, and the light-hearted maidens went gaily singing on their way.

When they had gone some way, Siloane suddenly remembered she had left the magic cap on the grave where she had been sitting. Afraid to face her mother without it, she asked her companions to wait for her while she hurried back to fetch it.

Long the maidens waited, amusing themselves by telling stories and singing songs in the moonlight, but Siloane returned not. At length two girls set out to look for her, but when they reached the spot, no trace of her was to be found. Great was their dismay. How could they tell the news to her parents? Still there was nothing else to be done, and, with heavy hearts, they all returned to the village.

When Ma-Batu, the mother of Siloane, heard their story, she immediately set to work to make another magic cap, which she gave to her younger daughter Sieng, telling her to have it always by her, in case Siloane should need her help.

Meanwhile, Siloane had been taken captive by the giant as she was making her way back to recover her magic cap. When she felt Lelimo's heavy hand on her shoulder, she struggled frantically to get away, but her strength was as water against such a man, and he soon had her securely tied up in his big bag, made out of the skin of an ox.

Now when Lelimo saw Siloane, he was returning from a feast, and was very drunk, so that he mistook his way, and wandered long and far, until, in the morning, he came to a large hut, where he threw down the sack containing Siloane, and demanded a drink of the woman who stood in the door. She gave him some very strong 'juala' (beer), which made him more drunk than before. While he was drinking, Siloane called softly from the sack, for she had recognised her mother's voice talking to the giant, and knew that he had brought her in some wonderful way to her father's house. Again she called, and this time her sister heard her, and hastened to undo the sack. She then hid Siloane, and, by the aid of the magic cap, she filled the sack with bees and wasps and closed it firmly. When the giant came out from the hut, he picked up the sack and started for his own home. On his arrival there he again threw down the sack, and ordered his wife to kill and cook the captive girl he imagined he had brought home. His wife began to feel the sack in order to find out how big the girl was, but the bees became angry and stung her through the sack, which frightened her, and she refused to open it. Thereupon Lelimo called his son, but he also refused. In a great rage, the giant turned them both out of the house, and closed all the openings. He then made a great fire, and prepared to roast the girl.

When he opened the sack, the bees and wasps, who were by this time thoroughly furious, swarmed upon him, and stung him till he howled with agony, and, mad with pain, he broke down the door of the hut and rushed down to the river, into which he flung himself head first. In this position he was afterwards found by his wife, his feet resting on a rock above the water, his head buried in the mud of the river.

Such was the end of this wicked giant, who had been the terror of that part of the country for many, many years.

Untombinde and the Squatting Monster

A CHIEF'S DAUGHTER, Untombinde, goes, with a number of other girls, to bathe in the Ilulange, against the warnings of her parents: "To the Ilulange nothing goes and returns again; it goes there forever." The girls found, on coming out of the water, that the clothes and ornaments they had left on the bank had disappeared; they knew that the *isiququmadevu* must have taken them, and one after another petitioned politely for their return. Untombinde, however, said, "I will never beseech the *isiququmadevu*," and was immediately seized by the monster and dragged down into the water.

Her companions went home and reported what had happened. The chief, though he evidently despaired of recovering her ("Behold, she goes there forever!"), sent a troop of young men to fetch the *isiququmadevu*, which has killed Untombinde. The warriors found the monster squatting on the riverbank, and were swallowed up, everyone, before they could attack her. She then went on to the chiefs kraal, swallowed up all the inhabitants, with their dogs and their cattle, as well as all the people in the surrounding country.

Among the victims were two beautiful children, much beloved. Their father, however, escaped, took his two clubs and his large spear, and went his way, saying, "It is I who will kill the *isiququmadevu*."

By this time the monster had left the neighbourhood, and the man went on seeking her till he met with some buffaloes, whom he asked, "Whither has Usiququmadevu gone? She has gone away with my children!" The buffaloes directed him on his way, and he then came across some leopards, of whom he asked the same question, and who also told him to go forward. He next met an elephant, who likewise sent him on, and so at last he came upon the monster herself, and announced, "I am seeking Usiququmadevu, who is taking away my children!" Apparently she hoped to escape recognition, for she directed him, like the rest, to go forward. But the man was not to be deceived by so transparent a device: he came and stabbed the lump, and so the *isiququmadevu* died."

Then all the people, cattle, and dogs, and, lastly, Untombinde herself, came out unharmed, and she returned to her father.

Mishemokwa, or The Origin of the Small Black Bear

IN A REMOTE PART OF THE NORTH lived a great magician called Iamo, and his only sister, who had never seen a human being. Seldom, if ever, had the man any cause to go from home; for, as his wants demanded food, he had only to go a little distance from the lodge, and there, in some particular spot, place his arrows, with their barbs in the ground. Telling his sister where they had been placed, every morning she would go in search, and never fail of finding each struck through the heart of a deer. She had then only to drag them into the lodge and prepare their food. Thus she lived till she attained womanhood, when one day her brother said to her, "Sister, the time is near at hand when you will be ill. Listen to my advice. If you do not, it will probably be the cause of my death. Take the implements with which we kindle our fires. Go some distance from our lodge, and build a separate fire. When you are in want of food, I will tell you where to find it. You must cook for yourself, and I will for myself. When you are ill, do not attempt to come near the lodge, or bring any of the utensils you use. Be sure always to fasten to your belt the implements you need, for you do not know when the time will come. As for myself, I must do the best I can." His sister promised to obey him in all he had said.

Shortly after, her brother had cause to go from home. She was alone in her lodge, combing her hair. She had just untied the belt to which the implements were fastened, when suddenly the event, to which her brother had alluded, occurred. She ran out of the lodge, but in her haste forgot the belt. Afraid to return, she stood for some time thinking. Finally she decided to enter the lodge and get it. For, thought she, my brother is not at home, and I will stay but a moment to catch hold of it. She went back. Running in suddenly, she caught hold of it, and was coming out when her brother came in sight. He knew what was the matter. "Oh," he said, "did I not tell you to take care? But now you have killed me." She was going on her way, but her brother said to her, "What can you do there now? the accident has happened. Go in, and stay where you have always stayed. And what will become of you? You have killed me."

He then laid aside his hunting dress and accoutrements, and soon after both his feet began to inflame and turn black, so that he could not move. Still he directed his sister where to place the arrows, that she might always have food. The inflammation continued to increase, and had now reached his first rib; and he said, "Sister, my end is near. You must do as I tell you. You see my medicine-sack, and my war-club tied to it. It contains all my medicines, and my war-plumes, and my paints of all colors. As soon as the inflammation reaches my breast, you will take my war-club. It has a sharp point, and you will cut off my head. When it is free from my body, take it, place its neck in the sack, which you must open at one end. Then hang it up in its former place. Do not forget my bow and arrows. One of the last you will take to procure food. The remainder tie to my sack, and then hang it up, so that I can look towards the door. Now and then I will speak to you, but not often." His sister again promised to obey.

In a little time his breast was affected. "Now," said he, "take the club and strike off my head." She was afraid, but he told her to muster courage. "Strike," said he, and a smile was on his face. Mustering all her courage, she gave the blow and cut off the head. "Now," said the head, "place me where I told you." And fearfully she obeyed it in all its commands. Retaining its animation, it looked around the lodge as usual, and it would command its sister to go to such places as it thought would procure for her the flesh of different animals she needed. One day the head said, "The time is not distant when I shall be freed from this situation, but I shall have to undergo many sore evils. So the Superior Manito decrees, and I must bear all patiently." In this situation we must leave the head.

In a certain part of the country was a village inhabited by a numerous and warlike band of Indians. In this village was a family of ten young men – brothers. It was in the spring of the year that the youngest of these blackened his face and fasted. His dreams were propitious. Having ended his fast, he sent secretly for his brothers at night, so that none in the village could overhear or find out the direction they intended to go. Though their drum was heard, yet that was a common occurrence. Having ended the usual formalities, he told them how favorable his dreams were, and that he had called them together to know if they would accompany him in a war excursion. They all answered they would. The third brother from the eldest, noted for his oddities, coming up with his war-club when his brother had ceased speaking, jumped up, "Yes," said he, "I will go, and this will be the way I will treat those we are going to fight;" and he struck the post in the centre of the lodge, and gave a yell. The others spoke to him, saying, "Slow, slow, Mudjikewis, when you are in other people's lodges." So he sat down. Then, in turn, they took the drum, and sang their songs, and closed with a feast. The youngest told them not to whisper their intention even to their wives, but secretly to prepare for their journey. They all promised obedience, and Mudjikewis was the first to say so.

The time for their departure drew near. Word was given to assemble on a certain night, when they would depart immediately. Mudjikewis was loud in his demands for his moccasins. Several times his wife asked him the reason. "Besides," said she, "you have a good pair on." "Quick, quick," he said, "since you must know, we are going on a war excursion. So be quick." He thus revealed the secret. That night they met and started. The snow was on the ground, and they travelled all night, lest others should follow them. When it was daylight, the leader took snow and made a ball of it; then tossing it into the air, he said, "It was in this way I saw snow fall in my dream, so that I could not be tracked." And he told them to keep close to each other for fear of losing themselves, as the snow began to fall in very large flakes. Near as they walked, it was with difficulty they could see each other. The snow continued falling all that day and the following night. So it was impossible to track them.

They had now walked for several days, and Mudjikewis was always in the rear. One day, running suddenly forward, he gave the Saw-saw-quan, and struck a tree with his war-club, which broke into pieces as if struck with lightning. "Brothers," said he, "this will be the way I will serve those whom we are going to fight." The leader answered, "Slow, slow, Mudjikewis. The one I lead you to is not to be thought of so lightly." Again he fell back and thought to himself, "What, what: Who can this be he is leading us to?" He felt fearful, and was silent. Day after day they travelled on, till they came to an extensive plain, on the borders of which human bones were bleaching in the sun. The leader spoke. "They are the bones of those who have gone before us. None has ever yet returned to tell the sad tale of their fate." Again Mudjikewis became restless, and, running forward, gave the accustomed yell. Advancing to a large rock which stood above the ground, he struck it, and it fell to pieces. "See, brothers," said he, "thus will I treat those whom we are going to fight." "Still, still," once more said the leader; "he to whom I am leading you is not to be compared to that rock."

Mudjikewis fell back quite thoughtful, saying to himself, "I wonder who this can be that he is going to attack." And he was afraid. Still they continued to see the remains of former warriors, who had been to the place where they were now going, some of whom had retreated as far back as the place where they first saw the bones, beyond which no one had ever escaped. At last they came to a piece of rising ground, from which they plainly distinguished, sleeping on a distant mountain, a mammoth bear.

The distance between them was great, but the size of the animal caused him plainly to be seen. "There," said the leader, "it is he to whom I am leading you; here our troubles only will commence, for he is a Mishemokwa and a Manito. It is he who has that we prize so dearly (i.e., wampum), to obtain which, the warriors whose bones we saw sacrificed their lives. You must not be fearful. Be manly. We shall find him asleep." They advanced boldly till they came near, when they stopped to view him more closely. He was asleep. Then the leader went forward and touched the belt around the animal's neck. "This," he said, "is what we must get. It contains the wampum." They then requested the eldest to try and slip the belt over the bear's head, who appeared to be fast asleep, as he was not in the least disturbed by the attempt to obtain it. All their efforts were in vain, till it came to the one next the youngest. He tried, and the belt moved nearly over the monster's head, but he could get it no further. Then the youngest one and leader made his attempt, and succeeded. Placing it on the back of the oldest, he said, "Now we must run," and off they started. When one became fatigued with its weight, another would relieve him. Thus they ran till they had passed the bones of all former warriors, and were some distance beyond, when, looking back, they saw the monster slowly rising. He stood some time before he missed his wampum. Soon they heard his tremendous howl, like distant thunder, slowly filling all the sky; and then they heard him speak and say, "Who can it be that has dared to steal my wampum? Earth is not so large but that I can find them." And he descended from the hill in pursuit. As if convulsed, the earth shook with every jump he made. Very soon he approached the party. They however kept the belt, exchanging it from one to another, and encouraging each other. But he gained on them fast. "Brothers," said the leader, "has never any one of you, when fasting, dreamed of some friendly spirit who would aid you as a guardian?" A dead silence followed. "Well," said he, "fasting, I dreamed of being in danger of instant death, when I saw a small lodge, with smoke curling from its top. An old man lived in it, and I dreamed he helped me. And may it be verified soon," he said, running forward and giving the peculiar yell, and a howl as if the sounds came from the depths of his stomach, and which is called Checau-dum. Getting upon a piece of rising ground, behold! a lodge, with smoke curling from its top, appeared. This gave them all new strength, and they ran forward and entered it. The leader spoke to the old man who sat in the lodge saying, "Nemesho, help us. We claim your protection, for the great bear will kill us." "Sit down and eat, my grandchildren," said the old man. "Who is a great Manito?" said he, "there is none but me; but let me look," and he opened the door of the lodge, when lo! at a little distance he saw the enraged animal coming on, with slow but powerful leaps. He closed the door. "Yes," said he, "he is indeed a great Manito. My grandchildren, you will be the cause of my losing my life. You asked my protection, and I granted it; so now come what may, I will protect you. When the bear arrives at the door, you must run out of the other end of the lodge." Then putting his hand to the side of the lodge where he sat, he brought out a bag, which he opened. Taking out two small black dogs, he placed them before him. "These are the ones I use when I fight," said he; and he commenced patting, with both hands, the sides of one of them, and they began to swell out, so that he soon filled the lodge by his bulk. And he had great strong teeth. When he attained his full size he growled, and from that moment, as from instinct, he jumped out at the door and met the bear, who in another leap would have reached the lodge. A terrible combat ensued. The skies rang with the howls of the fierce monsters. The remaining dog soon took the field. The brothers, at the onset, took the advice of the old man, and escaped through the opposite side of the lodge. They had not proceeded far before they heard the dying cry of one of the dogs, and soon after of the other. "Well," said the leader, "the old man will share their fate; so run, run, he will soon be after us." They started with fresh vigor, for they had received food from the old man; but very soon the bear came in sight, and again was fast gaining upon them. Again the leader asked the brothers if they could do nothing for their safety. All were silent. The leader, running forward, did as before. "I dreamed," he cried, "that, being in great trouble, an old man helped me who was a Manito. We shall soon see his lodge." Taking courage, they still went on. After going a short distance they saw the lodge of the old Manito. They entered immediately and claimed his protection, telling him a Manito was after them. The old man, setting meat before them, said, "Eat. Who is a Manito? there is no Manito but me. There is none whom I fear." And the earth trembled as the monster advanced. The old man opened the door and saw him coming. He shut it slowly, and said, "Yes, my grandchildren, you have brought trouble upon me." Procuring his medicine sack, he took out his small war-clubs of black stone, and told the young men to run through the other side of the lodge. As he handled the clubs they became very large, and the old man stepped out just as the bear reached the door. Then striking him with one of the clubs, it broke in pieces. The bear stumbled. Renewing the attempt with the other war-club, that also was broken, but the bear fell senseless. Each blow the old man gave him sounded like a clap of thunder, and the howls of the bear ran along till they filled the heavens.

The young men had now ran some distance, when they looked back. They could see that the bear was recovering from the blows. First he moved his paws, and soon they saw him rise on his feet. The old man shared the fate of the first, for they now heard his cries as he was torn in pieces. Again the monster was in pursuit, and fast overtaking them. Not yet discouraged, the young men kept on their way; but the bear was now so close, that the leader once more applied to his brothers, but they could do nothing. "Well," said he, "my dreams will soon be exhausted. After this I have but one more." He advanced, invoking his guardian spirit to aid him. "Once," said he, "I dreamed that, being sorely pressed, I came to a large lake, on the shore of which was a canoe, partly out of water, having ten paddles all in readiness. Do not fear," he cried, "we shall soon get to it." And so it was, even as he had said. Coming to the lake, they saw the canoe with ten paddles, and immediately they embarked. Scarcely had they reached the centre of the lake, when they saw the bear arrive at its borders. Lifting himself on his hind legs, he looked all around. Then he waded into the water; then losing his footing, he turned back, and commenced making the circuit of the lake. Meanwhile, the party remained stationary in the centre to watch his movements. He travelled around, till at last he came to the place from whence he started. Then he commenced drinking up the water, and they saw the current fast setting in towards his open mouth. The leader encouraged them to paddle hard for the opposite shore. When only a short distance from land, the current had increased so much, that they were drawn back by it, and all their efforts to reach it were vain.

Then the leader again spoke, telling them to meet their fates manfully. "Now is the time, Mudjikewis," said he, "to show your prowess. Take courage, and sit in the bow of the canoe; and when it approaches his mouth, try what effect your club will have on his head." He obeyed, and stood ready to give the blow; while the leader, who steered, directed the canoe for the open mouth of the monster.

Rapidly advancing, they were just about to enter his mouth, when Mudjikewis struck him a tremendous blow on the head, and gave the saw-saw-quan. The bear's limbs doubled under him, and he fell stunned by the blow. But before Mudjikewis could renew it the monster disgorged all the water he had drank, with a force which sent the canoe with great velocity to the opposite shore. Instantly leaving the canoe, again they fled, and on they went till they were completely exhausted. The earth again shook, and soon they saw the monster hard after them. Their spirits drooped, and they felt discouraged. The leader exerted himself, by actions and words, to cheer them up; and once more he asked them if they thought of nothing, or could do nothing for their rescue; and, as before, all were silent. "Then," he said, "this is the last time I can apply to my guardian spirit. Now if we do not succeed, our fates are decided." He ran forward, invoking his spirit with great earnestness, and gave the yell. "We shall soon arrive," said he to his brothers, "to the place where my last guardian spirit dwells. In him I place great confidence. Do not, do not be afraid, or your limbs will be fear-bound. We shall soon reach his lodge. Run, run," he cried.

They were now in sight of the lodge of Iamo, the magician of the undying head – of that great magician whose life had been the forfeit of the kind of necromantic leprosy caused by the careless steps of the fatal curse of uncleanliness in his sister. This lodge was the sacred spot of expected relief to which they had been fleeing, from the furious rage of the giant Bear, who had been robbed of her precious boon, the magis-sauniqua. For it had been the design of many previous war parties to obtain this boon.

In the mean time, the undying head of Iamo had remained in the medicine sack, suspended on the sides of his wigwam, where his sister had placed it, with its mystic charms, and feathers, and arrows. This head retained all life and vitality, keeping its eyes open, and directing its sister, in order to procure food, where to place the magic arrows, and speaking at long intervals. One day the sister saw the eyes of the head brighten, as if through pleasure. At last it spoke. "Oh! sister," it said, "in what a pitiful situation you have been the cause of placing me. Soon, very soon, a party of young men will arrive and apply to me for aid; but, alas! how can I give what I would have done with so much pleasure. Nevertheless, take two arrows, and place them where you have been in the habit of placing the others, and have meat prepared and cooked before they arrive. When you hear them coming and calling on my name, go out and say, 'Alas! it is long ago that an accident befell him; I was the cause of it.' If they still come near, ask them in and set meat before them. And now you must follow my directions strictly. When the bear is near, go out and meet him. You will take my medicine sack, bows and arrows, and my head. You must then untie the sack, and spread out before you my paints of all colors, my war eagle feathers, my tufts of dried hair, and whatever else it contains. As the bear approaches, you will take all these articles, one by one, and say to him, 'This is my deceased brother's paint,' and so on with all the other articles, throwing each of them as far from you as you can. The virtues contained in them will cause him to totter; and, to complete his destruction, you will take my head, and that too you will cast as far off as you can, crying aloud, 'See, this is my deceased brother's head.' He will then fall senseless. By this time the young men will have eaten, and you will call them to your assistance. You must then cut the carcass into pieces, yes, into small pieces, and scatter them to the four winds; for, unless you do this, he will again revive." She promised that all should be done as he said. She had only time to prepare the meat, when the voice of the leader was heard calling upon Iamo for aid. The woman went out and invited them in as her brother had directed. But the war party, being closely pursued, came promptly up to the lodge. She invited them in, and placed the meat before them. While they were eating they heard the bear approaching. Untying the medicine sack and taking the head, she had all in readiness for his approach. When he came up, she did as she had been told. "Behold, Mishemokwa," she cried, "this is the meda sack of Iamo. These are war eagle's feathers of Iamo (casting them aside). These are magic arrows of Iamo (casting them down). These are the sacred paints and magic charms of Iamo. These are dried tufts of the hair of furious beasts. And this (swinging it with all her might) is his undying head." The monster began to totter, as she cast one thing after the other on the ground, but still recovering strength, came close up to the woman till she flung the head. As it rolled along the ground, the blood, excited by the feelings of the head in this terrible scene, gushed from the nose and mouth. The bear, tottering, soon fell with a tremendous noise. Then she cried for help, and the young men came rushing out, having partially regained their strength and spirits.

Mudjikewis, stepping up, gave a yell, and struck the monster a blow upon the head. This he repeated till it seemed like a mass of brains; while the others, as quick as possible, cut him into very small pieces, which they then scattered in every direction. While thus employed, happening to look around where they had thrown the meat, wonderful to behold! they saw, starting up and running off in every direction, small black bears, such as are seen at the present day. The country was soon overspread with these black animals. And it was from this monster that the present race of bears, the mukwahs, derived their origin.

Having thus overcome their pursuer, they returned to the lodge. In the mean time, the woman, gathering the implements she had scattered, and the head, placed them again in the sack. But the head did not speak again.

The war party were now triumphant, but they did not know what use to make of their triumph. Having spent so much time, and traversed so vast a country in their flight, the young men gave up the idea of ever returning to their own country, and game being plenty, they determined to remain where they now were, and make this their home. One day they moved off some distance from the lodge for the purpose of hunting, having left the wampum captured with the woman. They were very successful, and amused themselves, as all young men do when alone, by talking and jesting with each other. One of them spoke and said, "We have all this sport to ourselves; let us go and ask our sister if she will not let us bring the head to this place, as it is still alive. It may be pleased to hear us talk and be in our company. In the mean time, we will take food to our sister." They went, and requested the head. She told them to take it, and they took it to their hunting-grounds, and tried to amuse it, but only at times did they see its eyes beam with pleasure. One day, while busy in their encampment, they were unexpectedly attacked by unknown Indians. The skirmish was long contested and bloody. Many of their foes were slain, but still they were thirty to one. The young men fought desperately till they were all killed. The attacking party then retreated to a height of ground, to muster their men, and to count the number of missing and slain. One of their young men had strayed away, and, in endeavoring to overtake them, came to the place where the undying head was hung up. Seeing that alone retain animation, he eyed it for some time with fear and surprise. However, he took it down and opened the sack, and was much pleased to see the beautiful feathers, one of which he placed on his head.

Starting off, it waved gracefully over him till he reached his party, when he threw down the head and sack, and told them how he had found it, and that the sack was full of paints and feathers. They all looked at the head and made sport of it. Numbers of the young men took up the paint and painted themselves, and one of the party took the head by the hair and said, "Look, you ugly thing, and see your paints on the faces of warriors." But the feathers were so beautiful, that numbers of them also placed them on their heads. Then again they used all kinds of indignity to the head, for which they were in turn repaid by the death of those who had used the feathers. Then the chief commanded them to throw all away except the head. "We will see," said he, "when we get home, what we can do to it. We will try to make it shut its eyes."

When they reached their homes they took it to the council lodge, and hung it up before the fire, fastening it with raw hide soaked, which would shrink and become tightened by the action of the fire. "We will then see," they said, "if we cannot make it shut its eyes."

Meanwhile, for several days, the sister of Iamo had been waiting for the young men to bring back the head; till at last, getting impatient, she went in search of it. The young men she found lying within short distances of each other, dead, and covered with wounds. Various other bodies lay scattered in different directions around them. She searched for the head and sack, but they were nowhere to be found. She raised her voice and wept, and blackened her face. Then she walked in different directions, till she came to the place from whence the head had been taken. There she found the magic bow and arrows, where the young men, ignorant of their qualities, had left them. She thought to herself that she would find her brother's head, and came to a piece of rising ground, and there saw some of his paints and feathers. These she carefully put up, and hung upon the branch of a tree till her return.

At dusk she arrived at the first lodge of the enemy, in a very extensive village. Here she used a charm, common among Indians when they wish to meet with a kind reception. On applying to the old man and woman of the lodge, she was kindly received. She made known her errand. The old man promised to aid her, and told her that the head was hung up before the council fire, and that the chiefs of the village, with their young men, kept watch over it continually. The former are considered as Manitoes. She said she only wished to see it, and would be satisfied if she could only get to the door of the lodge. She knew she had not sufficient power to take it by force. "Come with me," said the Indian, "I will take you there." They went, and they took their seats near the door. The council lodge was filled with warriors, amusing themselves with games, and constantly keeping up a fire to smoke the head, as they said, to make dry meat. They saw the eyes move, and not knowing what to make of it, one spoke and said, "Ha! ha! it is beginning to feel the effects of the smoke." The sister looked up from the door, and as her eyes met those of her brother, tears rolled down the cheeks of the undying head. "Well," said the chief, "I thought we would make you do something at last. Look! look at it – shedding tears," said he to those around him; and they all laughed and passed their jokes upon it. The chief, looking around and observing the woman, after some time said to the old man who came with her, "Who have you got there? I have never seen that woman before in our village." "Yes," replied the man, "you have seen her; she is a relation of mine, and seldom goes out. She stays in my lodge, and asked me to allow her to come with me to this place." In the centre of the lodge sat one of those vain young men who are always forward, and fond of boasting and displaying themselves before others. "Why," said he, "I have seen her often, and it is to his lodge I go almost every night to court her." All the others laughed and continued their games. The young man did not know he was telling a lie to the woman's advantage, who by that means escaped scrutiny.

She returned to the old man's lodge, and immediately set out for her own country. Coming to the spot where the bodies of her adopted brothers lay, she placed them together, their feet toward the east. Then taking an axe which she had, she cast it up into the air, crying out, "Brothers, get up from under it, or it will fall on you." This she repeated three times, and the third time the brothers all arose and stood on their feet.

Mudjikewis commenced rubbing his eyes and stretching himself. "Why," said he, "I have overslept myself." "No, indeed," said one of the others, "do you not know we were all killed, and that is our sister who has brought us to life?" The young men took the bodies of their enemies and burned them. Soon after, the woman went to procure wives for them, in a distant country, they knew not where; but she returned with ten young females, which she gave to the young men, beginning with the eldest. Mudjikewis stepped to and fro, uneasy lest he should not get the one he liked. But he was not disappointed, for she fell to his lot. And they were well matched, for she was a female magician. They then all moved into a very large lodge, and their sister Iamoqua told them that the women must now take turns in going to her brother's head every night, trying to untie it. They all said they would do so with pleasure. The eldest made the first attempt, and with a rushing noise she fled through the air.

Towards daylight she returned. She had been unsuccessful, as she succeeded in untying only one of the knots. All took their turns regularly, and each one succeeded in untying only one knot each time. But when the youngest went, she commenced the work as soon as she reached the lodge; although it had always been occupied, still the Indians never could see any one, for they all possessed invisibility. For ten nights now, the smoke had not ascended, but filled the lodge and drove them out. This last night they were all driven out, and the young woman carried off the head.

The young people and the sister heard the young woman coming high through the air, and they heard her saying, "Prepare the body of our brother." And as soon as they heard it, they went to a small lodge where the black body of Iamo lay. His sister commenced cutting the neck part, from which the head had been severed. She cut so deep as to cause it to bleed; and the others who were present, by rubbing the body and applying medicines, expelled the blackness. In the mean time, the one who brought it, by cutting the neck of the head, caused that also to bleed.

As soon as she arrived, they placed that close to the body, and by the aid of medicines and various other means, succeeded in restoring Iamo to all his former beauty and manliness. All rejoiced in the happy termination of their troubles, and they had spent some time joyfully together, when Iamo said, "Now I will divide the wampum;" and getting the belt which contained it, he commenced with the eldest, giving it in equal proportions. But the youngest got the most splendid and beautiful, as the bottom of the belt held the richest and rarest.

They were told that, since they had all once died, and were restored to life, they were no longer mortals, but spirits, and they were assigned different stations in the invisible world. Only Mudjikewis's place was, however, named. He was to direct the west wind, hence generally called Kabeyun, the father of Manabozho, there to remain forever. They were commanded, as they had it in their power, to do good to the inhabitants of the earth; and forgetting their sufferings in procuring the wampum, to give all things with a liberal hand. And they were also commanded that it should also be held by them sacred; those grains or shells of the pale hue to be emblematic of peace, while those of the darker hue would lead to evil and to war.

The spirits, then, amid songs and shouts, took their flight to their respective abodes on high; while Iamo, with his sister Iamoqua, descended into the depths below.

The Island of Skeletons

BIG WAVE and his little nephew, Red Shell, lived together in a deep forest. The boy was the only relative that the old man had, and he was very fond of him. He had brought Red Shell and his sister, Wild Sage, to his home some years before, just after the great plague had killed most of his tribe, among them the father and mother of the children. But they had not been many months in the forest before Wild Sage was stolen by a giant who lived on the Island of Skeletons.

Big Wave warned the boy never to go towards the east; for, if by any chance, he should cross a certain magic line of sacred meal that Big Wave had drawn, he would be at the mercy of the giant.

The boy obeyed for a time; but by and by he grew tired of playing in one place, so he went towards the east, not noticing when he crossed the magic line, till he came to the shore of a great lake.

He amused himself for a while, throwing pebbles into the water, and shooting arrows. A man came up to him, and said, "Well, boy, where is your lodge?"

Red Shell told him. Then the man proposed shooting arrows to see who could shoot the higher. Red Shell had had much practice, and though he was only a boy, his arm was strong, and he drew the bow far back and sent the arrow much higher than the man did.

The man laughed and said, "You are a brave boy; now let us see whether you can swim as well as you can shoot."

They jumped into the water and tried holding their breath while swimming. Again the boy proved himself the victor.

When they were again on land, the man said to him, "Will you go with me in my canoe? I am on my way to an island where there are pretty birds, and you can shoot as many as you please."

Red Shell said he would go, and looked about for a canoe. The man began singing, and presently there appeared a canoe drawn by six white swans, three on either side. The boy and his companion stepped in and the man guided the swans by singing.

The island was so long that he could not see the end of it, but it was not very wide. It was thickly wooded and there was so much undergrowth that the ground could hardly be seen, but Red Shell noticed heaps of bones under the bushes, and asked what they were. He was told that the island had once been a famous hunting-ground and these were the bones of the animals that had been killed.

After wandering about for some time, the man proposed another swim. They had been in the water but a few minutes when the boy heard singing, and looking around he saw the man going off in the canoe and taking his own and Red Shell's clothes with him. He shouted, but neither the man nor the birds paid any attention to him.

Thus he was left alone and naked, and it was fast growing dark. Then he remembered his uncle's warnings, and was so miserable from cold, hunger and fear, that at last he sat down and cried.

By-and-by he heard a voice calling to him, "Hist! keep still."

He looked round and saw a skeleton lying on the ground not far from him. It beckoned to him and said, "Poor boy, it was the same with me, but I will help you if you will do me a service. Go to that tree" (pointing to one close by) "dig on the west side of it, and you will find a pouch of smoking mixture and a pipe. Bring them to me. You can get a flint on the shore. Bring that also."

The boy was terribly frightened, but the skeleton spoke kindly, and not as though he meant to do harm. Red Shell therefore went to the tree, and brought the pipe and smoking mixture. Then he found a flint and on being asked to do so struck fire, lit the pipe and handed the same to the skeleton.

It smoked quickly, drawing the smoke into the mouth and letting it escape between the ribs. Red Shell watched and saw mice run out from between the bones. When the skeleton was rid of them it said: "Now I feel better, and can tell you what to do to escape my fate. A giant is coming to-night with three dogs, to hunt you and kill you for his supper. You must lose the trail for them by jumping into the water many times on your way to a hollow tree, which you will find on the other side of the island. In the morning after they have gone, come to me."

Red Shell thanked the skeleton and started at once to find the tree. It was quite dark, so he could see nothing, but he ran from tree to tree, climbing hallway up each one, and running into the water many times before he found the place where he had been told to sleep.

Towards morning he heard the splash of a canoe in the water, and soon a giant followed by three large dogs, strode into the forest.

"You must hunt this animal," the giant said to the dogs.

They scented the trail and dashed through the bushes. They rushed up one tree and then another, and at last came back to the giant with their tails between their legs, for they had found nothing.

He was so angry that he struck the foremost animal with his war-club and killed it on the spot. He skinned it and ate it raw. Then he drove the two others down to the canoe, jumped in and went away.

When they were out of sight of the island, Red Shell crept from his hiding place and went back to the skeleton.

"You are still alive?" it asked in surprise. "You are a brave boy. To-night the man who brought you here will come to drink your blood. You must go down to the shore before the darkness comes and dig a pit in the sand. Lie down in it and cover yourself with sand. When he leaves his canoe, get into it and say 'Come swans, let us go home.' If the man calls you, you must not turn round or look at him. When you are free, do not forget the skeleton."

Red Shell promised to come back to the island and to do all that he could for the poor bones. He went down to the shore and dug the pit deep enough so that when he stood in it his head was on a level with the water. When he heard the song in the distance he knew the swans were coming; so he covered his head with sand and waited till he heard a footstep on the dry leaves.

Then he crept out stealthily, stepped into the canoe and whispered to the swans, "Come, let us go home." He began the song that he had heard their master sing to them, and the canoe glided from the shore.

The swans carried him down the lake to a large cleft rock in the center. They drew the canoe through the opening and through the cave till they came to a stone door. Red Shell tried to open it, but could not. Then he turned the canoe around and struck the door with the stern.

The door flew open and Red Shell found himself in a fine lodge. He saw his own clothes and many others heaped in a corner near the fire which was burning brightly. A kettle of soup was steaming over it and there were some potatoes in the ashes on the hearth.

Seeing no one, the boy ate supper and then lay down to sleep on a couch of wild-cat skins.

In the morning he went out and stepping into the canoe, said, "Come, swans, let us go to the island."

He saw the two dogs lying asleep in the sun and, on landing, found that then had killed their master.

The skeleton was delighted to see him and praised him for his courage and for being true to his word. But he said to him, "You must not go home yet. Travel toward the east three days and you will come to some huge rocks. There you will see a young girl drawing water from a spring. She is your sister, Wild Sage, whom the giant stole many moons since, and whom you believed dead. You will be able to get her away. When you have done so, come back to me."

Red Shell at once set out for the east and in three days he found the rocks of which he had been told. As he came near them he saw a lovely girl drawing water. "Sister," he said, going up to her, "you must come home with me."

She was frightened and tried to run away. Looking back, she saw that it was really her brother, when she was even more afraid, though she turned and spoke to him. "Hist," said she, "a giant keeps me here. Go before he sees you or he will kill you."

Red Shell did not move.

"Go," said Wild Sage.

"No," he answered, "not till you go with me. Take me to your lodge."

The giant had gone to a cranberry swamp, and Wild Sage knew that he would not return until the evening; so she ventured to take her brother home with her. She dug a pit in one corner of the lodge, told him to get into it, and then covered it with her bed of buffalo skins.

Just before the darkness came the giant's dogs rushed in, barking furiously. "Who?" said the giant, "is hidden here?"

"No one," said Wild Sage.

"There is, there is," said the giant, "or the dogs would not bark like that."

They did not discover Red Shell, however, so the giant sat down to his supper.

"This boy is not tender, he is not cooked enough, get up and cook him more," said the giant.

"Cook it yourself, if it doesn't suit you," she answered.

The giant took no notice of her answer, but called to her to come and take off his moccasins.

"Take them off yourself," she said.

"Kaw," thought the giant, "now I know she has some one hidden. I will kill him in the morning."

Early the next day the giant said he was going to the cranberry swamp to get some children for his dinner. He did not go far from the lodge, but hid himself in some bushes close to the shore.

He saw Wild Sage and her brother get into a canoe, and threw a hook after them, which caught the boat and drew it towards the shore. But Red Shell took up a stone and broke the hook, and they floated off once more.

The giant was in a terrible rage. He lay down flat on the ground, and, putting his mouth to the water, drank so fast that the canoe was drawn close to the shore He began to swell from drinking such a quantity, and could not move. Red Shell took another stone and threw it at him. It struck him and he snapped in two, and the water he had swallowed flowed back into the lake.

Red Shell and his sister then sailed to the island, where the two dogs who had eaten their master rushed down to meet them. The boy raised his hand threateningly, and said: "Off to the woods as wolves. You no longer deserve to be dogs."

The animals slunk away growling, and as they disappeared were seen to change into lean and hungry wolves.

Red Shell went to the skeleton, who commanded him to gather all the bones that he could find on the island and to lay them side by side in one place. Then he was to say to them, "Dead folk, arise!"

It took him and his sister many days, for there were bones everywhere. When all had been arranged in one place, Red Shell stood off at a little distance and called loudly, "Dead folk, arise!" The bones raised themselves and took human form. All the men had bows and arrows, but some had only one arm, and others only one leg. The skeleton whom Red Shell had first met became a tall, handsome warrior, perfect in every limb. He saluted Red Shell as Chief, and the others did the same.

Then the boy and his sister crossed the lake and traveled westward till they came to their uncles' lodge. He was very old, his fire was out and he was still mourning for his nephew. But as he listened to the story of the lad's adventures, and realized that he had come back unhurt, some of his years left him.

They built a long lodge with many fireplaces; then Red Shell returned to the island and brought back those who had been skeletons. The handsome brave, who was known as White Eagle, married Wild Sage, and they all dwelt together in peace to the end of their lives.

The Bended Rocks

BENDING WILLOW was the most beautiful girl in a tribe noted for its handsome women. She had many suitors, but she refused them all; for her love was given to a young warrior of a distant nation, who, she felt sure, would some day return to throw a red deer at her feet in token that he wished to marry her.

Among her suitors was a hideous old Indian, a chief who was very rich. He was scarred and wrinkled and his hair was as gray as the badger that burrows in the forest. He was cruel also, for when the young men were put to the torture to prove themselves worthy to be warriors, he devised tests more dreadful than any that the tribe had ever known. But the chief, who was rightly named No Heart, declared that he would marry Bending Willow, and, as he was powerful, her parents did not dare to refuse him. Bending Willow begged and pleaded in vain.

On the night before the day set for the marriage, she went into the woods, and throwing herself on the ground, sobbed as if her heart would break. All night she lay there, listening to the thunder of the great cataract of Niagara, which was but a woman's journey from the village. At last it suggested to her a sure means of escape.

Early in the morning before any one was stirring, she went back to her father's wigwam, took his canoe and dragged it to the edge of the river. Then stepping into it she set it adrift and it headed quickly towards the Falls. It soon reached the rapids and was tossed like a withered branch on the white-crested billows, but went on, on, swiftly and surely to the edge of the great fall.

For a moment only, she saw the bright, green water, and then she felt herself lifted and was borne on great, white wings which held her above the rocks. The water divided and she passed into a dark cave behind the rainbow.

The spirit of Cloud and Rain had gone to her rescue and had taken her into his lodge. He was a little, old man, with a white face and hair and beard of soft, white mist, like that which rises day and night from the base of the Falls. The door of his lodge was the green wave of Niagara, and the walls were of gray rock studded with white stone flowers.

Cloud and Rain gave her a warm wrapper and seated her on a heap of ermine skins in a far corner of the lodge where the dampness was shut out by a magic fire. This is the fire that runs beneath the Falls, and throws its yellow-and-green flames across the water, forming the rainbow.

He brought her dainty fish to eat and delicate jelly made from mosses which only the water spirits can find or prepare.

When she was rested he told her that he knew her story, and if she would stay with him he would keep her until her ugly old suitor was dead. "A great serpent," added he, "lies beneath the village, and is even now poisoning the spring from which No Heart draws all the water that he uses, and he will soon die."

Bending Willow was grateful, and said that she would gladly remain all her life in such a beautiful home and with such a kind spirit.

Cloud and Rain smiled; but he knew the heart of a young girl would turn towards her own home when it was safe for her to return. He needed no better proof of this than the questions she asked about the serpent which caused so much sickness among her people.

He told her that this serpent had lain there many years. When he once tasted human blood he could never be satisfied. He crept beneath a village and cast a black poison into the springs from which people drew water. When any one died the serpent stole out at night and drank his blood. That made him ravenous for more. So when one death occurred more followed until the serpent was gorged and went to sleep for a time.

"When you return," said Cloud and Rain, "persuade your people to move their camp. Let them come near me, and should the serpent dare to follow I will defend them."

Bending Willow stayed four months with Cloud and Rain, and he taught her much magic, and showed her the herbs which would cure sickness.

One day when he came in from fishing he said to her: "No Heart is dead. This night I will throw a bridge from the foot of the waters across the Falls to the high hills. You must climb it without fear, for I will hold it firmly until you are on the land."

When the moon rose and lighted all the river, Cloud and Rain caused a gentle wind to raise the spray until it formed a great, white arch reaching from his cave to the distant hills. He led Bending Willow to the foot of this bridge of mist and helped her to climb until she was assured of her safety and could step steadily.

All the tribe welcomed her, and none were sorry that she had not married No Heart. She told them of the good spirit, Cloud and Rain, of his wonderful lodge, of his kindness, and of the many things he had taught her.

At first they would not entertain the idea of moving their village, for there were pleasant fishing-grounds where they lived, and by the Falls none but spirits could catch the fish. But when strong men sickened and some of the children of the Chief died, they took down their lodge poles and sought the protection of the good spirit.

For a long time they lived in peace and health; but after many moons the serpent discovered their new camp and made his way thither.

Cloud and Rain was soon aware of his arrival, and was very angry because the serpent dared to come so near his lodge. He took a handful of the magic fire and molded it into thunderbolts which he hurled at the monster. The first stunned him, the second wounded him severely, and the third killed him.

Cloud and Rain told them to drag the body to the rapids and hurl it into the water. It took all the women of the tribe to move it, for it was longer than the flight of twenty arrows. As it tossed upon the water, it looked as though a mountain had fallen upon the waves, and it drifted but slowly to the edge of the Great Fall. There it was drawn between the rocks and became wedged so firmly that it could not be dislodged, but coiled itself as if it had lain down to sleep. Its weight was so great that it bent the rocks, and they remain curved like a drawn bow to this day. The serpent itself was gradually washed to pieces and disappeared.

In the Moon of Flowers the young warrior whom Bending Willow loved came and cast a red deer at her feet, and they were happy ever after.

The Magic Feather

I

IN THE DEPTHS OF THE FOREST in the land of the Dacotahs stood a wigwam many leagues distant from any other. The old man who had been known to live in it was supposed to have died; but he kept himself in hiding for the sake of his little grandson, whose mother had brought him there to escape the giants.

The Dacotahs had once been a brave and mighty people. They were swift runners and proud of their fleetness. It had been told among the nations for many generations that a great chief should spring from this tribe, and that he should conquer all his enemies, even the giants who had made themselves strong by eating the flesh of those they took in battle and drinking their blood. This great chief should wear a white feather and should be known by its name.

The giants believed the story and sought to prevent it coming true. So they said to the Dacotahs: "Let us run a race. If you win you shall have our sons and our daughters to do with them as you please, and if we win we will take yours."

Some of the wise Indians shook their heads and said: "Suppose the giants win; they will kill our children and will serve them as dainty food upon their tables." But the young men answered: "Kaw: who can outrun the Dacotahs? We shall return from the race with the young giants bound hand and foot, to fetch and carry for us all our days." So they agreed to the wager and ran with the giants.

Now, it was not to be supposed that the giants would act fairly. They dug pitfalls on the prairie, covering them with leaves and grass, which caused the runners to stumble, and lose the race.

The Dacotahs, therefore, had to bring out their children and give them to the giants. When they were counted one child was missing. The giants roared with anger and made the whole tribe search for him, but he could not be found. Then the giants killed the father instead and ate his flesh, grumbling and muttering vengeance with every mouthful.

This was the child whose home was in the forest. When he was still a very little fellow his grandfather made him a tiny bow and some smooth, light arrows, and taught him how to use them.

The first time he ventured from the lodge he brought home a rabbit, the second time a squirrel, and he shot a fine, large deer long before he was strong enough to drag it home.

One day when he was about fourteen years old, he heard a voice calling to him as he went through the thick woods:

Come hither, you wearer of the white feather. You do not yet wear it, but you are worthy of it."

He looked about, but at first saw no one. At last he caught sight of the head of a little old man among the trees. On going up to it he discovered that the body from the heart downwards was wood and fast in the earth. He thought some hunter must have leaped upon a rotten stump and, it giving way, had caught and held him fast; but he soon recognized the roots of an old oak that he well knew. Its top had been blighted by a stroke of lightning, and the lower branches were so dark that no birds built their nests on them, and few even lighted upon them.

The boy knew nothing of the world except what his grandfather had taught him. He had once found some lodge poles on the edge of the forest and a heap of ashes like those about their own wigwam, by which he guessed that there were other people living. He had never been told why he was living with an old man so far away from others, or of his father, but the time had come for him to know these things.

The head which had called him, said as he came near: "Go home, White Feather, and lie down to sleep. You will dream, and on waking will find a pipe, a pouch of smoking mixture, and a long white feather beside you. Put the feather on your head, and as you smoke you will see the cloud which rises from your pipe pass out of the doorway as a flock of pigeons." The voice then told him who he was, and also that the giants had never given up looking for him. He was to wait for them no longer, but to go boldly to their lodge and offer to race with them. "Here," said the voice, "is an enchanted vine which you are to throw over the head of every one who runs with you."

White Feather, as he was thenceforth called, picked up the vine, went quickly home and did as he had been told. He heard the voice, awoke and found the pouch of tobacco, the pipe, and the white feather. Placing the feather on his head, he filled the pipe and sat down to smoke.

His grandfather, who was at work not far from the wigwam, was astonished to see flocks of pigeons flying over his head, and still more surprised to find that they came from his own doorway. When he went in and saw the boy wearing the white feather, he knew what it all meant and became very sad, for he loved the boy so much that he could not bear the thought of losing him.

The next morning White Feather went in search of the giants. He passed through the forest, out upon the prairie and through other woods across another prairie, until at last he saw a tall lodge pole in the middle of the forest. He went boldly up to it, thinking to surprise the giants, but his coming was not unexpected, for the little spirits which carry the news had heard the voice speaking to him and had hastened to tell those whom it most concerned.

The giants were six brothers who lived in a lodge that was ill-kept and dirty. When they saw the boy coming they made fun of him among themselves; but when he entered the lodge they pretended that they were glad to see him and flattered him, telling him that his fame as a brave had already reached them.

White Feather knew well what they wanted. He proposed the race; and though this was just what they had intended doing, they laughed at his offer. At last they said that if he would have it so, he should try first with the smallest and weakest of their number.

They were to run towards the east until they came to a certain tree which had been stripped of its bark, and then back to the starting point, where a war-club made of iron was driven into the ground. Whoever reached this first was to beat the other's brains out with it.

White Feather and the youngest giant ran nimbly on, and the giants, who were watching, were rejoiced to see their brother gain slowly but surely, and at last shoot ahead of White Feather. When his enemy was almost at the goal, the boy, who was only a few feet behind, threw the enchanted vine over the giant's head, which caused him to fall back helpless. No one suspected anything more than an accident, for the vine could not be seen except by him who carried it.

After White Feather had cut off the giant's head, the brothers thought to get the better of him, and begged him to leave the head with them, for they thought that by magic they might bring it back to life, but he claimed his right to take it home to his grandfather.

The next morning he returned to run with the second giant, whom he defeated in the same manner; the third morning the third, and so on until all but one were killed.

As he went towards the giant's lodge on the sixth morning he heard the voice of the old man of the oak tree who had first appeared to him. It came to warn him. It told him that the sixth giant was afraid to race with him, and would therefore try to deceive him and work enchantment on him. As he went through the wood he would meet a beautiful woman, the most beautiful in the world. To avoid danger he must wish himself an elk and he would be changed into that animal. Even then he must keep out of her way, for she meant to do him harm.

White Feather had not gone far from the tree when he met her. He had never seen a woman before, and this one was so beautiful that he wished himself an elk at once for he was sure she would bewitch him. He could not tear himself away from the spot, however, but kept browsing near her, raising his eyes now and then to look at her.

She went to him, laid her hand upon his neck and stroked his sides. Looking from him she sighed, and as he turned his head towards her, she reproached him for changing himself from a tall and handsome man to such an ugly creature. "For," said she, "I heard of you in a distant land, and, though many sought me, I came hither to be your wife."

As White Feather looked at her he saw tears shining in her eyes, and almost before he knew it he wished himself a man again. In a moment he was restored to his natural shape, and the woman flung her arms about his neck and kissed him.

By and by she coaxed him to lie down on the ground and put his head on her lap. Now, this beautiful woman was really the giant in disguise; and as White Feather lay with his head on her knee, she stroked his hair and forehead, and by her magic put him to sleep. Then she took an ax and broke his back. This done, she changed herself into the giant, turned White Feather into a dog, and bade him follow to the lodge.

The giant took the white feather and placed it on his own head, for he knew there was magic in it; and he wished to make the tribes honor him as the great warrior they had long expected.

II

In a little village but a woman's journey from the home of the giants lived a chief named Red Wing. He had two daughters, White Weasel and Crystal Stone, each noted for her beauty and haughtiness, though Crystal Stone was kind to every one but her lovers, who came from far and near, and were a constant source of jealousy to White Weasel, the elder. The eldest of the giants was White Weasel's suitor, but she was afraid of him, so both the sisters remained unmarried.

When the news of White Feather's race with the giants came to the village, each of the maidens determined that she would win the young brave for a husband. White Weasel wanted some one who would be a great chief and make all the tribes afraid of him. Crystal Stone loved him beforehand, for she knew he must be good as well as brave, else the white feather would not have been given to him. Each kept the wish to herself and went into the woods to fast, that it might come true.

When they heard that White Feather was on his way through the forest, White Weasel set her lodge in order and dressed herself gaily, hoping thereby to attract his attention. Her sister made no such preparation, for she thought so brave and wise a chief would have too good sense to take notice of a woman's finery.

When the giant passed through the forest, White Weasel went out and invited him into her lodge. He entered and she did not guess that it was the giant of whom she had been in such fear.

Crystal Stone invited the dog into her lodge—her sister had shut him out—and was kind to it, as she had always been to dumb creatures. Now, although the dog was enchanted and could not change his condition, he still had more than human sense and knew all the thoughts of his mistress. He grew to love her more and more every day and looked about for some way to show it.

One day when the giant was hunting on the prairie, the dog went out to hunt also; but he ran down to the bank of the river. He stepped cautiously into the water and drew out a large stone, which was turned into a beaver as soon as it touched the ground. He took it home to his mistress, who showed it to her sister and offered to share it with her. White Weasel refused it, but told her husband he had better follow the dog and discover where such fine beavers could be had.

The giant went, and hiding behind a tree, saw the dog draw out a stone, which turned into a beaver. After the animal had gone home he went down to the water and drew out a stone, which likewise turned into a beaver. He tied it to his belt and took it home, throwing it down at the door of the lodge.

When he had been at home a little while, he told his wife to go and bring in his belt. She did so, but there was no beaver tied to it, only a large, smooth stone such as he had drawn out of the water.

The dog, knowing that he had been watched, would not go for more beavers; but the next day went through the woods until he came to a charred tree. He broke off a small branch, which turned into a bear as soon as he took hold of it to carry it home. The giant, who had been watching him, also broke off a branch, and he, too, secured a bear; but when he took it home and told his wife to fetch it in, she found only a black stick.

Then White Weasel became very angry and scoffed at her husband, asking him if this was the way he had done the wonderful things that had made his fame. "Ugh!" she said, "you are a coward, though you are so big and great."

The next day, after the giant had gone out, she went to the village to tell her father, Red Wing, how badly her husband treated her in not bringing home food. She also told him that her sister, who had taken the dog into her wigwam, always had plenty to eat, and that Crystal Stone pitied the wife of the wearer of the white feather, who often had to go hungry.

Red Wing listened to her story and knew at once that there must be magic at work somewhere. He sent a company of young men and women to the lodge of Crystal Stone to see if White Weasel's story were true, and if so to bring his younger daughter and the dog to his wigwam.

Meanwhile the dog had asked his mistress to give him a bath such as the Indians take. They went down to the river, where he pointed out a spot on which she was to build him a lodge. She made it of grass and sticks, and after heating some large stones laid them on the floor, leaving only just enough room for the dog to crawl in and lie down. Then she poured water on the stones, which caused a thick steam that almost choked him. He lay in it for a long time, after which, raising himself, he rushed out and jumped into a pool of water formed by the river. He came out a tall, handsome man, but without the power of speech.

The messengers from Red Wing were greatly astonished at finding a man instead of the dog that they had expected to see, but had no trouble in persuading him and Crystal Stone to go with them.

Red Wing was as much astonished as his messengers had been, and called all the wise men of the tribe to witness what should take place, and to give counsel concerning his daughters.

The whole tribe and many strangers soon assembled. The giant came also and brought with him the magic pipe that had been given to White Feather in his dream. He smoked it and passed it to the Indians to smoke, but nothing came of it. Then White Feather motioned to them that he wished to take it. He also asked for the white feather, which he placed on his head; when, at the first whiff from the pipe, lo! clouds of blue and white pigeons rushed from the smoke.

The men sprang to their feet, astonished to see such magic. White Feather's speech returned, and in answer to the questions put to him, he told his story to the chief.

Red Wing and the council listened and smoked for a time in silence. Then the oldest and wisest brave ordered the giant to appear before White Feather, who should transform him into a dog. White Feather accomplished this by knocking upon him the ashes from the magic pipe. It was next decreed that the boys of the tribe should take the war-clubs of their fathers and, driving the animal into the forest, beat him to death.

White Feather wished to reward his friends, so he invited them to a buffalo hunt, to take place in four days' time, and he bade them prepare many arrows. To make ready for them, he cut a buffalo robe into strips, which he sowed upon the prairie.

On the day appointed the warriors found that these shreds of skin had grown into a large herd of buffaloes. They killed as many as they pleased, for White Feather tipped each arrow with magic, so that none missed their aim.

A grand feast followed in honor of White Feather's triumph over the giants and of his marriage with Crystal Stone.

How Setanta Won the Name of Cúchulainn

WITHIN THE COURT OF EMAIN MACHA, there existed an élite group of boy athletes whose outstanding talents filled the King with an overwhelming sense of pride and joy. It had become a regular part of Conchobar's daily routine to watch these boys at their various games and exercises, for nothing brought him greater pleasure than to witness their development into some of the finest sportsmen in Erin. He had named the group the Boy-Corps, and the sons of the most powerful chieftains and princes of the land were among its members, having proven their skill and dexterity in a wide and highly challenging range of sporting events.

Before Setanta had grown to the age of six, he had already expressed his desire before the King to be enrolled in the Boy-Corps. At first, Conchobar refused to treat the request seriously, since his nephew was a great deal younger than any other member, but the boy persisted, and the King at last agreed to allow him to try his hand. It was decided that he should join in a game of hurling one morning, and when he had dressed himself in the martial uniform of the Boy-Corps, he was presented with a brass hurley almost his own height off the ground.

A team of twelve boys was assembled to play against him and they sneered mockingly at the young lad before them, imagining they would have little difficulty keeping the ball out of his reach. But as soon as the game started up, Setanta dived in among the boys and took hold of the ball, striking it with his hurley and driving it a powerful distance to the other end of the field where it sailed effortlessly through the goal-posts. And after this first onslaught, he made it impossible for his opponents to retrieve the ball from him, so that within a matter of minutes he had scored fifty goals against the twelve of them. The whole corps looked on in utter amazement and the King, who had been eagerly following the game, was flushed with excitement. His nephew's show of prowess was truly astonishing and he began to reproach himself for having originally set out to humour the boy.

"Have Setanta brought before me," he said to his steward, "for such an impressive display of heroic strength and impertinent courage deserves a very special reward."

Now on that particular day, Conchobar had been invited to attend a great feast at the house of Culann, the most esteemed craftsman and smith in the kingdom. A thought had suddenly entered Conchobar's head that it would be a very fitting reward for Setanta to share in such a banquet, for no small boy had ever before accompanied the King and the Knights of the Red Guard on such a prestigious outing. It was indeed a great honour and one Setanta readily acknowledged. He desperately wanted to accept the invitation, but only one thing held him back. He could not suppress the desire of a true sportsman to conclude the game he had begun and pleaded with the King to allow him to do so:

"I have so thoroughly enjoyed the first half of my game with the Boy-Corps," he told the King, "that I am loathe to cut it short. I promise to follow when the game is over if you will allow me this great liberty."

And seeing the excitement and keenness shining in the boy's eyes, Conchobar was more than happy to agree to this request. He instructed Setanta to follow on before nightfall and gave him directions to the house of Culann. Then he set off for the banquet, eager to relate the morning's stirring events to the rest of Culann's house guests.

It was early evening by the time the royal party arrived at the dwelling place of Culann. A hundred blazing torches guided them towards the walls of the fort and a carpet of fresh green rushes formed a mile-long path leading to the stately entrance. The great hall was already lavishly prepared for the banquet and the sumptuous aroma of fifty suckling pigs turning on the spit filled every room of the house. Culann himself came forward to greet each one of his guests and he bowed respectfully before the King and led him to his place of honour at the centre of the largest table. Once his royal guest had taken his seat, the order was given for the wine to be poured and the laughter and music followed soon afterwards. And when it was almost time for the food to be served, Culann glanced around him one last time to make certain that all his visitors had arrived.

"I think we need wait no longer," he said to the King. "My guests are all present and it will now be safe to untie the hound who keeps watch over my home each night. There is not a hound in Erin who could equal mine for fierceness and strength, and even if a hundred men should attempt to do battle with him, every last one would be torn to pieces in his powerful jaws."

"Release him then, and let him guard this place," said Conchobar, quite forgetting that his young nephew had not yet joined the party. "My men are all present and our appetites have been whetted by our long journey here. Let us delay no longer and begin the feasting at once."

And after the gong had been sounded, a procession of elegantly-clad attendants entered the room carrying gilded trays of roasted viands and freshly harvested fruit and vegetables, which they set down on the table before the King and the hungry warriors of the Red Guard.

It was just at this moment that the young Setanta came to the green of Culann's fort carrying with him the hurley and the ball that had brought him victory against the

Boy-Corps. As the boy drew nearer to the entrance of the fort, the hound's ears pricked up warily and it began to growl and bark in such a way as to be heard throughout the entire countryside. The whole company within the great hall heard the animal snarling ferociously and raced outdoors to discover what exactly it was that had disturbed the creature. They saw before them a young boy, who showed little sign of fear as he stood facing the fierce dog with gaping jaws. The child was without any obvious weapon of defence against the animal, but as it charged at him, he thrust his playing ball forcefully down its throat causing it to choke for breath. Then he seized the hound by the hind legs and dashed its head against a rock until blood spewed from its mouth and the life had gone out of it.

Those who witnessed this extraordinary confrontation hoisted the lad triumphantly into the air and bore him on their shoulders to where Conchobar and Culann stood waiting. The King, although more than gratified by the boy's demonstration of courage, was also much relieved to know that Setanta was safe. Turning to his host, he began to express his joy, but it was immediately apparent that Culann could share none of Conchobar's happiness. He walked instead towards the body of his dead hound and fell into a mournful silence as he stroked the lifeless form, remembering the loyal and obedient animal who had given its life to protect its master's property. Seeing Culann bent over the body of his faithful dog, Setanta came forward without hesitation and spoke the following words of comfort to him:

"If in all of Erin there is a hound to replace the one you have lost, I will find it, nurture it and place it in your service when it is fit for action. But, in the meantime, I myself will perform the duty of that hound and will guard your land and your possessions with the utmost pride."

There was not one among the gathering who remained unmoved by this gesture of contrition and friendship. Culann, for his part, was overcome with gratitude and appreciation and declared that Setanta should bear the name of Cúchulainn, 'Culann's Hound', in remembrance of his first great act of valour. And so, at the age of six, the boy Setanta was named Cúchulainn, a name by which he was known and feared until the end of his days.

The Rise of Finn to Leadership of the Fianna

AFTER FINN HAD EATEN of the Salmon of Fec which gave him all the gifts of wisdom, he had only to put his thumb in his mouth and whatever he wished to discover was immediately revealed to him. He knew beyond all doubt that he had been brought into the world to take the place of Cumall as head of the Fianna, and was confident at last that he had learned from Finnegas all that he would ever need to know. Turning his back on the valley of the Boyne, he set off to join Crimall and his followers in the forests of Connacht once more in order to plan in earnest for his future. He had by now become the most courageous of warriors, yet this quality was tempered by a remarkable generosity and gentleness of spirit that no man throughout the length and breath of the country could ever hope to rival. Finn was loved and admired by every last one of his comrades and they devoted their lives to him, never once slackening in their efforts to prove themselves worthy of his noble patronage.

It was decided among this loyal group that the time had come for Finn to assert his claim to the leadership of the Fianna and they went and pledged him their support and friendship in this bravest of quests. For it was well known that the Clan of Morna, who continued to rule the Fenian warriors, would not surrender their position without a bitter struggle. Finn now believed himself ready for such a confrontation and the day was chosen when he and his army would march to the Hill of Tara and plead their case before Conn Céadchathach, the High King of Erin.

As it was now the month of November and the Great Assembly of Tara was once more in progress, a period of festivity and good-will, when every man was under oath to lay aside his weapon. Chieftains, noblemen, kings and warriors all journeyed to Tara for the splendid event and old feuds were forgotten as the wine and mead flowed freely and the merry-making and dancing lasted well into the small hours. It was not long before Finn and his band of followers had arrived at Tara and they proceeded at once to the main banqueting hall where they were welcomed by the King's attendants and seated among the other Fenian warriors. As soon as he had walked into the hall, however, all eyes had been turned towards Finn, and a flurry of hushed enquiries circulated around the room as to the identity of the golden-haired youth. The King too, was quick to acknowledge that a stranger had entered his court, and he picked up a goblet of wine and instructed one of his servants to present it to the young warrior. At this gesture of friendship, Finn felt reassured in approaching the King, and he walked forward to the royal table and introduced himself to one and all.

"I am Finn, son of Cumall," he declared, "and I have come to take service with you, High King of Erin, just as my father did before me as head of the Fianna."

And when he heard these words, Goll mac Morna, who sat at the King's right hand, grew pale in anger, and shuddered to hear the King respond favourably to the young warrior:

"I would be honoured to have you serve in my ranks," replied Conn Céadchathach. "If you are the son of Cumall, son of Trenmor, then you are also a friend of mine."

After this, Finn bound himself in loyalty to the King, and his own band of men followed his example, and each was presented with a sword of the Fianna which they accepted with great pride and humility.

Everybody in the kingdom had either heard of Aillen the goblin or seen the creature with their own eyes. Every year during the Great Assembly, Conn Céadchathach increased the number of men guarding the royal city, but still the goblin managed to pass undetected through the outer gates, moving swiftly towards the palace and setting it alight with its flaming breath. Not even the bravest of warriors could prevent Aillen from reeking havoc on Tara, for he carried with him a magic harp and all who heard its fairy music were gently lulled to sleep. The King lived in hope however, that one day the goblin would be defeated and he adamantly refused to be held to ransom by the creature, insisting that the annual festivities take place as normal. A handsome reward awaited that warrior who could capture or destroy Aillen, but none had yet succeeded in doing so. It was at this time that Goll mac Morna conceived of his wicked plan to belittle his young rival before the King, for he could see that Conn Céadchathach secretly entertained the hope that Finn would rescue

Tara from further destruction. He called the young warrior to him and told him of the one true way to win the King's favour, being careful not to mention the enchanting harp or the difficulty of the task that lay ahead:

"Go and bind yourself before the King to rid this city of the terrible goblin who every year burns it to the ground," said Goll. "You alone possess the courage to do this Finn, and you may name your price if you are successful."

So Finn went before the King and swore that he would not rest in peace until he had slain Aillen the goblin.

"And what would you have as your reward?" asked the King.

"If I manage to rid you of the goblin," Finn replied, "I should like to take up my rightful position as captain of the Fianna. Will you agree, under oath, to such a reward?"

"If this is what you desire," answered the King, "then I bind myself to deliver such a prize."

Satisfied with these words, Finn took up his weapon and ventured out into the darkness to begin his lonely vigil over the palace.

As night fell and the November mists began to thicken round the hill of Tara, Finn waited anxiously for the goblin to appear. After some time, he saw an older warrior enter the courtyard and make his way towards him. He noticed that the warrior held in his hand a long, pointed spear, protected by a case of the soft, shining leather.

"I am Fiacha," said the warrior gently, "and I was proud to serve under your father, Cumall, when he was leader of the Fianna. The spear I carry is the spear of enchantment which Cumall placed in my charge upon his death.

"Take this weapon," he added, "and as soon as you hear the fairy music, lay its blade against your forehead and you will not fall under the melody's spell."

Finn thanked the warrior for his gift and turned it over to inspect it, admiring its shining handle of Arabian gold and the sharp steel body of the blade that glinted challengingly in the moonlight. Then he began to roam the ramparts once more, straining his ear to catch the first notes of the magic harp. He gazed out over the wide, frosty plains of Meath but still there was no sign of the evil goblin. He had almost given up hope that Aillen would appear and had sat down wearily on the hard, frozen earth, when he caught sight of a shadowy, phantom-like figure in the distance, floating eerily over the plain towards the royal palace. At first the strange music that wafted through the air was scarcely audible, but as the goblin drew nearer, the sweet sound of the harp strings filled the air like a potent fragrance, intoxicating the senses and inducing a warm, drowsy feeling. Finn was immediately enraptured by the sound and his eyelids slowly began to droop as the music weaved its magic spell over him. But something within him struggled against the opiate of the melody and his fingers searched for the spear of enchantment. Releasing the weapon from its leather shroud, he lay the cold steel blade against his forehead and drew a long, deep breath as he allowed its rejuvenating strength to flow through his tired limbs.

As soon as Aillen had reached the crest of the Hill of Tara he began to spit blazing fireballs through the palace gates, unaware that Finn had escaped the enchantment of the harp. Now Aillen had never before come face to face with an alert and animate mortal, and the sudden appearance of the young warrior quenching the flames with the cloak off his back prompted a shriek of terror and alarm. Turning swiftly around in the direction he had come from, Aillen fled for his safety, hoping to reach the fairy mound at Sliabh Fuaid before Finn could overtake him. But the young warrior was far too fleet of foot and before the goblin had managed to glide through the entrance of the mound, Finn had cast his spear, striking down the goblin with a single fatal blow through the chest. Then Finn bent over the corpse and removed Aillen's head and carried it back to the palace so that all were made aware that he had put an end to the reign of destruction.

When the sun had risen on the following morning, the King was overjoyed to discover that his kingdom remained untouched by the goblin's flame. He knew at once that Finn must have fulfilled his promise and was eager to express his gratitude. He called together all the men of the Fianna and sent his messenger to Finn's chamber requesting him to appear before him. Then the King stood Finn at his right hand and addressed his audience slowly and solemnly with the following words:

"Men of Erin," said the King, "I have pledged my word to this young warrior that if he should ever destroy the goblin Aillen, he would be granted leadership of the Fianna. I urge you to embrace him as your new leader and to honour him with your loyalty and service. If any among you cannot agree to do this, let him now resign his membership of the Fianna."

And turning to face Goll mac Morna, the King asked him:

"Do you swear service to Finn mac Cumaill, or is it your decision to quit the Fianna?"

"The young warrior has risen nobly to his position," replied Goll, "and I now bow to his superiority and accept him as my captain."

Then Goll mac Morna swore allegiance to Finn and each warrior came forward after him and did the same in his turn. And from this day onwards it was deemed the highest honour to serve under Finn mac Cumaill, for only the best and bravest of Erin's warriors were privileged to stand alongside the most glorious leader the Fianna had ever known.

How Fin Went to the Kingdom of the Big Men

FIN[1] AND HIS MEN were in the Harbour of the Hill of Howth on a hillock, behind the wind and in front of the sun, where they could see every person, and nobody could see them, when they saw a speck coming from the west. They thought at first it was the blackness of a shower; but when it came nearer, they saw it was a boat. It did not lower sail till it entered the harbour. There were three men in it; one for guide in the bow, one for steering in the stern, and one for the tackle in the centre. They came ashore, and drew it up seven times its own length in dry grey grass, where the scholars of the city could not make it stock for derision or ridicule.

They then went up to a lovely green spot, and the first lifted a handful of round pebbles or shingle, and commanded them to become a beautiful house, that no better could be found in Ireland; and this was done. The second one lifted a slab of slate, and commanded it to be slate on the top of the house, that there was not better in Ireland; and this was done. The third one caught a bunch of shavings and commanded them to be pine-wood and timber in the house, that there was not in Ireland better; and this was done.

1 Fin M'Coul a.k.a Finn mac Cumaill of Fenian legend

This caused much wonder to Fin, who went down where the men were, and made inquiries of them, and they answered him. He asked whence they were, or whither they were going. They said, "We are three Heroes whom the King of the Big Men has sent to ask combat of the Fians." He then asked, "What was the reason for doing this?" They said they did not know, but they heard that they were strong men, and they came to ask combat of Heroes from them. "Is Fin at Home?" "He is not." (Great is a man's leaning towards his own life). Fin then put them under crosses and under enchantments, that they were not to move from the place where they were till they saw him again.

He went away and made ready his coracle, gave its stern to land and prow to sea, hoisted the spotted towering sails against the long, tough, lance-shaped mast, cleaving the billows in the embrace of the wind in whirls, with a soft gentle breeze from the height of the sea-coast, and from the rapid tide of the red rocks, that would take willom from the hill, foliage from the tree, and heather from its stock and roots. Fin was guide in her prow, helm in her stern, and tackle in her middle; and stopping of head or foot he did not make till he reached the Kingdom of the Big Men. He went ashore and drew up his coracle in grey grass. He went up, and a Big Wayfarer met him. Fin asked who he was. "I am," he said, "the Red-haired Coward of the King of the Big Men; and," said he to Fin, "you are the one I am in quest of. Great is my esteem and respect towards you; you are the best maiden I have ever seen; you will yourself make a dwarf for the King, and your dog (this was Bran) a lapdog. It is long since the King has been in want of a dwarf and a lapdog." He took with him Fin; but another Big Man came, and was going to take Fin from him. The two fought; but when they had torn each other's clothes, they left it to Fin to judge. He chose the first one. He took Fin with him to the palace of the King, whose worthies and high nobles assembled to see the little man. The king lifted him upon the palm of his hand, and went three times round the town with Fin upon one palm and Bran upon the other. He made a sleeping-place for him at the end of his own bed. Fin was waiting, watching, and observing everything that was going on about the house. He observed that the King, as soon as night came, rose and went out, and returned no more till morning. This caused him much wonder, and at last he asked the King why he went away every night and left the Queen by herself. "Why," said the King, "do you ask?" "For satisfaction to myself," said Fin; "for it is causing me much wonder." Now the King had a great liking for Fin; he never saw anything that gave him more pleasure than he did; and at last he told him. "There is," he said, "a great Monster who wants my daughter in marriage, and to have half my kingdom to himself; and there is not another man in the kingdom who can meet him but myself; and I must go every night to hold combat with him." "Is there," said Fin, "no man to combat with him but yourself?" "There is not," said the King, "one who will war with him for a single night." "It is a pity," said Fin, "that this should be called the Kingdom of the Big Men. Is he bigger than yourself?" "Never you mind," said the King. "I will mind," said Fin; "take your rest and sleep tonight, and I shall go to meet him." "Is it you?" said the King; "you would not keep half a stroke against him."

When night came, and all men went to rest, the King was for going away as usual; but Fin at last prevailed upon him to allow himself to go. "I shall combat him," said he, "or else he knows a trick." "I think much," said the King, "of allowing you to go, seeing he gives myself enough to do." "Sleep you soundly tonight," said Fin, "and let me go; if he comes too violently upon me, I shall hasten home."

Fin went and reached the place where the combat was to be. He saw no one before him, and he began to pace backwards and forwards. At last he saw the sea coming in kilns of fire and as a darting serpent, till it came down below where he was. A Huge Monster came up and looked towards him, and from him. "What little speck do I see there?" he said. "It is I," said Fin. "What are you doing here?" "I am a messenger from the King of the Big Men; he is under much sorrow and distress; the Queen has just died, and I have come to ask if you will be so good as to go home tonight without giving trouble to the kingdom." "I shall do that," said he; and he went away with the rough humming of a song in his mouth.

Fin went home when the time came, and lay down in his own bed, at the foot of the King's bed. When the King awoke, he cried out in great anxiety, "My kingdom is lost, and my dwarf and my lapdog are killed!" "They are not," said Fin; "I am here yet; and you have got your sleep, a thing you were saying it was rare for you to get." "How," said the King, "did you escape, when you are so little, while he is enough for myself, though I am so big." "Though you," said Fin, "are so big and strong, I am quick and active."

Next night the King was for going; but Fin told him to take his sleep tonight again. "I shall stand myself in your place, or else a better hero than yonder one must come." "He will kill you," said the King. "I shall take my chance," said Fin.

He went, and as happened the night before, he saw no one; and he began to pace backwards and forwards. He saw the sea coming in fiery kilns and as a darting serpent; and that Huge Man came up. "Are you here tonight again?" said he. "I am, and this is my errand: when the Queen was being put in the coffin, and the King heard the coffin being nailed, and the joiner's stroke, he broke his heart with pain and grief; and the *Parliament* has sent me to ask you to go home tonight till they get the King buried." The Monster went this night also, roughly humming a song; and Fin went home when the time came.

In the morning the King awoke in great anxiety, and called out, "My kingdom is lost, and my dwarf and my lapdog are killed!" and he greatly rejoiced that Fin and Bran were alive, and that he himself got rest, after being so long without sleep.

Fin went the third night, and things happened as before. There was no one before him, and he took to pacing to and fro. He saw the sea coming till it came down below him: the Big Monster came up; he saw the little black speck, and asked who was there, and what he wanted. "I have come to combat you," said Fin.

Fin and Bran began the combat. Fin was going backwards, and the Huge Man was following. Fin called to Bran, "Are you going to let him kill me?" Bran had a venomous shoe; and he leaped and struck the Huge Man with the venomous shoe on the breast-bone, and took the heart and lungs out of him. Fin drew his sword, Mac-a-Luin, cut off his head, put it on a hempen rope, and went with it to the Palace of the King. He took it into the *Kitchen*, and put it behind the door. In the morning the servant could not turn it, nor open the door. The King went down; he saw the Huge Mass, caught it by the top of the head, and lifted it, and knew it was the head of the Man who was for so long a time asking combat from him, and keeping him from sleep. "How at all," said he, "has this head come here? Surely it is not my dwarf that has done it." "Why," said Fin, "should he not?"

Next night the King wanted to go himself to the place of combat; "because," said he, "a bigger one than the former will come tonight, and the kingdom will be destroyed, and you yourself killed; and I shall lose the pleasure I take in having you with me." But Fin went, and that Big Man came, asking vengeance for his son, and to have the kingdom for himself, or equal combat. He and Fin fought; and Fin was going backwards. He spoke to Bran, "Are you going to allow him to kill me?" Bran whined, and went and sat down on the beach. Fin was ever being driven back, and he called out again to Bran. Then Bran jumped and struck the Big Man with the venomous shoe, and took the heart and the lungs out of him. Fin cut the head off, and took it with him, and left it in front of the house. The King awoke in great terror, and cried out, "My kingdom is lost, and my dwarf and my lapdog are killed!" Fin raised himself up and said, "They are not"; and the King's joy was not small when he went out and saw the head that was in front of the house.

The next night a Big Hag came ashore, and the tooth in the door of her mouth would make a distaff. She sounded a challenge on her shield: "You killed," she said, "my husband and my son." "I did kill them," said Fin. They fought; and it was worse for Fin to guard himself from the tooth than from the hand of the Big Hag. When she had nearly done for him Bran struck her with the venomous shoe, and killed her as he had done to the rest. Fin took with him the head, and left it in front of the house. The King awoke in great anxiety, and called out, "My kingdom is lost, and my dwarf and my lapdog are killed!" "They are not," said Fin, answering him; and when they went out and saw the head, the King said, "I and my kingdom will have peace ever after this. The mother herself of the brood is killed; but tell me who you are. It was foretold for me that it would be Fin-mac-Coul that would give me relief, and he is only now eighteen years of age. Who are you, then, or what is your name?" "There never stood," said Fin, "on hide of cow or horse, one to whom I would deny my name. I am Fin, the Son of Coul, son of Looach, son of Trein, son of Fin, son of Art, son of the young High King of Erin; and it is time for me now to go home. It has been with much wandering out of my way that I have come to your kingdom; and this is the reason why I have come, that I might find out what injury I have done to you, or the reason why you sent the three heroes to ask combat from me, and bring destruction on my Men." "You never did any injury to me," said the King; "and I ask a thousand pardons. I did not send the heroes to you. It is not the truth they told. They were three men who were courting three fairy women, and these gave them their shirts; and when they have on their shirts, the combat of a hundred men is upon the hand of every one of them. But they must put off the shirts every night, and put them on the backs of chairs; and if the shirts were taken from them they would be next day as weak as other people."

Fin got every honour, and all that the King could give him, and when he went away, the King and the Queen and the people went down to the shore to give him their blessing.

Fin now went away in his coracle, and was sailing close by the side of the shore, when he saw a young man running and calling out to him. Fin came in close to land with his coracle, and asked what he wanted. "I am," said the young man, "a good servant wanting a master." "What work can you do?" said Fin. "I am," said he, "the best soothsayer that there is." "Jump into the boat then." The soothsayer jumped in, and they went forward.

They did not go far when another youth came running. "I am," he said, "a good servant wanting a master." "What work can you do?" said Fin. "I am as good a thief as there is." "Jump into the boat, then"; and Fin took with him this one also. They saw then a third young man running and calling out. They came close to land. "What man are you?" said Fin. "I am," said he, "the best climber that there is. I will take up a hundred pounds on my back in a place where a fly could not stand on a calm summer day." "Jump in"; and this one came in also. "I have my pick of servants now," said Fin; "it cannot be but these will suffice."

They went; and stop of head or foot they did not make till they reached the Harbour of the Hill of Howth. He asked the soothsayer what the three Big Men were doing. "They are," he said, "after their supper, and making ready for going to bed."

He asked a second time. "They are," he said, "after going to bed; and their shirts are spread on the back of chairs."

After a while, Fin asked him again, "What are the Big Men doing now?" "They are," said the soothsayer, "sound asleep." "It would be a good thing if there was now a thief to go and steal the shirts." "I would do that," said the thief, "but the doors are locked, and I cannot get in." "Come," said the climber, "on my back, and I shall put you in." He took him up upon his back to the top of the chimney, and let him down, and he stole the shirts.

Fin went where the Fian band was; and in the morning they came to the house where the three Big Men were. They sounded a challenge upon their shields, and asked them to come out to combat.

They came out. "Many a day," said they, "have we been better for combat than we are today," and they confessed to Fin everything as it was. "You were," said Fin, "impertinent, but I will forgive you"; and he made them swear that they would be faithful to himself ever after, and ready in every enterprise he would place before them.

The Shee An Gannon and the Gruagach Gaire

THE SHEE AN GANNON was born in the morning, named at noon, and went in the evening to ask his daughter of the king of Erin.

"I will give you my daughter in marriage," said the king of Erin; "you won't get her, though, unless you go and bring me back the tidings that I want, and tell me what it is that put a stop to the laughing of the Gruagach Gaire, who before this laughed always, and laughed so loud that the whole world heard him. There are twelve iron spikes out here in the garden behind my castle. On eleven of the spikes are the heads of kings' sons who came seeking my daughter in marriage, and all of them went away to get the knowledge I wanted. Not one was able to get it and tell me what stopped the Gruagach Gaire from laughing. I took the heads off them all when they came back without the tidings for which they went, and I'm greatly in dread that your head'll be on the twelfth spike, for I'll do the same to you that I did to the eleven kings' sons unless you tell what put a stop to the laughing of the Gruagach."

The Shee an Gannon made no answer, but left the king and pushed away to know could he find why the Gruagach was silent.

He took a glen at a step, a hill at a leap, and travelled all day till evening. Then he came to a house. The master of the house asked him what sort was he, and he said: "A young man looking for hire."

"Well," said the master of the house, "I was going tomorrow to look for a man to mind my cows. If you'll work for me, you'll have a good place, the best food a man could have to eat in this world, and a soft bed to lie on."

The Shee an Gannon took service, and ate his supper. Then the master of the house said: "I am the Gruagach Gaire; now that you are my man and have eaten your supper, you'll have a bed of silk to sleep on."

Next morning after breakfast the Gruagach said to the Shee an Gannon: "Go out now and loosen my five golden cows and my bull without horns, and drive them to pasture; but when you have them out on the grass, be careful you don't let them go near the land of the giant."

The new cowboy drove the cattle to pasture, and when near the land of the giant, he saw it was covered with woods and surrounded by a high wall. He went up, put his back against the wall, and threw in a great stretch of it; then he went inside and threw out another great stretch of the wall, and put the five golden cows and the bull without horns on the land of the giant.

Then he climbed a tree, ate the sweet apples himself, and threw the sour ones down to the cattle of the Gruagach Gaire.

Soon a great crashing was heard in the woods, – the noise of young trees bending, and old trees breaking. The cowboy looked around and saw a five-headed giant pushing through the trees; and soon he was before him.

"Poor miserable creature!" said the giant; "but weren't you impudent to come to my land and trouble me in this way? You're too big for one bite, and too small for two. I don't know what to do but tear you to pieces."

"You nasty brute," said the cowboy, coming down to him from the tree, "'tis little I care for you;" and then they went at each other. So great was the noise between them that there was nothing in the world but what was looking on and listening to the combat.

They fought till late in the afternoon, when the giant was getting the upper hand; and then the cowboy thought that if the giant should kill him, his father and mother would never find him or set eyes on him again, and he would never get the daughter of the king of Erin. The heart in his body grew strong at this thought. He sprang on the giant, and with the first squeeze and thrust he put him to his knees in the hard ground, with the second thrust to his waist, and with the third to his shoulders.

"I have you at last; you're done for now!", said the cowboy. Then he took out his knife, cut the five heads off the giant, and when he had them off he cut out the tongues and threw the heads over the wall.

Then he put the tongues in his pocket and drove home the cattle. That evening the Gruagach couldn't find vessels enough in all his place to hold the milk of the five golden cows.

But when the cowboy was on the way home with the cattle, the son of the king of Tisean came and took the giant's heads and claimed the princess in marriage when the Gruagach Gaire should laugh.

After supper the cowboy would give no talk to his master, but kept his mind to himself, and went to the bed of silk to sleep.

On the morning the cowboy rose before his master, and the first words he said to the Gruagach were:

"What keeps you from laughing, you who used to laugh so loud that the whole world heard you?"

"I'm sorry," said the Gruagach, "that the daughter of the king of Erin sent you here."

"If you don't tell me of your own will, I'll make you tell me," said the cowboy; and he put a face on himself that was terrible to look at, and running through the house like a madman, could find nothing that would give pain enough to the Gruagach but some ropes made of untanned sheepskin hanging on the wall.

He took these down, caught the Gruagach, fastened him by the three smalls, and tied him so that his little toes were whispering to his ears. When he was in this state the Gruagach said: "I'll tell you what stopped my laughing if you set me free."

So the cowboy unbound him, the two sat down together, and the Gruagach said:

"I lived in this castle here with my twelve sons. We ate, drank, played cards, and enjoyed ourselves, till one day when my sons and I were playing, a slender brown hare came rushing in, jumped on to the hearth, tossed up the ashes to the rafters and ran away.

"On another day he came again; but if he did, we were ready for him, my twelve sons and myself. As soon as he tossed up the ashes and ran off, we made after him, and followed him till nightfall, when he went into a glen. We saw a light before us. I ran on, and came to a house with a great apartment, where there was a man named Yellow Face with twelve daughters, and the hare was tied to the side of the room near the women.

"There was a large pot over the fire in the room, and a great stork boiling in the pot. The man of the house said to me: "There are bundles of rushes at the end of the room, go there and sit down with your men!"

"He went into the next room and brought out two pikes, one of wood, the other of iron, and asked me which of the pikes would I take. I said, "I'll take the iron one;" for I thought in my heart that if an attack should come on me, I could defend myself better with the iron than the wooden pike.

"Yellow Face gave me the iron pike, and the first chance of taking what I could out of the pot on the point of the pike. I got but a small piece of the stork, and the man of the house took all the rest on his wooden pike. We had to fast that night; and when the man and his twelve daughters ate the flesh of the stork, they hurled the bare bones in the faces of my sons and myself. We had to stop all night that way, beaten on the faces by the bones of the stork.

"Next morning, when we were going away, the man of the house asked me to stay a while; and going into the next room, he brought out twelve loops of iron and one of wood, and said to me: "Put the heads of your twelve sons into the iron loops, or your own head into the wooden one;" and I said: "I'll put the twelve heads of my sons in the iron loops, and keep my own out of the wooden one."

"He put the iron loops on the necks of my twelve sons, and put the wooden one on his own neck. Then he snapped the loops one after another, till he took the heads off my twelve sons and threw the heads and bodies out of the house; but he did nothing to hurt his own neck.

"When he had killed my sons he took hold of me and stripped the skin and flesh from the small of my back down, and when he had done that he took the skin of a black sheep that had been hanging on the wall for seven years and clapped it on my body in place of my own flesh and skin; and the sheepskin grew on me, and every year since then I shear myself, and every bit of wool I use for the stockings that I wear I clip off my own back."

When he had said this, the Gruagach showed the cowboy his back covered with thick black wool.

After what he had seen and heard, the cowboy said: "I know now why you don't laugh, and small blame to you. But does that hare come here still?"

"He does indeed," said the Gruagach.

Both went to the table to play, and they were not long playing cards when the hare ran in; and before they could stop him he was out again.

But the cowboy made after the hare, and the Gruagach after the cowboy, and they ran as fast as ever their legs could carry them till nightfall; and when the hare was entering the castle where the twelve sons of the Gruagach were killed, the cowboy caught him by the two hind legs and dashed out his brains against the wall; and the skull of the hare was knocked into the chief room of the castle, and fell at the feet of the master of the place.

"Who has dared to interfere with my fighting pet?" screamed Yellow Face.

"I," said the cowboy; "and if your pet had had manners, he might be alive now."

The cowboy and the Gruagach stood by the fire. A stork was boiling in the pot, as when the Gruagach came the first time. The master of the house went into the next room and brought out an iron and a wooden pike, and asked the cowboy which would he choose.

"I'll take the wooden one," said the cowboy; "and you may keep the iron one for yourself."

So he took the wooden one; and going to the pot, brought out on the pike all the stork except a small bite, and he and the Gruagach fell to eating, and they were eating the flesh of the stork all night. The cowboy and the Gruagach were at home in the place that time.

In the morning the master of the house went into the next room, took down the twelve iron loops with a wooden one, brought them out, and asked the cowboy which would he take, the twelve iron or the one wooden loop.

"What could I do with the twelve iron ones for myself or my master?

I'll take the wooden one."

He put it on, and taking the twelve iron loops, put them on the necks of the twelve daughters of the house, then snapped the twelve heads off them, and turning to their father, said: "I'll do the same thing to you unless you bring the twelve sons of my master to life, and make them as well and strong as when you took their heads."

The master of the house went out and brought the twelve to life again; and when the Gruagach saw all his sons alive and as well as ever, he let a laugh out of himself, and all the Eastern world heard the laugh.

Then the cowboy said to the Gruagach: "It's a bad thing you have done to me, for the daughter of the king of Erin will be married the day after your laugh is heard."

"Oh! then we must be there in time," said the Gruagach; and they all made away from the place as fast as ever they could, the cowboy, the Gruagach, and his twelve sons.

They hurried on; and when within three miles of the king's castle there was such a throng of people that no one could go a step ahead. "We must clear a road through this," said the cowboy.

"We must indeed," said the Gruagach; and at it they went, threw the people some on one side and some on the other, and soon they had an opening for themselves to the king's castle.

As they went in, the daughter of the king of Erin and the son of the king of Tisean were on their knees just going to be married. The cowboy drew his hand on the bride-groom, and gave a blow that sent him spinning till he stopped under a table at the other side of the room.

"What scoundrel struck that blow?" asked the king of Erin.

"It was I," said the cowboy.

"What reason had you to strike the man who won my daughter?"

"It was I who won your daughter, not he; and if you don't believe me, the Gruagach Gaire is here himself. He'll tell you the whole story from beginning to end, and show you the tongues of the giant."

So the Gruagach came up and told the king the whole story, how the Shee an Gannon had become his cowboy, had guarded the five golden cows and the bull without horns, cut off the heads of the five-headed giant, killed the wizard hare, and brought his own twelve sons to life. "And then," said the Gruagach, "he is the only man in the whole world I have ever told why I stopped laughing, and the only one who has ever seen my fleece of wool."

When the king of Erin heard what the Gruagach said, and saw the tongues of the giant fitted in the head, he made the Shee an Gannon kneel down by his daughter, and they were married on the spot.

Then the son of the king of Tisean was thrown into prison, and the next day they put down a great fire, and the deceiver was burned to ashes.

The wedding lasted nine days, and the last day was better than the first.

The Lad with the Goat-Skin

LONG AGO, a poor widow woman lived down near the iron forge, by Enniscorth, and she was so poor she had no clothes to put on her son; so she used to fix him in the ash-hole, near the fire, and pile the warm ashes about him; and according as he grew up, she sunk the pit deeper. At last, by hook or by crook, she got a goat-skin, and fastened it round his waist, and he felt quite grand, and took a walk down the street. So says she to him next morning, "Tom, you thief, you never done any good yet, and you six foot high, and past nineteen; – take that rope and bring me a faggot from the wood."

"Never say't twice, mother," says Tom – "here goes."

When he had it gathered and tied, what should come up but a big giant, nine foot high, and made a lick of a club at him. Well become Tom, he jumped a-one side, and picked up a ram-pike; and the first crack he gave the big fellow, he made him kiss the clod.

"If you have e'er a prayer," says Tom, "now's the time to say it, before I make fragments of you."

"I have no prayers," says the giant; "but if you spare my life I'll give you that club; and as long as you keep from sin, you'll win every battle you ever fight with it."

Tom made no bones about letting him off; and as soon as he got the club in his hands, he sat down on the bresna, and gave it a tap with the kippeen, and says, "Faggot, I had great trouble gathering you, and run the risk of my life for you, the least you can do is to carry me home." And sure enough, the wind o' the word was all it wanted. It went off through the wood, groaning and crackling, till it came to the widow's door.

Well, when the sticks were all burned, Tom was sent off again to pick more; and this time he had to fight with a giant that had two heads on him. Tom had a little more trouble with him – that's all; and the prayers he said, was to give Tom a fife; that nobody could help dancing when he was playing it. Begonies, he made the big faggot dance home, with himself sitting on it. The next giant was a beautiful boy with three heads on him. He had neither prayers nor catechism no more nor the others; and so he gave Tom a bottle of green ointment, that wouldn't let you be burned, nor scalded, nor wounded. "And now," says he, "there's no more of us. You may come and gather sticks here till little Lunacy Day in Harvest, without giant or fairy-man to disturb you."

Well, now, Tom was prouder nor ten paycocks, and used to take a walk down street in the heel of the evening; but some o' the little boys had no more manners than if they were Dublin jackeens, and put out their tongues at Tom's club and Tom's goat-skin. He didn't like that at all, and it would be mean to give one of them a clout. At last, what should come through the town but a kind of a bellman, only it's a big bugle he had, and a huntsman's cap on his head, and a kind of a painted shirt. So this – he wasn't a bellman, and I don't know what to call him – bugleman, maybe, proclaimed that the King of Dublin's daughter was so melancholy that she didn't give a laugh for seven years, and that her father would grant her in marriage to whoever could make her laugh three times.

"That's the very thing for me to try," says Tom; and so, without burning any more daylight, he kissed his mother, curled his club at the little boys, and off he set along the yalla highroad to the town of Dublin.

At last Tom came to one of the city gates, and the guards laughed and cursed at him instead of letting him in. Tom stood it all for a little time, but at last one of them – out of fun, as he said – drove his bayonet half an inch or so into his side. Tom done nothing but take the fellow by the scruff o' the neck and the waistband of his corduroys, and fling him into the canal. Some run to pull the fellow out, and others to let manners into the vulgarian with their swords and daggers; but a tap from his club sent them headlong into the moat or down on the stones, and they were soon begging him to stay his hands.

So at last one of them was glad enough to show Tom the way to the palace-yard; and there was the king, and the queen, and the princess, in a gallery, looking at all sorts of wrestling, and sword-playing, and long-dances, and mumming, all to please the princess; but not a smile came over her handsome face.

Well, they all stopped when they seen the young giant, with his boy's face, and long black hair, and his short curly beard – for his poor mother couldn't afford to buy razors – and his great strong arms, and bare legs, and no covering but the goat-skin that reached from his waist to his knees. But an envious wizened bit of a fellow, with a red head, that wished to be married to the princess, and didn't like how she opened her eyes at Tom, came forward, and asked his business very snappishly.

"My business," says Tom, says he, "is to make the beautiful princess,

God bless her, laugh three times."

"Do you see all them merry fellows and skilful swordsmen," says the other, "that could eat you up with a grain of salt, and not a mother's soul of 'em ever got a laugh from her these seven years?"

So the fellows gathered round Tom, and the bad man aggravated him till he told them he didn't care a pinch o' snuff for the whole bilin' of 'em; let 'em come on, six at a time, and try what they could do.

The king, who was too far off to hear what they were saying, asked what did the stranger want.

"He wants," says the red-headed fellow, "to make hares of your best men."

"Oh!" says the king, "if that's the way, let one of 'em turn out and try his mettle."

So one stood forward, with sword and pot-lid, and made a cut at Tom. He struck the fellow's elbow with the club, and up over their heads flew the sword, and down went the owner of it on the gravel from a thump he got on the helmet. Another took his place, and another, and another, and then half a dozen at once, and Tom sent swords, helmets, shields, and bodies, rolling over and over, and themselves bawling out that they were kilt, and disabled, and damaged, and rubbing their poor elbows and hips, and limping away. Tom contrived not to kill any one; and the princess was so amused, that she let a great sweet laugh out of her that was heard over all the yard.

"King of Dublin," says Tom, "I've quarter your daughter."

And the king didn't know whether he was glad or sorry, and all the blood in the princess's heart run into her cheeks.

So there was no more fighting that day, and Tom was invited to dine with the royal family. Next day, Redhead told Tom of a wolf, the size of a yearling heifer, that used to be serenading about the walls, and eating people and cattle; and said what a pleasure it would give the king to have it killed.

"With all my heart," says Tom; "send a jackeen to show me where he lives, and we'll see how he behaves to a stranger."

The princess was not well pleased, for Tom looked a different person with fine clothes and a nice green birredh over his long curly hair; and besides, he'd got one laugh out of her.

However, the king gave his consent; and in an hour and a half the horrible wolf was walking into the palace-yard, and Tom a step or two behind, with his club on his shoulder, just as a shepherd would be walking after a pet lamb.

The king and queen and princess were safe up in their gallery, but the officers and people of the court that wor padrowling about the great bawn, when they saw the big baste coming in, gave themselves up, and began to make for doors and gates; and the wolf licked his chops, as if he was saying, "Wouldn't I enjoy a breakfast off a couple of yez!"

The king shouted out, "O Tom with the Goat-skin, take away that terrible wolf, and you must have all my daughter."

But Tom didn't mind him a bit. He pulled out his flute and began to play like vengeance; and dickens a man or boy in the yard but began shovelling away heel and toe, and the wolf himself was obliged to get on his hind legs and dance 'Tatther Jack Walsh,' along with the rest. A good deal of the people got inside, and shut the doors, the way the hairy fellow wouldn't pin them; but Tom kept playing, and the outsiders kept dancing and shouting, and the wolf kept dancing and roaring with the pain his legs were giving him; and all the time he had his eyes on Redhead, who was shut out along with the rest. Wherever Redhead went, the wolf followed, and kept one eye on him and the other on Tom, to see if he would give him leave to eat him. But Tom shook his head, and never stopped the tune, and Redhead never stopped dancing and bawling, and the wolf dancing and roaring, one leg up and the other down, and he ready to drop out of his standing from fair tiresomeness.

When the princess seen that there was no fear of any one being kilt, she was so divarted by the stew that Redhead was in, that she gave another great laugh; and well become Tom, out he cried, "King of Dublin, I have two halves of your daughter."

"Oh, halves or alls," says the king, "put away that divel of a wolf, and we'll see about it."

So Tom put his flute in his pocket, and says he to the baste that was sittin' on his currabingo ready to faint, "Walk off to your mountain, my fine fellow, and live like a respectable baste; and if ever I find you come within seven miles of any town, I'll –"

He said no more, but spit in his fist, and gave a flourish of his club. It was all the poor divel of a wolf wanted: he put his tail between his legs, and took to his pumps without looking at man or mortal, and neither sun, moon, or stars ever saw him in sight of Dublin again.

At dinner every one laughed but the foxy fellow; and sure enough he was laying out how he'd settle poor Tom next day.

"Well, to be sure!" says he, "King of Dublin, you are in luck. There's the Danes moidhering us to no end. Deuce run to Lusk wid 'em! and if any one can save us from 'em, it is this gentleman with the goat-skin. There is a flail hangin' on the collar-beam, in hell, and neither Dane nor devil can stand before it."

"So," says Tom to the king, "will you let me have the other half of the princess if I bring you the flail?"

"No, no," says the princess; "I'd rather never be your wife than see you in that danger."

But Redhead whispered and nudged Tom about how shabby it would look to reneague the adventure. So he asked which way he was to go, and Redhead directed him.

Well, he travelled and travelled, till he came in sight of the walls of hell; and, bedad, before he knocked at the gates, he rubbed himself over with the greenish ointment. When he knocked, a hundred little imps popped their heads out through the bars, and axed him what he wanted.

"I want to speak to the big divel of all," says Tom: "open the gate."

It wasn't long till the gate was thrune open, and the Ould Boy received Tom with bows and scrapes, and axed his business.

"My business isn't much," says Tom. "I only came for the loan of that flail that I see hanging on the collar-beam, for the king of Dublin to give a thrashing to the Danes."

"Well," says the other, "the Danes is much better customers to me; but since you walked so far I won't refuse. Hand that flail," says he to a young imp; and he winked the far-off eye at the same time. So, while some were barring the gates, the young devil climbed up, and took down the flail that had the handstaff and booltheen both made out of red-hot iron. The little vagabond was grinning to think how it would burn the hands o' Tom, but the dickens a burn it made on him, no more nor if it was a good oak sapling.

"Thankee," says Tom. "Now would you open the gate for a body, and I'll give you no more trouble."

"Oh, tramp!" says Ould Nick; "is that the way? It is easier getting inside them gates than getting out again. Take that tool from him, and give him a dose of the oil of stirrup."

So one fellow put out his claws to seize on the flail, but Tom gave him such a welt of it on the side of the head that he broke off one of his horns, and made him roar like a devil as he was. Well, they rushed at Tom, but he gave them, little and big, such a thrashing as they didn't forget for a while. At last says the ould thief of all, rubbing his elbow, "Let the fool out; and woe to whoever lets him in again, great or small."

So out marched Tom, and away with him, without minding the shouting and cursing they kept up at him from the tops of the walls; and when he got home to the big bawn of the palace, there never was such running and racing as to see himself and the flail. When he had his story told, he laid down the flail on the stone steps, and bid no one for their lives to touch it. If the king, and queen, and princess, made much of him before, they made ten times more of him now; but Redhead, the mean scruff-hound, stole over, and thought to catch hold of the flail to make an end of him. His fingers hardly touched it, when he let a roar out of him as if heaven and earth were coming together, and kept flinging his arms about and dancing, that it was pitiful to look at him. Tom run at him as soon as he could rise, caught his hands in his own two, and rubbed them this way and that, and the burning pain left them before you could reckon one. Well the poor fellow, between the pain that was only just gone, and the comfort he was in, had the comicalest face that you ever see, it was such a mixtherum-gatherum of laughing and crying. Everybody burst out a laughing – the princess could not stop no more than the rest; and then says Tom, "Now, ma'am, if there were fifty halves of you, I hope you'll give me them all."

Well, the princess looked at her father, and by my word, she came over to Tom, and put her two delicate hands into his two rough ones, and I wish it was myself was in his shoes that day!

Tom would not bring the flail into the palace. You may be sure no other body went near it; and when the early risers were passing next morning, they found two long clefts in the stone, where it was after burning itself an opening downwards, nobody could tell how far. But a messenger came in at noon, and said that the Danes were so frightened when they heard of the flail coming into Dublin, that they got into their ships, and sailed away.

Well, I suppose, before they were married, Tom got some man, like Pat Mara of Tomenine, to learn him the 'principles of politeness,' fluxions, gunnery, and fortification, decimal fractions, practice, and the rule of three direct, the way he'd be able to keep up a conversation with the royal family. Whether he ever lost his time learning them sciences, I'm not sure, but it's as sure as fate that his mother never more saw any want till the end of her days.

Conall Yellowclaw

CONALL YELLOWCLAW WAS A STURDY TENANT in Erin: he had three sons. There was at that time a king over every fifth of Erin. It fell out for the children of the king that was near Conall, that they themselves and the children of Conall came to blows. The children of Conall got the upper hand, and they killed the king's big son. The king sent a message for Conall, and he said to him – "Oh, Conall! what made your sons go to spring on my sons till my big son was killed by your children? but I see that though I follow you revengefully, I shall not be much better for it, and I will now set a thing before you, and if you will do it, I will not follow you with revenge. If you and your sons will get me the brown horse of the king of Lochlann, you shall get the souls of your sons."

"Why," said Conall, "should not I do the pleasure of the king, though there should be no souls of my sons in dread at all. Hard is the matter you require of me, but I will lose my own life, and the life of my sons, or else I will do the pleasure of the king."

After these words Conall left the king, and he went home: when he got home he was under much trouble and perplexity. When he went to lie down he told his wife the thing the king had set before him. His wife took much sorrow that he was obliged to part from herself, while she knew not if she should see him more.

"Oh, Conall," said she, "why didst not thou let the king do his own pleasure to thy sons, rather than be going now, while I know not if ever I shall see thee more?"

When he rose on the morrow, he set himself and his three sons in order, and they took their journey towards Lochlann, and they made no stop but tore through ocean till they reached it. When they reached Lochlann they did not know what they should do. Said the old man to his sons, "Stop ye, and we will seek out the house of the king's miller."

When they went into the house of the king's miller, the man asked them to stop there for the night. Conall told the miller that his own children and the children of his king had fallen out, and that his children had killed the king's son, and there was nothing that would please the king but that he should get the brown horse of the king of Lochlann.

"If you will do me a kindness, and will put me in a way to get him, for certain I will pay ye for it."

"The thing is silly that you are come to seek," said the miller; "for the king has laid his mind on him so greatly that you will not get him in any way unless you steal him; but if you can make out a way, I will keep it secret."

"This is what I am thinking," said Conall, "since you are working every day for the king, you and your gillies could put myself and my sons into five sacks of bran."

"The plan that has come into your head is not bad," said the miller.

The miller spoke to his gillies, and he said to them to do this, and they put them in five sacks. The king's gillies came to seek the bran, and they took the five sacks with them, and they emptied them before the horses. The servants locked the door, and they went away.

When they rose to lay hand on the brown horse, said Conall, "You shall not do that. It is hard to get out of this; let us make for ourselves five hiding holes, so that if they hear us we may go and hide." They made the holes, then they laid hands on the horse. The horse was pretty well unbroken, and he set to making a terrible noise through the stable. The king heard the noise. "It must be my brown horse," said he to his gillies; "find out what is wrong with him."

The servants went out, and when Conall and his sons saw them coming they went into the hiding holes. The servants looked amongst the horses, and they did not find anything wrong; and they returned and they told this to the king, and the king said to them that if nothing was wrong they should go to their places of rest. When the gillies had time to be gone, Conall and his sons laid their hands again on the horse. If the noise was great that he made before, the noise he made now was seven times greater. The king sent a message for his gillies again, and said for certain there was something troubling the brown horse. "Go and look well about him." The servants went out, and they went to their hiding holes. The servants rummaged well, and did not find a thing. They returned and they told this.

"That is marvellous for me," said the king: "go you to lie down again, and if I notice it again I will go out myself."

When Conall and his sons perceived that the gillies were gone, they laid hands again on the horse, and one of them caught him, and if the noise that the horse made on the two former times was great, he made more this time.

"Be this from me," said the king; "it must be that some one is troubling my brown horse." He sounded the bell hastily, and when his waiting-man came to him, he said to him to let the stable gillies know that something was wrong with the horse. The gillies came, and the king went with them. When Conall and his sons perceived the company coming they went to the hiding holes.

The king was a wary man, and he saw where the horses were making a noise.

"Be wary," said the king, "there are men within the stable, let us get at them somehow."

The king followed the tracks of the men, and he found them. Every one knew Conall, for he was a valued tenant of the king of Erin, and when the king brought them up out of the holes he said, "Oh, Conall, is it you that are here?"

"I am, O king, without question, and necessity made me come. I am under thy pardon, and under thine honour, and under thy grace." He told how it happened to him, and that he had to get the brown horse for the king of Erin, or that his sons were to be put to death. "I knew that I should not get him by asking, and I was going to steal him."

"Yes, Conall, it is well enough, but come in," said the king. He desired his look-out men to set a watch on the sons of Conall, and to give them meat. And a double watch was set that night on the sons of Conall.

"Now, O Conall," said the king, "were you ever in a harder place than to be seeing your lot of sons hanged tomorrow? But you set it to my goodness and to my grace, and say that it was necessity brought it on you, so I must not hang you. Tell me any case in which you were as hard as this, and if you tell that, you shall get the soul of your youngest son."

"I will tell a case as hard in which I was," said Conall. "I was once a young lad, and my father had much land, and he had parks of year-old cows, and one of them had just calved, and my father told me to bring her home. I found the cow, and took her with us. There fell a shower of snow. We went into the herd's bothy, and we took the cow and the calf in with us, and we were letting the shower pass from us. Who should come in but one cat and ten, and one great one-eyed fox-coloured cat as head bard over them. When they came in, in very deed I myself had no liking for their company. 'Strike up with you,' said the head bard, 'why should we be still? and sing a cronan to Conall Yellowclaw.' I was amazed that my name was known to the cats themselves. When they had sung the cronan, said the head bard, 'Now, O Conall, pay the reward of the cronan that the cats have sung to thee.' 'Well then,' said I myself, 'I have no reward whatsoever for you, unless you should go down and take that calf.' No sooner said I the word than the two cats and ten went down to attack the calf, and in very deed, he did not last them long. 'Play up with you, why should you be silent? Make a cronan to Conall Yellowclaw,' said the head bard. Certainly I had no liking at all for the cronan, but up came the one cat and ten, and if they did not sing me a cronan then and there! 'Pay them now their reward,' said the great fox-coloured cat. 'I am tired myself of yourselves and your rewards,' said I. 'I have no reward for you unless you take that cow down there.' They betook themselves to the cow, and indeed she did not last them long.

"'Why will you be silent? Go up and sing a cronan to Conall Yellowclaw,' said the head bard. And surely, oh king, I had no care for them or for their cronan, for I began to see that they were not good comrades. When they had sung me the cronan they betook themselves down where the head bard was. 'Pay now their reward, said the head bard; and for sure, oh king, I had no reward for them; and I said to them, 'I have no reward for you.' And surely, oh king, there was catterwauling between them. So I leapt out at a turf window that was at the back of the house. I took myself off as hard as I might into the wood. I was swift enough and strong at that time; and when I felt the rustling toirm of the cats after me I climbed into as high a tree as I saw in the place, and one that was close in the top; and I hid myself as well as I might. The cats began to search for me through the wood, and they could not find me; and when they were tired, each one said to the other that they would turn back. 'But,' said the one-eyed fox-coloured cat that was commander-in-chief over them, 'you saw him not with your two eyes, and though I have but one eye, there's the rascal up in the tree.' When he had said that, one of them went up in the tree, and as he was coming where I was, I drew a weapon that I had and I killed him. 'Be this from me!' said the one-eyed one – 'I must not be losing my company thus; gather round the root of the tree and dig about it, and let down that villain to earth.' On this they gathered about the tree, and they dug about the root, and the first branching root that they cut, she gave a shiver to fall, and I myself gave a shout, and it was not to be wondered at.

"There was in the neighbourhood of the wood a priest, and he had ten men with him delving, and he said, 'There is a shout of a man in extremity and I must not be without replying to it.' And the wisest of the men said, 'Let it alone till we hear it again.' The cats began again digging wildly, and they broke the next root; and I myself gave the next shout, and in very deed it was not a weak one. 'Certainly,' said the priest, 'it is a man in extremity – let us move.' They set themselves in order for moving. And the cats arose on the tree, and they broke the third root, and the tree fell on her elbow. Then I gave the third shout. The stalwart men hastened, and when they saw how the cats served the tree, they began at them with the spades; and they themselves and the cats began at each other, till the cats ran away. And surely, oh king, I did not move till I saw the last one of them off. And then I came home. And there's the hardest case in which I ever was; and it seems to me that tearing by the cats were harder than hanging tomorrow by the king of Lochlann."

"Och! Conall," said the king, "you are full of words. You have freed the soul of your son with your tale; and if you tell me a harder case than that you will get your second youngest son, and then you will have two sons."

"Well then," said Conall, "on condition that thou dost that, I will tell thee how I was once in a harder case than to be in thy power in prison tonight."

"Let's hear," said the king.

"I was then," said Conall, "quite a young lad, and I went out hunting, and my father's land was beside the sea, and it was rough with rocks, caves, and rifts. When I was going on the top of the shore, I saw as if there were a smoke coming up between two rocks, and I began to look what might be the meaning of the smoke coming up there. When I was looking, what should I do but fall; and the place was so full of heather, that neither bone nor skin was broken. I knew not how I should get out of this. I was not looking before me, but I kept looking overhead the way I came – and thinking that the day would never come that I could get up there. It was terrible for me to be there till I should die. I heard a great clattering coming, and what was there but a great giant and two dozen of goats with him, and a buck at their head. And when the giant had tied the goats, he came up and he said to me, 'Hao O! Conall, it's long since my knife has been rusting in my pouch waiting for thy tender flesh.' 'Och!' said I, 'It's not much you will be bettered by me, though you should tear me asunder; I will make but one meal for you. But I see that you are one-eyed. I am a good leech, and I will give you the sight of the other eye.' The giant went and he drew the great caldron on the site of the fire. I myself was telling him how he should heat the water, so that I should give its sight to the other eye. I got heather and I made a rubber of it, and I set him upright in the caldron. I began at the eye that was well, pretending to him that I would give its sight to the other one, till I left them as bad as each other; and surely it was easier to spoil the one that was well than to give sight to the other.

"When he saw that he could not see a glimpse, and when I myself said to him that I would get out in spite of him, he gave a spring out of the water, and he stood in the mouth of the cave, and he said that he would have revenge for the sight of his eye. I had but to stay there crouched the length of the night, holding in my breath in such a way that he might not find out where I was.

"When he felt the birds calling in the morning, and knew that the day was, he said – 'Art thou sleeping? Awake and let out my lot of goats.' I killed the buck. He cried, 'I do believe that thou art killing my buck.'

"'I am not,' said I, 'but the ropes are so tight that I take long to loose them.' I let out one of the goats, and there he was caressing her, and he said to her, 'There thou art thou shaggy, hairy white goat; and thou seest me, but I see thee not.' I kept letting them out by the way of one and one, as I flayed the buck, and before the last one was out I had him flayed bag-wise. Then I went and I put my legs in place of his legs, and my hands in place of his forelegs, and my head in place of his head, and the horns on top of my head, so that the brute might think that it was the buck. I went out. When I was going out the giant laid his hand on me, and he said, 'There thou art, thou pretty buck; thou seest me, but I see thee not.' When I myself got out, and I saw the world about me, surely, oh, king! joy was on me. When I was out and had shaken the skin off me, I said to the brute, 'I am out now in spite of you.'

"'Aha!' said he, 'Hast thou done this to me. Since thou wert so stalwart that thou hast got out, I will give thee a ring that I have here; keep the ring, and it will do thee good.'

"'I will not take the ring from you,' said I, 'but throw it, and I will take it with me.' He threw the ring on the flat ground, I went myself and I lifted the ring, and I put it on my finger. When he said me then, 'Is the ring fitting thee?' I said to him, 'It is.' Then he said, 'Where art thou, ring?' And the ring said, 'I am here.' The brute went and went towards where the ring was speaking, and now I saw that I was in a harder case than ever I was. I drew a dirk. I cut the finger from off me, and I threw it from me as far as I could out on the loch, and there was a great depth in the place. He shouted, 'Where art thou, ring?' And the ring said, 'I am here,' though it was on the bed of ocean. He gave a spring after the ring, and out he went in the sea. And I was as pleased then when I saw him drowning, as though you should grant my own life and the life of my two sons with me, and not lay any more trouble on me.

"When the giant was drowned I went in, and I took with me all he had of gold and silver, and I went home, and surely great joy was on my people when I arrived. And as a sign now look, the finger is off me."

"Yes, indeed, Conall, you are wordy and wise," said the king. "I see the finger is off you. You have freed your two sons, but tell me a case in which you ever were that is harder than to be looking on your son being hanged tomorrow, and you shall get the soul of your eldest son."

"Then went my father," said Conall, "and he got me a wife, and I was married. I went to hunt. I was going beside the sea, and I saw an island over in the midst of the loch, and I came there where a boat was with a rope before her, and a rope behind her, and many precious things within her. I looked myself on the boat to see how I might get part of them. I put in the one foot, and the other foot was on the ground, and when I raised my head what was it but the boat over in the middle of the loch, and she never stopped till she reached the island. When I went out of the boat the boat returned where she was before. I did not know now what I should do. The place was without meat or clothing, without the appearance of a house on it. I came out on the top of a hill. Then I came to a glen; I saw in it, at the bottom of a hollow, a woman with a child, and the child was naked on her knee, and she had a knife in her hand. She tried to put the knife to the throat of the babe, and the babe began to laugh in her face, and she began to cry, and she threw the knife behind her. I thought to myself that I was near my foe and far from my friends, and I called to the woman, 'What are you doing here?' And she said to me, 'What brought you here?' I told her myself word upon word how I came. 'Well then,' said she, 'it was so I came also.' She showed me to the place where I should come in where she was. I went in, and I said to her, 'What was the matter that you were putting the knife on the neck of the child?' 'It is that he must be cooked for the giant who is here, or else no more of my world will be before me.' Just then we could be hearing the footsteps of the giant, 'What shall I do? What shall I do?' cried the woman. I went to the caldron, and by luck it was not hot, so in it I got just as the brute came in. 'Hast thou boiled that youngster for me?' he cried. 'He's not done yet,' said she, and I cried out from the caldron, 'Mammy, mammy, it's boiling I am.' Then the giant laughed out HAI, HAW, HOGARAICH, and heaped on wood under the caldron.

"And now I was sure I would scald before I could get out of that. As fortune favoured me, the brute slept beside the caldron. There I was scalded by the bottom of the caldron. When she perceived that he was asleep, she set her mouth quietly to the hole that was in the lid, and she said to me 'was I alive?' I said I was. I put up my head, and the hole in the lid was so large, that my head went through easily. Everything was coming easily with me till I began to bring up my hips. I left the skin of my hips behind me, but I came out. When I got out of the caldron I knew not what to do; and she said to me that there was no weapon that would kill him but his own weapon. I began to draw his spear and every breath that he drew I thought I would be down his throat, and when his breath came out I was back again just as far. But with every ill that befell me I got the spear loosed from him. Then I was as one under a bundle of straw in a great wind for I could not manage the spear. And it was fearful to look on the brute, who had but one eye in the midst of his face; and it was not agreeable for the like of me to attack him. I drew the dart as best I could, and I set it in his eye. When he felt this he gave his head a lift, and he struck the other end of the dart on the top of the cave, and it went through to the back of his head. And he fell cold dead where he was; and you may be sure, oh king, that joy was on me. I myself and the woman went out on clear ground, and we passed the night there. I went and got the boat with which I came, and she was no way lightened, and took the woman and the child over on dry land; and I returned home."

The king of Lochlann's mother was putting on a fire at this time, and listening to Conall telling the tale about the child.

"Is it you," said she, "that were there?"

"Well then," said he, "'twas I."

"Och! och!" said she, "'twas I that was there, and the king is the child whose life you saved; and it is to you that life thanks should be given." Then they took great joy.

The king said, "Oh, Conall, you came through great hardships. And now the brown horse is yours, and his sack full of the most precious things that are in my treasury."

They lay down that night, and if it was early that Conall rose, it was earlier than that that the queen was on foot making ready. He got the brown horse and his sack full of gold and silver and stones of great price, and then Conall and his three sons went away, and they returned home to the Erin realm of gladness. He left the gold and silver in his house, and he went with the horse to the king. They were good friends evermore. He returned home to his wife, and they set in order a feast; and that was a feast if ever there was one, oh son and brother.

The Sea-Maiden and the Laidly Beast

THERE WAS ONCE a poor old fisherman, and one year he was not getting much fish. On a day of days, while he was fishing, there rose a sea-maiden at the side of his boat, and she asked him, "Are you getting much fish?" The old man answered and said, "Not I." "What reward would you give me for sending plenty of fish to you?" "Ach!" said the old man, "I have not much to spare." "Will you give me the first son you have?" said she. "I would give ye that, were I to have a son," said he. "Then go home, and remember me when your son is twenty years of age, and you yourself will get plenty of fish after this." Everything happened as the sea-maiden said, and he himself got plenty of fish; but when the end of the twenty years was nearing, the old man was growing more and more sorrowful and heavy hearted, while he counted each day as it came.

He had rest neither day nor night. The son asked his father one day, "Is any one troubling you?" The old man said, "Some one is, but that's nought to do with you nor any one else." The lad said, "I must know what it is." His father told him at last how the matter was with him and the sea-maiden. "Let not that put you in any trouble," said the son; "I will not oppose you." "You shall not; you shall not go, my son, though I never get fish any more." "If you will not let me go with you, go to the smithy, and let the smith make me a great strong sword, and I will go seek my fortune."

His father went to the smithy, and the smith made a doughty sword for him. His father came home with the sword. The lad grasped it and gave it a shake or two, and it flew into a hundred splinters. He asked his father to go to the smithy and get him another sword in which there should be twice as much weight; and so his father did, and so likewise it happened to the next sword – it broke in two halves. Back went the old man to the smithy; and the smith made a great sword, its like he never made before. "There's thy sword for thee," said the smith, "and the fist must be good that plays this blade." The old man gave the sword to his son; he gave it a shake or two. "This will do," said he; "it's high time now to travel on my way."

On the next morning he put a saddle on a black horse that his father had, and he took the world for his pillow. When he went on a bit, he fell in with the carcass of a sheep beside the road. And there were a great black dog, a falcon, and an otter, and they were quarrelling over the spoil. So they asked him to divide it for them. He came down off the horse, and he divided the carcass amongst the three. Three shares to the dog, two shares to the otter, and a share to the falcon. "For this," said the dog, "if swiftness of foot or sharpness of tooth will give thee aid, mind me, and I will be at thy side." Said the otter, "If the swimming of foot on the ground of a pool will loose thee, mind me, and I will be at thy side." Said the falcon, "If hardship comes on thee, where swiftness of wing or crook of a claw will do good, mind me, and I will be at thy side."

On this he went onward till he reached a king's house, and he took service to be a herd, and his wages were to be according to the milk of the cattle. He went away with the cattle, and the grazing was but bare. In the evening when he took them home they had not much milk, the place was so bare, and his meat and drink was but spare that night.

On the next day he went on further with them; and at last he came to a place exceedingly grassy, in a green glen, of which he never saw the like.

But about the time when he should drive the cattle homewards, who should he see coming but a great giant with his sword in his hand? "HI! HO!! HOGARACH!!!" says the giant. "Those cattle are mine; they are on my land, and a dead man art thou." "I say not that," says the herd; "there is no knowing, but that may be easier to say than to do."

He drew the great clean-sweeping sword, and he neared the giant. The herd drew back his sword, and the head was off the giant in a twinkling. He leaped on the black horse, and he went to look for the giant's house. In went the herd, and that's the place where there was money in plenty, and dresses of each kind in the wardrobe with gold and silver, and each thing finer than the other. At the mouth of night he took himself to the king's house, but he took not a thing from the giant's house. And when the cattle were milked this night there *was* milk. He got good feeding this night, meat and drink without stint, and the king was hugely pleased that he had caught such a herd. He went on for a time in this way, but at last the glen grew bare of grass, and the grazing was not so good.

So he thought he would go a little further forward in on the giant's land; and he sees a great park of grass. He returned for the cattle, and he put them into the park.

They were but a short time grazing in the park when a great wild giant came full of rage and madness. "HI! HAW!! HOGARAICH!!!" said the giant. "It is a drink of thy blood that will quench my thirst this night." "There is no knowing," said the herd, "but that's easier to say than to do." And at each other went the men. *There* was shaking of blades! At length and at last it seemed as if the giant would get the victory over the herd. Then he called on the dog, and with one spring the black dog caught the giant by the neck, and swiftly the herd struck off his head.

He went home very tired this night, but it's a wonder if the king's cattle had not milk. The whole family was delighted that they had got such a herd.

Next day he betakes himself to the castle. When he reached the door, a little flattering carlin met him standing in the door. "All hail and good luck to thee, fisher's son; 'tis I myself am pleased to see thee; great is the honour for this kingdom, for thy like to be come into it – thy coming in is fame for this little bothy; go in first; honour to the gentles; go on, and take breath."

"In before me, thou crone; I like not flattery out of doors; go in and let's hear thy speech." In went the crone, and when her back was to him he drew his sword and whips her head off; but the sword flew out of his hand. And swift the crone gripped her head with both hands, and puts it on her neck as it was before. The dog sprung on the crone, and she struck the generous dog with the club of magic; and there he lay. But the herd struggled for a hold of the club of magic, and with one blow on the top of the head she was on earth in the twinkling of an eye. He went forward, up a little, and there was spoil! Gold and silver, and each thing more precious than another, in the crone's castle. He went back to the king's house, and then there was rejoicing.

He followed herding in this way for a time; but one night after he came home, instead of getting 'All hail' and 'Good luck' from the dairymaid, all were at crying and woe.

He asked what cause of woe there was that night. The dairymaid said "There is a great beast with three heads in the loch, and it must get some one every year, and the lot had come this year on the king's daughter, and at midday tomorrow she is to meet the Laidly Beast at the upper end of the loch, but there is a great suitor yonder who is going to rescue her."

"What suitor is that?" said the herd. "Oh, he is a great General of arms," said the dairymaid, "and when he kills the beast, he will marry the king's daughter, for the king has said that he who could save his daughter should get her to marry."

But on the morrow, when the time grew near, the king's daughter and this hero of arms went to give a meeting to the beast, and they reached the black rock, at the upper end of the loch. They were but a short time there when the beast stirred in the midst of the loch; but when the General saw this terror of a beast with three heads, he took fright, and he slunk away, and he hid himself. And the king's daughter was under fear and under trembling, with no one at all to save her. Suddenly she sees a doughty handsome youth, riding a black horse, and coming where she was. He was marvellously arrayed and full armed, and his black dog moved after him. "There is gloom on your face, girl," said the youth; "what do you here?"

"Oh! that's no matter," said the king's daughter. "It's not long I'll be here, at all events."

"I say not that," said he.

"A champion fled as likely as you, and not long since," said she.

"He is a champion who stands the war," said the youth. And to meet the beast he went with his sword and his dog. But there was a spluttering and a splashing between himself and the beast! The dog kept doing all he might, and the king's daughter was palsied by fear of the noise of the beast! One of them would now be under, and now above. But at last he cut one of the heads off it. It gave one roar, and the son of earth, echo of the rocks, called to its screech, and it drove the loch in spindrift from end to end, and in a twinkling it went out of sight.

"Good luck and victory follow you, lad!" said the king's daughter. "I am safe for one night, but the beast will come again and again, until the other two heads come off it." He caught the beast's head, and he drew a knot through it, and he told her to bring it with her there tomorrow. She gave him a gold ring, and went home with the head on her shoulder, and the herd betook himself to the cows. But she had not gone far when this great General saw her, and he said to her, "I will kill you if you do not say that 'twas I took the head off the beast." "Oh!" says she, "'tis I will say it; who else took the head off the beast but you!" They reached the king's house, and the head was on the General's shoulder. But here was rejoicing, that she should come home alive and whole, and this great captain with the beast's head full of blood in his hand. On the morrow they went away, and there was no question at all but that this hero would save the king's daughter.

They reached the same place, and they were not long there when the fearful Laidly Beast stirred in the midst of the loch, and the hero slunk away as he did on yesterday, but it was not long after this when the man of the black horse came, with another dress on. No matter; she knew that it was the very same lad. "It is I am pleased to see you," said she. "I am in hopes you will handle your great sword today as you did yesterday. Come up and take breath." But they were not long there when they saw the beast steaming in the midst of the loch.

At once he went to meet the beast, but *there* was Cloopersteich and Claperstich, spluttering, splashing, raving, and roaring on the beast! They kept at it thus for a long time, and about the mouth of night he cut another head off the beast. He put it on the knot and gave it to her. She gave him one of her earrings, and he leaped on the black horse, and he betook himself to the herding. The king's daughter went home with the heads. The General met her, and took the heads from her, and he said to her, that she must tell that it was he who took the head off the beast this time also. "Who else took the head off the beast but you?" said she. They reached the king's house with the heads. Then there was joy and gladness.

About the same time on the morrow, the two went away. The officer hid himself as he usually did. The king's daughter betook herself to the bank of the loch. The hero of the black horse came, and if roaring and raving were on the beast on the days that were passed, this day it was horrible. But no matter, he took the third head off the beast, and drew it through the knot, and gave it to her. She gave him her other earring, and then she went home with the heads. When they reached the king's house, all were full of smiles, and the General was to marry the king's daughter the next day. The wedding was going on, and every one about the castle longing till the priest should come. But when the priest came, she would marry only the one who could take the heads off the knot without cutting it. "Who should take the heads off the knot but the man that put the heads on?" said the king.

The General tried them; but he could not loose them; and at last there was no one about the house but had tried to take the heads off the knot, but they could not. The king asked if there were any one else about the house that would try to take the heads off the knot. They said that the herd had not tried them yet. Word went for the herd; and he was not long throwing them hither and thither. "But stop a bit, my lad," said the king's daughter; "the man that took the heads off the beast, he has my ring and my two earrings." The herd put his hand in his pocket, and he threw them on the board. "Thou art my man," said the king's daughter. The king was not so pleased when he saw that it was a herd who was to marry his daughter, but he ordered that he should be put in a better dress; but his daughter spoke, and she said that he had a dress as fine as any that ever was in his castle; and thus it happened. The herd put on the giant's golden dress, and they married that same day.

They were now married, and everything went on well. But one day, and it was the namesake of the day when his father had promised him to the sea-maiden, they were sauntering by the side of the loch, and lo and behold! she came and took him away to the loch without leave or asking. The king's daughter was now mournful, tearful, blind-sorrowful for her married man; she was always with her eye on the loch. An old soothsayer met her, and she told how it had befallen her married mate. Then he told her the thing to do to save her mate, and that she did.

She took her harp to the sea-shore, and sat and played; and the sea-maiden came up to listen, for sea-maidens are fonder of music than all other creatures. But when the wife saw the sea-maiden she stopped. The sea-maiden said, "Play on!" but the princess said, "No, not till I see my man again." So the sea-maiden put up his head out of the loch. Then the princess played again, and stopped till the sea-maiden put him up to the waist. Then the princess played and stopped again, and this time the sea-maiden put him all out of the loch, and he called on the falcon and became one and flew on shore. But the sea-maiden took the princess, his wife.

Sorrowful was each one that was in the town on this night. Her man was mournful, tearful, wandering down and up about the banks of the loch, by day and night. The old soothsayer met him. The soothsayer told him that there was no way of killing the sea-maiden but the one way, and this is it – "In the island that is in the midst of the loch is the white-footed hind of the slenderest legs and the swiftest step, and though she be caught, there will spring a hoodie out of her, and though the hoodie should be caught, there will spring a trout out of her, but there is an egg in the mouth of the trout, and the soul of the sea-maiden is in the egg, and if the egg breaks, she is dead."

Now, there was no way of getting to this island, for the sea-maiden would sink each boat and raft that would go on the loch. He thought he would try to leap the strait with the black horse, and even so he did. The black horse leaped the strait. He saw the hind, and he let the black dog after her, but when he was on one side of the island, the hind would be on the other side. "Oh! would the black dog of the carcass of flesh were here!" No sooner spoke he the word than the grateful dog was at his side; and after the hind he went, and they were not long in bringing her to earth. But he no sooner caught her than a hoodie sprang out of her. "Would that the falcon grey, of sharpest eye and swiftest wing, were here!" No sooner said he this than the falcon was after the hoodie, and she was not long putting her to earth; and as the hoodie fell on the bank of the loch, out of her jumps the trout. "Oh! that thou wert by me now, oh otter!" No sooner said than the otter was at his side, and out on the loch she leaped, and brings the trout from the midst of the loch; but no sooner was the otter on shore with the trout than the egg came from his mouth. He sprang and he put his foot on it. 'Twas then the sea-maiden appeared, and she said, "Break not the egg, and you shall get all you ask." "Deliver to me my wife!" In the wink of an eye she was by his side. When he got hold of her hand in both his hands, he let his foot down on the egg, and the sea-maiden died.

Peredur the Son of Evrawc Slays the Addanc and the Serpent

ARTHUR WAS IN CAERLLEON upon Usk; and he went to hunt, and Peredur went with him. And Peredur let loose his dog upon a hart, and the dog killed the hart in a desert place. And a short space from him he saw signs of a dwelling, and towards the dwelling he went, and he beheld a hall, and at the door of the hall he found bald swarthy youths playing at chess. And when he entered, he beheld three maidens sitting on a bench, and they were all clothed alike, as became persons of high rank. And he came, and sat by them upon the bench; and one of the maidens looked steadfastly upon Peredur, and wept. And Peredur asked her wherefore she was weeping. "Through grief, that I should see so fair a youth as thou art, slain." "Who will slay me?" inquired Peredur. "If thou art so daring as to remain here tonight, I will tell thee." "How great soever my danger may be from remaining here, I will listen unto thee." "This Palace is owned by him who is my father," said the maiden, "and he slays every one who comes hither without his leave." "What sort of a man is thy father, that he is able to slay every one thus?" "A man who does violence and wrong unto his neighbours, and who renders justice unto none." And hereupon he saw the youths arise and clear the chessmen from the board. And he heard a great tumult; and after the tumult there came in a huge black one-eyed man, and the maidens arose to meet him. And they disarrayed him, and he went and sat down; and after he had rested and pondered awhile, he looked at Peredur, and asked who the knight was. "Lord," said one of the maidens, "he is the fairest and gentlest youth that ever thou didst see. And for the sake of Heaven, and of thine own dignity, have patience with him." "For thy sake I will have patience, and I will grant him his life this night." Then Peredur came towards them to the fire, and partook of food and liquor, and entered into discourse with the ladies. And being elated with the liquor, he said to the black man, "It is a marvel to me, so mighty as thou sayest thou art, who could have put out thine eye." "It is one of my habits," said the black man, "that whosoever puts to me the question which thou hast asked, shall not escape with his life, either as a free gift or for a price." "Lord," said the maiden, "whatsoever he may say to thee in jest, and through the excitement of liquor, make good that which thou saidst and didst promise me just now." "I will do so, gladly, for thy sake," said he. "Willingly will I grant him his life this night." And that night thus they remained.

And the next day the black man got up, and put on his armour, and said to Peredur, "Arise, man, and suffer death." And Peredur said unto him, "Do one of two things, black man; if thou wilt fight with me, either throw off thy own armour, or give arms to me, that I may encounter thee." "Ha, man," said he, "couldst thou fight, if thou hadst arms? Take, then, what arms thou dost choose." And thereupon the maiden came to Peredur with such arms as pleased him; and he fought with the black man, and forced him to crave his mercy. "Black man, thou shalt have mercy, provided thou tell me who thou art, and who put out thine eye." "Lord, I will tell thee; I lost it in fighting with the Black Serpent of the Carn. There is a mound, which is called the Mound of Mourning; and on the mound there is a carn, and in the carn there is a serpent, and on the tail of the serpent there is a stone, and the virtues of the stone are such, that whosoever should hold it in one hand, in the other he will have as much gold as he may desire. And in fighting with this serpent was it that I lost my eye. And the Black Oppressor am I called. And for this reason I am called the Black Oppressor, that there is not a single man around me whom I have not oppressed, and justice have I done unto none." "Tell me," said Peredur, "how far is it hence?" "The same day that thou settest forth, thou wilt come to the Palace of the Sons of the King of the Tortures." "Wherefore are they called thus?" "The Addanc of the Lake slays them once every day. When thou goest thence, thou wilt come to the Court of the Countess of the Achievements." "What achievements are there?" asked Peredur. "Three hundred men there are in her household, and unto every stranger that comes to the Court, the achievements of her household are related. And this is the manner of it, – the three hundred men of the household sit next unto the Lady; and that not through disrespect unto the guests, but that they may relate the achievements of the household. And the day that thou goest thence, thou wilt reach the Mound of Mourning, and round about the mound there are the owners of three hundred tents guarding the serpent." "Since thou hast, indeed, been an oppressor so long," said Peredur, "I will cause that thou continue so no longer." So he slew him.

Then the maiden spoke, and began to converse with him. "If thou wast poor when thou camest here, henceforth thou wilt be rich through the treasure of the black man whom thou hast slain. Thou seest the many lovely maidens that there are in this Court; thou shalt have her whom thou best likest for the lady of thy love." "Lady, I came not hither from my country to woo; but match yourselves as it liketh you with the comely youths I see here; and none of your goods do I desire, for I need them not." Then Peredur rode forward, and he came to the Palace of the Sons of the King of the Tortures; and when he entered the Palace, he saw none but women; and they rose up, and were joyful at his coming; and as they began to discourse with him, he beheld a charger arrive, with a saddle upon it, and a corpse in the saddle. And one of the women arose, and took the corpse from the saddle, and anointed it in a vessel of warm water, which was below the door, and placed precious balsam upon it; and the man rose up alive, and came to the place where Peredur was, and greeted him, and was joyful to see him. And two other men came in upon their saddles, and the maiden treated these two in the same manner as she had done the first. Then Peredur asked the chieftain wherefore it was thus. And they told him, that there was an Addanc in a cave, which slew them once every day. And thus they remained that night.

And next morning the youths arose to sally forth, and Peredur besought them, for the sake of the ladies of their love, to permit him to go with them; but they refused him, saying, "If thou shouldst be slain there, thou hast none to bring thee back to life again." And they rode forward, and Peredur followed after them; and, after they had disappeared out of his sight, he came to a mound, whereon sat the fairest lady he had ever beheld. "I know thy quest," said she; "thou art going to encounter the Addanc, and he will slay thee, and that not by courage, but by craft. He has a cave, and at the entrance of the cave there is a stone pillar, and he sees every one that enters, and none see him; and from behind the pillar he slays every one with a poisonous dart. And if thou wouldst pledge me thy faith to love me above all women, I would give thee a stone, by which thou shouldst see him when thou goest in, and he should not see thee." "I will, by my troth," said Peredur, "for when first I beheld thee I loved thee; and where shall I seek thee?" "When thou seekest me, seek towards India." And the maiden vanished, after placing the stone in Peredur's hand.

And he came towards a valley, through which ran a river; and the borders of the valley were wooded, and on each side of the river were level meadows. And on one side of the river he saw a flock of white sheep, and on the other a flock of black sheep. And whenever one of the white sheep bleated, one of the black sheep would cross over and become white; and when one of the black sheep bleated, one of the white sheep would cross over and become black. And he saw a tall tree by the side of the river, one half of which was in flames from the root to the top, and the other half was green and in full leaf. And nigh thereto he saw a youth sitting upon a mound, and two greyhounds, white-breasted and spotted, in leashes, lying by his side. And certain was he that he had never seen a youth of so royal a bearing as he. And in the wood opposite he heard hounds raising a herd of deer. And Peredur saluted the youth, and the youth greeted him in return. And there were three roads leading from the mound; two of them were wide roads, and the third was more narrow. And Peredur inquired where the three roads went. "One of them goes to my palace," said the youth; "and one of two things I counsel thee to do; either to proceed to my palace, which is before thee, and where thou wilt find my wife, or else to remain here to see the hounds chasing the roused deer from the wood to the plain. And thou shalt see the best greyhounds thou didst ever behold, and the boldest in the chase, kill them by the water beside us; and when it is time to go to meat, my page will come with my horse to meet me, and thou shalt rest in my palace tonight." "Heaven reward thee; but I cannot tarry, for onward must I go." "The other road leads to the town, which is near here, and wherein food and liquor may be bought; and the road which is narrower than the others goes towards the cave of the Addanc." "With thy permission, young man, I will go that way."

And Peredur went towards the cave. And he took the stone in his left hand, and his lance in his right. And as he went in he perceived the Addanc, and he pierced him through with his lance, and cut off his head. And as he came from the cave, behold the three companions were at the entrance; and they saluted Peredur, and told him that there was a prediction that he should slay that monster. And Peredur gave the head to the young men, and they offered him in marriage whichever of the three sisters he might choose, and half their kingdom with her. "I came not hither to woo," said Peredur, "but if peradventure I took a wife, I should prefer your sister to all others." And Peredur rode forward, and he heard a noise behind him. And he looked back, and saw a man upon a red horse, with red armour upon him; and the man rode up by his side, and saluted him, and wished him the favour of Heaven and of man. And Peredur greeted the youth kindly. "Lord, I come to make a request unto thee." "What wouldest thou?" "That thou shouldest take me as thine attendant." "Whom then should I take as my attendant, if I did so?" "I will not conceal from thee what kindred I am of. Etlym Gleddyv Coch am I called, an Earl from the East Country." "I marvel that thou shouldest offer to become attendant to a man whose possessions are no greater than thine own; for I have but an earldom like thyself. But since thou desirest to be my attendant, I will take thee joyfully."

And they went forward to the Court of the Countess, and all they of the Court were glad at their coming; and they were told it was not through disrespect they were placed below the household, but that such was the usage of the Court. For, whoever should overthrow the three hundred men of her household, would sit next the Countess, and she would love him above all men. And Peredur having overthrown the three hundred men of her household, sat down beside her, and the Countess said, "I thank Heaven that I have a youth so fair and so valiant as thou, since I have not obtained the man whom best I love." "Who is he whom best thou lovest?" "By my faith, Etlym Gleddyv Coch is the man whom I love best, and I have never seen him." "Of a truth, Etlym is my companion; and behold here he is, and for his sake did I come to joust with thy household. And he could have done so better than I, had it pleased him. And I do give thee unto him." "Heaven reward thee, fair youth, and I will take the man whom I love above all others." And the Countess became Etlym's bride from that moment.

And the next day Peredur set forth towards the Mound of Mourning. "By thy hand, lord, but I will go with thee," said Etlym. Then they went forwards till they came in sight of the mound and the tents. "Go unto yonder men," said Peredur to Etlym, "and desire them to come and do me homage." So Etlym went unto them, and said unto them thus, – "Come and do homage to my lord." "Who is thy lord?" said they. "Peredur with the long lance is my lord," said Etlym. "Were it permitted to slay a messenger, thou shouldest not go back to thy lord alive, for making unto Kings, and Earls, and Barons so arrogant a demand as to go and do him homage." Peredur desired him to go back to them, and to give them their choice, either to do him homage, or to do battle with him. And they chose rather to do battle. And that day Peredur overthrew the owners of a hundred tents; and the next day he overthrew the owners of a hundred more; and the third day the remaining hundred took counsel to do homage to Peredur. And Peredur inquired of them, wherefore they were there. And they told him they were guarding the serpent until he should die. "For then should we fight for the stone among ourselves, and whoever should be conqueror among us would have the stone." "Await here," said Peredur, "and I will go to encounter the serpent." "Not so, lord," said they; "we will go altogether to encounter the serpent." "Verily," said Peredur, "that will I not permit; for if the serpent be slain, I shall derive no more fame therefrom than one of you." Then he went to the place where the serpent was, and slew it, and came back to them, and said, "Reckon up what you have spent since you have been here, and I will repay you to the full." And he paid to each what he said was his claim. And he required of them only that they should acknowledge themselves his vassals. And he said to Etlym, "Go back unto her whom thou lovest best, and I will go forwards, and I will reward thee for having been my attendant." And he gave Etlym the stone. "Heaven repay thee and prosper thee," said Etlym.

And Peredur rode thence, and he came to the fairest valley he had ever seen, through which ran a river; and there he beheld many tents of various colours. And he marvelled still more at the number of water-mills and of wind-mills that he saw. And there rode up with him a tall auburn-haired man, in workman's garb, and Peredur inquired of him who he was. "I am the chief miller," said he, "of all the mills yonder." "Wilt thou give me lodging?" said Peredur. "I will, gladly," he answered. And Peredur came to the miller's house, and the miller had a fair and pleasant dwelling. And Peredur asked money as a loan from the miller, that he might buy meat and liquor for himself and for the household, and he promised that he would pay him again ere he went thence. And he inquired of the miller, wherefore such a multitude was there assembled. Said the miller to Peredur, "One thing is certain: either thou art a man from afar, or thou art beside thyself. The Empress of Cristinobyl the Great is here; and she will have no one but the man who is most valiant; for riches does she not require. And it was impossible to bring food for so many thousands as are here, therefore were all these mills constructed." And that night they took their rest.

And the next day Peredur arose, and he equipped himself and his horse for the tournament. And among the other tents he beheld one, which was the fairest he had ever seen. And he saw a beauteous maiden leaning her head out of a window of the tent, and he had never seen a maiden more lovely than she. And upon her was a garment of satin. And he gazed fixedly on the maiden, and began to love her greatly. And he remained there, gazing upon the maiden from morning until midday, and from midday until evening; and then the tournament was ended and he went to his lodging and drew off his armour. Then he asked money of the miller as a loan, and the miller's wife was wroth with Peredur; nevertheless, the miller lent him the money. And the next day he did in like manner as he had done the day before. And at night he came to his lodging, and took money as a loan from the miller. And the third day, as he was in the same place, gazing upon the maiden, he felt a hard blow between the neck and the shoulder, from the edge of an axe. And when he looked behind him, he saw that it was the miller; and the miller said to him, "Do one of two things: either turn thy head from hence, or go to the tournament." And Peredur smiled on the miller, and went to the tournament; and all that encountered him that day he overthrew. And as many as he vanquished he sent as a gift to the Empress, and their horses and arms he sent as a gift to the wife of the miller, in payment of the borrowed money. Peredur attended the tournament until all were overthrown, and he sent all the men to the prison of the Empress, and the horses and arms to the wife of the miller, in payment of the borrowed money. And the Empress sent to the Knight of the Mill, to ask him to come and visit her. And Peredur went not for the first nor for the second message. And the third time she sent a hundred knights to bring him against his will, and they went to him and told him their mission from the Empress. And Peredur fought well with them, and caused them to be bound like stags, and thrown into the mill-dyke. And the Empress sought advice of a wise man who was in her counsel; and he said to her, "With thy permission, I will go to him myself." So he came to Peredur, and saluted him, and besought him, for the sake of the lady of his love, to come and visit the Empress. And they went, together with the miller. And Peredur went and sat down in the outer chamber of the tent, and she came and placed herself by his side. And there was but little discourse between them. And Peredur took his leave, and went to his lodging.

And the next day he came to visit her, and when he came into the tent there was no one chamber less decorated than the others. And they knew not where he would sit. And Peredur went and sat beside the Empress, and discoursed with her courteously. And while they were thus, they beheld a black man enter with a goblet full of wine in his hand. And he dropped upon his knee before the Empress, and besought her to give it to no one who would not fight with him for it. And she looked upon Peredur. "Lady," said he, "bestow on me the goblet." And Peredur drank the wine, and gave the goblet to the miller's wife. And while they were thus, behold there entered a black man of larger stature than the other, with a wild beast's claw in his hand, wrought into the form of a goblet and filled with wine. And he presented it to the Empress, and besought her to give it to no one but the man who would fight with him. "Lady," said Peredur, "bestow it on me." And she gave it to him. And Peredur drank the wine, and sent the goblet to the wife of the miller. And while they were thus, behold a rough-looking, crisp-haired man, taller than either of the others, came in with a bowl in his hand full of wine; and he bent upon his knee, and gave it into the hands of the Empress, and he besought her to give it to none but him who would fight with him for it; and she gave it to Peredur, and he sent it to the miller's wife. And that night Peredur returned to his lodging; and the next day he accoutred himself and his horse, and went to the meadow and slew the three men. Then Peredur proceeded to the tent, and the Empress said to him, "Goodly Peredur, remember the faith thou didst pledge me when I gave thee the stone, and thou didst kill the Addanc." "Lady," answered he, "thou sayest truth, I do remember it." And Peredur was entertained by the Empress fourteen years, as the story relates.

The Story Of Lludd And Llevelys

BELI THE GREAT, the son of Manogan, had three sons, Lludd, and Caswallawn, and Nynyaw; and according to the story he had a fourth son called Llevelys. And after the death of Beli, the kingdom of the Island of Britain fell into the hands of Llud his eldest son; and Lludd ruled prosperously, and rebuilt the walls of London, and encompassed it about with numberless towers. And after that he bade the citizens build houses therein, such as no houses in the kingdoms could equal. And moreover he was a mighty warrior, and generous and liberal in giving meat and drink to all that sought them. And though he had many castles and cities this one loved he more than any. And he dwelt therein most part of the year, and therefore was it called Caer Lludd, and at last Caer London. And after the stranger-race came there, it was called London, or Lwndrys.

Lludd loved Llevelys best of all his brothers, because he was a wise and discreet man. Having heard that the king of France had died, leaving no heir except a daughter, and that he had left all his possessions in her hands, he came to Lludd his brother, to beseech his counsel and aid. And that not so much for his own welfare, as to seek to add to the glory and honour and dignity of his kindred, if he might go to France to woo the maiden for his wife. And forthwith his brother conferred with him, and this counsel was pleasing unto him.

So he prepared ships and filled them with armed knights, and set forth towards France. And as soon as they had landed, they sent messengers to show the nobles of France the cause of the embassy. And by the joint counsel of the nobles of France and of the princes, the maiden was given to Llevelys, and the crown of the kingdom with her. And thenceforth he ruled the land discreetly, and wisely, and happily, as long as his life lasted.

After a space of time had passed, three plagues fell on the Island of Britain, such as none in the islands had ever seen the like of. The first was a certain race that came, and was called the Coranians; and so great was their knowledge, that there was no discourse upon the face of the Island, however low it might be spoken, but what, if the wind met it, it was known to them. And through this they could not be injured.

The second plague was a shriek which came on every May-eve, over every hearth in the Island of Britain. And this went through people's hearts, and so scared them, that the men lost their hue and their strength, and the women their children, and the young men and the maidens lost their senses, and all the animals and trees and the earth and the waters, were left barren.

The third plague was, that however much of provisions and food might be prepared in the king's courts, were there even so much as a year's provision of meat and drink, none of it could ever be found, except what was consumed in the first night. And two of these plagues, no one ever knew their cause, therefore was there better hope of being freed from the first than from the second and third.

And thereupon King Lludd felt great sorrow and care, because that he knew not how he might be freed from these plagues. And he called to him all the nobles of his kingdom, and asked counsel of them what they should do against these afflictions. And by the common counsel of the nobles, Lludd the son of Beli went to Llevelys his brother, king of France, for he was a man great of counsel and wisdom, to seek his advice.

And they made ready a fleet, and that in secret and in silence, lest that race should know the cause of their errand, or any besides the king and his counsellors. And when they were made ready, they went into their ships, Lludd and those whom he chose with him. And they began to cleave the seas towards France.

And when these tidings came to Llevelys, seeing that he knew not the cause of his brother's ships, he came on the other side to meet him, and with him was a fleet vast of size. And when Lludd saw this, he left all the ships out upon the sea except one only; and in that one he came to meet his brother, and he likewise with a single ship came to meet him. And when they were come together, each put his arms about the other's neck, and they welcomed each other with brotherly love.

After that Lludd had shown his brother the cause of his errand, Llevelys said that he himself knew the cause of the coming to those lands. And they took counsel together to discourse on the matter otherwise than thus, in order that the wind might not catch their words, nor the Coranians know what they might say. Then Llevelys caused a long horn to be made of brass, and through this horn they discoursed. But whatsoever words they spoke through this horn, one to the other, neither of them could hear any other but harsh and hostile words. And when Llevelys saw this, and that there was a demon thwarting them and disturbing through this horn, he caused wine to be put therein to wash it. And through the virtue of the wine the demon was driven out of the horn. And when their discourse was unobstructed, Llevelys told his brother that he would give him some insects whereof he should keep some to breed, lest by chance the like affliction might come a second time. And other of these insects he should take and bruise in water. And he assured him that it would have power to destroy the race of the Coranians. That is to say, that when he came home to his kingdom he should call together all the people both of his own race and of the race of the Coranians for a conference, as though with the intent of making peace between them; and that when they were all together, he should take this charmed water, and cast it over all alike. And he assured him that the water would poison the race of the Coranians, but that it would not slay or harm those of his own race.

"And the second plague," said he, "that is in thy dominion, behold it is a dragon. And another dragon of a foreign race is fighting with it, and striving to overcome it. And therefore does your dragon make a fearful outcry. And on this wise mayest thou come to know this. After thou hast returned home, cause the Island to be measured in its length and breadth, and in the place where thou dost find the exact central point, there cause a pit to be dug, and cause a cauldron full of the best mead that can be made to be put in the pit, with a covering of satin over the face of the cauldron. And then, in thine own person do thou remain there watching, and thou wilt see the dragon fighting in the form of terrific animals. And at length they will take the form of dragons in the air. And last of all, after wearying themselves with fierce and furious fighting, they will fall in the form of two pigs upon the covering, and they will sink in, and the covering with them, and they will draw it down to the very bottom of the cauldron. And they will drink up the whole of the mead; and after that they will sleep. Thereupon do thou immediately fold the covering around them, and bury them in a kistvaen, in the strongest place thou hast in thy dominions, and hide them in the earth. And as long as they shall bide in that strong place no plague shall come to the Island of Britain from elsewhere.

"The cause of the third plague," said he, "is a mighty man of magic, who take thy meat and thy drink and thy store. And he through illusions and charms causes every one to sleep. Therefore it is needful for thee in thy own person to watch thy food and thy provisions. And lest he should overcome thee with sleep, be there a cauldron of cold water by thy side, and when thou art oppressed with sleep, plunge into the cauldron."

Then Lludd returned back unto his land. And immediately he summoned to him the whole of his own race and of the Coranians. And as Llevelys had taught him, he bruised the insects in water, the which he cast over them all together, and forthwith it destroyed the whole tribe of the Coranians, without hurt to any of the Britons.

And some time after this, Lludd caused the Island to be measured in its length and in its breadth. And in Oxford he found the central point, and in that place he caused the earth to be dug, and in that pit a cauldron to be set, full of the best mead that could be made, and a covering of satin over the face of it. And he himself watched that night. And while he was there, he beheld the dragons fighting. And when they were weary they fell, and came down upon the top of the satin, and drew it with them to the bottom of the cauldron. And when they had drunk the mead they slept. And in their sleep, Lludd folded the covering around them, and in the securest place he had in Snowdon, he hid them in a kistvaen. Now after that this spot was called Dinas Emreis, but before that, Dinas Ffaraon. And thus the fierce outcry ceased in his dominions.

And when this was ended, King Lludd caused an exceeding great banquet to be prepared. And when it was ready, he placed a vessel of cold water by his side, and he in his own proper person watched it. And as he abode thus clad with arms, about the third watch of the night, lo, he heard many surpassing fascinations and various songs. And drowsiness urged him to sleep. Upon this, lest he should be hindered from his purpose and be overcome by sleep, he went often into the water. And at last, behold, a man of vast size, clad in strong, heavy armour, came in, bearing a hamper. And, as he was wont, he put all the food and provisions of meat and drink into the hamper, and proceeded to go with it forth. And nothing was ever more wonderful to Lludd, than that the hamper should hold so much.

And thereupon King Lludd went after him and spoke unto him thus. "Stop, stop," said he, "though thou hast done many insults and much spoil erewhile, thou shalt not do so any more, unless thy skill in arms and thy prowess be greater than mine."

Then he instantly put down the hamper on the floor, and awaited him. And a fierce encounter was between them, so that the glittering fire flew out from their arms. And at the last Lludd grappled with him, and fate bestowed the victory on Lludd. And he threw the plague to the earth. And after he had overcome him by strength and might, he besought his mercy. "How can I grant thee mercy," said the king, "after all the many injuries and wrongs that thou hast done me?" "All the losses that ever I have caused thee," said he, "I will make thee atonement for, equal to what I have taken. And I will never do the like from this time forth. But thy faithful vassal will I be." And the king accepted this from him.

And thus Lludd freed the Island of Britain from the three plagues. And from thenceforth until the end of his life, in prosperous peace did Lludd the son of Beli rule the Island of Britain. And this Tale is called the Story of Lludd and Llevelys. And thus it ends.

Bhima and the Fair Demon

THE PANDAVAS, having escaped through the subterranean passage, travelled southwards and entered the forest, which was full of reptiles and wild animals and with ferocious man-eating Asuras and gigantic Rakshasas. Weary and sore, they were overcome with tiredness and fear. So the mighty Bhima lifted up all the others and hastened on through the darkness: he took his mother on his back, and Madri's sons on his shoulders, and Yudhishthira and Arjuna under his arms.

He went swifter than the wind, breaking down trees by his breast and furrowing the ground that he stamped on. After some time the Pandavas found a place to rest in safety; and they all lay down to sleep under a great and beautiful Banyan tree, except mighty Bhima who kept watch over them.

Now in the forest there lived a ferocious Rakshasa named Hidimva. He was terrible to behold; his eyes were red, and he was red-haired and red-bearded; his mouth was large, with long, sharp-pointed teeth, which gleamed in darkness; his ears were shaped like arrows; his neck was as broad as a tree, his belly was large, and his legs were long.

The monster was exceedingly hungry on that fateful night. Scenting human flesh in the forest, he yawned and scratched his grizzly beard, and spoke to his sister, saying: "I smell excellent food, and my mouth waters; tonight I will devour warm flesh and drink hot, frothy blood. Hurry now and bring the sleeping men to me; we will eat them together, and afterwards dance merrily in the wood."

So the Rakshasa woman went towards the place where the Pandavas slept. When she saw Bhima, the long-armed one, clad in royal garments and wearing his jewels, she immediately fell in love with him, and said to herself: "This man with the shoulders of a lion and eyes like lotus blooms is worthy to be my husband. I will not slay him for my evil brother."

She transformed herself into a beautiful woman; her face became as fair as the full moon; on her head was a garland of flowers, her hair hung in ringlets; and she wore rich ornaments of gold with many gems.

Timidly she approached Bhima and said: "Oh bull among men, who are you and where did you come from? Who are these fair ones sleeping there? Know that this forest is the abode of the wicked chief of the Rakshasas. He is my brother, and he has sent me here to kill you all for food, but I want to save you. Be my husband. I will take you to a secret place among the mountains, for I can speed through the air at will."

Bhima said: "I cannot leave my mother and my brothers to become food for a Rakshasa."

The woman said: "Let me help you. Awaken your mother and your brothers and I will rescue you all from my fierce brother."

To which Bhima replied: "I will not wake them, because I do not fear a Rakshasa. You can go as it pleases you, and I care not if you send your brother to me."

Meantime the Rakshasa chief had grown impatient. He came down from his tree and went after his sister, with gaping mouth and head thrown back.

The Rakshasa woman said to Bhima: "He comes here in anger. Wake up your family, and I will carry you all through the air to escape him."

"Look at my arms," said Bhima. "They are as strong as the trunks of elephants; my legs are like iron maces, and my chest is powerful and broad. I will slay this man-eater, your brother."

The Rakshasa chief heard Bhima's boast, and he fumed with rage when he saw his sister in her beautiful human form. He said to her: "I will slay you and those whom you would help against me." Then he rushed at her, but Bhima cried: "You will not kill a woman while I am near. I challenge you to single combat now. Tonight your sister will see you slain by me as an elephant is slain by a lion."

The Rakshasa replied: "Boast not until you are the victor. I will kill you first of all, then your friends, and last of all my treacherous sister."

Having said this, he rushed towards Bhima, who nimbly seized the monster's outstretched arms and, wrestling violently, cast him on the ground. Then as a lion drags off his prey, Bhima dragged the struggling Rakshasa into the depths of the forest, so that his yells should not wake his sleeping family. There they fought together like furious bull elephants, tearing down branches and overthrowing trees.

Eventually the clamour woke the Pandavas, and they gazed with wonder at the beautiful woman who kept watch in Bhima's place.

Pritha said to her: "Oh celestial being, who are you? If you are the goddess of woods or an Apsara, tell me why you linger here?"

The fair demon said: "I am the sister of the chief of the Rakshasas, and I was sent here to slay you all; but when I saw your mighty son the love god wounded me, and I chose him for my husband. Then my brother followed angrily, and your son is fighting with him. They are filling the forest with their shouting."

All the brothers rushed to Bhima's aid, and they saw the two wrestlers struggling in a cloud of dust, and they appeared like two high cliffs shrouded in mist.

Arjuna cried out: "Bhima, I am here to help you. Let me slay the monster."

Bhima answered: "Fear not, but look on. The Rakshasa will not escape from my hands."

"Do not keep him alive too long," Said Arjuna. "We must act quickly. The dawn is near, and Rakshasas become stronger at daybreak; they exercise their powers of deception during the two twilights. Do not play with him, therefore, but kill him quickly."

At these words Bhima became as strong as Vayu, his father, when he is angered. Raising the Rakshasa aloft, he whirled him round and round, crying: "In vain have you gorged on unholy food. I will rid the forest of you. No longer will you devour human beings."

Then, dashing the monster to the ground, Bhima seized him by the hair and by the waist, laid him over a knee, and broke his back. The Rakshasa was slain.

Day was breaking, and Pritha and her sons immediately turned away to leave the forest. The Rakshasa woman followed them, and Bhima cried to her: "Be gone! Or I will send you after your brother."

Yudhishthira then spoke to Bhima, saying: "It is unseemly to slay a woman. Besides, she is the sister of that Rakshasa, and even although she became angry, what harm can she do us?"

Kneeling at Pritha's feet, the demon wailed: "Oh illustrious and blessed lady, you know the sufferings women endure when the love god wounds them. Have pity on me now, and command your son to take me for his bride. If he continues to scorn me, I will kill myself. Let me be your slave, and I will carry you all wherever you desire and protect you from perils."

Pritha heard her with compassion, and persuaded Bhima to take her for his bride. So the two were married by Yudhishthira; then the Rakshasa took Bhima on her back and sped through the air to a lonely place among the mountains which is sacred to the gods. They lived together beside silvery streams and lakes sparkling with lotus blooms; they wandered through woods of blossoming trees where birds sang sweetly, and by celestial sea-beaches covered with pearls and nuggets of gold. The demon bride had assumed celestial beauty, and often played sweet music. She made Bhima happy.

In time the woman became the mother of a mighty son; his eyes were fiercely bright, his ears were like arrows, and his mouth was large; he had copper-brown lips and long, sharp teeth. He grew to be a youth an hour after he was born. His mother named him Ghatotkacha.

Bhima then returned to his mother and his brothers with his demon bride and her son. They lived together for a time in the forest; then the Rakshasa bade all the Pandavas farewell and left with Ghatotkacha, who promised to come to the Pandavas' aid whenever they called on him.

The King of the Asuras

ONE DAY THEREAFTER Vyasa appeared before the Pandavas and told them to go to the city of Ekachakra and to live there for a time in the house of a Brahman. Then he vanished from sight, promising to come again.

So the Pandavas went to Ekachakra and lived with a Brahman who had a wife and a daughter and an infant son. Disguised as holy men, the brothers begged for food. Every evening they brought home what they had obtained, and Pritha divided it into two portions; one half she gave to wolf-bellied Bhima, and the rest she kept for his brothers and herself.

Now the city of Ekachakra was protected against every enemy by a forest-dwelling Rakshasa named Vaka, who was king of the Asuras. Each day the people had to supply him with food, which consisted of a cartload of rice, two bullocks, and the man who carried the meal to him.

One morning a great wailing broke out in the Brahman's house because the holy man had been chosen to supply the demon's feast. He was too poor to purchase a slave, so he said he would deliver himself to Vaka. "Although I reach Heaven," he cried, "I will have no joy, because my family will perish when I am gone." His wife and his daughter pleaded to take his place, and the three wept together. Then the little boy plucked a long spear of grass, and with glowing eyes he spoke sweetly and said: "Do not weep, Father; do not weep, Mother; do not weep, Sister. With this spear I will slay the demon who devours human beings."

Pritha was deeply moved by the grief of the Brahman family, and she said: "Sorrow not. I will send my son Bhima to slay the Asura king."

The Brahman answered her, saying: "That cannot be. Your sons are Brahmans and are under my protection. If I go, I will be obeying the king; if I send your son, I will be guilty of his death. The gods hate the man who causes a guest to be slain, or permits a Brahman to perish."

To this Pritha said: "Bhima is strong and mighty. A demon cannot do him any harm. He will kill this bloodthirsty Rakshasa and return again safely. But, Brahman, you must not reveal to anyone who has performed this mighty deed, so that the people do not trouble my son and try to obtain the secret of his power."

So Bhima collected the rice and drove the bullocks towards the forest. When he got near to the appointed place, he began to eat the food himself, and called the Rakshasa's name over and over again. Vaka heard and came through the trees towards him. Red were his eyes, and his hair and his beard were red also; his ears were pointed like arrows; he had a mouth like a cave, and his forehead was puckered in three lines. He was terrible to look at; his body was huge, indeed.

The Rakshasa saw Bhima eating his meal, and approached angrily, biting his lower lip. "Fool," he cried, "would you devour my food before my very eyes?"

Bhima smiled, and continued eating with his face averted. The demon struck him, but the hero only glanced round as if someone had touched his shoulder, and he went on eating as before.

Raging furiously, the Rakshasa tore up a tree, and Bhima rose leisurely and waited until it was flung at him. When that was done, he caught the trunk and hurled it back. Many trees were uprooted and flung by one at the other. Then Vaka attacked, but the Pandava overthrew him and dragged him round and round until the demon gasped with fatigue. The earth shook; trees were splintered into pieces. Then Bhima began to strike the monster with his iron fists, and he broke Vaka's back across his knee. Terrible were the loud screams of the Rakshasa while Bhima was bending him double. He died howling.

All the other Asuras were terror-stricken, and, bellowing horribly, they rushed towards Bhima and bowed before him. Bhima made them take vows never to eat human flesh again or to oppress the people of the city. They promised to do so, and he allowed them to depart.

Afterwards Pritha's son dragged the monster's body to the main gate of Ekachakra. He entered the city secretly and hurried to the Brahman's house, and he told Yudhishthira all that had taken place.

When the people of the city discovered that the Asura king was dead, they rejoiced, and hurried towards the house of the Brahman. But the holy man was evasive, saying that his deliverer was a certain high-souled Brahman who had offered to supply food to the demon. The people established a festival in honour of Brahmans.

Arjuna's Celestial Gifts

NOW THE PANDAVAS NEEDED celestial weapons, because these were owned by Drona, Bhishma and Karna. In time, therefore, the holy sage Vyasa appeared before Arjuna and told him to go to Mount Kailasa, the high seat of the gracious god Shiva, and to perform penances there with deep devotion in order to obtain gifts of arms. So Arjuna went on his way, and when he reached the mountain of Shiva he went through great austerities: he raised his arms in the air and, leaning on nothing, stood on his tiptoes; for food he ate withered leaves at first, then he fed on air alone.

The Rishis pleaded with Shiva, fearing disaster from the penances of Arjuna. Then the god assumed the form of a hunter and went towards Indra's warrior son, whom he challenged to single combat. First they fought with weapons; then they wrestled one another fiercely. In the end Arjuna fell to the ground. When that brave Pandava regained consciousness he made a clay image of Shiva, threw himself down in worship, and made an offering of flowers. Soon afterwards he saw his opponent wearing the garland he had given, and he knew that he had wrestled with Shiva himself. Arjuna fell down before him, and the god gave him a celestial weapon named Pasupata. Then a great storm broke out, and the earth shook, and the spirit of the weapon stood beside Arjuna, ready to obey his will.

Next appeared Indra, king of gods, Varuna, god of waters, Yama, king of the dead, and Kuvera, lord of treasures, and they stood on the mountain summit in all their glory; to Arjuna they gave gifts of other celestial weapons.

Afterwards Indra transported his son to his own bright city, the celestial Swarga, where the flowers always bloom and sweet music is forever wafted on fragrant winds. There he saw sea-born Apsaras, the heavenly brides of gods and heroes, and music-loving Gandharvas, who sang songs and danced merrily in their joy. Urvasi, a beautiful Apsara with bright eyes and silken hair, looked with love at Arjuna; but she sought in vain to subdue him, at which she scornfully said: "Kama, god of love, has wounded me with his arrows, yet you scorn me. For this, Arjuna, you will live for a season as a dancer and musician, ignored by women." Arjuna was troubled by this, but Indra told him that this curse would work in his favour. So Arjuna remained in Indra's fair city for five years. He achieved great skill in music, in dance and song. He was also trained to wield the celestial weapons which the gods had given to him.

Now the demons and giants who are named the Daityas and Danavas were the ancient enemies of Indra. They hailed from the lowest division of the underworld beneath the ocean floor, in a place called Patala. And a day came when Arjuna waged war with them. He rode away in Indra's great car, which sailed through the air like a bird, driven by Matali. When he reached the shore of the sea, the waves rose against him like great mountains, and the waters were divided; he saw demon fish and giant tortoises, and vessels laden down with rubies. But he did not pause, as he was without fear. Arjuna was eager for battle, and he blew a mighty blast on his war shell: the Daityas and Danavas heard him and quaked with terror. Then the demons beat their drums and blew their trumpets, and amid the dreadful racket the wallowing sea monsters rose up and leapt over the waves against Indra's great son. But Arjuna chanted mantras; he shot clouds of bright arrows; he fought with his bright celestial weapons, and the furies were thwarted and beaten back. They then sent fire against him and water, and they flung huge rocks; but he fought on until in the end he triumphed, killing all that stood against him.

Afterwards the valiant hero quickly rode towards the city of demons and giants which is named Hiranyapura. The women came out to lure him, calling aloud. He heard them but did not pause. All these evil giant women fled in confusion, terrified by the noise of Indra's celestial car and the driving of Matali, and their earrings and necklaces fell from their bodies like boulders tumbling and thundering down mountain slopes.

When Arjuna entered the city of Hiranyapura he gazed with wonder at the mighty chariots with ten thousand horses, which were stately and proud. And he wrecked the dwellings of the Daityas and Danavas.

Indra praised his warrior son for his valour in overcoming the demons and giants of the ocean, and he gave him a chain of gold, a bright crown, and the war shell which gave a mighty, thunderous blast.

The Goblin of Oeyama

IN THE REIGN OF THE EMPEROR ICHIJO many dreadful stories were current in Kyoto in regard to a demon that lived on Mount Oye. This demon could assume many forms. Sometimes appearing as a human being, he would steal into Kyoto, and leave many a home destitute of well-loved sons and daughters. These young men and women he took back to his mountain stronghold, and, sad to narrate, after making sport of them, he and his goblin companions made a great feast and devoured these poor young people. Even the sacred Court was not exempt from these awful happenings, and one day Kimitaka lost his beautiful daughter. She had been snatched away by the Goblin King, Shutendoji.

When this sad news reached the ears of the Emperor he called his council together and consulted how they might slay this dreadful creature. His ministers informed his Majesty that Raiko was a doughty knight, and advised that he should be sent with certain companions on this perilous but worthy adventure.

Raiko accordingly chose five companions and told them what had been ordained, and how they were to set out upon an adventurous journey, and finally to slay the King of the Goblins. He explained that subtlety of action was most essential if they wished for success in their enterprise, and that it would be well to go disguised as mountain priests, and to carry their armour and weapons on their backs, carefully concealed in unsuspicious-looking knapsacks. Before starting upon their journey two of the knights went to pray at the temple of Hachiman, the God of War, two at the shrine of Kwannon, the Goddess of Mercy, and two at the temple of Gongen.

When these knights had prayed for a blessing upon their undertaking they set out upon their journey, and in due time reached the province of Tamba, and saw immediately in front of them Mount Oye. The Goblin had certainly chosen the most formidable of mountains. Mighty rocks and great dark forests obstructed their path in every direction, while almost bottomless chasms appeared when least expected.

Just when these brave knights were beginning to feel just a little disheartened, three old men suddenly appeared before them. At first these newcomers were regarded with suspicion, but later on with the utmost friendliness and thankfulness. These old men were none other than the deities to whom the knights had prayed before setting out upon their journey. The old men presented Raiko with a jar of magical *sake* called Shimben-Kidoku-Shu ('a cordial for men, but poison for goblins'), advising him that he should by strategy get Shutendoji to drink it, whereupon he would immediately become paralysed and prove an easy victim for the final despatch. No sooner had these old men given the magical *sake* and proffered their valuable advice than a miraculous light shone round them, and they vanished into the clouds.

Once again Raiko and his knights, much cheered by what had happened, continued to ascend the mountain. Coming to a stream, they noticed a beautiful woman washing a blood-stained garment in the running water. She was weeping bitterly, and wiped away her tears with the long sleeve of her *kimono*. Upon Raiko asking who she was, she informed him that she was a princess, and one of the miserable captives of the Goblin King. When she was told that it was none other than the great Raiko who stood before her, and that he and his knights had come to kill the vile creature of that mountain, she was overcome with joy, and finally led the little band to a great palace of black iron, satisfying the sentinels by telling them that her followers were poor mountain priests who sought temporary shelter.

After passing through long corridors Raiko and his knights found themselves in a mighty hall. At one end sat the awful Goblin King. He was of gigantic stature, with bright red skin and a mass of white hair. When Raiko meekly informed him who they were, the Goblin King, concealing his mirth, bade them be seated and join the feast that was about to be set before them. Thereupon he clapped his red hands together, and immediately many beautiful damsels came running in with an abundance of food and drink, and as Raiko watched these women he knew that they had once lived in happy homes in Kyoto.

When the feast was in full progress Raiko took out the jar of magic *sake*, and politely begged the Goblin King to try it. The monster, without demur or suspicion, drank some of the *sake*, and found it so good that he asked for a second cup. All the goblins partook of the magic wine, and while they were drinking Raiko and his companions danced.

The power of this magical drink soon began to work. The Goblin King became drowsy, till finally he and his fellow goblins fell fast asleep. Then Raiko sprang to his feet, and he and his knights rapidly donned their armour and prepared for war. Once more the three deities appeared before them, and said to Raiko: "We have tied the hands and feet of the Demon fast, so you have nothing to fear. While your knights cut off his limbs do you cut off his head: then kill the rest of the *oni* (evil spirits) and your work will be done." Then these divine beings suddenly disappeared.

Raiko Slays the Goblin

Raiko and his knights, with their swords drawn, cautiously approached the sleeping Goblin King. With a mighty sweep Raiko's weapon came crashing down on the Goblin's neck. No sooner was the head severed than it shot up into the air, and smoke and fire poured out from the nostrils, scorching the valiant Raiko. Once more he struck out with his sword, and this time the horrible head fell to the floor, and never moved again. It was not long before these brave knights despatched the Demon's followers also.

There was a joyful exit from the great iron palace. Raiko's five knights carried the monster head of the Goblin King, and this grim spectacle was followed by a company of happy maidens released at last from their horrible confinement, and eager to walk once again in the streets of Kyoto.

The Ogre of Rashomon, or Watanabe Defeats the Ibaraki-doji

LONG, LONG AGO IN KYOTO, the people of the city were terrified by accounts of a dreadful ogre, who, it was said, haunted the Gate of Rashomon at twilight and seized whoever passed by. The missing victims were never seen again, so it was whispered that the ogre was a horrible cannibal, who not only killed the unhappy victims but ate them also. Now everybody in the town and neighbourhood was in great fear, and no one durst venture out after sunset near the Gate of Rashomon.

Now at this time there lived in Kyoto a general named Raiko, who had made himself famous for his brave deeds. Some time before this he made the country ring with his name, for he had attacked Oeyama, where a band of ogres lived with their chief, who instead of wine drank the blood of human beings. He had routed them all and cut off the head of the chief monster.

This brave warrior was always followed by a band of faithful knights. In this band there were five knights of great valour. One evening as the five knights sat at a feast quaffing *sake* in their rice bowls and eating all kinds of fish, raw, and stewed, and broiled, and toasting each other's healths and exploits, the first knight, Hojo, said to the others:

"Have you all heard the rumour that every evening after sunset there comes an ogre to the Gate of Rashomon, and that he seizes all who pass by?"

The second knight, Watanabe, answered him, saying:

"Do not talk such nonsense! All the ogres were killed by our chief Raiko at Oeyama! It cannot be true, because even if any ogres did escape from that great killing they would not dare to show themselves in this city, for they know that our brave master would at once attack them if he knew that any of them were still alive!"

"Then do you disbelieve what I say, and think that I am telling you a falsehood?"

"No, I do not think that you are telling a lie," said Watanabe; "but you have heard some old woman's story which is not worth believing."

"Then the best plan is to prove what I say, by going there yourself and finding out yourself whether it is true or not," said Hojo.

Watanabe, the second knight, could not bear the thought that his companion should believe he was afraid, so he answered quickly:

"Of course, I will go at once and find out for myself!"

So Watanabe at once got ready to go – he buckled on his long sword and put on a coat of armor, and tied on his large helmet. When he was ready to start he said to the others:

"Give me something so that I can prove I have been there!"

Then one of the men got a roll of writing paper and his box of Indian ink and brushes, and the four comrades wrote their names on a piece of paper.

"I will take this," said Watanabe, "and put it on the Gate of Rashomon, so tomorrow morning will you all go and look at it? I may be able to catch an ogre or two by then!" and he mounted his horse and rode off gallantly.

It was a very dark night, and there was neither moon nor star to light Watanabe on his way. To make the darkness worse a storm came on, the rain fell heavily and the wind howled like wolves in the mountains. Any ordinary man would have trembled at the thought of going out of doors, but Watanabe was a brave warrior and dauntless, and his honour and word were at stake, so he sped on into the night, while his companions listened to the sound of his horse's hoofs dying away in the distance, then shut the sliding shutters close and gathered round the charcoal fire and wondered what would happen – and whether their comrade would encounter one of those horrible Oni.

At last Watanabe reached the Gate of Rashomon, but peer as he might through the darkness he could see no sign of an ogre.

"It is just as I thought," said Watanabe to himself; "there are certainly no ogres here; it is only an old woman's story. I will stick this paper on the gate so that the others can see I have been here when they come tomorrow, and then I will take my way home and laugh at them all."

He fastened the piece of paper, signed by all his four companions, on the gate, and then turned his horse's head towards home.

As he did so he became aware that someone was behind him, and at the same time a voice called out to him to wait. Then his helmet was seized from the back. "Who are you?" said Watanabe fearlessly. He then put out his hand and groped around to find out who or what it was that held him by the helmet. As he did so he touched something that felt like an arm – it was covered with hair and as big round as the trunk of a tree!

Watanabe knew at once that this was the arm of an ogre, so he drew his sword and cut at it fiercely.

There was a loud yell of pain, and then the ogre dashed in front of the warrior.

Watanabe's eyes grew large with wonder, for he saw that the ogre was taller than the great gate, his eyes were flashing like mirrors in the sunlight, and his huge mouth was wide open, and as the monster breathed, flames of fire shot out of his mouth.

The ogre thought to terrify his foe, but Watanabe never flinched. He attacked the ogre with all his strength, and thus they fought face to face for a long time. At last the ogre, finding that he could neither frighten nor beat Watanabe and that he might himself be beaten, took to flight. But Watanabe, determined not to let the monster escape, put spurs to his horse and gave chase.

But though the knight rode very fast the ogre ran faster, and to his disappointment he found himself unable to overtake the monster, who was gradually lost to sight.

Watanabe returned to the gate where the fierce fight had taken place, and got down from his horse. As he did so he stumbled upon something lying on the ground.

Stooping to pick it up he found that it was one of the ogre's huge arms which he must have slashed off in the fight. His joy was great at having secured such a prize, for this was the best of all proofs of his adventure with the ogre. So he took it up carefully and carried it home as a trophy of his victory.

When he got back, he showed the arm to his comrades, who one and all called him the hero of their band and gave him a great feast. His wonderful deed was soon noised abroad in Kyoto, and people from far and near came to see the ogre's arm.

Watanabe now began to grow uneasy as to how he should keep the arm in safety, for he knew that the ogre to whom it belonged was still alive. He felt sure that one day or other, as soon as the ogre got over his scare, he would come to try to get his arm back again. Watanabe therefore had a box made of the strongest wood and banded with iron. In this he placed the arm, and then he sealed down the heavy lid, refusing to open it for anyone. He kept the box in his own room and took charge of it himself, never allowing it out of his sight.

Now one night he heard someone knocking at the porch, asking for admittance.

When the servant went to the door to see who it was, there was only an old woman, very respectable in appearance. On being asked who she was and what was her business, the old woman replied with a smile that she had been nurse to the master of the house when he was a little baby. If the lord of the house were at home she begged to be allowed to see him.

The servant left the old woman at the door and went to tell his master that his old nurse had come to see him. Watanabe thought it strange that she should come at that time of night, but at the thought of his old nurse, who had been like a foster-mother to him and whom he had not seen for a long time, a very tender feeling sprang up for her in his heart. He ordered the servant to show her in.

The old woman was ushered into the room, and after the customary bows and greetings were over, she said:

"Master, the report of your brave fight with the ogre at the Gate of Rashomon is so widely known that even your poor old nurse has heard of it. Is it really true, what everyone says, that you cut off one of the ogre's arms? If you did, your deed is highly to be praised!"

"I was very disappointed," said Watanabe, "that I was not able take the monster captive, which was what I wished to do, instead of only cutting off an arm!"

"I am very proud to think," answered the old woman, "that my master was so brave as to dare to cut off an ogre's arm. There is nothing that can be compared to your courage. Before I die it is the great wish of my life to see this arm," she added pleadingly.

"No," said Watanabe, "I am sorry, but I cannot grant your request."

"But why?" asked the old woman.

"Because," replied Watanabe, "ogres are very revengeful creatures, and if I open the box there is no telling but that the ogre may suddenly appear and carry off his arm. I have had a box made on purpose with a very strong lid, and in this box I keep the ogre's arm secure; and I never show it to anyone, whatever happens."

"Your precaution is very reasonable," said the old woman. "But I am your old nurse, so surely you will not refuse to show *me* the arm. I have only just heard of your brave act, and not being able to wait till the morning I came at once to ask you to show it to me."

Watanabe was very troubled at the old woman's pleading, but he still persisted in refusing. Then the old woman said:

"Do you suspect me of being a spy sent by the ogre?"

"No, of course I do not suspect you of being the ogre's spy, for you are my old nurse," answered Watanabe.

"Then you cannot surely refuse to show me the arm any longer." entreated the old woman; "for it is the great wish of my heart to see for once in my life the arm of an ogre!"

Watanabe could not hold out in his refusal any longer, so he gave in at last, saying:

"Then I will show you the ogre's arm, since you so earnestly wish to see it. Come, follow me!" and he led the way to his own room, the old woman following.

When they were both in the room Watanabe shut the door carefully, and then going towards a big box which stood in a corner of the room, he took off the heavy lid. He then called to the old woman to come near and look in, for he never took the arm out of the box.

"What is it like? Let me have a good look at it," said the old nurse, with a joyful face.

She came nearer and nearer, as if she were afraid, till she stood right against the box. Suddenly she plunged her hand into the box and seized the arm, crying with a fearful voice which made the room shake:

"Oh, joy! I have got my arm back again!"

And from an old woman she was suddenly transformed into the towering figure of the frightful ogre!

Watanabe sprang back and was unable to move for a moment, so great was his astonishment; but recognizing the ogre who had attacked him at the Gate of Rashomon, he determined with his usual courage to put an end to him this time. He seized his sword, drew it out of its sheath in a flash, and tried to cut the ogre down.

So quick was Watanabe that the creature had a narrow escape. But the ogre sprang up to the ceiling, and bursting through the roof, disappeared in the mist and clouds.

In this way the ogre escaped with his arm. The knight gnashed his teeth with disappointment, but that was all he could do. He waited in patience for another opportunity to dispatch the ogre. But the latter was afraid of Watanabe's great strength and daring, and never troubled Kyoto again. So once more the people of the city were able to go out without fear even at night time, and the brave deeds of Watanabe have never been forgotten!

The Legend of Tawhaki

TAWHAKI WAS THE SON of Hema and Urutonga, and he had a younger brother named Karilii. Tawhaki having taken Hinepiri-piri as a wife, he went one day with his brothers-in-law to fish, from a flat reef of rocks which ran far out into the sea; he had four brothers-in-law, two of these when tired of fishing returned towards their village, and he went with them; when they drew near the village, they attempted to murder him, and thinking they had slain him, buried him; they then went on their way to the village, and when they reached it, their young sister said to them: 'Why, where is your brother-in-law?' and they replied: 'Oh, they're all fishing.' So the young wife waited until the other two brothers came back, and when they reached the village they were questioned by their young sister, who asked: 'Where is your brother-in-law?' and the two who had last arrived, answered her: 'Why, the others all went home together long since.' So the young wife suspected that they had killed her husband, and ran off at once to search for him; and she found where he had been buried, and on examining him ascertained that he had only been insensible, and was not quite dead; then with great difficulty she got him upon her back, and carried him home to their house, and carefully washed his wounds, and staunched the bleeding.

Tawhaki, when he had a little recovered, said to her: 'Fetch some wood, and light a fire for me'; and as his wife was going to do this, he said to her, 'if you see any tall tree growing near you, fell it, and bring that with you for the fire.' His wife went, and saw a tree growing such as her husband spoke of; so she felled it, and put it upon her shoulder, and brought it along with her; and when she reached the house, she put the whole tree upon the fire without chopping it into pieces; and it was this circumstance that led her to give the name of Wahieroa (long-log-of-wood-for-the-fire) to their first son, for Tawhaki had told her to bring this log of wood home, and to call the child after it, that the duty of avenging his father's wrongs might often be recalled to his mind.

As soon as Tawhaki had recovered from his wounds, he left the place where his faithless brothers-in-law lived, and went away taking all his own warriors and their families with him, and built a fortified village upon the top of a very lofty mountain, where he could easily protect himself; and they dwelt there. Then he called aloud to the Gods, his ancestors, for revenge, and they let the floods of heaven descend, and the earth was overwhelmed by the waters and all human beings perished, and the name given to that event was 'The overwhelming of the Mataaho,' and the whole of that race perished.

When this feat was accomplished, Tawhaki and his younger brother next went to seek revenge for the death of their father. It was a different race who had carried off and slain the father of Tawhaki; the name of that race was the Ponaturi – the country they inhabited was underneath the waters, but they had a large house on the dry land to which they resorted to sleep at night; the name of that large house was 'Manawa-Tane'.

The Ponaturi had slain the father of Tawhaki and carried off his body, but his father's wife they had carried off alive and kept as a captive. Tawhaki and his younger brother went upon their way to seek out that people and to revenge themselves upon them. At length they reached a place from whence they could see the house called Manawa–Tane. At the time they arrived near the house there was no one there but their mother, who was sitting near the door; but the bones of their father were hung up inside the house under its high sloping roof. The whole tribe of the Ponaturi were at that time in their country under the waters, but at the approach of night they would return to their house, to Manawa-Tane.

Whilst Tawhaki and his younger brother Karihi were coming along still at a great distance from the house, Tawhaki began to repeat an incantation, and the bones of his father, Hema, felt the influence of this, and rattled loudly together where they hung under the roof of the house, for gladness, when they heard Tawhaki repeating his incantations as he came along, for they knew that the hour of revenge had now come. As the brothers drew nearer, their mother, Urutonga, heard the voice of Tawhaki, and she wept for gladness in front of her children, who came repeating incantations upon their way. And when they reached at length the house, they wept over their mother, over old Urutonga. When they had ended weeping, their mother said to them:

'My children, hasten to return hence, or you will both certainly perish. The people who dwell here are a very fierce and savage race.' Karihi said to her: 'How low will the sun have descended when those you speak of return home?' And she replied: 'They will return here when the sun sinks beneath the ocean.' Then Karihi asked her: 'What did they save you alive for?' And she answered: 'They saved me alive that I might watch for the rising of the dawn; they make me ever sit watching here at the door of the house, hence this people have named me "Tatau", or "the door"; and they keep on throughout the night calling out to me: "Ho, Tatau, there! is it dawn yet?" And then I call out in answer: "No, no, it is deep night – it is lasting night – it is still night; compose yourselves to sleep, sleep on."'

Karihi then said to his mother: 'Cannot we hide ourselves somewhere here?'

Their mother answered: 'You had better return; you cannot hide yourselves here, the scent of you will be perceived by them.'

'But ', said Karihi, 'we will hide ourselves away in the thick thatch of the house.'

Their mother, however, answered: ''Tis of no use, you cannot hide yourselves there.'

All this time Tawhaki sat quite silent; but Karihi said: 'We will hide ourselves here, for we know incantations which will render us invisible to all.'

On hearing this, their mother consented to their remaining, and attempting to avenge their father's death. So they climbed up to the ridge-pole of the house, upon the outside of the roof, and made holes in the thick layers of reeds which formed the thatch of the roof, and crept into them and covered themselves up; and their mother called to them, saying: 'When it draws near dawn, come down again, and stop up every chink in the house, so that no single ray of light may shine in.'

At length the day closed, and the sun sank below the horizon, and the whole of that strange tribe left the water in a body, and ascended to the dry land; and, according to their custom from time immemorial, they sent one of their number in front of them, that he might carefully examine the road, and see that there were no hidden foes lying in wait for them either on the way or in their house. As soon as this scout arrived at the threshold of the house, he perceived the scent of Tawhaki and Karihi; so he lifted up his nose and turned sniffing all round the inside of the house. As he turned about, he was on the point of discovering that strangers were hidden there, when the rest of the tribe (whom long security had made careless) came hurrying on, and crowding into the house in thousands, so that from the denseness of the crowd the scent of the strange men was quite lost. The Ponaturi then stowed themselves away in the house until it was entirely filled up with them, and by degrees they arranged themselves in convenient places, and at length all fell fast asleep.

At midnight Tawhaki and Karihi stole down from the roof of the house, and found that their mother had crept out of the door to meet them, so they sat at the doorway whispering together.

Karihi then asked his mother: 'Which is the best way for us to destroy these people who are sleeping here?' And their mother answered: 'You had better let the sun kill them, its rays will destroy them.'

Having said this, Tatau crept into the house again; presently an old man of the Ponaturi called out to her: 'Ho, Tatau, Tatau, there; is it dawn yet?' And she answered: 'No, no, it is deep night – it is lasting night; 'tis still night; sleep soundly, sleep on.'

When it was very near dawn, Tatau whispered to her children, who were still sitting just outside the door of the house: 'See that every chink in the doorway and window is stopped, so that not a ray of light can penetrate here.'

Presently another old man of the Ponaturi called out again: 'Ho, Tatau there, is not it near dawn yet?' And she answered: 'No, no, it is night; it is lasting night; 'tis still night; sleep soundly, sleep on.'

This was the second time that Tatau had thus called out to them.

At last dawn had broken – at last the sun had shone brightly upon the earth, and rose high in the heavens; and the old man again called out: 'Ho, Tatau there; is not it dawn yet?' And she answered: 'Yes.' And then she called out to her children: 'Be quick, pull out the things with which you have stopped up the window and the door.'

So they pulled them out, and the bright rays cf the sun came streaming into the house, and the whole of the Ponaturi perished before the light; they perished not by the hand of man, but withered before the sun's rays.

When the Ponaturi had been all destroyed, Tawhaki and Karihi carefully took down their father's bones from the roof of the house, and burnt them with fire, and together with the bodies of all those who were in the house, who had perished, scorched by the bright rays of the sun; they then returned again to their own country, taking with them their mother, and carefully carrying the bones of their father.

The fame of Tawhaki's courage in thus destroying the race of Ponaturi, and a report also of his manly beauty, chanced to reach the ears of a young maiden of the heavenly race who live above in the skies; so one night she descended from the heavens to visit Tawhaki, and to judge for herself, whether these reports were true. She found him lying sound asleep, and after gazing on him for some time, she stole to his side and laid herself down by him. He, when disturbed by her, thought that it was only some female of this lower world, and slept again; but before dawn the young girl stole away again from his side, and ascended once more to the heavens. In the early morning Tawhaki awoke and felt all over his sleeping place with both his hands, but in vain, he could nowhere find the young girl.

From that time Tangotango, the girl of the heavenly race, stole every night to the side of Tawhaki and lo, in the morning she was gone, until she found that she had conceived a child, who was afterwards named Arahuta; then full of love for Tawhaki, she disclosed herself fully to him and lived constantly in this world with him, deserting, for his sake, her friends above; and he discovered that she who had so loved him belonged to the race whose home is in the heavens.

Whilst thus living with him, this girl of the heavenly race, his second wife, said to him: 'Oh, Tawhaki, if our baby so shortly now to be born, should prove a son, I will wash the little tiling before it is baptized; but if it should be a little girl then you shall wash it.' When the time came Tangotango had a little girl, and before it was baptized Tawhaki took it to a spring to wash it, and afterwards held it away from him as if it smelt badly, and said: 'Faugh, how badly the little thing smells.' Then Tangotango, when she heard this said of her own dear little baby, began to sob and cry bitterly, and at last rose up from her place with her child, and began to take flight towards the sky, but she paused for one minute with one foot resting upon the carved figure at the end of the ridge-pole of the house above the door. Then Tawhaki rushed forward, and springing up tried to catch hold of his young wife, but missing her, he entreatingly besought her: 'Mother of my child, oh return once more to me?' But she in reply called down to him: 'No, no, I shall now never return to you again.'

Tawhaki once more called up to her: 'At least, then, leave me some one remembrance of you.'

Then his young wife called down to him: 'These are my parting words of remembrance to you – take care that you lay not hold with your hands of the loose root of the creeper, which dropping from aloft sways to and fro in the air; but rather lay fast hold on that which hanging down from on high has again struck its fibres into the earth.' Then she floated up into the air, and vanished from his sight.

Tawhaki remained plunged in grief, for his heart was torn by regrets for his wife and his little girl. One moon had waned after her departure, when Tawhaki, unable longer to endure such sufferings, called out to his younger brother, to Karihi, saying: 'Oh, brother, shall we go and search for my little girl?' And Karihi consented, saying: 'Yes, let us go.' So they departed, taking two slaves with them as companions for their journey.

When they reached the pathway along which they intended to travel, Tawhaki said to the two slaves who were accompanying himself and his brother: 'You being unclean or unconsecrated persons must be careful when we come to the place where the road passes the fortress of Tongameha, not to look up at it for it is enchanted, and some evil will befall you if you do.' They then went along the road, and when they came to the place mentioned by Tawhaki, one of the slaves looked up at the fortress, and his eye was immediately torn out by the magical arts of Tongameha, and he perished. Tawhaki and Karihi then went upon the road accompanied by only one slave. They at last reached the spot where the ends of the tendrils which hung down from heaven reached the earth, and they there found an old ancestress of theirs who was quite blind, and whose name was Matakerepo. She was appointed to take care of the tendrils, and she sat at the place where they touched the earth, and held the ends of one of them in her hands.

This old lady was at the moment employed in counting some taro roots, which she was about to have cooked, and as she was blind she was not aware of the strangers who stole quietly and silently up to her. There were ten taro roots lying in a heap before her. She began to count them, one, two, three, four, five, six, seven, eight, nine. Just at this moment Tawhaki quietly slipped away the tenth, the old lady felt about everywhere for it, but she could not find it. She thought she must have made some mistake, and so began to count her taro over again very carefully. One, two, three, four, five, six, seven, eight. Just then Tawhaki had slipped away the ninth. She was now quite surprised, so she counted them over again quite slowly, one, two, three, four, five, six, seven, eight; and as she could not find the two that were missing, she at last guessed that somebody was playing a trick upon her, so she pulled her weapon out, which she always sat upon to keep it safe, and standing up turned round, feeling about her as she moved, to try if she could find Tawhaki and Karihi; but they very gently stooped down to the ground and lay close there, so that her weapon passed over them, and she could not feel anybody; when she had thus swept her weapon all round her, she sat down and put it under her again. Karihi then struck her a blow upon the face, and she, quite frightened, threw up her hands to her face, pressing them on the place where she had been struck, and crying out: 'Oh! who did that?' Tawhaki then touched both her eyes, and, lo, she was at once restored to sight, and saw quite plainly, and she knew her grandchildren and wept over them.

When the old lady had finished weeping over them, she asked: 'Where are you going to?' And Tawhaki answered: 'I go to seek my little girl.' She replied: 'But where is she?' He answered: 'Above there, in the skies.' Then she replied: 'But what made her go to the skies?' And Tawhaki answered: 'Her mother came from heaven. She was the daughter of Watitiri-mata-ka-taka.' The old lady then pointed to the tendrils, and said to them: 'Up there, then, lies your road; but do not begin the ascent so late in the day, wait until tomorrow, for the morning, and then commence to climb up.' He consented to follow this good advice, and called out to his slave: 'Cook some food for us.' The slave began at once to cook food, and when it was dressed, they all partook of it and slept there that night.

At the first peep of dawn Tawhaki called out to his slave: 'Cook some food for us, that we may have strength to undergo the fatigues of this great journey'; and when their meal was finished, Tawhaki took his slave, and presented him to Matakerepo, as an acknowledgment for her great kindness to them.

His old ancestress then called out to him, as he was starting: 'There lies the ascent before you, lay fast hold of the tendrils with your hands, and climb on; but when you get midway between heaven and earth, take care not to look down upon this lower world again, lest you become charmed and giddy, and fall down. Take care, also, that you do not by mistake lay hold of a tendril which swings loose; but rather lay hold of one which hanging down from above, has again firmly struck root into the earth.'

Just at that moment Karihi made a spring at the tendrils to catch them, and by mistake caught hold of a loose one, and away he swung to the very edge of the horizon, but a blast of wind blew forth from thence, and drove him back to the other side of the skies; on reaching that point, another strong land wind swept him right up heavenwards, and down he was blown again by the currents of air from above: then just as he reached near the earth again, Tawhaki called out: 'Now, my brother, loose your hands: now is the time!' – and he did so, and, lo, he stood upon the earth once more; and the two brothers wept together over Karihi's narrow escape from destruction. And when they had ceased lamenting, Tawhaki, who was alarmed lest any disaster should overtake his younger brother, said to him: 'It is my desire that you should return home, to take care of our families and our dependants.' Thereupon Karihi at once returned to the village of their tribe, as his eldest brother directed him.

Tawhaki now began to climb the ascent to heaven, and his old ancestress, Matakerepo, called out to him as he went up: 'Hold fast, my child; let your hands hold tight.' And Tawhaki made use of, and kept on repeating, a powerful incantation as he climbed up to the heavens, to preserve him from the dangers of that difficult and terrible road.

At length he reached the heavens, and pulled himself up into them, and then by enchantments he disguised himself, and changed his handsome and noble appearance, and assumed the likeness of a very ugly old man, and he followed the road he had at first struck upon, and entered a dense forest into which it ran, and still followed it until he came to a place in the forest where his brothers-in-law, with a party of their people, were hewing canoes from the trunks of trees; and they saw him, and little thinking who he was, called out: 'Here's an old fellow will make a nice slave for us'; but Tawhaki went quietly on, and when he reached them he sat down with the people who were working at the canoes.

It now drew near evening, and his brothers-in-law finished their work, and called out to him: 'Ho! old fellow, there! – you just carry these heavy axes home for us, will you?' He at once consented to do this, and they gave him the axes. The old man then said to them: 'You go on in front, do not mind, I am old and heavy laden, I cannot travel fast.' So they started off, the old man following slowly behind. When his brothers-in-law and their people were all out of sight, he turned back to the canoe, and taking a axe just adzed the canoe rapidly along from the bow to the stern, and lo, one side of the canoe was finished. Then he took the adze again, and ran it rapidly along the other side of the canoe, from the bow to the stem, and lo, that side also was beautifully finished.

He then walked quietly along the road again, like an old man, carrying the axes with him, and went on for some time without seeing anything; but when he drew near the village, he found two women from the village in the forest gathering firewood, and as soon as they saw him, one of them observed to her companion: 'I say here is a curious-looking old fellow, is he not?' – and her companion exclaimed: 'He shall be our slave'; to which the first answered: 'Make him carry the firewood for us, then.' So they took Tawhaki, and laid a load of firewood upon his back, and made him carry that as well as the axes, so was this mighty chief treated as a slave, even by female slaves.

When they all reached the village, the two women called out: 'We've caught an old man for a slave.' Then Tangotango exclaimed in reply: 'That's right bring him along with you, then; he'll do for all of us.' Little did his wife Tangotango think that the slave they were so insulting, and whom she was talking about in such a way, was her own husband Tawhaki.

When Tawhaki saw Tangotango sitting at a fireplace near the upper end of the house with their little girl, he wont straight up to the place, and all the persons present tried to stop him, calling out: 'Ho! ho! take care what you are doing; do not go there; you will become tapued from sitting near Tangotango.' But the old man, without minding them, went rapidly straight on, and carried his load of firewood right up to the very fire of Tangotango. Then they all said: 'There, the old fellow is tapu; it is his own fault.' But Tangotango had not the least idea that this was Tawhaki; and yet there were her husband and herself seated, the one upon the one side, the other upon the opposite side of the very same fire.

They all stopped in the house until the sun rose next morning; then at daybreak his brothers-in-law called out to him: 'Holloa, old man, you bring the axes along, do you hear.' So the old man took up the axes, and started with them, and they all went off together to the forest, to work at dubbing out their canoes. When they reached them, and the brothers-in-law saw the canoe which Tawhaki had worked at, they looked at it with astonishment, saying: 'Why, the canoe is not at all as we left it; who can have been working at it?' At last, when their wonder was somewhat abated, they all sat down, and set to work again to dub out another canoe, and worked until evening, when they again called out to the old man as on the previous one: 'Holloa, old fellow, come here, and carry the axes back to the village again.' As before, he said: 'Yes', and when they started he remained behind, and after the others were all out of sight he took an axe, and began again to adze away at the canoe they had been working at; and having finished his work ho returned again to the village, and once more walked straight up to the fire of Tangotango, and remained there until the sun rose upon the following morning.

When they were all going at early dawn to work at their canoes as usual, they again called out to Tawhaki: 'Holloa, old man, just bring these axes along with you'; and the old man went patiently and silently along with them, carrying the axes on his shoulder. When they reached the canoe they were about to work at, the brothers-in-law were quite astonished on seeing it, and shouted out: 'Why, here again, this canoe, too, is not at all as it was when we left it; who can have been at work at it?' Having wondered at this for some time, they at length sat down and set to again to dub out another canoe, and laboured away until evening, when a thought came into their minds that they would hide themselves in the forest, and wait to see who it was came every evening to work at their canoe; and Tawhaki overheard them arranging this plan.

They therefore started as if they were going home, and when they had got a little way they turned off the path on one side, and hid themselves in the thick clumps of bushes, in a place from whence they could see the canoes. Then Tawhaki, going a little way back into the forest, stripped off his old cloaks, and threw them on one side, and then repeating the necessary incantations he put off his disguise, and took again his own appearance, and made himself look noble and handsome, and commenced his work at the canoe. Then his brothers-in-law, when they saw him so employed, said one to another: 'Ah, that must be the old man whom we made a slave of who is working away at our canoe'; but again they called to one another and said: 'Come here, come here, just watch, why he is not in the least like that old man.' Then they said amongst themselves: 'This must be a demi-god'; and, without showing themselves to him, they ran off to the village, and as soon as they reached it they asked their sister Tangotango to describe her husband for them; and she described his appearance as well as she could, representing him just like the man they had seen: and they said to her: 'Yes, that must be he; he is exactly like him you have described to us.' Their sister replied: 'Then that chief must certainly be your brother-in-law.'

Just at this moment Tawhaki reappeared at the village, having again disguised himself, and changed his appearance into that of an ugly old man. But Tangotango immediately questioned him, saying: 'Now tell me, who are you?' Tawhaki made no reply, but walked on straight towards her. She asked him again: 'Tell me, are you Tawhaki?' He murmured 'Humph!' in assent, still walking on until he reached the side of his wife, and then he snatched up his little daughter, and, holding her fast in his arms, pressed her to his heart. The persons present all rushed out of the court-yard of the house to the neighbouring court-yards, for the whole place was made tapu by Tawhaki, and murmurs of gratification and surprise arose from the people upon every side at the splendour of his appearance, for in the days when he had been amongst them as an old man his figure was very different from the resplendent aspect which he presented on this day.

Then he retired to rest with his wife, and said to her: 'I came here that our little daughter might be made to undergo the ceremonies usual for the children of nobles, to secure them good fortune and happiness in this life'; and Tangotango consented.

When in the morning the sun arose, they broke out an opening through the end of the house opposite to the door, that the little girl's rank might be seen by her being carried out that way instead of through the usual entrance to the house; and they repeated the prescribed prayers when she was carried through the wall out of the house.

The prayers and incantations being finished, lightnings flashed from the arm-pits of Tawhaki; then they carried the little girl to the water, and plunged her into it, and repeated a baptismal incantation over her.

Tawhaki is said to still dwell in the skies, and is worshipped as a god, and thunder and lightning are said to be caused by his footsteps when he moves.

Monstrous Gods & Divine Monsters

Introduction

'OUR INTEREST'S ON THE DANGEROUS EDGE of things,' wrote Robert Browning (1812–89): 'the honest thief, the tender murderer.' It is human, the English poet felt, to find more fascination in moral ambiguity than in either pure perfection or outright villainy.

He overstates his case a little: we've already found in earlier sections here that the clash of good and evil can be completely riveting. Traditional storytellers had many ways of making their narratives interesting, emotionally compelling and symbolically convincing. They didn't depend on the kind of close psychological study or subtle moral searching that the novelists of Browning's age were becoming famous for.

They could of course still appreciate the complexities of life, a fact reflected in the make-up of their gods and goddesses, who are frequently more like mortal men and women in their limitations. Historians have often associated monotheism with modernity. Religions like Judaism, Christianity and Islam, with their all-powerful, universally benevolent deities, are seen as an advance on the polytheistic paganisms that went before. In some respects they may have been, offering perspectives beyond believers' immediate natural environment and opening up opportunities for scientific and economic progress. But the supreme beings in such systems are just about by definition distant, abstract figures – far less colourful than the pagan deities, with all their vices and their follies. Or, correspondingly, their monsters, which may be more morally nuanced than the downright demonic beasts of more recent myths. At times they may be positively divine.

Athena and Arachne

IN THIS STORY from the ancient Roman poet Ovid's *Metamorphoses*, Arachne, vain-glorious of her ingenuity, challenges Minerva (the Roman equivalent of Athena) to a contest of skill in her art. The Goddess accepts the challenge, and, being enraged to see herself outdone, strikes her rival with her shuttle; upon which, Arachne, in her distress, hangs herself. Minerva, touched with compassion, transforms her into a spider:

Tritonia (an epithet of Athena) turns her mind to the fate of the Mæonian Arachne; who, as she had heard, did not yield to her in the praises of the art of working in wool. She was renowned not for the place of her birth, nor for the origin of her family, but for her skill alone. Idmon, of Colophon, her father, used to dye the soaking wool in Phocæan purple. Her mother was dead; but she, too, was of the lower rank, and of the same condition with her husband. Yet Arachne, by her skill, had acquired a memorable name throughout the cities of Lydia; although, born of a humble family, she used to live in the little town of Hypæpæ. Often did the Nymphs desert the vineyards of their own Tymolus, that they might look at her admirable workmanship; often did the Nymphs of the river Pactolus forsake their streams. And not only did it give them pleasure to look at the garments when made, but even, too, while they were being made, so much grace was there in her working. Whether it was that she was rolling the rough wool into its first balls, or whether she was unravelling the work with her fingers, and was softening the fleeces worked over again with long drawings out, equalling the mists in their fineness; or whether she was moving the smooth round spindle with her nimble thumb, or was embroidering with the needle, you might perceive that she had been instructed by Pallas (another epithet of Athena).

This, however, she used to deny; and, being displeased with a mistress so famed, she said, "Let her contend with me. There is nothing which, if conquered, I should refuse to endure." Pallas impersonates an old woman; she both places false gray hair on her temples, and supports as well her infirm limbs by a staff. Then thus she begins to speak: "Old age has not everything which we should avoid; experience comes from lengthened years. Do not despise my advice; let the greatest fame for working wool be sought by thee among mortals. But yield to the Goddess, and, rash woman, ask pardon for thy speeches with suppliant voice. She will grant pardon at my entreaty." The other beholds her with scowling eyes, and leaves the threads she has begun; and scarcely restraining her hand, and discovering her anger by her looks, with such words as these does she reply to the disguised Pallas: "Thou comest here bereft of thy understanding, and worn out with prolonged old age; and it is thy misfortune to have lived too long. If thou hast any daughter-in-law, if thou hast any daughter of thy own, let her listen to these remarks. I have sufficient knowledge for myself in myself, and do not imagine that thou hast availed anything by thy advice; my opinion is still the same. Why does not she come herself? why does she decline this contest?"

Then the Goddess says, "Lo! she is come;" and she casts aside the figure of an old woman, and shows herself as Pallas. The Nymphs and the Mygdonian matrons venerate the Goddess.

The virgin alone is not daunted. But still she blushes, and a sudden flush marks her reluctant features, and again it vanishes; just as the sky is wont to become tinted with purple, when Aurora is first stirring, and after a short time to grow white from the influence of the Sun. She persists in her determination, and, from a desire for a foolish victory, she rushes upon her own destruction.

Nor, indeed, does the daughter of Jupiter decline it, or advise her any further, nor does she now put off the contest. There is no delay; they both take their stand in different places, and stretch out two webs on the loom with a fine warp. The web is tied around the beam; the sley separates the warp; the woof is inserted in the middle with sharp shuttles, which the fingers hurry along, and being drawn within the warp, the teeth notched in the moving sley strike it. Both hasten on, and girding up their garments to their breasts, they move their skilful arms, their eagerness beguiling their fatigue. There both the purple is being woven, which is subjected to the Tyrian brazen vessel, and fine shades of minute difference; just as the rainbow, with its mighty arch, is wont to tint a long tract of the sky by means of the rays reflected by the shower: in which, though a thousand different colors are shining, yet the very transition eludes the eyes that look upon it; to such a degree is that which is adjacent the same; and yet the extremes are different. There, too, the pliant gold is mixed with the threads, and ancient subjects are represented on the webs.

Pallas embroiders the rock of Mars in Athens, the citadel of Cecrops, and the old dispute about the name of the country. Twice six celestial Gods are sitting on lofty seats in august state, with Jupiter in the midst. His own proper likeness distinguishes each of the Gods. The form of Jupiter is that of a monarch. She makes the God of the sea to be standing there, and to be striking the rugged rocks with his long trident, and a wild horse to be springing forth out of the midst of the opening of the rock; by which pledge of his favor he lays claim to the city. But to herself she gives the shield, she gives the lance with its sharp point; she gives the helmet to her head, and her breast is protected by the Ægis. She there represents, too, the earth struck by her spear, producing a shoot of pale olive with its berries, and the Gods admiring it. Victory is the end of her work. But that the rival of her fame may learn from precedents what reward to expect for an attempt so mad, she adds, in four different parts, four contests bright in their coloring, and distinguished by diminutive figures. One corner contains Thracian Rhodope and Hæmus, now cold mountains, formerly human bodies, who assumed to themselves the names of the supreme Gods. Another part contains the wretched fate of the Pygmæan matron. Her, overcome

in a contest, Juno commanded to be a crane, and to wage war against her own people. She depicts, too, Antigone, who once dared to contend with the wife of the great Jupiter; and whom the royal Juno changed into a bird; nor did Ilion protect her, or her father Laomedon, from assuming wings, and as a white crane, from commending herself with her chattering beak. The only corner that remains, represents the bereft Cinyras; and he, embracing the steps of a temple, once the limbs of his own daughters, and lying upon the stone, appears to be weeping. She surrounds the exterior borders with peaceful olive. That is the close; and with her own tree she puts an end to the work.

The Mæonian Nymph delineates Europa, deceived by the form of the bull; and you would think it a real bull, and real sea. She herself seems to be looking upon the land which she has left, and to be crying out to her companions, and to be in dread of the touch of the dashing waters, and to be drawing up her timid feet. She drew also Asterie, seized by the struggling eagle; and made Leda, reclining beneath the wings of the swan. She added, how Jupiter, concealed under the form of a Satyr, impregnated Antiope, the beauteous daughter of Nycteus, with a twin offspring; how he was Amphitryon, when he beguiled thee, Tirynthian dame; how, turned to gold, he deceived Danaë; how, changed into fire, the daughter of Asopus; how, as a shepherd, Mnemosyne; and as a speckled serpent, Deois. She depicted thee too, Neptune, changed into a fierce bull, with the virgin daughter of Æolus. Thou, seeming to be Enipeus, didst beget the Aloïdæ; as a ram, thou didst delude Theophane, the daughter of Bisaltis. Thee too the most bounteous mother of corn, with her yellow hair, experienced as a steed; thee, the mother of the winged horse, with her snaky locks, received as a bird; Melantho, as a dolphin. To all these did she give their own likeness, and the real appearance of the various localities. There was Phœbus, under the form of a rustic; and how, besides, he was wearing the wings of a hawk at one time, at another the skin of a lion; how, too, as a shepherd, he deceived Isse, the daughter of Macareus. How Liber deceived Erigone, in a fictitious bunch of grapes; and how Saturn begot the two-formed Chiron, in the form of a horse. The extreme part of the web, being enclosed in a fine border, had flowers interwoven with the twining ivy.

Pallas could not blame that work, nor could Envy censure it. The yellow-haired Virgin grieved at her success, and tore the web embroidered with the criminal acts of the Gods of heaven. And as she was holding her shuttle made of boxwood from Mount Cytorus, three or four times did she strike the forehead of Arachne, the daughter of Idmon. The unhappy creature could not endure it; and being of a high spirit, she tied up her throat in a halter. Pallas, taking compassion, bore her up as she hung; and thus she said: "Live on indeed, wicked one, but still hang; and let the same decree of punishment be pronounced against thy race, and against thy latest posterity, that thou mayst not be free from care in time to come." After that, as she departed, she sprinkled her with the juices of an Hecatean herb; and immediately her hair, touched by the noxious drug, fell off, and together with it her nose and ears. The head of herself, now small as well throughout her whole body, becomes very small. Her slender fingers cleave to her sides as legs; her belly takes possession of the rest of her; but out of this she gives forth a thread; and as a spider, she works at her web as formerly.

The Weighing of the Heart of Ani

ANCIENT EGYPTIANS BELIEVED that the fate of the dead was decided in the Hall of Osiris. Here the gods sat in judgement while the dead person's heart, the seat of human conscience, was weighed against a feather. Upholding the fateful Balance (a contrivance used to weigh commodities in commercial transactions) was the dog-headed ape who was also a manifestation of Thoth, the divine scribe, while jackal-headed Anubis made sure that everything about the Balance was in its correct setting. If the heart proved heavier than a feather, the soul owning it was destroyed by the monster Ammit (or Amemet), the 'Devourer' or 'Eater of the Dead', described as standing behind Thoth. The following passages from the Papyrus of Ani illuminate some of this process and provide a description of this hybrid monster.

I. The names of the Gods of the Great Company : 1. Ra Harmakhis, the Great God in his boat. 2. Temu. 3. Shu. 4. Tefnut. 5. Keb. 6. Nut, the Lady of Heaven. 7. Isis. 8. Nephthys. 9. Horus, the Great God. 10. Hathor, Lady of Amentet. II. H11. 12. Sa.

II. The Prayer of Ani. [Chapter XXXb]: My heart, my mother; my heart, my mother! My heart whereby I came into being! May nought stand up to oppose me at [my] judgment, may there be no opposition to me in the presence of the Chiefs (Tchatchau); may there be no parting of thee from me in the presence of him that keepeth the Balance! Thou art my Ka, which dwelleth in my body; the god Khnemu who knitteth together and strengtheneth my limbs. Mayest thou come forth into the place of happiness whither we go. May the Sheniu officials, who make the conditions of the lives of men, not cause my name to stink, and may no lies be spoken against me in the presence of the God. [Let it be satisfactory unto us, and let the Listener god be favourable unto us, and let there be joy of heart (to us) at the weighing of words. Let not that which is false be uttered against me before the Great God, the Lord of Amentet. Verily, how great shalt thou be when thou risest in triumph.] [*These last sentences are added from the Papyrus of Nebseni.*]

III. The Speech of Thoth: Thoth, the judge of right and truth of the Great Company of the Gods who are in the presence of Osiris, saith: Hear ye this judgment. The heart of Osiris hath in very truth been weighed, and his Heart-soul hath borne testimony on his behalf; his heart hath been found right by the trial in the Great Balance. There hath not been found any wickedness in him; he hath not wasted (or stolen) the offerings which have been made in the temples; he hath not committed any evil act; and he hath not set his mouth in motion with words of evil whilst he was upon earth.

IV. Speech of the Dweller in the Embalmment Chamber (i.e., Anubis): Pay good heed, O righteous Judge to the Balance to support [the testimony] thereof. Variant: Pay good heed (or, turn thy face) to the weighing in the Balance of the heart of the Osiris, the singing- woman of Amen, Anhai, whose word is truth, and place thou her heart in the seat of truth in the presence of the Great God.

V. The Speech of the Gods: The Great Company of the Gods say to Thoth who dwelleth in Khemenu (Hermopolis): That which cometh forth from thy mouth shall be declared true. The Osiris the scribe Ani, whose word is true, is holy and righteous. He hath not committed any sin, and he hath done no evil against us. The devourer Ammit shall not be permitted to prevail over him. Meat offerings and admittance into the presence of the god Osiris shall be granted unto him, together with an abiding habitation in the Field of Offerings (Sekhet-hetepet), as unto the Followers of Horus. [*These were a number of beings who formed the body-guard of Horus the Elder. The name 'Shemsu Heru' was also given to the great king Horus who conquered Egypt, and later still to the bodyguard of Horus, the son of Isis, who vanquished Set, the murderer of Osiris.*]

VI. The Speech of Horus to Osiris in introducing Ani to him: Horus, the son of Isis, saith: I have come to thee, O Un-Nefer, and I have brought unto thee the Osiris Ani. His heart is righteous, and it hath come forth from the Balance; it hath not sinned against any god or any goddess. Thoth hath weighed it according to the decree pronounced unto him by the Company of the Gods, and it is most true and righteous. Grant thou that cakes and ale may be given unto him, and let him appear in the presence of the god Osiris, and let him be like unto the Followers of Horus for ever and ever.

VII. The Speech of Ani: And the Osiris Ani saith: Behold, I am in thy presence, O Lord of Amentet. There is no sin in my body. I have not spoken that which is not true knowingly, nor have I done anything with a false heart. Grant thou that I may be like unto those favoured ones who are in thy following, and that I may be an Osiris greatly favoured of the beautiful god, and beloved of the Lord of the Two Lands (i.e., the king of Egypt), I who am a veritable royal scribe who loveth thee, Ani, whose word is true before the god Osiris.

VIII. Description of the beast Ammit: Her forepart is like that of a crocodile, the middle of her body is like that of a lion, her hind quarters are like those of a hippopotamus.

The Legend of Horus of Behutet

THE GREAT HISTORICAL FACT underlying this legend is the conquest of Egypt by some very early king who invaded Egypt from the south, and who succeeded in conquering every part of it, even the northern part of the Delta. The events described are supposed to have taken place whilst Ra was still reigning on the earth.

The legend states that in the three hundred and sixty-third year of the reign of Ra-Harmakhis, the ever living, His Majesty was in Ta-sti (i.e. the Land of the Bow, or Nubia) with his soldiers; the enemy had reviled him, and for this reason the land is called 'Uauatet' to this day. From Nubia Ra sailed down the river to Apollinopolis (Edfu), and Heru-Behutet, or Horus of Edfu, was with him. On arriving there Horus told Ra that the enemy were plotting against him, and Ra told him to go out and slay them. Horus took the form of a great winged disk, which flew up into the air and pursued the enemy, and it attacked them with such terrific force that they could neither see nor hear, and they fell upon each other, and slew each other, and in a moment not a single foe was left alive. Then Horus returned to the Boat of Ra-Harmakhis, in the form of the winged disk which shone with many colours, and said, "Advance, Oh Ra, and look upon your enemies who are lying under you in this land." Ra set out on the journey, taking with him the goddess Ashtoreth, and he saw his enemies lying on the ground, each of them being fettered. After looking upon his slaughtered foes Ra said to the gods who were with him, "Behold, let us sail in our boat on the water, for our hearts are glad because our enemies have been overthrown on the earth."

So the Boat of Ra moved onwards towards the north, and the enemies of the god who were on the banks took the form of crocodiles and hippopotami, and tried to frighten the god, for as his boat came near them they opened their jaws wide, intending to swallow it up together with the gods who were in it. Among the crew were the Followers of Horus of Edfu, who were skilled workers in metal, and each of these had in his hands an iron spear and a chain. These 'Blacksmiths' threw out their chains into the river and allowed the crocodiles and hippopotami to entangle their legs in them, and then they dragged the beasts towards the bows of the Boat, and driving their spears into their bodies, slew them there. After the slaughter the bodies of six hundred and fifty-one crocodiles were brought and laid out before the town of Edfu. When Thoth saw these he said, "Let your hearts rejoice, Oh gods of heaven, Let your hearts rejoice, Oh gods who dwell on the earth. The Young Horus comes in peace. On his way he has made manifest deeds of valour, according to the Book of slaying the Hippopotamus." And from that day they made figures of Horus in metal.

Then Horus of Edfu took the form of the winged disk, and set himself on the prow of the Boat of Ra. He took with him Nekhebet, goddess of the South, and Uatchet, goddess of the North, in the form of serpents, so that they might make all the enemies of the Sun-god to quake in the South and in the North. His foes who had fled to the north doubled back towards the south, for they were in deadly fear of the god. Horus pursued and overtook them, and he and his blacksmiths had in their hands spears and chains, and they slew large numbers of them to the south-east of the town of Thebes in Upper Egypt. Many succeeded in escaping towards the north once more, but after pursuing them for a whole day Horus overtook them, and made a great slaughter among them. Meanwhile the other foes of the god, who had heard of the defeats of their allies, fled into Lower Egypt, and took refuge among the swamps of the Delta. Horus set out after them, and came up with them, and spent four days in the water slaying his foes, who tried to escape in the forms of crocodiles and hippopotami. He captured one hundred and forty-two of the enemy and a male hippopotamus, and took them to the fore part of the Boat of Ra. There he hacked them in pieces, and gave their inward parts to his followers, and their mutilated bodies to the gods and goddesses who were in the Boat of Ra and on the river banks in the town of Heben.

Then the remnant of the enemy turned their faces towards the Lake of the North, and they attempted to sail to the Mediterranean in boats; but the terror of Horus filled their hearts, and they left their boats and fled to the district of Mertet-Ament, where they joined themselves to the worshippers of Set, the god of evil, who dwelt in the Western Delta. Horus pursued them in his boat for one day and one night without seeing them, and he arrived at the town of Per-Rehui.

At length he discovered the position of the enemy, and he and his followers fell upon them, and slew a large number of them; he captured three hundred and eighty-one of them alive, and these he took to the Boat of Ra, then, having slain them, he gave their carcasses to his followers or bodyguard, who presumably devoured them. The custom of eating the bodies of enemies is very old in Egypt, and survives in some parts of Africa to this day.

Then Set, the great antagonist of Horus, came out and cursed him for the slaughter of his people, using most shameful words of abuse. Horus stood up and fought a duel with Set, the 'Stinking Face,' as the text calls him, and Horus succeeded in throwing him to the ground and spearing him. Horus smashed his mouth with a blow of his mace, and having fettered him with his chain, he brought him into the presence of Ra, who ordered that he was to be handed over to Isis and her son Horus, that they might work their will on him. Here we must note that the ancient editor of the legend has confounded Horus the ancient Sun-god with Horus, son of Isis, son of Osiris. Then Horus, the son of Isis, cut off the heads of Set and his followers in the presence of Ra, and dragged Set by his feet round about throughout the district with his spear driven through his head and back, according to the order of Ra. The form which Horus of Edfu had at that time was that of a man of great strength, with the face and back of a hawk; on his head he wore the Double Crown, with feathers and serpents attached, and in his hands he held a metal spear and a metal chain. And Horus, the son of Isis, took upon himself a similar form, and the two Horuses slew all the enemies on the bank of the river to the west of the town of Per-Rehui. This slaughter took place on the seventh day of the first month of the season Pert (about the middle of November), which was ever afterwards called the 'Day of the Festival of Sailing'.

Now, although Set in the form of a man had been slain, he reappeared in the form of a great hissing serpent, and took up his abode in a hole in the ground without being noticed by Horus. Ra, however, saw him, and gave orders that Horus, the son of Isis, in the form of a hawk-headed staff, should set himself at the mouth of the hole, so that the monster might never reappear among men. This Horus did, and Isis his mother lived there with him. Once again it became known to Ra that a remnant of the followers of Set had escaped, and that under the direction of the Smait fiends, and of Set, who had reappeared, they were hiding in the swamps of the Eastern Delta. Horus of Edfu, the winged disk, pursued them, speared them, and finally slew them in the presence of Ra. For the moment, there were no more enemies of Ra to be found in the district on land, although Horus passed six days and six nights in looking for them; but it seems that several of the followers of Set in the forms of water reptiles were lying on the ground under water, and that Horus saw them there. At this time Horus had strict guard kept over the tomb of Osiris in Anrutef (a district of Herakleopolis), because he learned that the Smait fiends wanted to come and wreck both it and the body of the god. Isis, too, never ceased to recite spells and incantations in order to keep away her husband's foes from his body. Meanwhile the 'blacksmiths' of Horus, who were in charge of the 'middle regions' of Egypt, found a body of the enemy, and attacked them fiercely, slew many of them, and took one hundred and six of them prisoners. The 'blacksmiths' of the west also took one hundred and six prisoners, and both groups of prisoners were slain before Ra. In return for their services Ra bestowed dwelling-places upon the 'blacksmiths', and allowed them to have temples with images of their gods in them, and arranged for offerings and libations to be made to them by properly appointed priests of various classes.

Shortly after these events Ra discovered that a number of his enemies were still at large, and that they had sailed in boats to the swamps that lay round about the town of Tchal, or Tchar, better known as Zoan or Tanis. Once more Horus unmoored the Boat of Ra, and set out against them; some took refuge in the waters, and others landed and escaped to the hilly land on the east. For some reason, which is not quite apparent, Horus took the form of a mighty lion with a man's face, and he wore on his head the triple crown. His claws were like flints, and he pursued the enemy on the hills, and chased them hither and thither, and captured one hundred and forty-two of them. He tore out their tongues, and ripped their bodies into strips with his claws, and gave them over to his allies in the mountains, who, no doubt, ate them. This was the last fight in the north of Egypt, and Ra proposed that they should sail up the river and return to the south. They had traversed all Egypt, and sailed over the lakes in the Delta, and down the arms of the Nile to the Mediterranean, and as no more of the enemy were to be seen the prow of the boat of Ra was turned southwards. Thoth recited the spells that produced fair weather, and said the words of power that prevented storms from rising, and in due course the Boat reached Nubia. When it arrived, Horus found in the country of Uauatet men who were conspiring against him and cursing him, just as they had at one time blasphemed Ra. Horus, taking the form of the winged disk, and accompanied by the two serpent-goddesses, Nekhebet and Uatchet, attacked the rebels, but there was no fierce fighting this time, for the hearts of the enemy melted through fear of him. His foes cast themselves before him on the ground in submission, they offered no resistance, and they died straightway. Horus then returned to the town of Behutet (Edfu), and the gods acclaimed him, and praised his prowess. Ra was so pleased with him that he ordered Thoth to have a winged disk, with a serpent on each side of it, placed in every temple in Egypt in which he (i.e. Ra) was worshipped, so that it might act as a protector of the building, and drive away any and every fiend and devil that might wish to attack it. This is the reason why we find the winged disk, with a serpent on each side of it, above the doors of temples and religious buildings throughout the length and breadth of Egypt.

Apep, Chaos Deity and Monster Serpent

THE THIRD SECTION of the Papyrus Bremner–Rhind in the British Museum, is called, according to E.A. Wallis Budge, the 'Book of overthrowing Apep, the Enemy of Ra, the Enemy of Un-Nefer' (i.e., Osiris), and 'contains a series of spells which were recited during the performance of certain prescribed ceremonies, with the object of preventing storms, and dispersing rain-clouds, and removing any obstacle, animate or inanimate, which could prevent the rising of the sun in the morning, or obscure his light during the day. The Leader-in Chief of the hosts of darkness was a fiend called Apep who appeared in the sky in the form of a monster serpent, and, marshalling all the fiends of the Tuat, attempted to keep the Sun-god imprisoned in the kingdom of darkness.' Budge also gives us translations of spells found on the Metternich Stele, including these particularly evocative incantations against Apep:

Incantations Against Reptiles and Noxious Creatures In General

Get thee back, Apep, thou enemy of Ra, thou winding serpent in the form of an intestine, without arms [and] without legs. Thy body cannot stand upright so that thou mayest have therein being, long is thy tail in front of thy den, thou enemy; retreat before Ra. Thy head shall be cut off, and the slaughter of thee shall be carried out. Thou shalt not lift up thy face, for his (i.e., Ra's) flame is in thy accursed soul. The odour which is in his chamber of slaughter is in thy members, and thy form shall be overthrown by the slaughtering knife of the great god. The spell of the Scorpion-goddess Serq driveth back thy might. Stand still, stand still, and retreat through her spell.

Be vomited, O poison, I adjure thee to come forth on the earth. Horus uttereth a spell over thee, Horus hacketh thee in pieces, he spitteth upon thee; thou shalt not rise up towards heaven, but shalt totter downwards, O feeble one, without strength, cowardly, unable to fight, blind, without eyes, and with thine head turned upside down. Lift not up thy face. Get thee back quickly, and find not the way. Lie down in despair, rejoice not, retreat speedily, and show not thy face because of the speech of Horus, who is perfect in words of power. The poison rejoiced, [but] the heart[s] of many were very sad thereat. Horus hath smitten it with his magical spells, and he who was in sorrow is [now] in joy. Stand still then, O thou who art in sorrow, [for] Horus hath been endowed with life. He coineth charged, appearing himself to overthrow the Sebiu fiends which bite. All men when they see Ra praise the son of Osiris. Get thee back, Worm, and draw out thy poison which is in all the members of him that is under the knife. Verily the might of the word of power of Horus is against thee. Vomit thou, O Enemy, get thee back, O poison.

The Story of Adapa and the South Wind

HERE IS THE STORY OF ADAPA, the son of Ea, who, but for his obedience to his father's command, might have attained deification and immortality.

One day when Adapa was out in his boat fishing the South Wind blew with sudden and malicious violence, upsetting the boat and flinging the fisherman into the sea. When he succeeded in reaching the shore Adapa vowed vengeance against the South Wind, which had used him so cruelly.

"Shutu, thou demon," he cried, "I will stretch forth my hand and break thy wings. Thou shalt not go unpunished for this outrage!"

The hideous monster laughed as she soared in the air above him, flapping her huge wings about her ungainly body. Adapa in his fury leapt at her, seized her wings, and broke them, so that she was no longer able to fly over the broad earth. Then he went his way, and related to his father what he had done.

Seven days passed by, and Anu, the lord of heaven, waited for the coming of the South Wind. But Shutu came not; the rains and the floods were delayed, and Anu grew impatient. He summoned to him his minister Ilabrat.

"Wherefore doth Shutu neglect her duty?" he asked. "What hath chanced that she travels not afield?"

Ilabrat bowed low as he made answer: "Listen, O Anu, and I will tell thee why Shutu flieth not abroad. Ea, lord of the deep and creator of all things, hath a son named Adapa, who hath crushed and broken the wings of thy servant Shutu, so that she is no more able to fly."

"If this be true," said Anu, "summon the youth before me, and let him answer for his crime."

"Be it so, O Anu!"

When Adapa received the summons to appear in heaven he trembled greatly. It was no light thing to answer to the great gods for the ill-usage of their servant, the demon Shutu. Nevertheless he began to make preparations for his journey, and ere he set out his father Ea instructed him as to how he should comport himself in the assembly of the gods.

"Wrap thyself not in a vesture of gold, O my son, but clothe thee in the garments of the dead. At the gates of heaven thou wilt find Tammuz and Gishzida guarding the way. Salute the twain with due respect, I charge thee, baring thy head and showing all deference to them. If thou dost find favour in their eyes they will speak well of thee before Anu. And when thou standest within the precincts of heaven, don the garment that is given thee to wear, and anoint thy head with the oil that is brought thee. But when the gods offer thee food and drink, touch them not; for the food will be the 'Meat of Death', and the drink the 'Water of Death'; let neither pass within thy lips. Go now, my son, and remember these my instructions. Bear thyself with humility, and all will be well."

Adapa bade his father farewell and set out on his journey to heaven. He found all as his father had predicted; Tammuz and Gishzida received him at the portals of the divine dwelling, and so humble was Adapa's attitude that they were moved with compassion towards him. They led him into the presence of Anu, and he bowed low before the great god.

"I am come in answer to thy summons," said he. "Have mercy upon me, O thou Most High!"

Anu frowned upon him.

"It is said of thee," he made answer, "that thou hast broken the wings of Shutu, the South Wind. What manner of man art thou, who darest destroy Shutu in thy wrath? Knowest thou not that the people suffer for lack of nourishment; that the herb droopeth, and the cattle lie parched on the scorching ground? Tell me why hast thou done this thing?"

"I was out on the sea fishing," said Adapa, "and the South Wind blew violently, upsetting my boat and casting me into the water. Therefore I seized her wings and broke them. And lo! I am come to seek thy pardon."

Then Tammuz and Gishzida, the deities whose favour Adapa had won at the gates of heaven, stepped forth and knelt at the feet of their king.

"Be merciful, O Anu! Adapa hath been sorely tried, and now is he truly humble and repentant. Let his treatment of Shutu be forgotten."

Anu listened to the words of Tammuz and Gishzida, and his wrath was turned away.

"Rise, Adapa," he said kindly; "thy looks please me well. Thou hast seen the interior of this our kingdom, and now must thou remain in heaven for ever, and we will make thee a god like unto us. What sayest thou, son of Ea?"

Adapa bowed low before the king of the gods and thanked him for his pardon and for his promise of godhead.

Anu therefore commanded that a feast be made, and that the 'Meat of Life' and the 'Water of Life' be placed before Adapa, for only by eating and drinking of these could he attain immortality.

But when the feast was spread Adapa refused to partake of the repast, for he remembered his father's injunctions on this point. So he sat in silence at the table of the gods, whereupon Anu exclaimed:

"What now, Adapa? Why dost thou not eat or drink? Except thou taste of the food and water set before thee thou canst not hope to live for ever."

Adapa perceived that he had offended his divine host, so he hastened to explain. "Be not angry, most mighty Anu. It is because my lord Ea hath so commanded that I break not bread nor drink water at thy table. Turn not thy countenance from me, I beseech thee."

Anu frowned. "Is it that Ea feared I should seek thy life by offering thee deadly food? Truly he that knows so much, and hath schooled thee in so many different arts, is for once put to shame!"

Adapa would have spoken, but the lord of heaven silenced him.

"Peace!" he said; then to his attendants – "Bring forth a garment that he may clothe himself, and oil bring also to anoint his head."

When the King's command had been carried out Adapa robed himself in the heavenly garment and anointed his head with the oil. Then he addressed Anu thus:

"O Anu, I salute thee! The privilege of godhead must I indeed forego, but never shall I forget the honour that thou wouldst have conferred upon me. Ever in my heart shall I keep the words thou hast spoken, and the memory of thy kindness shall I ever retain. Blame me not exceedingly, I pray thee. My lord Ea awaits my return."

"Truly," said Anu, "I censure not thy decision. Be it even as thou wilt. Go, my son, and peace go with thee!"

And thus Adapa returned to the abode of Ea, lord of the dead, and there for many years he lived in peace and happiness.

Gods Once Demons

MANY OF THE BABYLONIAN GODS retained traces of their primitive demoniacal characteristics, and this applies to the great triad, Ea, Anu, and En-lil, who probably evolved into godhead from an animistic group of nature spirits. Each of these gods was accompanied by demon groups. Thus the disease-demons were 'the beloved sons of Bel', the fates were the seven daughters of Anu, and the seven storm-demons the children of Ea. In a magical incantation describing the primitive monster form of Ea it is said that his head is like a serpent's, the ears are those of a basilisk, his horns are twisted into curls, his body is a sun-fish full of stars, his feet are armed with claws, and the sole of his foot has no heel.

Ea was 'the great magician of the gods'; his sway over the forces of nature was secured by the performance of magical rites, and his services were obtained by human beings who performed requisite ceremonies and repeated appropriate spells. Although he might be worshipped and propitiated in his temple at Eridu, he could also be conjured in mud huts. The latter, indeed, as in Mexico, appear to have been the oldest holy places.

The Legend of Ura

It is told that Ura, the dread demon of disease, once made up his mind to destroy mankind. But Ishnu, his counsellor, appeased him so that he abandoned his intention, and he gave humanity a chance of escape. Whoever should praise Ura and magnify his name would, he said, rule the four quarters of the world, and should have none to oppose him. He should not die in pestilence, and his speech should bring him into favour with the great ones of the earth. Wherever a tablet with the song of Ura was set up, in that house there should be immunity from the pestilence.

The Great Wizard

TANGLED-HAIR, son of the West-wind, was a giant in size and his face was as black as the feathers of the crow. His hair was of twisted snakes, gray, black and spotted, with an adder raising its copper-colored head for his crown, while a rattlesnake spread itself across his shoulders. He was the greatest of all wizards, and could change himself into any bird or beast at will, could disguise his voice, and did both good and evil as he felt inclined.

He lived with his grandmother, who had been thrown from the moon by a jealous rival. Their lodge was on the edge of the prairie not far from the Big Sea Water.

He himself did not know his power until one day while playing with a beautiful snake, whose colors were brighter than any of those upon his head, he found that by means of it he could do magic. He had caught the snake and kept it in a bowl of water, feeding it every day on birds and insects. By chance he let fall some seeds, which were turned into birds as they touched the water, and the snake greedily devoured them. Then he discovered that everything he put into the water became alive.

He went to the swamp where he had caught the snake, for others, which he put into the bowl. Happening to rub his eyes while his fingers were still wet he was surprised to find how much clearer things at a distance appeared.

He gathered some roots, powdered them, and put them into the water. Then he took a little of the water into his mouth and blew it out in spray which made a bright light. When he put the water on his eyes he could see in the dark. By bathing his body with it he could pass through narrow or slippery places. A feather dipped into it would shoot any bird at which it was aimed, and would enter its body like an arrow.

He was able to heal wounds and sicknesses and to conquer all his enemies, but for all this he was a bad spirit nearly all his life.

His father, the West-wind, had intrusted Tangled Hair's brothers with the care of three-fourths of the earth, the north, the south, and the east; but gave nothing to him, the youngest. When he was old enough to know how he had been slighted, he was very angry and sought to fight his father.

He took his bearskin mittens and dipped them into the snake-water, thereby making them strong with magic, so that he could break off great boulders by merely striking them. He chased his father across the mountains, hurling boulder after boulder at him until he drove him to the very edge of the earth. He would have killed the West-wind if he had dared, but he was afraid of his brothers, who were friendly to one another, and he knew that he could not stand against the three. So he compelled his father to give him power over serpents, beasts and monsters of all kinds, and to promise him a place in his own kingdom after he should have rid the earth of them.

Having thus secured his share, he returned to his lodge, where he was sick for a long time from the wounds that he had received.

One of his first adventures after he had recovered was capturing a great fish, from which he took so much oil, that when he poured it into a hollow in the woods, it formed a small lake, to which he invited all the animals for a feast.

As fast as they arrived he told them to jump in and drink. The bear went in first, followed by the deer and the oppossum. The moose and the buffalo were late and did not get as much as the others. The partridge looked on until nearly all the oil was gone, while the hare and the marten were so long in coming, that they did not get any. That is why animals differ so much in fatness.

When they had done feasting, Tangled Hair took up his drum, beat upon it, and invited his guests to dance. He told them to pass round him in a circle, keeping their eyes shut all the time.

When he saw a fat fowl pass by him he wrung its neck, beating loudly on his drum to drown its cries, and the noise of its fluttering. After killing each one, he would call out, "That's the way, my brothers, that's the way!"

At last a small duck, being suspicious of him, opened one eye, and seeing what he was doing, called as loudly as she could, "Tangled Hair is killing us," and jumped and flew towards the water.

Tangled Hair followed her, and just as she was getting into the water, gave her a kick which flattened her back, and straightened her legs out backward, so that she can no longer walk on land, and her tail-feathers are few to this day.

The other birds took advantage of the confusion to fly away, and the animals ran off in all directions.

After this Tangled Hair set out to travel, to see if there were any wizards greater than himself. He saw all the nations of red men, and was returning quite satisfied, when he met a great magician in the form of an old wolf, who was journeying with six young ones.

As soon as the wolf saw him, he told the whelps to keep out of the way, for Tangled Hair's fame for cruelty and wickedness had been carried everywhere by the animals and birds he had tried to kill.

As the young wolves were running off, Tangled Hair said to them, "My grandchildren, where are you going? Stop and I will go with you."

The old wolf was watching him and came up in time to answer, "We are going to a place where we can find most game, where we may pass the winter."

Tangled Hair said he would like to go with them and asked the old wolf to change him into a wolf. Now this was very foolish, for he thereby lost his power, whereas if he had changed himself into one he might still have kept it, but even the greatest wizard did not know everything.

The old wolf was only too glad to grant his wish, and changed him into a wolf like himself. Tangled Hair was not satisfied and asked to be made a little larger. The wolf made him larger; and as he was still dissatisfied, he made him twice as large as the others.

Tangled Hair was better pleased, but he still thought he might be improved, so he said to the old wolf, "Do, please make my tail a little larger and more bushy."

The wolf did this, and Tangled Hair found a large tail very heavy to drag about with him.

Presently they came to the bottom of a ravine up which they rushed into the thick woods where they discovered the track of a moose. The young wolves followed it, while the old wolf and Tangled Hair walked on after them, taking their time.

"Which do you think is the swiftest runner among my whelps?" said the wolf.

"Why the foremost one, that takes such long leaps," said Tangled Hair.

The old wolf laughed sneeringly.

"You are mistaken," he said, "he will soon tire out. The one who seems to be slowest will capture the game."

Shortly afterward they reached a place where one of the young wolves had dropped a small bundle.

"Pick it up," said the wolf to Tangled Hair.

"No," replied he, "what do I want with a dirty dog-skin?"

The wolf took it up and it was turned into a beautiful robe.

"I will carry it now," said Tangled Hair.

"Oh, no," said the wolf, "I cannot trust you with a robe of pearls," and immediately the robe shone, for nothing could be seen but pearls.

They had gone about six arrow-flights farther when they saw a broken tooth that one of the young wolves had dropped in biting at the moose as it passed.

"Tangled Hair," said the wolf, "one of the children has shot at the game, pick up his arrow."

"No," he replied, "what do I want with a dirty dog's tooth?"

The old wolf took it up, and it became a beautiful silver arrow.

They found that the young wolves had killed a very fat moose. Tangled Hair was hungry, but the wolf charmed him so that he saw nothing but the bones picked bare. After a time the wolf gave him a heap of fresh ruddy meat cut, so it seemed to Tangled Hair, from the skeleton.

"How firm it is!" he exclaimed.

"Yes," answered the wolf, "our game always is. It is not a long tail that makes the best hunter."

Tangled Hair was a good hunter when he was not too lazy to undertake the chase. One day he went out and killed a large fat moose, but having lived well in the wolf's lodge he was not very hungry, and so turned the carcass from side to side, uncertain where to begin. He had learned to dread the ridicule of the wolves, who were always showing him how little he knew as a wolf, yet he could not change himself into a man again.

"If I begin at the head," he said, "they will say I ate it backwards. If I cut the side first, they will say I ate it sideways." He turned it round so that the hindquarter was in front of him. "If I begin here, they will say I ate it forwards." But he began to be hungry, so he said, "I will begin here, let them say what they will."

He cut a piece off the flank and was just about to put it into his mouth when he heard the branches of a large tree creaking. "Stop, stop," he said to the tree, for the sound annoyed him. The tree paid no attention to him, so he threw down his meat, exclaiming, "I cannot eat with such a noise about!"

He climbed the tree and was pulling at the branch which by rubbing against another had caused the creaking, when it was suddenly blown towards him and his paw was caught so that he could not get it out. Pretty soon a pack of wolves came along and he called out to them,

"Go away, go away!"

The chief of the wolves knew Tangled Hair's voice and said to the others, "Let us go on, for I am sure he has something there he does not want us to see."

They found the moose and began eating it. Tangled Hair could not get to them, so they finished the animal, leaving nothing but the bones. After they had gone a storm arose which blew the branches of the trees apart, and Tangled Hair was able to get out, but he had to go home hungry.

The next day the old wolf said to him, "My brother, I am going to leave you, for we cannot live together always."

"Let me have one of your children for my grandson," said Tangled Hair.

The old wolf left the one who was the best hunter, and also the lodge.

Tangled Hair was disenchanted after the wolves had gone, and when he assumed his natural shape, his power as a wizard came back. He was very fond of his grandson and took good care of him, giving much thought night and day to his welfare. One day he said to him, "My grandson, I dreamed of you last night, and I feel that trouble will come to you unless you will heed what I say. You must not cross the lake that lies in the thick woods. No matter what may the need or how tired you may be, go around it, even though the ice looks strong and safe."

In the early spring when the ice was breaking up on the lakes and rivers, the little wolf came to the edge of the water late in the evening. He was tired and it was such a long way round. He stood and thought to himself, "My grandfather is too cautious about this lake," and he tried the ice with his foot, pressing his weight upon it. It seemed strong to him, so he ventured to cross. He had not gone half way, however, when it broke and he fell in, and was seized by the serpents whose lodge was under the water.

Tangled Hair guessed what had happened to him when night came and again the day and he did not return. He mourned many days first in his lodge, and then by a small brook that ran into the lake.

A bird that had been watching him said, "What are you doing here?"

"Nothing," said Tangled Hair, "but can you tell me who lives in this lake?"

"Yes," said the bird, "the Prince of Serpents lives here, and I am set by him to watch for the body of Tangled Hair's grandson, whom they killed three moons since. You are Tangled Hair, are you not?"

"No," was the answer, "Why do you think he would wish to come here? Tell me about these serpents."

The bird pointed to a beautiful beach of white sand where he said the serpents came just after mid-day to bask in the sun. "You may know when they are coming," said he, "because all the ripples will disappear and the water will be smooth and still before they rise.

"Thank you," said Tangled Hair, "I am the wizard Tangled Hair. Do not fear me. Come and I will give you a reward."

The bird went to him and Tangled Hair placed a white medal round his neck, which the Kingfisher wears to this day. While putting it on he tried to wring the bird's neck. He did this for fear it might go to the serpents and tell them he was watching for them. It escaped him, however, with only the crown feathers ruffled.

He went to the beach of white sand and changing himself into an oak stump waited for the serpents. Before long the water became smooth as the lake of oil he himself had once made. Soon hundreds of serpents came crawling up on the beach. The Prince was beautifully white, the others were red and yellow.

The Prince spoke to the others and said, "I never saw that black stump there before; it may be the wizard, Tangled Hair."

Then one of the largest serpents went to the stump and coiled itself round the top, pressing it very hard. The greatest pressure was on Tangled Hair's throat, and he was just ready to cry out when the serpent let go. Eight of the others did the same to him, but each let go just in time. They then coiled themselves up on the beach near their Prince, and after a long time fell asleep.

Tangled Hair was watching them closely, and when he saw the last one breathing heavily in sleep, he took his bow and arrows and stepped cautiously about until he was near the Prince, whom he shot and wounded.

The serpents were roused by his cry, and plunging into the water, they lashed the waves so that a great flood was raised and Tangled Hair was nearly drowned. He climbed into a tall tree, and when the water was up to his chin he looked about for some means of escape. He saw a loon and said to him, "Dive down, my brother, and bring up some earth so that I can make a new world."

The bird obeyed him, but came up lifeless. He next asked the muskrat to do him the service, and promised him if he succeeded, a chain of beautiful little lakes surrounded by rushes for his lodge in future. The muskrat dived down, but floated up senseless. Tangled Hair took the body and breathed into the nostrils, which restored the animal to life. It tried again and came up the second time senseless, but it had some earth in its paws.

Tangled Hair charmed the earth till it spread out into an island, and then into a new world. As he was walking upon it, he met an old woman, the mother of the Prince of Serpents, looking for herbs to cure her son. She had a pack of cedar cords on her back. In answer to his questions she said she intended it for a snare for Tangled Hair.

Having found out all he wished, Tangled Hair killed her, took off her skin, wrapped it about him, and placing the cedar cord on his back, went to her lodge.

There he saw the skin of his beloved grandson hanging in the doorway. This made him so angry that he could hardly keep up the disguise. He sat down outside the door and began weaving a snare of the cedar cord, rocking himself to and fro and sobbing like an old woman. Some one called to him to make less noise and to come and attend to the Prince.

He put down the snare, and wiping his eyes, went in, singing the songs the old woman had told him would cure her son.

No one suspected him, and he pretended to make ready to pull out the arrow which he found was not deeply embedded in the Prince's side. Instead of pulling it out he gave it a sudden thrust and killed the Prince; but he had used so much force that he burst the old woman's skin. The serpents hissed and he fled quickly from the place.

He took refuge with the badger, and with its help he threw a wall of earth against the opening of their lodge so that no one could get at him. They had another opening behind the rock, through which they could bring in food so that they could not be starved out by the serpents.

Tangled Hair soon grew tired of living under ground, so he started to go out, and, as the badger stood in his way, and did not move quickly enough to please him, he kicked the poor animal and killed him.

He then ran back towards the serpent's lodge, and finding the dead body of the Prince, which the serpents in their haste to follow him had left unburied, he put the skin around him and went boldly up to the serpent tribe. They were so frightened that they fell into the lake and never again ventured forth.

After many years of wickedness, Tangled Hair repented, and traveled to the end of the earth, where he built himself a lodge, and tried, by good deeds, to rid himself of remembrances. But even there he was a terror to men and beasts.

Having shown, however, that he was really sorry for his misdeeds, his father, the West-wind gave him a part of his kingdom. He went to live beyond the Rocky mountains, and took the name of the North-west wind.

The Island of Eagles

AT A SHORT DISTANCE below the Falls of St. Anthony, there is a small rocky island, covered with huge trees, oak, pine, and cypress, its water-fretted shores and steep cliffs formed of ragged rocks, against which the waves of the cataract dash and foam in vain endeavours to overwhelm it. This little island, so annoyed by the mighty and wrathful fiends who sit in that surge, is famous throughout the Indian nations for being the abode of the spirits of the warriors of the Andirondacks – a tribe which no longer exist – who, once upon a time, many ages ago, warring against the spirits of the cataract, were completely overthrown, and by the power of their enemies transformed into eagles. As a punishment, they were bidden to dwell for ever on that misty, foggy, and noisy island; doomed to a nicer perception of hearing than belongs to mortals, that their fate might be the more awful. If my brother wishes to hear the tradition, let him open wide the doors of his understanding, and be silent.

The tribe of the Andirondacks were the mightiest tribe of the land – neither in numbers nor in valour had they their equal – their rule stretched from the broad Lake Huron to the river of the Osages, from the Alleghany to the Mississippi. All the tribes which dwelt in their neighbourhood were compelled to bow down their heads and pay them tribute. The Hurons sent them beaver-skins; the Eries wove them wampum; even the Iroquois, that haughty and warlike nation, who lorded it over their eastern neighbours with the ferocity of wolves, bowed to those mighty warriors, the Andirondacks, whose number was greater than that of the flights of pigeons in the month before the snows, and who wielded spears, and bent bows, and shouted their war-cry with more power than any other tribe or people in the land. Some of the more distant tribes, to secure themselves against invasion, sent ambassadors with the pipe of peace wrapped in soft furs as a present; others offered their most beautiful women for wives to the 'lords of the land' – all, by various means, and in various ways, testified their inability to cope with them in war, and their anxiety to become friends and neighbours. If the proud Andirondacks granted the boon of peace, it was always with some hard condition annexed to it; not always did a favour granted by them prove a favour in the end.

So long and uninterrupted a course of prosperity begot pride and arrogance in the bosom of the Andirondacks, and they forgot the Being who had bestowed so many blessings upon them, making their wives fertile as a vine in a rich soil, giving them victory over all their enemies, and health, and bounteous harvests, and successful hunts. They paid no more worship to that Great Being; no more offered him the juicy fruits of their hunt; no more ascended the high hills at the rising or setting of the sun, with their heads anointed with clay, to pour out their souls in the song of gratitude for past, or in a prayer of supplication for future, favours; they no more scarified their bodies in deprecation of his anger, but, believing themselves – vain fools! – able to do without his aid, they shook off their duty and allegiance to him, and bade him, if not in words at least in their deeds, defiance. Pride now possessed their souls, and hardness their hearts.

It need not be told my brother that the Great Spirit is slow to anger. Knowing his power to crush with a wink of his eye every living creature; to rend asunder the mightiest hills, yea, shake to its centre the very earth with a puff of his breath; he is loth to put forth his powers or to call into action the whirlwinds of his wrath. He suffers men to revile him long before he attempts to punish them; he permits them to raise the finger of defiance many times before he strikes it down, and the tongue to utter many a scornful word before he dooms it to the silence of death. It is so with the creatures of this world, as my brother must know. The strongest man – he who feels most confident of his power to repel aggression, and to command respect and obedience, is slowest to provocation, and, when excited to anger, the easiest to be soothed and calmed. The prairie-dog oftener shows his teeth than the wolf; the imbecile adder than the death-dealing rattlesnake. And my pale-faced brother has told us the wondrous tale, that, in his own land beyond the Great Waters, the mighty animal which is called the King of Beasts is, save only when he lacks food, as mild as the dove or the song-sparrow. And thus it was with the Great Spirit, as regarded the scoffing and wickedness of the Andirondacks. Long he resisted the importunities of the subordinate Manitous, that the haughty tribe might be punished for their insolence; long he waited with the hope that their eyes might be opened, and repentance seize their hearts, and amendment ensue. He waited in vain, each day they grew worse, until at length they brought down upon their heads the vengeance which could be no longer delayed.

There was among the Andirondacks a youth who, from the moment of his birth, was the favourite of the being who rules the world. While yet an unfledged bird, his words were the words of grey-headed wisdom; while yet a boy his arm was the arm of a strong man, his eye the eye of a cool man, and his heart like the heart of a brave man. He was as cool as a warrior who has lived to be aged in scenes of war. While he sat in his cradle of woven willow, his father chanced to speak in his hearing of an expedition which the Braves were about to undertake against the distant Coppermines, who had their lodges on the skirts of the sea of eternal ice. The wise child bade the father call the chiefs and counsellors of the nation around him, and to them he said, "You will not succeed in this war. The Coppermines dwell in the regions of great cold; before they can be met, icy hills and frozen lakes, and stormy winds and bleak tempests, must be encountered. If you meet them, success would be doubtful, for they are on their own hills, with nerves fitted to endure the searching cold, and possessed of that which the Andirondacks want – a thorough knowledge of every path that crosses their snow-clad vales and ice-bound waters. Stay at home, Braves, help your women to plant corn, and cut up the buffalo-meat, rather than go upon an expedition from which you will never return. Do I not see the torturing fires lighted, and Braves wearing the Andirondack mocassins bound to the stake of death? Do not mine ears hear a death-song in the Andirondack tongue? And are not these fearless sounds which come to mine ears the cries of the vulture and the wolf, fighting for the remains of a human carcase, which hath the Andirondack tuft of hair? Stay at home, Andirondacks, help your women to plant corn, and cut up the buffalo-meat, rather than go upon an expedition from which you will never return."

But the young and ardent warriors said this was the speech of a boy, and they would not listen to them. They said that, were the words of Piskaret the words of a man, they might hearken to them, but was he, who sat in his willow cradle, a fit counsellor to gray-headed sages, or even to young Braves, who had eaten the bitter root, and put on new war-shoes, and fasted for six suns, and been made men. In vain did the boy assure them that his medicine, the Great White Owl, had revealed to him many strange things, and among others this – that if the Andirondacks engaged in a war against the Coppermines, the wrath of the Great Spirit, whose worship they had forsaken, would be upon them, and of those who went not one should ever return. They laughed at his words, treating them as they would the song of a bird that has flown over. They bound on their mocassins, and, taking their spears, and bows and arrows, bade adieu to the land of their fathers' bones. Did these valiant youths return, and did the words of the prophet-boy fall to the ground? Let the wolf, and the vulture, and the mountain-cat, answer the question. They will tell my brother that their voracious tribes held a feast in the far country of the Coppermines, and that the remains of that feast were a huge heap of human bones. Were they the bones of Andirondacks? They were, and thus were the prophetic words of the wise boy rendered true, and his reputation was established throughout the land.

And when years came over him, and the fire of early manhood beamed in his eye, the same signs of his being favoured of Heaven were displayed. He needed no practice to enable him to conquer in all the sports and exercises which are indulged in by the boys of his nation. He went beyond them in all which bespoke possession of the skill and courage necessary to make a patient and expert hunter, or a brave and successful warrior. In the game of archery, his arrow was ever nearest the clout, and in hurling the spear, his oftenest clove asunder the reed which was fixed as the mark. Ere he had seen fifteen harvestings of the maize, he could throw the stoutest man of the tribe in the wrestle, and his feet in the race were swifter than the deer in its flight from the steps of the red hunter. When grey-headed men assembled in the council to deliberate upon the affairs of the tribe, their invasions, or their projected removals to other hunting-grounds, they asked "Where is the wise boy?" If he were not present, he was sent for, and no determination was made till he came, and had delivered his thoughts. And thus grew up the young Piskaret, till he had reached his twentieth spring.

There was in the neighbouring nation of Ottawas a maiden who was as much celebrated for her beauty, and her charms, and her wit, as the Andirondack youth was for strength, and wisdom, and prudence. Her Indian name was Menana, which means the Daughter of the Flood. She had reached the sixteenth summer of her residence among the Ottawas, the gentlest and lightest hearted, the mildest and sweetest maiden, that ever gazed on the pale full moon, or the glittering stars, or listened to the song of the sparrow, or the waterfall. She knew how to do every thing that was beautiful, or useful. If you saw a piece of gorgeously dyed wampum, or a robe curiously plaited of the bark of the mulberry, or the feathers of the canieu or war-eagle, you needed not ask who did it – you might be sure it was Menana. Her voice was the sweetest thing ever heard, her face the most beautiful ever seen – the first had in it the melody of birds, with the expression they can never have till they are gifted with the reason given to man – the last – but what is so beautiful as the face of a beautiful woman! And then her laugh was as joyous as a dance of warriors after a great victory, and her foot was the speediest foot that ever brushed the dew from the grass. Every body loved her, and she loved every body. So kind, and so good, and so sweet-tempered, and so beautiful a maiden, was never known among the Ottawas, famed as they are throughout the land for kind, and good, and sweet-tempered, and beautiful maidens.

She was not the daughter of an Ottawa woman, or any other woman, nor was her father an Ottawa man, or any other man. She was the daughter of the mighty cataract. The moon in which she came to the land of the Ottawas was the moon in which the forest trees put forth their earliest buds, and the blooming takes place of the little blue flower, which our forest maidens love to twine with their hair, and our forest boys to gather as the harbinger of returning warmth, and joy, and gladness. She came not at first to the village of the Ottawas in the perfect shape of a human being. It was many years before that, one morning, as the head warrior of the nation went out, as was his wont, to look abroad on the early sky, he found sitting at his door a little creature of a form such as he had never beheld, nor ever dreamed of. Woman she seemed from her waist upward, but fish or rather two fishes below. Her face was that of a most beautiful maiden in the charming hours when she begins to dream of tall youths; her eyes were blue as the deepest tinge of the water, and mild as a summer morning, her teeth white as the teeth of a salmon, and her locks fell sweeping the very earth. Her hands and arms were perfectly shaped, but they were covered with scales, and here and there tinted with red, which glittered like the evening sun on the folds of a cloud. Her height was about that of a small child who is just beginning to use its feet. The strange little creature did not stir as the warrior approached it, but suffered him to survey it unmoved, and, when he kindly wiped the dew from its waving locks, bent its eyes upon him with the deepest gratitude depicted in its countenance. As an Indian believes that every thing, even trees, and rivers, and mountains, have souls, or spirits, and are all worthy to be adopted as his protecting okkis, the warrior addressed the strange creature, and besought it to become his intercessor with the Great Spirit, his okki in peace and war. What was his surprise when it made reply to him, in a tone very nearly like the tone of a human being, and in a dialect of the Ottawas, as follows!

"I cannot be thy guardian spirit, for I am about to throw off my spiritual nature, and to become as thou art, a mortal, or rather I am to assume my former nature and state. Though I wear a form which is neither fish nor flesh, yet have I not always been thus. Once, many years ago, I was a human being. Gazing one evening on the blue sky, filled with shining lights, a passion came over my soul to behold them nearer. I besought the Master of Life to suffer me to ascend to the land of those bright things, and to visit the beautiful rainbows which had been equally the objects of my fond contemplation. My prayer was heard; I fell asleep, and, when I awoke, found myself where I wished to be. I was among the stars, sailing with them as an eagle or a cloud is wafted along on the winds which sweep the lower world. I beheld them glorious as you behold them from the earth, bright, round, and twinkling balls of every size, all endued with life, and all busily engaged in dancing their intricate dances, to music which came from unseen hands. My words cannot describe the splendour of the scene. Yet shall I tell the Ottawa warrior that the scene and the dances soon ceased to give pleasure. Who would wish to gaze for ever on the sun, bright and dazzling though he be? What one of all the fair things of the earth may be looked on for ever with delight? Its lakes, its rivers, its mountains, its bold youths, and lovely maidens, and many other things, are very fair, but each would tire were the eye to be chained to that alone. I was soon tired of the splendour of the starry world, and wished myself again upon the earth. I asked the Master of all for permission to return. He said, ''Thou hast been disembodied, thy flesh is decayed – thou art but a spirit, it may not be.' 'May I not,' said I, 're-animate some form from which the breath has just departed? may I not enter the corse of some child, and live out the remainder of the days of a favoured mortal?'

"The Great Spirit answered, 'It cannot be. But if thou art content to return to the earth and assume a form which shall be neither mortal nor immortal, neither man nor beast, be it so. Remember thou shalt not be endowed with the shape of a human being till thou shalt hear in the cataract, where I doom thee to dwell, the voice of one crying, 'Now is the time.' Then shalt thou leave the flood, repair to the land of my beloved people, the Ottawas, and there gradually return to the shape which once was thine. But, an immortal soul shalt thou not possess till thy bosom shall be lit up by the flame of love.'

"Thus spake the Great Being, and in a breath I found myself descending from the land of the stars upon the glorious rainbow. Speedy and uninterrupted was my descent, till I came to the mighty cataract; its capacious and stormy bosom received me, and there have I dwelt with the Spirits of the Flood, the adopted daughter of their chief, till now. Lo, Ottawa! I am at thy door, a strange creature, but demanding hospitality and protection from thee. Wilt thou give it me till I am permitted to take that form which shall give me the powers of a human being, and feel my bosom lit up by that flame which may give me one bound to feed and protect me?"

The Ottawa answered, that "his cabin had a quiet corner, and there should the strange maiden – if, indeed, she were a woman – rest; his house was always the abode of plenty, and of that should the stranger partake." So the creature, who was neither fish nor flesh, continued to reside in the cabin of the Ottawa warrior.

But each day was she observed to be assuming more and more the appearance of a mortal maiden. The scales fell from her arms and hands, which lost their red tints, and became soft and fair as the flesh of a new-born child. The two fishes gradually became two well proportioned legs. But though she had now become identified in form with the human race, she retained many of the propensities of that with which she had formerly dwelt. She loved to sport in the cataract, and lave herself in the lakes and rivers. Often would she fly from the company of the Ottawas to that of her old friends, the Spirits of the Flood. How her eyes would glow with childish delight, when the rain dashed from the clouds in torrents, and how mirthful she would be when the spring thaws swelled the noise and the volume of the cataract! And she better loved to feed on the ooze and the seeds of the grass, which were found in the torrent, and on those species of fish which are made the prey of the larger, than on the food prepared on the hearth of the Ottawa. Gradually, however, and at length fully, did her tastes conform to the tastes of those with whom she dwelt.

Yet she had no soul – the spirit of a fish was in her, but not the spirit of a mortal. She could not weep with the afflicted, nor laugh with the joyful. She knew indeed her Creator, for all things, whether animate or inanimate, know Him; but the worship paid by her was not the worship of one who has reason for what he does, but of one who follows the prompting of instinct. She still retained her passion for the evening, and the bright balls which light it, but better loved to see their reflection in the water, than to behold them dancing about in the blue sky.

At length, there arose a black cloud in the atmosphere – the Andirondacks and the Ottawas were no longer friends. A little thing breeds a quarrel among the sons of the wilderness. A word lightly spoken, a deer stricken an arrow's flight over a certain limit, an insult of old date, but unavenged, a woman borne away from an approved lover, are each deemed of sufficient importance to enlist all the energies of a nation in the purpose of revenge. A deputation of Andirondacks came to the chief village of the Ottawas, demanding satisfaction for a trespass on their hunting-ground, and for doing the foolish thing, so much reprobated by the red men of the forest as to occasion frequent wars – the slaying of beasts of venery out of season. Among the chiefs was the youth Piskaret, who, although he had but just reached his twentieth summer, was, as I have before said, counted the strongest, the wisest, and, by anticipation, the bravest, man of the nation. And with him came his aged father, the great chief of the Andirondacks.

The feast was made and eaten, the dance was concluded, and the chiefs, and counsellors, and warriors, were smoking in the great pipe of peace, when the beautiful maiden, who bore the name of Menana, entered the council cabin. She had now lost all traces of her origin from the waters, and to all appearance was a mortal woman. She entered without that timid step which mortal maidens have when they find themselves suddenly cast into a crowd of the other sex, with none of their own to give them countenance. But Menana was not versed in the ways of mortals, and had none of the feelings which send the blush to the cheek and trembling to the heart of the maidens of the world. After surveying the stern array of warriors for a moment, with a curious and enquiring look, she walked up to the youthful Piskaret, and said to him in a sweet and soft tone, "Thou art very beautiful. Tell me if I may not win thy love?"

The Brave, who was smitten with the charms of the fair creature, pressing to her side, whispered that he loved her better than all the world, and wished her to become the wife of his bosom. Then he painted, to her willing ear, the charms of his native land, and spoke of the tall old oaks which threw their giant shade over the banks of the gentle and placid river, and the many thick glades filled with lusty deer, and lakes stocked with delicious wild fowl, which were to be found within the hunting-grounds of his nation. He told her of the plenty that reigned in the cabins of the Andirondacks, and how much better their women fared than those of the surrounding tribes. The Daughter of the Flood smiled sweetly on the youth, and tears, the first she had ever shed – and sighs, the first she had ever breathed – proofs of her having acquired a human soul – stole to her heart and her eyes.

And now she had received a soul, and become possessed of those faculties which confer pleasure and pain, and create for their possessor happiness and misery, and joy and sorrow. She was now alive to the hopes and fears which exalt or depress existence – had tears for those that wept, and a laugh for those that laughed. She, who entered that assembly of warriors, fearless as an eagle seated on the top of a lofty pine, now at once, in the twinkling of an eye, became filled with trembling, and alarm, and apprehension, and strove to hide her blushes by half hiding her face in the bosom of him she loved.

But pride, which has often interrupted the course of love, as well as led to the downfall of nations, crept into the councils of the Andirondacks, and they refused to permit the young warrior to take to wife the maiden who was not of mortal parentage. They said that she was of the blood of the spirits of the cataract, of a race who had delighted to shed a cold and pestilential vapour over the villages of their nation, and had destroyed several Andirondacks, whose blood remained unrevenged. In vain did the youth plead his love; in vain did he show, that if the spirits of the flood warred on their neighbours, who were unable to inflict a wound on their adversaries, it furnished no reason why the beautiful maiden, so lovely and so inoffensive, should be banned. She had not injured, then why should she be spurned? But his argument availed not to influence the warriors, or to bend their stern hearts to pity. They drove the fair Menana from the arms of him she loved best, and, exerting the authority, so potent among the red men of the wilderness, of a father, and of chiefs, and of elders, they carried away the lover from the village of the Ottawas, thus dividing those whom the Great Being had so clearly created for each other.

But my brother asks what became of the beautiful maiden. Let him listen, and I will tell him. She pined away with grief at being separated from the man she loved. She sang not the sweet song which young maidens sing, who know neither love nor care – but her song was lonely and sad, as that of the bird of night. She wandered by herself in the dark and gloomy woods, as the bird flits when deprived of its mate, or the deer which carries its death-wound from the shaft of the hunter. Each day her eye lost a portion of its light, and her step of its buoyancy. She laughed no more, nor joined the dance of maidens, nor went with them to gather wild flowers; but her amusements, if amusements they could be called, were to weep and sigh, to wander alone with listless step, and to sit by the edge of the cataract, telling her sad story to the spirits of the flood. The Great Spirit, seeing her grief, and knowing that a heart that is broken hath no more business among the things of this world, bade her rejoin her friends in the surge of the cataract. She heard the well-known and well-remembered voice, and prepared to obey. Calling around her the friends whom her sweetness and good-humour had won her, she bade them a tearful adieu, and received the like tribute of kindness. The young Braves, who had before attempted to win her love, crowded around her to catch her last farewell, anxious yet fearing to attempt to change a resolution which had been dictated by the Great Spirit. They had tough spears in their hands, and well filled quivers at their shoulders, and their cheeks and brows were stained with the hue of wrath, for they were prepared to avenge on the haughty Andirondacks the slight and injury done the beauteous Menana. The maidens came to witness her departure, with tears bedewing their cheeks. All accompanied her to the brink of the cataract, and beheld her throw herself into its fearful bosom.

No sooner had she reached the waters of that boiling torrent, than uprose from its bosom the grisly heads of the fell spirits, who were its inhabitants. Rage filled their countenances, and horrid imprecations burst from their lips, as they vowed to be avenged on that arrogant and wicked people, the Andirondacks, who had inflicted misery upon an adopted and cherished daughter of the flood. The last the Ottawas saw of them, they were soothing and comforting the beautiful Menana, whom, after sustaining for a few moments upon the surface of the water, they bore to their crystal dwelling beneath the foaming torrent. They first, however, employed an Ottawa messenger to bear their defiance to their enemies, and to assure them of their eternal hatred.

It was not long after that a large war-party of the Andirondacks, composed of the flower of that nation, and headed by Piskaret, ascended the Mississippi, to make an incursion into the territories of a nation who dwelt upon its borders above the Falls. It is the custom of the tribes, when travelling upon the river, to approach to the verge of the cataract, and then transport their canoes around it. The Andirondacks were within a bow-shot of the cataract, when all at once the surface of the water became covered with grisly heads, which grinned hatred and defiance upon the Andirondacks, who, though filled with courage to dare encounter with men of their own form and nature, shook with a new sense of fear, as they beheld the hideous countenances and uplifted arms of the spirits of the flood. In the centre of the array of water spirits, they beheld the face of the beautiful Menana, still shining in all its former beauty, her eyes lit up by the fires of an unquenched and unquenchable love. Raising their dreadful shout of vengeance, the spirits now gathered about the canoes of the paralysed Andirondacks, and commenced their work of destruction. But one was protected by a being of their own order – the brave and youthful Piskaret found himself, ere an arrow had been impelled, or a thrust given by a spear, caught and shielded by the arms of his faithful Menana. While the water-spirits were employed in dealing death among their enemies, whose resistance availed not, the beautiful maiden drew her lover from his seat in his canoe, and disappeared with him beneath the waters. The moment the lovers had sunk into the flood, the spirits, with a dreadful shout, sunk also, leaving but few of the Andirondacks survivors of their attack. Nearly the whole had perished from the assaults of beings against whom human weapons were useless – who laughed at the puny resistance of mortals, and feared their battle less than the carcajou fears the mouse, or the canieu the humming-bird.

The Great Being, at the prayer of the water-spirits, bade the souls of the slaughtered Andirondacks assume the shape of eagles, commanding them to dwell for ever on the little island which stands just below the cataract, and within the full hearing of its incessant and tremendous roar. That they might receive the full reward of their arrogance, and pride, and cruelty, he so refined their sense of hearing, that the shaking of the wings of the bat was to them as loud as the thunder of the hills to a man having but the usual ear. What then must be the noise of the mighty cataract, which, leaping over a precipice of rocks, upon a stony bed, flies back again in foam and spray, higher than an arrow impelled by the toughest bow, bent by the strongest arm!

If my brother believes my story the song of a bird, let him visit the cataract, and use his own eyes and ears. If he do not behold that little island covered with eagles, whose wings never cleave any other air than its own; if he do not hear the angry voice of the spirits in the boiling waters, ay, and if he do not see them after night-fall; then let him call me a liar.

I have no more to say.

The Diamond Kings of Heaven

ON THE RIGHT AND LEFT SIDES of the entrance hall of Buddhist temples, two on each side, are the gigantic figures of the four great Ssu Ta Chin-kang or T'ien-wang, the Diamond Kings of Heaven. They are the protectors or governors of the continents lying in the direction of the four cardinal points from Mount Sumeru, the centre of the world. They are four brothers named respectively Mo-li Ch'ing (Pure), or Tseng Chang, Mo-li Hung (Vast), or Kuang Mu, Mo-li Hai (Sea), or To Wen, and Mo-li Shou (Age), or Ch'ih Kuo. They are said to bestow all kinds of happiness on those who honour the Three Treasures, Buddha, the Law and the Priesthood.

Kings and nations who neglect the Law lose their protection. They are described as follows:

Mo-li Ch'ing, the eldest, is twenty-four feet tall. He has a beard, the hairs of which are like copper wire. He carries a magnificent jade ring and a spear and always fights on foot. He also has a magic sword, 'Blue Cloud', on the blade of which are engraved the characters Ti, Shui, Huo, Feng (Earth, Water, Fire, Wind). When brandished, the magic sword causes a black wind which produces tens of thousands of spears. These spears pierce the bodies of men and turn them to dust. The wind is followed by a fire which fills the air with tens of thousands of golden fiery serpents. A thick smoke also rises out of the ground which blinds and burns men, none being able to escape.

Mo-li Hung carries in his hand an umbrella called the Umbrella of Chaos, formed of pearls with spiritual properties. Opening this marvellous implement causes the heavens and earth to be covered with thick darkness. Turning it upside down produces violent storms of wind and thunder and universal earthquakes.

Mo-li Hai holds a four-stringed guitar, the twanging of which supernaturally affects the earth, water, fire or wind. When it is played all the world listens and the camps of the enemy take fire.

Mo-li Shou has two whips and a panther-skin bag, the home of a creature resembling a white rat, known as Hua-hu Tiao. When at large this creature assumes the form of a white winged elephant, which devours men. He sometimes also has a snake or other man-eating creature, always ready to obey his commands.

The legend of the Four Diamond Kings goes that at the time of the consolidation of the Chou dynasty in the twelfth and eleventh centuries BC, Chiang Tzu-ya (chief counsellor to Wen Wang) and General Huang Fei-hu were defending the town and mountain of Hsi-ch'i. The supporters of the house of Shang appealed to the four genii Mo, who lived at Chia-meng Kuan, praying for them to come to their aid. They agreed and raised an army of one hundred thousand celestial soldiers. They travelled through towns, fields and mountains and arrived at the north gate of Hsi-ch'i in less than a day, where Mo-li Ch'ing pitched his camp and entrenched his soldiers.

Hearing of this, Huang Fei-hu hurried to warn Chiang Tzu-ya of the danger that threatened him. "The four great generals who have just arrived at the north gate," he said, "are marvellously powerful genii, experts in all the mysteries of magic and use of wonderful charms. It is feared that we will not be able to resist them."

Many fierce battles ensued. At first these went in favour of the Chin-kang, thanks to their magical weapons and especially to Mo-li Shou's Hua-hu Tiao, who terrorized the enemy by devouring their bravest warriors.

Unfortunately for the Chin-kang, the brute attacked and swallowed Yang Chien, the nephew of Yu Huang. This genie, on entering the body of the monster, split his heart apart and cut him in two. Then, as he could transform himself at will, he assumed the shape of Hua-hu Tiao and went off to Mo-li Shou, who unsuspectingly put him back into his bag.

The Four Kings held a festival to celebrate their triumph and having drunk copiously soon fell asleep. During the night Yang Chien came out of the bag with the intention stealing the three magical weapons of the Chin-kang. But he succeeded only in carrying off the umbrella of Mo-li Hung. In a subsequent battle No-cha, the son of Vadjrâ-pani (the God of Thunder), broke the jade ring of Mo-li Ch'ing. Misfortune followed misfortune. Deprived of their magical weapons, the Chin-kang began to lose heart. To complete their embarrassment, Huang T'ien Hua brought a matchless magical weapon to the attack called the 'Heart-piercer'. This was a spike seven-and-a-half inches long, enclosed in a silk sheath. It projected a ray of light so strong that eyes were blinded by it.

Huang T'ien Hua, hard pressed by Mo-li Ch'ing, drew the mysterious spike from its sheath and hurled it at his adversary. It entered his neck and with a deep groan the giant fell dead.

Mo-li Hung and Mo-li Hai hastened to avenge their brother, but before they could come within striking distance of Huang Ti'en Hua his formidable spike reached their hearts and they lay prone at his feet.

The one remaining hope for the sole survivor was in Hua-hu Tiao. Mo-li Shou, not knowing that the creature had been slain, put his hand into the bag to pull him out. Immediately after which Yang Chien, who had re-entered the bag, bit his hand off at the wrist. There remained nothing but a stump of bone. In this moment of intense agony Mo-li Shou fell an easy prey to Huang T'ien Hua. The magical spike pierced his heart and he fell bathed in his own blood. So perished the last of the Chin-kang.

The Slaughter of the Sea Serpent

ORIBE SHIMA had offended the great ruler Hojo Takatoki, and was in consequence banished to Kamishima, one of the Oki Islands, and forced to leave his beautiful daughter Tokoyo, whom he deeply loved.

At last Tokoyo was unable to bear the separation any longer, and she was determined to find her father. She therefore set out upon a long journey, and arriving at Akasaki, in the province of Hoki, from which coast town the Oki Islands are visible on a fine day, she besought many a fisherman to row her to her destination. But the fisher-folk laughed at Tokoyo, and bade her relinquish her foolish plan and return home. The maiden, however, would not listen to their advice, and at nightfall she got into the lightest vessel she could find, and by dint of a fair wind and persistent rowing the brave girl came to one of the rocky bays of the Oki Islands.

That night Tokoyo slept soundly, and in the morning partook of food. When she had finished her meal she questioned a fisherman as to where she might find her father. "I have never heard of Oribe Shima," replied the fisherman, "and if he has been banished, I beg that you will desist from further search, lest it lead to the death of you both."

That night the sorrowful Tokoyo slept beneath a shrine dedicated to Buddha. Her sleep was soon disturbed by the clapping of hands, and looking up she saw a weeping maiden clad in a white garment with a priest standing beside her. Just as the priest was about to push the maiden over the rocks into the roaring sea, Tokoyo sprang up and held the maiden's arm.

The priest explained that on that night, the thirteenth of June, the Serpent God, known as Yofune-Nushi, demanded the sacrifice of a young girl, and that unless this annual sacrifice was made the God became angry and caused terrible storms.

"Good sir," said Tokoyo, "I am glad that I have been able to save this poor girl's life. I gladly offer myself in her place, for I am sad of heart because I have been unable to find my father. Give him this letter, for my last words of love and farewell go to him."

Having thus spoken, Tokoyo took the maiden's white robe and clad herself in it, and having prayed to the image of Buddha, she placed a small dagger between her teeth and plunged into the tempestuous sea. Down she went through the moonlit water till she came to a mighty cave where she saw a statue of Hojo Takatoki, who had sent her poor father into exile. She was about to tie the image on her back when a great white serpent crept out from the cave with eyes gleaming angrily. Tokoyo, realising that this creature was none other than Yofune-Nushi, drew her dagger and thrust it through the right eye of the God. This unexpected attack caused the serpent to retire into the cave, but the brave Tokoyo followed and struck another blow, this time at the creature's heart. For a moment Yofune-Nushi blindly stumbled forward, then with a shriek of pain fell dead upon the floor of the cavern.

During this adventure the priest and the maiden stood on the rocks watching the spot where Tokoyo had disappeared, praying fervently for the peace of her sorrowful soul. As they watched and prayed they saw Tokoyo come to the surface of the water carrying an image and a mighty fish-like creature. The priest hastily came to the girl's assistance, dragged her upon the shore, placed the image on a high rock, and secured the body of the White Sea Serpent.

In due time the remarkable story was reported to Tameyoshi, lord of the island, who in turn reported the strange adventure to Hojo Takatoki. Now Takatoki had for some time been suffering from a disease which defied the skill of the most learned doctors; but it was observed that he regained his health precisely at the hour when his image, which had been cursed and thrown into the sea by some exile, had been restored. When Hojo Takatoki heard that the brave girl was the daughter of the exiled Oribe Shima, he sent him back with all speed to his own home, where he and his daughter lived in peace and happiness.

Kauhuhu, The Shark-God of Molokai

THE STORY OF the shark-god Kauhuhu has been told under the legend of 'Aikanaka (Man-eater),' which was the ancient name of the little harbor Pukoo, which lies at the entrance to one of the beautiful valleys of the island of Molokai. The better way is to take the legend as revealing the great man-eater in one of his most kindly aspects. The shark-god appears as the friend of a priest who is seeking revenge for the destruction of his children. Kamalo was the name of the priest. His heiau, or temple, was at Kaluaaha, a village which faced the channel between the islands of Molokai and Maui. Across the channel the rugged red-brown slopes of the mountain Eeke were lost in the masses of clouds which continually hung around its sharp peaks. The two boys of the priest delighted in the glorious revelations of sunrise and sunset tossed in shattered fragments of cloud color, and revelled in the reflected tints which danced to them over the swift channel-currents. It is no wonder that the courage of sky and sea entered into the hearts of the boys, and that many deeds of daring were done by them. They were taught many of the secrets of the temple by their father, but were warned that certain things were sacred to the gods and must not be touched. The high chief, or alii, of that part of the island had a temple a short distance from Kaluaaha, in the valley of the harbor which was called Aikanaka. The name of this chief was Kupa. The chiefs always had a house built within the temple walls as their own residence, to which they could retire at certain seasons of the year. Kupa had two remarkable drums which he kept in his house at the heiau. His skill in beating his drums was so great that they could reveal his thoughts to the waiting priests.

One day Kupa sailed far away over the sea to his favorite fishing-grounds. Meanwhile the boys were tempted to go to Kupa's heiau and try the wonderful drums. The valley of the little harbor Aikanaka bore the musical name Mapulehu. Along the beach and over the ridge hastened the two sons of Kamalo. Quickly they entered the heiau, found the high chief's house, took out his drums and began to beat upon them. Some of the people heard the familiar tones of the drums. They dared not enter the sacred doors of the heiau, but watched until the boys became weary of their sport and returned home.

When Kupa returned they told him how the boys had beaten upon his sacred drums. Kupa was very angry, and ordered his mu, or temple sacrifice seekers, to kill the boys and bring their bodies to the heiau to be placed on the altar. When the priest Kamalo heard of the death of his sons, in bitterness of heart he sought revenge. His own power was not great enough to cope with his high chief; therefore he sought the aid of the seers and prophets of highest repute throughout Molokai. But they feared Kupa the chief, and could not aid him, and therefore sent him on to another kaula, or prophet, or sent him back to consult some one the other side of his home. All this time he carried with him fitting presents and sacrifices, by which he hoped to gain the assistance of the gods through their priests. At last he came to the steep precipice which overlooks Kalaupapa and Kalawao, the present home of the lepers. At the foot of this precipice was a heiau, in which the great shark-god was worshipped. Down the sides of the precipice he climbed and at last found the priest of the shark-god. The priest refused to give assistance, but directed him to go to a great cave in the bold cliffs south of Kalawao. The name of the cave was Anao-puhi, the cave of the eel. Here dwelt the great shark-god Kauhuhu and his guardians or watchers, Waka and Mo-o, the great dragons or reptiles of Polynesian legends. These dragons were mighty warriors in the defence of the shark-god, and were his kahus, or caretakers, while he slept, or when his cave needed watching during his absence.

Kamalo, tired and discouraged, plodded along through the rough lava fragments piled around the entrance to the cave. He bore across his shoulders a black pig, which he had carried many miles as an offering to whatever power he could find to aid him. As he came near to the cave the watchmen saw him and said:

"E, here comes a man, food for the great Mano. Fish for Kauhuhu." But Kamalo came nearer and for some reason aroused sympathy in the dragons. "E hele! E hele!" they cried to him. 'Away, away! It is death to you. Here's the tabu place." "Death it may be – life it may be. Give me revenge for my sons – and I have no care for myself." Then the watchmen asked about his trouble and he told them how the chief Kupa had slain his sons as a punishment for beating the drums. Then he narrated the story of his wanderings all over Molokai, seeking for some power strong enough to overcome Kupa. At last he had come to the shark-god – as the final possibility of aid. If Kauhuhu failed him, he was ready to die; indeed he had no wish to live. The mo-o assured him of their kindly feelings, and told him that it was a very good thing that Kauhuhu was away fishing, for if he had been home there would have been no way for him to go before the god without suffering immediate death. There would have been not even an instant for explanations. Yet they ran a very great risk in aiding him, for they must conceal him until the way was opened by the favors of the great gods. If he should be discovered and eaten before gaining the aid of the shark-god, they, too, must die with him. They decided that they would hide him in the rubbish pile of taro peelings which had been thrown on one side when they had pounded taro. Here he must lie in perfect silence until the way was made plain for him to act. They told him to watch for the coming of eight great surf waves rolling in from the sea, and then wait from his place of concealment for some opportunity to speak to the god because he would come in the last great wave. Soon the surf began to roll in and break against the cliffs.

Higher and higher rose the waves until the eighth reared far above the waters and met the winds from the shore which whipped the curling crest into a shower of spray. It raced along the water and beat far up into the cave, breaking into foam, out of which the shark-god emerged. At once he took his human form and walked around the cave. As he passed the rubbish heap he cried out: "A man is here. I smell him." The dragons earnestly denied that any one was there, but the shark-god said, "There is surely a man in this cave. If I find him, dead men you are. If I find him not, you shall live." Then Kauhuhu looked along the walls of the cave and into all the hiding-places, but could not find him. He called with a loud voice, but only the echoes answered, like the voices of ghosts. After a thorough search he was turning away to attend to other matters when Kamalo's pig squealed. Then the giant shark-god leaped to the pile of taro leavings and thrust them apart. There lay Kamalo and the black pig which had been brought for sacrifice.

Oh, the anger of the god!

Oh, the blazing eyes!

Kauhuhu instantly caught Kamalo and lifted him from the rubbish up toward his great mouth. Now the head and shoulders are in Kauhuhu's mouth. So quickly has this been done that Kamalo has had no time to think. Kamalo speaks quickly as the teeth are coming down upon him. "E Kauhuhu, listen to me. Hear my prayer. Then perhaps eat me." The shark-god is astonished and does not bite. He takes Kamalo from his mouth and says: "Well for you that you spoke quickly. Perhaps you have a good thought. Speak." Then Kamalo told about his sons and their death at the hands of the executioners of the great chief, and that no one dared avenge him, but that all the prophets of the different gods had sent him from one place to another but could give him no aid. Sure now was he that Kauhuhu alone could give him aid. Pity came to the shark-god as it had come to his dragon watchers when they saw the sad condition of Kamalo. All this time Kamalo had held the hog which he had carried with him for sacrifice. This he now offered to the shark-god. Kauhuhu, pleased and compassionate, accepted the offering, and said: "E Kamalo. If you had come for any other purpose I would eat you, but your cause is sacred. I will stand as your kahu, your guardian, and sorely punish the high chief Kupa."

Then he told Kamalo to go to the heiau of the priest who told him to see the shark-god, take this priest on his shoulders, carry him over the steep precipices to his own heiau at Kaluaaha, and there live with him as a fellow-priest. They were to build a tabu fence around the heiau and put up the sacred tabu staffs of white tapa cloth. They must collect black pigs by the four hundred, red fish by the four hundred, and white chickens by the four hundred. Then they were to wait patiently for the coming of Kauhuhu. It was to be a strange coming. On the island Lanai, far to the west of the Maui channel, they should see a small cloud, white as snow, increasing until it covers the little island. Then that cloud shall cross the channel against the wind and climb the mountains of Molokai until it rests on the highest peaks over the valley where Kupa has his temple. "At that time," said Kauhuhu, "a great rainbow will span the valley. I shall be in the care of that rainbow, and you may clearly understand that I am there and will speedily punish the man who has injured you. Remember that because you came to me for this sacred cause, therefore I have spared you, the only man who has ever stood in the presence of the shark-god and escaped alive." Gladly did Kamalo go up and down precipices and along the rough hard ways to the heiau of the priest of the shark-god. Gladly did he carry him up from Kalaupapa to the mountain-ridge above. Gladly did he carry him to his home and there provide for him while he gathered together the black pigs, the red fish, and the white chickens within the sacred enclosure he had built. Here he brought his family, those who had the nearest and strongest claims upon him. When his work was done, his eyes burned with watching the clouds of the little western island Lanai. Ah, the days passed by so slowly! The weeks and the months came, so the legends say, and still Kamalo waited in patience. At last one day a white cloud appeared. It was unlike all the other white clouds he had anxiously watched during the dreary months. Over the channel it came. It spread over the hillsides and climbed the mountains and rested at the head of the valley belonging to Kupa. Then the watchers saw the glorious rainbow and knew that Kauhuhu had come according to his word.

The storm arose at the head of the valley. The winds struggled into a furious gale. The clouds gathered in heavy black masses, dark as midnight, and were pierced through with terrific flashes of lightning. The rain fell in floods, sweeping the hillside down into the valley, and rolling all that was below onward in a resistless mass toward the ocean. Down came the torrent upon the heiau belonging to Kupa, tearing its walls into fragments and washing Kupa and his people into the harbor at the mouth of the valley. Here the shark-god had gathered his people. Sharks filled the bay and feasted upon Kupa and his followers until the waters ran red and all were destroyed. Hence came the legendary name for that little harbor – Aikanaka, the place for man-eaters.

It is said in the legends that "when great clouds gather on the mountains and a rainbow spans the valley, look out for furious storms of wind and rain which come suddenly, sweeping down the valley." It also said in the legends that this strange storm which came in such awful power upon Kupa also spread out over the adjoining lowlands, carrying great destruction everywhere, but it paused at the tabu staff of Kamalo, and rushed on either side of the sacred fence, not daring to touch any one who dwelt therein. Therefore Kamalo and his people were spared. The legend has been called 'Aikanaka' because of the feast of the sharks on the human flesh swept down into that harbor by the storm, but it seems more fitting to name the story after the shark-god Kauhuhu, who sent mighty storms and wrought great destruction.

Puna and the Dragon

TWO IMAGES of goddesses were clothed in yellow kapa cloth and worshipped in the temples. One was Kiha-wahine, a noted dragon-goddess, and the other was Haumea, who was also known as Papa, the wife of Wakea, a great ancestor-god among the Polynesians.

Haumea is said to have taken as her husband, Puna, a chief of Oahu. He and his people were going around the island. The surf was not very good, and they wanted to find a better place. At last they found a fine surf-place where a beautiful woman was floating on the sea.

She called to Puna, "This is not a good place for surf." He asked, "Where is there a place?" She answered, "I know where there is one, far outside." She desired to get Puna. So they swam way out in the sea until they were out of sight nor could they see the sharp peaks of the mountains. They forgot everything else but each other. This woman was Kiha-wahine.

The people on the beach wailed, but did not take canoes to help them. They swam over to Molokai. Here they left their surf-boards on the beach and went inland. They came to the cave house of the woman. He saw no man inside nor did he hear any voice, all was quiet.

Puna stayed there as a kind of prisoner and obeyed the commands of the woman. She took care of him and prepared his food. They lived as husband and wife for a long time, and at last his real body began to change.

Once he went out of the cave. While standing there he heard voices, loud and confused. He wanted to see what was going on, but he could not go, because the woman had laid her law on him, that if he went away he would be killed.

He returned to the cave and asked the woman, "What is that noise I heard from the sea?" She said: "Surf-riding, perhaps, or rolling the maika stone. Some one is winning and you heard the shouts." He said, "It would be fine for me to see the things you have mentioned." She said, "Tomorrow will be a good time for you to go and see."

In the morning he went down to the sea to the place where the people were gathered together and saw many sports.

While he was watching, one of the men, Hinole, the brother of his wife, saw him and was pleased. When the sports were through he invited Puna to go to their house and eat and talk.

Hinole asked him, "Whence do you come, and what house do you live in?" He said, "I am from the mountains, and my house is a cave." Hinole meditated, for he had heard of the loss of Puna at Oahu. He loved his brother-in-law, and asked, "How did you come to this place?" Puna told him all the story. Then Hinole told him his wife was a goddess. "When you return and come near to the place, go very easily and softly, and you will see her in her real nature, as a mo-o, or dragon; but she knows all that you are doing and what we are saying. Now listen to a parable. Your first wife, Haumea, is the first born of all the other women. Think of the time when she was angry with you. She had been sporting with you and then she said in a tired way, 'I want the water.' You asked, 'What water do you want?' She said, 'The water from Poliahu of Mauna Kea.' You took a water-jar and made a hole so that the water always leaked out, and then you went to the pit of Pele. That woman Pele was very old and blear-eyed, so that she could not see you well, and you returned to Haumea. She was that wife of yours. If you escape this mo-o wife she will seek my life. It is my thought to save your life, so that you can look into the eyes of your first wife."

The beautiful dragon-woman had told him to cry with a loud voice when he went back to the cave. But when Puna was going back he went slowly and softly, and saw his wife as a dragon, and understood the words of Hinole. He tried to hide, but was trembling and breathing hard.

His wife heard and quickly changed to a human body, and cursed him, saying: "You are an evil man coming quietly and hiding, but I heard your breath when you thought I would not know you. Perhaps I will eat your eyes. When you were talking with Hinole you learned how to come and see me."

The dragon-goddess was very angry, but Puna did not say anything. She was so angry that the hair on her neck rose up, but it was like a whirlwind, soon quiet and the anger over. They dwelt together, and the woman trusted Puna, and they had peace.

One day Puna was breathing hard, for he was thirsty and wanted the water of the gods.

The woman heard his breathing, and asked, "Why do you breathe like this?" He said: "I want water. We have dwelt together a long time and now I need the water." "What water is this you want?" He said, "I must have the water of Poliahu of Mauna Kea, the snow covered mountain of Hawaii."

She said, "Why do you want that water?" He said: "The water of that place is cold and heavy with ice. In my youth my good grandparents always brought water from that place for me. Wherever I went I carried that water with me, and when it was gone more would be brought to me, and so it has been up to the time that I came to dwell with you. You have water and I have been drinking it, but it is not the same as the water mixed with ice, and heavy. But I would not send you after it, because I know it is far away and attended with toil unfit for you, a woman."

The woman bent her head down, then lifted her eyes, and said: "Your desire for water is not a hard thing to satisfy. I will go and get the water."

Before he had spoken of his desire he had made a little hole in the water-jar, as Hinole had told him, that the woman might spend a long time and let him escape.

She arose and went away. He also arose and followed. He found a canoe and crossed to Maui. Then he found another boat going to Hawaii and at last landed at Kau.

He went up and stood on the edge of the pit of Pele. Those who were living in the crater saw him, and cried out, "Here is a man, a husband for our sister." He quickly went down into the crater and dwelt with them. He told all about his journey. Pele heard these words, and said: "Not very long and your wife will be here coming after you, and there will be a great battle, but we will not let you go or you will be killed, because she is very angry against you. She has held you, the husband of our sister Haumea. She should find her own husband and not take what belongs to another. You stay with us and at the right time you can go back to your wife."

Kiha-wahine went to Poliahu, but could not fill the water-jar. She poured the water in and filled the jar, but when the jar was lifted it became light. She looked back and saw the water lying on the ground, and her husband far beyond at the pit of Pele. Then she became angry and called all the dragons of Molokai, Lanai, Maui, Kahoolawe, and Hawaii.

When she had gathered all the dragons she went up to Kilauea and stood on the edge of the crater and called all the people below, telling them to give her the husband. They refused to give Puna up, crying out: "Where is your husband? This is the husband of our sister; he does not belong to you, O mischief-maker."

Then the dragon-goddess said, "If you do not give up this man, of a truth I will send quickly all my people and fill up this crater and capture all your fires." The dragons threw their drooling saliva in the pit, and almost destroyed the fire of the pit where Pele lived, leaving Ka-moho-alii's place untouched.

Then the fire moved and began to rise with great strength, burning off all the saliva of the dragons. Kiha-wahine and the rest of the dragons could not stand the heat even a little while, for the fire caught them and killed a large part of them in that place. They tried to hide in the clefts of the rocks. The earthquakes opened the rocks and some of the dragons hid, but fire followed the earthquakes and the fleeing dragons. Kiha-wahine ran and leaped down the precipice into a fish-pond called by the name of the shadow, or aka, of the dragon, Loko-aka (the shadow lake).

So she was imprisoned in the pond, husbandless, scarcely escaping with her life. When she went back to Molokai she meant to kill Hinole, because she was very angry for his act in aiding Puna to escape. She wanted to punish him, but Hinole saw the trouble coming from his sister, so arose and leaped into the sea, becoming a fish in the ocean.

When he dove into the sea Kiha-wahine went down after him and tried to find him in the small and large coral caves, but could not catch him. He became the Hinalea, a fish dearly loved by the fishermen of the islands. The dragon-goddess continued seeking, swimming swiftly from place to place.

Ounauna saw her passing back and forth, and said, "What are you seeking, O Kiha-wahine?" She said, "I want Hinole." Ounauna said: "Unless you listen to me you cannot get him, just as when you went to Hawaii you could not get your husband from Pele. You go and get the vine inalua and come back and make a basket and put it down in the sea. After a while dive down and you will find that man has come inside. Then catch him."

The woman took the vine, made the basket, came down and put it in the sea. She left it there a little while, then dove down. There was no Hinole in the basket, but she saw him swimming along outside of the basket. She went up, waited awhile, came down again and saw him still swimming outside. This she did again and again, until her eyes were red because she could not catch him. Then she was angry, and went to Ounauna and said: "O slave, I will kill you to-day. Perhaps you told the truth, but I have been deceived, and will chase you until you die."

Ounauna said: "Perhaps we should talk before I die. I want you to tell me just what you have done, then I will know whether you followed directions. Tell me in a few words. Perhaps I forgot something."

The dragon said, "I am tired of your words and I will kill you." Then Ounauna said, "Suppose I die, what will you do to correct any mistakes you have made?"

Then she told how she had taken vines and made a basket and used it. Ounauna said: "I forgot to tell you that you must get some sea eggs and crabs, pound and mix them together and put them inside the basket. Put the mouth of the basket down. Leave it for a little while, then dive down and find your brother inside. He will not come out, and you can catch him." This is the way the Hinalea is caught to this day.

After she had caught her brother she took him to the shore to kill him, but he persuaded her to set him free. This she did, compelling him ever after to retain the form of the fish Hinalea.

Kiha-wahine then went to the island Maui and dwelt in a deep pool near the old royal town of Lahaina.

After Pele had her battle with the dragons, and Puna had escaped according to the directions of Hinole, he returned to Oahu and saw his wife, Haumea, a woman with many names, as if she were the embodiment of many goddesses.

After Puna disappeared, Kou became the new chief of Oahu. Puna went to live in the mountains above Kalihi-uka. One day Haumea went out fishing for crabs at Heeia, below the precipice of Koolau, where she was accustomed to go.

Puna came to a banana plantation, ate, and lay down to rest. He fell fast asleep and the watchmen of the new chief found him. They took his loin-cloth, and tied his hands behind his back, bringing him thus to Kou, who killed him and hung the body in the branches of a breadfruit-tree. It is said that this was at Wai-kaha-lulu just below the steep diving rocks of the Nuuanu stream.

When Haumea returned from gathering moss and fish to her home in Kalihi-uka, she heard of the death of her husband. She had taken an akala vine, made a pa-u, or skirt, of it, and tied it around her when she went fishing, but she forgot all about it, and as she hurried down to see the body of her husband, all the people turned to look at her, and shouted out, "This is the wife of the dead man."

She found Puna hanging on the branches. Then she made that breadfruit-tree open. Leaving her pa-u on the ground where she stood, she stepped inside the tree and bade it close about her and appear the same as before. The akala of which the pa-u had been made lay where it was left, took root and grew into a large vine.

The fat of the body of Puna fell down through the branches and the dogs ate below the tree. One of these dogs belonged to the chief Kou. It came back to the house, played with the chief, then leaped, caught him by the throat and killed him.

Note. – This is the same legend as 'The Wonderful Breadfruit Tree' published in the 'Legends of Old Honolulu,' but the names are changed and the time is altered from the earliest days of Hawaiian lore to the almost historic period of King Kakuhihewa, whose under-chief mentioned in this legend gave the name to Old Honolulu, as for centuries it bore the name 'Kou.' The legend is new, however, in so far as it gives the account of the infatuation of Puna for Kiha-wahine, the dragon-goddess, and his final escape from her.

The Dragon Ghost-Gods

DRAGONS WERE among the ghost-gods of the ancient Hawaiians. These dragons were called mo-o. The New Zealanders used the same names for some of their large reptile gods. They, however, spelled the word with a 'k,' calling it mo-ko, and it was almost identical in pronunciation as in meaning with the Hawaiian name. Both the Hawaiians and New Zealanders called all kinds of lizards mo-o or mo-ko; and their use of this word in traditions showed that they often had in mind animals like crocodiles and alligators, and sometimes they referred the name to any monster of great mythical powers belonging to a man-destroying class.

Mighty eels, immense sea-turtles, large fish of the ocean, fierce sharks, were all called mo-o. The most ancient dragons of the Hawaiians are spoken of as living in pools or lakes. These dragons were known also as kupuas, or mysterious characters who could appear as animals or human beings according to their wish. The saying was: 'Kupuas have a strange double body.'

There were many other kupuas besides those of the dragon family. It was sometimes thought that at birth another natural form was added, such as an egg of a fowl or a bird, or the seed of a plant, or the embryo of some animal, which when fully developed made a form which could be used as readily as the human body. These kupuas were always given some great magic power. They were wonderfully strong and wise and skilful.

Usually the birth of a kupua, like the birth of a high chief, was attended with strange disturbances in the heavens, such as reverberating thunder, flashing lightning, and severe storms which sent the abundant red soil of the islands down the mountain-sides in blood-red torrents known as ka-ua-koko (the blood rain). This name was also given to misty fine rain when shot through by the red waves of the sun.

By far the largest class of kupuas was that of the dragons. These all belonged to one family. Their ancestor was Mo-o-inanea (The Self-reliant Dragon), who figured very prominently in the Hawaiian legends of the most ancient times, such as 'The Maiden of the Golden Cloud.'

Mo-o-inanea (The Self-reliant Dragon) brought the dragons, the kupua dragons, from the 'Hidden Land of Kane' to the Hawaiian Islands. Mo-o-inanea was apparently a demi-goddess of higher power even than the gods Ku, Kane, or Kanaloa. She was the great dragon-goddess of the Hawaiians, coming to the islands in the migration of the gods from Nuu-mea-lani and Kuai-he-lani to settle. The dragons and other kupuas came as spirit servants of the gods.

For a while this Mo-o-inanea lived with her brothers, the gods, at Waolani, but after a long time there were so many dragons that it was necessary to distribute them over the islands, and Mo-o-inanea decided to leave her brothers and find homes for her numerous family. So she went down to Puunui in the lower part of Nuuanu Valley and there made her home, and it is said received worship from the men of the ancient days. Here she dwelt in her dual nature – sometimes appearing as a dragon, sometimes as a woman.

Very rich clayey soil was found in this place, forced out of the earth as if by geyser action. It was greatly sought in later years by the chiefs who worshipped this goddess. They made the place tabu, and used the clay, sometimes eating it, but generally plastering the hair with it. This place was made very tabu by the late Queen Kaahumanu during her lifetime.

Mo-o-inanea lived in the pit from which this clay was procured, a place called Lua-palolo, meaning pit-of-sticky-clay. After she had come to this dwelling-place the dragons were sent out to find homes. Some became chiefs and others servants, and when by themselves were known as the evil ones. She distributed her family over all the islands from Hawaii to Niihau. Two of these dragon-women, according to the legends, lived as guardians of the pali (precipice) at the end of Nuuanu Valley, above Honolulu. After many years it was supposed that they both assumed the permanent forms of large stones which have never lost their associations with mysterious, miraculous power.

Even as late as 1825, Mr. Bloxam, the chaplain of the English man-of-war, recorded in 'The Voyage of the Blonde' the following statement:

"At the bottom of the Parre (pali) there are two large stones on which even now offerings of fruits and flowers are laid to propitiate the Aku-wahines, or goddesses, who are supposed to have the power of granting a safe passage."

Mr. Bloxam says that these were a kind of mo-o, or reptile, goddesses, and adds that it was difficult to explain the meaning of the name given to them, probably because the Hawaiians had nothing in the shape of serpents or large reptiles in their islands.

A native account of these stones says: "There is a large grove of hau-trees in Nuuanu Valley, and above these lie the two forest women, Hau-ola and Ha-puu. These are now two large stones, one being about three feet long with a fine smooth back, the other round with some little rough places. The long stone is on the seaward side, and this is the Mo-o woman, Hau-ola; and the other, Ha-puu. The leaves of ferns cover Hau-ola, being laid on that stone. On the other stone, Ha-puu, are lehua flowers. These are kupuas."

Again the old people said that their ancestors had been accustomed to bring the navel cords of their children and bury them under these stones to insure protection of the little ones from evil, and that these were the stone women of Nuuanu.

Ala-muki lived in the deep pools of the Waialua River near the place Ka-mo-o-loa, which received its name from the long journeys that dragon made over the plains of Waialua. She and her descendants guarded the paths and sometimes destroyed those who travelled that way.

One dragon lived in the Ewa lagoon, now known as Pearl Harbor. This was Kane-kua-ana, who was said to have brought the pipi (oysters) to Ewa. She was worshipped by those who gathered the shell-fish. When the oysters began to disappear about 1850, the natives said that the dragon had become angry and was sending the oysters to Kahiki, or some far-away foreign land.

Kilioe, Koe, and Milolii were noted dragons on the island of Kauai. They were the dragons of the precipices of the northern coast of this island, who took the body of the high chief Lohiau and concealed it in a cave far up the steep side of the mountain. There is a very long interesting story of the love between Lohiau and Pele, the goddess of fire. In this story Pele overcame the dragons and won the love of the chief. Hiiaka, the sister of the fire-goddess, won a second victory over them when she rescued a body from the cave and brought it back to life.

On Maui, the greatest dragon of the island was Kiha-wahine. The natives had the saying, "Kiha has mana, or miraculous power, like Mo-o-inanea." She lived in a large deep pool on the edge of the village Lahaina, and was worshipped by the royal family of Maui as their special guardian.

There were many dragons of the island of Hawaii, and the most noted of these were the two who lived in the Wailuku River near Hilo. They were called 'the moving boards' which made a bridge across the river.

Sometimes they accepted offerings and permitted a safe passage, and sometimes they tipped the passengers into the water and drowned them. They were destroyed by Hiiaka.

Sacred to these dragons who were scattered over all the islands were the mo-o priests and the sorcerers, who propitiated them with offerings and sacrifices, chanting incantations.

Beastly Beings, Malign & Benign

Introduction

TO AN EXTENT that would surely have surprised our ancestors, we've come to see grotesqueness as next to goodness. We take it almost as read that a monster is less malevolent than misunderstood. Like the lumbering 'Creature' in *Frankenstein* by Mary Shelley (1797–1859) or the hideous Quasimodo in *The Hunchback of Notre Dame* by Victor Hugo (1802–85).

Both those examples belong to a Romantic age in which introspection was encouraged and individuals were quick to see the darkness – even the monstrosity – in themselves. Where once they might have seen the monster as an utterly alien and external enemy, they were more inclined to interpret it as expressing something in themselves. Once that insight had been gained, it wasn't possible to forget it: we remain Romantics, in this respect, even if our attitudes have changed in many other ways.

The resentments of Shakespeare's Caliban (in *The Tempest*, c. 1610) 200 years before Romanticism make it clear that a more complex view of the monster was always possible. Even so, the idea that he's essentially sympathetic, a victim of oppression, is a wholly modern one (which depends on our overlooking a considerable capacity for violence and cruelty).

The stories that follow show us mythic monsters of every sort. Some are simply terrifying: rapacious and destructive. Others, though, are capable of kindness, loyalty, justice and honour.

The Giants

AS WE HAVE ALREADY SEEN, the Northern races imagined that the giants were the first creatures who came to life among the icebergs which filled the vast abyss of Ginnunga-gap. These giants were from the very beginning the opponents and rivals of the gods, and as the latter were the personifications of all that is good and lovely, the former were representative of all that was ugly and evil.

When Ymir, the first giant, fell lifeless on the ice, slain by the gods, his progeny were drowned in his blood. One couple only, Bergelmir and his wife, effected their escape to Jotunheim, where they took up their abode and became the parents of all the giant race. In the North the giants were called by various names, each having a particular meaning. Jotun, for instance, meant 'the great eater,' for the giants were noted for their enormous appetites as well as for their uncommon size. They were fond of drinking as well as of eating, wherefore they were also called Thurses, a word which some writers claim had the same meaning as thirst; but others think they owed this name to the high towers ('turseis') which they were supposed to have built. As the giants were antagonistic to the gods, the latter always strove to force them to remain in Jotunheim, which was situated in the cold regions of the Pole. The giants were almost invariably worsted in their encounters with the gods, for they were heavy and slow-witted, and had nothing but stone weapons to oppose to the Aesir's bronze. In spite of this inequality, however, they were sometimes greatly envied by the gods, for they were thoroughly conversant with all knowledge relating to the past. Even Odin was envious of this attribute, and no sooner had he secured it by a draught from Mimir's spring than he hastened to Jotunheim to measure himself against Vafthrudnir, the most learned of the giant brood. But he might never have succeeded in defeating his antagonist in this strange encounter had he not ceased inquiring about the past and propounded a question relating to the future.

Of all the gods Thor was most feared by the Jotuns, for he was continually waging war against the frost and mountain giants, who would fain have bound the earth for ever in their rigid bands, thus preventing men from tilling the soil. In fighting against them, Thor, as we have already seen, generally had recourse to his terrible hammer Miolnir.

According to German legends the uneven surface of the earth was due to the giants, who marred its smoothness by treading upon it while it was still soft and newly created, while streams were formed from the copious tears shed by the giantesses upon seeing the valleys made by their husbands' huge footprints. As such was the Teutonic belief, the people imagined that the giants, who personified the mountains to them, were huge uncouth creatures, who could only move about in the darkness or fog, and were petrified as soon as the first rays of sunlight pierced through the gloom or scattered the clouds.

This belief led them to name one of their principal mountain chains the Riesengebirge (giant mountains). The Scandinavians also shared this belief, and to this day the Icelanders designate their highest mountain peaks by the name of Jokul, a modification of the word 'Jotun.' In Switzerland, where the everlasting snows rest upon the lofty mountain tops, the people still relate old stories of the time when the giants roamed abroad; and when an avalanche came crashing down the mountain side, they say the giants have restlessly shaken off part of the icy burden from their brows and shoulders.

As the giants were also personifications of snow, ice, cold, stone, and subterranean fire, they were said to be descended from the primitive Fornjotnr, whom some authorities identify with Ymir. According to this version of the myth, Fornjotnr had three sons: Hler, the sea; Kari, the air; and Loki, fire. These three divinities, the first gods, formed the oldest trinity, and their respective descendants were the sea giants Mimir, Gymir, and Grendel, the storm giants Thiassi, Thrym, and Beli, and the giants of fire and death, such as the Fenris wolf and Hel.

As all the royal dynasties claimed descent from some mythical being, the Merovingians asserted that their first progenitor was a sea giant, who rose out of the waves in the form of an ox, and surprised the queen while she was walking alone on the seashore, compelling her to become his wife. She gave birth to a son named Meroveus, the founder of the first dynasty of Frankish kings.

Many stories have already been told about the most important giants. They reappear in many of the later myths and fairy-tales, and manifest, after the introduction of Christianity, a peculiar dislike to the sound of church bells and the singing of monks and nuns.

The Scandinavians relate, in this connection, that in the days of Olaf the Saint a giant called Senjemand, dwelt on the Island of Senjen, and he was greatly incensed because a nun on the Island of Grypto daily sang her morning hymn. This giant fell in love with a beautiful maiden called Juterna-jesta, and it was long ere he could find courage to propose to her. When at last he made his halting request, the fair damsel scornfully rejected him, declaring that he was far too old and ugly for her taste.

In his anger at being thus scornfully refused, the giant swore vengeance, and soon after he shot a great flint arrow from his bow at the maiden, who dwelt eighty miles away. Another lover, Torge, also a giant, seeing her peril and wishing to protect her, flung his hat at the speeding arrow. This hat was a thousand feet high and proportionately broad and thick, nevertheless the arrow pierced the headgear, falling short, however, of its aim. Senjemand, seeing that he had failed, and fearing the wrath of Torge, mounted his steed and prepared to ride off as quickly as possible; but the sun, rising just then above the horizon, turned him into stone, together with the arrow and Torge's hat, the huge pile being known as the Torghatten mountain. The people still point to an obelisk which they say is the stone arrow; to a hole in the mountain, 289 feet high and 88 feet wide, which they say is the aperture made by the arrow in its flight through the hat; and to the horseman on Senjen Island, apparently riding a colossal steed and drawing the folds of his wide cavalry cloak closely about him. As for the nun whose singing had so disturbed Senjemand, she was petrified too, and never troubled any one with her psalmody again.

Another legend relates that one of the mountain giants, annoyed by the ringing of church bells more than fifty miles away, once caught up a huge rock, which he hurled at the sacred building. Fortunately it fell short and broke in two. Ever since then, the peasants say that the trolls come on Christmas Eve to raise the largest piece of stone upon golden pillars, and to dance and feast beneath it. A lady, wishing to know whether this tale were true, once sent her groom to the place. The trolls came forward and hospitably offered him a drink from a horn mounted in gold and ornamented with runes. Seizing the horn, the groom flung its contents away and dashed off with it at a mad gallop, closely pursued by the trolls, from whom he escaped only by passing through a stubble field and over running water. Some of their number visited the lady on the morrow to claim this horn, and when she refused to part with it they laid a curse upon her, declaring that her castle would be burned down every time the horn should be removed. The prediction has thrice been fulfilled, and now the family guard the relic with superstitious care. A similar drinking vessel, obtained in much the same fashion by the Oldenburg family, is exhibited in the collection of the King of Denmark.

The giants were not supposed to remain stationary, but were said to move about in the darkness, sometimes transporting masses of earth and sand, which they dropped here and there. The sandhills in northern Germany and Denmark were supposed to have been thus formed.

A North Frisian tradition relates that the giants possessed a colossal ship, called Mannigfual, which constantly cruised about in the Atlantic Ocean. Such was the size of this vessel that the captain was said to patrol the deck on horseback, while the rigging was so extensive and the masts so high that the sailors who went up as youths came down as gray-haired men, having rested and refreshed themselves in rooms fashioned and provisioned for that purpose in the huge blocks and pulleys.

By some mischance it happened that the pilot once directed the immense vessel into the North Sea, and wishing to return to the Atlantic as soon as possible, yet not daring to turn in such a small space, he steered into the English Channel. Imagine the dismay of all on board when they saw the passage growing narrower and narrower the farther they advanced. When they came to the narrowest spot, between Calais and Dover, it seemed barely possible that the vessel, drifting along with the current, could force its way through. The captain, with laudable presence of mind, promptly bade his men soap the sides of the ship, and to lay an extra-thick layer on the starboard, where the rugged cliffs of Dover rose threateningly. These orders were no sooner carried out than the vessel entered the narrow space, and, thanks to the captain's precaution, it slipped safely through. The rocks of Dover scraped off so much soap, however, that ever since they have been particularly white, and the waves dashing against them still have an unusually foamy appearance.

This exciting experience was not the only one through which the Mannigfual passed, for we are told that it once, nobody knows how, penetrated into the Baltic Sea, where, the water not being deep enough to keep the vessel afloat, the captain ordered all the ballast to be thrown overboard. The material thus cast on either side of the vessel into the sea formed the two islands of Bornholm and Christiansoë.

In Thuringia and in the Black Forest the stories of the giants are legion, and one of the favourites with the peasants is that about Ilse, the lovely daughter of the giant of the Ilsenstein. She was so charming that far and wide she was known as the Beautiful Princess Ilse, and was wooed by many knights, of whom she preferred the Lord of Westerburg. But her father did not at all approve of her consorting with a mere mortal, and forbade her to see her lover. Princess Ilse was wilful, however, and in spite of her sire's prohibition she daily visited her lover. The giant, exasperated by her persistency and disobedience, finally stretched out his huge hands and, seizing the rocks, tore a great gap between the height where he dwelt and the castle of Westerburg. Upon this, Princess Ilse, going to the cleft which parted her from her lover, recklessly flung herself over the precipice into the raging flood beneath, and was there changed into a bewitching undine. She dwelt in the limpid waters for many a year, appearing from time to time to exercise her fascinations upon mortals, and even, it is said, captivating the affections of the Emperor Henry, who paid frequent visits to her cascade. Her last appearance, according to popular belief, was at Pentecost, a hundred years ago; and the natives have not yet ceased to look for the beautiful princess, who is said still to haunt the stream and to wave her white arms to entice travellers into the cool spray of the waterfall.

The giants inhabited all the earth before it was given to mankind, and it was only with reluctance that they made way for the human race, and retreated into the waste and barren parts of the country, where they brought up their families in strict seclusion. Such was the ignorance of their offspring, that a young giantess, straying from home, once came to an inhabited valley, where for the first time in her life she saw a farmer ploughing on the hillside. Deeming him a pretty plaything, she caught him up with his team, and thrusting them into her apron, she gleefully carried them home to exhibit to her father. But the giant immediately bade her carry peasant and horses back to the place where she had found them, and when she had done so he sadly explained that the creatures whom she took for mere playthings, would eventually drive the giant folk away, and become masters of the earth.

The Dwarfs

EARLIER WE SAW HOW the black elves, dwarfs, or Svart-alfar, were bred like maggots in the flesh of the slain giant Ymir. The gods, perceiving these tiny, unformed creatures creeping in and out, gave them form and features, and they became known as dark elves, on account of their swarthy complexions. These small beings were so homely, with their dark skin, green eyes, large heads, short legs, and crow's feet, that they were enjoined to hide underground, being commanded never to show themselves during the daytime lest they should be turned into stone. Although less powerful than the gods, they were far more intelligent than men, and as their knowledge was boundless and extended even to the future, gods and men were equally anxious to question them.

The dwarfs were also known as trolls, kobolds, brownies, goblins, pucks, or Huldra folk, according to the country where they dwelt.

These little beings could transport themselves with marvellous celerity from one place to another, and they loved to conceal themselves behind rocks, when they would mischievously repeat the last words of conversations overheard from such hiding-places. Owing to this well-known trick, the echoes were called dwarfs' talk, and people fancied that the reason why the makers of such sounds were never seen was because each dwarf was the proud possessor of a tiny red cap which made the wearer invisible. This cap was called Tarnkappe, and without it the dwarfs dared not appear above the surface of the earth after sunrise for fear of being petrified. When wearing it they were safe from this peril.

Helva, daughter of the Lord of Nesvek, was loved by Esbern Snare, whose suit, however, was rejected by the proud father with the scornful words: "When thou shalt build at Kallundborg a stately church, then will I give thee Helva to wife."

Now Esbern, although of low estate, was proud of heart, even as the lord, and he determined, come what might, to find a way to win his coveted bride. So off he strode to a troll in Ullshoi Hill, and effected a bargain whereby the troll undertook to build a fine church, on completion of which Esbern was to tell the builder's name or forfeit his eyes and heart.

Night and day the troll wrought on, and as the building took shape, sadder grew Esbern Snare. He listened at the crevices of the hill by night; he watched during the day; he wore himself to a shadow by anxious thought; he besought the elves to aid him. All to no purpose. Not a sound did he hear, not a thing did he see, to suggest the name of the builder.

Meantime, rumour was busy, and the fair Helva, hearing of the evil compact, prayed for the soul of the unhappy man.

Time passed until one day the church lacked only one pillar, and worn out by black despair, Esbern sank exhausted upon a bank, whence he heard the troll hammering the last stone in the quarry underground. "Fool that I am," he said bitterly, "I have builded my tomb."

Just then he heard a light footstep, and looking up, he beheld his beloved. "Would that I might die in thy stead," said she, through her tears, and with that Esbern confessed how that for love of her he had imperilled eyes and heart and soul.

Then fast as the troll hammered underground, Helva prayed beside her lover, and the prayers of the maiden prevailed over the spell of the troll, for suddenly Esbern caught the sound of a troll-wife singing to her infant, bidding it be comforted, for that, on the morrow, Father Fine would return bringing a mortal's eyes and heart.

Sure of his victim, the troll hurried to Kallundborg with the last stone. "Too late, Fine!" quoth Esbern, and at the word, the troll vanished with his stone, and it is said that the peasants heard at night the sobbing of a woman underground, and the voice of the troll loud with blame.

The dwarfs, as well as the elves, were ruled by a king, who, in various countries of northern Europe, was known as Andvari, Alberich, Elbegast, Gondemar, Laurin, or Oberon. He dwelt in a magnificent subterranean palace, studded with the gems which his subjects had mined from the bosom of the earth, and, besides untold riches and the Tarnkappe, he owned a magic ring, an invincible sword, and a belt of strength. At his command the little men, who were very clever smiths, would fashion marvellous jewels or weapons, which their ruler would bestow upon favourite mortals.

We have already seen how the dwarfs fashioned Sif's golden hair, the ship Skidbladnir, the point of Odin's spear Gungnir, the ring Draupnir, the golden-bristled boar Gullin-bursti, the hammer Miolnir, and Freyia's golden necklace Brisinga-men. They are also said to have made the magic girdle which Spenser describes in his poem of the 'Faerie Queene,' – a girdle which was said to have the power of revealing whether its wearer were virtuous or a hypocrite.

The dwarfs also manufactured the mythical sword Tyrfing, which could cut through iron and stone, and which they gave to Angantyr. This sword, like Frey's, fought of its own accord, and could not be sheathed, after it was once drawn, until it had tasted blood. Angantyr was so proud of this weapon that he had it buried with him; but his daughter Hervor visited his tomb at midnight, recited magic spells, and forced him to rise from his grave to give her the precious blade. She wielded it bravely, and it eventually became the property of another of the Northern heroes.

Another famous weapon, which according to tradition was forged by the dwarfs in Eastern lands, was the sword Angurvadel which Frithiof received as a portion of his inheritance from his fathers. Its hilt was of hammered gold, and the blade was inscribed with runes which were dull until it was brandished in war, when they flamed red as the comb of the fighting-cock.

The dwarfs were generally kind and helpful; sometimes they kneaded bread, ground flour, brewed beer, performed countless household tasks, and harvested and threshed the grain for the farmers. If ill-treated, however, or turned to ridicule, these little creatures would forsake the house and never come back again. When the old gods ceased to be worshipped in the Northlands, the dwarfs withdrew entirely from the country, and a ferryman related how he had been hired by a mysterious personage to ply his boat back and forth across the river one night, and at every trip his vessel was so heavily laden with invisible passengers that it nearly sank. When his night's work was over, he received a rich reward, and his employer informed him that he had carried the dwarfs across the river, as they were leaving the country for ever in consequence of the unbelief of the people.

According to popular superstition, the dwarfs, in envy of man's taller stature, often tried to improve their race by winning human wives or by stealing unbaptized children, and substituting their own offspring for the human mother to nurse. These dwarf babies were known as changelings, and were recognisable by their puny and wizened forms. To recover possession of her own babe, and to rid herself of the changeling, a woman was obliged either to brew beer in egg-shells or to grease the soles of the child's feet and hold them so near the flames that, attracted by their offspring's distressed cries, the dwarf parents would hasten to claim their own and return the stolen child.

The troll women were said to have the power of changing themselves into Maras or nightmares, and of tormenting any one they pleased; but if the victim succeeded in stopping up the hole through which a Mara made her ingress into his room, she was entirely at his mercy, and he could even force her to wed him if he chose to do so. A wife thus obtained was sure to remain as long as the opening through which she had entered the house was closed, but if the plug were removed, either by accident or design, she immediately effected her escape and never returned.

Naturally, traditions of the little folk abound everywhere throughout the North, and many places are associated with their memory. The well-known Peaks of the Trolls (Trold-Tindterne) in Norway are said to be the scene of a conflict between two bands of trolls, who in the eagerness of combat omitted to note the approach of sunrise, with the result that they were changed into the small points of rock which stand up noticeably upon the crests of the mountain.

Some writers have ventured a conjecture that the dwarfs so often mentioned in the ancient sagas and fairy-tales were real beings, probably the Phoenician miners, who, working the coal, iron, copper, gold, and tin mines of England, Norway, Sweden, etc., took advantage of the simplicity and credulity of the early inhabitants to make them believe that they belonged to a supernatural race and always dwelt underground, in a region which was called Svartalfaheim, or the home of the black elves.

Babylonian Demons

BABYLONIAN DEMONS WERE LEGION and most of them exceedingly malevolent. The Utukku was an evil spirit that lurked generally in the desert, where it lay in wait for unsuspecting travellers, but it did not confine its haunts to the more barren places, for it was also to be found among the mountains, in graveyards, and even in the sea. An evil fate befell the man upon whom it looked.

The Rabisu is another lurking demon that secretes itself in unfrequented spots to leap upon passers-by. The Labartu, which has already been alluded to, is, strangely enough, spoken of as the daughter of Anu. She was supposed to dwell in the mountains or in marshy places, and was particularly addicted to the destruction of children. Babylonian mothers were wont to hang charms round their children's necks to guard them against this horrible hag.

The Sedu appears to have been in some senses a guardian spirit and in others a being of evil propensities. It is often appealed to at the end of invocations along with the Lamassu, a spirit of a similar type. These malign influences were probably the prototypes of the Arabian jinn, to whom they have many points of resemblance.

Many Assyrian spirits were half-human and half-supernatural, and some of them were supposed to contract unions with human beings, like the Arabian jinn. The offspring of such unions was supposed to be a spirit called Alu, which haunted ruins and deserted buildings and indeed entered the houses of men like a ghost to steal their sleep. Ghosts proper were also common enough, as has already been observed, and those who had not been buried were almost certain to return to harass mankind. It was dangerous even to look upon a corpse, lest the spirit or edimmu of the dead man should seize upon the beholder. The Assyrians seemed to be of the opinion that a ghost like a vampire might drain away the strength of the living, and long formulae were in existence containing numerous names of haunting spirits, one of which it was hoped would apply to the tormenting ghost, and these were used for the purposes of exorcism. To lay a spirit the following articles were necessary: seven small loaves of roast corn, the hoof of a dark-coloured ox, flour of roast corn, and a little leaven. The ghosts were then asked why they tormented the haunted man, after which the flour and leaven were kneaded into a paste in the horn of an ox and a small libation poured into a hole in the earth. The leaven dough was then placed in the hoof of an ox, and another libation poured out with an incantation to the god Shamash. In another case figures of the dead man and the living person to whom the spirit has appeared are to be made and libations poured out before both of them, then the figure of the dead man is to be buried and that of the living man washed in pure water, the whole ceremony being typical of sympathetic magic, which thus supposed the burial of the body of the ghost and the purification of the living man. In the morning incense was to be offered up before the sun-god at his rising, when sweet woods were to be burned and a libation of sesame wine poured out.

If a human being was troubled by a ghost, it was necessary that he should be anointed with various substances in order that the result of the ghostly contact might be nullified.

An old text says, "When a ghost appeareth in the house of a man there will be a destruction of that house. When it speaketh and hearkeneth for an answer the man will die, and there will be lamentation."

Babylonian Vampires

IN ALL LANDS AND EPOCHS the grisly conception of the vampire has gained a strong hold upon the imagination of the common people, and this was no less the case in Babylonia and Assyria than elsewhere.

There have not been wanting those who believed that vampirism was confined to the Slavonic race alone, and that the peoples of Russia, Bohemia, and the Balkan Peninsula were the sole possessors of the vampire legend. Recent research, however, has exposed the fallacy of this theory and has shown that, far from being the property of the Slavs or even of Aryan peoples, this horrible belief is or was the possession of practically every race, savage or civilized, that is known to anthropology. The seven evil spirits of Assyria are, among other things, vampires of no uncertain type. An ancient poem which was chanted by them commences thus (note the last lines in particular):

Seven are they! Seven are they!
In the ocean deep, seven are they!
Battening in heaven, seven are they!
Bred in the depths of the ocean;
Not male nor female are they,
But are as the roaming wind-blast.
No wife have they, no son can they beget;
Knowing neither mercy nor pity,
They hearken not to prayer, to prayer.
They are as horses reared amid the hills,
The Evil Ones of Ea;
Throne-bearers to the gods are they,
They stand in the highway to befoul the path;
Evil are they, evil are they!
Seven are they, seven are they,
Twice seven are they!

Destructive storms (and) evil winds are they,
An evil blast that heraldeth the baneful storm,
An evil blast, forerunner of the baleful storm.
They are mighty children, mighty sons,
Heralds of the Pestilence.
Throne-bearers of Ereskigal,
They are the flood which rusheth through the land.
Seven gods of the broad earth,
Seven robber(?)-gods are they,
Seven gods of might,
Seven evil demons,
Seven evil demons of oppression,
Seven in heaven and seven on earth.

Spirits that minish heaven and earth,
That minish the land,
Spirits that minish the land,
Of giant strength,
Of giant strength and giant tread,
Demons (like) raging bulls, great ghosts,
Ghosts that break through all houses,
Demons that have no shame,
Seven are they!
Knowing no care, they grind the land like corn;
Knowing no mercy, they rage against mankind,
They spill their blood like rain,
Devouring their flesh (and) sucking their veins.

Where the images of the gods are, there they quake (?)
In the Temple of Nabu, who fertilises the shoots (?) of wheat.
They are demons full of violence, ceaselessly devouring blood.

Gihilihili: The Snake-man

THERE WAS ONCE a middle-aged woman living in a small village who for many years had tried to conceive a child. At last, when she had almost abandoned all hope, she discovered she was pregnant. The news filled her with great joy and she longed for the day when she could sit proudly amongst the other women holding her new-born infant in her arms.

But when nine months had passed and the time arrived for the woman to deliver her child, there was no sign of it emerging, and for several more years the infant remained within her womb, refusing to show itself. Eventually however, the woman began to suffer labour pains and was taken to her bed where she gave birth after a long and painful ordeal. She was surprised that her husband did not bring the infant to her and when she looked in his direction she saw that his eyes were filled with horror. Then she searched for the child, but no child lay on the bed. Instead she saw a long, thick-necked snake coiled up beside her, its body warm and glistening, its head lifted affectionately towards her.

Suddenly her husband grabbed hold of a shovel from a corner of the hut and began striking the snake furiously. But the woman cried out for him to stop at once:

"Do not harm the creature," she pleaded, "treat it with respect and gentleness. No matter what you may think of it, that snake is still the fruit of my womb."

The man lowered his shovel and went outdoors. Soon he returned to the hut accompanied by a group of village elders. They gathered around the bed and began to examine the snake more closely. At length, the wisest among them spoke to the husband and wife:

"We have no reason to treat this creature unkindly," he told them. "Take it to the forest and build a house for it there. Let it be free to do as it pleases. Let it grow to maturity unharmed so that it may shed its skin in the normal way."

The husband carried the snake to the heart of the forest and left it there as the elders had ordered him, making certain that it had a comfortable home to live in and a plentiful supply of food to survive on.

The years passed by quickly, and the snake grew to an impressive size, ready for the day when its old skin would be replaced by a new one. And as it wandered deeper into the forest the most wonderful transformation began to occur. The old skin started to shrink away to reveal a young man, tall, strong and handsome. The young man stood up and glanced around him. Then, lifting the snakeskin from the ground, he took a deep breath and followed the path through the forest back towards his parents' home.

Both mother and father were overjoyed to discover that the snake-creature they had abandoned so many years before had changed into such a fine and handsome youth. All the other members of the family were invited to assemble at the hut to admire their beautiful son and a great feast was held to welcome him into the community.

After their son had been with them several weeks, the father sat down with him one evening to discuss who would make the best wife for him.

"I have already chosen the daughter of Bwenge to be my wife," the young man told his father. "Even while I crawled on my belly through the forests I knew I would one day marry her. Each time she came to gather wood, I sat and watched and my love went out to her. Each time she came to get water, my love went out to her. Each time she came to cut grass for the young cattle, my love went out to her."

"You are not rich enough for such a match," his father replied. "We are poor people, and she is the daughter of a noble chief."

But the son said nothing further on the subject and called for a great fire to be made. As soon as the flames had grown quite tall, he cast the snakeskin which once covered his body into the centre of the fire, calling for his father and mother to keep a careful watch on it. They looked on in amazement as the skin crackled noisily and transformed itself into an array of valuable objects. Cattle, sheep and fowls began to leap from the flames. Drums, calabashes and churns began to appear, together with all other kinds of wealthy possessions.

Next morning the father and his son went in search of the daughter of Bwenge and presented to the chief a selection of these goods. The chief was more than satisfied by all that he saw and arranged for his daughter to be married immediately. The young man led his new wife back to his village where he made a home for them both. They were very happy together and lived long and fruitful lives, enriched by the birth of many healthy children.

The Snake-man grew old among the people who came to regard him as a man of profound wisdom and courage. Whenever there was trouble they turned to him for advice, and even after he died, his words lived on in their memory and they often recounted the story of his birth, mindful of what he had told them.

"Never allow yourself to be destroyed by misfortune," he had said.

"Never despair of yourself or of others. And above all, never condemn a person for his appearance."

The Sultan's Snake-child

ONCE UPON A TIME there was a Sultan and his Wazir, and those two men were very rich with much wealth, but neither had a son.

They took counsel together, "How will it be when we die? Who shall we leave all this wealth to and we are without children?"

The Sultan said to the Wazir, "We must go to a far country and look for some wise man who will tell us what to do."

So they went away, and wandered on and on for three years, till at last they met an old woman, bent with the weight of many years.

That woman said to them, "My grandsons, I know what you have come for."

Then she sank down to the bottom of a big lake, and when she came up again out of the water she brought in her hands two charms, which were two slimy roots; one for the Sultan and one for the Wazir. And she said, "Take these, and when you return home you will find that your wish has already been accomplished; but to these charms I give you there are conditions attached. When you arrive in your town, you must tell no man about it, and take heed that in the way you neither chirrup nor look back."

Then she shook her withered hand and said, "It has taken you three years to come; you will return in one month. Farewell."

Then the Sultan and the Wazir set off home.

In the way the Wazir said, "Allah be praised that our wish has been granted." The Sultan, forgetting the old woman's warning, chirruped, as much as to say, "I will believe when I see."

After one month they came to the gate of their town, and as they entered the cannons sounded and the news spread forth, "There is an heir in the palace of the Sultan, and there is an heir in the house of the Wazir."

The Wazir returned to his house swiftly, and there he found a most beautiful boy.

The Sultan came to the palace, and there he found a snake.

When he heard that the Wazir had a lovely child he was very pleased, and he used to go every day to the Wazir's house to see that child, but he told his people to throw that snake out of the palace.

Now there was a slave girl in the palace called Mizi, and when she saw them taking that snake to throw it in the river she said, "Give me that snake, that I may bring him up as my child."

So Mizi took that snake and wore him round her neck till he grew, and then she came to the Sultan and said, "Build me a grass hut, that I may live there with my child, the snake."

So a hut was built for her, and she stayed there by herself with that snake. She took her cooking pots there, and cooked food for herself and the snake. Every day she fed that snake, and it grew and grew, till at last it filled up the whole hut.

Then that snake said to Mizi, "Go and tell the Sultan that his little snake wants a stone house of seven storeys in which to live. He must look for craftsmen who are not afraid, to come and build the house, and what they ask must be given them."

So Mizi came and told those words to the Sultan, and craftsmen who had no fear were sought for. They came and built a house of seven storeys in the space of seven days, and the wages they asked for were given them.

When the house was finished, they said, "Go and tell the little snake that the house is ready."

Then Mizi and the snake moved into that house and lived there. Till one day the snake said to Mizi, "Go and look for a sage who will teach me learning, but he must be master of his heart and unafraid. He must come of his own free will."

So she went and sought a man of learning, but everyone she asked to come replied, "I am not going so as to be swallowed whole by that snake."

At last she found a sage who said, "I will go, for I see that Mizi lives with this snake and is not devoured, so why should I be eaten?"

So that professor came and taught the snake learning of every kind, and when he had finished he went to the Sultan and received the pay he asked for.

So the snake and Mizi lived together, till one day that snake said to her, "Now you must go and look for a wife for me; but she must come of her own free will, and what money she wants she must have."

So a wife for the snake was sought for in all the land, but none was found; all said, "Who wants to go and be swallowed whole by a big snake?"

Now in that country was a very poor man who had seven daughters. When the news came to them all refused, till the seventh and youngest was asked, and she replied, "We are very poor; I will go and be eaten by that snake. What matter?"

So that girl was taken and decked out with pearls and precious stones and clothes of silk, and then Mizi was called and told, "This is the wife of your master, the snake. Take her."

So Mizi took her and brought her to the snake, and he said, "Arrange everything for her comfort."

When night had come, Mizi slept with that girl till, when twelve o'clock came, that snake came out from inside his skin. He put on wooden sandals and went to the bathroom and made his ablutions. When he had finished washing he took his prayer mat and spread it out and prayed and read the Koran.

After that he came and sat near that girl and looked at her and said, "My wife is beautiful; she has beautiful eyes, lovely ears and long straight hair. Hhum! Poor me, who am a snake. Sleep, my beautiful wife."

Then he entered his skin again and slept.

Seven days passed in this way, and on the eighth Mizi said to that girl, "I will fasten a thread to your thumb; when I pull it open your eyes and look at him."

That night, at twelve o'clock, the snake came out of his skin, and then Mizi pulled the thread and that girl awoke and opened her eyes and saw a wondrously handsome Arab youth: in all that country there was no youth so handsome as that son of the Sultan.

The snake went to the bathroom and made his ablutions, and then returned and prayed and read the Koran.

At the time of the before dawn breezes he came and looked at his wife and then returned to his skin. When dawn came Mizi and that girl took counsel together, and then Mizi went to the Sultan and said to him, "Give me three tins of oil and ten maunds of firewood."

When she had got them she had them brought to the house.

Then she said to that girl, "Now we must dig a pit here in the other room."

So they dug a pit and put in it the firewood and then poured the oil over it.

That night they watched till after midnight. When the youth went to the bathroom they got up and seized on the skin and tried to drag it into the pit, but it was too heavy for them. So they exerted all their strength, till at last they managed to drag it into the pit. After that they set fire to the wood and the oil.

When its owner in the bathroom heard the skin crackling he ran in and said to Mizi, "What have you done, taking away my clothes to put in the fire?" Then he fell down, and did not regain consciousness till three o'clock next day, for that youth did not know the world outside of his skin.

When he recovered Mizi cooked porridge for him, and when he had eaten it he said to Mizi, "Go to the Sultan and tell him to make offerings, nine shells full of alms; for the day after tomorrow I will go out."

So Mizi went with the news to the Sultan, but he replied, "Go back and get eaten by that snake. We do not want any more of your folly; for you have taken the poor man's daughter and brought her to the snake, and she has already been swallowed up. Now you in your turn will be eaten, and today, I suppose, you have come to take leave of us."

Mizi returned and said to that youth, "He will not give the offering."

He replied, "Then leave him; he who has had no luck does not trust to luck. On Friday I will come forth by the power of Allah, alone."

When Friday came he decked his horse with pearls and precious stones and rode off to the mosque to pray amongst all the people; but the Sultan did not know that it was his son.

Then Mizi came forth and trilled and shouted for joy, and told everyone in the mosque: "Look at me today, for it is today that my son, the snake, has come to life."

Many people thought that Mizi had gone mad. When the Sultan had finished praying he came forth, and Mizi said to him, "Today my child has come forth."

The Sultan said, "Peace be upon you;" and he followed that youth on his horse and knew that it was his son, and rejoiced greatly.

He said to his slaves, "Run to the palace, spread out diamonds and cushions, carpets and mats; do not leave anything of any value, but spread everything out."

Then was the wedding of that girl, the poor man's daughter, and the snake held with great festivity. So that snake and Mizi lived happily, and he loved her as if she had been his own mother. When he became Sultan he gave the kingdom to her, he gave Mizi what spoke and what did not speak; it became her country, because she had nurtured that snake from its infancy until it became a full-grown man of wisdom.

Morongoe the Snake

MOKETE WAS A CHIEF'S DAUGHTER, but she was also beautiful beyond all the daughters of her father's house, and Morongoe the brave and Tau the lion both desired to possess her, but Tau found not favour in the eyes of her parents, neither desired she to be his wife, whereas Morongoe was rich and the son of a great chief, and upon him was Mokete bestowed in marriage.

But Tau swore by all the evil spirits that their happiness should not long continue, and he called to his aid the old witch doctor, whose power was greater than the tongue of man could tell; and one day Morongoe walked down to the water and was seen no more. Mokete wept and mourned for her brave young husband, to whom she had been wedded but ten short moons, but Tau rejoiced greatly.

When two more moons had waned, a son was born to Mokete, to whom she gave the name of Tsietse (sadness). The child grew and throve, and the years passed by, but brought no news of Morongoe.

One day, when Tsietse was nearly seven years old, he cried unto his mother, saying, "Mother, how is it that I have never seen my father? My companions see and know their fathers, and love them, but I alone know not the face of my father, I alone have not a father's protecting love."

"My son," replied his mother, "a father you have never known, for the evil spirits carried him from amongst us before ever you were born." She then related to him all that had happened.

From that day Tsietse played no more with the other boys, but wandered about from one pool of water to another, asking the frogs to tell him of his father.

Now the custom of the Basuto, when anyone falls into the water and is not found, is to drive cattle into the place where the person is supposed to have fallen, as they will bring him out. Many cattle had been driven into the different pools of water near Morongoe's village, but as they had failed to bring his father, Tsietse knew it was not much use looking near home. Accordingly, one day he went to a large pond a long distance off, and there he asked the frogs to help him in his search. One old frog hopped close to the child, and said, "You will find your father, my son, when you have walked to the edge of the world and taken a leap into the waters beneath; but he is no longer as you are, nor does he know of your existence."

This, at last, was the information Tsietse had longed for, now he could begin his search in real earnest. For many days he walked on, and ever on. At length, one day, just as the sun was setting, he saw before him a large sea of water of many beautiful colours. Stepping into it, he began to ask the same question; but at every word he uttered, the sea rose up, until at length it covered his head, and he began falling, falling through the deep sea. Suddenly he found himself upon dry ground, and upon looking round he saw flocks and herds, flowers and fruit, on every side. At first he was too much astonished to speak, but after a little while he went up to one of the herd boys and asked him if he had ever seen his (Tsietse's) father. The herd boy told him many strangers visited that place, and he had better see the chief, who would be able to answer his question.

When Tsietse had told his story to the chief, the old man knew at once that the great snake which dwelt in their midst must be the child's father; so, bidding the boy remain and rest, he went off to consult with the snake as to how they should tell Tsietse the truth without frightening him; but as they talked, Tsietse ran up to them, and, seeing the snake, at once embraced it, for he knew it was his father.

Then there was great joy in the heart of Morongoe, for he knew that by his son's aid he should be able to overcome his enemy, and return at length to his wife and home. So he told Tsietse how Tau had persuaded the old witch doctor to turn him into a snake, and banish him to this world below the earth. Soon afterwards Tsietse returned to his home, but he was no longer a child, but a noble youth, with a brave, straight look that made the wicked afraid. Very gently he told his mother all that had happened to him, and how eager his father was to return to his home. Mokete consulted an old doctor who lived in the mountain alone, and who told her she must get Tsietse to bring his father to the village in the brightness of the day-time, but that he must be so surrounded by his followers from the land beyond that none of his own people would be able to see him.

Quickly the news spread through the village that Morongoe had been found by his son and was returning to his people.

At length Tsietse was seen approaching with a great crowd of followers, while behind them came all the cattle which had been driven into the pools to seek Morongoe. As they approached Mokete's house the door opened and the old doctor stood upon the threshold.

Making a sign to command silence, he said: – "My children, many years ago your chief received a grievous wrong at the hand of his enemy, and was turned into a snake, but by the love and faithfulness of his son he is restored to you this day, and the wiles of his enemy are made of no account. Cover, then, your eyes, my children, lest the Evil Eye afflict you."

He then bade the snake, which was in the centre of the crowd, enter the hut, upon which he shut the door, and set fire to the hut. The people, when they saw the flames, cried out in horror, but the old doctor bade them be still, for that no harm would come to their chief, but rather a great good. When everything was completely burnt, the doctor took from the middle of the ruins a large burnt ball; this he threw into the pool near by, and lo! from the water up rose Morongoe, clad in a kaross, the beauty of which was beyond all words, and carrying in his hand a stick of shining black, like none seen on this earth before, in beauty, or colour, or shape. Thus was the spell broken through the devotion of a true son, and peace and happiness restored, not only to Mokete's heart, but to the whole village.

The Maid and Her Snake-lover

WHEN OUR FATHERS' FATHERS WERE CHILDREN, there lived in the valley of the rivers two chiefs, who governed their people wisely and with great kindness. The name of the one was Mopeli, and of the other Khosi.

Now Mopeli had a son whom he loved as his own heart, a youth, tall and brave, and fearless as the young lion. To him was given the name of Tsiu. When Tsiu was able to stand alone, and to play on the mat in front of his father's dwelling, a daughter was born unto the chief Khosi, to whom was given the name of Tebogo. The years passed, and Tsiu and Tebogo grew and thrived. Often the youth drove his father's cattle down towards the lands where Tebogo and her father's maidens worked, and many happy days were spent, while the love each bore the other grew and strengthened, even as they themselves grew older.

When the time came for Tsiu to take a wife, he went to his father and asked that Tebogo might be given him, for none other could he wed. Gladly the parents consented, and preparations were made for the wedding.

Now Tebogo had another lover, upon whom she looked with scorn, but who had vowed that never, never should she be the bride of Tsiu; so he consulted a witch doctor, who promised to aid him. Imagine then his joy when, ere the wedding feast had begun, he heard that Tsiu had disappeared. "Now," thought he, "Tebogo shall be mine;" but the maiden turned from him in anger, nor would her parents listen to his suit.

Meanwhile desolation hung over the home of the chief Mopeli. "My son, my son," cried the unhappy father; but no voice replied, no son came back to rejoice his father's heart.

When the moon had once more grown great in the heavens, an old man came to the village of Mopeli, and called the chief to him. Long they talked, and greatly the people wondered. At length they arose, and, saluting each other, parted at the door of the chief's dwelling. Mopeli then departed for the village of Chief Khosi, where he remained all night. The next day he returned to his own village, and bade his people prepare a great feast.

In the village of the Chief Khosi, also, much wonder filled the people's minds, for they, likewise, were commanded to make ready a marriage feast, for the chief's daughter, the lovely Tebogo, was about to be married, but none knew to whom.

Calling his daughter to him, Khosi said, "My child, your lover Tsiu has been taken from you, so it is my wish that you should marry one who has found favour in my eyes."

"Tell me, my father," replied Tebogo, "who is the man you have chosen for me? Let me at least know his name."

"Nay, my child, that I cannot do," answered Khosi, and with this the maiden was obliged to be content. Behold then her horror when she was brought forth to meet her bridegroom, to find not a man, but a snake. All the people cried "shame" upon the parents who could be so cruel as to wed their daughter to a reptile.

With cries and tears Tebogo implored her parents to spare her; in vain were her entreaties. She was told to take her reptile husband home to the new hut which had been built for them, near the large pool where the cattle drank. Tremblingly she obeyed, followed by her maidens, the snake crawling by her side. When she entered the hut, she tried to shut out the snake, but it darted half its body through the door, and so terrified her that she ran to the other end of the hut.

The snake followed, and began lashing her with its tail, till she ran out of the hut down to the clump of willows which grew by the side of the pool. Here she found an old doctor sitting, and to him she told her trouble. "My daughter," he said, "return to your hut. Do not let the snake see you, but close the door very softly from the outside, and set fire to the hut. When it is all burnt down, you will find the ashes of the snake lying in a little heap in the centre of the hut. Bring them here, and cast them into the water."

Tebogo did as the old doctor directed her, and while the hut was burning, many people ran from both the villages to see what had happened; but Tebogo called to them to keep away, as she was burning the snake. When all was destroyed, she went up, took the ashes of the snake, which she found in the middle of the ruins, and, putting them into a pitcher, ran with them down to the pool and threw them in. No sooner had she done so, than from the water arose, not a snake, but her lover Tsiu. With a joyful cry, she flung herself into his arms, and a great shout went up from all the people gathered there.

As the lightning darts across the heaven, so the news of Tsiu's return spread from hut to hut, and great was the people's wonderment. The story of how he had been turned into a snake, and banished to the pool, until he could find a maiden whose parents would bestow her upon him in marriage, and of how the good old doctor Int had revealed the secret to Mopeli, was soon told. For many days there was feasting and merry-making in the homes of Mopeli the chief and of Khosi, while in the hearts of Tsiu and his bride Tebogo there dwelt a great content; but the wicked lover fled to the mountains, where he cherished a bitter hatred in his heart against Tebogo and her husband, and longed for the time when he could be revenged.

Ali of the Crooked Arm

LONG AGO IN OLDEN DAYS there was a country, and the Sultan of that country had seven wives and the Wazir also had seven wives.

And the seven wives of the Sultan had seven children, and the seven wives of the Wazir had seven children, all boys.

The seventh child of the Sultan had only one eye, but the seventh child of the Wazir was wondrously beautiful. They called him Ali; but oh, misfortune, one arm was crooked.

Now all these fourteen children were brought up together till, by the power of Allah, they grew up into youths.

That seventh child of the Sultan, his companion was always Ali, the seventh child of the Wazir.

So those children grew up, and they were sent to school until they finished learning.

The Wazir's seventh child said to his father, "Buy me a white horse;" and the Sultan's seventh son said to his father, "Buy me a white horse."

So each one had a white horse given him with fine trappings.

Then one day the crier was sent forth to beat his horn and proclaim, "On Friday there is a meeting at the Sultan's. Everyone must bring his horse. There will be racing between the Sultan's son and the Wazir's son."

So people came with their horses, and the Wazir's son said, "I will go first," and the Sultan's son said, "I will go first," till grown-up men said, "Do not contend one against another like that."

So the Sultan's son went first, and the Wazir's son followed behind him. Then all who were present followed, every man on his horse, but the horses of the Wazir's son and the Sultan's son leaped and soared like kites, higher and higher.

At half-past six o'clock they all returned safely.

Next day Ali said to the Sultan's son, "Let us first go to the plantation, and remain in the garden till four o'clock, and then let us both go and play on horseback."

So they went into the garden at noon and gathered pomegranates and ate.

The Sultan's son said, "Let each one of us pluck a pomegranate and put it in his pocket."

So they each picked a pomegranate, but behold, in that one which Ali took was living the Jin of Jehan, who carries off children from year to year.

After this they returned to the palace and found their horses already saddled.

They mounted, and the Wazir's son struck his horse with his whip, and it soared over the clouds like a kite. And the Sultan's son followed his companion, his horse leaping. He saw his friend soaring and flying away in front till, as six o'clock struck, he saw him no more, so he returned weeping and in great distress.

Ali flew away on his horse till he found himself in the Jin's house, and he lifted up his voice and cried, "Alas, I am already lost."

That Jin sought a house, and told Ali, "Put your horse in here and fasten it apart."

On the second day he said to him, "Ali, do you see this big cooking-pot? Your work will be to keep up the fire under it."

On the third day the Jin gave into his hands all the keys of his house, seven in all, and he said to him, "You may open this one room, but these other six you may not open."

The demon then set out to go and walk about, saying to Ali as he left, "Today I am going out to walk, and tomorrow I will return. You are to look after this pot, but you must not lift the lid to see what is in it."

When the demon had gone Ali lifted up the lid to see what was in the pot, and he saw human flesh stewing.

Then Ali said to himself, "Ah! My father, the demon, eats human flesh." Then he thought, "I, too, will be eaten. Whatever God wishes is best." As he thought he played with a knife in his hand and cut his finger.

In the evening the old demon returned and called out, "Hi, Ali!" and he answered him, "Here, father."

When he came to him the demon said, "Oh dog, what have you done to your finger?"

Ali said, "Father, why are you angry and speaking fiercely to me? I am afraid."

So the Jin said to him, "Come now, undo your finger that I may see." Then he touched it and healed it up.

They slept that night, and in the morning the Jin said to him, "Ali, I am going out to walk about for the space of fourteen days, and then I will return."

Ali said to him, "Very good, father."

When the Jin had gone Ali sat and thought out different plans, and he said to himself, "My father, the demon, said that I must not open all the rooms, but today I will open them and see what is in them."

So he went and opened the first room, and saw an enormous horse, most wondrously beautiful.

When the horse saw Ali he neighed, and said to him, "What plan have you? Father said goodbye to you like that, saying that he would return on the fourteenth day, to deceive you. He will come back to eat you on the eighth day."

Then he said, "Go and open all the rooms, and then return here that I may advise you."

Ali went and opened the second room, and saw seven maidens, sitting each one in a box and reading a Koran. Their hair was long and very beautiful.

Ali asked them, "How now?"

Those maidens answered him, "We have been put here so that we may be eaten together with you. We have been lost to our parents many years."

He locked that room and went and opened the third. There he found swords with jewelled hilts fighting in the air by themselves, and he was very astonished.

Ali locked up the third room again, and now there were three rooms he had not yet opened.

He opened the fourth room, and found it filled from top to bottom with precious stones. Then he opened the fifth room, and found it full of grain; this was the horse's food.

He then went and unlocked the sixth room, and there he found the horse's saddle and bridle, adorned with jewels, and he found seven bottles; the first was full of sun, the second of rain, the third of needles, the fourth of hail, the fifth of thorns, the sixth of mud, and the seventh of sea.

Then he returned to the horse's room, and when he saw Ali he neighed and shook his head.

The horse said to Ali, "We who are in this house are as if we were already dead; we will all be eaten alike."

Then he said, "Open the wheat store quickly, that I may eat, for the time is nearly spent when that evil-disposed Jin will return."

Ali went and brought a sack of grain and opened it, and the horse ate and said, "Bring me a second sack, for I am not yet satisfied."

He brought a second, and the horse ate and finished it, and said, "Bring a third, for I am not yet full."

So he ate a third sack, and then he said, "Bring a bucket of water, stir it up with sugar, for that is the kind of water that I drink, and mix me up another bucket with bhang."

Then he said, "Now I am satisfied. Bring my saddle and the seven bottles, and take bags and fill them with precious stones and fasten them on quickly, that we may go."

So Ali put all the valuables in the house in bags, and he took those seven maidens and placed them in bags, and he saddled the horse and fastened those bags on to him.

Then the horse said, "Strap me up tight and with all your strength."

So Ali strapped him up as tight as he could, till the horse said, "Stop now; mount me for a little to try me."

So Ali mounted and smacked him, and he soared up over the clouds. Then he returned and said, "Now bring out another sack of grain, that I may eat and be satisfied."

So he gave him another sack, and then he said, "Now fasten another sack of grain on to me, lest I grow hungry in the way."

So Ali fastened on a sack of grain, and then the horse said, "Take a crow-bar and dig there in the floor of the house."

So Ali dug there and found more precious stones, and he put them in bags, and brought them and fastened them to the saddle.

Then the horse said, "Come on, Ali, mount me. We are going now, and this advice I give you before we go. In the way we will meet with great strife, so listen well, and do as I tell you."

Then Ali mounted and smacked him, and the horse soared up over the clouds, higher and higher.

When they had gone a little way they met the Jin and a host of his fellow demons, whom he had brought to feast on those eight people in his house. One was taking an axe to chop up the meat, others carried firewood and pots and water with which to cook the flesh.

When those demons saw them they called out, "Look, there is the flesh going off."

The horse said to Ali, "Take the bottle of sun and break it." So Ali broke it, and the sun shone on the demons and scorched them.

But they pursued them, crying, "Our meat is going away, our meat is going away."

They ran after them, and as they came near the horse said, "Break the bottle of rain." So Ali broke the bottle and rain poured on them, but still they pursued.

Ali looked round and said, "They are coming." So the horse said, "Break the bottle of needles."

Ali broke the bottle, and many got needles in their feet and could not run quickly, but many escaped and came on swiftly, crying, "Hi there! Hi there! our meat is escaping."

Then the horse said, "Break the bottle of hail." So Ali broke the bottle, and the hail poured down on them, and knocked many of them over, but they got up again and ran on.

The horse said, "Break the bottle of thorns." So Ali broke the bottle, and the thorns got in their feet and delayed many of them, but the rest came on. Ali called out, "There they come," and the horse said, "Break the bottle of mud."

So he broke the bottle, and the demons went slipping and falling about in the mud till they got across it, and still pursued them.

Then the horse said, "Break the bottle of sea." So Ali broke the bottle, and the demons rushed into the sea, where many were drowned, and the rest were unable to cross and turned back.

The horse flew across to the opposite side and alighted, and said to Ali, "Let us rest here now that we have crossed safely."

Then he said, "Take out the sack of grain, for hunger is paining me."

So Ali gave him the grain, and he ate till he could eat no more, and he did not finish it, because he was so tired.

Then he said, "When we have nearly arrived, stand in the midst of the way, that I may give you advice."

Ali replied to him, "Very good, father."

After that they went on till they were nearly at their journey's end, and then Ali stood still in the middle of the way, and the horse stood still and said to Ali, "The first counsel I give you, that you must take it to heart, is that when you arrive home you must speak to no one for the space of seven days. If you want to do anything, first ask me, that I may advise you whether to do it or not; and if you want to marry a wife and place her in your house, you must first ask me.

"And if, when you arrive home, you want to walk abroad, you must first ask me, for I know all things great and small. If you walk out without telling me, that Jin of Jehan will take you; you will return home no more."

Ali replied, "It is well, father; I have heard."

Then they journeyed on and went their way.

At three o'clock the people of that town saw a dust coming.

There in the Wazir's house the Wazir himself was on the roof looking out, and his middle son was there with him upstairs; he and his father were looking out at that road by which Ali had been lost to them.

That Wazir, his hair covered his face, as he had not cut it, and he could not see for weeping for his son.

Then the people of that town saw a wondrously big horse soaring and soaring like a kite.

Ali entered the town, but he spoke to no one.

The door of his house had been left open since the day he had set out, and he passed in, he and the horse, but he spoke to no one, and there were great rejoicings at his return.

Ali stayed for the space of seven days, neither speaking to anyone, nor drinking water, nor bathing, for fear of being bewitched by that Jin. If he wanted food it was the horse who brought it to him, and if he wanted water it was the horse who gave it to him.

When the eighth day came there was a big festival at the Wazir's and at the Sultan's, for the child who had been dead was alive, he who had been lost to sight was restored to view.

If Ali wanted to walk out it was necessary for him first to take counsel of the horse. On the tenth day Ali brought all his riches downstairs and filled ninety-nine store-rooms full.

So Ali lived, he did not marry nor did he want a wife, and those seven sisters of his, whom he had brought away from amongst the Jins, they did not marry, but they read their Korans night and day.

He built a house of seven storeys, and, in this house he put his seven sisters who had come with him from the Jins.

This is the end of the fable.

Ryangombe and Binego

RYANGOMBE'S FATHER WAS BABINGA, described as the 'king of the ghosts (*imandwa*)'; his mother, originally called Kalimulore, was an uncomfortable sort of person, who had the power of turning herself into a lioness, and took to killing her father's cattle, till he forbade her to herd them, and sent someone else in her place. She so frightened her first husband that he took her home to her parents and would have no more to do with her. After her second marriage, to Babinga, there seems to have been no further trouble.

When Babinga died, his son, Ryangombe, announced that he was going to take his father's place. This was disputed by one of Babinga's followers named Mpumutimuchuni, and the two agreed to decide the question by a game of *kisoro*, which Ryangombe lost.

Ryangombe passed some time in exile. He went out hunting, and heard a prophecy from some herd-lads which led to his marriage. After some difficulties with his parentsin-law he settled down with his wife, and had a son, Binego, but soon left them and returned to his own home.

As soon as Binego was old enough, his mother's brother set him to herd the cattle; he speared a heifer the first day, a cow and her calf the next, and when his uncle objected he speared him too. He then called his mother, and they set out for Ryangombe's place, which they reached in due course, Binego having, on the way, killed two men who refused to leave their work and guide him, and a baby, for no particular reason.

When he arrived, he found his father playing the final game with Mpumutimuchuni. The decision had been allowed to stand over during the interval, and Ryangombe, if he lost this game, was not only to hand over the kingdom, but to let his opponent shave his head – that is, deprive him of the crest of hair which marked his royal rank. Binego went and stood behind his father to watch the game, suggested a move which enabled him to win, and when Mpumutimuchuni protested, stabbed him. Thus he secured his father in the kingship, which, apparently, was so far counted to him for righteousness as to outweigh all the murders he had committed. Ryangombe named him, first as his second-in-command and afterwards as his successor, and Binego, as will be seen, avenged his death. Like all the *imandwa*, with the exception of Ryangombe himself, who is uniformly kind and beneficent, Binego is mischievous and cruel.

Ryangombe's Death

The story of his death is as follows.

Ryangombe one day went hunting, accompanied by his sons, Kagoro and Ruhanga, two of his sisters, and several other *imandwa*. His mother tried to dissuade him from going, as during the previous night she had had four strange dreams, which seemed to her prophetic of evil. She had seen, first, a small beast without a tail; then an animal all of one colour; thirdly, a stream running two ways at once; and, fourthly, an immature girl carrying a baby without a *ngobe* (the skin in which an African woman carries a baby on her back; the Zulus call it *imbeleko*). She was very uneasy about these dreams, and begged her son to stay at home, but, unlike most Africans, who attach great importance to such things, he paid no attention to her words, and set out. Before he had gone very far he killed a hare, which, when examined, was found to have no tail. His personal attendant at once exclaimed that this was the fulfilment of Nyiraryangombe's dream, but Ryangombe only said, "Don't repeat a woman's words while we are after game."

Soon after this they encountered the second and third portents (the "animal all of one colour" was a black hyena), but Ryangombe still refused to be impressed. Then they met a young girl carrying a baby, without the usual skin in which it is supported. She stopped Ryangombe and asked him to give her a *ngobe*. He offered her the skin of one animal after another; but she refused them all, till he produced a buffalo hide. Then she said she must have it properly dressed, which he did, and also gave her the thongs to tie it with. Thereupon she said, "Take up the child." He objected, but gave in when she repeated her demand, and even, at her request, gave the infant a name. Finally, weary of her importunity, he said, "Leave me alone!" and the girl rushed away, was lost to sight among the bushes, and became a buffalo. Ryangombe's dogs, scenting the beast, gave chase, one after the other, and when they did not return he sent his man, Nyarwambali, to see what had become of them. Nyarwambali came back and reported: "There is a beast here which has killed the dogs." Ryangombe followed him, found the buffalo, speared it, and thought he had killed it, but just as he was shouting his song of triumph it sprang up, charged, and gored him. He staggered back and leaned against a tree; the buffalo changed into a woman, picked up the child, and went away.

At the very moment when he fell, a bloodstained leaf dropped out of the air on his mother's breast. She knew then that her dream had in fact been a warning of disaster; but it was not till a night and a day had passed that she heard what had happened. Ryangombe, as soon as he knew he had got his death-wound, called all the *imandwa* together, and told first one and, on his refusal, another to go and call his mother and Binego. One after another all refused, except the maidservant, Nkonzo, who set off at once, travelling night and day, till she came to Nyiraryangombe's house and gave her the news. She came at once with Binego, and found her son still living. Binego, when he had heard the whole story, asked his father in which direction the buffalo had gone; having had it pointed out, he rushed off, overtook the woman, brought her back, and killed her, with the child, cutting both in pieces. So he avenged his father.

Ryangombe then gave directions for the honours to be paid him after his death; these are, so to speak, the charter of the Kubandwa society which practises the cult of the *imandwa*. He specially insisted that Nkonzo, as a reward for her services, should have a place in these rites. Then at the moment when his throat tightened, he named Binego as his successor, and so died.

Hlakanyana's Precocious Development and Mischievous Pranks

THEY SAID THAT "Uhlakanyana is a very cunning man; he is also very small, of the size of a weasel", "it is as though he really was of that genus; he resembles it in all respects" – hence his other name *icakide*.

Hlakanyana was a chief's son. Like Ryangombe, he spoke before he was born; in fact, he repeatedly declared his impatience to enter the world. No sooner had he made his appearance than he walked out to the cattle kraal, where his father had just slaughtered some oxen, and the men were sitting round, ready for a feast of meat. Scared by this portent – for they had been waiting for the birth to be announced – they all ran away, and Hlakanyana sat down by the fire and began to eat a strip of meat which was roasting there. They came back, and asked the mother whether this was really the expected baby. She answered, "It is he"; whereupon they said, "Oh, we thank you, our queen. You have brought forth for us a child who is wise as soon as he is born. We never saw a child like this child. This child is fit to be the great one among all the king's children, for he has made us wonder by his wisdom."

But Hlakanyana, thinking that his father did not take this view, but looked upon him as a mere infant, asked him to take a leg of beef and throw it downhill, over the kraal fence (the gateway being on the upper side). All the boys and men present were to race for it, and "he shall be the man who gets the leg." They all rushed to the higher opening, but Hlakanyana wormed his way between the stakes at the lower end of the kraal, picked up the leg, and carried it in triumph to meet the others, who were coming round from the farther side. He handed it over to his mother, and then returned to the kraal, where his father was distributing the rest of the meat. He offered to carry each man's share to his hut for him, which he did, smeared some blood on the mat (on which meat is laid to be cut up), and then carried the joint to his mother. He did this to each one in turn, so that by the evening no house had any meat except that of the chiefs wife, which was overstocked. No wonder that the women cried out, "What is this that has been born today? He is a prodigy, a real prodigy!" His next feat was to take out all the birds which had been caught in the traps set by the boys, and bring them home, telling his mother to cook them and cover the pots, fastening down the lids. He then went off to sleep in the boys' house (*ilau*), which he would not ordinarily have entered for several years to come, and overbore their objections, saying, "Since you say this I shall sleep here, just to show you!" He rose early in the morning, went to his mother's house, got in without waking her, opened the pots, and ate all the birds, leaving only the heads, which he put back, after filling the lower half of the pots with cow dung, and fastened down the lids. Then he went away for a time, and came back to play Huveane's trick on his mother. He pretended to have come in for the first time, and told her that the sun had risen, and that she had slept too long – for if the birds were not taken out of the pot before the sun was up they would turn into dung. So he washed himself and sat down to his breakfast, and when he opened the pots it was even as he had said, and his mother believed him. He finished up the heads, saying that, as she had spoilt his food she should not have even these, and then announced that he did not consider himself her child at all, and that his father was a mere man, one of the people and nothing more. He would not stay with them, but would go on his travels. So he picked up his stick and walked out, still grumbling about the loss of his birds.

He Goes on His Travels

When he had gone some distance and was beginning to get hungry he came upon some traps with birds in them and, beginning to take them out, found himself stuck fast. The owner of the traps was a 'cannibal' – or, rather, an ogre – who, finding that birds had more than once disappeared from his traps, had put sticks smeared with birdlime in front of them. Now he came along to look at them, and found Hlakanyana, who, quite undisturbed, addressed him thus: "Don't beat me, and I will tell you. Take me out and cleanse me from the birdlime and take me home with you. Have you a mother?" The ogre said he had. Hlakanyana, evidently assuming that he was to be eaten, said that if he were beaten and killed at once his flesh would be ruined for the pot. "I shall not be nice; I shall be bitter. Cleanse me and take me home with you, that you may put me in your house, that I may be cooked by your mother. And do you go away and just leave me at your home. I cannot be cooked if you are there; I shall be bad; I cannot be nice."

The ogre, a credulous person, like most of his kind, did as he was asked, and handed Hlakanyana over to his mother, to be cooked next morning.

When the ogre and his younger brother were safely out of the way, Hlakanyana proposed to the old woman that they should "play at boiling each other." He got her to put on a large pot of water, made up the fire under it, and when it was beginning to get warm he said, "Let us begin with me." She put him in and covered the pot. Presently he asked to be taken out, and then, saying that the fire was not hot enough, made it up to a blaze and began, very rudely, to unfasten the old woman's skin petticoat. When she objected he said: "What does it matter if I have unfastened your dress, I who am mere game, which is about to be eaten by your sons and you?" He thrust her in and put on the lid. No sooner had he done so than she shrieked that she was being scalded; but he told her that could not be, or she would not be able to cry out. He kept the lid on till the poor creature's cries ceased, and then put on her clothes and lay down in her sleeping place. When the sons came home he told them to take their 'game' and eat; he had already eaten, and did not mean to get up. While they were eating he slipped out at the door, threw off the clothes, and ran away as fast as he could. When he had reached a safe distance he called out to them, "You are eating your mother, you cannibals!" They pursued him hot-foot; he came to a swollen river and changed himself into a piece of wood. They came up, saw his footprints on the ground, and, as he was nowhere in sight, concluded he had crossed the river and flung the piece of wood after him. Safe on the other bank, he resumed his own shape and jeered at the ogres, who gave up the pursuit and turned back.

He Kills a Hare, Gets a Whistle and Is Robbed of It

Hlakanyana went on his way, and before very long he spied a hare. Being hungry, he tried to entice it within reach by offering to tell a tale, but the hare would not be beguiled. At last, however (this part of the story is not very clear, and the hare must have been a different creature from the usual

Bantu hare!), he caught it, killed it, and roasted it, and, after eating the flesh, made one of the bones into a whistle. He went on, playing his whistle and singing:

"I met Hloya's mother,
And we cooked each other.
I did not burn;
She was done to a turn."

In time he came to a large tree on the bank of a river, overhanging a deep pool. On a branch of the tree lay an iguana, who greeted him, and Hlakanyana responded politely. The iguana said, "Lend me your whistle, so that I can hear if it will sound." Hlakanyana refused, but the iguana insisted, promising to give it back. Hlakanyana said, "Come away from the pool, then, and come out here on to the open ground; I am afraid near a pool. I say you might run into the pool with my whistle, for you are a person that lives in deep water." The iguana came down from his tree, and when Hlakanyana thought that he was at a safe distance from the river he handed him the whistle. The iguana tried the whistle, approved the sound, and wanted to take it away with him. Hlakanyana would not hear of this, and laid hold of the iguana as he was trying to make off, but received such a blow from the powerful tail that he had to let go, and the iguana dived into the river, carrying the whistle with him.

Hlakanyana again went on till he came to a place where a certain old man had hidden some bread. He ran off with it, but not before the owner had seen him; the old man evidently knew him, for he called out, "Put down my bread, Hlakanyana." Hlakanyana only ran the faster, the old man after him, till, finding that the latter was gaining on him, he crawled into a snake's hole. The old man put in his hand and caught him by the leg. Hlakanyana cried, laughing, *"He! He!* you've caught hold of a root!" So the old man let go, and, feeling about for the leg, caught a root, at which Hlakanyana yelled, "Oh! oh! you're killing me!" The old man kept pulling at the root till he was tired out and went away. Hlakanyana ate the bread in comfort, and then crawled out and went on his way once more.

The Ogre Husband

THERE WAS A GIRL NAMED MBODZE, who had a younger sister, Matsezi, and a brother, Nyange. She went one day, with six other girls, to dig clay – either for plastering the huts or for making pots, which is usually women's work. There was a stone in the path, against which one after the other stubbed her toes; Mbodze, coming last, picked up the stone and threw it away. It must be supposed that the stone was an ogre who had assumed this shape for purposes of his own; for when the girls came back with their loads of clay they found that the stone had become a huge rock, so large that it shut out the view of their village, and they could not even see where it ended. When they found that they could not get past it the foremost in the line began to sing:

"Stone, let me pass, O stone! It is not I who threw you away, O stone!
She who threw you away is Mbodze, Matsezi's sister,
And Nyange is her brother."

The rock moved aside just enough to let one person pass through, and then closed again. The second girl sang the same words, and was allowed to pass, and so did the rest, till it came to Mbodze's turn. She, too, sang till she was tired, but the rock did not move. At last the rock turned into a *zimwi* (ogre) – or, rather, we may suppose, he resumed his proper shape – seized hold of Mbodze, and asked her, "What shall I do with you? Will you be my child, or my wife, or my sister, or my aunt?" She answered, "You may do what you like with me." So he said, "I will make you my wife"; and he carried her off to his house.

There was a wild fig tree growing in front of the *zimwi's* house. Mbodze climbed up into it, and sang:

"Matsezi, come, come! Nyange, come, come!"

But Matsezi and Nyange could not hear her.

She lived there for days and months, and the *zimwi* kept her well supplied with food, till he thought she was plump enough to be eaten. Then he set out to call the other ogres, who lived a long way off and were expected to bring their own firewood with them. No sooner had he gone than there appeared a *chitsimbakazi* (sprite), who, by some magic art, put Mbodze into a hollow bamboo and stopped up the opening with wax. She then collected everything in the house except a cock, which she was careful to leave behind, spat in every room, including the kitchen, and on both the doorposts, and started.

Before she had gone very far she met the ogres, coming along the path in single file, each one carrying his log of wood on his head. The first one stopped her, and asked, "Are you Marimira's wife?" – Marimira being the ogre, Mbodze's husband.

She sang in answer, "I am not Marimira's wife: Marimira's wife has not a swollen mouth [like me]. *Ndi ndi!* This great bamboo!"

At each *ndi* she struck the bamboo on the ground, to show that it was hollow, and the ogre, seeing that the upper end was closed with wax, suspected nothing and passed on.

The other ogres now passed her, one after another. The second was less easily satisfied than the first had been, and insisted on having the bamboo unstopped, but when he heard a great buzzing of bees he said hastily, "Close it! Close it!" The same happened with all the rest, except the last, who was Marimira himself. He asked the same question as the others, and was answered in the same way, and then said, "What are you carrying in that stick? Unstop it and let me see!" The sprite, recognizing him, said to herself, "Now this is the end! It is Marimira; I must be very cunning," and she sang:

"I am carrying honey, ka-ya-ya!
I am carrying honey, brother, ka-ya-ya!
Ndi ndi! This great bamboo!"

But he kept on insisting that he must see, and at last she took out the wax: the bees swarmed out and began to settle upon him, and he cried in a panic, "*Funikia! Funikia!* Shut them up!"

So he passed on with his guests, and the sprite went on her way.

The ogres reached Marimira's house, and he called out, "*Mbodze!*" The spittle by the doorposts answered, "He-e!" He then cried, "Bring some water!" and a voice from inside answered, "Presently!" He got angry, and, leaving the others seated on the mats, went in and searched through the whole house, finding no one there and hearing nothing but the buzzing of flies. Terrified at the thought of the guests who would feel themselves to have been brought on false pretences, he dug a hole to hide in and covered himself with earth – but his one long tooth projected above the soil.

It will be remembered that a cock had been left in the house when everything else was removed; and this cock now began to crow, "*Kokoi koko-o-o!* Father's tooth is outside!"

The guests, waiting outside, wondered. "Hallo! Listen to that cock. What is he saying? "Come! Go in and see what Marimira is doing in there, for the sun is setting, and we have far to go!" So they searched the house, and, coming upon the tooth, dug him up and dragged him outside, where they killed, roasted, and ate him – all but his head. While doing so they sang:

"Him who shall eat the head, we will eat him too."

After a while one of them bit off a piece from the head; the others at once fell upon him and ate him. This went on till only one was left. He fixed up a rope to make a swing and climbed into it, but the rope was not strong enough; it broke, and he fell into the fire. And he began to cry out, "*Maye! Maye!* [Mother!] I'm dying!" And he started to chew himself there in the fire, and so perished.

Meanwhile the *chitsimbakazi* had reached Mbodze's home. A little bird flew on ahead, perched outside the house, and sang:

"Mother, sweep the yard! Mbodze is coming!"

The mother said, "Just listen to that bird! What does it say? It is telling us to sweep the yard, because Mbodze is coming." So she set to work at once, and presently the sprite arrived and said, "Let me have a bath, and then I will give you your daughter."

She gave her a bath and rubbed her with oil and cooked gruel for her. The sprite said, "Don't pour it into a big dish for me; put it into a coconut shell," which the woman did. When the *chitsimbakazi* had eaten she unstopped the bamboo and let Mbodze out, to the great joy of the whole family, who could not do enough to show their gratitude.

The Were-wolf Husband

THERE WAS ONCE A GIRL who refused to marry. Her parents, too, discouraged all wooers who presented themselves, as they said they would not give their daughter to any common man.

On a certain day the sword dance was going on at this girl's village, and men came from the whole countryside to take part in it. Among the dancers there appeared a tall and handsome young man, wearing a broad ring like a halo round his head, who drew all eyes by his grace and noble bearing. The maiden fell in love with him at first sight, and her parents also approved of him. The dancing went on for several days, during which time she scarcely took her eyes off him. But one day, as he happened to turn his back, she caught sight of a second mouth behind his head, and said to her mother, "That man is a *rimu*!" They would not believe it. "That fine fellow a *rimu*! Nonsense! Just you go with him and let him eat you, that's all!"

The suitor presented himself in due course, and the marriage took place. After spending some days with the bride's parents the couple left for their home. But her brothers, knowing the husband to be a *rimu*, felt uneasy, and followed them, without their knowledge, keeping in the bushes alongside the path. When they had gone some distance the husband stopped and said, "Look back and tell me if you can still see the smoke from your father's hut." She looked, and said that she could. They went on for another hour or two, and then he asked her if she could see the hills behind her home. She said yes, and again they went on. At last he asked her again if she could see the hills, and when he found that she could not said, "What will you do now? I am a *rimu*. Climb up into this tree and weep your last tears, for you must die!"

But her brothers, watching their chance, shot him with poisoned arrows, and he died. She came down from the tree, and the brothers took her home.

The Girl Who Married a Lion

A LION WENT TO A VILLAGE of human beings and married. And the people thought that maybe it was but a man and not a wild creature.

In due course the couple had a child. Some time after this the husband proposed that they should visit his parents, and they set out, accompanied by the wife's brother. In several parallel stories a younger brother or sister of the bride desires to go with her, and when she refuses follows the party by stealth, but there is no indication of this here.

At the end of the first day's journey they all camped in the forest, and the husband cut down thorn bushes and made a kraal (*mutanda*), after which he went away, saying that he was going to catch some fish in the river. When he was gone the brother said to his sister, "He has built this kraal very badly," and he took his axe and cut down many branches, with which to strengthen the weak places.

Meanwhile the husband had gone to seek out his lion relations, and when they asked him, "How many animals have you killed?" he replied, "Two and a young one." When darkness fell he had become a huge male lion, and led the whole clan (with a contingent of hyenas) to attack his camp. Those inside heard the stealthy footfalls and sat listening. The lions hurled themselves on the barrier, trying to break through, but it was too strong, and they fell back, wounded with the thorns. He who by day had been the husband growled: "M . . .," and the baby inside the kraal responded: "M . . .". Then the mother sang:

> *"The child has bothered me with crying; watch the dance!*
> *Walk with a stoop; watch the dance!"*

The were-lion's father, quite disgusted, said, "You have brought us to a man who has built a strong kraal; we cannot eat him." And as day was beginning to break they all retired to the forest.

When it was light the husband came back with his fish, and said that he had been detained, adding, "You were nearly eaten," meaning that his absence had left them exposed to danger. It seems to be implied that the others were taken in by his excuses, but the brother, at any rate, must have had his suspicions. When the husband had gone off again, ostensibly to fish, he said, "See, it was that husband of yours who wanted to eat us last night." So he went and walked about, thinking over the position. Presently he saw the head of a gnome (*akachekulu*) projecting from a deft in a tree; it asked him why he had come, and, on being told, said, "You are already done for; your brother-in-law is an ogre that has finished off all the people in this district." The creature then asked him to sweep out the midden inside his house – and after he had done so told him to cut down the tree, which it then hollowed out and made into a drum, stretching two prepared skins over the ends. It then slung the drum round the man's waist, and said, "Do as if you were going to do this" – that is, raise himself from the ground. And, behold, he found himself rising into the air, and he reached the top of a tree. The gnome told him to jump down, and he did so quite easily. Then it said, "Put your sister in the drum and go home." So he called her, and, having stowed her in it, with the baby, rose up and sat in the tree-top, where he began to beat the drum. The lion, hearing the sound, followed it, and when he saw the young man in the tree said, "Brother-in-law, just beat a little"; so the man beat the drum and sang:

"Boom, boom sounds the little drum
Of the sounding drum, sounds the little drum!
Ogre, dance, sounds the little drum
Of the sounding drum, sounds the little drum!"

The lion began to dance, and the skins he was wearing fell off and were blown away by the wind, and he had to go back and pick them up. Meanwhile the drum carried the fugitives on, and the lion pursued them as soon as he had recovered his skins. Having overtaken them, he called up into the tree, "Brother-in-law, show me my child!" and the following dialogue took place:

"What, you lion, am I going to show you a relation of mine?"

"Would I eat my child?" conveniently ignoring the fact that he had himself announced the killing of the young one.

"How about the night you came? You would have eaten us!"

Again the brother-in-law beat the drum, and the lion danced (apparently unable to help himself), and as before lost his skins, stopped to pick them up, and began the chase again, while the man went springing along the tree-tops like a monkey. At last he reached his own village, and his mother saw as it were a swallow settle in the courtyard of his home. She said, "Well, I never! Greeting, my child!" and asked where his sister was. He frightened her at first by telling her that she had been eaten by her husband, who was really a lion, but afterwards relented and told her to open the drum. Her daughter came out with the baby, safe and sound, and the mother said, praising her son, "You have grown up; you have saved your sister!" She gave him five slave girls.

The lion had kept up the pursuit, and reached the outskirts of the village, but, finding that his intended victims were safe within the stockade, he gave up and returned to the forest.

The Hyena Bridegroom

THERE WAS A GIRL in a certain village who refused all suitors, though several very decent young men had presented themselves. Her parents remonstrated in vain; she only said, "I don't like the young men of our neighbourhood; if one came from a distance I might look at him!" So they left off asking for her, and she remained unmarried for an unusually long time.

One day a handsome stranger arrived at the village and presented himself to the girl's parents. He had all the appearance of a rich man; he was wearing a good cloth, had ivory bracelets on his arms, and carried a gun and a powder-horn curiously ornamented with brass wire. The maiden exclaimed, on seeing him, "This is the one I like!" Her father and mother were more doubtful, as was natural, since no one knew anything about him; but in spite of all they could say she insisted on accepting him. He was, in fact, a hyena, who had assumed human shape for the time being. The usual marriage ceremonies took place, and the husband, in accordance with Yao and Nyanja custom, settled down at the village of his parents-in-law, and made himself useful in the gardens for the space of several months. At the end of that time he said that he had a great wish to visit his own people. His wife, whom he had purposely refrained from asking, begged him to let her accompany him. When all was ready for the journey her little brother, who was suffering from sore eyes, said he wanted to go too; but his sister, ashamed to be seen in company with such an object, refused him sharply. He waited till they had started, and then followed, keeping out of sight, till he was too far from home to be sent back.

They went on for many days, and at last arrived at the hyenas' village, where the bride was duly welcomed by her husband's relations. She was assigned a hut to sleep in, but, to keep her brother out of the way, she sent him into the hen house.

In the middle of the night, when she was asleep, the people of the village took their proper shape and, called together by the hyena husband, marched round the hut, chanting:

"Let us eat the game, but it is not fat yet."

The little boy in the hen-house was awake and heard them; his worst fears were confirmed. In the morning he told his sister what he had heard, but she would not believe him. So he told her to tie a string to her toe and put the end outside where he could get it. This he drew into the hen house, and that night, when the hyenas began their march, he pulled the string, and awakened his sister. She was now thoroughly frightened, and when he asked her next morning, "Did you hear them, sister?" she had nothing more to say.

The boy then went to his brother-in-law and asked him for the loan of an axe and an adze. The man (as he appeared to be), who had no notion that he was detected and every reason to show himself good-natured, consented at once, and watched him going off into the bush, well pleased that the child should amuse himself.

The latter soon found and cut down a tree such as he needed, and then began to shape a thing which he called *nguli* – something in the nature of a small boat. When he had finished it he got into it and sang:

"My boat! swing! swing!"

And the *nguli* began to rise up from the earth. As he went on singing it rose higher and higher, till it floated above the tops of the tallest trees. The hyena-villagers all rushed out to gaze at this wonder, and the boy's sister came with them. Then he sang once more:

"My boat! come down! down, de-de! come down!"

And it floated gently down to the ground. The people were delighted, and cried out to him to go up again. He made some excuse for a little delay, and whispered to his sister to get her bundle (which, no doubt, she had ready) and climb in. She did so, and when both were safely stowed he sang his first song once more. Again the vessel rose, and this time did not come down again. The spectators, after waiting in vain, began to suspect that their prey was escaping, and shouted to the boy to come back, but no attention was paid to them, and the *nguli* quickly passed out of sight. Before the day was out they found themselves above the courtyard of their home, and the boy sang the words which caused them to descend, so that they alighted on their mother's grain mortar. The whole family came running out and overwhelmed them with questions; the girl could not speak for crying with joy and relief, and her brother told the whole story, winding up with: "Look here, sister, you thought I was no good, because I had sore eyes – but who was it heard them singing, 'Let us eat her!' and told you about it?" The parents, too, while praising the boy, did not fail to point the moral for the benefit of their foolish daughter, who, some say, had to remain unmarried to the end of her days.

Khodumodumo, or Kammapa, the Swallowing Monster

ONCE UPON A TIME there appeared in our country a huge, shapeless thing called Khodumodumo (but some people call it Kammapa). It swallowed every living creature that came in its way. At last it came through a pass in the mountains into a valley where there were several villages; it went to one after another, and swallowed the people, the cattle, the goats, the dogs, and the fowls. In the last village was a woman who had just happened to sit down on the ash-heap. She saw the monster coming, smeared herself all over with ashes, and ran into the calves' pen, where she crouched on the ground. Khodumodumo, having finished all the people and animals, came and looked into the place, but could see nothing moving, for, the woman being smeared with ashes and keeping quite still, it took her for a stone. It then turned and went away, but when it reached the narrow pass (or *nek*) at the entrance to the valley it had swelled to such a size that it could not get through, and was forced to stay where it was.

Meanwhile the woman in the calves' pen, who had been expecting a baby shortly, gave birth to a boy. She laid him down on the ground and left him for a minute or two, while she looked for something to make a bed for him. When she came back she found a grown man sitting there, with two or three spears in his hand and a string of divining bones (*ditaola*) round his neck. She said, "Hallo, man! Where is my child?" and he answered, "It is I, Mother!" Then he asked what had become of the people, and the cattle, and the dogs, and she told him.

"Where is this thing, Mother?"

"Come out and see, my child."

So they both went out and climbed to the top of the wall surrounding the calves' kraal, and she pointed to the pass, saying, "That object which is filling the *nek*, as big as a mountain, that is Khodumodumo."

Ditaolane got down from the wall, fetched his spears, sharpened them on a stone, and set off to the end of the valley, where Khodumodumo lay. The beast saw him, and opened its mouth to swallow him, but he dodged and went round its side – it was too unwieldy to turn and seize him – and drove one of his spears into it. Then he stabbed it again with his second spear, and it sank down and died.

He took his knife, and had already begun to cut it open, when he heard a man's voice crying out, "Do not cut me!" So he tried in another place, and another man cried out, but the knife had already slashed his leg. Ditaolane then began cutting in a third place, and a cow lowed, and someone called out, "Don't stab the cow!" Then he heard a goat bleat, a dog bark, and a hen cackle, but he managed to avoid them all, as he went on cutting, and so, in time, released all the inhabitants of the valley.

There was great rejoicing as the people collected their belongings, and all returned to their several villages praising their young deliverer, and saying, "This young man must be our chief." They brought him gifts of cattle, so that, between one and another, he soon had a large herd, and he had his choice of wives among their daughters. So he built himself a fine kraal and married and settled down, and all went well for a time.

But the unintentionally wounded man never forgot his grudge, and long after his leg was healed began, when he noticed signs of discontent among the people, to drop a cunning word here and there and encourage those who were secretly envious of Ditaolane's good fortune, as well as those who suspected him because, as they said, he could not be a normal human being, to give voice to their feelings.

So before long they were making plans to get rid of their chief. They dug a pit and covered it with dry grass – just as the Bapedi did in order to trap Huveane – but he avoided it. They kindled a great fire in the courtyard, intending to throw him into it, but a kind of madness seized them; they began to struggle with each other, and at last threw in one of their own party. The same thing happened when they tried to push him over a precipice; in this case he restored to life the man who was thrown over and killed.

Next they got up a big hunt, which meant an absence of several days from the village. One night when the party were sleeping in a cave they induced the chief to take the place farthest from the entrance, and when they thought he was asleep stole out and built a great fire in the cave mouth. But when they looked round they saw him standing among them.

After this, feeling that nothing would soften their inveterate hatred, he grew weary of defeating their stratagems, and allowed them to kill him without offering any resistance. Some of the Basuto, when relating this story, add, "It is said that his heart went out and escaped and became a bird."

The Devouring Pumpkin

SOME LITTLE BOYS, playing in the gardens outside their village, noticed a very large gourd, and said, "Just see how big that gourd is getting!" Then the gourd spoke and said, "If you pluck me I'll pluck you!" They went home and told what they had heard, and their mother refused to believe them, saying, "Children, you lie!" But their sisters asked to be shown the place where the boys had seen the talking gourd. It was pointed out to them, and they at once went there by themselves, and said, as their brothers had done, "Just see how big that gourd is getting!" But nothing happened. They went home, and, of course, said that the boys had been making fun of them. Then the boys went again and heard the gourd speak as before. But when the girls went it was silent.

The gourd continued to grow: it became as big as a house, and began swallowing all the people in the village. Only one woman escaped – we are not told how. Having swallowed everyone within reach, the gourd made its way into a lake and stayed there.

In a short time, the woman bore a boy, and, apparently, they lived on together on the site of the ruined village. When the boy had grown older he asked his mother one day where his father was. She said, "He was swallowed up by a gourd which has gone into the lake." So he went forth, and when he came to a lake he called out, "Gourd, come out! Gourd, come out!" There was no answer, and he went on to another lake and repeated his command. He saw one ear of the gourd come out of the water (by which it would appear that the gourd had by this time assumed some sort of animal shape), and climbed a tree, where he kept on shouting, "Gourd, come out!" At last the gourd came out and set off in pursuit of him; but he ran home and asked his mother for his bow and quiver. He hastened back, and when he came in sight of the monster, loosed an arrow and hit it. He shot again and again, till, wounded by the tenth arrow, it died, roaring so that it could be heard from here to Vuga. The boy then called to his mother to bring a knife, cut open the gourd and liberated all the people.

The Broken Promise

AT THE HEART OF A SOLITARY FOREST, a hunter had built for himself and his family a small wooden lodge, having decided once and for all to withdraw from the company of his tribe. Their deceit and cruelty had caused him to turn from them and he had chosen the loneliest spot he could find, adamant that his three young children should never fall under their poisonous influence.

The years passed by and the family remained happy and peaceful in their new home until, one day, the father fell gravely ill, and took to his couch with little or no hope of a recovery. Day and night the family lovingly attended the sick man, exhausting all of their simple medicines on him, yet never failing to whisper words of encouragement in his ear. But at last, they resigned themselves to the fact that he would not regain his health and gathered around him in the dimly lit room, awaiting the departure of his spirit.

As death drew near, the sick man called for the skin door of the lodge to be thrown open so that he might witness the sun sinking in the evening sky one last time. Then he motioned to his eldest son to raise him up in the bed and with these words he addressed his grieving family:

"I must leave you very shortly," he said, "but I am satisfied that I have been a good father and that I have provided you with ample food and protected you from the storms and cold of our harsh climate.

"You, my partner in life," he continued, casting his eyes upon his wife, "you, I can leave behind with an easy conscience, for you do not have much longer here and will soon join me in the Isle of the Blessed. But oh, my children who have only just set off on life's great journey, you have every wickedness before you from which I can no longer offer you protection. The unkindness and ingratitude of men caused me to abandon my tribe, and while we have lived here in peace and harmony, those very men have caused the forests to echo with the cries of war.

"My wish for you is that you remain pure at heart and never follow the evil example of such men. I will go tranquilly to my rest only if I am certain that you will always cherish one other.

"My eldest son, my eldest daughter, promise to obey my dying command and never forsake your younger brother, for he is most in need of your care."

The sick man then closed his eyes and spoke no more, and after a few minutes' silence, when his family came to his bedside and called him by name, they found that his spirit did not answer, for it was already well on its way to the Land of Souls. After eight months, the mother sadly passed away also, but in her last moments she was careful to to remind the two eldest children of the promise they had made to their father. During the winter that followed her death, they could not have been more attentive to the delicate younger child, but as soon as the winter had passed, the older brother became restless and struggled increasingly to conceal his uneasy mood. Before long, he had reached a decision to break his promise to his father and to search out the village of his father's tribe.

"I am lonely and wretched here," he told his sister one morning. "Must I forever pretend that we are the only people in the world and sacrifice my youth to this miserable existence? No! I am determined to seek out the society of our fellow-men and nothing you can say will prevent me leaving."

"My brother," replied his sister, "I do not blame you for harbouring these desires, but we have made a solemn promise to cherish each other always and to protect the youngest of our family from all harm. Neither pleasure nor pain should separate us, for if we follow our own inclinations, he will surely become a victim of our neglect."

The young man made no reply to this and for some weeks afterwards continued on with his work as normal, every day exerting himself in the hunt to supply the wants of the family. But then, one evening, he failed to return home and when she searched his corner of the lodge, his sister found that all of his possessions had vanished. Turning aside from her little brother, she began to weep silently, knowing in her heart that he might never return and that, from now on, she would carry the burden of responsibility her father had placed upon them.

Five moons had waned, during which the young girl tenderly watched over her younger brother, feeding him, clothing him, and building a great fire every day to protect them both from the bitter winds. But soon the solitude of her life began to weary her unspeakably. She had nobody to converse with save the birds and beasts about her, nothing ever to look forward to and she felt at the bottom of her heart that she was entirely alone. Her younger brother was the only obstacle preventing her enjoying the companionship of others and there were times when she wished him dead so that she might escape and have a new life of her own.

At last, when she felt her patience had been entirely exhausted, she gathered into the lodge a large store of food and firewood and announced to her little brother: "My child, I must go in search of our older brother, but I have provided for you until my return. Do not leave the lodge until I reappear and you will remain safe."

Then she embraced the young boy warmly and set off with her bundle in search of the village of her father's tribe. Soon she had arrived at her destination and found her brother nicely settled with a wife of his own and two healthy sons. She had been prepared to chastize him severely, but she discovered quite quickly that there was much about the village that appealed to her own starved curiosity. Within a few weeks she had accepted a proposal of marriage from one of the most handsome warriors of the tribe and abandoned all thought of ever returning to the solitary lodge in the forest.

The poor younger brother had fully expected his sister to return, but the months passed by and soon he discovered he had eaten all of the food she had provided him with. Forced to trudge through the woods in search of food, he began picking whatever berries he could find and digging up roots with his pale, slender hands. These satisfied his hunger as long as the weather remained mild, but winter arrived briskly and now the berries were blighted by frost or hidden from view by a thick carpet of snow.

With each new day he was obliged to wander farther and farther from the lodge, sometimes spending the night in the clefts and hollows of old trees, glad of the opportunity to scavenge any scraps of food the wolves might leave for him.

At first fearful of these animals, in time he grew so desperate for food that he would sit waiting a few feet from their circle watching while they devoured their meat, patiently awaiting his share. The wolves themselves became accustomed to the sight of him, and seeming to understand his plight, developed a habit of leaving something behind for him to eat. In this way the little boy lived on through the savage winter, saved from starvation by the generosity of the wild beasts of the woods.

When spring had come and the ice sheets on the Great Lake began melting slowly, the boy followed the wolf pack to the pebbled shore. It so happened that on the same day he arrived, the older brother, whom he had almost entirely forgotten about, was fishing on the lake in his canoe and, hearing the cry of a child, stood up and listened with all his attention, wondering how any human creature could survive in such a bleak and hostile environment. Again, he heard the cry, but this time it sounded very familiar and so he hastened to the shore to confront its source. Here he came face to face with his little brother who had begun singing a mournful little song:

"Nesia, Nesia, shug wuh, gushuh!
Ne mien gun-iew! Ne mien gun-iew!
My brother, my brother,
I am almost a wolf!
I am almost a wolf!"

The wailing voice touched him deeply and as the song drew to a close, the young boy howled long and loudly, exactly like a wolf. Approaching closer to the spot, the elder brother was startled to see that the little fellow had indeed half changed into a wolf.

"My brother, my brother, come to me," he pleaded, but the boy fled, leaving behind paw-prints in the sand while he continued to sing:

"Ne mien gun-iew! Ne mien gun-iew!
I am almost a wolf."

The more eagerly the older brother called, the faster his brother fled from him and the more rapidly the change continued, until with a prolonged, mournful howl, his whole body was transformed.

The elder brother, sick with remorse, and hearing again the voice of his dying father, continued to cry out in anguish: "My brother! my brother!"

But the young boy leaped upon a bank and looking back, his eyes filled with a deep reproach, exclaimed: "I am a wolf!"

Then he bounded swiftly away into the depths of the forest and was never heard of again.

The Serpent-Men

AFTER OVER A MONTH on the war-path, an eminent band of Sioux warriors accompanied by their chief, were returning home to their encampment in the hills. When they were still quite a long way off, they were suddenly gripped by a savage hunger and decided amongst themselves to scatter in search of wild game to sustain them on the rest of their journey. Some dispersed to the woodlands while others headed for the plains, agreeing that the first to locate an animal should signal to the others to join in the pursuit, for no great warrior could ever enjoy the flesh of a creature he had not helped to track down.

They had been on the hunt for some time without having anything to show for their efforts when suddenly one of the braves, placing his ear to the ground, declared that he could hear a herd of buffalo approaching in the distance. The prospect of such an enjoyable chase greatly cheered the young warriors and they gathered around their chief, anxious to assist in the plan to intercept the animals.

Closer and closer came the sound of the herd. The chief and his men lay very still in the undergrowth, their arrows poised and ready to shoot as soon as the buffalo came into view. Suddenly, their target appeared, but to their absolute horror the group came face to face, not with the four-legged animals they had been expecting, but with a gigantic snake, its rattle held menacingly in the air, as large as a man's head. Although almost paralysed with terror, the chief somehow managed to raise his weapon and shot an arrow through the air which lodged itself in the snake's throat. The huge creature immediately keeled over and lay squirming and hissing in the earth for some minutes until all life had passed out of it.

Even though it lay dead, the Sioux warriors did not dare to approach the snake for quite some time but remained instead at a safe distance, debating what they should do with the carcass. Hunger beckoned once more and for the first time the chief was struck by the thought that they had, in fact, provided themselves with a perfectly good, if unusual, meal. He called up his men and ordered them to build a fire and soon they were helping themselves to a delicious stew, as flavoursome as the tenderest buffalo meat. Only one brave refused to partake of the meal. Even his extreme hunger could not conquer his scruples and he remained adamant that he would not join the others in tasting the body of a great rattling snake.

When the meal was over, the warriors felt both satisfied and drowsy and lay down beside the camp-fire for a brief rest in preparation for their ongoing journey. It was several hours before the chief awoke, but as he slowly opened his eyes, he imagined he must still be dreaming, for he observed that all around him, his men had turned to snakes. Then he gazed at his own body and cried out in alarm, for he himself was already half snake, half man. Hastily, he slithered towards his transformed warriors and observed that only one among them had not suffered the same fate as the others – the young brave who had earlier refused to try any of the food.

The serpent-men and their chief placed themselves under the protection of the young brave, requesting that he gather them together in a large robe and carry them to the summit of the high hill overlooking their village. Terrified by the sight of them and fearing he might soon be attacked, the boy raced all the way to the hill-top and flung the robe beneath some trees. But the snakes broke free quickly and, moving towards him, coiled themselves around his ankles. They had no wish to harm him, they assured him, and soon he discovered that they treated him very kindly, sharing with him their strange wisdom and their many mysterious charms.

"You must return to the village and visit our families for us," they said to him. "Tell the people not to be afraid, and say to our wives and children that we shall visit them in the summer when they should come out to greet us."

The young brave readily agreed to deliver this message and set off homewards without further delay. Tears filled the eyes of every villager as he informed them of the fate of their chief and the other great warriors of the tribe, but the people were determined not to let grief destroy them, and took some comfort in the news that they would at least see their loved ones again.

It was a hot summer's morning when the snakes arrived at the little village, striking up a loud, hissing chorus that immediately attracted the attention of every man, woman and child. Abruptly, the villagers gathered together and walked cautiously in the direction of the snakes, taking with them moccasins, leggings, saddles and weapons that once belonged to the missing warriors. Their hearts were filled with fear as they drew closer to the creatures and they stood, still at a safe distance, fully prepared to turn on their heels. But the chief, who sat at the centre of the serpent-men, rose up from the earth and spoke to his people reassuringly: "Do not be afraid of us," he called to them. "Do not flee from us, we mean you no harm."

From that moment, the people grew in confidence and moving boldly forwards, they formed a circle around the serpent-men and chatted to them long into the evening.

In the winter the snakes vanished altogether, but every summer, for as long as the villagers could remember, they returned, wearing a new and brilliant coat. The villagers always treated them with the greatest respect and taught their children to revere the serpent, so that even today if a snake appears in the pathway of a tribal warrior, he will always stop and talk to it, offering it some token of his friendship and regard.

The Man-Fish

A VERY GREAT WHILE AGO the ancestors of the Shawanos nation lived on the other side of the Great Lake, half-way between the rising sun and the evening star. It was a land of deep snows and much frost, of winds which whistled in the clear, cold nights, and storms which travelled from seas no eyes could reach. Sometimes the sun ceased to shine for moons together, and then he was continually before their eyes for as many more. In the season of cold the waters were all locked up, and the snows overtopped the ridge of the cabins. Then he shone out so fiercely that men fell stricken by his fierce rays, and were numbered with the snow that had melted and run to the embrace of the rivers. It was not like the beautiful lands – the lands blessed with soft suns and ever-green vales – in which the Shawanos now dwell, yet it was well stocked with deer, and the waters with fat seals and great fish, which were caught just when the people pleased to go after them. Still, the nation were discontented, and wished to leave their barren and inhospitable shores. The priests had told them of a beautiful world beyond the Great Salt Lake, from which the glorious sun never disappeared for a longer time than the duration of a child's sleep, where snow-shoes were never wanted – a land clothed with perpetual verdure, and bright with never-failing gladness. The Shawanos listened to these tales till they came to loathe their own simple comforts; all they talked of, all they appeared to think of, was the land of the happy hunting-grounds.

Once upon a time the people were much terrified at seeing a strange creature, much resembling a man, riding along the waves of the lake on the borders of which they dwelt. He had on his head long green hair; his face was shaped like that of a porpoise, and he had a beard of the colour of ooze.

If the people were frightened at seeing a man who could live in the water like a fish or a duck, how much more were they frightened when they saw that from his breast down he was actually fish, or rather two fishes, for each of his legs was a whole and distinct fish. When they heard him speak distinctly in their own language, and when he sang songs sweeter than the music of birds in spring, or the whispers of love from the lips of a beautiful maiden, they thought it a being from the Land of Shades – a spirit from the happy fishing-grounds beyond the lake of storms.

He would sit for a long time, his fish-legs coiled up under him, singing to the wondering ears of the Indians upon the shore the pleasures he experienced, and the beautiful and strange things he saw in the depths of the ocean, always closing his strange stories with these words, shouted at the top of his voice:

"Follow me, and see what I will show you."

Every day, when the waves were still and the winds had gone to their resting-place in the depths of the earth, the monster was sure to be seen near the shore where the Shawanos dwelt. For a great many suns they dared not venture upon the water in quest of food, doing nothing but wander along the beach, watching the strange creature as he played his antics upon the surface of the waves, listening to his songs and to his invitation:

"Follow me, and see what I will show you."

The longer he stayed the less they feared him. They became used to him, and in time looked upon him as a spirit who was not made for harm, nor wished to injure the poor Indian. Then they grew hungry, and their wives and little ones cried for food, and, as hunger banishes all fear, in a few days three canoes with many men and warriors ventured off to the rocks in quest of fish.

When they reached the fishing-place, they heard as before the voice shouting:

"Follow me, and see what I will show you."

Presently the man-fish appeared, sitting on the water, with his legs folded under him, and his arms crossed on his breast, as they had usually seen him. There he sat, eying them attentively. When they failed to draw in the fish they had hooked, he would make the water shake and the deep echo with shouts of laughter, and would clap his hands with great noise, and cry:

"Ha, ha! there he fooled you."

When a fish was caught he was very angry. When the fishers had tried long and patiently, and taken little, and the sun was just hiding itself behind the dark clouds which skirted the region of warm winds, the strange creature cried out still stronger than before:

"Follow me, and see what I will show you."

Kiskapocoke, who was the head man of the tribe, asked him what he wanted, but he would make no other answer than:

"Follow me."

"Do you think," said Kiskapocoke, "I would be such a fool as to go I don't know with whom, and I don't know where?"

"See what I will show you," cried the man-fish.

"Can you show us anything better than we have yonder?" asked the warrior.

"I will show you," replied the monster, "a land where there is a herd of deer for every one that skips over your hills, where there are vast droves of creatures larger than your sea-elephants, where there is no cold to freeze you, where the sun is always soft and smiling, where the trees are always in bloom."

The people began to be terrified, and wished themselves on land, but the moment they tried to paddle towards the shore, some invisible hand would seize their canoes and draw them back, so that an hour's labour did not enable them to gain the length of their boat in the direction of their homes. At last Kiskapocoke said to his companions:

"What shall we do?"

"Follow me," said the fish.

Then Kiskapocoke said to his companions:

"Let us follow him, and see what will come of it."

So they followed him – he swimming and they paddling, until night came. Then a great wind and deep darkness prevailed, and the Great Serpent commenced hissing in the depths of the ocean. The people were terribly frightened, and did not think to live till another sun, but the man-fish kept close to the boats, and bade them not be afraid, for nothing should hurt them.

When morning came, nothing could be seen of the shore they had left. The winds still raged, the seas were very high, and the waters ran into their canoes like melted snows over the brows of the mountains, but the man-fish handed them large shells, with which they baled the water out. As they had brought neither food nor water with them, they had become both hungry and thirsty. Kiskapocoke told the strange creature they wanted to eat and drink, and that he must supply them with what they required.

"Very well," said the man-fish, and, disappearing in the depths of the water, he soon reappeared, bringing with him a bag of parched corn and a shell full of sweet water.

For two moons and a half the fishermen followed the man-fish, till at last one morning their guide exclaimed:

"Look there!"

Upon that they looked in the direction he pointed out to them and saw land, high land, covered with great trees, and glittering as the sand of the Spirit's Island. Behind the shore rose tall mountains, from the tops of which issued great flames, which shot up into the sky, as the forks of the lightning cleave the clouds in the hot moon. The waters of the Great Salt Lake broke in small waves upon its shores, which were covered with sporting seals and wild ducks pluming themselves in the beams of the warm and gentle sun. Upon the shore stood a great many strange people, but when they saw the strangers step upon the land and the man-fish, they fled to the woods like startled deer, and were no more seen.

When the warriors were safely landed, the man-fish told them to let the canoe go; "for," said he, "you will never need it more." They had travelled but a little way into the woods when he bade them stay where they were, while he told the spirit of the land that the strangers he had promised were come, and with that he descended into a deep cave near at hand. He soon returned, accompanied by a creature as strange in appearance as himself. His legs and feet were those of a man. He had leggings and moccasins like an Indian's, tightly laced and beautifully decorated with wampum, but his head was like a goat's. He talked like a man, and his language was one well understood by the strangers.

"I will lead you," he said, "to a beautiful land, to a most beautiful land, men from the clime of snows. There you will find all the joys an Indian covets."

For many moons the Shawanos travelled under the guidance of the man-goat, into whose hands the man-fish had put them, when he retraced his steps to the Great Lake. They came at length to the land which the Shawanos now occupy. They found it as the strange spirits had described it. They married the daughters of the land, and their numbers increased till they were so many that no one could count them. They grew strong, swift, and valiant in war, keen and patient in the chase. They overcame all the tribes eastward of the River of Rivers, and south to the shore of the Great Lake.

Manabozho the Wolf

MANABOZHO SET OUT TO TRAVEL. He wished to outdo all others, and see new countries, but after walking over America, and encountering many adventures, he became satisfied as well as fatigued. He had heard of great feats in hunting, and felt a desire to try his power in that way.

One evening, as he was walking along the shores of a great lake, weary and hungry, he encountered a great magician in the form of an old wolf, with six young ones, coming towards him. The wolf, as soon as he saw him, told his whelps to keep out of the way of Manabozho.

"For I know," said he, "that it is he we see yonder."

The young wolves were in the act of running off, when Manabozho cried out:

"My grandchildren, where are you going? Stop, and I will go with you."

He appeared rejoiced to see the old wolf, and asked him whither he was journeying. Being told that they were looking out for a place where they could find the most game, and best pass the winter, he said he should like to go with them, and addressed the old wolf in these words:

"Brother, I have a passion for the chase. Are you willing to change me into a wolf?"

The old wolf was agreeable, and Manabozho's transformation was effected.

He was fond of novelty. He found himself a wolf corresponding in size with the others, but he was not quite satisfied with the change, crying out:

"Oh! make me a little larger."

They did so.

"A little larger still," he cried.

They said:

"Let us humour him," and granted his request.

"Well," said he, "that will do." Then looking at his tail:

"Oh!" cried he, "make my tail a little longer and more bushy."

They made it so, and shortly after they all started off in company, dashing up a ravine. After getting into the woods some distance, they fell in with the tracks of moose. The young wolves went after them, Manabozho and the old wolf following at their leisure.

"Well," said the wolf, "who do you think is the fastest of my sons? Can you tell by the jumps they take?"

"Why," replied he, "that one that takes such long jumps; he is the fastest, to be sure."

"Ha, ha! You are mistaken," said the old wolf. "He makes a good start, but he will be the first to tire out. This one who appears to be behind will be the first to kill the game."

Soon after they came to the place where the young ones had killed the game. One of them had dropped his bundle there.

"Take that, Manabozho," said the old wolf.

"Esa," he replied, "what will I do with a dirty dog-skin?"

The wolf took it up; it was a beautiful robe.

"Oh! I will carry it now," said Manabozho.

"Oh no," replied the wolf, who at the moment exerted his magic power. "It is a robe of pearls."

From that moment he lost no opportunity of displaying his superiority, both in the hunter's and magician's art, over his conceited companion.

Coming to a place where the moose had lain down, they saw that the young wolves had made a fresh start after their prey.

"Why," said the wolf, "this moose is poor. I know by the tracks, for I can always tell whether they are fat or not."

They next came to a place where one of the wolves had tried to bite the moose, and, failing, had broken one of his teeth on a tree.

"Manabozho," said the wolf, "one of your grandchildren has shot at the game. Take his arrow. There it is."

"No," replied he, "what will I do with a dirty tooth?"

The old wolf took it up, and, behold! it was a beautiful silver arrow.

When they overtook the young ones, they found they had killed a very fat moose. Manabozho was very hungry, but, such is the power of enchantment, he saw nothing but bones, picked quite clean. He thought to himself:

"Just as I expected. Dirty, greedy fellows!"

However, he sat down without saying a word, and the old wolf said to one of the young ones:

"Give some meat to your grandfather."

The wolf, coming near to Manabozho, opened his mouth wide as if he had eaten too much, whereupon Manabozho jumped up, saying:

"You filthy dog, you have eaten so much that you are ill. Get away to some other place."

The old wolf, hearing these words, came to Manabozho, and, behold! before him was a heap of fresh ruddy meat with the fat lying all ready prepared. Then Manabozho put on a smiling-face.

"Amazement!" cried he, "how fine the meat is!"

"Yes," replied the wolf; "it is always so with us. We know our work, and always get the best. It is not a long tail that makes a hunter."

Manabozho bit his lip.

They then commenced fixing their winter quarters, while the young ones went out in search of game, of which they soon brought in a large supply. One day, during the absence of the young wolves, the old one amused himself by cracking the large bones of a moose.

"Manabozho," said he, "cover your head with the robe, and do not look at me while I am at these bones, for a piece may fly in your eye."

Manabozho covered his head, but, looking through a rent in the robe, he saw all the other was about. At that moment a piece of bone flew off and hit him in the eye. He cried out:

"Tyau! Why do you strike me, you old dog!"

The wolf said:

"You must have been looking at me."

"No, no," replied Manabozho; "why should I want to look at you?"

"Manabozho," said the wolf, "you must have been looking, or you would not have got hurt."

"No, no," said Manabozho; and he thought to himself, "I will repay the saucy wolf for this."

Next day, taking up a bone to obtain the marrow, he said to the old wolf:

"Cover your head, and don't look at me, for I fear a piece may fly in your eye."

The wolf did so. Then Manabozho took the leg-bone of the moose, and, looking first to see if the old wolf was well covered, he hit him a blow with all his might. The wolf jumped up, and cried out:

"Why do you strike me so?"

"Strike you?" exclaimed Manabozho. "I did not strike you!"

"You did," said the wolf.

"How can you say I did, when you did not see me. Were you looking?" said Manabozho.

He was an expert hunter when he undertook the work in earnest, and one day he went out and killed a fat moose. He was very hungry, and sat down to eat, but fell into great doubts as to the proper point in the carcass to begin at.

"Well," said he, "I don't know where to commence. At the head? No. People would laugh, and say, 'He ate him backward!'"

Then he went to the side.

"No," said he, "they will say I ate him sideways."

He then went to the hind-quarter.

"No," said he, "they will say I ate him forward."

At last, however, seeing that he must begin the attack somewhere, he commenced upon the hind-quarter. He had just got a delicate piece in his mouth when the tree just by began to make a creaking noise, rubbing one large branch against another. This annoyed him.

"Why!" he exclaimed, "I cannot eat when I hear such a noise. Stop, stop!" cried he to the tree.

He was again going on with his meal when the noise was repeated.

"I cannot eat with such a noise," said he; and, leaving the meal, although he was very hungry, he went to put a stop to the noise. He climbed the tree, and having found the branches which caused the disturbance, tried to push them apart, when they suddenly caught him between them, so that he was held fast. While he was in this position a pack of wolves came near.

"Go that way," cried Manabozho, anxious to send them away from the neighbourhood of his meat. "Go that way; what would you come to get here?"

The wolves talked among themselves, and said, "Manabozho wants to get us out of the way. He must have something good here."

"I begin to know him and all his tricks," said an old wolf. "Let us see if there is anything."

They accordingly began to search, and very soon finding the moose made away with the whole carcass. Manabozho looked on wistfully, and saw them eat till they were satisfied, when they left him nothing but bare bones. Soon after a blast of wind opened the branches and set him free. He went home, thinking to himself:

"See the effect of meddling with frivolous things when certain good is in one's possession!"

The Chenoo, or the Story of a Cannibal with an Icy Heart

AN INDIAN, with his wife and their little boy, went one autumn far away to hunt in the northwest. And having found a fit place to pass the winter, they built a wigwam. The man brought home the game, the woman dressed and dried the meat, the small boy played about shooting birds with bow and arrow; in Indian-wise all went well.

One afternoon, when the man was away and the wife gathering wood, she heard a rustling in the bushes, as though some beast were brushing through them, and, looking up, she saw with horror something worse than the worst she had feared. It was an awful face glaring at her – a something made of devil, man, and beast in their most dreadful forms. It was like a haggard old man, with wolfish eyes; he was stark naked; his shoulders and lips were gnawed away, as if, when mad with hunger, he had eaten his own flesh. He carried a bundle on his back. The woman had heard of the terrible Chenoo, the being who comes from the far, icy north, a creature who is a man grown to be both devil and cannibal, and saw at once that this was one of them.

Truly she was in trouble; but dire need gives quick wit, as it was with this woman, who, instead of showing fear, ran up and addressed him with fair words, as "My dear father," pretending surprise and joy, and, telling him how glad her heart was, asked where he had been so long. The Chenoo was amazed beyond measure at such a greeting where he expected yells and prayers, and in mute wonder let himself be led into the wigwam.

She was a wise and good woman. She took him in; she said she was sorry to see him so woe-begone; she pitied his sad state; she brought a suit of her husband's clothes; she told him to dress himself and be cleaned. He did as she bade. He sat by the side of the wigwam, and looked surly and sad, but kept quiet. It was all a new thing to him.

She arose and went out. She kept gathering sticks.

The Chenoo rose and followed her. She was in great fear. "Now," she thought, "my death is near; now he will kill and devour me."

The Chenoo came to her. He said, "Give me the axe!" She gave it, and he began to cut down the trees. Man never saw such chopping! The great pines fell right and left, like summer saplings; the boughs were hewed and split as if by a tempest. She cried out, "Noo, tabeagul boohsoogul!" "My father, there is enough!" He laid down the axe; he walked into the wigwam and sat down, always in grim silence. The woman gathered her wood, and remained as silent on the opposite side.

She heard her husband coming. She ran out and told him all. She asked him to do as she was doing. He thought it well. He went in and spoke kindly. He said, "N'chilch," "My father-in-law," and asked where he had been so long. The Chenoo stared in amazement, but when he heard the man talk of all that had happened for years his fierce face grew gentler.

They had their meal; they offered him food, but he hardly touched it. He lay down to sleep. The man and his wife kept awake in terror. When the fire burned up, and it became warm, the Chenoo asked that a screen should be placed before him. He was from the ice; he could not endure heat.

For three days he stayed in the wigwam; for three days he was sullen and grim; he hardly ate. Then he seemed to change. He spoke to the woman; he asked her if she had any tallow. She told him they had much. He filled a large kettle; there was a gallon of it. He put it on the fire. When it was scalding hot he drank it all off at a draught.

He became sick; he grew pale. He cast up all the horrors and abominations of earth, things appalling to every sense. When all was over he seemed changed. He lay down and slept. When he awoke he asked for food, and ate much. From that time he was kind and good. They feared him no more.

They lived on meat such as Indians prepare. The Chenoo was tired of it. One day he said, "N'toos" (my daughter), "have you no pela weoos?" (fresh meat). She said, "No." When her husband returned the Chenoo saw that there was black mud on his snow-shoes. He asked him if there was a spring of water near. The friend said there was one half a day's journey distant. "We must go there to-morrow," said the Chenoo.

And they went together, very early. The Indian was fleet in such running. But the old man, who seemed so wasted and worn, went on his snow-shoes like the wind. They came to the spring. It was large and beautiful; the snow was all melted away around it; the border was flat and green.

Then the Chenoo stripped himself, and danced around the spring his magic dance; and soon the water began to foam, and anon to rise and fall, as if some monster below were heaving in accord with the steps and the song. The Chenoo danced faster and wilder; then the head of an immense Taktalok, or lizard, rose above the surface. The old man killed it with a blow of his hatchet. Dragging it out he began again to dance. He brought out another, the female, not so large, but still heavy as an elk. They were small spring lizards, but the Chenook had conjured them; by his magic they were made into monsters.

He dressed the game; he cut it up. He took the heads and feet and tails and all that he did not want, and cast them back into the spring. "They will grow again into many lizards," he said. When the meat was trimmed it looked like that of the bear. He bound it together with withes; he took it on his shoulders; he ran like the wind; his load was nothing.

The Indian was a great runner; in all the land was not his like; but now he lagged far behind. "Can you go no faster than that?" asked the Chenoo. "The sun is setting; the red will be black anon. At this rate it will be dark ere we get home. Get on my shoulders."

The Indian mounted on the load. The Chenoo bade him hold his head low, so that he could not be knocked off by the branches. "Brace your feet," he said, "so as to be steady." Then the old man flew like the wind – nebe sokano'v'jal samastukteskugul chel wegwasumug wegul; the bushes whistled as they flew past them. They got home before sunset.

The wife was afraid to touch such meat. But her husband was persuaded to eat of it. It was like bear's meat. The Chenoo fed on it. So they all lived as friends.

Then the spring was at hand. One day the Chenoo told them that something terrible would soon come to pass. An enemy, a Chenoo, a woman, was coming like wind, yes – on the wind – from the north to kill him. There could be no escape from the battle. She would be far more furious, mad, and cruel than any male, even one of his own cruel race, could be. He knew not how the battle would end; but the man and his wife must be put in a place of safety. To keep from hearing the terrible war-whoops of the Chenoo, which is death to mortals, their ears must be closed. They must hide themselves in a cave.

Then he sent the woman for the bundle which he had brought with him, and which had hung untouched on a branch of a tree since he had been with them. And he said if she found aught in it offensive to her to throw it away, but to certainly bring him a smaller bundle which was within the other. So she went and opened it, and that which she found therein was a pair of human legs and feet, the remains of some earlier horrid meal. She threw them far away. The small bundle she brought to him.

The Chenoo opened it and took from it a pair of horns – horns of the chepitchcalm, or dragon. One of them has two branches; the other is straight and smooth. They were golden-bright. He gave the straight horn to the Indian; he kept the other. He said that these were magical weapons, and the only ones of any use in the coming fight. So they waited for the foe.

And the third day came. The Chenoo was fierce and bold; he listened; he had no fear. He heard the long and awful scream – like nothing of earth – of the enemy, as she sped through the air far away in the icy north, long ere the others could hear it. And the manner of it was this: that if they without harm should live after bearing the first deadly yell of the enemy they could take no harm, and if they did but hear the answering shout of their friend all would be well with them. But he said, "Should you hear me call for help, then hasten with the horn, and you may save my life."

They did as he bade: they stopped their ears; they hid in a deep hole dug in the ground. All at once the cry of the foe burst on them like screaming thunder; their ears rang with pain: they were well-nigh killed, for all the care they had taken. But then they heard the answering cry of their friend, and were no longer in danger from mere noise.

The battle begun, the fight was fearful. The monsters, by their magic with their rage, rose to the size of mountains. The tall pines were torn up, the ground trembled as in an earthquake, rocks crashed upon rocks, the conflict deepened and darkened; no tempest was ever so terrible. Then the male Chenoo was heard crying: "N'loosook! choogooye! abog unumooe!" "My son-in-law, come and help me!"

He ran to the fight. What he saw was terrible! The Chenoos, who upright would have risen far above the clouds as giants of hideous form, were struggling on the ground. The female seemed to be the conqueror. She was holding her foe down, she knelt on him, she was doing all she could to thrust her dragon's horn into his ear. And he, to avoid death, was moving his head rapidly from side to side, while she, mocking his cries, said, "You have no son-in-law to help you." Neen nabujjeole, "I'll take your cursed life, and eat your liver." The Indian was so small by these giants that the stranger did not notice him. "Now," said his friend, "thrust the horn into her ear" He did this with a well-directed blow; he struck hard; the point entered her head. At the touch it sprouted quick as a flash of lightning, it darted through the head, it came out of the other ear, it had become like a long pole. It touched the ground, it struck downward, it took deep and firm root.

The male Chenoo bade him raise the other end of the horn and place it against a large tree. He did so. It coiled itself round the tree like a snake, it grew rapidly; the enemy was held hard and fast. Then the two began to dispatch her. It was long and weary work. Such a being, to be killed at all, must be hewed into small pieces; flesh and bones must all be utterly consumed by fire. Should the least fragment remain unburnt, from it would spring a grown Chenoo, with all the force and fire of the first.

The fury of battle past, the Chenoos had become of their usual size. The victor hewed the enemy to small pieces, to be revenged for the insult and threat as to eating his liver. He, having roasted that part of his captive, ate it before her; while she was yet alive he did this. He told her she was served as she would have served him.

But the hardest task of all was to come. It was to burn or melt the heart. It was of ice, and more than ice: as much colder as ice is colder than fire, as much harder as ice is harder than water. When placed in the fire it put out the flame, yet by long burning it melted slowly, until they at last broke it to fragments with a hatchet, and then melted these. So they returned to the camp.

Spring came. The snows of winter, as water, ran down the rivers to the sea; the ice and snow which had encamped on the inland hills sought the shore. So did the Indian and his wife; the Chenoo, with softened soul, went with them. Now he was becoming a man like other men. Before going they built a canoe for the old man: they did not cover it with birch bark; they made it of moose-skin. In it they placed a part of their venison and skins. The Chenoo took his place in it; they took the lead, he followed.

And after winding on with the river, down rapids and under forest-boughs, they came out into the sunshine, on a broad, beautiful lake. But suddenly, when midway in the water, the Chenoo laid flat in the canoe, as if to hide himself. And to explain this he said that he had just then been discovered by another Chenoo, who was standing on the top of a mountain, whose dim blue outline could just be seen stretching far away to the north. "He has seen me," he said, "but he cannot see you. Nor can he behold me now; but should he discover me again, his wrath will be roused. Then he will attack me; I know not who might conquer. I prefer peace."

So he lay bidden, and they took his canoe in tow. But when they had crossed the lake and come to the river again, the Chenoo said that he could not travel further by water. He would walk the woods, but sail on streams no more. So they told him where they meant to camp that night. He started over mountains and through woods and up rocks, a far, round-about journey. And the man and his wife went down the river in a spring freshet, headlong with the rapids. But when they had paddled round the point where they meant to pass the night, they saw smoke rising among the trees, and on landing they found the Chenoo sleeping soundly by the fire which had been built for them.

This he repeated for several days. But as they went south a great change came over him. He was a being of the north. Ice and snow had no effect on him, but he could not endure the soft airs of summer. He grew weaker and weaker; when they had reached their village he had to be carried like a little child. He had grown gentle. His fierce and formidable face was now like that of a man. His wounds had healed; his teeth no longer grinned wildly all the time. The people gathered round him in wonder.

He was dying. This was after the white men had come. They sent for a priest. He found the Chenoo as ignorant of all religion as a wild beast. At first he would repel the father in anger. Then he listened and learned the truth. So the old heathen's heart changed; he was deeply moved. He asked to be baptized, and as the first tear which he had ever shed in all his life came to his eyes he died.

Snowbird and the Water-Tiger

SNOWBIRD was the much-loved wife of Brown Bear, the brave hunter whose home was on the shore of the Great Lake. He kept the wigwam well supplied with food; and Snowbird's moccasins were the finest in the tribe, save only those of the Chief's daughters. Even those owed much of their beauty to the lovely feathers that Snowbird had given them. If you had asked her where she got them she would have answered proudly, "My husband brought them from the chase."

Besides Brown Bear and his wife, there lived in the wigwam their own, dear, little papoose whom they called "Pigeon," because he was always saying, "Goo, goo;" but they hoped that he would win a nobler name some day, when he should fight the enemy, or kill some beast that was a terror to the tribe, and so take its name for his own.

These three would have been a very happy family; nor would the little orphan boy whom they had adopted long before Pigeon was born, have made them any trouble; he was a great help to them. But there was still another inmate, Brown Bear's mother, a wicked, old squaw, whom none of the other sons' wives would have in their wigwams. Brown Bear was her youngest son, and had always been her favorite. She was kind to him when she was not to any one else; and he loved her and took good care of her, just as much after he brought Snowbird home to be his wife, as he had done before. But the old woman was jealous; and when Brown Bear brought in dainty bits, such as the moose's lip and the bear's kidney, and gave them to his wife, she hated her and grumbled and mumbled to herself in the corner by the fire.

Day after day she sat thinking how she could get rid of the "intruder," as she called her daughter-in-law. She forgot how she had married the only son of a brave Chief and had gone to be the mistress of his wigwam; and he had been as kind and good to her as her son was to Snowbird.

One day when the work was all done, the old woman asked her daughter-in-law to go out to see a swing she had found near the Great Lake. It was a twisted grapevine, that hung over a high rock; but it was stout and strong, for it had been there many years and was securely fastened about the roots of two large trees. The old woman got in first and grasping the vine tightly, swung herself further and further until she was clear out over the water. "It is delightful," said she; "just try it."

So Snowbird got into the swing. While she was enjoying the cool breeze that rose from the lake, the old woman crept behind the trees, and, as soon as the swing was in full motion, and Snowbird was far out over the water, she cut the vine and let her drop down, down, down, not stopping to see what became of her.

She went home and putting on her daughter-in-law's clothes sat in Snowbird's place by the fire, hiding her face as much as possible, so that no one should see her wrinkles.

When Brown Bear came home he gave her the dainties, supposing she was his wife; and she ate them greedily, paying no attention to the baby, who was crying as if its heart would break.

"Why does little Pigeon cry so?" asked the father.

I don't know," said the old woman, "I suppose he's hungry."

Thereat, she picked up the baby, shook it soundly and made believe to nurse it. It cried louder than ever. She boxed its ears and stuffed something into its mouth to keep it quiet.

Brown Bear thought his wife very cross, so he took his pipe and left the wigwam.

The orphan boy had watched all these doings and had grown suspicious. Going to the fire he pretended to brush away the ashes; and, when he thought the old woman was not looking at him, he stirred the logs and made a bright flame leap up so that he could plainly see her face. He was sure there was something wrong.

"Where is Snowbird?" asked he.

"Sh–!" said the old woman; "she is by the lake, swinging." The boy said no more, but went out of the wigwam and down to the lake. There he saw the broken swing, and guessing what had happened, he went in search of Brown Bear and told him what he had discovered.

Brown Bear did not like to think any wrong of his mother, and therefore asked her no questions. Sadly he paced up and down outside the door of his wigwam. Then taking some black paint he smeared his face and body with it as a sign of mourning. When this was done he turned his long spear upside down, and pressing it into the earth, prayed for lightning, thunder and rain, so that his wife's body might rise from the lake.

Every day he went thither, but saw no sign of his dear Snowbird, though the thunder rolled heavily and the lightning had split a great oak near the wigwam from the top to the base. He watched in the rain, in the sunlight, and when the great, white moon shone over the lake, but he saw nothing.

Meanwhile the orphan boy looked after little Pigeon, letting him suck the dantiest, juiciest bits of meat, and bringing him milk to drink. On bright afternoons he would take the baby to the lake shore and amuse him by throwing pebbles into the water. Little Pigeon would laugh and crow and stretch out his tiny hands, then taking a pebble would try to throw it into the water himself, and, though it always dropped at his feet, he was just as well pleased.

One day as they were playing in this manner they saw a white gull rise from the center of the lake and fly towards the part of the shore where they were. When it reached them it circled above their heads, flying down close to them until little Pigeon could almost touch its great, white wings. Then, all of a sudden, it changed to a woman— Snowbird, little Pigeon's mother!

The baby crowed with delight and caught at two belts, one of leather and one of white metal, that his mother wore about her waist. She could not speak; but she took the baby in her arms, fondled it and nursed it. Then she made signs to the boy by which he understood that he was to bring the child there every day.

When Brown Bear came home that night the boy told him all that had happened.

The next afternoon when the baby cried for food the boy took him to the lake shore, Brown Bear following and hiding behind the bushes. The boy stood where he had before, close to the water's edge, and, choosing a smooth, round pebble, raised his arm slowly and with careful aim threw it far out into the lake.

Soon the gull, with a long, shining belt around its body, was seen rising from the water. It came ashore, hovered above them a moment, and, as on the previous day, changed into a woman and took the child in her arms.

While she was nursing it her husband appeared. The black paint was still on his body, but he held his spear in his hand.

"Why have you not come home?" he cried, and sprang forward to embrace her.

She could not speak, but pointed to the shining belt she wore.

Brown Bear raised his spear carefully and struck a great blow at the links. They were shivered to fragments and dropped on the sands, where any one seeing them would have supposed they were pieces of a large shell.

Then Snowbird's speech returned and she told how when she fell into the lake, a water-tiger seized her and twisting his tail around her waist, drew her to the bottom.

There she found a grand lodge whose walls were blue like the bluejay's back when the sun shines upon it, green like the first leaves of the maize and golden like the bright sands on the island of the Caribs; and the floor was of sand, white as the snows of winter. This was the wigwam of the Chief of the water-tigers, whose mother was the Horned Serpent and lived with him.

The Serpent lay on a great, white shell which had knobs of copper that shone like distant campfires. But these were nothing to the red stone that sparkled on her forehead. It was covered with a thin skin like a man's eyelid, which was drawn down when she went to sleep. Her horns were very wonderful, for they were possessed of magic. When they touched a great rock the stone fell apart and there was a pathway made through it wherever the Serpent wanted to go.

There were forests in the Water-Tiger's country, trees with leaves like the willow, only longer, finer and broader, bushes and clumps of soft, dark grass.

When night came and the sun no longer shone down into the lodge and the color went out of the walls, there were fireflies—green, blue, crimson, and orange—that lighted on the bushes outside the Water-Tiger's wigwam; and the most beautiful s of them passed inside and fluttered about the throne of the Serpent, standing guard over her while the purple snails, the day sentinels, slept.

Snowbird trembled when she saw these things and fell down in a faint before the great Horned Serpent. But the Water-Tiger soothed her, for he loved her and wanted her to become his wife. This she consented to do at last on condition that she should be allowed to go back sometimes to the lake shore to see her child.

The Water-Tiger consulted his mother, who agreed to lend him a sea-gull's wing which should cover his wife all over and enable her to fly to the shore. He was told, however, to fasten his tail securely about her waist, lest she should desert him when she found herself near her old home. He did so, taking care to put a leather belt around her, for fear the links of white metal might hurt her delicate skin.

So she lived with the Water-Tiger, kept his lodge in order and made moccasins for the little water-tigers out of beaver skin and dried fish scales, and was as happy as she could have been anywhere away from her own Brown Bear and Little Pigeon.

When the old woman, Brown Bear's mother, saw them at the door of the wigwam, she leaped up and flew out of the lodge and was never seen again.

Nanahboozhoo, Nahpootee and the Windegoos

And Why the Kingfisher Wears a White Collar

"WHO WAS THIS NANAHBOOZHOO that we are hearing so much about?"

Thus was the old story-teller addressed by Sagastao, who always was anxious to learn about those who interested him.

The old man began in this way:

"When the great mountains are wrapped in the clouds we do not see them very well. So it is with Nanahboozhoo. The long years that have passed since he lived have, like the fogs and mists, made it less easy to say exactly who he really was, but I will try to tell you. Nanahboozhoo was not from one tribe only, but from all the Indians. Hence it is that his very name is so different.

"The Ojibway call him Mishawabus—Great Rabbit; the Menomini call him Manabush. He had other names also. One tribe called him Jouskeha, another Messou, another Manabozho, and another Hiawatha. His father was Mudjekeewis, the West Wind. There was an old woman named Nokomis, the granddaughter of the moon, who had a daughter whose name was Wenonah. She was the mother of twin boys, but at their birth she died and so did one of the boys. Nokomis wrapped the living child in soft dry grass, laid it on the ground at one end of her wigwam, and placed over it a great wooden bowl to protect it from harm. Then in her grief she took up the body of Wenonah, her daughter, and buried it, with the dead child, at some distance from her wigwam. When she returned from thus laying away her dead she sat down in her wigwam, and for four days mourned her loss. At the end of that time she heard a slight noise in her wigwam, which she soon found came from that wooden bowl. Then as the bowl moved she suddenly remembered the living child, which she had forgotten in her great grief at the loss of its mother. When she removed the bowl from its place, instead of there being the baby boy she had placed there she beheld a little white rabbit, and on taking it up she said, 'O my dear little rabbit, my Manabush!' Nokomis took great care of it and it grew very rapidly.

"One day, when Manabush was quite large, it sat up on its haunches and hopped slowly across the floor of the wigwam, and caused the earth to tremble.

"When the bad Windegoos, or evil spirits who dwell underground, felt the earth to thus tremble they said, 'What is the matter? What has happened? A great Munedoo (spirit) is born somewhere.' And at once they began to devise means by which they might kill Manabush, or Nanahboozhoo, as he was now called, when they should find him.

"But Nanahboozhoo did not long continue to look like a rabbit. As he was superior to other people he could change himself to any form he liked. He was most frequently seen as a fine strong young Indian hunter. He called the people his uncles. When he grew up he said to his grandmother, the old Nokomis, that the time had come when he should prepare himself to go and help his uncles, the people, to better their condition. This he was able to do, seeing he was more than human, for his father was the West Wind and his mother a great-granddaughter of the moon. Sometimes he was the beautiful white rabbit; then he would be a wolf or a wolverine; then he would be a lovely bird. He could even change himself to look like a dry old stump or a beautiful tree. Sometimes he would be like a little half-frozen rabbit; then he would be a mighty magician, and often a little snake. He was just as changeable in his disposition as in his outward appearance. Sometimes he was doing the best things imaginable for his uncles, the Indian people, and at other times he was full of mischief and trickery. But on the whole he was a friend, and although quick-tempered and fiery yet he did lots of fine things for the people, for he was really one of the best of the Munedoos of the early times.

"When the time came for him to leave his grandmother's wigwam he built one for himself, and then he asked Nokomis to prepare for him the sacred magical musical sticks which she alone could make. His grandmother made him four sticks, and with these he used to beat time when singing his queer songs. Some of them were very queer, and ended up with 'He! he! ho! ho! ha! ha! hi! hi!' Others were in reference to some special benefits he would confer on his uncles. In one of them, referring to his going to steal the fire for them, he sings:

"'Help to my uncles I'm bringing,
Their sorrows I'll change into singing.
From their enemies the fire I'll steal,
That its warmth the children may feel.
"'Disguised will be Nanahboozhoo,
That his work may the better be done;
But his jolly deeds ever will tell who
Has been sporting around in his fun.'

"At first he was a jolly fellow, full of fun, and did lots of good things for his uncles. He showed them the plants and roots good for food, and taught them the arts of surgery and medicine, but as the years went by he did some things that caused him to be feared very much. His uncles always went to him when they got into trouble, but whether he would help them or not depended much on the humor he was in when they came.

"After he had lived for years in the first wigwam which he had built, and taught the people of the earth many things, his father, the West Wind, held a council with the North Wind and the South Wind and the East Wind, and as Nanahboozhoo was never married, and was living such a lonely life, they determined to restore to life, and give to reside with him, his twin brother who had died at his birth. The name of this brother was Nahpootee, which means the Skillful Hunter. Nanahboozhoo was very fond of him, and took great care of him. He grew very rapidly, and he and Nanahboozhoo were very great friends. Like Nanahboozhoo, Nahpootee could disguise himself in any form he chose. One favorite form he often assumed was that of a wolf, as he was often away on hunting excursions. The evil spirits, or Windegoos, who dwell under the land and sea, had never been able to do much harm to Nanahboozhoo, he was too clever for them; and although they often tried he generally worsted them. Now they were doubly angry when they heard that Nahpootee had been restored to life and was living with him. Nanahboozhoo warned his brother of their enmity, and of the necessity of being on his guard against them.

"These brothers moved far away and built their wigwam in a lonely country on the shore of a great lake which is now called Mirror Lake, because of its beautiful reflections. Here, as he was a hunter, Nahpootee was kept busy supplying the wigwam with food. Once, while he was away hunting, Nanahboozhoo discovered that some of the evil Munedoos dwelt in the bottom of the very lake on the shores of which they had built their wigwam. So he warned his brother, Nahpootee, never to cross that lake, but always to go around on the shore, and for some time he remembered this warning and was not attacked. But one cold winter day, when he had been out for a long time hunting, he found himself exactly on the opposite side of the lake from the wigwam. The ice seemed strong, and as the distance was shorter he decided that, rather than walk around on the shore, he would cross on the ice. When about half-way across the lake the ice broke, he was seized by the evil Munedoos and drowned.

"When Nahpootee failed to return to the wigwam Nanahboozhoo was filled with alarm and at once began searching everywhere for his loved, lost brother. One day when he was walking under some trees at the lake he beheld, high up among the branches, Ookiskimunisew, the kingfisher.

"'What are you doing there?' asked Nanahboozhoo.

"'The bad Munedoos have killed Nahpootee,' Ookiskimunisew replied, 'and soon they are going to throw his body up on the shore and I am going to feast on it!'

"This answer made Nanahboozhoo very angry, but he concealed his feelings.

"'Come down here, handsome bird,' he said, 'and I'll give you this collar to hang on your neck.'

"The kingfisher suspected that the speaker was Nanahboozhoo, the brother of Nahpootee, and he was afraid to descend.

"'Come down, and have no fear,' said Nanahboozhoo, in a friendly tone. 'I only want to give you this beautiful necklace to wear, with the white shell hanging from it.'

"On hearing this the kingfisher came down, but suspecting that Nanahboozhoo would be up to some of his tricks he kept a sharp watch on him. Nanahboozhoo placed the necklace about the neck of the bird so that the beautiful white shell should be over the breast. Then he pretended to tie the ends behind, but just as he had made a half knot in the cord, and was going to tighten it and strangle the bird, the latter was too quick for him and suddenly slipped away and escaped. He kept the necklace, however, and the white spot may be seen on the breast of the kingfisher to this day.

"Soon after this the shade or ghost of Nahpootee appeared to Nanahboozhoo and told him that, as his death was the result of his own carelessness, in not keeping on the land, he would not be restored to live here, but was even now on his way to the Happy Hunting Grounds, in the Land of the Setting Sun, beyond the Great Mountains.

"Nanahboozhoo was deeply moved by the loss of his brother, who had been such a pleasant companion to him. So great was his grief that at times the earth trembled and the evil spirits dwelling under the land or water were much terrified, for they knew they would be terribly punished by Nanahboozhoo if he should ever get them in his power. But it was a long time before he had an opportunity to get his revenge on them for the death of his brother. How he did it I will tell you at some future time."

The Pöokónghoyas and the Cannibal Monster

A VERY LONG TIME AGO a large monster, whom our forefathers called Shíta, lived somewhere in the west, and used to come to the village of Oraíbi and wherever it would find children it would devour them. Often also grown people were eaten by the monster. The people became very much alarmed over the matter, and especially the village chief was very much worried over it. Finally he concluded to ask the Pöokónghoyas for assistance. These latter, namely Pöokónghoya and his younger brother Balö'ngahoya, lived north of and close to the village of Oraíbi. When the village chief asked them to rid them of this monster they told him to make an arrow for each one of them. He did so, using for the shaft feathers, the wing feathers of the bluebird. These arrows he brought to the little War Gods mentioned. They said to each other: "Now let us go and see whether such a monster exists and whether we can find it." So they first went to Oraíbi and kept on the watch around the village. One time, when they were on the east side of the village at the edge of the mesa, they noticed something approaching from the west side. They at once went there and saw that it was the monster that they were to destroy. When the monster met the two brothers it said to them: "I eat you" (Shíta). Both brothers objected. The monster at once swallowed the older one and then the other one. They found that it was not dark inside of the monster, in fact, they found themselves on a path which the younger brother, who had been swallowed last, followed, soon overtaking his older brother. The two brothers laughed and said to each other: "So this is the way we find it here. We are not going to die here." They found that the path on which they were going was the œsophagus of the monster, which led into its stomach. In the latter they found a great many people of different nationalities which the monster had devoured in different parts of the earth; in fact, they found the stomach to be a little world in itself, with grass, trees, rock, etc.

Before the two brothers had left their home on their expedition to kill the monster, if possible, their grandmother had told them that in case the monster should swallow them too, to try to find its heart; if they could shoot into the heart the monster would die. So they concluded that they would now go in search of the heart of the monster. They finally found the path which led out of the stomach, and after following that path quite a distance they saw way above them hanging something which they at once concluded must be the heart of the monster. Pöokónghoya at once shot an arrow at it, but failed to reach it, the arrow dropping back. Hereupon his younger brother tried it and his arrow pierced the heart, whereupon the older brother also shot his arrow into the heart. Then it became dark and, the people noticed that the monster was dying. The two brothers called all the people together and said to them: "Now let us get out." They led them along the path to the mouth of the monster, but found that they could not get out because the teeth of the monster had set firmly in death. They tried in vain to open the mouth but finally discovered a passage leading up into the nose. Through this they then emerged.

It was found that a great many people assembled there north of the village. The village chief had cried out that a great many people had arrived north of the village and asked his people to assemble there too. They did so and many found their children and relatives that had been carried off by the monster, and were very glad to have them back again.

The two brothers then said to the others that they should now move on and try to find their own homes where they had come from, which they did, settling down temporarily at different places, which accounts for the many small ruins scattered throughout the country The old people say that this monster was really a world or a country, as some call it, similar to the world that we are living in.

The Sprightly Tailor

A SPRIGHTLY TAILOR was employed by the great Macdonald, in his castle at Saddell, in order to make the laird a pair of trews, used in olden time. And trews being the vest and breeches united in one piece, and ornamented with fringes, were very comfortable, and suitable to be worn in walking or dancing. And Macdonald had said to the tailor, that if he would make the trews by night in the church, he would get a handsome reward. For it was thought that the old ruined church was haunted, and that fearsome things were to be seen there at night.

The tailor was well aware of this; but he was a sprightly man, and when the laird dared him to make the trews by night in the church, the tailor was not to be daunted, but took it in hand to gain the prize. So, when night came, away he went up the glen, about half a mile distance from the castle, till he came to the old church. Then he chose him a nice gravestone for a seat and he lighted his candle, and put on his thimble, and set to work at the trews; plying his needle nimbly, and thinking about the hire that the laird would have to give him.

For some time he got on pretty well, until he felt the floor all of a tremble under his feet; and looking about him, but keeping his fingers at work, he saw the appearance of a great human head rising up through the stone pavement of the church. And when the head had risen above the surface, there came from it a great, great voice. And the voice said: "Do you see this great head of mine?"

"I see that, but I'll sew this!" replied the sprightly tailor; and he stitched away at the trews.

Then the head rose higher up through the pavement, until its neck appeared. And when its neck was shown, the thundering voice came again and said: "Do you see this great neck of mine?"

"I see that, but I'll sew this!" said the sprightly tailor; and he stitched away at his trews.

Then the head and neck rose higher still, until the great shoulders and chest were shown above the ground. And again the mighty voice thundered: "Do you see this great chest of mine?"

And again the sprightly tailor replied: "I see that, but I'll sew this!" and stitched away at his trews.

And still it kept rising through the pavement, until it shook a great pair of arms in the tailor's face, and said: "Do you see these great arms of mine?"

"I see those, but I'll sew this!" answered the tailor; and he stitched hard at his trews, for he knew that he had no time to lose.

The sprightly tailor was taking the long stitches, when he saw it gradually rising and rising through the floor, until it lifted out a great leg, and stamping with it upon the pavement, said in a roaring voice: "Do you see this great leg of mine?"

"Aye, aye: I see that, but I'll sew this!" cried the tailor; and his fingers flew with the needle, and he took such long stitches, that he was just come to the end of the trews, when it was taking up its other leg. But before it could pull it out of the pavement, the sprightly tailor had finished his task; and, blowing out his candle, and springing from off his gravestone, he buckled up, and ran out of the church with the trews under his arm. Then the fearsome thing gave a loud roar, and stamped with both his feet upon the pavement, and out of the church he went after the sprightly tailor.

Down the glen they ran, faster than the stream when the flood rides it; but the tailor had got the start and a nimble pair of legs, and he did not choose to lose the laird's reward. And though the thing roared to him to stop, yet the sprightly tailor was not the man to be beholden to a monster. So he held his trews tight, and let no darkness grow under his feet, until he had reached Saddell Castle. He had no sooner got inside the gate, and shut it, than the apparition came up to it; and, enraged at losing his prize, struck the wall above the gate, and left there the mark of his five great fingers. Ye may see them plainly to this day, if ye'll only peer close enough.

But the sprightly tailor gained his reward: for Macdonald paid him handsomely for the trews, and never discovered that a few of the stitches were somewhat long.

Tarbh Na Leòid and the Water-Horse

ON THE ISLAND OF HEISKER, just west of Uist, lies an enchanted loch. Here lived a water-horse who was so terrible that everyone feared he would enter the village and destroy them all. And so it was that an old man in the village who knew of such things advised his neighbours to raise a bull, one to each household, and never let it out until it was needed.

For many years, the village was safe. Women washed their clothes at the loch in pairs, for everyone knew that the water-horse would only strike if you ventured to the loch alone. And every household had a bull, never let out in the event that it would be needed. But so it was one year, that the villagers had become a wee bit complacent about the water-horse, and women began to be a little less careful about doing their laundry in pairs. And one day, for whatever the reason, a woman washed alone there, and when she finished, she laid down on the banks of the river and slept there.

The sun was high in the sky, and she was warmed into a deep slumber. When she woke, she saw a magnificent man standing there, the sun glinting on his golden hair, and lighting his clear blue eyes. He spoke to her then, about the fineness of the afternoon, and she spoke back.

"You must be very tired, after all that washing," he said kindly, and the woman blushed, for the men of Heisker never cared much about a woman's tiredness, or about the washing.

"I am indeed," she stammered.

"Do you mind if I join you there?" He smiled at her. "Because I am pretty tired myself."

"Oh, no," she said sweetly, and made room beside her.

Now that fine young man sat down beside her, and then spoke again.

"Do you mind if I lay my head in your lap?" he whispered, and the woman flushed again and shook her head.

And so it was that this young woman was sitting by the sunny banks of the loch with the head of a handsome young man in her lap. And as she gazed down, hardly believing her good fortune, she noticed sea-dirt in his hair, and weeds, and bits of water-moss. And only then did she notice his hooves, which lay crossed in slumber.

The water-horse.

And carefully, ever so gently, the woman took from her washing bag a pair of sharp scissors, and cutting a hole in her coat where the water-horse's head lay, she slipped out from under him, leaving a bit of her coat behind.

And then she ran back to the village, and as the fear struck her, she shrieked to the villagers, "Help, it's the water-horse."

There was a neighing behind her, and the sound of hooves on gravel, and she ran all the faster, calling for help.

Now the old man heard her first, and he called out to his neighbour, a man named MacLeod, whose bull was the closest. The bull was called Tarbh na Leòid, and he was a fierce creature, all the more so for being kept inside all his life.

"Let loose Tarbh na Leòid," cried the woman, rushing into the village. "Turn him loose!"

And so the bull was let loose, and he threw himself at the water-horse and there ensued a fight so horrific that the villagers could hardly watch. And it carried on for hours, and then days, and finally the bull beat that water-horse back to the loch, and they both disappeared.

The woman returned to her home, and she laid down on her bed, never to rise again. Nor did the bull or the water-horse, although it is said that the horn of Tarbh na Leòid rose to the surface of the water one fine day, many years later. It's still there, they say, guarding the path to the loch of the water-horse.

Nuckelavee

NUCKELAVEE WAS A MONSTER of unmixed malignity, never willingly resting from doing evil to mankind. He was a spirit in flesh. His home was the sea; and whatever his means of transit were in that element, when he moved on land he rode a horse as terrible in aspect as himself. Some thought that rider and horse were really one, and that this was the shape of the monster. Nuckelavee's head was like a man's, only ten times larger, and his mouth projected like that of a pig, and was enormously wide. There was not a hair on the monster's body, for the very good reason that he had no skin.

If crops were blighted by sea-gust or mildew, if live stock fell over high rocks that skirt the shores, or if an epidemic raged among men, or among the lower animals, Nuckelavee was the cause of all. His breath was venom, falling like blight on vegetable, and with deadly disease on animal life. He was also blamed for long-continued droughts; for some unknown reason he had serious objections to fresh water, and was never known to visit the land during rain.

I knew an old man who was credited with having once encountered Nuckelavee, and with having made a narrow escape from the monster's clutches. This man was very reticent on the subject. However, after much higgling and persuasion, the following narrative was extracted:

Tammas, like his namesake Tam o' Shanter, was out late one night. It was, though moonless, a fine starlit night. Tammas's road lay close by the seashore, and as he entered a part of the road that was hemmed in on one side by the sea, and on the other by a deep fresh-water loch, he saw some huge object in front of, and moving towards him. What was he to do? He was sure it was no earthly thing that was steadily coming towards him. He could not go to either side, and to turn his back to an evil thing he had heard was the most dangerous position of all; so Tammie said to himself, "The Lord be aboot me, any tak' care o' me, as I am oot on no evil intent this night!" Tammie was always regarded as rough and foolhardy. Anyway, he determined, as the best of two evils, to face the foe, and so walked resolutely yet slowly forward. He soon discovered to his horror that the gruesome creature approaching him was no other than the dreaded Nuckelavee. The lower part of this terrible monster, as seen by Tammie, was like a great horse with flappers like fins about his legs, with a mouth as wide as a whale's, from whence came breath like steam from a brewing-kettle. He had but one eye, and that as red as fire. On him sat, or rather seemed to grow from his back, a huge man with no legs, and arms that reached nearly to the ground. His head was as big as a clue of simmons (a clue of straw ropes, generally about three feet in diameter), and this huge head kept rolling from one shoulder to the other as if it meant to tumble off. But what to Tammie appeared most horrible of all, was that the monster was skinless; this utter want of skin adding much to the terrific appearance of the creature's naked body – the whole surface of it showing only red raw flesh, in which Tammie saw blood, black as tar, running through yellow veins, and great white sinews, thick as horse tethers, twisting, stretching, and contracting as the monster moved.

Tammie went slowly on in mortal terror, his hair on end, a cold sensation like a film of ice between his scalp and his skull, and a cold sweat bursting from every pore. But he knew it was useless to flee, and he said, if he had to die, he would rather see who killed him than die with his back to the foe. In all his terror Tammie remembered what he had heard of Nuckelavee's dislike of fresh water, and, therefore, took that side of the road nearest to the loch. The awful moment came when the lower part of the head of the monster got abreast of Tammie. The mouth of the monster yawned like a bottomless pit. Tammie found its hot breath like fire on his face: the long arms were stretched out to seize the unhappy man. To avoid, if possible, the monster's clutch, Tammie swerved as near as he could to the loch; in doing so one of his feet went into the loch, splashing up some water on the foreleg of the monster, whereat the horse gave a snort like thunder and shied over to the other side of the road, and Tammie felt the wind of Nuckelavee's clutches as he narrowly escaped the monster's grip. Tammie saw his opportunity, and ran with all his might; and sore need had he to run, for Nuckelavee had turned and was galloping after him, and bellowing with a sound like the roaring of the sea. In front of Tammie lay a rivulet, through which the surplus water of the loch found its way to the sea, and Tammie knew, if he could only cross the running water, he was safe; so he strained every nerve. As he reached the near bank another clutch was made at him by the long arms. Tammie made a desperate spring and reached the other side, leaving his bonnet in the monster's clutches. Nuckelavee gave a wild unearthly yell of disappointed rage as Tammie fell senseless on the safe side of the water.

Sam-Chung And The Water Demon

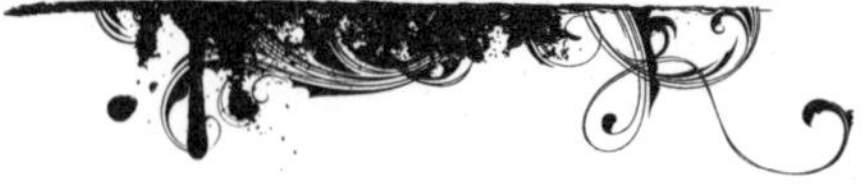

SAM-CHUNG WAS ONE of the most famous men in the history of the Buddhist Church, and had distinguished himself by the earnestness and self-denial with which he had entered on the pursuit of eternal life. His mind had been greatly exercised and distressed at the pains and sorrows which mankind were apparently doomed to endure. Even those, however, terrible as they were, he could have managed to tolerate had they not ended, in the case of every human being, in the crowning calamity which comes upon all at the close of life.

Death was the great mystery which cast its shadow on every human being. It invaded every home. The sage whose virtues and teachings were the means of uplifting countless generations of men came under its great law. Men of infamous and abandoned character seemed often to outlive the more virtuous of their fellow-beings; but they too, when the gods saw fit, were hurried off without any ceremony. Even the little ones, who had never violated any of the laws of Heaven, came under this universal scourge; and many of them, who had only just commenced to live were driven out into the Land of Shadows by this mysterious force which dominates all human life.

Accordingly Sam-Chung wanted to be freed from the power of death, so that its shadow should never darken his life in the years to come.

After careful enquiry, and through friendly hints from men who, he had reason to believe, were fairies in disguise and had been sent by the Goddess of Mercy to help those who aspired after a higher life, he learned that it was possible by the constant pursuit of virtue to arrive at that stage of existence in which death would lose all its power to injure, and men should become immortal. This boon of eternal life could be won by every man or woman who was willing to pay the price for so precious a gift. It could be gained by great self-denial, by willingness to suffer, and especially by the exhibition of profound love and sympathy for those who were in sorrow of any kind. It appeared, indeed, that the one thing most imperatively demanded by the gods from those who aspired to enter their ranks was that they should be possessed of a divine compassion, and that their supreme object should be the succouring of distressed humanity. Without this compassion any personal sacrifice that might be made in the search for immortality would be absolutely useless.

Sam-Chung was already conscious that he was a favourite of the gods, for they had given him two companions, both with supernatural powers, to enable him to contend against the cunning schemes of the evil spirits, who are ever planning how to thwart and destroy those whose hearts are set upon higher things.

One day, accompanied by Chiau and Chu, the two attendants commissioned by the Goddess of Mercy to attend upon him, Sam-Chung started on his long journey for the famous Tien-ho river, to cross which is the ambition of every pilgrim on his way to the land of the Immortals. They endured many weeks of painful travelling over high mountains and through deep valleys which lay in constant shadow, and across sandy deserts where men perished of thirst or were struck down by the scorching heat of the sun, before they met any of the infernal foes that they expected to be lying in wait for them.

Weary and footsore, they at last arrived one evening on the shores of the mighty Tien-ho, just as the sun was setting. The glory of the clouds in the west streamed on to the waters of the river, and made them sparkle with a beauty which seemed to our wearied travellers to transform them into something more than earthly. The river here was so wide that it looked like an inland sea. There was no sign of land on the distant horizon, nothing but one interminable vista of waters, stretching away as far as the eye could reach.

One thing, however, greatly disappointed Sam-Chung and his companions, and that was the absence of boats. They had planned to engage one, and by travelling across the river during the night, they hoped to hurry on their way and at the same time to rest and refresh themselves after the fatigues they had been compelled to endure on their long land journey.

It now became a very serious question with them where they were to spend the night. There was no sign of any human habitation round about. There was the sandy beach along which they were walking, and there was the wide expanse of the river, on which the evening mists were slowly gathering; but no appearance of life. Just as they were wondering what course they should pursue, the faint sound of some musical instruments came floating on the air and caught their ear. Hastening forward in the direction from which the music came, they ascended a piece of rising ground, from the top of which they were delighted to see a village nestling on the hillside, and a small temple standing on the very margin of the river.

With hearts overjoyed at the prospect of gaining some place where they could lodge for the night, they hurried forward to the hamlet in front of them. As they drew nearer, the sounds of music became louder and more distinct. They concluded that some festival was being observed, or that some happy gathering amongst the people had thrown them all into a holiday mood. Entering the village, they made their way to a house which stood out prominently from the rest, and which was better built than any others they could see. Besides, it was the one from which the music issued, and around its doors was gathered a number of people who had evidently been attending some feast inside.

As the three travellers came up to the door, a venerable-looking old man came out to meet them. Seeing that they were strangers, he courteously invited them to enter; and on Sam-Chung asking whether they could be entertained for the night, he assured them that there was ample room for them in the house, and that he gladly welcomed them to be his guests for as long as it was their pleasure to remain.

"In the meanwhile you must come in," he said, "and have some food, for you must be tired and hungry after travelling so far, and the tables are still covered with the good things which were prepared for the feast to-day."

After they had finished their meal, they began to talk to the old gentleman who was so kindly entertaining them. They were greatly pleased with his courtesy and with the hearty hospitality which he had pressed upon them. They noticed, however, that he was very absent-minded, and looked as if some unpleasant thought lay heavy on his heart.

"May I ask," said Sam-Chung, "what was the reason for the great gathering here to-day? There is no festival in the Chinese calendar falling on this date, so I thought I would take the liberty of enquiring what occasion you were really commemorating."

"We were not commemorating anything," the old man replied with a grave face. "It was really a funeral service for two of my grand-children, who, though they are not yet dead, will certainly disappear out of this life before many hours have passed."

"But how can such a ceremony be performed over persons who are still alive?" asked Sam-Chung with a look of wonder in his face.

"When I have explained the circumstances to you, you will then be no longer surprised at this unusual service," replied the old man.

"You must know," he continued, "that this region is under the control of a Demon of a most cruel and bloodthirsty disposition. He is not like the ordinary spirits, whose images are enshrined in our temples, and whose main aim is to protect and guard their worshippers. This one has no love for mankind, but on the contrary the bitterest hatred, and his whole life seems to be occupied in scheming how he may inflict sorrow and disaster on them. His greatest cruelty is to insist that every year just about this time two children, one a boy and the other a girl, shall be conveyed to his temple by the river side to be devoured by him. Many attempts have been made to resist this barbarous demand, but they have only resulted in increased suffering to those who have dared to oppose him. The consequence is that the people submit to this cruel murder of their children, though many a heart is broken at the loss of those dearest to them."

"But is there any system by which the unfortunate people may get to know when this terrible sacrifice is going to be demanded from them?" asked Sam-Chung.

"Oh yes," replied the man. "The families are taken in rotation, and when each one's turn comes round, their children are prepared for the sacrifice. Moreover, that there may be no mistake, the Demon himself appears in the home a few days before, and gives a threatening command to have the victims ready on such a date. Only the day before yesterday, this summons came to us to have our children ready by tomorrow morning at break of day. That is why we had a feast to-day, and performed the funeral rites for the dead, so that their spirits may not be held under the control of this merciless Damon, but may in time be permitted to issue from the Land of Shadows, and be born again under happier circumstances into this world, which they are leaving under such tragic circumstances."

"But what is the Demon like?" enquired Sam-Chung.

"Oh, no one can ever tell what he is like," said the man. "He has no bodily form that one can look upon. His presence is known by a strong blast of wind which fills the place with a peculiar odour, and with an influence so subtle that you feel yourself within the grip of a powerful force, and instinctively bow your head as though you were in the presence of a being who could destroy you in a moment were he so disposed."

"One more question and I have finished," said Sam-Chung. "Where did this Demon come from, and how is it that he has acquired such an overmastering supremacy over the lives of men, that he seems able to defy even Heaven itself, and all the great hosts of kindly gods who are working for the salvation of mankind?"

"This Demon," the man replied, "was once an inhabitant of the Western Heaven, and under the direct control of the Goddess of Mercy. He must, however, have been filled with evil devices and fiendish instincts from the very beginning, for he seized the first opportunity to escape to earth, and to take up his residence in the grottoes and caverns that lie deep down beneath the waters of the Tien-ho. Other spirits almost as bad as himself have also taken up their abode there, and they combine their forces to bring calamity and disaster upon the people of this region."

Sam-Chung, whose heart was filled with the tenderest feelings of compassion for all living things, so much so that his name was a familiar one even amongst the Immortals in the far-off Western Heaven, felt himself stirred by a mighty indignation when he thought of how innocent childhood had been sacrificed to minister to the unnatural passion of this depraved Demon. Chiau and Chu were as profoundly indignant as he, and a serious consultation ensued as to the best methods to be adopted to save the little ones who were doomed to destruction on the morrow, and at the same time to break the monster's rule so that it should cease for ever.

Chiau, who was the more daring of the two whom I the goddess had deputed to protect Sam-Chung, at length cried out with flashing eyes, "I will personate the boy, Chu shall act the girl, and together we will fight the Demon and overthrow and kill him, and so deliver the people from his dreadful tyranny."

Turning to the old man, he said, "Bring the children here so that we may see them, and make our plans so perfect that the Demon with all his cunning will not be able to detect or frustrate them."

In a few moments the little ones were led in by their grandfather. The boy was seven and the girl was one year older. They were both of them nervous and shy, and clung timidly to the old man as if for protection.

They were very interesting-looking children. The boy was a proud, brave-spirited little fellow, as one could see by the poise of his head as he gazed at the strangers. If anything could be predicted from his looks, he would one day turn out to be a man of great power, for he had in his youthful face all the signs which promise a life out of the common. The girl was a shy little thing, with her hair done up in a childlike fashion that well became her. She was a dainty little mortal. Her eyes were almond-shaped, and with the coyness of her sex she kept shooting out glances from the corners of them at the three men who were looking at her. Her cheeks were pale, with just a suspicion of colour painted into them by the deft hand of nature; whilst her lips had been touched with the faintest dash of carmine, evidently just a moment ago, before she left her mother's side.

"Now, my boy," said Chiau to the little fellow, "keep your eyes fixed on me, and never take them from me for a moment; and you, little sister," addressing the girl, "do the same to the man next to me, and you will see something that will make you both laugh."

The eyes of them both were at once riveted on the two men, and a look of amazement slowly crept into their faces. And no wonder, for as they gazed they saw the two men rapidly changing, and becoming smaller and smaller, until they were the exact size and image of themselves. In their features and dress, and in every minute detail they were the precise pattern of the children, who with staring eyes were held spellbound by the magic change which had taken place in front of them.

"Now," said Chiau to the old gentleman, "the transformation is complete. Take the children away and hide them in the remotest and most inaccessible room that you have in your house. Let them be seen by no chattering woman or servant who might divulge our secret, so that in some way or other it might reach the ears of the Demon, and put him on his guard. Remember that from this moment these little ones are not supposed to exist, but that we are your grand-children who are to be taken to the temple tomorrow morning at break of day."

Just as the eastern sky showed the first touch of colour, two sedan-chairs were brought up to the door to carry the two victims away to be devoured by the Demon. A few frightened-looking neighbours peered through the gloom to catch a last glimpse of the children, but not one of them had the least suspicion that the boy and girl were really fairies who were about to wage a deadly battle with the Demon in order to deliver them from the curse under which they lived.

No sooner had the children been put into the temple, where a dim rush-light did but serve to disclose the gloom, and the doors had been closed with a bang, than the chair-bearers rushed away in fear for their very lives.

An instant afterwards a hideous, gigantic form emerged from an inner room and advanced towards the children. The Demon was surprised, however, to find that on this occasion the little victims did not exhibit any signs of alarm, as had always been the case hitherto, but seemed to be calmly awaiting his approach. There was no symptom of fear about them, and not a cry of terror broke from their lips; but with a fearless and composed mien they gazed upon him as he advanced.

Hesitating for a moment, as if to measure the foe which he began to fear might lie concealed beneath the figures of the boy and girl before him, the Demon's great fiery eyes began to flash with deadly passion as he saw the two little ones gradually expand in size, until they were transformed into beings as powerful and as mighty as himself. He knew at once that he had been outwitted, and that he must now battle for his very life; so, drawing a sword which had always stood him in good stead, he rushed upon the two who faced him so calmly and with such apparent confidence in themselves.

Chiau and Chu were all ready for the fray, and with weapons firmly gripped and with hearts made strong by the consciousness of the justice of their cause, they awaited the onslaught of the Demon.

And what a battle it was that then ensued in the dim and shadowy temple! It was a conflict of great and deadly significance, waged on one side for the deliverance of helpless childhood, and on the other for the basest schemes that the spirits of evil could devise. It was a battle royal, in which no quarter was either asked or given. The clash of weapons, and sounds unfamiliar to the human ear, and groans and cries which seemed to come from a lost soul, filled the temple with their hideous uproar.

At last the Demon, who seemed to have been grievously wounded, though by his magic art he had caused his wounds to be instantly healed, began to see that the day was going against him. One more mighty lunge with his broadsword, and one more furious onset, and his craven heart failed him. With a cry of despair he fled from the temple, and plunged headlong into the river flowing by its walls.

Great were the rejoicings when Chiau and Chu returned to report to Sam-Chung the glorious victory they had gained over the Demon. Laughter and rejoicing were heard in every home, and men and women assembled in front of their doors and at the corners of the narrow alley-ways to congratulate each other on the great deliverance which that day had come to them and to their children. The dread of the Demon had already vanished, and a feeling of freedom so inspired the men of the village that as if by a common impulse, they rushed impetuously down to where the temple stood, and in the course of a few hours every vestige of it had disappeared beneath the waters into which the Demon had plunged.

After his great defeat the baffled spirit made his way to the grotto beneath the waters, where he and the other demons had taken up their abode. A general council was called to devise plans to wipe out the disgrace which had been sustained, and to regain the power that had slipped from the Demon's grasp. They wished also to visit Sam-Chung with condign punishment which would render him helpless for the future.

"We must capture him," said one wicked-looking imp, who always acted as counsellor to the rest. "I have been told that to devour some of his flesh would ensure the prolongation of life for more than a thousand years."

The suggestion to seize Sam-Chung was unanimously accepted as a very inspiration of genius, and the precise measures which were to be adopted in order to capture him were agreed to after a long discussion.

On the very next morning, a most violent snowstorm set in, so that the face of the river and the hills all round about, and the very heavens themselves were lost in the blinding snow-drifts that flew before the gale. Gradually the cold became so intense that the Ice King laid his grip upon the waters of the Tien-ho, and turned the flowing stream into a crystal highway, along which men might travel with ease and safety. Such a sight had never been seen before by any of the people who lived upon its banks, and many were the speculations as to what such a phenomenon might mean to the welfare of the people of the region. It never occurred to any one that this great snow-storm which had turned into ice a river that had never been known to freeze before, was all the work of demons determined on the destruction of Sam-Chung.

Next day the storm had passed, but the river was one mass of ice which gleamed and glistened in the morning rays. Much to the astonishment of Sam-Chung and his two companions, they caught sight of a number of people, who appeared to be merchants, moving about on the bank of the river, together with several mules laden with merchandise. The whole party seemed intent on their preparations for crossing the river, which they were observed to test in various places to make sure that it was strong enough to bear their weight. This they seemed satisfied about, for in a short time the men and animals set forward on their journey across the ice.

Sam-Chung immediately insisted upon following their example, though the plan was vigorously opposed by the villagers, who predicted all kinds of dangers if he entered on such an uncertain and hazardous enterprise. Being exceedingly anxious to proceed on his journey, however, and seeing no prospect of doing so if he did not take advantage of the present remarkable condition of the river, he hastened to follow in the footsteps of the merchants, who by this time had already advanced some distance on the ice.

He would have been less anxious to enter on this perilous course, had he known that the innocent-looking traders who preceded him were every one of them demons who had changed themselves into the semblance of men in order to lure him to his destruction.

Sam-Chung and his companions had not proceeded more than five or six miles, when ominous symptoms of coming disaster began to manifest themselves. The extreme cold in the air suddenly ceased, and a warm south wind began to blow. The surface of the ice lost its hardness. Streamlets of water trickled here and there, forming great pools which made walking exceedingly difficult.

Chiau, whose mind was a very acute and intelligent one, became terrified at these alarming symptoms of danger, especially as the ice began to crack, and loud and prolonged reports reached them from every direction. Another most suspicious thing was the sudden disappearance of the company of merchants, whom they had all along kept well in sight. There was something wrong, he was fully convinced, and so with all his wits about him, he kept himself alert for any contingency. It was well that he did this, for before they had proceeded another mile, the ice began to grow thinner, and before they could retreat there was a sudden crash and all three were precipitated into the water.

Hardly had Chiau's feet touched the river, than with a superhuman effort he made a spring into the air, and was soon flying with incredible speed in the direction of the Western Heaven, to invoke the aid of the Goddess of Mercy to deliver Sam-Chung from the hands of an enemy who would show him no quarter.

In the meanwhile Sam-Chung and Chu were borne swiftly by the demons, who were eagerly awaiting their immersion in the water, to the great cave that lay deep down at the bottom of the mighty river. Chu, being an immortal and a special messenger of the Goddess, defied all the arts of the evil spirits to injure him, so that all they could do was to imprison him in one of the inner grottoes and station a guard over him to prevent his escape. Sam-Chung, however, was doomed to death, and the Demon, in revenge for the disgrace he had brought upon him, and in the hope of prolonging his own life by a thousand years, decided that on the morrow he would feast upon his flesh. But he made his plans without taking into consideration the fact that Sam-Chung was an especial favourite with the Goddess.

During the night a tremendous commotion occurred. The waters of the river fled in every direction as before the blast of a hurricane, and the caverns where the demons were assembled were illuminated with a light so brilliant that their eyes became dazzled, and for a time were blinded by the sudden blaze that flashed from every corner. Screaming with terror, they fled in all directions. Only one remained, and that was the fierce spirit who had wrought such sorrow amongst the people of the land near by. He too would have disappeared with the rest, had not some supernatural power chained him to the spot where he stood.

Soon the noble figure of the Goddess of Mercy appeared, accompanied by a splendid train of Fairies who hovered round her to do her bidding. Her first act was to release Sam-Chung, who lay bound ready for his death, which but for her interposition would have taken place within a few hours. He and his two companions were entrusted to the care of a chosen number of her followers, and conveyed with all speed across the river.

The Goddess then gave a command to some who stood near her person, and in a moment, as if by a flash of lightning, the cowering, terrified Demon had vanished, carried away to be confined in one of the dungeons where persistent haters of mankind are kept imprisoned, until their hearts are changed by some noble sentiment of compassion and the Goddess sees that they are once more fit for liberty.

And then the lights died out, and the sounds of fairy voices ceased. The waters of the river, which had been under a divine spell, returned to their course, and the Goddess with her magnificent train of beneficent spirits departed to her kingdom in the far-off Western Heaven.

The Kingdom of the Ogres

IN THE LAND of Annam there once dwelt a man named Su, who sailed the seas as a merchant. Once his ship was suddenly driven on a distant shore by a great storm. It was a land of hills broken by ravines and green with luxuriant foliage, yet he could see something along the hills which looked like human dwellings. So he took some food with him and went ashore. No sooner had he entered the hills than he could see at either hand the entrances to caves, one close beside the other, like a row of beehives. So he stopped and looked into one of the openings. And in it sat two ogres, with teeth like spears and eyes like fiery lamps. They were just devouring a deer. The merchant was terrified by this sight and turned to flee; but the ogres had already noticed him and they caught him and dragged him into their cave. Then they talked to each other with animal sounds, and were about to tear his clothes from his body and devour him. But the merchant hurriedly took a bag of bread and dried meat out and offered it to them. They divided it, ate it up and it seemed to taste good to them. Then they once more went through the bag; but he gestured with his hand to show them that he had no more.

Then he said: "Let me go! Aboard my ship I have frying-pans and cooking-pots, vinegar and spices. With these I could prepare your food."

The ogres did not understand what he was saying, however, and were still ferocious. So he tried to make them understand in dumb show, and finally they seemed to get an idea of his meaning. So they went to the ship with him, and he brought his cooking gear to the cave, collected brush-wood, made a fire and cooked the remains of the deer. When it was done to a turn he gave them some of it to eat, and the two creatures devoured it with the greatest satisfaction. Then they left the cave and closed the opening with a great rock. In a short space of time they returned with another deer they had caught. The merchant skinned it, fetched fresh water, washed the meat and cooked several kettles full of it. Suddenly in came a whole herd of ogres, who devoured all he had cooked, and became quite animated over their eating. They all kept pointing to the kettle which seemed too small to them. When three or four days had passed, one of the ogres dragged in an enormous cooking-pot on his back, which was thenceforth used exclusively.

Now the ogres crowded about the merchant, bringing him wolves and deer and antelopes, which he had to cook for them, and when the meat was done they would call him to eat it with them.

Thus a few weeks passed and they gradually came to have such confidence in him that they let him run about freely. And the merchant listened to the sounds which they uttered, and learned to understand them. In fact, before very long he was able to speak the language of the ogres himself. This pleased the latter greatly, and they brought him a young ogre girl and made her his wife. She gave him valuables and fruit to win his confidence, and in course of time they grew much attached to each other.

One day the ogres all rose very early, and each one of them hung a string of radiant pearls about his neck. They ordered the merchant to be sure and cook a great quantity of meat. The merchant asked his wife what it all meant.

"This will be a day of high festival," answered she, "we have invited the great king to a banquet."

But to the other ogres she said: "The merchant has no string of pearls!"

Then each of the ogres gave him five pearls and his wife added ten, so that he had fifty pearls in all. These his wife threaded and hung the pearl necklace about his neck, and there was not one of the pearls which was not worth at least several hundred ounces of silver.

Then the merchant cooked the meat, and having done so left the cave with the whole herd in order to receive the great king. They came to a broad cave, in the middle of which stood a huge block of stone, as smooth and even as a table. Round it were stone seats. The place of honor was covered with a leopard-skin, and the rest of the seats with deerskins. Several dozen ogres were sitting around the cave in rank and file.

Suddenly a tremendous storm blew up, whirling around the dust in columns, and a monster appeared who had the figure of an ogre. The ogres all crowded out of the cave in a high state of excitement to receive him. The great king ran into the cave, sat down with his legs outstretched, and glanced about him with eyes as round as an eagle's. The whole herd followed him into the cave, and stood at either hand of him, looking up to him and folding their arms across their breasts in the form of a cross in order to do him honor.

The great king nodded, looked around and asked: "Are all the folk of the Wo-Me hills present?"

The entire herd declared that they were.

Then he saw the merchant and asked: "From whence does he hail?"

His wife answered for him, and all spoke with praise of his art as a cook. A couple of ogres brought in the cooked meat and spread it out on the table. Then the great king ate of it till he could eat no more, praised it with his mouth full, and said that in the future they were always to furnish him with food of this kind.

Then he looked at the merchant and asked: "Why is your necklace so short?"

With these words he took ten pearls from his own necklace, pearls as large and round as bullets of a blunderbuss. The merchant's wife quickly took them on his behalf and hung them around his neck; and the merchant crossed his arms like the ogres and spoke his thanks. Then the great king went off again, flying away like lightning on the storm.

In the course of time heaven sent the merchant children, two boys and a girl. They all had a human form and did not resemble their mother. Gradually the children learned to speak and their father taught them the language of men. They grew up, and were soon so strong that they could run across the hills as though on level ground.

One day the merchant's wife had gone out with one of the boys and the girl and had been absent for half-a-day. The north wind was blowing briskly, and in the merchant's heart there awoke a longing for his old home. He took his son by the hand and went down to the seashore. There his old ship was still lying, so he climbed into it with his boy, and in a day and a night was back in Annam again.

When he reached home he loosened two of his pearls from his chain, and sold them for a great quantity of gold, so that he could keep house in handsome style. He gave his son the name of Panther, and when the boy was fourteen years of age he could lift thirty hundred weight with ease. Yet he was rough by nature and fond of fighting. The general of Annam, astonished at his bravery, appointed him a colonel, and in putting down a revolt his services were so meritorious that he was already a general of the second rank when but eighteen.

At about this time another merchant was also driven ashore by a storm on the island of Wo-Me. When he reached land he saw a youth who asked him with astonishment: "Are you not from the Middle Kingdom?"

The merchant told him how he had come to be driven ashore on the island, and the youth led him to a little cave in a secret valley. Then he brought deer-flesh for him to eat, and talked with him. He told him that his father had also come from Annam, and it turned out that his father was an old acquaintance of the man to whom he was talking.

"We will have to wait until the wind blows from the North," said the youth, "then I will come and escort you. And I will give you a message of greeting to take to my father and brother."

"Why do you not go along yourself and hunt up your father?" asked the merchant.

"My mother does not come from the Middle Kingdom," replied the youth. "She is different in speech and appearance, so it cannot well be."

One day the wind blew strongly from the North, and the youth came and escorted the merchant to his ship, and ordered him, at parting, not to forget a single one of his words.

When the merchant returned to Annam, he went to the palace of Panther, the general, and told him all that had happened. When Panther listened to him telling about his brother, he sobbed with bitter grief. Then he secured leave of absence and sailed out to sea with two soldiers. Suddenly a typhoon arose, which lashed the waves until they spurted sky-high. The ship turned turtle, and Panther fell into the sea. He was seized by a creature and flung up on a strand where there seemed to be dwellings. The creature who had seized him looked like an ogre, so Panther addressed him in the ogre tongue. The ogre, surprised, asked him who he was, and Panther told him his whole story.

The ogre was pleased and said: "Wo-Me is my old home, but it lies about eight thousand miles away from here. This is the kingdom of the poison dragons."

Then the ogre fetched a ship and had Panther seat himself in it, while he himself pushed the ship before him through the water so that it clove the waves like an arrow. It took a whole night, but in the morning a shoreline appeared to the North, and there on the strand stood a youth on look-out. Panther recognized his brother. He stepped ashore and they clasped hands and wept. Then Panther turned around to thank the ogre, but the latter had already disappeared.

Panther now asked after his mother and sister and was told that both were well and happy, so he wanted to go to them with his brother. But the latter told him to wait, and went off alone. Not long after he came back with their mother and sister. And when they saw Panther, both wept with emotion. Panther now begged them to return with him to Annam.

But his mother replied: "I fear that if I went, people would mock me because of my figure."

"I am a high officer," replied Panther, "and people would not dare to insult you."

So they all went down to the ship together with him. A favorable wind filled their sails and they sped home swiftly as an arrow flies. On the third day they reached land. But the people whom they encountered were all seized with terror and ran away. Then Panther took off his mantle and divided it among the three so that they could dress themselves.

When they reached home and the mother saw her husband again, she at once began to scold him violently because he had said not a word to her when he went away. The members of his family, who all came to greet the wife of the master of the house, did so with fear and trembling. But Panther advised his mother to learn the language of the Middle Kingdom, dress in silks, and accustom herself to human food. This she agreed to do; yet she and her daughter had men's clothing made for them. The brother and sister gradually grew more fair of complexion, and looked like the people of the Middle Kingdom. Panther's brother was named Leopard, and his sister Ogrechild. Both possessed great bodily strength.

But Panther was not pleased to think that his brother was so uneducated, so he had him study. Leopard was highly gifted; he understood a book at first reading; yet he felt no inclination to become a man of learning. To shoot and to ride was what he best loved to do. So he rose to high rank as a professional soldier, and finally married the daughter of a distinguished official.

It was long before Ogrechild found a husband, because all suitors were afraid of their mother-in-law to be. But Ogrechild finally married one of her brother's subordinates. She could draw the strongest bow, and strike the tiniest bird at a distance of a hundred paces. Her arrow never fell to earth without having scored a hit. When her husband went out to battle she always accompanied him, and that he finally became a general was largely due to her. Leopard was already a field marshal at the age of thirty, and his mother accompanied him on his campaigns. When a dangerous enemy drew near, she buckled on armor, and took a knife in her hand to meet him in place of her son. And among the enemies who encountered her there was not a single one who did not flee from her in terror. Because of her courage the emperor bestowed upon her the title of "The Superwoman."

The Kappa's Promise

IN IZUMO the village people refer to the *Kappa* as *Kawako* ('The Child of the River'). Near Matsue there is a little hamlet called Kawachi-mura, and on the bank of the river Kawachi there is a small temple known as Kawako-no-miya, that is, the temple of the *Kawako* or *Kappa*, said to contain a document signed by this river goblin. Concerning this document the following legend is recorded.

In ancient days a *Kappa* dwelt in the river Kawachi, and he made a practice of seizing and destroying a number of villagers, and in addition many of their domestic animals. On one occasion a horse went into the river, and the *Kappa*, in trying to capture it, in some way twisted his neck, but in spite of considerable pain he refused to let his victim go. The frightened horse sprang up the river bank and ran into a neighbouring field with the Kappa still holding on to the terrified animal. The owner of the horse, together with many villagers, securely bound the Child of the River. "Let us kill this horrible creature," said the peasants, "for he has assuredly committed many horrible crimes, and we should do well to be rid of such a dreadful monster." "No," replied the owner of the horse, "we will not kill him. We will make him swear never to destroy any of the inhabitants or the domestic animals of this village." A document was accordingly prepared, and the *Kappa* was asked to peruse it, and when he had done so to sign his name. "I cannot write," replied the penitent *Kappa*, "but I will dip my hand in ink and press it upon the document." When the creature had made his inky mark, he was released and allowed to return to the river, and from that day to this the *Kappa* has remained true to his promise.

The Shōjō's White Sake

THE SHŌJŌ IS A SEA MONSTER with bright red hair, and is extremely fond of drinking large quantities of sacred white *sake*. The following legend will give some account of this creature and the nature of his favourite beverage.

We will refer later to the miraculous appearance of Mount Fuji. On the day following this alleged miracle a poor man named Yurine, who lived near this mountain, became extremely ill, and feeling that his days were numbered, he desired to drink a cup of *sake* before he died. But there was no rice wine in the little hut, and his boy, Koyuri, desiring if possible to fulfil his father's dying wish, wandered along the shore with a gourd in his hand. He had not gone far when he heard someone calling his name. On looking about him he discovered two strange-looking creatures with long red hair and skin the colour of pink cherry-blossom, wearing green seaweed girdles about their loins. Drawing nearer, he perceived that these beings were drinking white *sake* from large flat cups, which they continually replenished from a great stone jar.

"My father is dying," said the boy, "and he much desires to drink a cup of *sake* before he departs this life. But alas! we are poor, and I know not how to grant him his last request."

"I will fill your gourd with this white *sake*," replied one of the creatures, and when he had done so Koyuri ran with haste to his father.

The old man drank the white *sake* eagerly. "Bring me more," he cried, "for this is no common wine. It has given me strength, and already I feel new life flowing through my old veins."

So Koyuri returned to the seashore, and the red-haired creatures gladly gave him more of their wine; indeed, they supplied him with the beverage for five days, and by the end of that time Yurine was restored to health again.

Now Yurine's neighbour was a man called Mamikiko, and when he heard that Yurine had recently obtained a copious supply of *sake* he grew jealous, for above all things he loved a cup of rice wine. One day he called Koyuri and questioned him in regard to the matter, saying: "Let me taste the *sake*." He roughly snatched the gourd from the boy's hand and began to drink, making a wry face as he did so. "This is not *sake*!" he exclaimed fiercely; "it is filthy water," and having said these words, he began to beat the boy, crying: "Take me to those red people you have told me about. I will get from them fine *sake*, and let the beating I have given you warn you never again to play a trick upon me."

Koyuri and Mamikiko went along the shore together, and presently they came to where the red-haired creatures were drinking. When Koyuri saw them he began to weep.

"Why are you crying?" said one of the creatures. "Surely your good father has not drunk all the *sake* already?"

"No," replied the boy, "but I have met with misfortune. This man I bring with me, Mamikiko by name, drank some of the *sake*, spat it out immediately, and threw the rest away, saying that I had played a trick upon him and given him foul water to drink. Be so good as to let me have some more *sake* for my father."

The red-haired man filled the gourd, and chuckled over Mamikiko's unpleasant experience.

"I should also like a cup or *sake*" said Mamikiko. "Will you let me have some?"

Permission having been granted, the greedy Mamikiko filled the largest cup he could find, smiling over the delicious fragrance. But directly he tasted the *sake* he felt sick, and angrily remonstrated with the red-haired creature.

The red man thus made answer: "You are evidently not aware that I am a *Shōjō*, and that I live near the Sea Dragon's Palace. When I heard of the sudden appearance of Mount Fuji I came here to see it, assured that such an event was a good omen and foretold of the prosperity and perpetuity of Japan. While enjoying the beauty of this fair mountain I met Koyuri, and had the good fortune to save his honest father's life by giving him some of our sacred white *sake* that restores youth to human beings, together with an increase in years, while to *Shōjō* it vanquishes death. Koyuri's father is a good man, and the *sake* was thus able to exert its full and beneficent power upon him; but you are greedy and selfish, and to all such this *sake* is poison."

"*Poison*?" groaned the now contrite Mamikiko. "Good *Shōjō*, have mercy upon me and spare my life!"

The *Shōjō* gave him a powder, saying: "Swallow this in *sake* and repent of your wickedness."

Mamikiko did so, and this time he found that the white *sake* was delicious. He lost no time in making friends with Yurine, and some years later these men took up their abode on the southern side of Mount Fuji, brewed the *Shōjō's* white *sake*, and lived for three hundred years.

Text Sources & Biographies

The stories in this book derive from a multitude of original sources, often from the nineteenth century and often based on the writer's first-hand accounts of tales narrated to them by native and indigenous peoples, while others are their own retellings of traditional tales. Authors, works and contributors to this book include:

Liz Gloyn
Foreword
Dr Liz Gloyn is Reader in Classics at Royal Holloway, University of London, UK. Her many research interests include the reception of classics in popular culture, with a particular focus on film and children's literature. She has recently published *Tracking Classical Monsters in Popular Culture* (2019). As well as writing for publications like *History Today* and *Strange Horizons*, she tweets about her research at @lizgloyn.

Hartley Burr Alexander
Hartley Burr Alexander (1873–1939) was born and raised in Nebraska, where he developed an interest in native cultures. He attended the universities of Nebraska and Pennsylvania and obtained his doctorate from Columbia University in 1901. A writer, poet, scholar and philosopher, he was also a successful iconographer, his decorative schemes and inscriptions embellishing many buildings, including the Nebraska State Capitol. His written works range from *The Problem of Metaphysics* (1902) and *Poetry and the Individual* (1906) to the North American and Latin American volumes of *The Mythology of All Races* (1916 and 1920).

E. M. Berens
E.M. Berens was a scholar and author of classical mythology and folklore. His most important and well-known work is *Myths and Legends of Ancient Greece and Rome* (1894).

Abbie Farwell Brown
American author Abbie Farwell Brown (1871–1927) was born in Boston and attended the Girls' Latin School. While attending school she set up a school newspaper and also contributed articles to other magazines. Brown's books were most often retellings of old tales for children such as in *The Book of Saints and Friendly Beasts*. She also published a collection of tales from Norse mythology, *In the Days of Giants*, which became the common text held by many libraries for several generations.

E. A. Wallis Budge
Sir Ernest Alfred Thompson Wallis Budge (1857–1934) was an English Egyptologist, Orientalist, philologist and author. Born in 1857 in Bodmin, Cornwall, Budge would leave for London as a boy, to live with his aunt and grandmother. It was here, including at the British Museum, that he would be able, whilst working at the stationers W.H. Smith, to indulge is growing interest in languages, particularly Biblical Hebrew, Syriac and Assyrian. He studied Semitic languages at Cambridge and then worked at the British Museum in the Department of Egyptian and Assyrian Antiquities, part of which involved helping the museum to build it collection. He is best known today for his many publications on ancient Egyptian religion, history, culture and

hieroglyphics, from *The Dwellers On The Nile: Chapters on the Life, Literature, History and Customs of the Ancient Egyptians* (1885) to *The Literature of the Ancient Egyptians* (1914), and countless more.

Margaret Compton
Margaret Compton was born in 1852 and is best known as the author of *Snow Bird and the Water Tiger and other American Indian Tales*, a collection of Native American folk tales written for children and young adults that was based on authentic Native American lore. Originally published in 1895, the book was republished four years after Compton's death in 1903 under the new title *American Indian Fairy Tales*.

F. Hadland Davis
Frederick Hadland Davis was a writer and a historian – author of *The Land of the Yellow Spring and Other Japanese Stories* (1910) and *The Persian Mystics* (1908 and 1920). His books describe these cultures to the western world and tell stories of ghosts, creation, mystical creatures and more. He is best known for his book *Myths and Legends of Japan* (1912).

W. Dittmer
Wilhelm Dittmer (1866–1909) was a German artist and the author and illustrator of *Te Tohunga: The Ancient Legends and Traditions of the Maori*s (1907).

George Douglas
George Brisbane Scott Douglas (1856–1935) was a Scottish poet and writer, sometimes writing under the name of Sir George Douglas on account of his rank as baronet. In addition to his *Scottish Fairy and Folk Tales* of 1901, other publications of his include *Poems* (1880), *The Fireside Tragedy* (1896), *New Border Tales* (1892), *Poems of a Country Gentleman* (1897), *History of the Border Counties: Roxburgh, Selkirk and Peebles* (1899) and *Scottish Poetry: Drummond of Hawthornden to Fergusson* (1911).

Constance Goddard DuBois
Born in Zanesville, Ohio in 1869, Constance Godard DuBois was the author of six novels and a self-taught ethnographer. DuBois devoted a significant portion of her life to the study of Native American people in California, writing articles that revealed much about their lives, customs, traditions and myths, and working to preserve their way of life. Her work on Native Americans was published as *The Mythology of the Diegueños* (1901) and *The Dawn of the World: Myths and Weird Tales Told by the Miwok Indians of California* (1904–06). She died in 1934.

George Grey
Sir George Grey (1812–98) was a British soldier, explorer, colonial administrator and writer, who among various governing positions, was the eleventh prime minister of New Zealand. Among his many achievements, he became a pioneering scholar of Māori culture, publishing *Polynesian Mythology & Ancient Traditional History of the New Zealanders* in 1854.

H.A. Guerber
Hélène Adeline Guerber (1859–1929) was a British historian who published a large number of works, largely focused on myths and legends. Guerber's most famous publication is *Myths of the Norsemen: From the Eddas and Sagas*, a history of Germanic mythology. Her works continue

to be published today and include *The Myths of Greece and Rome*, *The Story of the Greeks* and *Legends of the Middle Ages*.

Lady Charlotte Guest
Lady Charlotte Elizabeth Guest (née Bertie; 1812–95), later Lady Charlotte Schreiber, was an English aristocrat who became a prominent figure in the study of literature, as well as a philanthropist, educator and collector. She is best known as the first publisher, in 1838–45, in modern print format in Welsh and English, of the Middle Welsh prose stories known as *The Mabinogion*.

Homer
(Text in this book translated by Samuel Butler; Roman names reverted to Greek)
Little is known for certain about the life of Homer, the Greek poet credited as the author of the great epic poems *The Iliad* and *The Odyssey*, although he is believed to have been born some time between the twelfth and eighth centuries BC. *The Odyssey*, generally considered one of the most fundamental works of the literary canon, describes the trials and tribulations of the hero Odysseus on his journey home to Ithaca following the Trojan War. It has had a huge influence on Western literature, inspiring extensive translations, poems, plays and novels.

Joseph Jacobs
Joseph Jacobs (1854–1916) was born in Australia and settled in New York. He is most famous for his collections of English folklore and fairy tales including 'Jack and the Beanstalk' and 'The Three Little Pigs'. He also published Celtic, Jewish and Indian fairy tales during his career. Jacobs was an editor for books and journals centred on folklore and a member of The Folklore Society in England.

James Athearn Jones
Born in the state of Massachusetts in 1790, James Athearn Jones would go on to work as a lawyer and editor. It is for his work collecting Native American legends that he is best remembered, however, beginning in 1820 with *Traditions of the North American Indians, or Tales of an Indian Camp*, which featured stories told to him by an Indian woman of the Gayhead tribe who was employed as his nurse. Jones would write three volumes in the *Traditions of the North American Indian* series prior to his death in 1853.

Katherine Berry Judson
Born in Poughkeepsie, New York in 1871, Katherine Berry Judson was the author of numerous books, including the novel *When the Forests Are Ablaze* and several works of non-fiction. She is perhaps best remembered for her series of *Myths and Legends* books published between 1910 and 1917, which collected folk tales and myths of Native American people from across the North American continent. She died in 1929.

Charles Kingsley
Charles Kingsley (1819–75) was an English priest, professor, social reformer, historian, novelist and poet, whose most famous works are probably the novels *Westward Ho!* (1855) and *The Water-Babies, A Fairy Tale for a Land Baby* (1863). Though he held some questionable views, his knack for storytelling is evident in *The Heroes, or Greek Fairy Tales* (1856).

Andrew Lang
Poet, novelist and anthropologist Andrew Lang (1844–1912) was born in Selkirk, Scotland. He is

now best known for his collections of fairy stories and publications on folklore, mythology and religion. Inspired by the traditional folklore tales of his home on the English-Scottish border, Lang complied twelve coloured fairy books which collected 798 stories from French, Danish, Russian and Romanian sources, amongst others. *The Grey Fairy Book* (1900) contains a lone African-inspired story of 'The Jackal and the Spring'. This hugely successful series further encouraged the increasing popularity of fairy tales in children's literature.

Charles Godfrey Leland
Charles Godfrey Leland (1824–1903) was a qualified lawyer, journalist and civil war veteran whose various interests saw him travel widely and write about many topics. Perhaps most notably, Leland's keen fascination with folklore would lead him to write many books on the subject, covering everything from pagan and Aryan traditions, to studies of Gypsies; his work on Native American tales was published in 1884 as *The Algonquin Legends of New England.*

Rev. J. Macgowan
John Macgowan (1835–1922) was born in Belfast and became a missionary to China with the London Missionary Society, where he helped to found the anti-footbinding Natural Foot Society. He was author of many books about Chinese culture and history. As well as *Chinese Folk-Lore Tales* (1910), his works include *English and Chinese Dictionary of the Amoy Dialect* (1883) and *Men and Manners of Modern China* (1912).

Eirikr Magnusson
Eirikr Magnusson (1833–1913) was an Icelandic scholar who worked during his life as a librarian at Cambridge University. He arrived in England in 1862 after being sent by the Icelandic Bible Society to translate Christian texts. Magnusson's most notable work was his teaching of Old Norse to William Morris and their collaborations on translations. Together they published numerous Icelandic sagas including *The Story of Grettir the Strong*, *Volsunga Saga* and *Heimskringl.* Magnusson and Morris also spent time traveling around Iceland to visit places which were of significance to the Icelandic sagas they translated.

Minnie Martin
Minnie Martin was the wife of a government official, who arrived in South Africa in 1891 and settled in Lesotho (at that time Basutoland). In her preface to *Basutoland: Its Legends and Customs* (1903) she explains that 'We both liked the country from the first, and I soon became interested in the people. To enable myself to understand them better, I began to study the language, which I can now speak fairly well.' And thus she wrote this work, at the suggestion of a friend. Despite the inaccuracies pointed out by E. Sidney Hartland in his review of her book, he deemed the work 'an unpretentious, popular account of a most interesting branch of the Southern Bantus and the country they live in.'

Frederick H. Martens
Frederick Herman Martens (1874–1932) was an author, lyricist and translator, whose work includes a translation of Pietro Yon's 1917 Christmas carol 'Gesu Bambino', a biography of the musician A.E. Uhe (1922), *A Thousand and One Nights of Opera* (1926), *Violin Mastery (Talks with Master Violinists and Teachers)* (1919), and fairy-tale translations in *The Chinese Fairy Book* (ed. Dr. R. Wilhelm).

Clinton Hart Merriam

Clinton Hart Merriam (1855–1942) was a zoologist, naturalist and doctor who conducted a number of expeditions to the American West in the latter half of the nineteenth century. Reliant on the knowledge of Native American guides in his surveys, Merriam would in later years become fascinated by their culture and abandon his zoological work to study the tribes of California, hoping to preserve their knowledge, language, customs and mythology before they were lost forever. This would lead to the publication of his book *The Dawn of the World: Myths and Weird Tales Told by the Miwok Indians of California* (1910).

William Morris

Textile designer, poet, novelist and translator William Morris (1834–96) was born in Essex and studied at Oxford University. Morris is best known for his textiles work as he created designs for wallpaper, stained glass windows and embroideries that are enduringly popular. Alongside this, Morris wrote poetry, fiction and essays and after befriending Eirikr Magnusson he helped to translate many Icelandic tales. In his final years Morris published fantasy fiction including *The Wood Beyond the World* and *The Well at the World's End* and these were the first fantasy books to be set in an imaginary world. His legacy is an important one as he was a major contributor to both textile arts and literature.

Ovid

A contemporary of Virgil and Horace and alongside them ranked as one of the three canonical poets of Latin literature, Publius Ovidius Naso (43 BC–17/18 AD) was a Roman poet during the reign of Augustus and is best known for his *Metamorphoses*, an epic narrative poem dealing with the transformations of characters from Greco-Roman myth.

Yei Theodora Ozaki

The translations of Japanese stories and fairy tales by Yei Theodora Ozaki (1871–1932) were, by her own admission, fairly liberal ('I have followed my fancy in adding such touches of local colour or description as they seemed to need or as pleased me'), and yet proved popular. They include *Japanese Fairy Tales* (1908), 'translated from the modern version written by Sadanami Sanjin', and *Warriors of Old Japan, and Other Stories* (1909).

Henry Rowe Schoolcraft

Henry Rowe Schoolcraft (1793–1865) devoted a significant portion of his life to interactions with Native American people. In 1822 he served as an Indian agent for the US government covering Michigan, Wisconsin and Minnesota, before later marrying Jane Johnston, who was herself the daughter of an Ojibwa war chief. From his wife Schoolcraft would learn the Ojibwa language and much about their history and way of life. He would go on to write extensively about the Native American people, with works including *The Myth of Hiawatha, and other Oral Legends, Mythologic and Allegoric, of the North American Indians* (1856) and a comprehensive six-volume series titled *Historical and Statistical Information Respecting the History, Condition, and Prospects of the Indian Tribes of the United States* that was published between 1851 and 1857.

Lewis Spence

James Lewis Thomas Chalmers Spence (1874–1955) was a scholar of Scottish and Mexican and Central American folklore, as well as that of Brittany, Spain and the Rhine. He was also a poet, journalist, author, editor and nationalist who would found the party that would become the Scottish

National Party. He was a Fellow of the Royal Anthropological Institute of Great Britain and Ireland, and Vice-President of the Scottish Anthropological and Folklore Society. He published many books, of which *Myths & Legends of Babylonia & Assyria* (1917) is one of relevance to this volume.

Henry M. Stanley

"Dr Livingstone, I presume?" Welshman Sir Henry Morton Stanley (1841–1904) is probably most famous for a line he may or may not have uttered, on encountering the missionary and explorer he had been sent to locate in Africa. He was also an ex-soldier who fought for the Confederate Army, the Union Army, and the Union Navy before becoming a journalist and explorer of central Africa. He joined Livingstone in the search for the source of the Nile and worked for King Leopold II of Belgium in the latter's mission to conquer the Congo basin. His works include *How I Found Livingstone* (1872), *Through the Dark Continent* (1878), *The Congo and the Founding of Its Free State* (1885), *In Darkest Africa* (1890) and *My Dark Companions* (1893).

Capt. C.H. Stigand

Chauncey Hugh Stigand (1877–1919) was a British army officer, colonial administrator and big game hunter who served in Burma, British Somaliland and British East Africa. He was in charge of the Kajo Kaji district of what is now South Sudan, and was later made governor of the Upper Nile province and then Mongalla Province before being killed during a 1919 uprising of the Aliab Dinka people. During his time in Africa he managed to write prolifically, from *Central African Game and its Spoor* (1906), through *Black Tales for White Children* (1914), to *A Nuer-English Vocabulary*, published posthumously in 1923.

Rachel Storm

Rachel Storm studied at Oxford University and the University of London and has written widely on religion, mysticism, mythology and ancient cultures. She is the author of several books, including *In Search of Heaven on Earth*, *Myths of the Near East* and *The Sacred Sea*.

H.R. Voth

Heinrich (Henry) Richert Voth (1855–1931) was an ethnographer and Mennonite missionary and minister, born in Alexanderwohl, Southern Russia, who would spend most of his life in the USA. He learnt the language and studied the culture and ceremonies of the Arapaho and the Hopi people, having been sent by the Mission Board of the General Conference Mennonite Church. His works include *The Traditions of the Hopi* (1905).

Alice Werner

Alice Werner (1859–1935) was a writer, poet and professor of Swahili and Bantu languages. She travelled widely in her early life but by 1894 had focused her writing on African culture and language, and later joined the School of Oriental Studies, working her way up from lecturer to professor. *Myths and Legends of the Bantu* (1933) was her last main work, but others on African topics include *The Language Families of Africa* (1915), *Introductory Sketch of the Bantu Languages* (1919), *The Swahili Saga of Liongo Fumo* (1926), *A First Swahili Book* (1927), *Swahili Tales* (1929), *Structure and Relationship of African Languages* (1930) and *The Story of Miqdad and Mayasa* (1932).

E.T.C. Werner

Edward Theodore Chalmers Werner (1864–1954) was a sinologist specializing in Chinese superstition, myths and magic. He worked as a British diplomat in China during the final imperial dynasty, working his way up to British Consul-General in 1911. Being posted to all four corners of China encouraged Werner's interest in the mythological culture of the land, and after retirement he was able to concentrate on his sinological studies, of which *Myths & Legends of China* (1922) was one result.

W.D. Westervelt

William Drake Westervelt (1849–1939) was a pastor from Ohio, who moved to Hawaii and became a prominent authority on the island's folklore, publishing numerous articles and works on Hawaiian history and legends, including *Legends of Maui* (1910), *Legends of Old Honolulu* (1915), *Legends of Gods and Ghost-Gods* (1915), *Hawaiian Legends of Volcanoes* (1916) and *Hawaiian Historical Legends* (1923).

Dr R. Wilhelm

Richard Wilhelm (1873–1930) was a German theologian, missionary and sinologist. He is best known for his works of translations of philosophical works from Chinese into German, including his translation of the *I Ching* and *The Secret of the Golden Flower*. He also edited *The Chinese Fairy Book* (1921).

Egerton R. Young

Initially starting out as a teacher, the Canadian author Egerton Ryerson Young (1840–1909) was ordained in the Wesleyan Methodist Church in 1867 and set out to work as a missionary among the Cree people. Encouraged to tell his stories of missionary life and of the cultures he learnt about, he produced a number of works, such as *By Canoe and Dog Train Among the Cree and Salteaux* (1890), *Stories from Indian Wigwams and Northern Camp-fires* (1893) and *Algonquin Indian Tales* (1903).

FLAME TREE PUBLISHING
Epic, Dark, Thrilling & Gothic

New & Classic Writing

Flame Tree's Gothic Fantasy books offer a carefully curated series of new titles, each with combinations of original and classic writing:

Chilling Horror • Chilling Ghost • Science Fiction
Murder Mayhem • Crime & Mystery • Swords & Steam
Dystopia Utopia • Supernatural Horror • Lost Worlds
Time Travel • Heroic Fantasy • Pirates & Ghosts • Agents & Spies
Endless Apocalypse • Alien Invasion • Robots & AI • Lost Souls
Haunted House • Cosy Crime • American Gothic • Urban Crime
Epic Fantasy • Detective Mysteries • Detective Thrillers • A Dying Planet
Footsteps in the Dark • Bodies in the Library • Strange Lands • Lovecraft Mythos

Also, new companion titles offer rich collections of classic fiction, myths and tales in the gothic fantasy tradition:

George Orwell Visions of Dystopia • H.G. Wells • Lovecraft
Sherlock Holmes • Edgar Allan Poe • Bram Stoker • Mary Shelley
African Myths & Tales • Celtic Myths & Tales • Greek Myths & Tales
Norse Myths & Tales • Chinese Myths & Tales • Japanese Myths & Tales
Native American Myths & Tales • Irish Fairy Tales • Heroes & Heroines Myths & Tales
Witches, Wizards, Seers & Healers Myths & Tales • One Thousand and One Arabian Nights
Hans Christian Andersen Fairy Tales • Alice's Adventures in Wonderland
King Arthur & The Knights of the Round Table • The Divine Comedy • Brothers Grimm
The Wonderful Wizard of Oz • The Age of Queen Victoria

GOTHIC FANTASY